Mario 6

Marked

Mario 6
Marked

by

George
Hatcher

Warning
Adult matter

This book is intended for adults. Violence and sexual antics are not intended for minors, sensitive readers, or people living in the real world where there are sexually transmitted diseases which are incurable. Mario is a work of fiction. The people in the book lived and died only in my imagination. Any resemblance to actual people will be only in your imagination. The story is purely a product of long, boring plane flights, random flights of fantasy, the wild goose-chasing of ideas like what if this (or that) happened on top of my experience in wrongful death cases. Like Mario, I am no lawyer. I do not employ nubile sex groupies, or toss people out of high rise buildings when they get on my nerves.

This is a work of fiction. All of the characters, organizations and events portrayed in this novel are either products of the author's imagination or used fictitiously. Any resemblance to actual events, to persons living or dead, is purely coincidental.

CasaHatcherPress is an imprint of
Pretty Face, Inc.
225 South Lake Avenue Suite 300
Pasadena, CA 91101

For details, contact:
CasaHatcherPress.
http://casahatcherpress.com
(818) 519-2976

Mario 6: Marked
Copyright © 2018 by George J. Hatcher

Mario 6: Marked by George J. Hatcher
First Edition November 2018
Library of Congress Cataloguing-In-Publication data on file
ISBN: 978-0-9983762-5-7 (hardback)
ISBN: 978-0-9983762-6-4 (paperback)
ISBN: 978-0-9983762-7-1 (ebook)
R:181124

George and Molly 1968

To my one and only, Molly.

You continue to be my inspiration to keep moving ahead. For 53 years now I have loved you. I am looking forward to our next 53.

I love you.

Acknowledgements

Jody Clinker, thanks for keeping your eagle eye sharp as always.

If it were up to my collaborator and editor, Allie Bates, this book would still be in edits. Balky once again. I had to pry it out of your grip while you were still marking it up. Now if only you would move a little faster....

Works by George Hatcher

One Wilshire

Fiction by George Hatcher

Ambulance Chaser Series
Mario 1: Woman in Jeopardy
Mario 2: Coming of Age
Mario 3: Risky Business
Mario 4: Free Fall
Mario 5: Afire
Mario 6: Marked

Independent Titles
Arabe (coming soon)
Pretty Face (coming soon)

Chapter 1
Jan 2, 1980
Shoot out

Mario

Pixie and Letty arrived, and scanned the lobby of the plush Huntington Hotel where I've been staying for the two weeks since my place was torched. I was with Tricia at the reception desk checking out when they came in, and they hadn't seen us yet. Once they were far enough from the entrance that the cold didn't wash over them with every entrance and exit, they stopped, resting their luggage on the marble floor. Each carried a suitcase, briefcase, carry-on, garment bag, and purse. We all tend to over-pack in cold weather.

Pixie

"Maybe we should go up to his suite. You sure he said to meet in the lobby?" I asked Letty, wondering if we should go check out his rooms.

"He's right there," Letty said, pointing. "Tricia got here first, or she slept with him. I knew I should have stayed like I usually do."

"Oh hush, already."

He towers head and shoulders above everybody, so he's easy to spot, even in a crowd. I waved at him as he walked toward us.

I hugged him. Letty joined in. You'd think we hadn't seen him in ages, but it was less than a day from when we were together in his suite.

I kissed Tricia on the cheek. Letty only smiled at her.

Tricia waved over the yawning, pizza-faced bellboy who lazily followed with his half-empty luggage trolley.

I've known Mario since we were kids growing up in ELA. He went to school, but as a corner girl, I ditched from middle school on. When I came to work for Mario, Jo pushed me to get a GED. She and Niley left to manage apartments for him, so I took over the team arrangements for travel and everything down to the details of how we dress when we work. Jo is a total control freak. I will never be as good as her, but I give it all I got.

I hate to say it, but I'm glad for the timing of this plane crash. Texas will be a good change of scene. Maybe Mario's head will switch gears, and he can stop torturing himself wondering who burned down his house.

Mario

We were coming together for the usual reason: a plane crash. A Lockheed Super Electra jet airliner flying from Miami to San Antonio had broken up in mid-air during a thunderstorm, leaving a debris field just outside of the San Antonio city limits. Usually the girls left their cars at Casa Luna—my house—and rode with me to the airport, but that was impossible now that there was nothing left of my place but the burnt bones. My Rolls had burned up, as well as Pixie's and Letty's cars, and my station wagon, which Letty used for shopping. Every vehicle had been replaced, but it would take years to rebuild the house. Everyone we talked to said it was a miracle we were alive. We'd all been asleep when the fire started.

Rarely did a crash have survivors, and this one was no exception. We were traveling from Pasadena to San Antonio to follow up with the families of the deceased on behalf of the Chicago law firm that I did business with. The law firm specialized in aviation litigation. It would be up to us to befriend the families of victims who needed a lawyer to look out for their interests. It's a slow process, and we didn't outright solicit the families—that was my rule, and, depending on what country we were in, the law. At fourteen I was running around finding car accident cases for a lawyer in East Los Angeles. You don't do that with plane crashes.

The plan had been for me to meet Pepe in Mexico City before heading back to San Antonio to join up with my team, but last night, Pepe called off our meeting. On his way to the airport in Bogota, someone tried to shoot him. He didn't explain much. The would-be shooter was dead. Pepe's voice was calm, like this was no big deal. After his call, I talked to his sister Camila who was somewhere in Europe, then his other sister Olga, who was in South America. Both seemed way too calm about the attempted shooting, and told me to not worry. Pepe had an army protecting him. With the meeting put off, I'd decided to travel to San Antonio with the team.

"I missed you last night," I told Letty, "and I love that suit." She was in something that looked like a man's tuxedo, but she couldn't look like a guy if she tried.

"So damn cold out there. I have on long-john thermals."

"You didn't say anything about my suit." Pixie did a circle. "Wanna see my long johns? Like, right here and now?" She giggled.

Pixie always gets a smile out of me. "Baby, as usual, you're hot." The cashmere top she wore looked like it was painted on.

"Are you armed?" Tricia asked, looking Pixie and Letty over.

The girls were a prosperous-looking bunch. Tricia's holstered gun was well concealed. At least, I couldn't see it.

Pixie indicated her purse and Letty's shoulder bag. "We decided to carry our guns on the plane. We can declare them at the airport."

Tricia nodded her understanding and gave them a thumbs up.

The bellboy pulled up with the trolley, looking from Pixie and Letty to their luggage.

"This too?" he asked, his adolescent voice breaking.

I nodded. "Thanks, kid."

I handed the kid a ten, earning a big grin and a burst of enthusiastic rearrangement. The boy hung the garment bags, meticulously aligning them with the others, and organized the suitcases like a jigsaw puzzle, with the smaller pieces wedged in the gaps, although there was plenty of room.

"Juan rented a big car and will pick us up at the airport in San Antonio," Pixie said. She handled getting us where we were going and back, as well as lodging and providing Juan with whatever he needed.

Juan, like Tricia, is a private eye. She's former military, and he's an excop. As my advance man, from his home in Puerto Rico, Juan flies in ahead of us to the city where the families of victims will gather, normally the departing city or the destination. By the time we arrive, Juan has ferreted out the details of where the families of crash victims are being housed by the airline operator. He also takes care of finding personnel at the hotel who would work with us behind the scenes, and he makes friends at the coroner's office. He has worked with me for years.

"Boss, I ordered a limo," Pixie said, looking at my car through the glass as we approached the front entrance.

"Some limo they sent—a VW van. I tipped the driver and sent him on his way. We're taking my car to the airport."

"I hope some jealous freak doesn't key your brand-new Rolls while we're in Texas for a month."

"Hey, have some faith," I said. "Besides, we don't know how long we're staying."

"Boss, airport parking sucks big time," Pixie argued.

"Hello, Boss, you listening?" Letty asked.

I ignored them.

The small swarm of hotel service staff fluttered around us as we headed outside into the cold. The valet had pulled up under the awning and left the car running. The doorman opened the car door with a smart bow. I gave the doorman and valet ten dollars each as Pixie got in the front passenger seat. It was a chilly night, but the car's heater was already starting to warm things up. Letty and Tricia got in the back while the bellboy piled luggage in the trunk.

"Nice wheels," the bellboy said.

"Thanks."

I waited till everyone was settled, then got going. Soon we were on the Pasadena Freeway.

"Your gun permits are probably not valid in Texas," I said. The girls' concealed weapon permits had been issued by the State of California.

"Sorry, Boss. We're packing." Pixie's voice was firm.

"No one is going to know unless we have to use the guns," Tricia said. "Besides, everyone carries a gun in Texas."

"Oh, they do not," Letty said, elbowing Tricia. "Bitch, don't lie."

With my criminal record, I couldn't buy or possess a gun unless the president gave me a pardon. That was never happening. Besides, as a karate and judo master, I didn't need a gun. I'd started martial arts at ten and just kept going with it, year after year. After I was kidnapped in Venezuela, I worried more about the girls' safety, so I pushed my team to take up karate. They had many levels to go, but they already had black belts. Martial arts only stop bullets in movies. If their guns make them feel safer, I am okay with them having them. Their gun coach was an ex-cop who had been training my team for seven years, ever since Melina had the bowling alley at her house renovated as a shooting gallery. I'd seen the girls' regular Wednesday-night practice session. Their drill instructor was a slave driver who never cracked a smile, but he'd polished their skills to competition-level on a large variety of handguns and rifles.

Letty expected lip from me about the guns, but it didn't happen.

"The new-car smell is making me cum," Pixie said.

Pixie always says stuff like that. I ignored her. Letty did not.

"Bitch, you're probably playing with yourself."

It had always been Jo who kept a watchful eye over Letty and Pixie's bickering, but Jo was back at the management office. Tricia stepped in.

"Behave, kids."

"Fuck you," I heard Letty say.

"Okay, show me your dick. Not taking my clothes off until I see it."

They laughed. I was glad to see their good mood and merged onto the Harbor Freeway. Familiar turf. Downtown Los Angeles on both sides. Traffic started to congest. A motorcycle appeared to the left, racing ahead and slowing several times in a way that snared my attention, as if the driver was trying to get aligned with the Rolls. The speeding and slowing and weaving continued. I breathed a sigh of relief when the biker swerved out of sight. But then he sped up and zigzagged too close again.

We had caught up to traffic and were nearly boxed in.

I wondered if the biker was drunk off his ass. I kept one eye on the road ahead and my right hand on the wheel, but I was getting more and more pissed. The biker was close enough that his handlebar was a hair from my side-view mirror. Traffic slowed to fifteen miles an hour, then ten. I got a good look at him then and ticked off the details. Gold jewelry. Tanned. Cheap amber-colored sunglasses. Black dragon painted on a red helmet that had no visor. Pockmarked skin. White streaks down the sides of his mouth through a black beard that was pointed like Lucifer's. Barbed-wire tattoo on his neck. Red ink. A gangie-looking scuzz-bucket.

"Fucker," I said, and opened the driver-side window. I stretched my left arm to take a punch at him, but the jerk accelerated again. Good riddance—but not for long. He accelerated then slowed till he was shoulder-to-shoulder with me. I felt the breeze as the rear window opened, saw the flash of light reflect on polished steel. I registered the biker's surprise.

"I got a picture of the scumbag; now I can shoot him," Letty growled behind me.

"Wait," Tricia said. "You can't just take a shot."

The biker twisted his body, reaching for something inside his leathers.

My hackles raised. He lifted the black barrel of a shotgun into my face. Instantly I lunged and grabbed it. I jerked, shoved, and jerked again, the tug of war throwing the Harley off balance.

Another light flashed. The firearm slipped out of the biker's gloved grip. I dropped it on the seat. Pixie moved the shotgun to the floorboard in front of her seat and pulled her gun.

"What the fuck?" The biker swore and struggled for balance. He was boxed in, a wall of traffic up ahead, me on his right, a beat-up Chevy truck on the left, a semi behind him.

The bike weaved and swayed, sideswiping the Chevy. From behind, the air brakes and horn of the semi blasted, braking metal squealing, even at our snail's pace. The sound vibrated the windows of the Rolls and buffeted the biker like a quake. I thought he was going down, but then he wobbled toward a gap in the wall of traffic ahead.

"Boss, you're blocking my shot," Tricia said. "Lean right. One o'clock."

"Boss, move," Letty said, simultaneously.

Pixie leaned forward, her gun fixed on the biker, then threw herself across me, aiming out my open window. Good thing we were hardly moving. It's not that easy to navigate with an armful of Pixie. I lifted my chin to see over her head.

"Don't shoot. He's already too far off. Don't want any innocents hurt," I said. All three of the girls had their guns targeted on the biker.

The biker swerved left, then shot through a space between the lanes.

Traffic slowed to a crawl. In my rear-view mirror, I saw that the side-swiped Chevy had stopped. Its driver was on the soft shoulder looking at the damage. The biker was long gone.

"I wasn't going to kill him, just take him down," Pixie said.

"I could have killed him," Letty said, "but Tricia stopped me. Bitch."

I turned around. Tricia and Letty's guns were still out, still pointed like Pixie's at the space the bike had disappeared into. The gap in traffic closed.

"He's gone."

With a fingertip, I gently moved Letty's barrel down, then Pixie's. "No one is shooting anybody. Put the guns away."

"I'm fucking pissed off," Tricia said, holstering her gun.

"One shot would have put that motherfucker on the pavement." Letty was shaking with emotion.

"That fucker was after you, Boss," Pixie said.

"He's not the one," I said slowly. I'd never forget that face. "He's nobody. But I bet he knows who's behind all this. I bet he takes orders from whoever is gunning for me, maybe from whoever torched the house."

Tricia said, "I don't think he was trying to kill you."

"What the fuck are you talking about?" Letty's voice was blistering.

"Of course he was trying to kill him!" Pixie exploded.

I snuck a glance at Tricia. "When I yanked the shotgun, he could have pulled the trigger. It was a stupid move on my part. Because..."

"But—" Pixie said.

I continued, "...he could have just taken a shot. That shotgun would spread a world of hurt."

No one spoke for a few seconds, then Tricia said, "Exactly. I agree, Boss. He could have blasted through the back window. He wanted you to see him. The fucker was out to scare you. That was a message. But who from?"

"If I see his face ever again, he's dead meat," Pixie said stiffly.

"Fuckin'-A," Letty agreed.

"I got two pictures of the son of a bitch. Just need to develop the film," Letty said.

We continued through heavy traffic. "If you're not up to it, we can fly another day."

"We're a go." Pixie turned around to face Tricia and Letty. High fives all around.

"In that case, I need to do some crazy driving so we don't miss our flight." My mind was not on the traffic but on the puzzle: What could I have done to get someone so pissed off? Was the biker connected to the fire and the murders of Jake and Oscar? What the fuck was going on?

I left the rifle in the trunk, called Jo from the airport, told her to get a locksmith in the morning, retrieve the shotgun, and take it to Mike Sanchez, a detective I met years ago when Tanis was killed. I realized that because I did not report the incident, Mike may not be able to do anything, but it was worth a try.

At noon in San Antonio, Jo called me. "Are you sure the shotgun was in your trunk?"

"Of course. Why?"

"In that case, I must have just broken into the wrong Rolls Royce."

"Jo, what are you talking about?"

"I'm at the airport with Jimmy, the locksmith. I know I have the right car. Brand new. Sticker on the front windshield. No rifle."

"What do you mean, no rifle?"

"Someone beat me here."

"I put it right in the center of the trunk.I didn't hide it."

"Boss, it's not there."

Letty

Pixie and I were in her bedroom at the Hyatt Regency. The bedroom was dark, but I could see her. We were on the bed, leaning against the headboard. Boss hinted that he wanted to be with Tricia. She's not into threesomes and foursomes like us. Pixie and me, we dig our quality time, and this was one of those times. But I had some bad news.

"What do you mean the fucking camera had no film?"

"Pixie, I had film in the carry-on with the camera but at the time, fuck, I didn't think about whether the camera was loaded or not."

"Oh, you dumbass!"

"I know. Go ahead, take a punch or two. I won't block."

"Fuck, fuck!"

"You can do that, too."

"You think this is funny?"

"Don't be stupid, I know it's not funny."

Pixie got quiet. If she threw a punch, I would block it; no way was she going to get one at me cold turkey. "I think the second flash threw the fucker off guard so that Boss could yank the shotgun away."

I felt better. "So maybe my fuckup isn't completely fucked up? Only fifty percent fucked."

Mario

For the past three weeks in San Antonio, our home away from home had been the Hyatt Regency on the River Walk that now connected the Alamo Plaza. During our early breakfast on the top-floor restaurant, the great view of the river below did not display the activity it would have later in the day when boats floated by filled with tourists. It was too cold to be out on the patio, even with the heaters.

Pixie forked a bite of salsa-covered scrambled eggs into her mouth, swallowed, sighed, and forked in another bite. "We have forty-one retainers, Boss. How many are we shooting for?"

I looked at Pixie. "Babies, if you're homesick, take a few days off. It's just a short jump home."

"I'm fine, Boss. I just hate this place."

"Boring, totally," Letty said.

I looked from Juan to Tricia. "You bored, too?"

Tricia just shook her head.

Juan piped up. "I fine, Boss. I do everything to do already. I think you are wasting money having me here now."

I'd known this for a week. "Juan, make reservations and go. No doubt Valita's anxious to have you home. Next time bring her."

"Yes, Boss, thanks."

"Anyone else?"

I looked around the table at the team. Even if we went home now, Gonor in Chicago would consider himself lucky to have signed so many families. A few were on the wire. I was waiting on them, then we could go home.

"One more week, max," I said.

"No sweat, Boss," Pixie said. "Sorry I bitched."

I leaned left and kissed her.

"No need to be sorry," Letty said. I leaned right and kissed her, too.

Tricia asked the waitress for the bill. It was early, but the hotel where the families of victims were staying was twenty minutes away. I put a twenty on the tray the waitress brought.

The restaurant had been empty on our arrival, but now it was packed. The clatter of silverware and conversation was a loud hum, punctuated by tinkling glasses and some faint, indistinguishable noise from a distant kitchen. Coffee and biscuits, bacon and sausage, and a faint undertone of cigarette smoke perfumed the air. We weaved through to the register where the exit was, the team leading the way as I followed across the red-patterned carpet.

So many tourists. Some of the groups were obviously families, but some were lone businessmen with briefcases, sipping coffee and going over their important papers. It was not the season for summer-casual; it was a winter crowd, and most were heavily dressed for their encounter with San Antonio, coats hanging on the back of their chairs, cameras, and some with the hotel's free city guides open on their tabletop. My attention skittered around, settling on nothing of particular interest. Then I saw a leather jacket, a flash of red. My eye moved on. I stopped, watching the girls draw away, and returned my attention to the man in the leather jacket. Across from him, another leather jacket. Both men were drinking coffee and looking out the window at the view. The second man did not have on his sunglasses, but the white-pointed Lucifer beard was indisputable. Beneath the jacket, he wore a collared shirt. Above it, the red barbed-wire tattoo was unmistakable.

I went from ice to boiling in a second. It could not be a coincidence that the biker had followed us to San Antonio. In a few steps, I was at their table. The tattooed guy came off of his chair, his stance alarmed. My hands were casually in my pockets. I head-butted him. Fucking hurt my head. On the bright side, the biker went down, flat on his back.

The restaurant fell silent, like someone had switched the volume off. All eyes were on me. Shit. I hadn't meant to hold a floor show.

The biker's companion reached into his jacket, presumably to draw a gun. Tricia was already there, her gun pressing into his neck. Her hammer clicked. He froze in place. I flashed Tricia a smile. She nodded.

"Just try me," she said to the guy.

One beat behind Tricia, Pixie and Letty flanked me, their guns aimed at the man on the floor. Juan took up the rear.

From somewhere in the silent, shocked crowd, a small child whispered loudly, "Is this the wild west, Mommy?"

I moved over to the biker, still on the floor, shaking his head, probably dizzy. Fucker.

"Hey, shithead, I have a fucking shotgun that belongs to you." If he got to my trunk before Jo, he would know I was lying and his expression confirmed it to me. He had gotten to my car or had it done. Had he doubled back and followed me to the airport?

There was no time for the shithead's comeback. Four hotel security guards appeared with guns drawn and leveled on me. Hell, why me? It was the girls who had three guns out. One of the security guards reached down and pulled up the biker, who stood unsteadily on his feet, shaking his head like a schnauzer with water in its ears. Tricia holstered her weapon. Pixie and Letty stashed their guns in their purses. Juan stepped into the group and casually put his arms over Pixie and Letty's shoulders.

The restaurant manager fluttered nervously, looking at his full crowd and the growing line of waiting customers. To security, he said in a low voice but loud enough for me to hear, "Just get rid of them. This is the breakfast rush. This is the Hyatt, not the O.K. Corral."

A guard asked, "Are you all right?" Not us. He asked the shithead.

"No harm done," the shithead said, then looked at me. "Crazy fucker."

"Are you going to press charges?" The manager picked up the five-dollar bill from their table and handed it back to the biker. "Breakfast is on us. We don't want any trouble here."

The biker said nothing, just looked at his companion. Both were inching away from their table now that no guns were on them.

My hands were still in my pockets. I turned toward the guards with no sign of aggression.

"Put your hands up."

I complied, slowly and calmly.

"Boss," Juan said, pointing as the biker and his companion slipped out.

I told the guards, "Stop that fucker. He tried to kill me."

One of the waitresses piped up. "That's not true. He attacked the man that just ran out. Next thing I knew, the poor man was on the floor."

"He attacked us. Not here," Tricia said. "Someplace else."

"We were there," Pixie said with attitude.

"All of us." Letty put her hands on her hips.

Juan flushed, but didn't disagree, although he hadn't been there.

The restaurant manager was still fluttering around, trying to shoo us away, and looking flustered until the security guards got into gear.

"You're all coming with us."

The guards herded us into a freight elevator, and then downstairs into a security office. We were held until two deputy sheriffs showed up.

"The victim disappeared without identifying himself. We aren't charging you," the deputy said, "but the hotel wants you out."

"We were ready to leave your boring hotel already," Pixie sniped.

"Shh," Letty said, not that she disagreed.

Tricia stayed with me as the girls and Juan went to our rooms. I am told that Pixie dialed a service and rented a limo and driver for the rest of the day while Letty packed. The bellboy picked up their luggage and loaded the limo, where Tricia and I were waiting under a security guard's watchful eye.

"We've been here nineteen days," I said once we were settled and on the way. "Have you seen either of those men here in San Antonio?"

No one had.

"Boss, he had to believe that you wouldn't recognize him. No way he'd be sitting in the restaurant like everything was okay unless he figured that," Pixie said.

"I believe that," Tricia said.

Letty said, "I don't believe it. He knows there were two flashes from a camera and that we have pictures of him. Even if we don't have them, he can't be that stupid."

"He very well could be that stupid," I said.

"Sure as hell broke up the boredom," Pixie said.

Letty cleared her throat, then said, "You just like to draw your gun."

"I do, and you know what? If I had fired and shot the ignorant fuck-trumpet, I would cum every time I thought about it," Pixie said dead seriously.

"Everything that comes out of your mouth is gushing with sex," Tricia said.

"Fuck you," Letty answered first.

"Don't be such a fuckmuppet, Tricia," Pixie said.

As we took several appointments at the hotel where the families of the victims were, our luggage, limo, and driver waited outside; then we went straight to the airport. Juan got a seat in coach to Puerto Rico, and the girls and I sat in first class to LAX. The two-hour-plus flight is hardly worth spending the money on first class, but I'm too tall for regular seats. Riding in coach would really be a sacrifice. All the way back, I brooded, furious at myself for losing control. If I'd handled it differently, I could have gotten the truth out of that guy. I could have made him confess who was pulling his strings. Missed opportunities suck.

At LAX, we ran into the usual mobs of overdressed planegoers. Crowds filled the halls, shops, stores, and restaurants.

"I can't hear myself think!" Tricia yelled.

"What?" I yelled over the dull roar, while pulling a valise off the carousel. "I sure miss flying private."

"Boss, if we had chartered, our tickets would have been three times as much," Pixie said.

"I would have pitched in." Letty made a face. "I hate LAX."

"Boss, I'll fetch the car and pick you guys up curbside." Tricia put her hand out.

"Deal. Meet you at the third sign." I poked through my jacket pockets, found the ticket for long-term parking, and handed it over with the keys.

Tricia was already headed for the exit. "I need to stretch my legs. I'll run."

Pixie, Letty, and I waited at the curb with the luggage.

A family came out, flagged down a taxi, and left. Dozens, maybe hundreds of people emerged from the door behind us, headed for the parking lots. The lines of cars inched through at a steady pace, puking out and collecting passengers. We waited a long time. I checked my Rolex. Ten minutes. Twenty minutes. Thirty minutes.

"She should have been here by now."

"Maybe she can't find the fucking car."

"Of course, Tricia can find the car. She's a fucking investigator," I said. So, I was agitated. What of it? It was cold.

"Then where the hell is she? Did something happen to her?"

"We can't just wait here like sheep."

"I'll go find her."

"Letty, relax. You stay right here. We don't split up."

"Tricia doesn't get lost."

I hailed the next security suit I saw. Before I had a chance to ask about Tricia, an airport security car pulled up directly in front of us, followed immediately by a small airport shuttle bus. Tricia emerged from the security car, followed by a security officer carrying a yellow envelope. Tricia was pale, her lips compressed as if she were upset.

I took an urgent step in her direction.

"Tricia?"

She put her hand on my forearm. "The Rolls was torched, Boss."

I tensed. In fact, tension shot through the team, like electricity sparking from lightning rods. I could practically see the sparks.

The uniformed officer asked Tricia, "Is this the owner?"

Tricia nodded.

The officer handed me the envelope. "Mr. Luna, two weeks ago, your car was burned. What was left was towed. The fire department determined that your car had been intentionally torched. Probably a Molotov cocktail." He indicated the envelope. "The report is in there. Also officers' names, contact information, our security records, and my card in case you need to reach me."

I said nothing. Though I could feel my face getting hot, I held my tongue. My temper had already screwed us once today. Pixie had no objection to killing the messenger. She was never one to hold back. She stepped between me and the airport crew.

"You'll be hearing from our lawyers," she snapped, looking from one guard to the other. "That was a brand-fucking-new Rolls Royce. And we had a ticket for long-term parking. That ticket said 'Not responsible for items left in vehicles.' It didn't say anything about getting fucking firebombed. You're going to pay, mister."

"We do our best," the guard said, admirably keeping his cool. "For now, I'm authorized to get you a ride home." He motioned to the bus, and a couple of airport employees began hauling our bags into the shuttle's luggage compartment.

The car must have been torched after Jo came with the locksmith. I was determined to get out of there gracefully and said nothing to the guard except to thank him for providing the ride. On the way to the Huntington Hotel, none of us uttered a word. We were all awake, alone with our thoughts. After the encounter with the biker and his shotgun, none of us had been shaken by the destruction of the car, but none of us wanted to talk in front of the airport driver and security guard riding shotgun, either. Too many threats, too many disasters over too long a time had toughened us to warnings. It was not that we were immune to caution; it was that there had been so much writing on the wall that danger had become the boy who cried wolf. Another day, another threat. At least that's how I felt. I'd be very surprised if the girls felt differently.

At the Huntington, Tricia and Pixie stowed their luggage in their trunks before they met Letty and me up in my suite, where it was a balmy seventy degrees and we could all defrost. That was after the hotel staff went on about my return like I was their long-lost brother. If the valet wondered where the Rolls went, he did not betray it. Gleaming smiles from the desk clerk, valets, and bellboys were my welcome, along with a gift of champagne from the manager, cards for free massages from the spa masseuse, extra candies on the pillows from housekeeping, and my favorite peanut butter ice cream from the concierge. With that kind of welcome, I should go away more often. Of course, my staying there in that big suite was sweet income for the hotel and sweet for me as well, since my house insurance was footing most of the bill.

"Anyone hungry? Room service?" I made the offer.

No one wanted food. The girls' minds were elsewhere.

"Home away from home again," I said, taking my familiar place on the loveseat in the sitting room, Tricia on one side, Pixie on the other, Letty perching on an ottoman and pulling my feet to her lap. She hummed the burlesque song "Take It Off" as she took off my shoes one at a time, dropped them to the floor, and started massaging my feet. I started to pull away, but Letty found a rhythm and got a sigh out of me. She smiled triumphantly, said nothing, and kept working my feet. Seriously, I could feel my bones melting—I was that relaxed.

"I'll call insurance about the car," Pixie said. "Then I'll sing you a song or two, instead of that humming." Tongue out at Letty.

"It will keep till tomorrow," I said, watching Letty. "If the one behind all this thinks I'm going to be scared off, they've got another thing coming." Scared off of what? If all this was a message, how about a note with a warning or something? A note saying 'Fuck you,' or 'Fuck you, I hate you.' All this and the puppeteer or puppeteers weren't taking any credit.

Pixie is no better at listening than I am. She got my insurance guy on the phone, covered the mouthpiece, and reported, "Another new Rolls will cost you the five-hundred deductible. He's going to put in the report right away. Needs a police report."

"Why are you being fingered, Boss? Who's doing it?" Tricia looked troubled.

"Fuck, that's what bugs me. I don't know who. I don't know why."

"It was that bastard biker," Pixie said, hanging up. "He followed us to the airport, got the trunk open, took his shotgun, then returned to torch the car, maybe on the day he flew to San Antonio to find us."

"He's a puppet. Who's pushing his buttons? And why? Same one who burned down my house?"

"We should stay," Tricia said, making moves like she was parking herself for the night to watch the door to the suite.

I didn't need a security guard half my size. "I'm fine, babies. Pixie, you got to hit your house. Tricia, go home. Get rested up."

I shuffled them out into the hallway and closed the door.

After they left, I let Letty undress me. She urged me on to the bed. She wasn't Betty, but she knows what I like. It was winter outside, but we were warm and naked on the slick sheets and she worked the stress from me.

"You really care, babies," I said softly into the pillow. I turned to one side. Letty took that as a sign and abandoned the massage. She reached over me, clicked the lamp off, and curled up against my back. She kissed the place on my neck where she herself liked to be kissed, and it drew from me a soft chuckle. The white noise of the hotel's heater kicked in, and we lay cocooned in the dark. I moved her arm from where it rested on my hip and folded it against my stomach, pulling her closer. Sleeping with Letty is nothing new, but that night, I felt the love.

Letty's Walther PPK was under her pillow.

When I'm not on a plane crash, I have a side job acquiring assets for LAI, a company controlled by Pepe Camacho and his sister Camila and adopted sister Olga. I don't know how big the company really is, but it's international and it is vast. I have free reign to buy anything I believe is a good deal, including small businesses, apartment buildings, office buildings, and shopping centers. I make a cool commission based on the price I pay for the business. Pepe wants to pay cash. I have to work the seller to accept full payment or partial payment in green cash. It doesn't always work the way we want, but if I like what we're buying enough, I do it like a regular sale, then Olga wires the money to an escrow and that's that.

The attempt on Pepe's life had cancelled our last meeting. If I had gone on to Mexico City, would the biker still have been after me? Would the shotgun have still disappeared? Would my car still have been torched? Fuck.

My shadow Letty was with me in the parlor of my suite at the Huntington when I called Pepe. I wondered if there was a connection between the attempt on his life on the way to the airport and the attempt on my life on the way to the airport. Pepe swam deep in the undercurrent of not-overly legal international business. If there was some plot underfoot, if Pepe's network did not know about it, they would find out. I tried not to think of the Camacho empire as a cartel. Pepe Camacho himself had told me only that he was in the family business, something he'd taken over and expanded upon when his father had died. Camila once told me that her father was the *jefe* of a cartel. Pepe had branched out into many enterprises in many countries, a web of enterprises that flew under the radar of government, taxes, and petty things like laws. We didn't discuss this, but I'd seen with my own eyes that the Camachos obeyed no law but their own. Pepe was an international businessman who avoided the US after he'd been arrested here and charged with what he claimed were his father's crimes.

This was our history: my good friend Oscar had gotten a jury to find Pepe not guilty on all counts, but the trial had taken a year. For Pepe, that had been a year in the LA County Jail with no bail. All this had been before we met. When I got kidnapped in Venezuela, Oscar had talked me up to Pepe, to the point that we were now fast friends. Oscar had talked Pepe into a rescue, though by the time his team got there, the fireworks were over, and it was pretty much just a helicopter ride home. I'd never in my life expected to be hanging with anybody with this kind of money. Before we ever met, it was his actions that got me out of the Venezuelan jungle. That counts for something.

While Letty ordered a late breakfast, I got through to Pepe Camacho in Bogota. Told him about the biker. Part one in LA. Part two in San Antonio, Texas.

Pepe said, "You been gone weeks and didn't tell me about this."

"I was busy with a case. I didn't want to bother you. You have enough on your plate. I didn't tell Camila or Olga either, and I talked to them regularly while I was gone. You got the shooter, but any luck finding who wanted to take you out?"

"Just a matter of time," Pepe said with certainty. "The biker makes no sense to me as a threat. No one took responsibility. If they were out to scare you, they would have let you know they were out there."

"No one claimed responsibility for burning down my house, either. But I agree, Pepe. I keep thinking someone would drop me a hint about why they're fucking with me."

"Burning your house, that was attempted murder. You were asleep. It's a good thing you had Fino's man on guard and he woke you."

I laughed, but it was no joke. "My alarm system woke us. The only thing Bruno did was let them burn down my house."

"Fino said you fired Bruno on the spot."

"The torching happened on his watch. Fucking firebugs managed to get on the property, get past him, get their cocktails into the house and cars, and get away scot-free. He fucked up big time."

I hung up as room service arrived. A waiter set up the table, and I sat down with Letty to eat.

"Did you talk to all of them?"

"Just Pepe," I said.

"Might as well hold off," Letty said, pushing away from the table, replacing the top of the chafing dish, and crossing her arms. She uncrossed her arms long enough to pour me a cup of coffee. "You know they always call in threes." She started counting off the seconds.

I sipped the coffee, black. Letty was right.

The Camacho sisters were quite a pair. Camila Camacho was the girl who owned everything now grown into the woman who owned everything. As the reigning queen of the Camacho family, she flew the world in her family's jets, money-laundering tens of millions of dollars made in her family's enterprises. Not that I have proof. It's just the hints I heard drop over the years, plus the need for Camacho properties to be bought from people who accept cash. Camila is a people-user. She is also beautiful, spoiled, flighty, impulsive, promiscuous, and drunk on the power of her limitless wealth, a woman-child who always gets what she wants. I am pretty sure that she has no clue what rules, or ethics, or law, or commitment, or love might be; but she is clear on one thing only—what Camila wants, Camila gets. And one of the things she wants is me. The rest of the world might be in awe of me, but I think Camila thinks of me as her boy toy. Sure, I'm willing to take advantage of that—when I feel like it. I know she's into my body, my sexual prowess, and she didn't mind cashing in on my ability to size up a deal. She likes being surrounded by beautiful people and isn't possessive or bothered with conventional morals. She's as happy in bed with my team and me, or Olga and me, as she is with me alone. Or Olga, for that matter.

When Olga's father died in service to Camila's father, Camila claimed her as a little sister. They'd both been girls, Olga just a little younger. To be honest, these days, I spend more time with Olga than Camila. Olga had always been well-to-do but had never known unlimited wealth until becoming a Camacho. She learned to live and think like Camila. Like Camila, Olga obeys no law other than her own will. She is outspoken about being grateful to Camila. It's no secret the family paid for her schooling. Olga found her place in the Camacho world, which is, as far as I can tell, picking up the pieces Camila leaves behind. Olga plays banker for the Camacho empire and runs things, so Camila doesn't have to. I've known her to cover things up when bad things happened. They were practically two halves of a single, interdependent, gorgeous whole.

At times I find myself bouncing between them like a volley ball. I count myself lucky. What man could resist the attention of two passionate Colombian beauties? Fielding their attention is like being in a circus, batted about by a couple of lionesses. Like the time one of them shot a couple of guys in the Bahamas, practically in front of me, just because a deal went bad. A helicopter scooped Camila, Olga, and me out of there in minutes. I forget that I can be as damaged by their claws as anyone, but for me, the danger is part of their allure. Sometimes I get drunk on them, their lifestyle, and their wealth. When I come home from seeing them, it's like a hangover. It takes days to learn to breathe real air and find my footing in real life again. But I am always glad to be home.

At the table, Letty counted to thirty-seven before the phone rang. Before my second sip of coffee. Letty flashed me a look. *Told you so*. She answered, handed over the receiver, and mouthed Camila's name. Smug.

"What is going on, Amor?" Camila sounded anxious.

"I know you've already talked to Pepe," I said. "Baby, this happened weeks ago; sorry that it upset you. I'm fine, really."

"When we're in Bogota, we have an army of guards around our house and around us when we're out of the house to protect us. I didn't think you'd need that in California."

"This bastard followed me to Texas," I said, "but he got to me in California first."

"Amor, I'm so sorry."

Then Olga's call. "Amor, I will send a plane, or come get you myself. Fly you away from the *pendejo* trying to hurt you."

"I'd love to see you, but I'm not running away, babies." Camila and Olga's voices were therapeutic, and not to my ears. "Besides, Baby, it happened weeks back. I'm over it. Pepe should have said so. I'm sorry you're upset."

"All the times we talked in Texas, you never told me."

"Why make you worry? I'm sorry, Baby. Send me a kiss so I can eat my breakfast without a guilty conscious."

Finally, I was free to chow down. I looked up at Letty, still sitting across from me waiting to take her first bite. "You're beautiful."

She blushed. "You too."

I first knew Jack Fino as a criminal attorney who represented Pixie on a bullshit charge, then as a financier who loaned money out to attorneys venturing into personal injury, then as a lunch companion because he has the kind of powerhouse pull that I like. I had been suspicious of Fino at first—something about his lending company requiring insurance policies on the borrowers—but the suspicion was something I got over.

"I found you the perfect place to rent while you rebuild or decide what you're going to do," Jack said. "Jerry Mills' place on Millionaire Row. It's just sitting there, totally furnished and in move-in condition."

"Fine. Good as done." I wanted out of the hotel. "You the man, Jack; no question."

Fino had been the matchmaker who hooked me up with the Gonor Firm in Chicago. He's older, but we have a lot in common. Like me, he lives in a big-ass house in Pasadena. Like me, he'd been raised by a single woman. After his father died, Fino's mother had taken in boarders and worked as a nanny. Like me, Jack started working young. Unlike me, he had clawed his way into a law degree. Jack was a hell of a dealmaker himself, the kind who always comes out on top. Like most of my more notorious friends, it is better to be on his good side. My team called Fino a mafioso, whatever that means.

"How did you do in San Antonio?" Jack asked.

"Signed a bunch."

Knowing Jack, he already knew from Gonor exactly how many cases we had signed. Fino was into everything. I brought Jack up to date about the biker.

Fino said, "Hire a badass investigator and get to the bottom of this once and for all. I know a guy. Retired FBI."

"I'll think about it." I wasn't too keen on having to tell the story all over again to a retired FBI agent. The last investigator Jack had recommended had been Bruno, who let my house get incinerated. "Anybody you recommend but Bruno."

Fino laughed. "You're too cruel, Mario."

Thanks to Jack's recommendation to the owner of the big house, I was able to write a check without any paperwork, just like that. I paid him twelve months in advance and he told me if I needed more time, our agreement could stand. He had no plans to use or sell the house. I made an immediate move from the hotel. The house was not like my torched house, but it was beautiful, including the expensive furniture. He had to be crazy to have a house like this just sitting unoccupied for three years since he moved to Beverly Hills. "If not for Fino telling me what a great friend you are of his, I wouldn't rent it," he said. He had sentimental reasons. I figured that no matter how much this lawyer was worth, a check as big as the one I gave him had him smiling all the way to the bank.

"I miss my giant bed and the mirror," I told Melina, but otherwise I knew I'd be fine there. The help could commute the short distance every day and go back to their quarters when they're done. My personnel's quarters were in a separate building and had not been damaged when the main house burned.

"Cuz, fuck, you scored," she said when she came over to check the house. "I love this place. I would buy it in a heartbeat."

"For the right price, right?"

"Of course. Smartass." She punched my stomach, and I crunched over a little as if it hurt. "I remember when I brought you to see my house for the first time that Sunday. The broker was downstairs reading the newspaper while we looked around. He found us fucking on the floor of the master bedroom. He was so freaked out, remember?"

We laughed.

"He ran out of the room and you yelled after him, 'Come back in here, haven't you ever seen anyone fuck before?'"

"I did say that, I remember," Melina said, laughing. "Which room should we break in, Cuz?"

Tricia

When we got back from San Antonio, I hired two artists on behalf of Boss and for two days Mario, Pixie, Letty, and I sat in the parlor of Mario's hotel suite describing the biker. The two renditions were practically identical. We agreed that the bearded biker on the freeway was the same dude that Mario took down at the Hyatt. After all that work and expense, Mario wouldn't let me submit a report to the police, said we had waited too long. Baloney. He just doesn't like to call the cops.

I got 5x7 and 8x10 copies done of the portraits, fifty of each. Not sure how he plans to use the pictures. One thing is for sure. None of us will ever forget that face.

Letty

If I had to live in my apartment and not with him, I could do it, but I'd miss just being with him, especially lying there next to him at night. Even if we aren't doing anything, it's satisfaction for me.

My apartment is unlived-in, but it's comfy—squeaky clean, as Boss would say. I still miss his house. His mansion, it was like paradise to me. Some fucking firebug torched paradise, and I miss it like some people would miss a good friend. The cops haven't come up with a fucking clue. You'd think they would be in touch with Boss, but I get more advice from my dead *Abuela Bela* than he gets from the cops.

The rented house is a big estate on Orange Grove where there's mansion after mansion behind gates and walls. It's a primo house, but it's no Casa Luna. That was the name of the house. Before the house, that was the name of his apartment in downtown Los Angeles. I wasn't around then, but Pixie has told me all about it. It's hard for me to see him as just a guy just starting out in his first apartment.

Pixie and I met at my apartment for her to play her guitar and try out her new songs on a small trusted audience—me. She could do the same at his house, but there are so many big echoey rooms, and always people there, and the intercom. She says she likes to be one-on-one with just me listening. We've all heard her sing. Her voice is beautiful. I listen to a lot of music, and I get ideas about songs and harmony and stuff. When we're alone, if it sucks, I tell her it sucks. It's little stuff like how she used to make a face when she sang high notes. I brought out a mirror and she was horrified to see the face she was making, but it still took a while to straighten it out. Now if she's singing in front of a crowd,

I can twist up my lips and it makes her pay attention or makes her laugh. If I tell her when she looks like her own music is putting her to sleep, she makes herself shine. I don't know how she does it.

"Are you tired or something? Look alive, girl. Get with it."

She stuck out her tongue and put down the guitar. She said, "Fuck you," and started singing again.

Her eyes sparkle when she sings.

In my small living room, she sat on a kitchen stool, singing "La Paloma." I've heard her do this song many times. She's so good. The way my ears hear her is different. No one does it like she does it. She stopped. Started over.

"I can't. I'm shy."

"That's a fucking laugh. There's not a shy bone in your body."

The idea is to stare at me, eye to eye. That helps her not be shy. I stare back, hard. Sometimes she's so pretty and her song is so much it makes my throat hurt, but I never want her to see me crying.

After the songs, this time, we talked about Boss. Nothing in my fridge but Cokes. We clicked away like we were drinking his expensive wine.

"I worry so much about him," Pixie said.

It's stupid. He's so big and powerful. Nobody is as big as he is, and when I'm there with him, I feel the same as Pixie, so I said, "Me too. I feel like I'm protecting him. When I'm there, he's safe."

Pixie said, "You are protecting him. He doesn't have a gun like you do."

"He killed four dudes without a gun. He doesn't need a gun."

Pixie counted them off on her fingers. The guy who shot him and Tanis—tossed off the motel balcony. The guy who broke into his high-rise in the middle of the night—tossed through the window. The crazy ambulance chaser who held the team hostage—tossed through the same window. One of the two follow-home guys who'd crashed our Christmas decorating party— karate-kicked into the hereafter.

"He's a fighting machine," Pixie said.

Pixie hugged me. Our drinks were going flat on the coffee table. I hugged her back.

"I love you," I said.

"Do you, really?"

"I do. I love him, too."

"We both love him."

"Are we gay?"

"Fuck you. We go either way, yeah? With the ones we love."

I put my arms around her, hugged her like she's all the world. Maybe she is. She and Mario, both. He's in my head even when he's not with me. But all I said was, "Yeah, that's how it is."

"Want to go back?" Pixie looked toward the bedroom.

"Check for yourself."

She touched me through my jeans. The jeans came off. The talk was done.

Trent Joel the contractor, aka TJ

Mario is family to me. He saved my ass when I had an unfinished high-rise in foreclosure in Westwood, California. He came by where I was staying and made a deal to take the building out of foreclosure and put up the money to finish construction. I got paid for running the job, plus 1.5 million when the build was complete. The money was his investor's. I didn't give a shit where it came from. As long as he kept coming up with cash to cover the build, I was his guy. Most financiers in construction, they promise a life raft and hand you an anvil, then laugh while you sink. Not Mario. He was the real deal. And then there was Jo.

His right-hand assistant Jo, well...I fell in love with her. By the time the building was complete, we were engaged. We got married soon after. The cash Mario paid as promised bounced me back into life. Ever since the high-rise, I've been up to my neck in construction jobs, busy as all hell. Jobs were falling in my lap. I have crews out the yin yang. When Mario's house got torched and he wanted to rebuild, he became my top priority.

After twenty revisions by him and Melina, thirteen months after the fire, I presented him the final plans that will go to the City of Pasadena for approval and building permits. It's no simple bungalow. The architect claimed he got ulcers and warned he might sue. Kidding about suing, but I believed the ulcers. The plans face public hearings. Even if things go smoothly, it will be a year before we get the green light to break ground on the four-story house that is taller than code allows, five thousand square feet on each floor. The first floor will have a glassed-in indoor Olympic swimming pool with electric shades throughout that control the sunlight. On the same floor, a gym, a karate workout room, a disco, a wine room with an entertainment area, an arcade, and a media room.

The second floor will have the main entry with a huge foyer, a living room, a family room, a kitchen with walk-in refrigerator and walk-in freezer, a breakfast room, a walk-in pantry, and a thirty-foot granite island with stools for casual dining when Mario wants to be close to the action in the kitchen.

The third floor has nine guest rooms with ensuite bathrooms plus two—a reading room and a den for guests.

Half of the fourth floor will be the master suite with a double king-size bed and a beveled mirror mounted above the bed, his-and-her bathrooms, his-and-her sitting rooms, and his-and-her walk-in closets off of the dressing rooms. Room for a hundred pairs of shoes each.

The other half of the fourth floor is the office. Conference room with work stations for four, with floor-to-ceiling bookcases with room for hundreds of books and several adjoining spaces: a hidden fire-safe room for three safes, soundproof room for the telex, and a connecting supply room. Mario's desk is in a separate room facing a glass wall view of the conference room with entry through double glass doors. At his back behind the desk, a hidden room, just for fun. On the roof right above his office, a helipad. He probably will not get a permit to land a helicopter there for years, but he wanted it.

He could save a bundle of money by putting the safes on the first floor. The floor to that room is going to be double reinforced to sustain the vaults. The wall around the property is twelve feet, but there's a fourteen-foot section that lets us squeak by codes, allowing the wall to be built up, grandfathered to the previous residence—a fourteen-foot block wall with gates in the front and same at the back of the property. The laundry and the pre-existing personnel housing is located three hundred feet behind the main house, hidden by a stand of trees. I'll be doing a little upgrade there too.

Much of the original landscaping and trees are still in place, and the outdoor swimming pool. A guardhouse will be built that cannot be seen from the street unless the front gates are open. The guardhouse is over a hundred feet from the entry to the main house. The help will have golf carts to commute between the two buildings. Three new fountains will be built, and a Japanese garden with a waterfall and a large pond for koi.

Pixie

I have two small apartment buildings, a duplex, and a four unit. I live in the four unit, a three-bedroom, three-bathroom that is perfect for my daughter Lainie, my live-in, and me. Years back, Boss kept on me until I bought the duplex, and, a year later, this one. Both buildings are in Monterey Hills, a great neighborhood in Monterey Park, about fifteen minutes from Casa Luna and only four minutes from Mario's Aunt Carmen's, where Lainie and I lived for years before I became a landlord. The best thing about having a place of your own is being able to change it how you want. I remodeled the shit out of this place, and to be honest, it's no Casa Luna, but I really like it. I park my new Corvette under a carport, just like the tenants.

Today my keys were in my right hand, my purse in my left. As I got close to my car, I saw glass all over the cement deck. My mirror and the driver-side T-Top was broken. I gripped the gun still in my purse, the business end facing where the vandal might be as I checked out the damage. I was ready to shoot straight through my purse, even though I seriously doubted the intruder was going to be waiting for me in the car. Nobody was there, so I pulled my hand free. Besides, I know karate. I don't need a gun to take on even a big perp. The door was locked, so I used my key to open the door. On my seat on top of a pile of shattered glass was a shotgun.

"What the actual fuck?"

It's been more than a year since the biker came after us on the freeway and Boss yanked the shotgun away from him. I barely saw it when I dropped it to the floor of the Rolls. Later, at the airport, Boss took the shotgun and put it in the trunk of his car. Could this be the same shotgun? What the fuck was it doing in my car? Did the biker do this? If so, why?

I took a hankie out of my purse, grabbed the shotgun, and went back into my apartment. By now, even the stupidest crook would have cleaned the gun of any evidence. My precaution about fingerprints was unnecessary but I was hoping the jerk who did this got careless. I called Boss and told him what I found.

"DoI call the cops?"

"Yes, but keep the shotgun out of the picture. After you make a report, call a tow truck to take the Corvette to the service department where you bought it. I'll send Tricia for you."

"Boss send Letty, or I'll ask Niley to take me. I don't want to listen to a bunch of dramatic scenarios from Tricia about who and why this happened."

"Letty it is, Pix. Are you okay?"

"Of course, but my baby, the car... fuck. I don't even have three hundred miles on it!"

I caught myself sniveling and cut it out before he could say anything. "Sorry, Boss, it's just my T-Top."

"Bring the shotgun," Boss said.

"Will do, Boss. Sorry to start your morning like this."

Boss laughed. "Fuck it, don't be sorry. It's the biker. Got to be."

"I agree, and I'm not sure how we'll ever prove it, but this gotta be the shotgun that went missing from your trunk."

"For sure," Boss said. "Are you sure you're okay?"

"Give me a break, Boss. Of course, I'm okay."

"You think you need to take any extra precautions for Lainie?"

"Nah, I think this limp microdick is just trying to show us how fucking smart he is. Lainie is right here with me. She ain't afraid."

Over the years, I've kicked some of the best female Asian ass myself, in matches of course. I have five belts. Lainie takes after me. She is shooting for her second karate belt. She's no Bruce Lee, but she can defend herself in competition with opponents twice her size. Lainie holds her own.

Mario

Pixie, Letty and Tricia were in the breakfast room with me, having breakfast for lunch. We had all seen Pixie come in with the shotgun.

"When we were in San Antonio and I put that turd on the floor, if he had any training at all, he would have fought back."

"What's that mean?" Pixie asked.

"It means that this guy depends on something to defend himself, not his skills."

"He's buff," Letty said, "but I agree, he should have fought back."

"If he was military, it wasn't special forces," Tricia said. "Boss, we can't keep that shotgun. It may have been involved in a crime, and I don't mean on you on the freeway."

"The serial number is ground off," Letty said.

"He has to be packing a gun, but so are we," Pixie said, grabbing the last piece of bacon and making short work of it.

"I seriously think someone has him intimidating you," Tricia said. "Or us, since he went for Pixie's car."

"I wouldn't call what happened on the freeway intimidation. He was ready to fire that fucking shotgun," said Pixie.

"We don't know that," I said.

"Boss, come on," Letty said.

"Look, he could have blasted through the back window and killed us all. He didn't do that. I just worry about you guys, and I worry about Lainie. The prick has shown us he knows where you live." I looked at Pixie.

"I believe I can speak for all of us. We got it covered. Don't worry, Boss," Tricia said.

"And I got your back, Boss, when the team is not here." Letty buttered a biscuit. She looked from the biscuit to me, and she flashed me a grin.

"I'll be so glad when my house is fucking finished. This place doesn't have security worth a shit. Wait till you see what TJ is going to build over there."

Pixie giggled aloud. "Boss, they haven't even broken ground."

"Maybe I need to make some improvements here," I said.

"Boss don't bother. It's not your house. And it isn't exactly sitting on the street; it has a tall fence and gates," Letty said. "Besides, I have eleven rifles and nine handguns in my room, and I'm a marksman with any of them."

"Show off, bitch. I have the same at home," Pixie snapped back.

"Okay, already," I said.

"The cops are not going to use their lab to figure out anything about this shotgun without a report on file," Tricia said.

"Bury it."

"Boss, I'll break it down and get rid of it. Let me handle it."

"You don't mind, Tricia?"

"My pleasure, Boss."

We all took a good look at the shotgun for the last time before Tricia took it away. There was no way to remember what the shotgun I'd grabbed from the biker looked like. A shotgun was a shotgun. At the time, we never looked for a serial number. It's possible it had already been ground off, assuming it was the same one. The bastard left the gun in Pixie's car to show us he had taken it from the Rolls and was now giving it back like it meant nothing that we had it.

Chapter 2
January 1983 (three years since the biker attack)
Ambushed

Mario

Tricia was out chauffeuring the rental's keys back to Jerry Mills. Today was the first day living in my new home. I was in my den thinking about what I wanted to buy to fill an empty bookcase when the doorbell chimed. I carefully replaced the autographed 1961 first edition of Harold Robbins' *The Carpetbaggers* on the side table. It had been a housewarming gift from Melina, who knew how I favor Harold Robbins. My newest staff member, Sunny, beat me to the door. She was a tall, blonde mouse of a woman, dressed in a gray skirt, white shirt, apron tied at the waist. She opened the door. I saw over her head, recognized the visitor, and saw red.

"That will be all," I snapped. My original staff would have known not to open the door to that scumbag.

Sunny winced and rushed off, her soft-heeled shoes barely making a sound on the marble floors.

"Hey, Boss. Fabulous pad, congratulations."

I frowned and said quietly, "Bruno, you aren't welcome here. Go away."

I moved to close the door, and Bruno stopped it with his hand. There was a moment of tension with both of us putting our weight into the door between us. I took a breath and controlled myself.

Bruno was a stocky man, every part of him muscled to the point of deformity. His face was clean-shaven, and what hair he still had was cut military style. His ill-fitting clothes were rumpled as if he'd slept in them: black pants, yellow turtleneck, yellow-patterned sweater vest, plaid sport jacket—underdressed for the weather. A strong scent of cigarettes and shaving lotion did not entirely block the faint odor of beer.

"I fired you, Bruno. My house burned down on your watch. Go home and finish drinking that case of Schlitz in your refrigerator. You and me, we got nothing going."

"Mario, I heard something. You need to listen—"

"Bruno, I said go away."

I gave a tap to Bruno's elbow, breaking his stance. His elbow folded up like a hinge, and I closed the door.

Anyone coming in from the front gates had to check in. I called the guardhouse located at the front of the grounds.

"Quito, how the fuck did that big guy get through without you calling up here?"

"Boss, no one has driven in, and no one has come through the gates since you got here."

"Are you sure?"

A guy Bruno's size didn't jump a fourteen-foot block wall, nor could he scale the front gates without Quito seeing him directly or in a video monitor. The gatehouse had been one of my property's improvements, looking like a purely decorative folly surrounded by a circular drive. The structure had been constructed to match the house and housed a bathroom and office area. Visitors passed the gatehouse window just as they did in a garage, and if their entry was rejected, they could easily circle out. If allowed in, they could continue up the drive to the main house. The torching of my home three years earlier had left me scarred and cautious. I want to think I am wiser now about my safety and the safety of my team and workers that live on the premises. It is too damn bad that I have to take such precautions.

Quito Vasquez was one of my security improvements—one of three guards on my payroll, all licensed to carry guns. They weren't live-ins, but they worked twelve-hour shifts in the guardhouse and took alternating days off. The double security gates were intricate pieces of art that only revealed the gatehouse when they were open. The guard controlled a wrought iron door off the left gate for a person to walk in or out. The only other entrance to the grounds was also double-gated, an entrance that opened up to access the personnel building three hundred feet behind the main house.

I paged Tricia, and she called back instantly.

"Handed over the keys, Boss."

"Good," I said. "Bruno got to the front door. I think he must have snuck through the personnel gate after someone opened it. See if there's something we missed back there. See if we need to adjust the view or add more security cameras. By the way, Memo is polishing up the Rolls even as we speak. I want everything perfect when you pick up my aunt."

Quito called me from the guardhouse. "Boss, I checked two hours of tape from the back gates and I don't see a stranger coming on the property. I checked the cameras in the front gates. Nothing."

"That son of a bitch is way too big to climb the wall."

"Boss, wish I had an answer for you."

"Let Tricia know."

"I just paged her. She's on the property."

Jake and Oscar had been shot. I wasn't taking chances. The security problem would be handled. If Bruno had climbed that fence, especially in broad daylight, I'd give him a medal if I didn't dislike him as much as I do.

Aunt Carmen

Mario insisted that I get the first tour of the place, so Tricia was driving me to Mario's. His home that burned was everything he wanted. It broke my heart that he lost it to arson. He's come so far, so fast. I delivered him from my sister Elena, just as I delivered hundreds of babies before and after him. She was my only family left. I have fought with myself for many years not to share with him the truth about his father and the death of his mother. The day he was born should have been a day to rejoice; instead, it was a day of horror and grief.

I remember when I cleaned him up and put him in Elena's arms. It took only seconds to roll back the messy sheets and toss them to the floor at the foot of the bed.

I looked at the baby in her arms. From where I was kneeling by the sheets, they seemed a holy sight. My throat caught, and my eyes filled with tears.

Elena said, "He is so beautiful. He sees me. Carmen, he sees me. He knows me."

"It is true," I agreed, not wanting to break the moment.

No Madonna and child painting was ever so lovely. Elena was glowing with love, and the baby gazed into her eyes with an expression of pure wonder, their faces inches apart. All the times I had been told that infants could not focus at that age, that their smiles were simply gas—it was not true. The vision was caught like a snapshot in my head, a lifetime of love trapped forever in that instant of recognition.

The moment was broken when Mario's father, staggered in, drunk, an empty tequila bottle clutched in his fist.

I knelt at the foot of the bed and bundled the dirty sheets while he waltzed around the room, staggering. Francisco kissed Elena and thanked her. Then he looked from Elena to the baby.

The baby's complexion was pale, paler even than Elena's. And he had green eyes.

Francisco screamed, "That is not my child! You betrayed me! You're a *puta*! This baby is a *huero*.[1] You betrayed me. You've been whoring around! This baby is not mine!"

Like in a nightmare, he grabbed his gun from the nightstand and shot Elena. She jerked from the impact and was still. The baby screamed. Elena's arm dropped against the pillow and the baby rolled face-down, his screams muffled.

Francisco, slobbering drunk, was standing with the gun still out. He hadn't moved; he was frozen, transfixed by the hole left by the bullet.

"Elena?" he had asked. "You can stop that now. I forgive you, even if you are a *puta*. Elena? We can try again, make another baby…"

My bastard brother-in-law had lost his mind. I kept waiting to wake up, because this had to be a nightmare. I was on my knees gathering up the linens. I dropped the sheets. Stood. I was like a doe in the woods but reversing the roles—the prey stalking the hunter. One step. Two. On the third step, I was around the other side of the bed, beside Francisco. He seemed to have forgotten me. I just reached over and took the gun. He was staring and gibbering at Elena. I didn't care if his condition was from the liquor, shock, or disbelief. For once in his life, he was vulnerable.

I turned the gun in my hand, stared at it. I'd never held one before, but I'd just seen him use it, not four feet away. I crossed to the other side of the bed, so the infant was between us. I pointed the barrel at Francisco, cocked, and fired. The first squeeze, I hadn't quite cocked it. Nothing happened. My first actual shot went wild and knocked me into the door. He didn't even look up. I squeezed the trigger again. I didn't mean to shut my eyes, but I did by reflex. This time, the shot actually hit him sideways through his paunch. I staggered. He looked down at his punctured beer belly as if it weren't part of him, turned to face me with the expression of a dumb animal, and pointed to Elena.

"Fix her," he said to me.

"I can't fix her, *desgraciado*. You broke her…you killed her, you bastard! But I'll fix you."

---

[1] Light-skinned, white

I aimed for his widest part and fired again and again until all the gun did was click and click. After I stopped clicking the gun, he was still standing, looking at me. Finally, he slumped to the floor like a marionette whose strings had been cut.

"Miss Carmen, we're here. Are you alright?" Tricia asked me. I blinked and returned to the present, at the doors of Casa Luna. The baby I had stolen that night has come so far.

Mario

I had been pacing ever since I sent Tricia to pick up Aunt Carmen for her first walk-through of the new house. No mortal man or beast could have made me feel this vulnerable. Only Aunt Carmen.

At fifty-nine, she was still a statuesque woman, her hair as black and her back just as straight as when she'd been a young girl in Arizona. The strong features that defined my face were gentled in hers. She wore a pair of huge round sunglasses and slid them to the top of her head as she gazed up at the Mediterranean modern façade. She froze on the step, half down, half up.

"Good God, boy, did you build a house or a hotel?"

"Just a house."

That night, Melina came by.

"First night in the house." Melina grinned.

"We've come a long way, Baby."

"You're still my hero, Cuz."

In December of 1972, Melina had had a car accident in downtown Los Angeles. We met when I pulled her out of the wreckage before it went up in flames. When I visited her tenth-floor Bunker Hill apartment, I loved the place so much that I leased an apartment next to hers and had lived next door ever since—except for the rental while my house was rebuilt. When she'd purchased her million-dollar place in Pasadena in 1976, I bought the big house across the street. A tour guide of the city would call these residences "mansions." I prefer "big house." Mansion sounds way out there for an ELA guy like me to be living in.

Pasadena was known for its inventory of huge old homes, some built in the 1800s and still looking grand and boisterous. Melina had worked her decorating magic on my first big house, and again after it was rebuilt. Not that it was just rebuilt. It was reimagined.

"You put so much energy and countless hours in this house for me. I continue to be indebted to you for life."

"It was a pleasure, Cuz. It broke my heart that you lost everything in the fire, but once I got past that, I had fun doing it, just like before."

"I love you," I said, kissing her.

"You love everyone," she teased, showing her beautiful teeth. "Where is everyone?"

"Jo and Niley stopped by for lunch, but they only stayed long enough to eat with Aunt Carmen and me. Pixie went off to sing. It's open-mic night somewhere. She's going straight home from there. Letty is up in her bedroom, no doubt still unpacking."

"A scout is going to hear Pixie one day and scoop her away."

I thought of Pixie going away to the world of entertainment. "I hope not, unless she really wants to be a rock star."

"Everyone wants to be a rock star."

Pixie's presence fills a room. There would be emptiness without Pixie around.

We sat down to eat in the formal dining room. Our settings were at one corner of the immense dining table made intimate by dimmed lights and flickering candlelight.

"A lot of firsts tonight. Our first dinner at this table." I wanted to talk to her about Bruno's surprise arrival but didn't want that disturbing visit to intrude on our tryst. I would tell her later.

Melina rarely indulged in mid-week visits. Her seven markets and more than seven hundred employees demanded more than a ninety-hour work week. They—plus me—are her life. Every location had been built from the ground up by a contractor who agreed in advance to work together with Melina on every aspect of the construction. By the time the second market was complete, the contractor's hair had gone from dark brown to gray. She had a lawyer's attention to detail.

Miguel came out of the kitchen with two steaks sizzling on their plates. It was a simple meal. Wine. Salad. Meat. Peanut butter ice cream for dessert.

I had too many women in my life, and Melina admitted she reached out to a man when she needed it. We had come close to getting married several times. Although sixties-era free love was gone, the seventies wife-swapping craze was dying down, and the free love movement was stopped dead in its tracks by the discovery of this deadly new scourge, AIDS, we still had an open relationship.

I lifted my wine glass.

"To Sunday," I said. We had made it a point to leave behind our busy lives and keep Sunday open to spend the entire day together. Our Sundays were sacred, but after three years of commuting to Sunday, finally, it was good to be back to being neighbors.

"To tonight," Melina said, though it was not Sunday. We touched glasses, linked arms, and drank from each other's cups.

Miguel brought in the ice cream, a perfect scoop in each glass. I stabbed a spoon into mine.

"Get your bowl," she said with a wicked and promising look. "Which room are we initiating first?"

Melina grabbed me by the hand. A spoonful of my ice cream went overboard, slid down the inside of her arm to the crease of her elbow, melting as it went. The skin of the inside of her arm is pale and sleek. I made eye contact as my lips touched the path of melted cream.

"My favorite flavor."

We smiled at each other.

"There are a whole lot of rooms." Raising my voice, I said, loud enough for Miguel to hear without the intercom, "We're going to need more ice cream."

The phone rang.

I let it ring. Melina and I were about to get busy. We carried our dishes down to the spa but encountered Sunny. She reminded me more than ever of a mouse, her small hands quickly rubbing each other in nervousness. She could barely manage to meet my eyes.

"Excuse me, Mr. Luna."

"Mario," I said. "Mr. Luna was my uncle."

"On the phone. It was Mr. Bruno."

"Really?" Melina said, with a bark of laughter. "Bruno Bruno? I haven't heard that name in ages."

"He says he has something important to tell you. He…he hung up already, but he said he'll meet you at The Pantry at one tomorrow."

"Thanks, Sunny." I let her walk away, then said, "That asshole had the gall to show up here. I shut the door in his face. Still not sure if he got in through the personnel gate or what."

"I think you should go see what he has to say. It's not like he personally torched your house. You fired him. He lost his job. What else do you want from him?"

"What I want is easy, same thing he did for three years—stay away from me."

"Cuz, don't be an asshole. He got fired, he paid."

"I prefer getting back to our monkey business. Want to check out the master bedroom?"

Melina licked her lips in that way that she knew turned me on. "I bet it's fabulous." She took my hand. "Yes, let's go look, Cuz."

Melina's taste and design talent were what made my master bedroom as special as it was, and it didn't stop with my bedroom—it spread to the entire house. Every custom-made piece of furniture was her creation.

Melina

The Pantry on 9th and Figueroa in Los Angeles is the busiest restaurant and the last place in the world to have a meeting, but Bruno had designated this place and here I was. I hadn't seen the guy for three years, when I met him briefly after Mario hired him.

There was a line with no less than fifty people waiting to get in. Those willing to sit at the counter could walk in a center door and wait around until there was a place to sit. I went through that door, and saw tables packed with casually dressed diners rubbing shoulders with suited-up men and women who probably worked in offices close by.

I spotted Bruno sitting at a table for two.

"Bruno." I extended my hand. "I'm Melina. You may not remember me."

Lots of chatter surrounded us. My eyes leveled on his as he got up. We shook hands; his hand was bigger than Mario's, and that's big. His clothes were neat and clean, if shabby. A missing button, faded plaid shirt, a mend on the sleeve in contrasting thread.

"Why didn't he come?" he asked.

"He doesn't know I'm here. I was at his house when you left the message to meet you."

Bruno was drinking a cup of coffee. The waiter appeared, probably anxious to get us to eat and get out so another couple could sit down. "I'll have coffee, black," I said.

"Food is good here," Bruno said. He winked at me. He was a rough-looking mess, unshorn, and unshaven, but he had relatively handsome features. The face didn't match the body. He was on the burly side. I mean, he was massive in a way that stands out. Mario's chef Miguel is a weightlifter, but nothing like this guy.

"Just coffee," I said.

Bruno ordered a six egg omelet, a double side of bacon, and a double side of ham. It was my turn to smile at him.

The waiter went away.

"Look, I don't practice law. I've always been an advisor and I have handled delicate matters for Mario. Please confide in me so I can get you together with him. What is it you have to tell him?"

Bruno grinned. Ignored my question. "I read about you before I met him. He saved you when your car caught fire after an accident over there by Grand Central Market."

"That was a long time ago, but that was me." Eye contact good. He did not look away.

Bruno got serious, drank a couple gulps of the coffee he'd already had when I sat down. The Pantry mugs have the restaurant name painted on the heavy pottery.

"I'm getting out of LA, going to Florida, and I need money. Don't take me wrong, I'm not trying to hold him up or anything. If I didn't need the money, I'd just dump what I have to say and be done with it."

"You know money is not a problem for Mario or for me," I said.

"I know that. I don't think it's proper for me to discuss what I have with you or talk about how much money I need. I'm not even sure how much I need. I just want enough to make the move, settle in Miami, and who knows, maybe I'll do better there as a PI than I'm doing here. Only PI work I do lately is serving lawsuits and subpoenas. Got nothing going anymore."

I extended my hand across the table and touched his left hand, which was resting next to his silverware.

Bruno smiled. "You are a lovely lady. Glad you came instead of him. I went to his house and he threw me out. He was furious at me. You'd think I burned his house down."

The waiter was on top of his game. He brought my coffee just as I was about to call for it, and refilled Bruno's cup.

"He doesn't hate you. He's really a kind and generous man."

"I thought so when he hired me, but that changed quickly when hours later he fired me on the spot when the house was burning."

"Bruno, let's cut to the chase. I'll give you whatever money you need, but you need to tell me what it is you know. Someone is hunting him. It's not just the house." I took out the picture of the biker. "This person tried to kill him on the freeway. Do you know who is behind this?"

Bruno looked at the picture and handed it back. "I never seen that man in my life. I believe I know who is behind the house fire and possibly anything else bad that has happened in the three years since I was fired. What I heard was recent."

"What do you know?"

"Miss Melina, I need to tell him personally what I heard."

"You heard it how?"

"I heard it with my own ears. Not hearsay either. I would feel bad saying something to you. It might make you a target."

The food was delivered, and I realized why the place I'd heard so much about was so popular—their servings were huge. The three plates of food they brought for Bruno took up much of the table, followed by another plate with sourdough toast piled high.

"Okay, I'll go back and talk to him. How do we let you know?"

"I have some things I need to do that have nothing to do with this, then I'll call him. If he wants to meet, he can tell me when I call."

I didn't push it. I got up, moved over to him, leaned over and kissed him on the cheek. He smelled like Dial soap. He started to get up. "Eat your food while it is hot," I said. "Bruno, be sure to call him."

"Count on it, Miss Melina." He smiled up at me.

I crossed the street to where my car was parked. Johnson saw me coming and had the door open when I got there.

"Which market, ma'am?"

I had tons of work to do, but I needed to see that stubborn man in person. "Take me to the house. You can get something to eat while I run across the street to see Mario, then we'll leave for Montebello."

"Yes, ma'am." Johnson was always formal with me. I stopped fighting him on what to call me years ago.

Mario would think I was coming for another round. I never visit him in the middle of the work day like this. Just remembering the night we'd had last night had my body halfway to another orgasm.

The gatekeeper alerted him that I was there. Mario was waiting at the front door with a shit-eating grin and a hungry twinkle in his eye.

"Back for seconds?"

"No time, Cuz, I'm here on serious business. Let's go to your office. It's important."

Mario saluted. "Yes, ma'am. Stairs or elevator?"

Pixie

When I called Jo and Niley to let them know about Melina meeting with Bruno, they already knew. Letty had told them. It had been a hectic day around here. At first, Boss seemed all tangled after he learned about the meeting, then he mellowed out and said that any call from Bruno should be given to him immediately.

If I had met with him instead of Melina, I would have forced him to take the money from me and tell me what he has. I got bread of my own. When I become a star, fuck me, I'll have so much bread I won't know what to do with it. I would have given Bruno the bread he wants, and head, right there at The Pantry, under the table. Melina just didn't try hard enough; I could tell when she was telling Boss about the meet. I remember when Bruno got hired, I saw him get a hard on, scoping me out with x-ray eyes. I remember him, big fucker, but I figured he was like other big ones. All muscle, no pecker.

Letty came in and sat across from me at the conference table. She had a fresh batch of telexes. "Give me some," I said to her.

I could cum just from thinking of me singing and banging away at my guitar or some other instrument. Crowd cheering me on. I know it will happen. I feel it.

"You looked spaced out," Letty said, and slid some paper to me.

"I was just thinking of when I get famous. You wouldn't understand." I was just kidding with her. I love Letty.

"Bitch, what do you mean I won't understand? Think I just fell off the truck or something?"

I stuck my tongue out at her and giggled. She returned the tongue thing and the laugh.

"I talked to Jo and Niley, told them about Bruno," she told me.

"Big mouth bitch, I called to tell them, and they already knew." I bunched up the top telex I had just read into a ball and threw it at her.

"I didn't tell anyone else." She ducked, and the paper ball smacked the wall and rolled on the floor.

"I'm bored," I told her.

"He's not at his desk. Where is he?"

"Maybe fucking Tricia somewhere in the house," I said with a giggle.

Letty laughed. "Want to go to the kitchen and bake cookies?"

"Fuck, I'm no baker. That's you."

"Okay then, come to the kitchen and watch me bake some."

We went down to the kitchen. Letty can bake like Betty Crocker. I'm so jealous of her skills. I said, "Make donuts, too. Want me to turn on the deep fryer for you?" I figured that's the least I can do.

"It'll have to be cake donuts. Yeast ones have to rise."

"You're the chef," I said. My mouth was already watering. We'd both have to do an extra hour of karate to burn it off, but it would be worth it.

"Cake donuts and cookies. Anything else?" Letty asked. "Just sit there. I'll handle the deep fryer when I'm ready."

She's the best.

Mario

Jack Fino and I met for one of our regular lunches at PDC. I had not called him about Bruno. It was noon and the place was busy, but I had a table that they'd saved for me with a one-hour notice. I figured I'd hold off on the Bruno questions till we had lunch.

"Here we are." Jack chuckled, raised the sparkling water glass the waiter had just poured for him, and we clicked a silent toast.

"Bruno still doing work for you?"

"On occasion. He's horrible with people, his manners are shit, and he looks like the Hulk, but he's a good investigator. There's a working brain under all that beef," Jack said. "Why do you ask?"

"The day I move in, Bruno comes over, sneaks past my gate. Has something on his mind, but I shut the door in his face. Anyway, he keeps calling. Leaves a message about meeting at The Pantry, but I didn't show. Melina showed for me."

Jack put down his glass and leaned forward, showing a keen interest. "What did he want?"

I told him the story. "Says he's moving to Miami, needs money."

Jack scooted his chair forward, his voice eager. "Give him the money."

"For starters, our actual meeting hasn't been set up. I'm waiting for him to call."

I'm no poker player, but if Jack was involved or knew anything of Bruno's intent, that knowledge was securely hidden behind his poker face. If Jack knew about this, nothing about him betrayed it. He was all eager curiosity.

"You want me to contact him and expedite the meeting?"

"Jack, please don't. If he's hungry, he'll surface."

"You're right. Wait for him to call," Jack said, focusing on the menu that we both knew from start to finish. His eyes were glued to the list of appetizers. "I haven't used him in a long time," Jack continued. "I'm not so hands-on lately, and I outsource some of the things I used to do personally. However, some of the work he's done for me over the years was delicate and sensitive. He always came through. I'm sorry my referral of him to you turned out the way it did."

In the three years since my house burned down on Bruno's watch, this was not the first time Jack had apologized.

"Jack, it's not your fault. Melina has hammered it in my head that it's not like Bruno torched the house intentionally. I'm pissed at his screw-up, but it was my fault for plugging a square peg in a round hole. Maybe he's good at investigations, but that doesn't make him a good security guard, especially with his drinking problem."

On the way home, I wondered what I would do with the information if I really got it from Bruno. Was the information just about the house fire, or did it have something to do with the biker and my torched car at the airport? Fuck, I wished he'd hurry up and call already. Was Oscar's death connected to this, and if so, would Bruno know that? Fuck.

My next step hinged on what he had to say. The cops had come up with nada. I knew I should probably call the arson investigator handling the house case and the Pasadena Police Department detective and give them the goods on Bruno.

But no, I wasn't going to do that because they had proved incompetent in chasing down the arsonists. I had no faith that the justice system would bring the guilty to justice. And if there were secrets to be had, I wanted to have them first. I listened for the phone for the rest of the day, waiting for the call from Bruno. I had waited days with no call, but I felt like Fino would get him to call me even though I'd told Fino not to.

The phone rang. I picked up and turned my chair to face the view out of my office window. Gray sky darkening to dusk. Nothing much to see but the reflection of the room in the plate glass, but I wasn't really looking. Bruno was on the phone, and he had a hundred percent of my attention.

"I have something to tell you."

"I hear you have something to sell."

"I need the bread. You need what I got. When I tell you what I heard and who it was, it will all fall together for you."

I wanted to tell him to come right over. "Be here at ten in the morning."

"I'll be there."

"Come through the front gate."

"Just like I did when you wouldn't see me."

I let it go. Maybe he was lying to keep me wondering how he got in without the guard seeing him. As soon as I hung up, I wondered if Jack had pushed Bruno to call me. I scooted the chair around and caught Pixie, Letty, and Tricia in the doorway, arms crossed, looking petulant like eavesdropping statues.

"Bravo, Boss," Pixie sang out.

"Why tomorrow? Why not right now?" Letty asked.

"He wants us to sit and wonder all day and tonight, that's why," Tricia said.

With that, they all filed back to the conference room. I was a little irritated that I can't keep anything secret from them. Their noses are into everything. But I called and brought Melina up to date. "Thanks for meeting with him," I said again. "Even if nothing comes out of this, thank you."

"Oh, please, Cuz. On Sunday you can do a payback."

"Do I have to wait that long?"

"Tomorrow's Thursday, almost the weekend. That's not long."

I hung up and joined the girls in their half of the office. Miguel brought us up a bucket of ice, glasses, a tray of sandwiches, a huge basket of fries, and warmed china plates to put the food on. We picked out canned sodas from the little office fridge and sat at the clear end of the conference table to eat and talk. I reached for the burger, but Pixie shook her head and grabbed it. I let her have it. If Pixie wanted the burger, it wasn't what it looked like. She was in a meatless phase. I'd already found out for myself that Miguel grinds up a patty that looks like beef but is actually some kind of veggie-bean concoction. Letty, Trish, and I pigged out on actual roast beef and sliced chicken. We all pigged out on the fries. Fresh, hot. It's good to have a personal chef.

"How creepy that he knows something when the cops and fire guys keep telling us they have nothing to report," Letty said, dipping her fry in ketchup.

"Melina said he overheard a conversation, not like he was investigating," Pixie said, dueling for her share of ketchup.

"If I get any inkling at all that he's snowing me, I'll throw him out," I said.

"Fuck, you should have told him to come right over," Tricia said between bites.

"Maybe I should have, but I didn't."

"Can we be here?" Pixie asked.

"Ten in the morning is during your work day, so you'll be here. Here, but not in the meeting."

"Fuck, not fair."

"I'll bug your office," Letty said, getting up as though about to do the bugging right there and then.

"Good idea." I looked at Tricia. "Can you handle it, Baby?"

"Probably, but we don't have what I need to do it," Tricia said.

The guardhouse had twenty monitors using the newest in CCTV technology, with overlapping viewing fields of the house's exterior. That had no connection with what went on in my office, and it was nonsense to bug it anyway.

Niley surprised us. "Hope you don't mind company. I wanted to see you guys."

Tricia was already gone, but Pixie and Letty greeted her with enthusiasm and I picked her up, cradled her, and kissed her. "I wish you were here with us every day."

"Just say the word, Boss."

I kissed her again. "Let's go to the wine room. We had enough sodas for dinner. Letty, get Miguel to put dinner together for Niley."

"No, I'm fine. I had dinner."

Betty came over to massage Letty and me. She didn't expect a crowd, but she was always game. The more work, the better.

"Baby, set up here, and let Niley go first. Just maybe we get lucky and she shows off her fine ass."

We were in the wine room, jukebox on, dimmed lighting, perfect ambiance. Niley was out of her clothes before Betty was done putting up the table and placing the linens.

"Boss, you want a close-up, or you okay from here?" Niley asked.

"Do a three-sixty," Letty chimed in.

"Yeah," Pixie agreed.

Niley did; she was beautiful.

"She has abs. Gorgeous abs," Letty said.

"You going to lose the abs if you don't work them out every day," Pixie warned.

"I can kick your ass, Pix. I may not be working my abs much, but I'm in fine shape, going for another belt." She positioned herself, ready to fight, jokingly, fully naked, no shame, as always.

She got on the table, face-down. I sipped my wine. "You're so hot," I said.

In the morning, we sat down to have breakfast. Even Betty had stayed the night, though Niley left without breakfast. Leaving, Niley said, "I have tons of work to do. Not fair I pile it all on Jo. I had a fabulous night. I love you all."

"You have a dozen people working for you and Jo. It's not like you can't take a day off," Pixie said.

Niley looked from Pixie to Letty. "I'll be back before long, I promise. I miss you. Last night was bitchin.'"

We found our way to my office and waited for the clock to show ten o'-clock.

Noon arrived. By that time, Melina had already called three times to check if Bruno had showed. I wasn't steaming or boiling, only disappointed. A big part of me had believed Bruno had something to say that would solve the mystery of who torched my house and hired the freeway shooter, and hopefully more.

Pixie and Letty wandered back to their usual spots, pouting with disappointment. They started reading print-outs across from each other on the conference table in my office.

I went down to the gym, stripped, and started the workout I had skipped that morning at five. An hour later, soaked in sweat, I went into the steam room to sweat some more. Thirty minutes later, I was upstairs in my office, feeling steam-cleaned.

"Did you get a good workout?" Pixie asked.

"I did. I'm starved."

"That's a good sign," Letty said, getting up to reach the intercom and buzz Miguel. "What would you like?"

A minute later, Miguel was across from my desk.

"Some soft tacos with your special hot sauce. Beef. Refried jalapeño beans with lots of cheese, and anything else you think I should have in order to get over today's disappointment."

"I got it, Boss."

"Hurry," Pixie said, "I just got hungry listening to the order."

"Me too," Letty said.

We ate again in my office at the conference table with the television tuned to the news.

A field reporter was on location in Chinatown. The camera started panning across an old Chevy and pulled back to focus on the reporter.

"Two witnesses reported to police that a motorcycle pulled up to the driver's side and fired at the driver." The camera did a slow scan of the wrecked car and the reporter continued. "The identity of the deceased is being withheld until relatives are notified."

Pixie's face went white. "Didn't Bruno used to live in Chinatown? Does he still live there?"

I didn't remember what kind of car Bruno drove. It had been three years since he worked for me, hired and fired so fast, and I had no paperwork on him. If I hadn't fired him, he'd have been living in the back with the rest of my house staff. I felt a sick sinking feeling in my gut. I didn't know, but I knew. I knew the dead person they were not showing on television was Bruno. Pixie and Letty both had the same shocked expression.

We were all thinking it. "I bet you that's Bruno," I said it aloud.

"Oh my God," Letty said, her eyes on the television. "Don't say that."

I wondered exactly when the shooting happened. I thought about the drive time from Chinatown to Pasadena. The report we were watching was not live. The shooting had occurred right about the time Bruno would have been headed to the house.

I dialed the direct number to a deputy coroner in downtown Los Angeles. I hadn't talked to him since I'd worked car crash cases, but his number had not changed. Neither had mine. We went way back. When I was chasing accident cases, Hank gave me the names of decedents who had died in or because of a vehicle. Many times, he also helped with names and addresses. I would then go hunt out the relatives. I told his answering machine, "Hank, this is Mario. Call me. Same number." If things were still working as they used to, Hank would now be connected to Carson, who had taken over my contacts after I sold them to Oscar.

In under thirty minutes, Hank called me back.

"I need a favor, man. Tell me that guy who got shot is not Bruno."

"I can't tell you that, preliminarily because Bruno is who I got," Hank said. "Need someone to ID him, then we can release his name. Sheriff is looking for next of kin." The case would be handled by the Los Angeles County Sheriff's Homicide Division. I always took good care of Hank. Even though we didn't talk anymore, and he didn't send me cases, he remembered my being generous. Hank was motivated by cash. "Homicide got everything," Hank said, "but I have a copy of his driver's license."

He read out the address, and I wrote it down.

"Eventually an inventory of personal property will show up from the sheriff's office, and I'll get a copy for you."

I told my team the news before I called Melina. I called Jo and Niley. We were dumbfounded by the news. Murder was a serious crime, but on top of that, I felt involved in this mess. Bruno was going to spill his guts to me and he got offed before he could.

"Who the fuck hates me so much to do this?"

"I know what you mean, but it seems to me it was Bruno who got the short end of the stick."

"You don't know, Boss. This could be a coincidence. Bruno is...was...entirely capable of pissing somebody off on his own. There was a reason he wanted to get out of Dodge," Tricia said.

"Give me a fucking break," Pixie said, anger in her voice, staring at Tricia.

"We don't know. We won't know until we have all the facts," Tricia said.

Letty decided to side with Pixie. "Fuck, Tricia, I thought you were smarter."

"He was probably going to give you a big fish, so he was silenced," Pixie said.

"You don't know how many times I had a case and things that looked one way turned into something entirely different. You know how they say when you hear hoofbeats, think horse, not zebra. But there are a hell of a lot of horses in this game. Somebody took him down. Might have been the same as who was after Mario. Maybe not. I doubt Bruno cared if he stepped on anybody's toes."

"It looks bad," I said. "Bruno was taken out, and I believe his murder could be connected to his plans to come over here to give me evidence. Hank will let me know what personal property was taken from the scene. I really would like to get my hands on his notes." I pushed the possibility of breaking and entering into the back of my mind.

I handed Tricia the Chinatown address.

"Trish, it's a homicide. Probably a bunch of cops are at his house. Go snoop around. Not even sure the address is his. Not even sure what we're looking for. He said he overheard a conversation."

"Got it, Boss. I always kept records. Maybe he did, too."

"Careful," Pixie said.

Letty said, "Call me if you need bail, bitch."

"Yeah, right," Tricia said. "You'd want payback with my body."

"That's we," said Pixie as Tricia walked out of my office.

By the time Tricia returned, we had moved to the wine room to sip Chateau Lafite Rothschild 1961. It was probably one of the most comfortable places in the house. Maybe it was the seating that I like so much.

"I thought you'd call," I said.

"I wanted to get back here fast." Tricia put a stack of pictures down and took a seat as Letty filled her glass. Pixie grabbed the pictures, looked them over and passed them on.

"No cops yet. Took me sixty seconds to pick the padlock. He lived in one room. Fucking trashy. A dump. Check the Polaroids."

"Anyone see you?"

"Come on, Boss. I'm a pro."

Pixie giggled. "A pro at what?"

Letty joined in. "I'm listening?"

Tricia and I ignored the two jokesters.

The stack of pictures got to me. Not much to see. Bruno had lived in a one-room walk-up. Gray painted wood floor, rough wood, with some gaps and lots of wear. An antique claw-footed tub was in the middle of the room, centered between a mattress on the floor on the window side and a smaller day bed that had probably come from someone's trash. A couple of window shutters were open, showing some plants on the sill struggling to live. I wasn't surprised to see he had a set of weights. Mail and books were piled on a tiny refrigerator in the corner. It was spotless, and it looked like someone had recently painted the plaster walls white. The big old house had been broken into apartments, and he was living in the original large bathroom. In spite of the paint, I could practically smell the mold and dry rot.

"Any tapes? Anything you would call evidence?"

"Not even a tape recorder. If he had one, maybe it was on him. No spy equipment. He barely owned anything. A clock radio. An old television. A few changes of clothes in an end table and in the closet, two sport jackets and one suit. Trash was full of beer cans, TV dinners, and take-out containers."

I felt a twinge of remorse, not only because he was dead, but because this barren room was the sum total of his life. If I had not fired him, he would have lived in the quarters behind my house. But there's no turning back the clock.

Bruno was a stranger to her, but when I called Melina, she cried, which wasn't like her.

"I feel horrible," she said between sniffs. "I picture him right now sitting across the table from me. He was a good person, Cuz. This is terrible."

"Pix, open another bottle. I should call Jack Fino," I said.

"Boss, let him call you. Let's see how long it takes for him to find out Bruno is dead." Letty tilted her head like a bird. "Or to tell you."

"It's on the news, not like it's a secret," I said. I didn't call him.

Pixie handed me the bottle that had been breathing. "Yeah. Why let him in on your coroner friend? You think Jack's showing you all of his cards? I bet not. He's too much of a lawyer for that." Pixie held out her glass for more.

I raised my glass. "Trish, you did good."

"I didn't find anything, so how good is that?"

"Don't be hard on yourself," Pixie said. "Fuck, you got in."

"How do we know it was his place?" Letty asked. "I mean, know for sure?"

"I took pictures of the box of bills. Gas and electric. His name. See the picture of his phone? His number is right there, typed in the center of the dialer. I picked it up and heard the dial tone, so I know it was live. I was wearing latex gloves, but I didn't move much around."

"We're back to square one," Letty said.

"We've been in square one for three years," Pixie said.

"A toast for square one." Letty raised her glass.

"Let's crash this somber fucking mood," I said. "Pix, roll a couple joints."

Pixie giggled. Only she could giggle like that. "I thought you'd never ask."

I hate to hide behind alcohol and weed, but fuck—I'm human.

I kept thinking how the news had affected Melina. If I could only go back to the fire, be reasonable and not fire him. If he hadn't possessed the secret he wanted to tell me, he'd probably be alive. I knew there was a connection. There had to be a connection. Now that it was too late, I believed that Bruno had something real to tell me.

Jack Fino

January 1983

"My bank account is close to empty," Janice said on the phone, "I thought you were coming over with cash."

"I don't want to go over there. You being drunk all the time gets old for me," I said.

"A hooker doesn't do what I do to you, bastard that you are."

Janice always punched low. "I remember when you were nice. Never heard you talk like that when Oscar was alive."

"I never had to worry about money when Oscar was alive. Blame that peasant, Mario. He did this to me. Oscar died broke. Left me in the street. The peasant lives in a mansion, all bought and paid for with my money."

"Come off it, Janice. I hear this every time we talk. Drop it. Oscar was a greedy bastard. He wanted more and more cases and was blinded by what he thought the cases would settle for. He could have told Mario that he didn't want more cases. Instead, he kept borrowing from me and from the banks, to pay for the new cases and the big office expense that went with it—"

Janice interrupted me. "You probably had him shot dead to collect the insurance and pay off the money he owed you. You're despicable! You always defend that peasant—you prick! When you get horny, let him rim you like you like. Let him suck your old fucking cock."

After she hung up on me, I saw the perch was empty, and went from room to room looking for Bogart and Cleo. I found them on the office perch by the cabinet that held the nutcracker bowl. I pulled it out and cracked a couple of walnuts, splitting the pieces between them. One for them, one for me.

"Bogart, that woman needs to go. Someday she's going to mouth off to the wrong person, and then what will I do?"

"Fuck her," Bogart said.

"Bad word, stupid," Cleo said.

"Fuck her," Bogart repeated.

Following that kind of advice is what got me into this mess. I put the nuts back in the cabinet. I needed something stronger, and reached for the brandy.

Mario

In the morning, I was up at five. Ten minutes later, without rousing Pixie and Letty, I was into my workout. The Bruno tragedy had made me maudlin. I wondered if Bruno had a family; I couldn't remember talking to him about anything personal when I hired him three years ago. I felt obligated to do something for him. Maybe a proper funeral. I hadn't yet heard from Fino, but that meant nothing.

After I showered, I almost dressed, but was lured back to bed with my two girls, who were still sound asleep. A few minutes later, Melina walked in.

"I figured you'd be up."

"I've been up, worked out, showered. Come get in bed with us."

"How can you think about sex when Bruno was killed?"

"I mourned yesterday like crazy. I feel bad, yes. If there's something I can do for him, his funeral, anything like that, I'm ready."

"I'm sorry, Cuz. Maybe I wouldn't feel as bad if my thirty minutes with him wasn't still fresh in my head. I liked him." She put on a smile. "Go ahead, go fuck the twins in your bed. I got to go to work."

"You're so dirty," I said.

"I wish I had time, I'd show you how dirty."

"Promises, promises."

Just before noon, Jack Fino called with the news. "Bruno was shot dead last night."

"I heard about the shooting on TV." I spoke too fast, without any explanation from Jack yet. I tried to cover up the blunder. "Was that him? When he didn't show up, I wondered about it. How did you find out?"

"His mother called me."

"His mother? You knew his mother?" I knew Bruno had been a friend, but not that he'd been a family friend.

"She used to be a client," Jack said.

I felt a jolt of tension hit. That's when I knew he was upset. He was close-mouthed when it came to clients. If she was a client, he would not normally say so.

"Bruno had been working for me when she got pulled over for drunk driving. He recommended me to her. I got the case dropped."

I was glad to hear she was a former client. That was better than a family friend. Not as close a tie. "I never got a chance to meet with him on that matter I told you about. He never showed up."

"I think the shooting was a random thing."

"Does he have a big family?"

"Just his mother. Father died a few years back. She's a nurse over at Veteran's Hospital. They never got along very well, but that's changed now that he's dead. She couldn't stop crying on the phone. Last night, a sheriff contacted her and told her about the shooting."

"If there's anything I can do, please tell me, Jack."

"I got it covered. I'm supposed to talk to her later today."

"Do you think there's a connection between whoever's stalking me and his getting offed?"

"My opinion? No. Some random shooter shot him. Some chump had your house burned and sent that biker after you. That's what I think."

I thought a moment. "Some chump had enough money to hire somebody to get the job done. The biker didn't follow me to San Antonio on his own dime. Some chump burned up my car at the airport."

"We don't know if the torching of your house and car and the biker are connected."

"Jack, a second ago you said you thought the chump who had my house burned sent the biker after me. Which is it?"

There was silence. I could hear Jack breathing, maybe upset about Bruno, more upset than I had figured.

"Bruno overheard a conversation proving who burned my house," I continued, "and it was connected with the biker on the freeway. Bruno was supposed to be here yesterday at ten in the morning to sell me the information."

More silence. "You didn't tell me that." Jack sounded rough, maybe irritated at being out of the loop.

"He called, and I told him to be at my house at ten. When we had lunch the other day, I told you I was waiting for him to call to arrange a meet."

"Yes, you told me that."

"I feel bad. It makes me feel like there's a connection."

Silence. "That's life, Mario. We feel bad after a person dies. Like his mother. Now she regrets everything she did and didn't do for him."

I felt like he had just taken a punch at me, but let it go. "I overreacted when I fired him. I know that now. I hired him to do work that I now have a three-man crew doing with the help of dozens of security cameras."

Jack was breathing heavy again. Sounded upset. "I'll call you later when I know what his mother is planning for him."

"I know you were close, Jack. My deepest condolences."

Jack didn't respond. He just hung up.

When I told Pixie and Letty about my talk with Fino, Pixie went off. "So now he's pissed at you for firing Bruno three fucking years ago?"

"Maybe. He was upset over something."

"He's probably taking his death hard," Letty said.

"Maybe we all are."

Pixie had stayed last night. I expected that she was planning to go home. "If you want to leave early, go, Baby."

"Lainie has karate tonight and Nanny Delores is there to monitor. Can I stay another night?"

Letty licked her lips. "Yeah, stay, and I'll—"

Pixie said, "I'll sit on your face, bitch."

"Promise," Letty said, bubbly as champagne.

"You don't need to ask. Stay as long as you want." I finally got a word in.

With the AIDS thing going around, I wasn't inclined to go out shopping for pussy, and I hated to be alone. Letty made sure I wasn't alone. When Pixie spent the night, it was more company. Great way to spend a night. Niley's surprise visit and stay-over was a treat. Having Betty there had made it perfect.

I tried hard to stay busy looking at properties and businesses for sale. Much of the material was from Tricia's hunting and research and from a broker friend who went back years with me. He'd sold me my first apartment building and kept egging me on and on until I amassed much of what I had today. No matter how I tried to concentrate, I kept looking at my watch, hoping it was time to call it a day. That was funny, since I was the boss.

It took more than a week for Hank to get back to me with the details of the personal property found in Bruno's possession and his car. There was a pocket tape recorder with a tape loaded. Bruno had three hundred and eighteen dollars in his wallet, and a driver's license. No credit cards. He had business cards in his wallet with his home phone number, which Tricia had taken a picture of. "Homicide has everything," Hank said.

"Any way at all to get a copy of the tape or a transcription?"

"I doubt it, but here are the names of the detectives handling the case."

I wrote down the names and telephone numbers, thanked Hank, and told him I'd catch up with him with the expected green he always got from me when he came through.

"There's a tape!" I told Pixie and Letty.

"Fuck me!" Pixie said with excitement.

"And me!" Letty said.

"Homicide has the tape and everything else," I said.

I called Melina and told her. She didn't say what the girls had said, but close. "Fuck!"

Later, when Tricia returned to the house, I told her.

"I been seeing this retired FBI," she said. "He's well connected, but not sure what he can do with this because it's not federal. Want me to check?"

"No," I said, "but thanks for the offer, Baby. I need to sit on this a bit."

"How long this been going on with you and the FED?" Pixie asked.

"It's nothing. I met him when I was checking on a building for sale."

"Have you dated?" Letty pressed.

"Stop it," I said. "Let Tricia have a life."

"He's just a friend. Yes, we dated twice."

"Did you fuck him?" Pixie wouldn't let up.

"Nope."

"I don't believe it," said Letty with a toothy smile.

"Boss, tell these two pests to stop."

"You calling us pests?"

We all laughed, Tricia too.

"No wonder you don't come to bed with us," Pixie said.

"I do, too."

"Barely," said Letty.

"Stop," I repeated. "Let's get serious. There's a tape out there. How do we get it?"

I learned after the fact that Bruno's mom had her son cremated. She told Fino there would be no service. I was tempted to call the detective in charge of my house torching, as well as the arson investigator. I wanted to tell them about Bruno's claim to know who burned down my house. Maybe the detectives or the sheriff could get a transcription of the tape, and what if they did, could there be something on the tape to hurt me? Their getting the tape didn't put it in my hands. In the end, I decided not to call them, just as I never reported the biker on the freeway. If there was anything in that tape with my name on it, the sheriff handling Bruno's homicide would certainly come see me. Best to wait and see.

Pixie

Letty and I were in her bedroom at Casa Luna.

"When I was a corner girl, there was this cop out of Hollenbeck Station that always gave me a bad time. He'd make me sit in his car and counsel me that I was too young to be doing what I was doing, and he threatened time and time again to turn me over to child services. He always stopped the counseling bullshit when I reached for his cock. Ten minutes later, he was out of my life till the next time he got horny."

"Did he at least pay you?" Letty asked.

"Get serious—fuck no, cops are cheap."

"So, what are you telling me the story for?"

"I'm thinking how I can get that tape from the cops who have it."

Letty laughed. She laughed so hard, I started laughing.

"Why the fuck are we laughing?" I finally asked Letty. Her eyes were all wet, but I don't think from laughing. She feels bad for how I grew up.

"You so crazy, Pix. How you plan to get to the cops?"

"Fuck you, bitch, at least I'm thinking how to help the cause."

We were fully clothed, lying on the bed, getting ready to go back to the fourth floor to work.

"Come over here and let me kiss some sense into you," Letty told me.

I did as she asked, my mind rolling around about how we could get the tape.

"You French-kiss so good," I told her.

I remember years ago when Mario kissed me like that, once I asked him to take a guess at how many cocks I'd sucked when I was a corner girl with the mouth his tongue was probing. I don't remember why I said it, probably feeling down because there's some shit you can't forget. He said my being experienced was hot, and kept kissing me. Funny how some guys can make you feel like dirt under their feet. Mario makes you feel like a fucking queen.

Mario

No one had taken potshots at us in three years. The shotgun on the seat was maybe two years ago. Nothing since. Maybe the sponsor of the terror went broke or had died and gone to hell. Maybe that's why everything had been quiet. Bruno being shot now made it all fresh again. The only thing I knew now is that it felt like a whole team of ghosts were walking on my grave.

Niley

Our management office is located in Monterey Park, California, five minutes from Mario's Aunt Carmen's house, seven minutes from Pixie's house, and less than twenty minutes to Casa Luna. After I spent the night with Boss, Pixie, Letty, and Betty, I realized how dumb it is that we go weeks without seeing each other. It's like Jo and I have been severed from the team.

Jo is married, meaning that she's not all hot and ready to spring over to his house to spend the night, but can't she come over just to visit? Then Jo can go home, and I can spend the night. Everything has become so formal. We send monthly reports of the rental income and expenses. Sometimes we send it by messenger, when it would be so easy to drop it off at the house. Damn it. I miss them. Jo and I are making so much money managing the apartments, it's a delight, but I'd give up my share to be back on the team, just to be there, around them. Being around them, I feel beautiful. I feel accepted, and part of something.

I see the way he looks at me. I feel the lust, same as I did when I first met him, years ago. It was a wild ride, first chasing car accidents, train and bus crashes, then plane crashes. I'm proud of all the stamps in my passport. I'm going to hate it when I renew, and they give me a new one that has no stamps. I would never have gone anywhere if it wasn't for him.

My sister Tanis was a nurse at a hospital in East Los Angeles. She had two kids; I had two kids. We lived together, and I took care of the kids. Mario and Tanis were occasional lovers. She used to say there were two good reasons to find a car accident case for Mario. The first was that he always gave her money for the lead. The second reason was that after he came over to get the details about the case and give her the money, they met at a motel, where they made the best love ever. One time when they spent the night together and were kissing goodbye outside the room they'd been in, a shooter came from behind Mario, and shot them both. Mario survived; she died. When I first met this man that Tanis had talked about so much, I was struggling to keep a roof over our heads, and he asked me to work with him. I never looked back. I always knew he saw Tanis in me. After she was gone, I ditched my glasses, so the resemblance showed more. We looked alike, though I always figured she was much prettier than me. For a long time, he'd accidentally call me Tanis, followed by an apology. It made me feel good, like she wasn't really gone. It was Mario who coached me to get a live-in for the kids then, Pixie and I worked out how to split Nanny Delores. It allowed me to try selling gift baskets, buy that ramshackle old house of mine, and then work for him and escape being cooped up at home with no way out. There is nothing I wouldn't do for him.

Chapter 3
February 1983
Trimming Loose Ends

Mario

The phone rang during a usual day in my home office. Pixie picked up.
"Matias on line one," she said over the intercom.

Matias was a lawyer I'd worked with before. I picked up, and we talked in Spanish for a few minutes. After some cordial remarks, Matias told me why he was calling.

"The case settled almost a year ago, and I don't have my cut of the attorney's fees. I'm sorry to bother you with this, but I've called Gonor's office three times and I'm getting nowhere."

Matias was a lawyer in Mexico City. I had just started with Gonor when the plane crash occurred there, and my team and I signed a number of families. Matias signed eight families who'd lost eight loved ones in the tragedy. I convinced Matias that it takes an expert in aviation litigation to maximize the compensation for the families, and most lawyers, including Matias, admitted he'd never handled a plane crash before.

I made a deal with Matias that Gonor would handle the case from start to finish and Matias would receive twenty-five percent of the attorney's fees that Gonor received when the case was concluded, either by settlement or by a court.

In addition, I paid Matias an advance of two thousand US dollars for each family. He had eight families, so I gave him sixteen thousand dollars. Matias was not the first attorney I had made a deal with like this. Before Gonor it was Oscar. Deals were not always identical, but all deals put the burden on the law firm I was representing to handle the case and pay up when the case settled.

Soon as I was off the phone with Matias, I called Gonor.

"I'll check on this," Gonor told me with concern. "I don't handle the accounting, but I'll get to the bottom of it and get a wire out to Matias."

I wondered if Matias was the only person not paid in the three years I had been doing business with Gonor.

"Do me a favor. Have someone call me when it's done. I'll call Matias to let him know he'll be getting a wire."

"Mario, I said I'd handle it, and I will. No need for you to messenger messages."

I heard irritation in his voice, and that irritated me all the more.

In a voice louder than normal, I said, "I want a call back letting me know it's handled. It's been a year since the case settled; Matias should have received his fees right after the clients got theirs."

Gonor hung up on me.

I called back and the receptionist, Lina, told me he was on a call. She swore it was true when I questioned her.

Ten minutes later, I called back. This time, Lina said he had just walked out the door and would be back shortly.

The next morning, I was in Chicago. I arrived at Gonor's office at eight in the morning, sharp. He was not in.

"Mario, how do you want your coffee?" Lina asked.

"Black, please."

"You can wait in the conference room. Let me show you in."

"It's okay," I said, "I know the way."

Just as I started to walk out of the reception area, the entry door to the suite opened and there was Gonor, all decked out in a sharp suit. He saw me, and it was like nothing had happened. He had his hand out as he walked over to me.

"What a surprise," he said.

I was going to slap his hand away, but that would have been stupid, especially since Lina was back with my coffee and there were two people waiting in the reception area. We shook hands, and I followed him into his office.

"What brings you here?" he asked.

The door shut behind me. We were alone. "I came here to kick your ass for hanging up on me," I said with whatever anger was left over from the day before.

"Come on, I hang up on my wife all the time and she doesn't beat me up. Sit down, let's talk."

I let the wife thing pass and took a seat across his desk. "When I'm in the field on a case and I make a deal with anyone on your behalf, that deal better be as solid as if I had made it on my own behalf."

Gonor was calm, sitting. I wasn't sure if his good humor was to cover up anxiety over me being in his face or if that was just him. I didn't know him that well. I rarely saw him, talked to him on phone all the time. Without face-to-face meets, sizing up a person is tough.

"I am not questioning any deal you ever made. I approved them all, even the one with Matias. Like yourself, I have a busy schedule. I just responded. I didn't feel an explanation was necessary."

"Explain now. I'm here."

"Mario, it takes a ton of money to operate a law firm. We have cases coming in all the time. Your caseload is huge and expensive. It's a godsend, but the balances fluctuate, and it can be difficult to stay afloat. I make certain that all clients get paid without delay when settlement funds come in, but there are delays paying association fees, delays with vendors who have liens. That doesn't mean I'm not going to pay. It's cash flow. As you know, I pay you immediately and always have. That's a big bite from my cash flow, especially when we have twenty or more clients that you sign. You know the size of your checks."

I felt myself calm down, and I didn't bother to interrupt him. He was giving it to me straight. I often wondered if my success at client development had not sent two other lawyers, including Oscar, to the poor house. Gonor might be on his way or already there. He just admitted he was borrowing from the client trust account, and even I know that's the quickest way to lose your license to practice law and even end up in jail.

Gonor continued. "I could tell you to stop sending cases, but that's hard to do. I keep hoping that our cash flow will improve by settling cases more quickly. Sometimes that happens. We coast for a while, get caught up, then wham—we're scratching again."

"It sounds like I need to pull out and let you breathe," I said. "You're paying me, but you aren't paying Matias. I hope he's the only person I'm hooked to that hasn't been paid."

"I don't know for sure, but I think Matias is the only one. I will get a wire out to him today, I promise."

"I'm going to hold you to that," I said, pointing my finger at him.

He grinned. "You're a big one. I don't want to mess with you, believe me. Fino has told me stories about you." He chuckled.

"Stories?"

"All good," Gonor said. "Fino thinks the world of you, and so do I."

"If that's true, don't ever hang up on me again. Just level with me. No bullshit."

Gonor got up, a signal we were done.

I remained seated. "Can you afford the next big case I bring you?"

"If I don't have the cash flow, I'll borrow the money. Don't worry about getting yours. I got you covered. Keep bringing them in."

I thought of Fino and how he loans money to lawyers. By the time the lawyer pays me for a case and covers the overhead and the high interest to Fino, is there anything left? I'm not Gonor's keeper. Is that even my problem?

"Just one thing I need assurance on," I said as I started for the door that would lead to reception.

"Matias' wire will be out of here in less than an hour," Gonor said, grasping my hand with both of his and putting a lot of emotion in that shake. He let go.

"Not that. Check with your accountant. If there are any other attorneys I brought you that haven't been paid on a settled case, you pay them right away."

Gonor extended his hand again, just one this time. "Deal, Mario. I'll do that today."

We shook hands.

"I'm not going to ask about the clients getting paid their settlements, because you said you take care of those payments right away, right?"

"Of course. Clients are paid, no exception." I turned for the door. He said, hesitantly, "I trust that the heart-to-heart talk we just had is our little secret?"

I turned to look him in the eye. "I'm not a snitch."

Two hours later, I was on a plane to Los Angeles.

Pixie had gone home. Miguel had the night off. That was okay for me, since Letty was great in the kitchen. It was eight at night. Letty had just made waffles and a dozen strips of crispy bacon. We stood around the large granite island and ate away.

"You are a great cook," I told her. I remembered when I used to live in my apartment and had to drive to PDC for breakfast and dinner.

"Waffles and bacon? That makes me a great cook?"

"You even heated the syrup," I said.

"You have a microwave for that."

I put my fork down and looked her in the face. She has a sweet face.

Her cheeks were rosy, perhaps because she'd spent too long standing over the waffle iron as it heated. There was a bit of flour on the tip of her nose. I wiped it off with my thumb.

"Have you ever tried Pixie's waffles? Or Jo's?"

Solemnly, she shook her head.

"Try them some time. They'd be good paddles for playing ping-pong."

"That bad?" she asked, trying not to laugh.

"Worse."

"I'm going to snitch you out and tell them what you said."

"They know."

I gave her a long hug. Our lips pressed against each other, sharing the flavor of syrup.

"I love you, Letty."

Her laugh was soft. We were close. Lip to lip.

"You love Melina, Pixie, Jo, Niley, and me."

"Yes."

"I love you, Boss." After a moment, she said, "Do we have any peanut butter?" She had a glint in her eye, and I knew she wasn't thinking of food.

"Of course," I said. "We should have a bunch."

"Been a long time since we had peanut butter. I know how you love it."

Had. The way she said it didn't mean peanut butter on toast. "Chunky or smooth?" I asked.

"Boss, we only have the one you like—chunky."

I abandoned my dinner and watched her walk to the pantry. She returned with a jar and dropped her jeans and panties right there on the kitchen floor. Letty was beautiful.

I'm much taller. It's something I hardly notice, but being naked in the kitchen, the difference is pretty noticeable. I lifted her on to the counter and applied the peanut butter to her anatomy.

"I want you right now. I can't wait. I'm so horny, I could scream." She wasn't screaming. Her words were coming out more like a moan.

"It's the peanut butter," I teased.

"It's your huge fingers."

My pants dropped to join hers. We gyrated against each other. Peanut butter was everywhere. She wrapped her legs around my waist. I cupped her bottom, her ass on my palms. I held her as she twisted and bounced, moving her body so that I was deep inside. Nothing existed but the feel of her.

Her ass bouncing on my hands.

Her legs gripping my waist.

The pressure thrummed until we were both spent. We went from the kitchen to the spa, where we showered in cool water, waiting for the steam room to heat up.

Then we lay on towels, head to head, fitted like puzzle pieces, with steam hissing around us, eucalyptus oil doing its thing. She was stretched out full length, going one way. My legs were bent, going the other.

"I'd be fucking lonely without you." It was so true.

"Got a secret," she whispered in my ear. "I look forward to when everyone goes home so I can have you all to myself."

"Thank you for the years you have been with me," I said. "You are so very special to me."

The steam was hot. I could barely see beyond her upside-down face.

"You're facing the wrong way," I said.

"That can be fixed," she said. She got up. I straightened my legs and rolled to my side to make room on the marble slab. She lay down beside me, skin to skin in a continuous embrace.

"Don't thank me, Boss."

Sometime later, we made it to my bedroom. I was sitting up in bed with the latest Robbins, and Letty had fallen asleep in my lap. I set the book aside, remembering when I'd hired her years ago, when Melina and I had first moved into the neighborhood. Melina had found me a chef, Miguel. Miguel was Letty's uncle, and they were a package deal. The two of them were estranged from their family—Miguel because he was gay, and Letty because she'd gone after her stepfather with a knife. While Letty was in juvenile detention, her stepfather's abuse ran off her mother. Afterward, only Miguel, fresh out of chef school, had been there for her. He was her mother's younger brother and stuck with her after.

Her sleeping self looks so young and naïve, it's difficult to think of what she'd been through before I hired them. She'd confessed early on that it had been so tight at one point that Miguel had tried robbing a liquor store with Letty in the getaway car, a terrifying unsuccessful jaunt into crime that they'd sworn never to repeat. I did not know everything about their lives before, only that they had moved all over, following Miguel's short-term gigs.

Luckily for me, Miguel had applied at Marron's Markets for a job that was already filled, then for a post at Melina's home. Melina, who already had a full crew, sent them to me. I had just moved into my house and hired a staff but had no cook. Miguel had been the perfect chef for me. At first, I had no idea what there was for Letty to do; but she found her place in my staff and in my bed, and eventually as part of my team. I could hardly imagine life without her now. She was as much a part of my life as Melina, Niley, Pixie, and Jo.

I talked to Fino on the phone and thought I would mention my trip to see Gonor, but I should have known—Fino knew everything.

"If I'm going to stay in this business," I said, "I need another lawyer or two who know aviation and can afford me."

"Gonor is still good for more; don't worry about getting paid."

"That's what he told me; said he'd borrow if he has to."

Fino laughed. "That's the lawyer answer to a money problem—borrow."

"That's good for you," I said.

"Yeah, but after they reach a certain peak, some can't afford to pay the monthly interest, then the interest starts accruing."

I thought about that for a few seconds. "How do you have the stomach for that?"

"Only a handful get to that point. Gonor is not there, and with any luck he'll make it through and straighten out his cash flow."

"Let's have lunch soon," I said.

"I'm looking forward to it," Fino said.

Then a siren's call from Olga.

"Amor, I just landed in Van Nuys, headed for New York. Want to come with me for a few days?"

I laughed. "I was just in Chicago."

"Drop whatever you got going and get over here. The crew is getting some sleep and we'll be off in five hours."

"Way too tempting," I said, getting up from my desk chair. "When do you want me there?"

"Soon as possible. We can roll around in bed while we wait."

"Where did you fly in from?"

"Colombia, non-stop. I slept for hours. Hurry, Amor. I so want to see you."

Two hours later, under a dull gray winter sky, I boarded the DC-9. I was casually dressed, jeans and a sweater layer. I'd packed a coat because New York was colder than Pasadena.

"Amor, shut the door and get your buns back here." Her voice came over the speakers and bounced off the fuselage. A minute later, I was in the bedroom on board where a very naked Olga was lying with her arms spread over her head.

"Come here, Papi."

Time flies, especially if you are having fun. We heard the crew arrive. At her insistence, we put on robes and went to the main cabin. The staff paid no attention to how we were dressed. In addition to the pilots, I saw three men who were stewards. The pilots wore captain's uniforms I recognized as AC— Pepe's airline, Aerolineas Colombia—in the same colors as the Colombian flag.

The stewards wore matching slacks and dress shirts. All of them were armed, their guns worn at the small of their backs, hooked in their waistband. If a gun went off accidentally, surely their asses would have been blown off, and we would be exploded through whatever hole they blew open. Seems a risky place to keep a firearm. I suppose they remove them when they are buckled in their jump seats.

The experience was almost déjà vu, since I'd been in this situation so many times before. I could recall entering this plane in all seasons, dressed in everything from a Hawaiian shirt and flip-flops to Armani in Ferragamo crocodile penny loafers.

One steward asked, "What's your pleasure?" He looked at Olga, then me, then back to her.

"I'll have a Merlot," I said.

"Same."

She smiled, and he went away.

We sat across from each other, a table between us, window on my left, window on her right. This cabin was decked out like a small living room.

"Thank you for coming with me, Amor."

"Are you on business?"

"A little business. If you have time, let's stay a couple days at the apartment. Si?"

I smiled. "Si." The stewards were not with us in the main cabin, but I wondered about them.

"I don't remember the stewards carrying guns."

"Pepe is being moody. After the shooter at the airport, he's being more careful. He decided I needed guns. Rare for him to do that. He always has an army, but normally not Camila and me. He's paranoid."

"He seemed calm when I talked to him," I said.

"Oh, he's calm. He's not scared. He just doesn't trust anyone right now."

"I'm glad he's got you guarded," I said. "You ain't getting no sympathy from me."

"As long as they give me breathing room, I don't care if they are there." She stretched like a cat and crossed her legs. "Pepe told me to say hi and give you a hug."

"You really deliver. That was more than a hug."

"Did you like?"

I turned that around. "Did you like?"

"No one fucks like you do. You so go out of your way to satisfy."

I could have said that I learned from Melina many years ago that it wasn't just about me getting off. I made sure that the girl—or the bed full of girls—I was with experienced memorable satisfaction. The truth is that I did not get around like I used to. I hadn't decided to cut back when the rumors started about a fatal venereal disease, but it had just sort of coincided with having a household that had everything—and everyone—I could possibly need. I wondered what Olga had heard of this epidemic.

"With this AIDS thing going around—"

She interrupted me. "Amor, the last person I fucked was you. Camila and other girls I may roll around with don't count."

"It's been more than a month since I saw you."

"Forty-six days," she said. "I could break it down to hours and minutes. Are you being careful?" she asked, uncrossing and crossing her long, tanned legs so that I could not miss them. Her long, slim feet were bare, the curve of her ankles a tender promise.

"Just my team. And Melina."

"This AIDS shit is fucking horrible."

"It is," I agreed.

"Amor, let's just get married."

"Baby, you don't want to get married."

Olga got out of her seat and straddled me, her face two inches from my face, her arms around me. "I'd marry you." We were not in turbulent weather, but the plane was bouncing a little. The seatbelt lights were on, but no one was going to say anything.

"I would be a terrible husband. You know how I fuck around."

She kissed me. Concentrated on the kiss.

"You could continue to fuck your team but no one else. Amor, sounds good to you?" She looked so serious. "Baby." She gave me a deep, wet kiss. "Let's go back to bed."

I spoke into her mouth. "Si, bed."

It was not the first time she brought up marriage, but she seemed more serious about it today. I stopped thinking. Olga always managed to consume my entire being with sex, including my brain. Afterward, we ate light, planning to eat a real meal somewhere in New York. As she showered, I glanced through the *New York Times*. Couldn't break the habit of scanning for plane crashes. I came across an article about the US DEA being in talks with Colombian officials, strategizing how to cut down the cartels. I knew that here in the states, the DEA confiscated property. Pepe's father had been a cartel heavyweight, according to Oscar and Camila. I had heard hints but had zero confirmation that Pepe himself was in that business. I thought he would not dirty his hands directly but put layers of hierarchy between himself and anything illegal. Still, he had money to burn, and it was coming from somewhere. Lots of somewheres. Then Olga was out of the shower in nothing but a shimmer of water on her skin and a towel around her hair. I put the newspaper aside. Thirty minutes later, we landed in New York.

As we reached the elevator, one of the three guards with us pulled out a walkie-talkie.

"I'm off. See you in eight," he said in Spanish. I was not close enough to make out the reply through the static, but I presumed his replacement was already somewhere in the building because a mobile radio like that only had a short range. As the elevator went up, one guard remained in the entry parlor of the building, and one stayed with us until he took his post just outside the apartment in the hallway.

"When do you sleep?" I asked him in Spanish.

Olga answered for him. "They rotate their shifts. Relief every four hours. Two of the five of them are always off duty."

"What about the guns? Are they licensed?"

"You don't see the guns, do you?"

I smiled, shrugged. "I get it."

The Camacho place was unlike Sami's penthouse in London, which took up the entire top floor. Several apartments were on this level. I seem to recall the hall having carpeting and heavy drapery, and I could see it had been redone. I did not remember the wooden floor being so finely polished, nor the uncovered windows at either end being quite so grand, or the mass of greenery clustered by the windows, east and west. Knowing Camila, she had probably ordered the changes. I felt a chuckle rise in my chest as I pictured Camila handling the demands of a homeowner's association.

I'd forgotten how great the New York apartment is. In the several years since I'd been here, there were a few differences. Some antiques. A massive buffet that had to be more than a hundred years old. Different paintings were hanging where others had been, no doubt assets purchased for LAI.

"Nice," I said, admiring one.

"I love it, too. Camila bought it at auction with four more last year. You have a good eye, Amor."

We were in the living room. Outside through the windows, I could see snow falling, but it was warm inside.

"Do you want to go out and feast?" she asked.

"Do you?" Standing by a window, I glanced at the condensation. Outside, the wind whistled and moaned like a wounded animal. She walked over and tucked her arm into mine. I tugged her into a kiss.

"Your call, Amor."

"What if we order in?"

She led me into the kitchen and opened a small drawer filled with printed sheets—many colors, many styles.

I reached in and pulled out a paper menu. They were all menus.

"Amor, perfect for me. I'd rather play right here. Take your pick. This is New York. They all deliver."

I woke to daylight showing through a gap in the blackout curtains though it was five California time—just my body alarm rousing me for my work-out. Through half-closed eyes, I watched Olga quietly get out of bed, leaving the curtains' electric remote sitting on the nightstand. The shower turned on. I was not inclined to remain in bed.

I showered in the other bathroom. Who knew why she was up so early, but if Olga was going out, I didn't plan on hanging out in the apartment. I layered for the outside—a t shirt over a long-sleeve thermal shirt and a cashmere sweater over that. She came out in a robe, her hair wrapped in a towel. Her face registered surprise when she saw me up.

"Amor, I'm sorry if I woke you."

My watch set on New York time said nine thirty. I kissed her. At home, by nine thirty, I would be deep into work after a long workout and one of Miguel's stellar breakfasts. "Good morning, Baby. This is early for you. You have business today?"

"Yes, an appointment this morning, then I'm free."

"Want me to go with you?"

In the walk-in closet, she dropped her robe, revealing her tall, willowy torso and long legs. She had the sleek, elegant physique of a model. I watched her open a drawer, inevitably feeling my appetite for her rise to the surface. She slipped her arms through a wispy piece of lace that did nothing to hide her assets.

"I'm only going to pay for a property that Camila bought. Are you sure you want to come along?" This wasn't news to me. Any time Camila purchased anything of significant value, it was Olga who came by at a later time to pay in cash.

She pulled on black pantyhose, more silky lingerie that belonged inside a men's magazine, and topped it with a sedate-looking business suit suitable for visiting an office.

"Unless you have an objection—"

She interrupted. "No objection. Come."

"Cool, Baby."

As coffee perked, Olga used a walkie-talkie to speak to one of the guards. I heard static. I filled our cups.

"Mario is coming with us. We'll be in the limo. The three of you follow in the Benz." She set the little radio aside. My house intercom had better reception.

"Baby, if you have to do all that just because I'm coming, I'll wait for you."

She took a sip of her coffee and tapped my lips with a fast kiss. "You're coming with me."

Thirty minutes later, Olga and I were in the limousine. On an empty seat were two of the Louis Vuitton suitcases that the Camachos must buy by the truckload. The 'boys' were behind us in a Mercedes.

"What did she buy?"

"A diamond."

I estimated two or three million per suitcase and split the difference. "Looks like five million," I said, gesturing to the luggage.

She smiled, shaking her head. "Amor, you missed it. Six million, five hundred thousand.[2]"

"Some diamond. What if you're getting ripped off?"

"No one would dare." She patted my hand as if assuring a small child. "I'm told it is gorgeous and worth twice as much." This came out of her mouth as casually as if she was talking about the ten-dollar tip she'd given the guy who'd

---

[2] $6,500,000.00 in 1983 had the same buying power as $16,418,094.26 in 2018

brought our dinner over last night.

Sitting in my safe in case I ever got married was the diamond ring that Sami had given me before she died. I had never had the huge stone appraised, but Melina said it would be worth more than a million. This diamond Olga was paying for must be something special.

"How do you know what it's worth? I mean, you have to be a jeweler."

Olga's laugh showed a flash of her beautiful teeth. "The diamond is worth more than I am paying."

Camila had told me before that she changed money to diamonds and used them to buy something else.

"Camila buys things with diamonds," I said.

"Camila wheels and deals," she laughed. "I don't think this diamond will be used as currency. At least not any time soon."

When the car pulled up to the Waldorf Astoria, we were wrapped up in each other. The driver stood outside until Olga gestured for him to open the door. I reached for the suitcases, but she said, "Amor, let the guard carry them."

I walked with her into the hotel, the guard tagging along behind us with the cash. The entry was the same as it had been the last time I was here, still owned by Hilton. The elegant shop that was our destination was in the lobby on the first floor. Ever since planning security for my rebuilt home, I'd been interested in security measures. I glanced to see if the storefront gate retracted into the ceiling or the wall and followed to join her in the jewelry store. Plate-glass windows, gold-painted lettering. Inside, there was a lot of marble, glass, platinum, and jewels, pretty much routine for a shop of this type.

A middle-aged man in a decent suit welcomed her by name. He came around the corner of the glass display cases and air-kissed her above both cheeks, European style. I didn't recognize his accent. He took the two suitcases from the guard with no word to me, as if I were not there. I figured each suitcase weighed about seventy pounds; he was in good shape. Olga made no introduction. Two guards remained in the car that was parked behind the limo at the hotel's front entrance. The one who had carried the bags returned to the car.

Olga went out the door. I stood there, stupidly waiting for the jeweler to bring her the stone. Olga opened the door from the lobby, peeked in, and gestured me outside. I followed.

"You didn't get the thing you bought."

"Amor, my job, I pay. Someone else will handle delivery. Let's go eat."

"All we had this morning is coffee. I'm starving! Smell that? Breakfast. Follow your nose," I said.

"I have somewhere else in mind," she said as we returned to the limo.

We pulled up in front of the Park Central Hotel. My favorite hotel in New York.

"Are we eating here?"

"Not if you don't want to, Amor."

"This is fine."

She told the driver to take an hour to eat and to pick up something for the guards, then she got me inside to a table. We ordered. The food was as good as I remembered, but what was running through my mind was the whole Camacho business. What a fucking operation. If Pepe was a cartel heavy, he sure did not keep a low profile. The Camachos certainly did fly around in jetliners doing their international doings. Maybe they believed their operations passed the smell test or that they had bribed all the wrong people in the right places. They were always running around with millions in US currency, like it was nothing. For years now, I have had millions of Camacho cash in my safes.

We ordered off the menu. A waitress brought coffee.

As we waited, I asked the question that had been on my mind since she refused my help outside the Waldorf.

"Why didn't you let me carry the suitcases? Don't you trust me?"

"Why involve you?" Olga asked.

That did not make much sense to me. I was already involved. My safe had seven million of Camacho cash, just waiting to be spent on some real estate deal I'd find. I was constantly reminded that there was plenty where that came from. I could not help remembering all the objections Melina had initially thrown up to my working with the Camachos. I was gearing up to argue with Olga over how involved I already was when our food arrived. By the time we were done eating, the subject had moved on, and I had thought better of rocking the boat. We had entered the Park Central Hotel at noon. It was two thirty when we left.

"We ate like piggies," Olga said, her fingers tugging at her waistband, though her torso was as lean as ever.

"No worries. We can fuck it off, Baby."

"I love it when you talk dirty to me."

The limo pulled up. Dirty talk was not Olga's thing. I was hit by a flashback. Sami always wanted me to talk dirty to her, and Sami had died almost four years ago.

The doorman opened the door, and we went inside, waiting in the lobby for the guards to catch up. The guards, the cash, the sense of secrecy. It was all part of Camacho business.

We got out of the elevator on the top floor and walked to the end of the hallway, where the double entry doors led to the apartment. A picture was duct-taped to the door. Olga and I saw it at the same time. The two guards were behind us, but I beat them to it and peeled it off the door. A 5x7 copy of the biker drawing. I recognized it instantly. It was without a doubt from the batch of pictures that Tricia had made three years ago from the artist portraits.

"That son of a bitch," I said.

"You know him?" Olga asked. One guard opened the door and went in to the apartment, and the other guard stood beside Olga standing watch.

"It's the fucking shooter from the freeway, the same bastard that followed me to San Antonio."

"How did he know about this apartment?" Olga asked, but I could not detect fear in her. "We should have left someone here," she said to the guard beside her.

We got the all clear to go inside. One guard wanted to stay inside the apartment, but Olga told him no. The way the apartment was laid out, I was confident that even if that ape managed to get in, I could take him on, even if he had a gun. Only one entranc. He certainly wasn't going to scale the building and come in by way of one of the balconies.

"I never told the cops about this guy," I said to Olga.

"I know, Amor, you told me. We're not going to report this."

"There's nothing to report," I said, not really meaning it, but in full agreement that we were not calling the police.

"Amor, this fool, whoever it is, is sending some kind of message. Maybe it's to me."

"No, you have nothing to do with it," I said.

"How did he get this picture? Did you pass these out? I remember the pictures," Olga said.

"I showed them to friends and gave out some, yes. It was like, 'Do you know this prick?'"

"Well, one of those pictures came back in a circle," Olga said. "I'd like a hit of a joint. Do you mind, Amor?"

"Light it, Baby."

I don't know one weed from another, but I know that Olga keeps my team stocked with marijuana. What we were smoking was powerful. It worked fast.

I did not call Letty or the others, but I did call Quito. "It's a long story, but I want you to glue your eyes open and have Pico walk the grounds with the dogs every hour until I get back."

"If the *puto* is here, why worry about home?" Olga asked.

"We don't know who put this picture on your door."

"Amor, right, I'm not thinking straight. I think you should call Letty; it's not right you don't tell her. That girl is not afraid of anything."

Minutes later, I was talking to Letty.

"Boss, I hope he gets in here. I promise I will blow a hole in him. I'm going to sleep with my .457 Magnum, don't you worry."

Letty

Pixie went home. All the help, including Miguel, were in their quarters. I was alone in Casa Luna, in the kitchen cutting up Hershey bars for righteous chunky chocolate chip cookies. The alarm was on, but I was tempted not to arm it. How stupid would that be? Two of my favorite guns, one for each hand, were on the counter.

In my head, I taunted the biker *Come and get me, bastard, whatever the fuck your name is. You'll need to be a ghost to get past the guards and dogs outside, but how neat would it be if you made it in here when I'm wide awake like I am right now?*

The phone rang, but with my sticky hands, I knew I'd mess up the receiver. I managed to poke the speaker button with a wooden spoon, and washed cookie dough off my fingers.

"You want me to come over?" Pixie asked.

"Who told you?"

"He called me, told me to check on you. Probably busy fucking her."

"I'm baking chunky cookies. I mean chunky chocolate."

"Umm, I should have stayed. Want me over? I can be there in a jiff."

"Pix get your rest, I can handle it. My sweethearts are on the counter."

Pixie giggled. "So cool."

"Love you, Pix. Go jack off and sleep."

"Bitch, I don't have a dick to jack off."

I laughed. "Whatever you call it, then. Got to get back to the cookies. Love you."

A few minutes later, Tricia called. She'd made more arrangements with Quito, and didn't want me accidentally blowing away Pico or one of the dogs or anybody on extra duty walking the property. I assured her I was totally fine. I hadn't put the cookie trays in the oven and Niley called; she wanted to come over. I got her off the phone, then Jo called; she didn't offer to come over—she had TJ to deal with—but she wanted to make sure I was okay.

"I'm totally fine. Love you for thinking of me," I told her. At last the phone stopped ringing, and I breathed a sigh of relief, only not really. It's like having four sisters, something precious I would never take for granted. Finally I got the cookies in the oven. The television mounted to one of the walls was on mute. I left it that way and danced to music being piped from the juke downstairs. Soon the kitchen smelled terrific. In ten minutes, I pulled out the first trays. Twenty-four cookies ready for someone to eat. They cooled on the counter, and I put in more trays, dancing another twenty minutes away till all the batter was done, and polishing up the disaster I'd made of Miguel's kitchen so he wouldn't bite my head off. Stashed the cookies in the cookie safe except for two.

I put out two napkins, one of them in front of Mario's chair. Put a cookie on each one. Put out two coffee cups, poured each half full of milk. I ate my cookie, drank my milk. If I didn't work out like I do, I'd be so fat. Fuck, I could never let myself go.

The kitchen was clean but so very quiet. Some Oliver and Hardy black and white flick was playing. The Boss always laughs at those. I took his cookie, dunked it and saluted him. I looked at the empty stool Mario was not sitting on.

"This one's for you, Boss." I ate the second cookie, chased it with milk, and stuck the glasses in the dishwasher.

Fifteen minutes later, I was in bed in the dark, my guns under the pillow, the dim glow of the bathroom nightlight enough for me to orient myself. I turned on my side and reached out for him, but he wasn't there. He was with her.

Mario

Just the smell of Olga drew me to her. We smoked the joint and went to bed. I sucked her neck and she laughed softly. A few minutes later, I lay back on the pillows as she did the same to me.

We lay exhausted on the bed, her head on my chest.

"Not sure I mentioned it, but we will probably move out of Colombia."

I looked down but could only see her outline in the dark.

"Say that again?"

"We are probably leaving Colombia. Pepe will settle in Rome or Milan. Camila will live here in New York. She's looking for a penthouse or an estate that isn't buried too far in the country. She likes the activity, the noise, the life, the flash of New York."

For years, Camila had been telling me she wanted to buy a house in Pasadena. That was how she got me started holding a stash of Camacho money—as the down payment on her eventual Los Angeles house. I didn't bring it up. I had not known this was coming, though it probably wouldn't change too much on my end of things. It's not like we regularly got together in Colombia.

"Interesting."

"None of us really want to leave. It's political. The government has changed. It can be dangerous to be an entrepreneur."

"Dangerous?"

She didn't explain her use of the word dangerous and I didn't ask. I didn't follow Colombian politics except in the slightest way, and only because I was friendly with the Camachos.

It was common knowledge that law enforcement everywhere was clamping down on the cartels. Drugs were the enemy. Maybe it was a tidal wave that started with Nancy Reagan just saying 'No.' But everybody knew the cartels were feeling the heat all over South America. Hell, it was in all the papers. That discussion belonged in the papers, not in Olga's bed. Pepe had a lot of powerful friends and was into a whole lot of things, but I didn't know if Pepe was in the drug business.

"So. Pepe in Italy, Camila here. What about you?"

"You tell me, Amor."

The question moved me. Not changing the position, we were in, I caressed her face. She took my hand, kissed my palm, then each finger, one by one.

"Your fingers smell like pussy."

We laughed, breaking the moment. She moved from where she was snuggled next to me on the pillow, so that we were facing each other.

"Do you like me just a little bit at least?"

I kissed her nose. "I love you, Olga."

I felt her hand on my neck as she kissed me.

"I get chills when you call me by my name."

I wanted to find out more about the move. I wondered about LAI. Was I still to find properties for them?

"What about Pepe's airline once you leave Colombia?"

"LAI owns the airline and our hub is in Lima, Peru. If Colombia makes any moves toward us, Pepe will simply cut that route. It will hurt all of Colombia. We service five major cities there. Passenger fares are lower than any other operator."

"What about the other businesses?"

"Amor, you are curious today. So many questions."

"Baby, how can I not wonder?"

She nodded. "I would ask, too. We've sold most of the real estate holdings in Colombia. You know how we are diversified over many countries. Nothing's left there, really, except for the family residences, Camila's house, and my house. I'm not sure I want to get rid of my house, and Camila feels the same about hers. Pepe is still hanging on to the big estate."

"Well, it must be serious if Pepe has practically liquidated."

"Most of the assets are not in Colombia. He's working with his people that are connected to the new government. We'll see if anything comes out of that. Maybe our departure will be delayed once again. This is not the first changing of the guard we have weathered in Colombia, but this is the first time we are ready to get out."

"I hope it's all good and works out the way you want it."

"Thank you, Amor."

She would have stopped at that, but I urged her to continue.

Olga told me about the house in Bogota. "It's worth millions of dollars, sits on over one hundred prime acres, and the government could take the position that Pepe's father bought the home decades ago with drug money, which is no doubt true. If the new government is as corrupt as the old one, we got nothing to worry about and Pepe may decide not to sell the two houses—until the next time."

Since she was answering questions, I wanted to ask about the cash. There was so much cash. The cash I used to buy properties. The cash Olga flew around to cover purchases that Camila made. Where did all the cash come from?

I didn't ask. In the years I had known them, I had never learned as much as in the last few minutes.

Blood pumped. My head was spinning. I sat up. My veins flooded with adrenaline. I wondered if my deal with them would be changed.

"Amor, are you curious or worried about the one who put that picture on my door a few hours ago?"

"Not at all. Are you?"

"No,"

I wondered at her change of topic but recognized the Olga tactic. She'd said all she was going to about Camacho doings.

She pulled me close and whispered in my ear.

"Fuck me, Amor." She reached for me and I felt myself grow hard again.

I don't think newlyweds would have spent as much time closeted in a small apartment in bed as we did in the four days that followed.

I called home each evening to speak to Letty. I'd ask if maybe Pixie should have stayed, or Tricia.

She always countered this. "Boss, I'm good. Stop worrying. Miss you. Enjoy New York." In the day, when they would be there working, I spoke with Pixie, Letty, and Tricia. I called them in the office, with them listening on speaker and gave them a warning. "I want you to be extra careful. This biker or someone connected with him could be close. Don't know if the picture on the door here was intended to be a distraction," I told them.

"Boss, don't worry," Tricia said. "Got it covered."

"Believe it, Boss," Pixie assured me.

The routine of life continued when I was not there. Betty gave Letty a massage every night before going over to do Melina at midnight when she arrived from work.

Olga kept me too busy to miss my girl, my house, or my team. At times when the light was good, I stared at Olga as she slept. I always had a mental argument with myself about whether Olga or Camila was lovelier. The two of them shared no blood but looked much alike, both with the same Latin look. Sometimes I wished that I could enter Olga's head just for a little while so that I could understand more about her. I didn't really care about her secrets, but I wanted to understand what and who she was. I felt close to her, but she was so much a mystery to me. I don't know if it was chemistry, love, or curiosity, but I would have pledged to be with her for the rest of my life. She had that power over me. Camila did not. Camila was too much like her brother Pepe. Though it was rarely directed at me, both Camila and Pepe had a forceful, sometimes childish will I had little patience for dealing with. But I cared for them, cared for them a lot, and accepted them as they were.

"When you leave Colombia, will you still be flying around for LAI like you do?"

"Probably for another three or four years."

"Why?"

Olga knew that question was coming, I could tell. She gave me a non-answer. "Because there's a lot of cash income that needs to be invested and banked."

"Sounds like I'll be buying property for a while for LAI?"

"Is that a question?"

"Yes."

"Of course. You will be buying for us as long as you want."

"Thanks," I said, feeling a little relief. "It's not like I'm hurting, but I'd be lying if I didn't admit I like doing what I'm doing for LAI. It's been a whole new world for me, having millions of dollars at my disposal to buy anything I consider a good asset for Pepe and the family."

"I know, my love." She kissed me. "Pepe loves you; the three of us love you. Why shouldn't you share in our good fortune? So now that I told you so much, will you marry me?"

"Why marriage? Is it something you believe you have to do?"

Olga frowned. She never frowns. "I want babies. Not for the next five years, but I want a family."

"In five years, I'll be five years older," I said. "Maybe too old to be a dad?"

"Old? You won't be old in five years." She laughed.

Then we were silent. It was my turn to kiss her. "Forget what I said about age, Baby, don't take offense. You know how fucking crazy I am. I know I would be a terrible husband. A worse father. Pepe would no doubt have me shot dead if he thought I was mistreating you."

"If you beat me up, he might have you shot dead, if I didn't beat him to it."

I kissed her nose. "I cannot strike a woman."

"Amor, I know."

I had never hit a woman in anger. Even in karate when I used to work out with female fighters as aggressive and good as me, I had trouble striking them.

"I'll go home and digest it. You do the same."

"Amor, I can make you very happy. I know you have money, but I have more money than we can spend in our lifetime and in our children's lifetime. Four more years tops, and I'll be free to live a life without always traveling on business. Everything is being sorted, management companies all over the world are managing LAI assets. One day all control will be out of Pepe and Camila's hands and I will no longer be needed to keep track of the money, the bank accounts, the payments, and the financial stuff that I do."

My feelings for this woman had nothing to do with money.

Camacho business broke our time together. Camila had made a purchase and Olga had to take care of the cash part of the deal. Three of the guards went ahead of us to the plane, and the other two guards waited for us then followed in another car. Olga insisted I fly home in Camila's Learjet.

"Her plane is just sitting here until the next time she needs it. Take the plane."

I packed for home. Olga packed for Berlin. What a life.

In the limousine headed to the airport, Olga held my hand. She was silent, in another world, her mind no doubt doing a marathon. I know mine was. As the driver made his way through the impossible Manhattan traffic, I watched Olga's face. She'd feel my gaze, turn to see me, smile. I knew she was way out there somewhere. Her face was so alive. The creamy skin, the dark flashing eyes, the sharp cheekbones, the wide, expressive mouth.

"We haven't really talked about the picture on the door," I said. "I need to know you are safe from him."

"Amor, I have my security, and as you would say, he's long gone. The boys were hoping he'd return during the past four days when we were inside the apartment, so they could give him a Colombian welcome. I have the picture in my purse."

"I have plenty where that came from."

"That man is dead," Olga said without expression. "I should have done something about it when he attacked you on the freeway. I'm sorry, Amor." She kissed me.

"Why sorry? What could you have done? We don't know anything about him."

The expressionless look on her face spoke for her. I felt a chill and changed the subject. "Where will I see you again?" I asked. It must have seemed like a crazy question. I never knew from one time to the next where or when we would meet. Mentally, I still felt like their home was in Rio, since that was the first of their estates that I had seen. Knowing that their home may no longer be in Colombia made me feel different. I'd always felt like even though all the Camachos were birds in flight, they were still rooted in Colombia.

"From now on, call and I'll come flying to you."

"Where will you live? You never said."

"Amor, Camila and I decided that if either one of us was going to have you, it would be me. So it is a done deal, yes?"

She laughed so I laughed. Inside, I felt something else. I wanted her, yes, but I wasn't a cake to be divided between the two of them at their whim.

"It's not a done deal, Olga. I do my own thinking. Make my own decisions."

"Amor, don't get angry, please."

I smiled to make the awkward moment go away. At least it chased the games away.

She said, "I'll buy a house in Pasadena. I'll bother you and bother you and bother you every day until you cave and marry me."

We laughed. I wondered what might happen to my Melina-Sundays if this LA house came to pass.

Before we got out of the car, our mouths locked.

"I want you, Amor. Even if we are apart, I want to know we are married."

The big plane she would be taking to Germany was sitting on a tarmac away from the terminal. Beside it, the Lear looked very small, but when I got aboard, the interior was as gorgeous as I remembered. It is amazing what you can do with little spaces when you have the money.

The stewardess approached as I sat on a club seat that had only a table in front of it with plenty of room for my long legs.

"Olga told me to take good care of you, Señor Mario. My name is Natalia."

"Call me Mario," I responded in Spanish.

Natalia held a walkie-talkie in her hand and gave it to me. Olga's voice.

"We're going out first. Safe travels, Amor."

"Safe travels to you, too, Olga."

"I got chills, Amor."

I looked out the window. I could see the plane, but there was no telling where she was inside the DC-9. "You have been a wonderful hostess. I enjoyed every minute."

"I loved every second. Think about our plans. Our marriage could be open. Amor, you know how I am when we are in a group. In four or five years, we'll be over the thrills of open sex. We can settle down, just the two of us, and the beautiful babies that you will produce in my body."

"Fuck," I said.

"What, Amor?"

"I just got chills."

I felt like ordering the door of the Lear open and running across the tarmac to take off with her wherever she was going.

Reality kicked in.

"We'll talk," I said. "Let's be in touch every day."

"Si, Amor." Her voice was tucked in my ear, even while the big plane carrying her began moving away.

I did eat a little from an assortment of appetizers. Less than an hour out, the stewardess opened a pullout bed in the rear compartment and I crashed. The pretty attendant that I didn't expect to have on the flight home put a pillow under my head and fastened my seat belt over the blanket she put over me while I was lying down. Natalia didn't have to do very much, at least not for me. I slept most of the way. I consumed no wine, no sodas, just water.

At Van Nuys Airport, not far from the runway, my Rolls was waiting for me. It was cold in Pasadena, but not as cold as New York had been. Pixie, Letty, and Tricia were standing beside the car. I ran down the mobile stairs with my duffle bag and the girls came running to me. Tricia got behind the wheel. I got in back with Pixie and Letty.

"Did the bitch leave anything for us?" Pixie asked, scowling, her expression reminding me of a wet cat.

Letty reached for my zipper.

Tricia was laughing, her eyes on the road, so different from the days when Pixie drove with her eyes more on me than on the other cars.

"I'm going to fuck all night," I promised, "but not till we get home."

"Great. I'm staying over," Pixie said.

"I'm staying over, too," Letty said.

"Bitch, you live with him." Pixie started up her usual routine. That mouth. Immediately she and Letty were bickering. They fake-punched at each other. It wasn't exactly dangerous, but I was between them and pulled them apart. Soon as we were on the freeway headed to Pasadena. I couldn't resist saying, "Keep the windows rolled up just in case the prick biker shows."

Seconds later, Pixie and Letty had their guns out. "This time, we shoot the prick."

I was back. My team was still my team. No question about it.

My front gates opened. Tricia drove in and waved at the guard in the guardhouse.

I glanced back and watched the gates close. Life was so strange. Thanks to Bruno's fuckup, I lived in a fortress. Not that I needed to be guarded like this.

I was a nobody, living behind a fourteen-foot wall with twenty-four-hour guards. I thought about the biker. Was he here somewhere? Where did he get his information? How did he know about the New York apartment?

"Wait, wait!" Letty said, running in the house first and shutting the door.

I looked at Pixie, wondering what was up. She shrugged.

I put my hand on the door, and it swung open. Letty, on the other side, leaped at me and gave me a serious hello.

"Welcome home, Boss," she whispered.

Tricia came in behind me. Pixie didn't have the patience for Letty's little performance.

"I hope you're hungry. I told Miguel to cook up a storm," Pixie said.

"If he's not hungry, I'll eat it all," Tricia said.

"Let me guess. It's either steak or Mexican."

"Of course," Letty said. "That's all you ever want to eat."

"You forgot the peanut butter," I said.

Letty winked at me and smiled.

Three hours after dinner, we were drinking wine and passing around a joint. Letty unpacked for me. "Olga sent a care package." Letty's teeth gleamed, and she held up a plastic baggie.

Camila loves pot. Olga less so, but she'd packed it for the team. Tricia hardly ever touches it. Melina doesn't like pot, but she loves wine. When Letty and Pixie get high, they giggle a lot. Maybe I do too.

In the wine room, I told them about Olga and her talk about marriage.

"Seems like she always gets around to talking marriage," Tricia said.

"We've heard it before," Pixie said.

"Hey, wait. Maybe Boss wants to marry her." Letty looked at me. "Do you?"

"Kiss-ass. He doesn't want to marry her. Do you, Boss?" Pixie frowned.

I remained quiet. Took a drink. Accepted the joint. Played with the lighter. Took a hit.

"Boss, answer me."

I looked over at Pixie.

"I don't know," I confessed. "It's never going to be Melina. She won't follow through."

"Fuck me," Pixie snarled. "Why does it have to be anyone? You don't want to get married."

"Fuck off," Letty said.

It was weird watching them get in a knock-down-drag-out catfight over whether or not I should marry a woman who was neither of them. Okay, no claws were involved, just words. But their words can get sharp enough to make anybody bleed.

"Girls, we're having a good time. Back off. He's not pregnant, and nobody's got a shotgun. Mellow out." Tricia had been sitting next to me, but she squeezed between Letty and Pixie and put her arms over their shoulders. She took the joint and blew some smoke at Pixie.

Pixie snatched it away and took a long drag, then a big swallow of her wine. She slammed the glass down on the table in front of her. I was relieved it did not shatter.

"Fuck me." Pixie was still using words like a weapon, and she'd aimed them not at me but Letty. Tricia leaned back, still between them, but turning left and right like she was watching a tennis match. It was like a game. I knew Pixie and Letty were not going at each other unless it was a workout in the gym with mats under them.

"You are using my words," Letty said. "Is that all you got? Words?"

"Fuck you."

"Okay," Letty said. "Wait till we get to a bed, and I will."

Tricia took that moment to fill the wine glasses.

Pixie stopped at Letty and went at Tricia. "Why you being so nice, pouring wine and even taking a few tokes with us?"

Tricia ignored her.

Letty said, "You going to swing with us tonight in bed?"

Tricia chugged her wine, set down the glass, and got up. "I'm out of here, Boss. I got a date."

"With the *FED*?" Pixie sang it like a song.

"Baby, don't let these two wildcats get to you. You know they love you," I said.

"I really got a date. Got to go." She leaned over to kiss me. She walked over to Pixie, kissed the top of her head, then did the same to Letty.

I love my team.

Almost a week in New York is enough to get settled into New York time. It was easier for me to adjust to European time than to deal with three hours' time change.

We did the spa, sauna, and wet steam, then took a dip in the icy pool spa. Betty gave the girls a thirty-minute massage right there in the spa, then we went up to the master bedroom. Betty took off to Melina's to do the usual midnight massage.

"Come back to sleep with us if you want," I said as Betty said her goodbyes.

"Deal," she said with a big smile. "Will there be anything left?"

"You can always give me head," Pixie said.

"And I'll watch," Letty bubbled out. She was high. We were all high.

Once in bed, we did more talking in the dark than we did anything sexual. We were like cats lying against each other, then across each other. They kept talking about marriage.

"I'm thirty-five already."

"It's not like you plan to give birth," Pixie said to me. "Your uterus is not on its final countdown."

That cracked Letty up, which turned into two minutes of pillow fighting, then it was back to snuggling. At two, Betty returned and walked over to the fire that was blazing perfectly. Backlit by the flames and a room full of candles, she took her clothes off. It could have been a sexy or romantic moment, but Letty and Pixie catcalled and whistled and turned it into a burlesque. I threatened to kick Pixie over to the couch when she threatened to wet the bed from laughing so hard.

Betty was standing naked, or as naked as you can be with nothing on but the big pink boa she carries in her massage kit. I know the boa very well. It must be twenty feet long. Betty's massages sometimes include textures.

"We've been talking," I told Betty. "We were waiting for you."

"Want your massage, Boss?" She stood with one hand on her waist, the other twirling the end of the boa.

"Nope, I just want your hot body over here with us."

"Hot is right," she said.

We all put our arms out, but she walked past us into the bathroom. I heard the shower start.

"Gonna be a long night, Boss," Pixie said, sounding wise.

She was right.

Olga

I landed in Geneva just in time to meet with the seller. I knew about the deal from Camila, but I was in and out in under twenty minutes. Camila had made a deal on a six-story office building that was fully occupied by architects and interior-design companies. One of my guards brought in two suitcases—four million US dollars. I had nothing to do with the paperwork or anything else regarding the deal.

An hour and a half after I left my plane, I was back aboard, taking off to Milan for a meeting with Camila and Pepe.

The pilots would have a shit fit if they knew I was in the shower as the plane ascended, but fuck the pilots, this was my plane.

The short flight gave me enough time to dry off, lie down, and nap for forty-five minutes, then get up and dress. I was so used to this. Lately I have been keeping my hair short and my makeup light as possible to lighten the routine. I put on the same suit I had on in Geneva. Forty minutes after we landed, I was at the Milan property.

I found Pepe and Camila in a sitting room by the dining room. I kissed them both. Pepe hugged me, hard as usual. He's not a blood brother, but I wish he would not go there. Too much water under the bridge between us.

"We are so hungry but we waited for you," Pepe said, headed to the dining room. The table was set for three; he sat at the head of one end of the table, Camila on his right and me on his left.

"Everything okay in Geneva?" Camila asked, beginning on a salad, a dozen different greens topped with sliced hearts of palms and tiny tomatoes arranged on a crystal plate that looked like a work of art.

"Went perfect."

"I'm told we can inject a lot of cash through that vehicle," Pepe said. He ground the mill fiercely, covering his clam chowder in pepper. He stirred it, gave it a taste, and slurped happily.

My chowder was unpeppered but with lots of saltines.

For Pepe, most things were vehicles. A building was a vehicle. A liquor store—Mario bought a lot of them—they were vehicles.

"I love the building," Camila said.

"The terms of all cash—perfect. You did good," Pepe said.

Camila always got the compliments. She made the deals; she deserved the compliments. I comfort myself and don't need compliments. All I did was pay. I had to be sure that there was always enough cash near me or on the plane. My primary duty was to get our bankers to keep accepting cash deposits for the least amount of payoff. Most of these bankers were old, but they like me. I'm not saying I'm beautiful, but even those that can't get it up anymore want to have sex. The good thing for me, if I go along with it, I am able to bring in suitcases filled with cash to deposit to LAI accounts. The other good thing is Pepe and Camila pay me bonuses based on how much money I bank in cash. The downside is if I have to pay the banker for the favor of letting me do it, it comes out of my bonus. Still, I make tons of money.

"Camila says you want to marry Mario?"

I confirmed it with a direct look into Pepe's eyes, then Camila's. Funny how they are the same eyes, but somehow different, angry and impatient on Pepe, beautiful on Camila.

"Yes. Even if we can't be together much, I want to be married to him. I love him."

"I thought you loved me," Camila teased, working on her swordfish.

I had a delectable lobster thermidor in front of me that I had barely started. I looked at my sister. "I do love you." I looked at Pepe. "And I love you."

"I was kidding you," Camila said. She looked at her brother. "Be happy for her, brother dear."

"I am happy if Olga is happy. But you know he's a playboy. I don't think he will ever settle down. Does that bother you?"

"Maybe someday, but not now. Besides, men are men."

"I'm a man. I don't get married, so there are no strings," Pepe said, carving his steak.

"Oh Pepe, you have so many girlfriends that think they are the only ones and you fool around on all of them," Camila said, then laughed.

I didn't laugh because I never know what mood Pepe is in. Mood can make a big difference with Pepe. He can blow up at the littlest things. Camila, she's the queen. He never gets rough with her—just words with her. With me, he has no such limits. Being his 'whipping girl' is painful. Soon after, he apologizes and leaves me a bundle of bills. I put that money away and I've never offered to give it back and never will. I hate it when Camila goads him on. She can say what she wants, but I tiptoe around or he will take it out on me. I have learned to keep my mouth shut.

Camila is also moody. I've seen her slap the help, but she's not ever laid a hand on me, and I know she never will.

The best time to talk with her is when we are totally into each other. After the last time he slapped me, I had to bring it up. Her legs were wrapped around my neck, my mouth on her pussy, and before she started moaning, I asked, "Is it possible that Pepe needs to see a doctor for his temper?"

"I'll talk to him, Amor, I promise. Don't stop, Amor, please."

Mario

I still made it up at five to do my workout. I slept an hour at most. Sometimes I wonder if I'm a nut case. I could have just stayed in bed and skipped a workout. It's like an obsession. I have to work out. If I don't, I just don't feel right. Sometimes I have a go in the morning, then again later in the day. The later-day workouts are never as good as the mornings. When I came out of the spa shower, I dried off, jumped into joggers, and headed up for coffee. A minute later, Melina walked in full of salt and vinegar. She joined me in the coffee room beside the kitchen.

"Asshole. You mess with that Colombian for a week in New York and don't even bother to call me. You have an orgy with the team. If it hadn't been for Betty, I wouldn't even know you were back."

In a flash I had her. I cradled her in my arms and bent down for a kiss. I got fists instead. She pounded my chest. I held her up until she started laughing. Her ribs are ticklish.

"I should have called, but I just never know what market you're in."

"Not good enough. Make a little more effort when you're away."

"I will, but you could have called me."

"Pixie told me about the bastard pasting a picture on the door of the apartment."

She caught me off guard. "It could have been anyone who put that picture on the door," I said. "But there's got to be a connection to that prick, no question."

"I worry about you, Cuz."

I kissed the tip of her nose. "Olga surrounds herself with five heavily armed guards," I laughed. "I was never in danger."

"Smartass," she said.

The coffee room had a small five-person table. Currently, three chairs were against the wall, with two strategically placed facing the bay window that revealed a winter garden. The chairs were upholstered and though they look lower than they are, are tall enough to be comfortable for me. The wall between this room and the kitchen had a Brazilwood counter, underneath which several stools were parked. I would have taken a stool, but the stools were too high to be comfortable for Melina. I put my hands on the back of a chair. She sat, then I did.

"Buy me a cup."

Miguel walked in. In a flash, we had full coffee cups and an assortment of pastries, including pan dulce.

"Who was it this time? Olga or Camila? Did you fuck day and night?"

"Letty must have told you it was Olga."

"She only said you were in New York at the Camacho apartment. Then Pixie called me to tell me about the prick biker."

I ignored the biker talk.

"You better latch onto me, Baby, because I am seriously getting interested in that babe."

Melina and I had come close to getting married at least three times. By close, I mean packed for Vegas with the chauffeur waiting, the car revved up and ready to go. Then she would chicken out, always blaming the fact that she is ten years older. Melina looks younger than me. No way does she look forty-five. She looked about twelve years old right now, with her hands around that big steamy latté cup. She'd taken to drinking lattés lately. The steamed milk in that cup was probably the only nutrition she'd have time for till mid-afternoon.

"Go ahead and marry her. I'll still be here. It won't last."

"Damn. Throwing salt in the wound."

"Why do you need to get married? Just shack up."

Miguel poured another round and brought Melina another little pitcher of steamed milk.

She flashed Miguel a smile. "When are you going to let me steal you away from here?" she asked.

Miguel grinned back and retreated to the kitchen.

"Maybe you're right," I said. "Last night, my bed was full of Pixie, Letty, and Betty. I'd never be able to do that married to Olga. But listen to this—she says it's okay for me to do what I'm doing with my team."

"Bull. That's what she says now. If you still want Pixie, Letty, and Betty in your bed, maybe you're not ready for tying the knot." She leaned closer. "Or maybe you should marry someone who's already in your bed who doesn't mind the crowd."

"Like you or Letty? You just are never going to marry me, are you?"

"Cuz, I'm too old for you. I love you, always will love you. I'm in for the long haul, Cuz, ring or not."

"I'm in it with you, Baby," I said.

"You better be, Cuz." We shared a coffee-flavored kiss. "I like Olga better than Camila. They are both beautiful, but Olga is more like us."

I wasn't sure what she meant by that and I didn't ask. I couldn't be sure if I hurt Melina by telling her what I did. She wasn't showing any hurt—but then maybe she wouldn't let me see that. Maybe she really only loved me like a brother, like a family member, except that we had our Sundays. Melina is special to me. In my heart, she is the queen of all the women I had. Ever since I met her, she's been a major part of my life. She's been with me, stuck with me through everything. Stood by me after I killed four human beings in self-defense, on four separate occasions. I never did anything for her that was even close to what she's done for me.

When Melina comes over for coffee, she's always in a hurry to leave for work.

"My bed is filled, but I have a bunch of guest rooms. Do we have time for a quickie?" I knew what her answer would be but asked anyway. She's been known to say yes.

Miguel was in the kitchen, baking something that smelled yeasty and wonderful. I didn't care if he heard.

"Asshole, you're a sex freak."

"Takes one to know one." I pushed all the mischief I had into my face and gave her a smile. "Dare you."

She put one finger up and chugged the rest of her coffee, leaving a touch of foam on her upper lip. She wiped it away with the back of her hand, put the empty cup on the table and popped out of the chair.

"I'm not taking off anything from the waist up."

She was off and running. Never made it to the stairs. I found her bottomless, standing on a daybed in the sunroom, and in a moment, I was right behind her.

Wednesday. I met Fino at the Pacific Dining Car in downtown Los Angeles for lunch.

"When are you coming over to see the house now that it's done?"

"Set the date," Jack said.

"This weekend. Saturday?"

"It's a deal."

I could see that Jack was relaxed. He'd finished off a Bloody Mary and was crunching away at the celery stick that had been in it. I knew the topic I was opening up would be a bombshell.

"I have it from a good source that Bruno had a tape recorder with a tape in it that is with the sheriff, along with his other personal property."

The crunching stopped. He dropped the small end of the celery to his bread plate and focused on me. "What source?"

"Jack, the source is solid."

"Then why doesn't he get the tape?"

"Because he's not with the sheriff." I took a drink of my Perrier. "I don't want the tape; I want a copy or a transcription, that's all."

Fino started laughing. I didn't laugh as hard as he did, but it was a hearty laugh that invited others around us to laugh. I laughed because it was irresistible, but nothing about it seemed funny to me.

Fino settled down after a while. "That's all you want, a copy or a transcription?"

"Yeah," I said. You'd think I was talking about Watergate or something.

Fino started laughing again. When we were done eating, Fino said, "I know a lot of people there, but what you want is so delicate I need to think about it."

Chapter 4
March 1983
Host

Mario

March arrived, and so did Fino. During construction he had walked through, but this was his first time in the finished house. Every room we went into earned a laudatory remark from him. By the time we were up to the top floor, I was getting embarrassed.

"How much you got in this house?"

"The insurance gave me just under three million. I dumped in another million and change."

"I would have guessed seven."

"I don't pay retail. Or I should say it was Melina that didn't pay retail. My contractor, TJ, delivered a Rolls Royce for the price of a Lincoln Continental."

Our Sundays had been starting at Saturday night, so I was only half-surprised when Melina showed up for dinner. The whole team was parked around my huge dining room table, including Jo and Niley; Pixie had brought her daughter Lainie along. I was surprised to see how grown-up she was getting. She was seventeen. Pixie had bought her a new Camaro for her birthday. She was beginning her third year of karate, her first year of shooting range training, her fifth year of singing lessons, and like her mother, there were very few music instruments she couldn't play by ear. Like her mother, she was beautiful. She reminded me so much of Pixie at that age, except that there was something in Pixie that always acted like a little girl, and Lainie had always been too serious. Aunt Carmen had told me once it was because Lainie knew her mother would always be a little girl, so she had always been the grown-up.

I kept an eye out for it, but the grumpiness that I'd detected in Fino right after Bruno got killed was gone. Jack presented a warm front, and everyone liked him. Something was off. He looked happy, he looked social, but there was a hesitation here and there, and an edge to his warmth that told me that Fino was feeling jealous. I don't know if it was the house, or if it was the boisterous team parked around my dining table. Maybe he was tipsy; he was drinking pretty good.

"What is it?" Melina asked me. I watched Fino and shook my head. Gave him a smile. Poured some table wine. My instincts were telling me something was off. I just couldn't put my finger on it.

But how could that be? Fino had more money than anyone, except maybe the Camacho family. His huge mansion was only ten minutes away from me in a pristine part of Pasadena. He joked with me about needing to remodel his place, but it was just joking around. He could afford any kind of living he wanted.

We moved from the dining room to the living room. Letty and Jo started bullying Pixie to pull out the guitar she had stashed in my house. Lainie ran to my den and took it from the place where it hung. Pixie was reluctant but was finally convinced. First, she sang alone—a Spanish ballad she'd written herself. It sounded amazing as she was accompanying herself with the twelve-string guitar; then she sang a pop ballad with Lainie—Bonnie Tyler's "Total Eclipse of the Heart."

When they were done, there wasn't a dry eye in the room. We were all quietly stunned. They were so good that clapping was almost like an insult.

"Incredible," I said, not much louder than a whisper, and gave Pixie and Lainie a big group hug. I could see Jack Fino watching intently, drinking from a glass of wine. He was in a wing chair near the fireplace where the girls were standing. I backed off and let the rest of the guests gather around. I saw Miguel sneaking back into the kitchen, wiping his eyes. They were that good.

"One day they will be discovered. One day you're going to lose them," Melina whispered to me. Not for the first time.

"That day is not today," I said.

Saturday night. Long past Saturday, actually, in the wee hours of Sunday morning, I was lying on my bed, watching Melina sleep. She'd had her hair cut short into a pixie, and it was frosted. I was fascinated by the way the firelight played with the highlights of her hair. I spread my fingers and ran them through the short cut.

I took my hand away, but she grabbed my wrist and put it back.

"Don't stop. That feels good."

I put my unused hand to my head and experimented for a second on how it felt and resumed rubbing her head. She made a soft, contented noise that stirred my overactive libido and off we went.

"Amor, congratulations," Camila said sweetly on the phone. "I hear you're going to get married to Olga."

"Baby, if I marry Olga, what about you and me?"

"You're not married yet," she said. Not that Camila would consider a wedding ring an obstacle. I knew she and Olga had already parceled me out like a pie. "I'm at the airport. I have twelve hours."

"Come over. See the house."

"I'll be there in an hour."

The guard called me at one when she was at the gate. Pixie, Letty, Tricia, and I opened the front door just as a uniformed driver held the passenger door open, a familiar suitcase resting on my driveway beside the driver's feet. She stepped out of the SUV wearing a huge conical red hat that had an Asian look, and a bulky sable coat. We met halfway across the driveway in a mass of hugs and kisses. I put my hands on her forearms and held her away from me for a second. I saw mostly hat, and just a hint of her chin, then whipped off the hat so I could see her face.

"There you are."

"Love the hat," Pixie said.

Camila put it on Pixie's head.

"It's yours."

Pixie squealed. "Are you sure?"

Camila's smile was her answer.

I released Camila's arm and looked her over. A new do, a lighter hair color, but she still looked as she did the day we met.

"Soon as the gates opened I began to see what was new. Love the nice guardhouse." She gave a hoarse laugh. "The guard inside isn't too bad either."

The girls laughed. I didn't. "That's Quito."

The limo driver handed me the suitcase.

Pixie reached for it.

"It's heavy," I told her.

"More than a hundred pounds?" she asked.

I hefted it and guessed it was close, maybe ninety. Probably four million inside.

"Not quite."

"That's nothing. Give me," she said.

The team had been working out, so I figured it was true. I handed it off to Pixie, who pretended she wasn't staggering as she carried it into the house to my office, and probably to a mirror to check out the hat.

Camila hooked her arm around mine and broke into chatter. She smelled expensive and exotic with a new unfamiliar perfume. Her fingers were painted fire-engine red and matched her lips, purse, and shoes, but the coat obscured the dress. She had on a dozen rings, at least.

"I'm excited. Now," she said in a bossy tone, "show me the house."

Once in the house, she gave the full-length sable to Sunny, who cradled it like it was a small child until she hung it in the front hall guest closet.

"Perfect temperature in here," she said.

Under the coat was a broad-shouldered jacket with a Chinese-style collar and a shiny red skirt that reached her knees, not the skinny pencil skirts the girls favored, but something that was bunched at the waist. Monochrome red to match the nails. I couldn't tell the fabric—either silk or whatever ribbons are made of. Five buttons down the center of the coat. Looked like onyx. It's not like I care that much about women's clothes, but she was dressed to the nines, and Melina would want a description. Pixie reappeared, carrying a Polaroid we kept up in the office. She had changed clothes, but still wore the hat. She was all in red to match her new hat.

"How is Melina?" Camila asked.

"Busy as always. Her markets are serious business."

"Maybe she wants to sell?"

That caught me off guard. I smiled. "I doubt it, but I'll ask her," I lied.

"They are Mexican markets," Camila said. "They would go with the tortilla factory and the bakery you found for us."

"I seriously doubt Melina would sell," Letty said.

Camila looked at her, then at me. "Everything has a price."

Miguel had prepared a tray of wine glasses, with white and red wines breathing. We fortified ourselves and took an hour for the tour, the team tagging along with us. Pixie took some pictures on the way. We found tapas waiting when we returned to the den. Miguel was cooking Colombian and Mexican for a late lunch at three.

After lunch, the teletype machine usually received. With some broad hints from me, the team went upstairs to work and left us in the living room.

Camila took out a joint, and asked, "Can I light up?"

"Of course."

"Olga is really mad at that *puto* who put the picture on the door in New York, and so am I and so is Pepe. We're looking for him."

"Ouch," I said with gusto. "I'd love it if you catch the fucker, so I can beat him to a pulp."

At five, the girls were still busy in the office. Camila and I went wild on my bed with no mention of Olga. No mention of the future move from Colombia. No mention of business. Just sex. Camila was venturous, and there is always something new to try.

"*Eres un toro,*[3]" Camila said. I was still hard.

At eight, Sunny brought back the coat. The team and I walked Camila to the waiting car. We kissed passionately as the driver held the door open for her. Then she was off for Bogota.

"Should I stay over?" Pixie asked. "Or is Boss pooped out?"

"Pooped would cover it."

"Sweet dreams." Tricia blew a kiss to everyone in general and headed for the door.

"I'm jealous," Pixie said, glaring at Letty, and slipping on her snow jacket, hat, and gloves.

"You're dressed for New York, not Pasadena."

"I should wear my mink," she said. "It's cold out there."

"Did you dig that sable she had on? She never wears anything twice," Letty said.

"We don't see her that often. Of course, she wears stuff twice." Pixie's cheeks flush when she gets her dander up. Her cheeks were bright, her hands parked on her hips. She was ready to do battle.

"Bitch," Letty said, then kissed Pixie on the lips before she left.

I got kisses too. Life was back to normal. The specter of marriage to

---

[3] Bull

Olga was vanishing. Olga was off doing her thing. Camila had come just to stir things up, or to mess up my mind with sex, or just to make the point she did whatever the hell she wanted to do. Didn't matter. The sex was damn good.

I thought of what Melina had said, to marry one of my own so that I didn't have to give up anything. I didn't believe Letty or Pixie would tolerate me if I was married to either one of them, and Melina—she was never going to marry me, no matter what. Why do I need to get married at all?

"Get Miguel to make me something simple," I told Letty.

"Steak?" she asked with a knowing smile.

"Good idea." I smiled back. "Meanwhile, I have to call Melina and tell her what Camila was wearing before I forget."

"Tell her Yves Saint Laurent," Letty said. "It was on the label in the hat she gave Pixie."

"I can't believe she wore that all day." I laughed. It looked like a cross between a giant red Frisbee and the red electric wok Miguel uses in the kitchen.

I didn't reach Melina but left a message. She had her secretary call back that she would come by after work. She made it over at eleven in the evening, early for her. Letty went off to her room as we shared a glass of wine.

"That was hostile," she said. "Everything about her coming here was vicious."

"What do you mean?" I asked. I thought Camila had been really nice the whole time.

"What Olga knows, Camila knows. Camila gave Olga permission to have you, then swooped in like a pigeon to shit on the relationship she'd permitted."

I laughed. "I've had them every which way, separately and together."

"Asshole."

I made a funny face. "I know. Baby, do you hear the drama in your voice? It's not unusual at all for Camila to come over or me to go to the airport when they stop over."

Melina left and, about two in the morning, when it was nine hours later in Spain, Olga called. I answered the phone.

"Amor, I thought you would be up."

"You lie," I said in a sleepy voice.

"Camila told me you gave her four hours of slam-slam. Notice how calm I am, not a jealous bone in my body."

"Baby, it wasn't four hours."

"It was five hours and she said you were hard as a bat. It wouldn't go down."

"Not true," I lied.

"Sleep tight, Amor. Pretend I'm sleeping there with you. I miss you."

"I miss you, too," I said.

Letty came into my dark room. "I heard the phone. Is everything alright, Boss?"

"It was Olga. She purposely woke me up."

"You want me to stay or go back to my room?"

"Take a wild guess?"

A minute later we were both tucked together.

Chapter 5
March 1983 (continued)
Puerto Rico

Mario

Juan called from his home to let us know that a tour helicopter had crashed in Puerto Rico. Nine dead. Three in the hospital. He gave me the details before the crash hit network news.

"Boss, I check. Hilton here books the tour flights. I think you can hook them for liability."

"Good work, Juan. You really got it together." My job was to sign new cases, not to figure out who would get hooked for the liability.

"I have good teacher, Boss."

"Give me five days. That will give the families time to arrive. Are they locals or tourists?"

"Too early to know, but the names look like tourists from everywhere."

"Put it together. It will be good to see you and Valita."

"I have it all together by the time you get here."

I told Gonor about the crash.

"I love the case already. Please sign it and let me have it."

He was as eager as when we first met, as if our blow-up had never happened. I was playing the same game, after all. I called him. I knew he didn't have the cash flow, that he may have to borrow or steal from the trust account to pay me, and I was keeping my eyes shut about it. I told myself it was his problem. As long as the clients got paid and as long as any and all deals I may have to make on his behalf were handled in a timely fashion, for now, that would keep me from looking more carefully.

We were booked to go commercial. Olga called mid-week, and when she learned we were going to Puerto Rico, she insisted on sending a Learjet.

"Not necessary," I told her.

"It is just sitting in New York getting dusty. It flies you there, and when you come back, you call me. We see what is available. Maybe I'll come get you in a big one."

I laughed.

"Get used to it, Amor. You and I are in it for life."

I got the chills that time.

"I need to cover the cost. Please."

"No," she said flatly.

The Learjet that flew us was not one I recognized. Not the one I knew was Camila's. It was plush and great, but it was a different jet. There is so much I don't know.

Pixie, Letty, and Tricia were on the Puerto Rico case. We made a fuel stop in Atlanta, Georgia, and from there flew direct to Puerto Rico. Juan and Valita picked us up in the limo Pixie had scheduled. Juan had finally managed to get Valita to marry him. She was as wildly primitive and as beautiful as ever, surprising me with a lusty kiss that reminded me of our time together in Venezuela. We gathered in my four-bedroom hotel suite to strategize, and to catch up on what they had learned of the passengers and their families.

"You have one family from Mexico who lost his wife and daughter. I talk to him, Boss. I did not push. He wants to talk to you right away."

"We need to wait until after the funerals."

Juan shook his head. "Tomorrow they release the bodies to him and he will go back to Guadalajara for burial."

I nodded. If he was flying back to Mexico tomorrow, it looked like we didn't have much wiggle room. "Arrange it."

Pixie called downstairs and got us a small conference room. The table took up most of the space. We catered. Nothing elaborate, just coffee and tea, and a tray of pastries since it was between meals.

When Luis arrived, each of us offered our condolences. We hugged as if we knew him. Funny how hugs break the ice and make an instant connection. Tears rolled, first from him, then from us.

Luis Amaral was in his mid-thirties, close to my age. He had thick dark brows that dominated his face, his eyes red and swollen as if he'd been crying for days, which he probably had. I gave him a quick glance and saw his stiff pair of new jeans that rasped when he moved, a black button-down shirt, a worn pair of well-made boots with new soles. His wife had been thirty, his daughter ten, and he was inconsolable. After a few minutes, we took our seats. I sat at the head and Luis took the seat to my right. Next to him, Pixie sat with a stack of documents in front of her. On my left, Letty, Tricia, and Juan. Tissue boxes were in easy reach, and we availed ourselves of them—all of us.

"Juan tells me you want to hire a lawyer."

"Yes." He nodded soberly. "Juan is correct."

"Luis, I very seldom talk to a family member until after a funeral, but I agreed to see you because you are leaving tomorrow."

He nodded again, settling into his chair, and resting his hands on the table, his gaze fixed on his left. He was still wearing his wedding ring, staring at it as if there were answers hidden inside.

Pixie slid the Spanish version of the Gonor Law Firm brochure in front of him, a book filled with pictures of aviation cases, closed and pending.

He looked up at her, a question in his sad eyes.

"For you to check later," Pixie told him. "It's the law firm."

He nodded.

"I have worked aviation tragedies all over the world for many years, and so has the law firm I am recommending."

The hand with the ring clutched at the spine of the book. Luis turned in his chair to meet my eyes squarely.

"I already trust you, Mario." He spoke in Spanish.

"Thank you."

I was about to open the book to give us something to talk about, but his words stopped me.

"How much will this cost?"

I was reluctant to talk money so soon after the tragedy, but his question made it easier.

"You pay the law firm one third of the settlement amount awarded by a court or reached through a settlement without court. Fees go up to forty percent once the case is filed in court. Most lawyers charge the same. This law firm has a flat fee of one third. You will also pay the expenses and costs that will be presented to you in detail at the time the case is closed."

His brow creased. "What if something happens and there is no settlement or award?"

"That's not going to happen," Pixie said, putting one hand over his.

"Good question," Letty said.

At the sound of her voice, he looked from Pixie at his right to Letty, who was across from him.

Letty met his eyes and continued. "That's not going to happen. But if it did happen, you pay nothing." Like Pixie's, her Spanish was perfect.

"What about the costs and expenses the attorney puts out?"

"If you get nothing, you pay nothing," Letty said.

"Luis, I feel terrible talking about money so soon, when your wife and daughter haven't been laid to rest."

He raised his palm, stopping me. "Rachel was very business-oriented. If I had died on that tour, she would have hired a lawyer immediately."

There was silence for a few seconds. "Thanks for telling me that," I said. "I feel better knowing that's what your wife would have wanted."

"Yes." As he spoke her name, his eyes filled. Two fat tears ran down his cheek. "Excuse me," he said, and reached for a tissue. "She was very smart."

"Luis, is it okay if I ask you some basic questions about your wife?" Pixie asked.

"Yes, it's okay."

Pixie pulled a pen from her pocket and turned the questionnaire so that Luis could see what she was writing.

"Her full name? Was she employed or self-employed?"

One hour later, Juan accompanied Luis to his hotel in a taxi. The girls and I went up to our suite.

Tricia sat stiffly on the loveseat, her stockinged feet squarely on the carpet, her eyes as pink as her socks. She swiped at her face with her arm. "I will never get used to this."

"None of us are used to it." Pixie spoke in a soft, battered voice she seldom used.

It is always hard. I'm no sensitive flower. A big guy like me, you'd think I could keep it cool, but sudden loss is agonizing. I identify so much with the family. When someone they love is ripped away, just gone, their lives are fractured. The wound is raw, feels like it will never heal. Sometimes it never does. We were all feeling sad from the case. Puerto Rico was all business. We came back from meetings and fortified ourselves quietly. Hugs, affection, huddled warm bodies. You'd be surprised how regenerative simple contact can be. You go to sleep feeling broken, but together; and in the morning, somehow, just by being together, you are renewed.

We don't always sign all the families, but this time we did—everyone but the pilots. The pilots were employees and covered by insurance; and if the cause was ruled pilot error, there could be conflict. There could also be a conflict of interest when you represent more than one family, but the retainers covered that possibility.

Camila called twice in the two weeks we were in Puerto Rico. I talked with Olga—not every day as we had agreed, but we did try to connect. It was more like every other day. When we did talk, she always wanted me. Always asked me to come to her. "Shall I send a plane for you today?"

I would look at the pile of work in front of me or at whatever was going on, and say no. By comparison to an airliner crash like we normally handled, this was a small case, but somehow it seemed more tormenting and more work than working with twenty, thirty, or more families like we did when a big one crashed.

"Be sure you let me know when to send a plane for you. Maybe I can pick you up and we can do it all the way to Los Angeles."

After we hung up, I wondered why marriage kept coming up. We could live together, have a ball together, and keep it open until she was done with LAI. Then if we were still happy and together, we could tie the knot. Why now?

Tricia went on to Chicago to deliver the retainers to Gonor. On the way home from Puerto Rico, we flew commercial to Miami and stayed for two days at the Delano Hotel, where Pixie had ordered the Presidential Suite for us. Two bedrooms.

Letty said, "That's one bedroom too many. We babes are sex-starved, Boss."

We would never find a bed as big as mine in a hotel, but a smaller bed can be fun when you have Pixie and Letty sleeping with you.

It was the end of March. Miami was sticky, but in the high seventies, lovely compared to March at home. We spent almost a whole day shopping and had to buy a suitcase for each one of us to handle our purchases, reminding me of all the Louis Vuitton suitcases back home that had been delivered full of cash.

At the airport, Pixie and Letty handled the check-in with six extra suitcases.

"We would not have been able to pack all that in the Learjet," Tricia said.

"Yeah, but it's so fucking cool to fly private," Letty said. "Boss, if you marry Olga or Camila, you'll have a plane at your fingertips."

"Yeah." Pixie nodded enthusiastically and grabbed my arm. "Do that. But you can't give up your right to have sex with us."

"I could buy my own Lear, but I don't want the maintenance and shit that comes with owning a plane."

Oscar's Learjet had been repossessed by the bank after he died. Sure, he'd lived extravagantly, and he had the lawyers on his payroll in two floors' worth of top-of-the-line high-dollar offices, but funding that high-maintenance bird had been one of the reasons he had died in debt, mortgaged to the hilt and cash broke.

No Lear for me.

The day we got home, two homicide detectives came to see me at the house. When they followed Pixie out of the elevator, I could see how they appreciated her fine ass, that is, until they noticed me standing beside my office door.

They sat down, and I faced them from across my desk. I hoped that Miguel had not noticed their arrival, and that he would not be sending up his usual smartass snack: pigs-in-blankets and doughnuts.

"I haven't seen Bruno in years. I fired him three years ago," I said, conveniently not mentioning when he snuck past the gates and guard and tried to push his way in to talk to me.

"Your phone number is on his phone bill a couple of times. One call the day before he was killed."

I said nothing.

"Why did you fire him?"

I told them about the fire but I didn't mention the biker. I told them how Bruno left me a message to meet him at The Pantry and how a friend met him instead. "He said he had overheard a conversation that would point to who was out to get me. He never said who it was—not to the staff member who took the message, not to my friend, and not to me when he called the night before he was killed. He wanted to get paid for the information."

"Do you think he knew something important? Something that got him killed?" asked one of the detectives.

I shrugged. "I didn't know Bruno well enough to know the answer to that. He worked for me about twenty-four hours before I fired him after the arson."

"Good possibility he was headed over here when he was taken out."

One detective was talking and the other was making notes.

"I don't know. Look, I cooperated with you; tell me, did he have anything in the car? Any tapes? A tape recorder?"

"Nothing like that. Why do you ask?"

I scratched my head, still probing for something about that tape. "He worked as a PI. Seems like he used to carry one." Immediately I knew something had gone terribly wrong. My buddy at the coroner's office said there was a tape recorder with a tape in it. These dudes were telling me nothing like that at all. Someone got the tape? I played it cool, though.

After they left, I called Melina and told her about the missing tape recorder. "Who knew about this?" she asked.

"Just the team...and I told Fino, actually. I asked him to find a friend or something that could get us access to the tape, a copy, or a transcription."

"I have more bad-vibe days about your friend Fino than good days," Melina said.

"I didn't know that. I thought you liked him?"

"On good days," she said. "Other times, I don't know. At dinner that night, he seemed, I don't know, jealous."

"He has so much money, it's crazy for him to be envious," I said, remembering his visit to the house.

"Maybe Fino got the tape for you. He hasn't called you?"

"You'd know if he called me," I said.

"Cuz, you shouldn't meet with cops again unless I'm there with you," Melina said sharply, concern heavy in her voice. I could hear lots of noise in the background. A voice on a loudspeaker asking for a price check. She must have been on the floor and taken the call where she was instead of going into her office. I heard several different people talking to her simultaneously and calling her name.

"Quiet!" she said sharply. "Not you, Mario. There are people here who can't wipe their ass without instructions."

I laughed. There was still a lot of background noise, but the voices stopped clamoring. "The detectives made no appointment. They just showed up."

"Well, it sounds like you handled it," she said begrudgingly.

"Of course I handled it. Besides, Baby, it's not like I killed Bruno."

"Of course you didn't kill him, but innocence is no protection from someone charging you."

"Give me a break."

"Don't get huffy, asshole, or I'll jump all over you," she threatened.

"Oh, that mouth. You sound like Pixie and Letty."

Chapter 6
April 1983
Wrecked

Mario

Pixie and Tricia left at six. The help dwindled one by one as they finished their work and went home. Miguel was the last to leave. The alarm was set throughout the house, and the guardhouse manned. Two German shepherds, trained guard dogs, accompanied the dog handler Pico when he did a walk of the grounds. Casa Luna certainly couldn't be compared to a prison, but once everything was locked down and we were in for the night, it reminded me of the ten days I spent at Terminal Island Prison. Well, maybe that's a stretch.

Letty and I were in the wine room, the television muted, the jukebox playing softly. Letty took a sip of the wine in my glass and wondered aloud, "Is this what married life is like?" She giggled and took a drag of the joint she was smoking.

It seemed to me that marriage was a topic on everybody's lips.

For this room, Melina had gotten a custom-made round sofa that went all the way around a table. Perfect for cuddling. I still missed my wine-room chairs, but they had burned in the fire.

Letty buried her face in my chest, one leg straight, one leg curled over my midsection. The wine glass she'd emptied sat on the table beside my half-full one. We were both relaxed. I didn't want to break the mood and send her the few feet away to the wine bar for a new bottle. I spoke through the joint between my lips. "Is this boring you?" I asked.

"How can you say that, Boss? I love it. Are you bored?"

"Never bored with you, Baby."

She snuggled tighter. "Me either."

At our ages, being single in Pasadena, we should be out clubbing. I suppose that living in this big house killed the urge to go out. While I was in the rented house, we'd gone out more. All of us, not just Letty and me. It had been a great house to stay in while this one was being built, but it had not been mine. It didn't have all the bells and whistles that this house has. My whole house is custom-fit to me. I have it all. The three years of living in the rented house and going out regularly—that burned us out, too. For now, we were happy to stay in.

"What are you thinking about?" Letty asked.

"You mentioned marriage." I was on my back. Her head moved from my chest to my arm, which was folded so that my hand rested over her hipbone. I slid my hand to her knee, which rested on me mid-chest. I repeated the motion as she settled closer to me. Her foot caressed my crotch, firming things up.

"I don't know what will happen to my life if I marry Olga. Or anyone else, for that matter. Look at us now. This would change."

She didn't comment. Time passed. Different songs played. We drank. We smoked.

I thought she'd gone to sleep, but she said, "You'll keep the team when you get married?"

"It's not when. It's if. I have no plans to give up my business."

"Oh, good." She stroked me with her foot. We couldn't get any closer than this.

I didn't want to get married. I didn't want to give up my team. I wanted

Olga. I wanted all of them.

I took another drag. I realized I was buzzed.

Letty giggled, sounding to me a lot like Pixie. She was buzzed too.

I could have taken the elevator, but I did not. I carried her to the fourth floor and placed her on my turned-down bed. I had no need to turn on a light. The fireplace was burning, creating a romantic ambiance.

"Boss, let's not go to sleep yet." Her voice was somewhere between a whisper and a giggle. She yawned hugely and eyed me in an impish fashion.

"Who said anything about sleep?"

Our clothes went flying.

When we were pooped out and on the verge of allowing sleep to take over, I said to Letty, "Would you marry me?"

I was hugging her from behind, my arms embracing her. I felt her hands touch my hands. "I won't marry you, but I will spend the rest of my life with you."

I kissed the back of her neck, her tight ass found a resting spot, and we went out.

For months I had been working on Lucas Salvador who owned a chain of liquor stores. I had already purchased liquor stores for LAI, but Lucas had a bunch of stores I wanted, sixty-one locations leased back to the corporation that owned the liquor store. In other words, he was renting to himself. He said it was a tax thing. I didn't care what it was.

"Lucas, half of your properties are in foreclosure. I don't blame you for not wanting to sell, but we can both see what's going to happen down the road. When you lose your ass, don't come running to me at the last minute. After the first property goes down at foreclosure, the rest will fall like dominoes."

"Mario, all you need is a mask. Your offer is highway robbery."

He owed four million[4] to pay off all the mortgage. He needed several

---

[4] $4,000,000.00 in 1983 had the same buying power as $10,103,442.62 in 2018

hundred thousand just to rescue the properties that were already in default. I'd had Tricia triple-check his finances and assets. He was buried. He'd mortgaged everything down to his underwear. He'd already hung himself. Interest on his mortgages and second mortgages was going to strangle him. It would not be long before his whole operation went down the tubes. I was surprised he'd kept it together as long as he had.

"I'm giving you one hundred thousand[5] per store, plus cash for each store's inventory. That's a good deal. It's a hell of a lot better than what you have going right now."

"What about my equity? What about that?"

"It's part of the deal. Lucas, my offer is a gift. You aren't making money. You aren't even close to breaking even. All you have are a bunch of stores, but if you don't act now, you are out, and you know it. You were smart enough to put all these stores on the map, so I know you aren't stupid. Your suppliers are leaving you like rats off a sinking ship. Before long, you won't have any product to sell, and you won't be able to buy more. I checked. I know."

Pepe never asked if a business was making money, and I understood why. He wanted to pump cash into the business—his way of laundering money. This was not common knowledge. He knew, the management company that managed the US properties I bought for him had to know, and I had guessed. He had never told me outright, but he didn't have to. His actions confirmed this more than his words. One thing was certain—LAI could work wonders with sixty-one liquor outlets.

If the agreement went through, LAI's bank account would pay off the mortgages. If he agreed to it, Lucas would get the settlement outside of escrow in cash.

"What the fuck am I going to do with that much cash?"

"Take less and I'll put all the money in escrow for you. But if you want what's on the table, it's cash."

---

[5] $100,000.00 in 1983 had the same buying power as $252,586.07 in 2018

I had read him from the beginning as being a seller who would appreciate cash. I think he wanted some leverage. That's why he was raising hell about it now.

"You are fucking killing me, Mario."

"Don't be stupid, Lucas. Take the deal. Walk away clean."

"On top of the mortgages, I have creditors. That amount you quote won't be what I walk away with."

I was growing impatient. Not much had happened in the five face-to-face meetings we'd had before this call, and it was difficult to deal on the phone, where I could not see his face.

"Tell you what, Lucas. I'll up the current offer ten thousand[6] per store. I pay off the mortgages through escrow and I will hand you the cash for the business and inventory. You need to find a way to get what you need to escrow to pay off the liens."

He exhaled and grabbed the deal.

"Let's get this motherfucker over with." Then he said, "Aren't you afraid that one day a seller like me is going to turn you in to the feds for making cash deals?"

Everything was perfect until he said that. I didn't show any anger, but he pissed me off. "Lucas, why don't you keep the stores, go to the feds, and explain to them what you think is illegal about paying cash for a bunch of shit stores and property."

"Hey, Mario, dn't mean anything. Sorry I said what I said—come on."

"Forget about me. I told you from the beginning, this is not my money. The person who it belongs to is not someone you want to cross. You got that, Lucas?"

"Loud and clear, man. Arrange for the cash and let's close the deal. And when you see me, take a punch at me for what my big mouth said. Go ahead."

---

[6] $10,000.00 in 1983 had the same buying power as $25,258.61 in 2018

While Pixie and Letty went out of town on two small single-engine plane crashes that claimed a total of five lives, Tricia stayed close. She read countless listings of commercial and apartment buildings. I was still going after foreclosures, but not only foreclosures. A good deal meant a lot of negotiating, especially for properties not in foreclosure. Listed properties were a lot easier than foreclosures, except for that messy hitch of finding someone who could take cash.

I'd found a local gas station chain called 'Cheap Gas.' Seventy-five locations, all in Los Angeles county cashed payroll checks free with a fill-up, and with a fee if there was no purchase. I envisioned LAI dropping off cash weekly by courier. Checks would be cashed and banked. I hadn't figured the angle yet of how the big corporation that owned the gas stations would be able to swing taking cash, but the business was a natural for the Camacho empire. I hadn't even broached the subject of cash to the seller, but the ongoing ability of cash moving to a bank account fit the Camacho niche. Cashing checks was a big deal. Most workers cashed their paychecks, purchased money orders to pay bills, and paid cash for their purchases. Melina's markets cashed payroll checks for customers free of charge. She often complained that she had almost a hundred thousand dollars tied up in ready cash for the markets, a sum she had nicknamed 'dead money.' Her markets would deposit the checks they cashed for customers then draw it back out in cash to have on hand to cash more checks. If LAI owned the gas stations, checks cashed would be deposited and fresh cash would arrive from the Camacho stash so that no cash had to be drawn back like Melina did with her markets.

"Can I come over?" Olga asked me on the phone from Van Nuys Airport.

"Are you serious?" I wanted to show off more than LAI's new gas stations and liquor stores.

When I first started with Pepe, we discussed details on the phone but now, I seldom discuss any pending deal with Pepe, at least not on the phone. I told details to Camila and Olga when they were around, in person, but I didn't trust phones. Oscar, my lawyer friend who introduced me to Pepe, used to tell me to use a pay phone when I talked to Pepe about anything. "And never use the same pay phone more than once." To this day, I don't know why I had to be so careful back then; our talks were never about business, because I had no business with him. The calls were social calls following my kidnapping and Pepe mobilizing my rescue from the kidnappers.

"Well, do you want me over or not? Hello?"

"I said are you serious?"

"Serious as a firecracker," she answered in Spanish.

"Get your fine ass over here," I said, and glanced over at Tricia, who was engrossed in a stack of real estate documents on the conference table. Pixie and Letty were on the way home from their separate appointments, both with retainers. Tricia could keep doing what she was doing. I had no problem with driving, especially if it was to get my Olga. "Want me to come fetch you?"

"Thanks, Amor, but I have a car picking me up in five minutes. I have the boys with me; they will follow, then find a place there in Pasadena."

"Great, so you're staying?"

"Yes, Amor."

At two in the afternoon, when the limo dropped her off, I met Olga at the door. It swung open and we fell together into a big hug. Pixie and Letty had just gotten back; they hung back with more discretion than they usually offer, but their manners did not last long, and in moments they engulfed Olga. I noticed the two suitcases at her side. Louis Vuitton of course, but unlike the ones she used for currency. She noticed that I noticed, gave me an uncertain look, and pointed at her suitcases.

"Cash?" Letty asked perkily from behind me.

It was the wrong kind of suitcase for that. I shook my head.

"Clothes," Olga said, answering Letty but looking at me. "Are you okay that I just invited myself, luggage and all?"

I felt a huge smile stretch across my face. "I may not let you leave." I pulled her back into another hug.

She whispered in my ear, "Promises, promises. I left the big plane in New York getting a seven-day service. I'm here in the Lear. I have a week. Are you sure it's okay? I am here for seven days if you'll have me."

I wanted to tell her she could stay forever. "You can stay a week?" This was a first. "I'm delighted to host for as long as you want, Baby. I'm so pleased that I have to—" I obeyed the surge of excitement that shot through me, picked her up right there in the front hall, and swung her around until she was laughing out loud, then I set her on her feet and looked her over. She was looking comfortable and touchable in jeans, a cashmere sweater, and sneakers. The denim was new and a little stiff, unlike the ones the girls wore, which had been washed to softness. Maybe her sense of style was changing, or maybe she was just feeling comfortable with me, and felt no need to dress up.

"I love you in jeans with that fine jeans ass."

She turned around, so I could get a good look and gestured like she was going to unbutton and drop them to her ankles.

I waved Caro over and pointed up the stairs. She nodded twice, once to show me her understanding, and once as a gesture to Olga, then took the bags to one of the third-floor guest rooms. The team trailed behind her, returning to the office.

Miguel delivered a platter of sandwiches to us in the wine room. Finger sandwiches with the crusts cut off, but there was a small mountain of them, all roast beef with a bowl of fragrant *au jus* for dipping. Beside the wine decanter, Miguel put two plates in front of us on the round table in the center of the sofa. The plates were flavored and decorated with bits of fresh cilantro, freesia, and other herbs, and a slice of cinnamon-jalapeño-spiced apple in some kind of pastry. I had whiled away a few nights here with Letty, but Olga's presence made the room her own.

"You look ravishing," I said to Olga when Miguel left.

"It's you who looks ravishing."

I shivered as she looked me over, feeling her gaze on my skin.

We kissed slowly and ate and drank red Argentinian wine. My brain and tongue knew the finely sliced roast beef was succulent, the *au jus* gravy salty and savory, but I only had appetite for Olga.

"What about the girls? Do they mind my being here?"

"My girls are fine."

"I don't know about that." She gave a little laugh. "I got the hugs and kisses, but Pixie and Letty stared at my luggage kind of strange."

"Baby, no. They love you."

"And I love them."

"They're probably excited and wondering if you're going to invite them to join us in bed."

"No problem, Amor. You know me."

I did know her. Neither she nor Camila objected to bedding their same sex.

"You don't need to invite them to our bed." I didn't want to add any pressure. Maybe I wanted her all to myself.

"Liar, you love it."

We kissed softly, the Merlot flavoring our lips, slickening the friction between us. Our lips were wet with shared wine.

"I do love it. I love being with you."

"Then why are we in the wine room?"

I spoke to her, still lip to lip. "Foreplay."

She snuck another little kiss. I caught my breath.

"Amor, you know I'm not jealous. I want you to do what you always do. I don't want to interfere."

"You're not interfering." I filled her glass. As she held it to her lips, I watched her, how the red of the wine reflected in her eyes, tinting them to burgundy, shades darker than her manicured nails. Though the room's lamps were on a rheostat, they were not dimmed, and the light softly caressed her face, lending a softness to it that matched her cashmere. Her fingers wrapped around the stem of the glass bore nearly as many rings as Camila's usually did, not all of them with stones. A thin silk scarf was wound around her head like a headband. I reached over, pulled it loose, and tossed it aside. It floated to drape over the couch's edge. I leaned close and nuzzled the hollow of her collar bone. She smelled spicy, like wine and something else, something exotic I had no words for.

She looked at me, startled, and put her hand to her hair, smoothing the pixie cut that emphasized her big eyes. I put my hand over hers.

"Music?" she asked.

"Anything you want."

I pointed to the stereo sitting in the built-in Formica cabinet set against one wall. With the press of a button, the music from any of a dozen house stereos could be pumped through the intercom. Olga did not know about it, but that was okay. This music was for us alone. She walked over to check out the hundreds of eight-track tapes Pixie had an addiction to buying, and picked one out. A Spanish pop song, one I hadn't heard before. She stalked toward me in time with the music and started dancing.

I leaned back, watching her, feeling the slow burn of arousal. She had her own unique way of moving, which I fully appreciated, but then she stopped.

"I'm not in this alone," she said, trying to pull me into the dance. We grinned at each other, but I don't dance, at least not standing up. I pulled her next to me. It was going to be a long week, and I had every intention of making the most of it.

Melina came over on Sunday. I heard the doorbell, but Olga and I were in the pool at the time. Someone let her in, probably Sunny, since it was Sunny who led her to where we were swimming indoors. I had not told Melina that

Olga was visiting. Olga climbed out of the pool with me behind her and gave her an air-kiss, respecting the designer dress Melina was wearing. Melina laughed and pulled her into a real hug, getting water all over the clothes.

"Don't stop swimming on my account. Get back in the water before you get cold." Without a bit of awkwardness, Melina took a seat on one of the patio chairs and conversed with us for a good thirty minutes. While Olga was telling some story about a fashion show in Milan, Melina's beeper went off. She didn't even glance at it but stood and said, "Duty calls." She left abruptly and did not return. She did not call me. I did not call her. I was consumed by Olga. Going back for years, I couldn't remember a Sunday when I was in town that I had not spent with Melina. Our Sundays were practically sacred. No doubt Melina was pissed off.

Olga stayed nine days and the team did not get invited to bed with us. Pixie and Letty said their goodbyes on that last day when we popped into my office on the top floor. It was April Fools' Day, and Pixie squirted me in the face with a plastic flower pinned on her shirt. I was not amused and told her no more pranks were allowed. Olga laughed at me.

"You don't know how Pixie is on April Fools' Day. I bet she has a hundred dollars' worth of stuff from the joke store that she plans to use on me."

Holding hands like teenagers, Olga and I took the elevator down, and I walked her to where Tricia was waiting in the driver's seat of my Rolls. Olga's luggage was already stowed. I kissed Olga as I held open the car door.

"Can I come back?"

"I don't want you to leave."

"Does that mean you want me to come back?"

Our lips touched. "Yes," I whispered in her ear. I palmed her face and kissed her.

"I'll return before you know it."

"Let's talk every day."

"You know I want that."

"I do too."

"Do you love me just a little?"

"No." I felt her nibble my lip. "I love you a lot."

"We need to be together," she said.

"I agree. We are better together."

"You're beautiful, Baby."

The Rolls pulled away. I watched the car disappear down the forested driveway toward the front entrance. After I could not see the car, I still stood there like a dummy. Olga was driving away and taking my heart with her. I had held her by the face and kissed her. I raised my hands to my nose. She was gone, but her scent remained on my palms, the feel of her in my fingertips.

I had not turned nor made a move for the front door. Maybe a minute had passed, and I was still mawkishly staring down the drive. Squeal of tires. Crunch of metal. Air brakes. A collision somewhere near the gates. No one knows the sound of a car crash better than I do. It sounded like a monster of a truck. I thought I heard a shot. My heart leaped into my throat.

"Olga," I said, my mouth dry, my voice a cracked whisper.

I took off running down the driveway. It wasn't just a wreck. I heard gunfire. Loud, rapid shots. I ran past the empty guardhouse through the front gates that were standing open. I saw Quito leaving the car, a red stain on his shoulder. The Rolls was crippled, rear-ended, twisted around the front of a truck that was still wedged into the trunk of the Rolls. The trunk lid was gnarled, the lock broken by the impact, gapped but not standing open. The seam between the trunk and the car was yawning, squashed like a soft clay model that had been squeezed and wedged under the truck's undamaged front. The rear end of the Rolls was crumpled and compacted, skid marks from the tires showing an angled path. Not a sound from Tricia. Not a sound from Olga. *Olga*. I smelled rubber, gas and smoke but saw no fire. Quito passed me at a run, panting. I saw blood on his uniform but did not know whose it was.

Without a break in his step, he yelled, "I'm calling paramedics, Boss."

We were running in opposite directions. I ran behind the truck, and my feet took me to the driver's door. It was standing open. Tricia slouched facing out, both feet on the pavement. Her right wrist was resting at an odd angle on the steering wheel, her hand just hanging there, the pistol in it loosely held. On the floor mat by the pedal, I saw another handgun.

"Tricia."

I knelt in front of her. Her head was slumped down. I could not see her face, just the top of her head. I reached for her chin to lift her face, and my hand came away wet. She was bleeding. I glimpsed a bloody lip.

"Going to be okay. Check Olga." She didn't move from the wilted position, her voice audible, but barely so. Clearly, she needed looking after, but I was desperate to find Olga. I did not see her on the seat. In the moment, I needed to be twins.

I tried the back door. Jammed. Ran to the other side. Both back doors were jammed, but at least I could see Olga on the floor, pale and still and silent. I gave the passenger door a desperate pull, and nothing. I stepped back and saw how the car's body had been shoved forward. I tried the handle a few more times, pulling with my full weight, and keeping a foot braced against the frame. The window cracked and half of it fell inside the door. I bent the hell out of the top part that framed the glass, but it creaked open enough for me to get a good grip on the door's skeleton. I pulled for all I was worth. The whole time, I was talking to Olga, telling her I was coming for her and I don't know what else. Olga said nothing. Neither did Tricia.

Seeing her like that, helpless and immobile, drove me to a herculean effort. I tried a couple of holds till I found the most effective one. The hinges protested in a shrill metal shriek. I levered myself in and hovered over her, helpless.

"Olga, Baby, can you hear me?"

No reply, but a groan. She did not open her eyes, but a groan was good.

A groan meant she was alive. They were both alive. They needed help. I was here, but what could I do? Here and helpless. I was afraid to touch her. Too many cases in my head. Too many stories of people getting fatal injuries while being assisted out of a car. I wanted to scream for the fucking ambulances and fire department. I had spent more time on the door than I'd thought. The sirens were already approaching. I felt sick with terror and worry, crouched over her, bracing my weight on the seat. The worst was the blood on her face. I could not see what had cut her, nor how bad it was.

"Olga, Baby."

I heard Quito saying something calming to Tricia.

"The paramedics are here. The police are here."

Quito was repeating himself. I guess I was too. Someone in uniform asked if I was hurt, asked if I was able to stand. I jabbered something about Olga, squeezed my way out of the back seat, moved aside for the paramedics. I stood next to the car, crazed, surrounded by firemen readying the Jaws of Life, caught in the dance of paramedics and firemen. It was like a nightmare I had visited too many times.

The stink of burning rubber was still in the air. I couldn't smell gasoline any more. Both of the doors to my back seat had been forced open, and the crowd of rescue workers who had maneuvered me aside were massed around the Rolls. I could not see what they were doing. Pixie and Letty were beside me looking pale and shocked. I had not noticed their arrival. I saw cops with clipboards walking alongside Tricia who was flat on her back on a stretcher.

"I'll ride with Tricia," Pixie said, as the paramedics moved Tricia's gurney into the ambulance.

The second ambulance was ready for the next patient.

"I'll meet you at the hospital. I'll get my car and everybody's stuff," Letty said, then ran to the house.

"Is she going to be okay?" I asked a paramedic.

"She'll be at Huntington Memorial."

The cluster of firemen and paramedics moved from the Rolls to the ambulance as they maneuvered Olga's gurney. I could not see her, but I knew she was alive. I got in the ambulance with her, sat in a jump seat while paramedics worked on Olga. The five-minute drive from my house to the hospital took three minutes in an ambulance.

In the emergency room, nurses and orderlies came around and made Olga comfortable. She was quiet but held my hand, just with her left. Her right arm was in a contraption the paramedics had put on her. It seemed like hours before a doctor came. He wanted to see her alone, so I walked across the hall to Tricia who was in better shape, but quiet. Pixie talked enough for them both, and explained Tricia had a split lip and bitten tongue. Her face was badly bruised. She was sitting up in the ER bed with an icepack to her split lip, and had been given a shot at some point before I came in. She was feeling no pain, but I didn't ask if it was a local or something like morphine. Letty was there too, carrying everyone's purses and coats. She handed me my leather jacket. Tricia didn't speak but gave me a peace sign and waved me back to Olga's room.

Both Olga and Tricia had broken noses. Olga had fractured her right elbow and wrist and had two serious cuts, one on her forehead and another on her chin. I was at the hospital bouncing between their rooms to various waiting rooms and being as supportive as possible. Both of them went straight from their ER beds to plastic surgeons who surgically dealt with their broken noses. Olga's surgery began first and took longer as her facial cuts were to be made invisible by the plastic surgeon's skilled stitching.

I reached Pepe at the Milan house. Ever since the FBI's beef with him, he did not travel to the US, but I believe if the injury had happened in any other country, he would have come to her no matter where. I told him that the preliminary x-rays did not reveal a concussion, that Olga's facial surgery had gone well, and that she was resting in recovery. Her right elbow and wrist might need future surgery, but a cast had been applied.

"Why didn't she have her guards with her?" Pepe asked. "They travel to protect her."

"The guards and pilots stayed in a hotel. Tricia was taking her to the airport, so Olga was having them meet her on the plane."

"She is very stupid about her own safety. The guards must stay with her."

"I'm sorry, Pepe."

"Keep me informed. The doctors expect her to recover?"

"Yes. She will stay at my house with a private nurse after they release her from the hospital. I will be at her side. Do you know where Camila is?"

Pepe said, "Camila was in Rio when the first officer let her know he called your house and found out there had been an accident. By now she is probably on her way to you."

I caught her minutes before she left the house.

"Amor, Letty brought me up to date. She's called me twice. Anything new?"

"She's in recovery. The plastic surgeon did good."

"I will see for myself. I am on my way."

"Looking forward to seeing you. Plan on staying at the house. Don't go to a hotel."

"Amor, thank you."

Once Olga was out of recovery and situated in a private room, we were given five minutes to see her. She was sedated but her smile worked. I gently kissed her. On the other side of the bed, Pixie and Letty kissed her too.

"I'm so glad to be alive, Amor." Tears appeared in her eyes. "I thought I was going to die."

Letty dabbed the tears with a tissue.

"You didn't die," Pixie said, rubbing Olga's belly through the sheet. "You are right here and soon we will take you home to recover."

Letty moved close to her ear. "When you feel up to it, I am going to give you the best head you ever had."

"Si," Olga said.

We were given the same amount of time with Tricia.

"My tongue," she said thickly, sounding like she had a mouth full of marbles. "So stupid."

I kissed her. "Don't talk."

"Have to," she lisped. "I'm dopey and I know I'm about to go out again."

Tricia told how she heard the truck roar toward her before it struck, how afterward, in the rear-view mirror, she saw the truck driver leap out of the truck. Behind him, a biker drove up, and squealed to a stop.

"I had hit my face. My eyes were tearing up. I don't know if I passed out or was in shock, but I blinked, and saw the biker peering in the back window. *The* biker," she said with emphasis.

"Biker?"

"The bastard from the freeway. The picture of him that we have. The asshole from the restaurant in San Antonio. That biker. He was staring through the window at Olga. He yelled out to the truck driver who was waiting on the motorcycle, 'He's not in here.' Then he was swearing his fucking head off. He was looking for you, and I'm sure he was pissed off because it was not you in the back seat of the car. He didn't even glance at me. Must have figured I was unconscious, or dead."

A nurse came in, interrupted Tricia's painful recital, gave her a fresh ice pack for her split lip, and scolded her for talking.

"Five more minutes and we're gone," I said to the nurse.

She fussed around the room a few minutes while we waited for her to leave.

When the door closed behind her, Tricia continued, "I pulled my gun. He double-timed it to the bike, climbed on, trucker behind him. I aimed for the tank and tires to disable their ride, then shot at the men. Emptied the clip and pulled the second gun. My eyes were bloody and blurry. Not sure how good a shot I got in. My eyes were screwed up." She raised her hand to touch her broken nose. "Think I got one of them, because he was yelling."

The doctors told the girls and me to go home and rest. Both patients would soon be over and out for at least eight hours. What they needed now was rest.

Letty drove us in her car, a two-seater Corvette like Pixie's. The top was off to give me head room. My first car had been one of these, but either I wasn't six feet five inches back then, or I was better at fitting in cramped spaces. The passenger seat pushed all the way back. My legs fit okay, but with Pixie on me, we were squeezed to say the least. April was cold with the T-Top off. Good thing Letty had brought coats.

"Take the streets," I told Letty. "If a cop sees us, you're getting a ticket."

"Worth it, this is fun."

Now that we knew the extent of the injuries, we felt better.

Pixie was getting excited. "If the girls weren't in the hospital, I'd tell you to slip it inside me, Boss," Pixie moved her ass on my lap. Her legs were wedged in a crossed position, resting on my upper calves with no room for her legs and feet.

"Oh, you are so bad," Letty said, taking a fast left that shifted our weight against the door.

As soon as we got home, we watched the security tapes. In the den, Quito had already fast-forwarded to the correct time stamp. The big truck had been parked along the curb since nine on the morning of the accident, two hours before the collision. A man with a hat, heavy jacket and dark pants twice got out and back in the truck, and a man on a motorcycle picked him up afterward. It was obvious the men knew the cameras were there and avoided showing their faces. We watched the sequences from several different camera angles.

"Boss, the police requested a copy of the tapes. Is it okay?"

I told him to do it. If we said no, they'd wonder and come back with a warrant.

There was nothing useful on the tape.

I woke at five but skipped the workout and fell back to sleep. About six, a guard notified me that Camila had arrived. I was in bed alone, Letty in her room, Pixie in a guest room.

I took the stairs to the second floor and found Camila in the kitchen. We hugged and kissed. I could see Camila was anxious over Olga's condition. Miguel had obviously been awake for a while. Racks of muffins and pastries were cooling on the kitchen counter. He had coffee going, and the oven was giving off the scent of something baked and delicious.

It's about ten hours from Rio to Miami, about six more from Miami to Pasadena. After the long flight from Brazil, even at this hour, Camila looked marvelous. As we stood at the kitchen island, Miguel moved silently, pouring us coffee. Camila already had a muffin on a plate. Caro whisked Camila's bags upstairs.

"I took a sleeping pill in Rio. When we fueled up in Miami, I barely could stay awake for customs. I got back in bed and slept until we were over Arizona."

"You look great."

"You are okay about Olga's condition?"

"She's going to be fine. They will watch her a couple days, do more tests to rule out a concussion, then I believe they will let her come home."

"When can we see her?"

"Visiting hours don't start till eight-thirty. I'll shower, and we can head over there."

"Tell me about the security video."

"Tricia had more to offer than the video. She recognized the biker bastard, same as in the picture someone pasted on your NY apartment door. That's the biker, same one that years back tried to shoot me on the freeway."

Camila's face went scarlet.

"He must die," she hissed in Spanish. "Did you tell Pepe this?"

"Not yet."

"My poor Olga." Tears ran down her face.

I tried to comfort her.

"Estoy Bien, Amor."[7] But her eyes were still worried.

Miguel slid a basket of muffins and pastries within reach. I saw Camila reach for one.

"Have a bite and get comfortable. Miguel will fix you anything you want. Caro, when Miss Camila is ready, show her to her room."

Pepe called me at home before Olga was released.

"Mario, I never ask you for a favor."

"Anything, my friend, what can I do?"

"Olga's security detail. If she is at your house, so are her guards. They stay till she departs. I don't care if they sleep in tents as long as they are on the property."

I didn't remind him that I already had security, or that after he heard what Tricia witnessed, Pepe himself had said that I was the target, not Olga.

"Of course, Pepe. Consider it done."

"I won't forget this favor," Pepe said graciously.

I wanted to laugh. After all he had done for me, he called this a favor.

When Olga was released, she returned to the guest room she used before. She and Tricia both refused hospital beds I was willing to put in for them. I had to threaten to fire Tricia to make her stay on the third floor till she was recovered. The nursing service Melina had arranged made sure our two invalids each had twenty-four-hour care.

Miguel was happy with so many people to feed. Of course, he said nothing, but he was always in the kitchen cooking, and humming, a grin on his face. It wasn't just Olga, the regular house staff, and four nurses, two of whom were always on duty. Olga's five guards now needed feeding too. Letty made room

---

[7] I'm fine, Love

for the guards. Rollaway beds in the common areas of the staff's quarters. My security guys took care of their own meals, but Olga's security ate at the house. With Olga's guards on the property, Camila's security stayed at a hotel.

Camila left the day after Olga was settled on the third floor. Camila's last words before she got in the limousine: "Amor, guard her with your life."

Inches behind the limo, a GMC Suburban followed with Camila's security detail. One of the guards rode in the front passenger side of Camila's limousine. The pilots and crew were already at the Ontario Airport. I thought back to the day of the accident. If Olga's security team had done the same, maybe the car riding shotgun in the back would have sustained the impact of the truck, instead of the Rolls Olga and Tricia were in.

I took a Wednesday lunch with Fino, our usual steaks and salads. I was seeing the biker in every shadow, so I stayed sober with sparkling water and a squeeze of lime. Fino swirled his snifter of brandy.

"I used to think this biker bastard was not really trying to kill me. Can't think that any longer," I told Fino. "That truck was a weapon of mass destruction. It is a miracle that Olga and Tricia are still breathing. They could have suffered tremendous injuries."

"I agree, Mario. I just don't understand why. Maybe you have some dark secrets I don't know about." He looked up at me and shook his head. "Secrets I don't need to know. Absent that, I'm at a loss."

"I have no dark secrets," I said. Who had I stepped on during my life that would be doing this?

Betty practically moved in. Olga was improving, and her massage sessions moved from thirty minutes to sixty minutes and eventually to two hours.

"Now I know why you guys always get massages," she said to me. "I totally love Betty working my body and I mean, she does all of my body."

I know I looked like a dunce when I said, "All of your body?"

It became a routine to have breakfast with her at a table in her room. I spent a lot of time with Olga.

"I'm so sorry that I am taking up so much of your time, but Amor, I adore you."

"Baby, I love you being here. Soon you will be totally recovered."

"Si, Amor." Her appetite was better now that she was no longer on a bland diet. She had dressed for breakfast in black lingerie.

Tricia poked her head in. She was wearing pink sweats.

"Boss, I don't want to interrupt, but Caro brought me the paper."

"No problem," I said. "Keep it, we have extra."

"Thanks, Boss," she said, returning to her room. I heard the door close.

Very softly, Olga said, "Tricia's boyfriend comes over to see her every day. Amor, don't take this wrong, but I feel very uncomfortable that he is former FBI and he is here every day."

I also felt uncomfortable, but I trusted Tricia so much that I couldn't see anything bad happening as a result of her bed partner, Bill Rush, being an ex-Fed. He seemed like a totally good guy. Had to be for Tricia to be drawn to him. She had survived a bad marriage. I wasn't sure she even divorced that asshole in Nevada. "Tricia got rid of her nurse and is aching to go home," I said. "Bear with this a little longer, Baby, *Si*?"

"*Si*, Amor, of course. I just had to tell you."

"Always be open with me," I said.

"We are open with each other, Amor. I adore you."

I met with Tricia in her room after breakfast. Bill was at her bedside. The bruises from her broken nose made her look a little like a raccoon. She wasn't a fussy type and didn't bother to try covering them up with makeup.

Tricia held up a sheet of paper. Though I didn't know what it was, I nodded. She handed it over to Bill.

"Boss, I gave Bill a picture of the biker. He's going to put some feelers out with some of his friends. I hope you don't mind."

I was a little alarmed by this. Maybe it showed on my face.

Bill said, "Mario, I know you didn't report the freeway incident. Don't worry about it. If I find out who it is, you have my word only you and Tricia will know."

We shook hands.

"Thanks, Bill. The freeway thing was three years ago."

"Yes, Tricia told me."

After that, Tricia went home. I insisted she take off until she was one hundred percent. Bill Rush agreed with me. At first, I was pissed that Tricia had given him the picture. What else might show up in her pillow talk? But I believed Bill's assurances. If he really cared for her, he had a personal reason to want to identify this mother fucker. We could proceed from there.

Detectives kept calling the house asking if Olga was well enough to meet with them. Eventually Olga told them to come over. We met in the conference room where the girls normally worked. Olga and me, and the two detectives. I didn't know them, but they felt familiar. Something about their short hair and cheap suits. One was about my age, the other old enough to be going gray.

Olga gave them her account of the events of April first. She had been taken by surprise when the truck slammed into the car. She'd seen no one.

To my surprise, one of the detectives took out two still shots and showed them to her. I was sitting beside her and saw them clearly, even before she slid them over to me. It was the biker. Not a good picture, but I recognized him instantly.

"Have you ever seen this man?" one detective asked Olga.

"I didn't see anyone."

"Did these come from my security tape?" I asked.

"They did. Only two halfway decent shots out of three tapes."

The detectives never asked me if I recognized the man in the picture. I'm not sure what my answer would have been. It is not as if I knew his identity.

"Do you have pictures of your injuries?"

"I have them," I said. "Give me your card. If Olga says okay, I'll send them to you."

"No problem by me. I don't look very nice in those pictures, sorry." She smiled at the two suits.

"What is your occupation?" They asked Olga.

"I'm a senior consultant and advisor to a global investment company."

"And the purpose of your visit?"

"I was here to see Mario. Here for nine days. Do you know who the truck belonged to?"

"It was stolen from a hauling company in Boyle Heights."

"I figured it was stolen," Olga said.

"The crash looks deliberate. It's too early to know who the target was. We may never know. It's possible you were not the target. The car you were in belonged to Mr. Luna."

The detective looked at me.

"I've thought of that," I said, "but I got no idea who would want to take me out. Seems like there has to be an easier way to get at me than to steal a truck and wait out in front of my house for two hours to ram my car."

"We're looking at it like that, too."

I could not answer the questions they had for me. Why did they figure I would be in the car that day, at that hour? Did I have a snitch in the house? A snitch in the house seemed unlikely. I'd had no plans of leaving that morning or the entire day for that matter.

"What's your phone number?"

"You can call her here. I'll get the message to her," I said handing them a couple of my business cards.

Olga made eye contact with both detectives sitting across from her.

"I will give you my business card too. The phone is monitored 24/7. Sorry, it's Italy, long distance."

"We can try you through Mr. Luna first. If we can't reach you here, we can call your office in Italy."

"Anything else?" Olga asked.

The men got up. "Not for now. We hope you recover soon."

The bruising on her face was gone, and she looked beautiful. I was sure the detectives were thinking the same.

Letty escorted them to the exit.

"The biker is in the open now," I said to Letty. "I should have checked those security tapes more closely."

"Amor, it's okay. They got his picture. So, what? They better get him before Pepe does."

"Or me," I added. "Want to go back to your room?"

"Absolutely not. I feel good, Amor. Let me stick around here for a while."

Without moving from her chair, she looked around like she had never seen the conference room before. Pixie walked in, and a few minutes later, Letty was back.

"If you are going to sit there young lady, you will have to start reading some telexes," Pixie said with a giggle. She pushed a stack of unread messages in front of Olga.

Letty sat next to Olga, took her hand and kissed it. "I'm so glad you are better."

"I love you, Letty," Olga said, then looked up at who had moved behind the chair. "I love you, Pixie."

"We love you, too," Pixie said.

"That's for sure," Letty echoed.

Melina had never practiced law, but she did have a license. On the phone, I told her, "We never mentioned anything about the freeway or anything about the picture pasted on the door in New York."

"I would have advised you to tell them the entire story. But what is done is done," Melina said. "Don't worry about it. How is Olga?"

"She's doing much better. Thanks for asking. She handled the interview perfectly."

"I need to get over there and visit. She must think I'm a bitch."

"You are a bitch, Baby, but she's never said that."

"Asshole."

"See? You're a bitch."

"Love you, Cuz. Got to get back to work. Miss you."

Melina knew Olga was staying in my house. She was smarter than smart. After that short call, I was convinced that Melina was receptive to the fact that going forward it was Olga and me as a couple. It pained me when I thought about it. Melina was very important to me. In our own ways, I in mine, she in hers, we loved each other, big time.

Tricia called daily. I told her the local cops had pulled two pictures from the security camera.

"I want to come back to work, Boss." She was getting paid as though she was working.

"Not until all the bruising is gone and you can pass a fitness test."

"A fitness test, Boss?"

I laughed. "Baby, I keep forgetting you have Bill now. You don't need me anymore."

"Boss, I'll bend over for you, any time. Just say the word."

"Stop talking like that. I just got hard."

"Boss, listen, Bill found nothing on this prick but all we have is the picture."

"Well, if the FBI can't find anything, then I doubt the locals are going to come up with a hit," I said.

"I know I got a shot in him. I just know it."

She had said that a hundred times. "I'm sure Bill has checked the hospitals."

"Bill works in secret. Sometimes I don't think the idea of retirement has really sunk in."

Maybe he didn't retire. Maybe he was a plant?

"I'm glad they have his picture."

"It's done, Baby. Call me tomorrow. Let's see how you feel by then."

"Boss, I'm ready to come back, already."

"Okay, Monday, come back."

"Deal," she said. "I'll call you tomorrow."

On her return, Tricia wanted to talk about Quito.

"He should have done something when he noticed that big truck sitting out there for two hours or more. He didn't scan the tapes properly. If he had, he would have found the biker picture like the cops did."

"Where are you going with this?"

"He fucked up."

I did not respond immediately. I don't know if my experience with Bruno had made me more compassionate, but I had not turned on Quito when this had happened. I don't know if that was because my head was full of Tricia's and Olga's conditions, or because I felt guilty at how Bruno had been living after I fired him. And to give credit where it was due, the assault on my vehicle had happened outside of my gates. Nothing had happened inside my gates since Quito had been working for me.

"Tricia, you can have a talk with him, but he gets a pass on this. Right after it happened, he came in to talk. He offered to quit. He said he realized he'd messed up not doing anything about the truck in the street."

"And?"

"I didn't want to mess with it at the time, and I don't want to mess with it now."

Tricia got up. "Okay, Boss."

"I thought you liked him?"

"I do like him."

I waited a little bit, looked up at her from my seated position behind my desk. "Let it go, Baby."

"Will do, Boss."

I gave her permission to increase the staff if she still felt it was necessary after Olga's security team went home.

The attack was a wakeup call, a kick in my gut, no question. It put all of us on edge, but at least we were all more careful outside the gates. The guards were following a revamped security routine, and Quito had become a harsh taskmaster. His new attention to detail didn't exactly make me rest easy, but when I had to fly to Mexico for a chopper crash that killed two Texas billionaires, and I was gone for five days, I was not up all night every night worrying the security of my home might be breached. You better believe that I was also counting on the heavy security detail that Olga had living at my house and helping my security people, day and night. When I was gone, Olga and I talked on the phone no less than six times a day.

"I didn't plan on being gone this long," I said.

"Amor, it's okay, I love living in your house. Maybe—someday—our house."

I talked to Camila one time while I was in Mexico City.

"Amor, you are supposed to be guarding Olga with your life. What are you doing so far away from her?"

Normally I would have growled back to a comment like that, but this was Camila.

"My security and Olga's security are on the house grounds. She's okay."

"No one is after Olga, I worry this bastard who is after you will try something again."

"I wasn't going to come on this case, but Olga insisted. If I believed she was unsafe, I would not have left. Pixie and Letty are staying inside the house. They are excellent fighters and marksmen. I –"

Camila interrupted me.

"I talk to her a number of times a day, but I worry. I don't worry when she is traveling around the world, but now I'm worried about her when she's at your house."

Chapter 7
May 1983
Down Time

Mario

Olga could have returned to work in under a month, but May came and went, and she was still in residence. Camila was not overly happy about the situation.

Camila called, talking first to me and then I passed the phone to Olga.

"I'm not used to all this work. I don't want to be the banker."

"Amorcito, I will be back soon," she said to her sister.

Olga's clothes were in her guest room, but she slept in my bed. Melina didn't come over any more for her daily coffee, and our Sundays were suspended by mutual consent.

I dropped in to the market closest to our houses a couple of times at different times of day. On the third trip, I struck pay dirt in an early morning visit. Melina was there. I joined her in her office for tea and pastries. The sofa used to face the glass wall that overlooked the store but had been moved against a brick wall. Her desk was on the wall opposite the glass, giving her a view of the store. Store-side, the glass was mirrored.

She offered me a Mexican beer, but it was seven in the morning, and I was fine with the tea. We sat on the couch that I knew from experience made into a bed, and before us was a wrought iron cart that held bowls of various hors d'oeuvres-sized *empanadas*. She pointed them out to me: picadillo steak and stilton, curried lamb, tortillas, shrimp, crab and a spicy vegetarian mixture. One had scrambled eggs, since this was breakfast, after all. Sopapillas were the only sweets. I knew the spread was for my benefit. She did not eat breakfast.

"I am here on a pretext," I told her as we munched away. "Miguel wants a case of live lobsters."

She didn't waste any time. She crossed her spacious office and bent over her desk.

"Send Mario a case of live lobsters," Melina said into her intercom. When her secretary confirmed the order, she returned to her seat beside me.

"Done," she said, getting one of the empanadas. Before she bit into it, she said, "The bitch is never leaving. Is this what it's going to be like if you marry her?"

"Who said anything about marriage? We don't even talk about that anymore."

She nodded. "Of course not. No need. She's already here, living like a wife."

I reached for her hand. "Baby, she could have been killed. She's okay now. Camila is calling her every day to come back to work. We can use the couch if you want a quickie," I offered.

"Asshole, I don't need you to service me."

"I don't think of sex between us as servicing you."

Expressionless, Melina looked at her watch. She reached across the metal lattice of the serving cart and grabbed a grocery bag. It took four seconds for her to snap lids on the bowls and two more to drop the containers into the paper bag. She snatched the pastry from my hand, and tossed it in the bag too, shoved it in my hand, then opened the door of her office. She stood there, waiting for me to leave.

Maybe she *was* mad.

I went home. It was after nine, and though the girls were already at work, I went straight to my bedroom to see if Olga was awake. She was lying in the bed on her back, her beautiful eyes open. When she saw me, she reached out.

"Amor, come back to bed. I'm okay, Amor. I am not so fragile. Get on me, Si?"

I stripped down to skin and joined her under the covers. We had been having sex nightly ever since the night nurse had been dismissed. I was careful of her arm in the cast, and especially her nose and face.

I loved her morning breath and told her so. "I love your scent. I don't want you to leave."

"Amor, I want to stay."

"Then stay."

"Camila is already bananas, having to do my work along with hers. I can travel and come here to you. We can live together, here or anywhere."

I did not mind that Olga did not mention marriage. I was okay with living together.

"This is home," I said. "Live here with me."

"Amor, Si, Please, Si. You make me so happy, Amor."

Her smile flashed, warming me.

It was close to eleven, but we had breakfast in bed. I don't know what he did with Melina's leftovers, but Miguel outdid himself. Olga feasted on eggs and tender filet, and I feasted on Olga. The team made no appearance, but I knew they were busy in my office, respecting my privacy.

Olga brought up the topic of money. "Amor, I have over ninety million dollars in banks, mostly in Switzerland. If I hold out another four years or so, I will have much more. I'll also have a brand new executive jet of my choice, and a banked reserve to operate the plane for ten years. I have the house in Brazil. I am buying a house in Mexico City that Pepe says I should not buy because he doesn't trust the government there, but I love the house. I am building a house in Rio. I must show it to you. Pepe is covering the cost of construction, his money, my house. You and me, we are set, Amor."

"Sounds like you have a retirement package all figured out."

"You better believe I have a plan. I work very hard for the money I'm paid. It's not even a drop in the bucket next to the hundreds of millions of dollars I handle for them."

I whistled. "That much?"

"More than you can imagine, Amor. I'm the person who picks the banks we deal with, the investment companies, and I carry and move the money. I'm good at what I do, Amor."

"I would cave if you ever got in trouble," I heard myself say.

I hadn't seen her smile that broadly in a long time. "Amor, never going to happen, I'm doing nothing illegal."

A short pause, a look at her face, a smile of my own. "I believe you, Baby."

We kissed.

"I plan to walk away with at least five hundred million." She smiled again. "I'm not just an accountant. With what I know about investments and the contacts I have made for LAI, the money I walk away with will be tenfold in five to seven years."

I whistled again. "Baby, I had no idea." I moved closer. I whispered in her ear, "Even if you had no money, I would love you."

She turned her face to look at me. "I adore you, Mario. What is mine is yours."

I have come a long way from being that kid upset that Dearden's Furniture Store repossessed my aunt's television set, the incident that had sent me out the door looking for a job at ten years old. My life had grown far beyond what I could have imagined back then. At times I still thought I might be dreaming, and if I was, I did not want to wake up.

A little after noon, we emerged. In my office, Pixie and Letty were poring through AP and UPI print-outs looking for crashes. Tricia was out looking at properties.

Pixie and Letty greeted us with big smiles.

"*Amores, como los amo con todo mi corazon,*"[8] Olga said.

"We love you, too," Letty replied, joining the hug.

Sunny came out of my room with an armful of blankets and sheets, heading down the stairs. Inside, Caro was making the bed with fresh sheets. I heard the vacuum running.

"Too much fuss is going on in my bedroom. We're heading down to Olga's room."

"Come get comfy with us," Olga said.

Olga's invitation took me by surprise. I had not anticipated it.

"Right on," Pixie said.

We took the elevator down one floor. I was all for whatever might happen. Actions speak louder than words. My team was catching on to the relationship developing between Olga and me. Any guilt I had was eased by Olga's handling of my team.

Melina was another story.

My insurance replaced my totaled Rolls within a few days after the accident. Olga purchased a new Mercedes that her guards could use when she was in Pasadena. The day before Olga went back to work, she took Pixie, Letty— and her five security guards—shopping in Beverly Hills. They were gone for hours. When they returned, her guards streamed in with their arms full of purchases.

"We could have paid for our own," Pixie said, "but Olga is bitchingly generous. We didn't spend a dime of our money. It's embarrassing how many gifts she bought for us. And wait till you see the lingerie Olga bought for herself.

---

[8] I love you with all my heart.

Fucking out of sight."

"And when Betty comes over and opens the gifts Olga got for her," Pixie said, "she's going to squat and cum for hours."

Olga clapped, and laughed, as Letty and Pixie went on and on.

We were in the living room. Bags and boxes on the floor, sofas, and chairs. I watched the goings-on with a big smile.

If anything, I wear a watch. I have some expensive pieces, some that I bought and some that others have bought for me. I sometimes wear a religious medal but nothing else. Olga gave me a small unwrapped box. The way the girls were egging me on to open it, they knew what was inside. Inside was a braided gold bracelet. Olga put it on me and I was surprised that it fit. I have big wrists.

"Wear it in the best of health," she said in Spanish.

I didn't say my usual, *you shouldn't*, or *it wasn't necessary*. I said, "I love it. Thank you, Baby!"

Letty hugged Olga. "Thank you so much for a wonderful day, and for all the fine clothes and all the fabulous goodies. I love you."

"You know I love you very much," Pixie told Olga. "Even before all the gifts."

"Not fair. I loved you before today." Letty giggled.

Jason called unexpectedly from London. Jason had been more than Sami's significant other. He was a lawyer who worked with insurance companies on plane crashes. My first thought at his call was that somewhere in the world, a big airliner had crashed.

"Just letting you know that even though I am retiring, my door is always open to you."

I was sad to hear his plans. He'd always been my secret weapon in the aviation business, alerting me soon after the crash happened and getting me a flight manifest from the big crashes. From now on, I would have to get the manifests on my own. Not wanting to seem too petty, I kept my feelings to myself, and congratulated him on his retirement. We chatted for a while longer. I asked about Ginger and Crispin. He asked about Pixie. I told him that she was waving to him from my office on the fourth floor. I recalled that the last few times we'd flown to London, Pixie had gone off with Jason. I put my hand over the mouthpiece.

"Hey Pixie!"

I handed her the phone.

"It's a friend of yours."

I went downstairs for a swim, and hit the spa, taking about two hours out of the day. I passed Miguel on the way up and asked him to send up a light lunch. When I got back to my office, I found Pixie stretched out on my couch, laughing, singing a song, one shapely leg stretched up and drawing circles in the air with her pointed toes. She was still on the phone with Jason.

Olga gave a spin, turning around and around again.

"Amor, no makeup. Look close, the scars are practically gone!"

"You're beautiful, Baby," I said, not wanting her to go.

But I let Tricia drive Olga to Ontario Airport, a burly guard next to her in the front passenger seat. A hired Lincoln Continental followed behind with her other four guards. Olga's new Mercedes was parked in my garage waiting for her return. I had offered to drive her, but this was the way she wanted it.

Pepe had given me fair warning that Olga was going to continue to travel heavily guarded, especially when she was around me or my house.

After all, Pepe had said, "I love you, but I love Olga more, you understand? When she's with you or at the house, her security must be there, *comprende?*"

Olga wasn't crazy about having security always invading her privacy, but she told me that Pepe was still angry at her for having sent the guards to the plane that day instead of accompanying her to the airport.

I was in love with her. I knew the threat to me had spilled over to her. I knew her connection to Pepe exposed her to more dangers I knew nothing about. I wanted her to be safe. Only I knew the pain I'd felt when I saw Olga lying on the floor of my car, motionless. I was terrified that I might lose her.

Jo's husband, my contractor, TJ, was putting in an addition to the personnel quarters to accommodate Olga's guards when she was in Pasadena. The remodel repurposed part of the common area but included a two-story addition of small kitchenette suites that more than doubled the building's occupancy and footprint. TJ said the city would no doubt sit on the plans for months before issuing building permits.

"Build it without permits, big deal. It's not like you're building another house."

As a contractor, TJ could get into trouble for building without a permit, but he laughed it off.

"How will anyone know what is going on behind the fourteen-foot wall?"

I gave him a thumbs up.

Olga and I didn't add any difficult contingencies to our relationship. She would be in touch every day and would fly back to me at every opportunity.

"You will see so much of me, you'll be tired of my presence."

"No way, Baby. I love you. I want you with me."

"She loves you, Boss. I know she does," Letty said after she was gone.

For once, Pixie did not wise off. "Boss, she's quite a chick."

I rode up the elevator with them. In my office, they sat down, shoulder to shoulder on the leather sofa. I sat behind my desk as we talked over plans for the day's work, but no one made a move to begin. The house felt still and silent without Olga in it.

"I miss her already," I said.

"I know," Letty said.

"I know, too," Pixie said, scooting away from Letty and patting the spot on the sofa she had just vacated.

I moved to sit between them, and put my arms over their shoulders, kissing Pixie, then Letty.

"I love you guys."

"We love you too, Boss. We will keep you company." Pixie moved to my lap. "Olga told us to take care of you."

Letty fit herself closer and put her hands on me.

"Boss, let's not work today. Let's call Betty to come over. She can spend the day pampering us, and Letty and I will pamper you."

"Sounds like a plan. I need a joint," I said.

"You got it, Boss." Pixie was off in a flash.

The phone rang. Letty jumped up and handed me the phone. It was Olga calling on the plane's radio phone.

"Amor, I'm on the plane headed to Zurich. You could have come along."

I chuckled. "Baby, don't tempt me."

"I told the girls to fuck your brains out."

I laughed. "Thanks for the warning."

"Amor. My pussy is yours."

"What about your heart?"

"Amor, my heart and my entire being is yours. I adore you."

I was moved by the word adore that she used.

I heard static, but she was still coming in. I don't know what she heard on her end, but there must have been a problem.

"I may lose you. We are beginning our take off roll."

"Safe travels, Baby. Please stay in touch."

"Si, Amor."

Camila

I had a long day in Santiago, Chile and closed a very big copper deal for ten million dollars. I was in my hotel suite, alone. Well, not really alone. I had two guards outside the door to my suite and four more security people some-where in the hotel, all charged with the responsibility of keeping me safe. I lit up a joint. In Santiago, you can go to jail for smoking a joint in a hotel like I'm in, but LAI owns this hotel, so I wasn't going anywhere, only to the clouds when the smoke hit me.

"'I've been calling you," Olga complained.

"Amor, I just got in. Took longer than I thought. Two days from now, you come here to pay."

"How much?"

"Ten."

"I'll be there."

"Amor, I'm so happy you are back."

"Amorcito, I'm glad to be back."

Olga is like my sister, always has been. "Are you feeling well?"

"Perfectly well. Next week the cast comes off. Maybe a little therapy then it's over."

"Amorcito, I hear your voice and I realize how much I wish you were here with me."

"You'll wake up one morning and find me in your bed," Olga said in a low sexy voice.

"I'm taking the edge off with a smoke."

I heard a little laugh. She said, "Sister enjoy your evening. I'm sure you have plans. It's early evening where you are."

I called Pepe to tell him the copper thing was done.

"I was waiting for your call. It should not be so hard to buy copper."

"It can be when it's state-owned. Let's not discuss it. Deal is done. She will be here in two days to pay."

"Do you think he is strong enough for her?"

I'm high but I know he just switched from talking copper to Mario and Olga.

"Amor, he killed four men with his bare hands, and you ask me if he's strong enough?"

I heard my brother sigh in frustration. I know him so well. "Not that kind of strong."

"Amor, can we discuss this another time? My day has been long. I'm so tired."

He ignored my words. "If they marry, will he become one of us or will he push her to leave? No one can manage our money like Olga. We need her."

I took a drag and held it. My reply is delayed.

"Are you there?"

I exhaled. "Amor, she has her own strength. She is not dependent on his strength."

"Will he push her to abandon her work with us?"

"Amor, you and I agreed to walk away in '88. That's less than five years from now. She's counting on that. Did you forget?"

He hung up on me. I know him. Tomorrow, he will say we got disconnected.

Pepe does not scare me. Our father scared me. By the time I was fifteen, he was raping me regularly. I lived scared. If I told on him, he would kill me. He was mean. My mother was part of his drug business, strong as him. If he slapped her, she slapped him back. Once after he hit her, I saw my mother grab a rolling pin from our cook and bash my father on the head. My brother and me, we thought he was dead.

One night when my mother caught my father naked in my bed on top of me, she shot him, then took her own life with the same gun. Pepe was just twenty. In all the years since, I have never been able to block out that horrible night and many of the days that followed as Pepe stepped in and began making his changes to our father's business.

I closed my eyes, and watched the colors floating inside my lids. The pot was getting into my head. The joint burned down, leaving me buzzed. The copper deal was behind me. Tomorrow I would fly out of here. When the doorbell rang, I knew it was Valentina. She'd been with me last night and the plan was for a repeat. Valentina is a gorgeous Chilean, twenty-three, hazel eyes, natural blonde hair, light-skinned. When I first met her, I thought she was American. When there's someone like Valentina around, I don't need a man.

In the morning, I woke with Valentina skin to skin with me.

"Te gusto todo lo que hicimos anoche?"

"Me Encanto, Amor. Sabes quieres ir conmigo a Bogota un par de dias?"[9]

For a lark, I decided to fly her home with me to Bogota. The paradise I own there will come as a surprise. She will not want to leave.

Betty

Mario went downstairs to work out or something, leaving me alone with Letty and Pixie and six boxes. I had no idea that Olga would leave me six presents, or why she did it, but that's what she did. Pixie and Letty made me open them right on the king-sized bed in Olga's guest room. To me, this room will always be hers. The small box held a solid gold lighter. The note said *for your joints.* A joke. I work joints to make people feel better. Olga smokes them, at least sometimes she does. Not as much as Camila. Camila smokes like pot is sugar candy and she's on a mission to get diabetes. The second box held three pieces, a Natori nightie, panties, and a matching robe, all pastel and lace. Gorgeous stuff I'd never be able to buy for myself. Lingerie for the eye of a lover.

"Don't cry," Letty said.

"Save it till you open them all." Pixie always joked around.

The bigger box was a little heavy. I left it on the chair where it was and opened it. A white leather jacket with mink on the shoulders and along the seam and around the sleeves. It's fucking beautiful. I had tears running down my face as I put on the jacket.

Pixie and Letty gave me a couple of wolf whistles. I spun in a circle like

---

[9] You liked everything we did last night?
I love it, Love. Do you want to go with me to Bogota for a couple of days?

a model, hands in my pockets. They clapped and catcalled till I went for the next box. In all my life, I never got more than one gift at a time except on Christmas and my birthday. Today was neither, not even a holiday. I spun again with a box clutched to my chest. I found a red cashmere sweater, a pullover. The fifth box was small. An eternity ring. It fit like it was made for my hand. The diamonds were brilliant and shine like, well, diamonds.

The sixth gift, a small box. Inside a stack of hundreds.

"Count it," Pixie ordered, laughing up a storm.

"Let me count it." Letty got up and grabbed the box.

Pixie's arm went around my shoulder. We watched Letty count, counting along in concert, though we'd lost track.

"Fifty," she finally says, "Five thousand bucks!"

I want to fucking faint.

"Why me?"

"Probably because you gave her a lot of head."

Pixie and her jokes. But it's true, I did give her head. She was broken in that bed, hurting, and drugged up. I did it when I massaged her, and she loved it. She told me so.

Pixie and Letty seem excited as I am. We were making so much noise, maybe that's what brought the Boss in. He didn't really know what was going on except he saw the wrapping paper, ribbon on the floor, boxes, like it's a holiday. He started laughing. Letty laughing, Pixie laughing. Me laughing. It's contagious.

Mario

She hadn't been gone that long, but it felt like forever.

Olga called at every chance. Each time I picked up and heard her voice, it was like coming alive again.

"I am so behind on everything. Camila complains that she's been doing my work and hers. She may have done hers, but not very much of mine."

"I love to hear your voice."

"Do I have an accent?"

"You should but you don't, and you know it."

Olga laughed like she was with me, next to me, but she was so far away. I didn't even know where.

"I'm leaving Sweden for Chile."

I felt a sudden urge to visit Chile. "I'd like to go there someday. Never had a case in Chile."

"You don't need a case. Come with me whenever you want. LAI has a hotel in Santiago. A big one."

"Do I get special rates?"

"Amor, for you, it's free. I heard about that plane crash yesterday."

I told her what I knew about the case. That I was waiting a few days to give the families time to settle in their hotels. The flight had been from Buenos Aires to Sao Paulo, Brazil. The families were probably from both countries and would probably be housed in Argentina since the plane crashed shortly after takeoff.

"I sent Juan to Buenos Aires to do the advance work before we fly in."

"Safe travels, Amor, do be careful. That bearded bastard is still out there."

I ignored the biker talk.

"I miss you," I said.

"My pussy trembles when I hear your voice."

"I just felt something move down there," I said.

As I expected, the families of victims were gathering in two Buenos Aires hotels. The plane had crashed six minutes after taking off for Sao Paulo, Brazil. I felt like I was working without a net, not having Jason advancing me the unpublished details about each passenger and their emergency contact information. The girls found passenger lists in AP print-outs from Brazilian and Argentinean news sources, but as resources they didn't compare to what I got from Jason for years. I presumed that most of passengers resided either in Argentina or Brazil. Because all of the families would have the opportunity to travel to Buenos Aires to claim the bodies of their loved ones, and the airline operators would host them until such time as the family wanted to return home, that would be the opportunity to connect with them. The team and I geared up for the hotel sit-in. We used variations of our well-practiced lines: "I consult for an American law firm, but it's too soon for me to talk to you about it. Tell me about your loved one that perished in this horrible crash." Our business was not immediately getting retainers; the immediate focus was making friends with as many families possible. Business talk waited until the bodies were recovered and turned over to the families, and that did not occur normally until after a funeral. However, once meeting us, it was rare that the families waited to take the body back home, have a funeral and for us to travel there if they wanted to talk. By the time they knew who we were, they were ready to sign. We may have been around them for weeks before the funeral happened, and most of them just wanted the whole business done with so they could move on with their altered lives. No matter where we were, there was competition. We weren't always retained.

Pixie and I were covering the same hotel. She was off somewhere with another family. I had made a connection with the new widow, Griselda Negro, and we were sitting down for breakfast in one of the hotel restaurants. She was a round woman of medium height, but in the weeks I'd known her, I'd seen a weight loss. We frequently met over plates of food, but rarely did she consume very much.

"I have so little appetite," she said, using the side of her fork to chase scrambled eggs around a plate. The sunglasses she was wearing hid eyes swollen from weeks of tears.

"Paulo would not want you to hurt yourself," I said, trying to coax her to eat the food rather than play with it.

She still did not eat. We sat companionably, and both drank the hotel's excellent coffee. I listened as she talked quietly of Paulo until the plates in our booth had been cleared. She would be traveling with her husband back to her home in Brazil, she in the cabin, he in a coffin in the luggage hold.

"You are going back home tomorrow?"

She nodded. In the absence of her plate, she had nothing to do with her hands. She picked up a fresh linen napkin and twisted it. "I am anxious to put him to rest."

"I can come see you after the funeral, if you want."

She reached for my hand across the table, first nodding, then shaking her head.

"Mario, tell me now about the contract I must sign with the American lawyer."

"Griselda, it can wait. A trip to Brazil for me is no trouble."

"I like you. I trust you. There is no need to put this off any longer," she said heavily. I could hear unfallen tears in her voice. "Tell me how this works, Mario."

For the next half hour, I told her about the retainer, the fees and costs and how she would not owe legal fees if no compensation was collected. I let her know that not collecting was highly unlikely. That afternoon, I met up with Pixie. We signed Pixie's client, and less than an hour later, we had a signed retainer for Paulo Negro.

Olga and I were in constant touch. When I missed her call, I was on the phone returning her call and vice versa. Olga could be anywhere in the world and thanks to LAI's 24/7 phone service, I could reach her any time except for when she was in flight.

I was sitting around with my team in our suite, a glass of wine in my hand. We were full of excellent beef and relaxing after a long day. It was nine Argentina time when she called, two in the morning in Berlin where she was.

She noticed that I seemed down.

"It's the job. It doesn't get easier."

"It must be like being a mortician or a funeral director, always having to listen to families that want to arrange a service and burial. It must be so depressing. Mario, why keep doing this? I know the money is good, but there are so many other things you could be doing. You make good money with LAI buying properties for us."

"Baby, I'm not a mortician. It's not just the money. What I do helps the families. And you are right, I do great with LAI."

The television was on, and the sound off ever since I'd picked up the phone. Pixie, Letty, and Tricia watched me curiously instead of the screen. Pixie kept filling my wine glass.

Silence hung between us for a moment, then she said, "By the way, I have some days off. I'm flying to Los Angeles."

"Baby, I'm swamped with appointments here. This will be your first time going home without me there."

"It will be exciting to have the place to myself. To go there and know I live there with you now."

I got a chill. "Is there anything I can do for you?"

"You could be there to make love to me."

I laughed.

Olga said, "Let everyone know I will be there in two days. I don't want my guards going to war with Quito and his guards."

"I will let Quito and Miguel know to be ready for you. By the way, you know TJ is doing the addition. In the meantime, Pixie got two modular homes like we used when the house was being rebuilt and the quarters were being remodeled. My entire staff moved in to the modular homes. Your guards should be comfortable."

"Wonderful, Amor, you are so thoughtful."

I laughed. "Pepe would have been okay with them in a tent."

When I hung up, the girls were all over me. They did not need Olga's side of the conversation to figure out what we were talking about.

"Fuck me," Letty said. "This is a total first."

"Sure is," Pixie took a swallow of her wine, emptying the glass.

"Look, I love the woman. What can I say?"

"Boss, get on a plane and go home. We can handle here," Letty said.

I shook my head. "If she wanted to, she could fly here in a heartbeat."

"Boss is right, she wants to be in his house while he's gone, to see how it feels." There was high drama in Pixie's voice, and not a single giggle.

"Betty will be delighted she's coming back so soon," Letty said. "She was so happy with all the gifts."

"Let her know she'll be there and to look after her," I said.

"I got it," Letty said.

Melina had apologized the day after she showed me the door at the market, but we had not seen each other since. While I had been in Argentina I talked to her three times. Short calls but in touch.

"Olga will be at my house while I'm over here in case you feel social."

"Oh please, asshole."

I laughed. "That's such a terrible thing to be calling me for all these years. I prefer Cuz."

"You're right, Cuz. I'll save it for when you piss me off. If I get the time, I'll swing over there but I don't think she's up as early as I am, and as you know I don't get home till almost midnight. I may just call her."

"Sure, that would be nice."

I talked about the case I was on. She talked about an empty lot she just purchased in Burbank where she planned to build another market.

I never knew if Melina was calm, cool, and collected or just pretending to be to demonstrate how jealous she wasn't. When I heard her voice, I realized I missed her. She made me laugh. She'd always been there for me. But at the moment, I missed Olga more. By the time I hung up, the girls had gone off to their beds. I was soon asleep.

The best food I had ever ate was in Bueno Aires. Maybe because I love steak, and if there's anything they have, it is great steak. We were there for six weeks.

By the time I was back in Pasadena, Olga had left again. When we got home, I told Miguel I didn't want to see a steak until further notice. I was exhausted, and jet lagged but I hit the gym and tried to make up for lost time. There is no such thing as making up six weeks in one workout.

On that first night back in Pasadena, Pixie and Tricia went home. Letty spent the night in her room on the third floor. I slept alone. I talked to Olga in Rome and let her know I was back.

"I have a surprise for you," she said.

"Are you pregnant?"

She laughed. "Amor, no."

"What is it?"

"I tell you when you are rested."

I didn't argue. I was more tird than curious, so I let the matter rest.

Chapter 8
June 1983
Quid Pro Quo

Mario

Melina was over in the morning. We had coffee on the patio overlooking the pool.

"Did Olga tell you?"

"Tell me what?"

"I sold her my house."

I spilled my coffee on my lap. "What did you say?"

Miguel ran out with a dish towel and a bunch of napkins. I dabbed. It was inadequate. Melina was all smiles over the deal, and I did not want to interrupt the moment, even if I was soaked to my shorts. She looked happy as could be. I was shocked that she sold her house to Olga.

"You're shitting me."

"No shit."

I heard a distant crack of thunder. We looked for the coming storm, but neither of us saw anything.

"That's my cue. Meet you inside," I said, getting up and slipping out of my coffee-soaked sweat pants. I changed and joined Melina in the breakfast room in record time. Melina was finishing up a pastry. It looked like she'd eaten all of it. Not like her, at all.

"Explain, Baby."

"I came over to say hello one night. Betty had just finished giving Olga a massage and was going over to my house. It was almost midnight. We spent an hour or so talking, and I went home. Next day, Olga invited me for a drink. I came over at eleven. Olga said she wanted to own a home near you. I invited her to come over and check out my house."

"And?"

"She fell in love with it. I said I'd sell if the price was right."

"That doesn't sound like you."

"Of course, it's me. I'm in retail. I told her I'd take six million as is where is, but she had to keep my help for at least three years, and she couldn't sell for five years."

"And?"

"Olga wrote me a check for six million. Said I can stay in the house until I find someplace else. She's very savvy about how we do it here. Her conditions were that I handle the escrow, pay the title insurance and escrow costs and she would let me know what name to use on title. She also said I could cash the check, didn't need to put it in escrow."

I ignored the title thing. That question was just whether or not the house would belong to Olga or LAI and that didn't matter. "What about me?" I felt excited and sad at the same time.

"What about you?"

"I mean, our Sundays?" It was more than Sundays. We'd lived practically side by side from the day we'd met. I had followed Melina to her apartment, and then to this house across the street from hers.

"Cuz, we haven't had a Sunday since Olga moved in. We will always be tight. For now, it's you and Olga. I'm not going to be a third wheel. Let's see what happens. I hope you get married and have kids and are happy. I'll put three million into another house, spend a bundle fixing it up and still come out miles ahead."

She stood and leaned over to kiss me.

"That's it?"

"What does that mean, Cuz?"

"I mean, you're leaving me?" I could not keep the shock out of my voice.

She laughed at me. I felt my face get hot.

"I'm not leaving you. I'm moving. I'm not moving this minute." She looked at her watch. "I need to hit the road. I have an appointment at the Echo Park store."

She departed without the usual kiss. I opened the door and she walked under my arm. I watched her leave, her quick pace eating up the ground to the car Johnson was waiting in, but my mind had jumped on the idea of Olga living across the street.

After Melina left, I realized that Olga had no plan to live across the street. I realized she had bought that house to get rid of Melina. She knew that Melina and I had come very close to getting married on more than one occasion. She knew Melina was a threat. So, then she called.

"Baby, tell me the surprise."

"You rascal," she said in Spanish with a cute ha-ha. "Melina already told you."

"So, you guys are pals now."

"Amor, I told you I'd buy a house in Pasadena. Remember, Camila wants one there, too."

"But you and I are going to be living together."

"Si, we are."

"Then why buy her house?"

"Her house is a good investment."

"It's a sitting asset. It's not like an apartment building or a business," I argued.

"You will get your ten percent," she said.

"I'm not looking to get paid on her house."

"Of course, you will. When you marry me, you'll need *mucha lana.*"[10]

"Why her house?"

She hesitated. "I'm not jealous of your team or my sister. But Melina is not like the others. I don't want her across the street. You almost married this woman how many times?"

"I can't believe you feel threatened by her."

"Do you want me to lie?"

On her return, Olga gave zero notice. Caro came running to say the guard called, Olga was driving in.

I didn't wait for the elevator. I ran down from the fourth-floor office with the team close behind, hitting the second-floor landing just as she was walking in. After I swung her around, and her legs wrapped around my waist and we shared a very long, wet, kiss, she got a rock star reception. Two of her guards brought in her luggage, said hello to me then headed back out the front entrance. I sent Memo after them to show them the modular buildings, so they could sort out their rooms.

Sunny and Caro took her luggage up in the elevator, leaving behind a Zero briefcase. I had never seen Olga with a metal suitcase.

"Letty, please put that in his office."

"Money?" Pixie winked.

"Si, money. It's your six hundred thousand for the house deal."

"No."

"We'll talk about it later," Olga said patiently.

I was happy to see her, but I let it pass only because I did not want to disagree with her in front of the team. She was a magnet for me. Yes, she's beautiful, but Pixie and Letty are beautiful. Why was I so infatuated with her? If I asked my Aunt Carmen a question like this, she would say Olga has me be-

---

[10] Lots of money

witched.

Olga did not stay long. As soon as she was off again, I took the suitcase to Melina and tried to give it to her.

Melina refused it. "I sold the house, got paid and besides, I wouldn't accept cash like that."

"I'll keep the cash and write you a check," I said quickly.

"I appreciate your offering it to me, but it's not necessary. I'm okay with what I got for the house. Six million is a damn good price."

"I don't want to make money off your house."

She smiled up at me, her eyes gleaming. She gave me a touch on the cheek. "Cuz, I'm happy. Don't mess with me."

I heard *Cuz* and figured we were okay.

"I miss you."

"I miss you, too."

We stood in her foyer, staring at each other. I kissed her. She kissed me. I walked back across the street to Casa Luna.

Olga returned with eight pieces of luggage and a tan.

"I hope you have enough closet space for me. I'm bringing more on each trip."

"I have plenty of room, Baby."

She shook her head. "I have a lot of clothes. When Melina moves, I can keep clothes over there, too." I got a kiss from her. "I want you to remember I live here with you. Lots of my clothes will keep reminding you."

I kissed her back. "Casa Luna has lots of closets, Baby."

After the news that she had sold her house, Melina and I had been talking on the phone more frequently than we'd been seeing each other since Olga moved in.

"Cuz, guess what?" Melina asked.

"You miss me and want to fuck?"

"No," replied Melina.

"You don't miss me, and you don't want to fuck?"

"I am buying the house you rented while they were rebuilding yours."

I was surprised at that. I'd tried to buy that house, but Jerry Mills had been too attached. "He'll never sell."

"Oh yes he will. We went out for dinner and made a deal. I'm going to escrow in the next couple days. I bought it with all the furniture, but I plan to revamp it top to bottom. I'm moving as soon as we close."

I felt a strong emotion in response to what she said but could not put my finger on what it was. "You don't need to move so fast. Olga doesn't need the house right now. Do your remodel and live where you are."

She was adamant. "The house is no longer mine. I'm out of there."

"Maybe you should have kept all your help. Tell Olga you want to take them with you."

"I'll hire new people except for Lucia. I want everything new."

The help Melina left behind would have nothing to do. I couldn't help but be reminded of Sami, my London friend who had died from fatal injuries from a terrorist bombing when the two of us were in a pub. While she'd been alive, Sami had purchased flats for her help, Crispin and Ginger. After she'd died, Jason, executor of the estate, kept them on to care for the lavish top floor penthouse, even though no one lived there. I didn't say any more about it.

"How much?"

"Cuz, I got it for 1.5 million."

"You are kidding. That's a steal for that property."

"I don't know if it's a steal. It needs a shitload of work."

"At least you are only going to be seven minutes away," I said. "So, are we ever going to do it anymore?"

"You mean, fuck?"

"Yeah, fuck."

"Not right away."

"What does that mean?"

"Just what I said."

"Baby, you are a smart ass."

"I'm not blind. Olga spent millions getting me away from you."

"Can't look at it like that," I said. "She got a house and everything in it for six million."

"Cuz, go cool off with the team till Olga returns. She must be out of town if you are hitting me up for a fuck."

Melina and me, we had to have fucked a thousand times over the years since we met. How could she talk like one more fuck was a big deal, like no more fucking would not change what we were?

We all wondered how Melina's house was going to be used. The girls—including Jo and Niley—were still meeting with their shooting coach there every other Wednesday night.

With no big crashes happening for a few months, I had down time, and the intermission was a timely opportunity to scout out and purchase a few properties for LAI. It also gave me the freedom to fly out and meet Olga twice in as many weeks just to overnight with her. One of those trips took me to Paris, where I spent a day visiting with Simone and Junon. Junon was small and round, with deep dimples. Simone was a tall blonde originally from Amsterdam, and a brilliant pastry chef. I'd been a silent partner in Simone's bakery for more than a decade. While I was there, I sold her my half of the business.

As always, the girls continued covering small crashes in the US, everything from private executive jets to medical evacuations to crop-dusting accidents. For anything not in the immediate area, they either flew commercial or chartered a small plane. I think we all preferred using a private plane. The girls had been nagging me for years to get one of my own. I guess we'd all been spoiled, thanks to Oscar who had always insisted I use his Lear when I flew around the country getting cases for him. The nagging had started years ago when the girls found out I declined when Oscar offered me his plane as part of my payment for a case I brought him.

My mindset had changed, and so had my circumstances. Then, I didn't have the money I have now, and I had been afraid of the expense involved, not just in flying but also in maintenance, keeping a crew. The thing is that the girls and I were flying somewhere every week. Olga was accustomed to having a plane handy. Camila had her own big jet. Pepe had a whole airline. Owning a plane didn't seem as daunting or extravagant as it used to. I asked Pepe to help me find a Lear to purchase.

A Lear wasn't practical for crossing oceans, but it was perfect for traveling within the states. On several occasions my team and I had crossed an ocean with Oscar's Lear, but fuel stops and crew rest stops are crazy with a small plane.

When I asked my CPA about it, he said, "It's a write-off, yes. Doesn't mean it's free." He was so conservative.

"Let me give you one of our planes to use," Pepe insisted.

"How would that work?"

"You pay the expense of the pilots and maintenance, fuel, and so forth. The plane remains the property of LAI."

"I don't see a gain for you, Pepe."

"We have three Lears. One of them is Camila's commuter plane. The other two have a lot of down time. Use one of them."

"Sell me one of them."

We were both dead-set on our positions, but after a few days, with some pressure, maybe from Olga, Pepe caved.

"Give me a million but not cash."

Under the circumstances, that coaxed a laugh out of me.

"That's a great deal. Pepe are you sure?"

"Write me a check and the plane is yours. I should give it to you. You're going to be my brother-in-law."

I did not contradict him. Though we were like a married couple, Olga and I never talked marriage anymore.

"Mario, when I send you the plane, get a full maintenance check on it. Going to cost just under a hundred thousand, but you need to do it. Never, ever put off maintenance."

"No way," I said in earnest. It's not like you can pull a disabled plane over on the nearest cloud and park on the soft shoulder.

Engines are the big expense on a plane like a Lear, but I can confirm that my past cautions over the expense had been justified. Owning a plane is expensive, and it's not just the fuel and the pilots.

Jack and I had our weekly lunch at PDC, and it was there that I broke the news to him that I had bought a plane.

"Join the club," Jack said, giving me a high five. It wasn't until that moment that I found out that Jack Fino kept a plane in the Van Nuys Airport hanger. I vaguely recalled Oscar once mentioning that he'd flown with Jack before, but I'd never really thought about it. It came as a surprise to me that Jack was a pilot who checked out not only on a Lear, but also several helicopters, and single engine planes.

"I had no idea you were a pilot."

Jack brushed it aside. "It's no big deal. It's just a fucking expense whether you use the plane or not. I could have saved you the money and offered you the use of mine whenever you wanted, but it never occurred to me."

"Thanks for the offer, Jack."

"You never have to thank me, my boy."

Jack had one of his secretaries give the girls his list of where to go for local plane-related staffing. I cut a deal to keep the Lear, a 25D, at Van Nuys Airport, and used the agency Jack recommended in Los Angeles to line up pilots when I needed to fly. Pepe sent me the plane the day after we made the deal. I had the entire interior redone and got the works on maintenance. I grew impatient waiting.

When I finally took possession of the plane, I invited the whole team for our virgin flight. They didn't say why, but Jo and Tricia opted out. Jo and Tricia were the only ones with serious relationships.

Olga was off on a business trip when my team and I took our maiden flight to New York. I can't describe the emotion I felt walking up to the plane, just knowing it was mine. Outside, it was white with a blue stripe, with three passenger windows on each side. Inside we sat on spacious new buttery-soft leather seats. The carpet was dark brown and plush, and inner fuselage walls were a creamy ivory, a perfect foil against the leather trim. The interior smelled like a leather orgasm. The sofa was long like the one in Camila's plane.

I sat in one of the seats and looked out the window. I owned that view. Pixie, Letty and Niley filled my ears with excited chatter. The plane was far from new but smelled like cars do as they are driven off the showroom floor. Especially the leather.

Once we were in New York, we stayed at the Camacho penthouse on Park Avenue. I had always thought of it as Camila's place, but Olga told me everything was owned by LAI except their personal bank accounts.

Camila called from Mexico City not long after I arrived. She was there on a marble-buying trip. She talked about marble, and the deal she was getting. I talked about the plane.

"Your apartment is gorgeous as always," I told her.

"I do love that place, but I am still looking for a big house in New York."

Olga called as soon as Camila hung up. She talked to Pixie, Letty, Niley, and finally to me.

I admitted to her, "I feel like I can walk on water." The flight had been that invigorating. "While I am here, I might look into some properties Camila might be interested in. Jack gave me the name of a local agent he's used before."

"Amor, we use the same broker. Enjoy yourself with the team."

"I should have known that if Jack knows the broker, you guys do too."

"I'll be home for a week in about a week," she said.

"I'll make sure I'm there, no matter what."

"I'll hold you to that, Amor."

Since we didn't see Niley very much, she became the center of attraction in New York. She reminded me very much of her sister, Tanis who had died in my arms.

Niley

Earlier he said to Pixie, "I didn't hear you come."

"Here, Boss, touch here and tell me if I came."

He can't call it quits until he knows everyone had a finish. Everyone fell asleep except for me. I don't want to waste the time I have with him sleeping. I want to be close to him. I got the lucky spot. He's sleeping between me and Pixie. Letty's on my left. Times like this, I long to return to the team. I miss being out like this. I miss the travel. I'm not getting any younger. I know I can never have him, but so what? I want to sleep with him like this. I love him. I love us all together.

Mario

As part of the home routine, Letty burns incense, lights candles, and dims the lights. She bought many plants and a bi-weekly service rotated plants that needed TLC in the green house. She had arranged for the plant service to deliver fresh flowers weekly. When we are gone on a case, the service people take care of business as usual. Life continued as usual. Pixie, Letty, and Tricia worked in my top floor office. Pixie and Tricia went home after work. When Olga was in Pasadena, Letty went to her apartment.

More than once I told her, "Baby, you don't live over there. You live here. You don't have to leave." Her room on the third floor was gorgeous, her description, not mine. Some of her things stayed there always.

"It's okay, Boss, Pixie is coming over."

Maybe she needed a break from the big house. I expect that one day she'd find a guy she'd fall for just as Tricia and Jo had. It would be a blow to me not to have Letty here.

Olga kept her promise to spend more time with me, but her stays were short with seldom more than a day's notice that she would be coming or going.

On her current visit home, Olga said, "Letty, I'm leaving day after tomorrow. Stay tonight."

"I don't want to be in the way."

"If you have something going tonight, split Baby," I said.

"Yes, of course," Olga said.

She blew a kiss at Olga and me and left.

When Letty wasn't around, Olga prepped the bedroom but not with Letty's magic touch.

Late in the afternoon, Olga asked Betty to be available for massage.

"Letty, you go first," Olga told her. The massage table was in the sitting room in view of the bed.

"Olga, no, you go first," Letty said.

"Amor, tell her to get her pretty ass up on the table and enjoy a ninety-minute massage."

"Go," I said to Letty though she was already naked and on the way to Betty.

"You always do so much for all of us. Enjoy, Amor," Olga said to her.

The entire scene was a turn on.

People said that 'free-love' would end with the Sixties. And when the Seventies were over, they said swinging, wife-swapping, and open sex would exit with the decade. I hadn't personally been to an open orgy in at least three years and didn't plan on it, but swinging was as hot as it ever was. The best orgies ever had been in London with Sami. May she rest in peace.

Letty

"I'm going to Stockholm, Munich, and probably Barcelona," Olga says, "then we come home. Ten days, tops. You come with me. What do you say?" Total surprise. She leaves tomorrow, and I'm invited.

I look at Mario. He has a big smile, like he's encouraging a yes out of me. But I think he likes having me around. Without me, who will be here with him after Pixie and Tricia leave every day? Who will take my place? I feel like he wants me to go, so I say, "Olga, that is so very generous of you. I'd love to go. I hope I can do some work for you to make up at least a little for the trip."

She laughs. She hugs me.

"I work like crazy on these trips," Olga says, "but I get lonely. I should pay you for going with me."

"Olga, how can you say that? Tell me what to pack. I know the weather in Barcelona this time of year but what about Stockholm and Munich?"

I like Olga. She gives me no reason not to, but we aren't really tight. She bought me a pile of gifts when we went shopping. She did that for everybody. She's cool. I hope I don't disappoint her.

So, last night I am getting a massage, stomach down. I face the bed and they're doing it, the Boss and Olga. She likes for him to get on top. He's so big his body covers her except her legs wrapped around him. Not the first time that I have seen him make love to Olga. I watch his body move on her. They finish, and Olga takes her massage. She eggs him on. She wants him to pretend she's out of town. Like me earlier, she's facing the bed, watching. The difference is I get on top and I fuck the living daylights out of Boss. If that doesn't make her jealous, nothing will. It's not like she's out of town. She's in the fucking room.

Olga finishes her massage. Boss has so much energy, it's crazy, but I have lots of energy too. It's Boss's turn on the table. Olga comes out of the shower wet, her hair wrapped in a towel. I go down on her and she goes crazy. It's good I like girls. She's not Melina, I am more than half in love with Melina. I get crazy in my head, I am all in love with Boss, so doing Olga, I am doing Boss. I get so far in the fantasy, I don't see how far hands on Betty goes. Betty is busy massaging Boss, but I feel her eyes on me. I know he's on the table watching, I can feel his eyes, but in my head he's Melina and Olga and coming in my mouth.

Five and a half hours gone, and Betty's the only one who doesn't get a turn on the table or the bed. I don't know where she gets the juice.

The next day, Boss drives us to Ontario Airport. One of Olga's guards rides up front with him. Olga, Pixie, Tricia and me are squeezed in the back seat, but I dig the squeeze. Behind us Olga's Mercedes follows with four of her guards like we're rock stars. Pixie has a big purse with two guns, I am packing two and Tricia holsters hers, plus has one of those worthless toy guns on her ankle.

Olga laughs at our firearms. Her guard gives us a thumbs up. Boss laughs, but he's bothered that all this protection is necessary.

The team comes aboard the big plane. Pixie doesn't mouth off. She gives me a big hug and kisses me so hard Olga's eyes narrow. Boss kisses Olga then gives me a peck, and they all leave. It's like watching my family go, but I know they'll be okay. Miguel promised me he'll take care of them.

Olga gives me the plane tour, even where the guards are in the front compartment.

"This is Sofia," Olga introduces the flight attendant. Sofia is all over the color of coffee. She's African, maybe a little Indian too. "Sofia you are gorgeous!" She smiles with perfect white teeth.

Olga says, "I tell her that all the time."

Sofia hands Olga and me silk pajamas. It is hot outside but the plane is freezing. I'm in sleeveless cotton and going commando, and it's so cold my nipples are making points through my shirt. The pjs are no warmer. The seats are like pillows, maybe the most comfortable I've ever been on a plane. The plane is like a flying hotel. Living room with seats for ten but it's just Olga and me. We sit facing each other, a window for her and one for me. I'm the one facing backward because without him around, she's the boss.

We have cokes. Once we are airborne, she moves to the center of the cabin. Sofia opens the table's leaves on both. I swivel to face the action as Olga spreads papers all over. Charts and tables and stacks of documents and notes. It looks like homework to me. Not that I went to high school. I got a GED thanks to the school of Jo.

"I need to look this over to be ready for my meeting in Stockholm."

"Anything I can do?"

"Maybe. Hang in there."

Sofia brings a list of films on tape, recent releases. We have them all at Casa Luna and I don't want to distract Olga by watching a movie. I close my eyes and don't open them again till the pilot says we are descending in New York. Olga is wearing glasses, quiet, intense. Studying, reading, writing. This side of her is new to me.

"Some help I am," I say, yawning.

"Amor, it's fine, I'm almost done. We're going to stop for fuel. We will stay on the plane."

Sofia feeds us hamburgers and chocolate ice cream shakes. Olga shows me closets of clothes that live in her plane. It's all business, but all designer. The style, the clothes remind me of Melina which makes me like Olga more. She picks out what she wants to wear in Stockholm. Clothes are gorgeous but more sedate than the dead sexy shit she wears around Boss. Sedate is the wrong word. These are business suits that give off a killer power vibe. I spray the suitcase and garment bag with her perfume first, just a hint of it, then pack the clothes for her.

She watches me closely, sees I pack like a champ. I know my way around a suitcase and fancy-ass clothes. Hey, I learned from the best.

"I used to do this for Camila," she says, sounding a little sad. We take off from New York.

"We can watch a movie in the bedroom," Olga says. She picks Tootsie.

The shades over the portholes are down but it is dark outside anyway. The bed is a giant pillow, big, fluffy comforters with gold points. Extra pillows, shams, all that shit, like a fancy hotel. I'm not surprised. I can't even picture Olga sleeping on bargain basement sheets. The extra pillows get tossed on the floor. We sit up against the padded headboard. The movie plays. Fifteen minutes in, Olga nods off. I get up to turn off the TV and lights. Two small night lights near the door of the bathroom keep glowing, reminding me this is a plane we are on. The engine is just a hum of white noise next to the soft whoosh of air conditioning. I guess at this altitude, it's heat. Olga slips under the covers. The night passes. It gets a little choppy. My eyes adjust to the dark. Her hand touches my face, though her eyes never open.

"Gracias Amor por estar aqui conmigo."[11]

Two cars are waiting for us in Stockholm, one for four guards, one for one guard and us. The pilots and Sofia are regular employees, not rentals like the Boss's plane crew. There's a car for them, too.

Our hotel pad is no flophouse. It's a two-bedroom suite, though I had expected we'd be sleeping in one bed. Top of the line, chocolate on the pillow, champagne in the fridge, concierge up Olga's ass like nothing I've ever seen, but I understand that better when one of the maids says Olga's family owns the hotel. Olga is hysterical with him, sends him fetching all kinds of random shit. I want to call Pixie and tell her about it.

I unpack her one suitcase, hang her garment bag.

"Gracias, Amor. Let's get some sleep, tomorrow will be busy. I will have one of the guards take you sightseeing while I go to my meeting."

"Olga, no worries. I'll take myself sightseeing. You keep the guards."

"Amor, I would take you with me but the banker I am meeting is sensitive, sensitive talk we will be having."

"No explanation needed. Thank you for having me here. I feel like a queen."

When she leaves, the concierge switches over to me. His name is Doug, and he promises that while I am here, he is my best friend. For the hell of it, I

---

[11] Thank you for being here with me my Love

send him out for the English Lavender soap I know Olga likes. He's a gas. I ask him about tours and he brings me so many brochures I wish we were staying longer. I put on jeans and tennis shoes and walk all over. I take a tour in a bus with a lot of tourists wearing cameras around their necks, but I am back at the hotel by dinner time. I pick from the room service menu but tell the concierge we won't be eating till Olga returns, and she gets champagne with dinner.

At midnight, we are wiped out. We sleep in our own beds.

I leave the bedroom door open. So, does she. I hear her talking to Boss in Pasadena. I think of calling him after, but I am over and out.

In the morning, the concierge delivers the breakfast I had set up.

"Amor, you are a jewel," Olga says. She doesn't eat all of it but has a bite of everything and does some hefty damage to a short stack of pancakes.

When she is ready to leave, I tell her, "Wow, Olga, you are dressed to the nines." It's the truth. She is drop dead gorgeous.

"Thank you, Amor. I need to get this banker to come around with what I need him to do," she winks. She has on jewelry I never had seen her wear before, a diamond ring as large as the one Sami gave Boss.

"Cash alone doesn't talk here, you need to dress the part," Olga says.

"You look fantastic. If that banker doesn't come around, he's dead."

"Will you be okay?"

"Totally," I say. "I got plans." I wave around the tour brochures and put on my walking shoes.

Mario

Letty called, so excited to be flying around in that big plane that I wasn't sure she'd ever again be content to sit at home reviewing telex communication tear-offs for potential cases.

The first night Letty was away, Pixie volunteered to take her place.

"Boss, I'm staying with you unless you have something planned."

"Baby, you got Lainie waiting at home."

"I got her covered. Believe me, she's not home waiting for mama to arrive. C'mon, Boss. Don't be such a pickle fucker."

I choked down a laugh and ended up snorting a nose full of my iced tea. "Stay, Baby. Let's hit a night club tonight. What do you say?"

"We got no driver. Tricia already split."

As I sat at my desk and pondered the possibilities of flipping a coin for whoever had to stay sober, Pixie moved up close. She gave a spin to the back of my chair and plopped down on my lap when I came around. She flung her arms around me.

"Boss, let's hang here. Miguel can fix us a cool dinner. I can even make it romantic if you want."

I have known her almost all of my life and I love her more than words could describe. Her giggle is irresistible.

"Do we fuck before or after dinner?" I asked with my own chuckle.

"Let's hit the spa." She wiggled her way to sitting across me, her left arm draped over my shoulder, her legs crossed and swinging, and hanging over the arm of the chair. One of her strappy tall heels went flying. She ticked off her to-do list items on the fingers of her right hand one by one. "We can stop by the kitchen and give Miguel a dinner challenge, do a quickie down there in the steam like you like, stuff our faces in the wine room, then come up to your bedroom and fuck all night."

She didn't have to offer twice. I was liking her itinerary for the night. I got up with her in my arms, and set her on her feet, waiting while she grabbed her escaped shoe. She didn't put it on but hobbled unbalanced down the hall with the shoe hanging from a fingertip. I put my arm over her shoulder. "I'm already hard, I hope I can make it to the spa."

With her free hand, she checked to see just exactly how hard. She gave me a wicked grin.

"Boss, let's take the elevator. I've never done it in there. Have you?"

Olga and Letty were gone thirteen days. On her return, Olga only stayed two days. Her life was on a plane.

Of Letty, Olga had nothing but praises to sing. "Amor, I love Letty all the more now. She was a great assistant and I loved her company. She's a classy lady."

Once Olga was gone, Letty told me the stories of their travels. I knew they had changed plans. Instead of Munich or Barcelona, they had gone from Stockholm to Paris, and from there, Monaco.

"In Paris, she buys me a fabulous business suit at the hotel, and I go with her to a meeting with a banker named Marshall Zeglin. He has dark blue eyes. I figured he was handsome—" She paused to sneak a teasing look at me, "—about fifty years ago. Anyway, a nice guy. In Stockholm I don't attend any meetings with Olga, but in Paris, she introduces me as her assistant. Dig this, Boss: Olga has a small foldout case with a collection of eye glasses in different shapes and sizes, but they are plain, no prescription." We laughed together.

"You got to be kidding," I said.

"Not kidding. Anyway, she selects a neat pair of glasses for me that almost match the color of my suit, a dark blue. I look at myself in the mirror, a fucking different person. Wish I had taken a picture."

"Before we head to the bank, Olga tells me, 'Now you look like an assistant but that won't stop Marshall from eyeing you. He likes pussy, but we aren't giving him any, understand?'"

"Baby, if there is anything you don't think you should tell me, don't," I said, even though I was enjoying the gossip.

"Way ahead of you. I asked Olga if there was anything at all about the trip that I could not share with you, and she says, 'no secrets from him, and I trust you.'"

"Okay, great, shoot," I said.

"Anyway, the guards bring four suitcases into Marshall's office, but not until we are almost ready to leave. He asks her how much is the deposit. She writes it on a piece of paper that's on his desk. He writes out a receipt and stamps it, I guess with a bank stamp or something."

I wanted to ask if he got any payoff, but I doubted she would know that.

Letty told me about a snobbish, intimidating male bank president they met the next day, also in Paris. "I knew they had done business before. He's an old guy, real old, but even though he's grumpy with her, the banter is like code because I am there or a precaution if the office might be bugged." Letty laughed at what she said, and I joined her.

"Later, Olga says to me, 'All that chatter was about how much he wanted to make on the deposit I proposed to make. It was either a night with her or me, or ten thousand dollars."

"This sounds like a movie," I said.

"I had so much fun, Boss. So, I tell Olga, 'Fuck, I would have jacked him off for half that much.' Olga said that she would too, but when it's possible, it is better to pay, and ten thousand is a bargain for the size of the deposit."

I nodded like I approved of Olga's thinking. Did I approve?

"She is so fucking smart, Boss. On the plane, she's always working charts and numbers. She's always on target. The bankers fire questions at her, and she fires answers right back. She's never at a loss. It's those charts. She says she's always prepared because of the charts. It has to do with how much interest the deposit demands, and the term of the deposit, like is it less than a year, more than a year. She showed me how she forecasts future interest rates based on two indexes she uses. Fuck, sorry, I'm so wordy, Boss."

She made me laugh again.

Chapter 9
July 1983
Under the Radar

Mario

"When I'm in a plane with her, I never see charts or numbers."

"You guys are balling all the time, calculating the best angles for friction, not computing cash flow or the rate of return so you can throw big numbers in the face of some obnoxious German financier who thinks you can't add two plus two because you happen to have a vagina."

I laughed again. She had to have gotten that line from Olga. I didn't know Olga thought like that. She never mentioned the downside of what she does. Maybe being a woman was not always good. An Olga secret.

Letty went into detail about Gerulf, a banking hot shot in Monaco who had insulted Olga. Olga had insulted him right back, and by the end of the meeting, he was begging Olga to open an account.

"Did she?"

"Yeah, but not till the next day. She says she has to sleep on it and we go. Next day, the guys bring the suitcases, she opens three accounts."

I shook my head in wonderment. How was it possible that she would be bold enough to walk in a bank and offer to open an account, but demand it has to be in cash? Not bold, if the money is clean. Why do I assume the money is not clean? Maybe the money is clean.

We were sitting on one of the balconies off of the master bedroom, overlooking grounds that were all lit up. It had been a hot day, but the temperature had dropped at sunset. We were both still in shorts. A little breeze ruffled Letty's pony tail wafting the fresh scent of her shampoo in my direction. She always walked in a cloud of sweetness. We were sipping sangria chilled iced cold the way Letty liked it. The backlight from one section of the garden was positioned perfectly so that every so often, she'd move, and her hair would light up like a halo. Even her long lashes were dripping with light. Four stories down, the sound of the waterfall into the koi pond was mesmerizing.

I stared at Letty in silhouette, at the delicate bones of her face, the slim long neck, the big eyes that were pools of midnight, that caught glimmers of light and reflected them back to me. She had a beauty all her own, and a good part of that beauty was her energy. The French doors to my bedroom were open. Inside, a couple of candles burned, but outside, we had only the stars, and the backlighting of the shrubbery.

"Boss, you are staring."

"I like staring at you."

"You're sweet."

"If I was sweet, I would ask you to marry me."

"You can't be that sweet to everybody. Besides, you belong to Olga," she said. "Only sometimes, like now, you're mine."

I took a hit of the joint and considered her words. The tip of the joint crackled, popped out a seed and glowed red as I inhaled.

"I don't say it in a possessive way, Boss."

"I know, Baby."

We were sitting shoulder to shoulder on the outdoor couch. The breeze was just a little cool, but where our skin met, warmth overflowed. She moved so slowly that I hadn't realized where she was going until she had worked her way between my legs. She reached for my zipper. I caught her hand and held her palm to my cheek.

"Baby, if you give me head, I give you head."

"You don't have to. Let me."

I was not going to waste the night exchanging words. I stood, picking her up and carrying her inside. It took thirty seconds for us to undress, thirty seconds until I fitted my mouth between her legs. I felt her mouth on me. Taunting, then rhythmic, then I don't know what. I held off till it was impossible not to, because I became music, turned into the notes that burst out of me. I don't perspire easy, but we were both slick with sweat when it was over.

And then, a thud. It was faint. If it had happened five minutes before, it is very possible that I would not have heard the very slight thump on the balcony. The double doors were wide open. I sat up in bed, directly facing the balcony where Letty and I had been earlier. I looked out but from that angle saw nothing. The doors did not encompass the entire width of the balcony.

Letty sat up. "What is it?" she whispered.

"I heard something," I whispered back.

In a flash I was out of bed. The room was only lit by candles. I stood there bare ass naked. On the other side of the bed, Letty stood, also naked, a gun in each hand.

When you've had karate and judo training for more than twenty years, your senses become keenly developed. I inched forward toward the door, all my nerves on full alert, screaming at me that something was up. I don't think Letty has been in martial arts long enough for that, but she knew what fear was and she was matching my pace. Six feet from the door, she moved to where I was and signaled to let her go first. I wanted to laugh for her being so brave. I ignored her signal. She continued closing in on the door. The balcony was deserted. The night was quiet. The light from the moon and the gardens was perfect, calm, almost magical but the hairs were still standing at attention on the back of my neck. I smelled a faint odor of sour sweat. I knew someone was out there and invisible. Out jumped this big guy, a hood over his face, his clothes black like a parody of a cat burglar.

"Boss, he has a gun!"

I kicked and connected with his arm. His rifle went airborne, arcing before it fell to the yard below. Clearly, we surprised the intruder. Letty shot once, twice in rapid succession. He fell to his knees screaming. No question, Letty had hit something. He was leaving a trail of liquid black. Had to be blood.

My reaction was too fast. I leaped at the figure on the floor, scooped him up and out to the balcony. He got to his feet, no longer screaming. He fastened his hands around my throat. I felt his gloved fingers. The hood had fallen backward. I jerked the cap off and tossed it away. No surprises there. I saw the face I expected to see. Our eyes met, his pain-maddened, or maybe just crazy. I peeled back his little finger—the glove was certainly no impediment—and heard the bone snap, loosening his grip. His eyes got even crazier. He made the mistake of removing that hand from my neck, and that's when I saw his handgun.

"I got him," Letty yelled, moving in close and chopping his gun hand so that his firearm fell to the balcony floor.

"Who sent you?" I hissed.

He didn't answer.

"Who fucking sent you? Why the fuck are you stalking me?"

Still no answer. There wasn't much light, but it was enough to see a half-smile cross his face. Smug bastard. Now I had him where I wanted him. I was getting answers.

I slammed his nose first. He put up a hand defensively over the nose, so then I went for his jaw. I heard the crunch of bone and cartilage. He covered the jaw and I went for the nose.

"Ready to talk?"

He was panting, and I had him on the ropes. I wasn't even close to being winded. I repeated that sequence twice more. Nose-jaw-nose-jaw.

He backed off from the last punch, backed over the railing, flipping down four floors, then I heard him splash in the koi pond.

Letty and I looked at each other for a split second. Her eyes flicked down my body. We realized simultaneously that we were bare ass naked. She hit the bedroom lights and punched the panic button that set off a loud siren throughout the house. I scrambled into my shorts and ran out of the bedroom, Letty a few seconds behind me in panties and my long sleeve shirt from yesterday. We took the staircase like sprinters with our asses on fire. I could hear the dogs now and see the outdoor flood lights through the windows as we hustled our way downstairs.

"Boss, it's the biker."

"It is. I saw him when I pulled off his cap. He didn't come up with one fucking answer. I hope he survived that fucking fall."

"No way, Boss. It's a long way down."

"He landed on lily pads," I said. You'd think we would be out of breath running and talking but we were not. This is when we got rewarded for daily workouts that sometimes pushed our bodies to extremes. I noticed that in her panties and my shirt, Letty was still packing heat.

"Baby, you don't need the guns."

"I may need them," Letty said.

"I hear a helicopter."

"That was fast," Letty said. "I just pushed the panic button twenty seconds ago."

We heard gunshots. The sound of the helicopter roared closer, closer, farther, distant, gone.

By the time we were outside, the sirens of police cars were screaming just outside my wall.

We caught up with Pico the dog handler in the back of the property. Both the dogs were barking their faces off.

"Boss, a helicopter hovered but it was for just a minute. Two guys hauled a third guy from over there." He pointed over my shoulder. "They took off at the end of a rope like circus performers. I fired off four shots. I know I hit the chopper, but it still flew off. They had raw steaks for the dogs, but they're well trained, didn't touch it. Boss, I'd like to see if that meat was doped or poisoned. I'd like to know how they knew about the dogs."

He was still talking when I ran to the koi pond. The grounds were lit with spotlights revealing there was no one in the pond. The lotus plants were in shallow pots around the edges, and some of them were turned over and their pots shattered, the water lilies in the pond's center, crushed, and there was a murky darkness floating in the water that was probably blood.

We heard a helicopter again. This time it was the police flying overhead with a spotlight searching the property from above. The entire staff had come out of their quarters to walk toward the main house, not in their golf carts. The rest of the staff was walking. Miguel was running towards us.

It took all night for the police to conjecture that the intruder had been delivered by a helicopter and lowered by hoist to the roof of my house. Once on the roof, the intruder used a rope to climb down to my balcony. Mine was the only bedroom on the fourth floor but there were four balconies: two balconies in my office and two balconies off my master bedroom. How did this man know which to lower himself to?

The police took the shotgun and a 38 revolver they found, but my bet was that no prints would be found. They took the rope he had left behind, the cap and fished one glove from the pond.

The police speculated that while the intruder was on the grounds, the chopper was airborne and in communication by walkie talkies. They talked about how high the helicopter had to be so that we didn't wake up.

One of the detectives wondered aloud, "How did this injured man manage to get to the helicopter so fast? It's a hundred feet or more from where the helicopter landed and the koi pond."

The biker and I had wrestled nose to nose before I got my punches in. I told the police I thought he looked like the pictures the detectives had gotten from my security cameras.

Letty only knew the guy had a beard. She wasn't sure it was the guy we called the biker.

"Why didn't you just shoot to kill?" the detective asked her.

"Just because I have guns and a permit to carry doesn't mean it's okay to commit murder, not when there's another way."

I could see the detective liked that answer.

"You didn't panic at all?"

"Panic, no, upset, yes. He interrupted a very intimate moment." She grinned suggestively.

I shrugged at the detective then looked at her with a smile. We both knew we had finished that intimate moment before the thump on the balcony sent us stalking the intruder like a couple of bare ass ninjas. I was certain someone had hired the biker. How could he have the cash to secure a helicopter to get him entry into my house? The biggest of all questions remained unanswered. Why?

Noon the next day, none of us had gotten any sleep. Letty was home of course, but Pixie, Tricia, Jo and Niley had come over for moral support. We sat at the dining table and Miguel served us what we ordered. The plates didn't come out simultaneously, but pretty fast. The egg dishes were out first.

Cold scrambled eggs are not good. I told everyone, "No waiting."

I got my steak and started in on it.

Melina brought a huge basket of fruit. She kissed everyone, stayed thirty minutes at most and ate nothing. Miguel managed to get her drinking a cup of coffee.

Six concerned neighbors that I did not socialize with but knew very well came over to hear the story that they could have read in the newspaper or three of the local television stations. They said they were going to call a neighborhood meeting to call for heightened security. The police had no clue yet if the helicopter was stolen or where it came from. They were quoted they were sure it had a hoist.

When Quito came inside to see me, I spoke before he did.

"There was no way you could have prevented this, so don't worry about it. What's done, is done. Letty and I are fine, and no one was hurt except for the intruder."

Pixie said, "I can't believe any criminal would have much of a brain in his head if he's dumb enough to hang out on Mario's fourth floor balcony. We all know how that story is going to end." She laughed maniacally for five minutes straight, then turned to Letty and said, "I would have put a bullet in his Koi-splatting ass. I can't believe you just went for the feet and didn't just shoot him dead."

"Oh please, Pix, how many times are you going to say that to me? I shot his ass. Twice. That's enough."

"His feet," Pixie said, teasing.

"You did the right thing," Tricia told her. "You're a hero."

"I agree, Baby. I owe you my life," I said with a wink.

"Oh bull," Letty giggled. "You kicked that shotgun right out of his hands. You slapped him so silly he backed his ass right off the edge."

Jo said, "I could say something about intruders flying out of windows, but I won't bring it up." She was joking, but it was the truth.

"Boy do I remember," Niley said. "That one time that asshole held us hostage."

"Hey, I didn't hear that one?" Letty lied.

"Oh, I told you," Pix shook her head. "You."

They went on and on. I kept thinking of the nerve of this bastard. Where was this guy getting inside information? Where the fuck did he get a chopper? Nine bedrooms on the third floor. How did he know I was sleeping in the only bedroom on the fourth floor? He came ready to spray us with that shotgun? Why?

Olga and Camila flew in. They arrived at different times, with ten security guards between them. TJ was almost done with the addition, but we still had the two modular homes out by the personnel quarters. The new build was only to accommodate five guards, Olga's security force. Maybe I'd have to keep the modular units. They weren't that ugly, and it was far enough from the house you couldn't see them through the trees around that area of the property.

"I'm surprised Pepe let you come over when things are this hot," I said to Olga. Camila was scheduled to arrive two hours later.

"Pepe can't tell me what to do in my personal life," Olga said, "I had to see you."

When Camila arrived, I told her the same thing. Her response was not unlike Olga's.

"Amor, Pepe is my brother, not my boss. Of course, I had to come. I was so worried, Amor."

As for Letty, well, she was a hero. Camila hugged her for a long time. Olga cried on my shoulder, then hugged Letty too. It was all very emotional. It would have been like Letty to say that she didn't save me at all. She had already said it once, but she knew it was best to say nothing. I think Camila and Olga were just proud that Letty disabled his gun hand with a chop, and used two guns on the bastard, stopping him without killing him.

After the rest of my team went home, Olga, Camila, Letty, and I went to bed in my bedroom on my very huge bed, and—check this out—there was no sex. I was too exhausted to sleep. We all smoked weed and drank wine, even Olga who doesn't smoke much. Even Camila drank wine instead of champagne. And another first. We fell asleep in sleepwear.

Detective Mullins, one of two detectives handling Olga and Tricia's case was assigned the intruder case.

Mullins said, "I have a body at the morgue I need you to I.D. for us."

"Who is it?"

"I think it's the guy you call the biker. If it's him, and I think by the pictures we have that it is him, his name is Luca Rossi."

"Damn," I said. "The fall killed him."

"Not sure what killed him yet. He was shot between the eyes. Looks like a professional hit. Can you come down?"

"The guy on my balcony was shot in the feet. We told you that."

"Luna, I know that. I need to I.D. this guy. I need to know if he's the man who broke in your house and I need Letty to tell me he's the one she shot two bullets into. I know who he is now that we got prints."

"Mullins, okay, we'll do the I.D. Tell me this, do his feet have wounds?"

"They do. Luna, when can you and Letty come down?"

"You haven't told me where he showed up?"

"He was found at Hollenbeck Park. Coroner doesn't think he was there more than an hour or two before he was discovered."

An hour later we were at the coroner's office in downtown Los Angeles. Pixie and Tricia insisted on coming along. They had seen the biker before and wanted to see if he was the dead guy.

The body was wheeled to a window and we stood on the other side when the attendant pulled back a sheet to reveal his face. It was definitely him, and he was not a pretty sight.

Letty nodded to the cop. "I didn't get a good look at his face in the dark, but I saw the beard. And this is the guy I saw before. This guy accosted on the freeway and stalked us at the Hyatt in San Antonio. We didn't report it because what could you do without proof? Anyway, how many people get shot in both feet? I did that."

Tricia and Pixie agreed and so did I.

"He's the one I fought with on the balcony," I said. The dead bastard sure as fuck wasn't talking now.

The curtain was shut on the window and we stood there together with Mullins.

Letty said, "I didn't shoot that dude between the eyes. All my guns are registered and available to you. It wasn't me."

"I believe you," Mullins said. I was surprised that a cop would say that.

Letty said, "Thanks. It's the truth."

"I'll arrange to have an expert come by and check your guns. This looks like a forty-five. We'll know soon," Mullins said.

"I have two forty five's, a black and a chrome that's never been shot."

Mullins smiled. "You have quite a gun collection."

Pixie waved her hand to indicate the girls. "Yeah, we do. We were trained by an expert on every gun we own. Except for Boss. The karate kid here doesn't know shit about guns."

Mullins said no more.

I dropped the girls off at home and dropped in to the market where Melina was working to tell her what we had learned. I wasn't surprised when she made an offer to represent Letty.

Melina hugged me fiercely. She said, "You have to wonder where this is coming from. This is some serious shit. An attempted hit on you is way the hell more sinister than pasting a picture on a door of an apartment twenty-eight hundred miles away. Think it out, Cuz. Who have you messed with that is trying to get back to you?"

It was not the first time she had said this to me. Hell, this was not the first time I'd said the same thing to myself.

"I've killed four times in self-defense. Maybe one or all of them have family out for revenge. Maybe it's the bastards that kidnapped me in Venezuela. Pepe said they burned to death at their plantation. If they survived, they'd be pissed off. They spent five years in prison because of me, because during my rescue the military claimed they found drugs and the kidnappers insisted the drugs were planted. I've always figured they didn't die."

"Maybe they died, maybe not. Maybe their relatives want vengeance."

More questions, no answers. Melina offered to represent Letty.

Soon as I got home, I called Fino. I had already talked to him twice since he had read the newspaper article about the intruder. I told him the identity of the biker and about his being shot between the eyes.

Fino volunteered his professional services. "I can call the detective and tell him I'm representing Letty."

"I'll bear that in mind, but with any luck it won't get to that. Thanks a lot for the offer."

As much as I love Melina, if it got serious I'd have to pick Fino. He's been a criminal lawyer for decades.

When Olga called from Punta del Este, South America, I told her about the home invasion, the body found in Hollenbeck Park, the holes in his feet that we'd known about, and the one between his eyes that had come as a surprise. Olga was back in Pasadena within twenty-four hours. What was significant to me was not what she said, but what she did not say. She did not engage in speculation over who might have been Luca Rossi's executioner. I wondered who that shooter might be, but my primary concern was to be there for Letty so that the shooting did not get pinned on her. We were all in the dark about who made the kill shot, who sent him and if it was the same person.

"I think you should get out of there for a while. Come fly with me, Amor."

"Tempting, but I have a number of deals going for LAI and I have things to do here."

"You just don't want to think you are running away, Amor."

I did not jump at her challenge.

"Amor?"

"I have to stay close to Letty until they finish investigating the shooting to the shithead's face."

"If she had shot him dead, it would have been self-defense. She has nothing to worry about."

"Baby, I know."

"I talked to Letty. She doesn't sound worried," said Olga, who wanted me to fly away with her, but that body was one more reason to stick around LA. LAI duty called, and she left a few days later.

We frequented the wine room at least once a day, even if we weren't there to drink wine. It was a great spot for talking, and convenient to the downstairs play areas. Tonight 'we' meant Letty, Pixie, me, wine and a tray of various jalapeño tapas that Miguel was testing out on us. We had been forewarned.

"Way I see it," Pixie said, gingerly holding a fried morsel to her nose and sneezing, "the freeway crime is solved, the biker is dead. I don't know if he's the one who left the shotgun in my car but I'm thinking it was him so that crime is solved with his death. The picture on the New York apartment door, even if he didn't paste the picture there, he probably had it done so that's solved, too."

Letty and I exchanged looks.

"What did I miss?" asked Pixie. She bit into the crunchy fried oval, whistled and swigged her wine. "Shitfire, that's hot." She held one out to me. "Bet you can't take it."

I accepted it and popped the whole thing in my mouth. The burn exploded, melted the roof of my mouth, my tongue and all of my teeth. I felt heat then cold seeping out of my ears. I did not let my face change expression. "Perfect," I said coolly, not waiting for the burn to subside. The four-year-old child in me wanted to run to the pool and swim twenty laps with my mouth open. "You missed the truck ramming my car with Olga and Tricia in it," I said.

"Fuck, of course, so that's solved, too." Pixie offered Letty a pepper bomb.

Wisely, Letty refused both the pepper and Pixie's hypothesis. "I don't think so," said Letty. "What about the guy driving the truck? Who was it, how is he connected to the biker? Or to whoever? Those guys did not come up with a helicopter on their own."

"I figure we're progressing," Pixie said, tipsy and getting tipsier. She swished wine around her mouth. "Want me to recite the solved crimes again for you?"

I suspected she was trying to cool her tongue. I shook my head and dunked one of her fingers in a bowl of sour cream. "Suck on that," I said. "It's more cooling than wine."

Olga was in for five days.

"I'm getting used to your regular visits," I told her.

"Amor, I miss you so much when I'm away. I love being around you," she hugged me, smothering me with kisses. It was afternoon and we were basking in the living room on a sofa. The phone rang.

I took a call from Ches, not his actual name, but a shortened version of it I could remember. It was something long and unpronounceable. I was in the market for his clubs. We had talked the deal through, and it looked to me like it was going to fly. I put my hand over the phone and told Olga I might take the call in my office.

"Stay," Olga said. "I like to watch."

"Even if we don't make this deal," I said, "I have a feeling we're going to be friends."

"Mario, need to make the deal. We're already friends, dude, you just not appreciating the gold mine my four clubs are."

The clubs, two in West Hollywood and two in Hollywood, were not what I would go to and leave my car out on the sidewalk like at Whisky Go-Go. I knew Letty liked the clubs. We'd done a drive by when I first started talking to Ches about buying. Ches had been in the car, and Letty had truly played the part of the quiet driver. The clubs weren't in the best locations, but there were lines to get in no matter the day of week. The books he had given me were trash, he knew it and I knew it. He claimed there was as much cash as what he showed on the books.

Four leases on the locations, rent wasn't bad, and the shortest lease had seven years to go. I offered him four hundred thousand.

Olga had moved to the couch across from me and was watching intently. I patted the warm spot on the couch where she had been. I preferred her cuddled next to me where she had been.

"I'll up it twenty-five each but the no competition clause extends from five miles to ten miles from each location for five years. Call me when you think about it."

"Mario, wait. I don't plan on opening clubs there no matter how many miles you want to add to the no competition clause. I want one fifty for each club. Give a brother a break, Mario, come on."

I watched Olga who seemed to be urging me to up it a little.

"Ches, the money is not mine. I just gave you every penny, nickel and dime I'm authorized to give you."

It was a good deal. LAI would pump in a bunch of cash and unlike Ches, bank it and report it on their tax returns.

"How soon can I have the bread?"

"Got to do a bulk sale in escrow, but I can advance you some money pending close."

"Thanks, brother, no need for advance. Here's what I want: Deposit two hundred in escrow and three hundred comes to me the other way."

"Deal," I said. "You got an escrow?"

"Make it close. Don't like to drive across town to sign documents, know what I mean?"

"Smart man, Ches. This is a good deal for you."

"They gold mines. I need the money, you stealing bread from my mouth."

"Don't lie," I countered. "You making out like a king."

When I hung up, I walked where Olga was sitting, the long corded phone trailing behind.

"One more call, Baby." I kissed her.

"The end number?"

"Five hundred, two in paper, three green."

Olga smiled. "You're so smart, Amor."

I called my broker who handled everything for me: escrows, running to make the deals close. This one was easy. LAI would have to assume the leases but that wouldn't be hard. They'd probably buy the properties. Good thing is I didn't handle any of that.

"Now you got my attention." I wrapped my arms around Olga.

Letty drove Olga and me for a night on the town. Olga wanted to go out and it was a perfect opportunity to let her check out what we were about to close. It was after nine on a Thursday, not the best party night of the week. Sure enough, the lines to get in were backed up down the block. We spun by all four to check them out.

"The lines don't mean they are making money," I said to Olga.

"That's not important, Amor, well done, fabulous deal."

After that, we went to The Factory where a live rock band was playing, and the one acre dance floor had ten acres of dancers gyrating on it. A twenty got us a table with only a five minute wait. Olga and I squeezed on to the floor for the one slow dance, then Olga would not quit. As much as I needed to polish up my fast dancing, it was so crowded it didn't matter. It was a crazy fun night, we laughed ourselves out of breath, and till my face hurt from smiling. Olga and I were pretty wasted when we made it back to the car, but the hilarity lasted all the way home. I was grateful Letty was driving stone cold sober. When I was a kid my Aunt Carmen would tell me that too much fun was followed by something sad or terrible. Truly, I did not believe that.

Letty

I love this funny chauffer hat that Boss hates so much. I think it's cute. He refuses to let me wear my blacks that I used to drive him around in, years ago. He didn't like them then either.

They're in there an hour. Plenty of people-watching to do here. Drunks coming out are funny. I think one guy's trying to pick up the lamp post, and some girl with pink panties is passing out on a bus bench. The cops pull through the parking lot twice. Olga looked sincere when she invited me to join them, but I figure, let them have their fun. I want him happy. If he's dancing in there, fuck, I'd love to take pictures. So hard to get him dancing. Full of excuses, that man. "I'm so tall, I feel awkward," Pixie and me, we get him up to dance sometimes. For three years in the rented house, we did all the good clubs. I don't miss them. I got nobody to impress.

Two hours. They're still in there. We got it all at Casa Luna, all we need to top this is a live band. Juke box and all the wall to wall stereo equipment, we do okay without a bunch of wasted musicians crapping up the place. Still, I bet it's a blast. It's pretty boring out here, just sitting. Parking lot is halfway lit. A chauffeur on the cute side is waiting for his riders, like me. I love his chauffeur's cap. So formal looking, like a real uniform. He's eyeing me from across a couple cars. Third cigarette in thirty minutes. He walks in my direction half way, then closer. What the hell. With a little luck, I can chew the fat to while away the next two hours. Finally, I get out of the car. I keep my hat on. I smile, he smiles, I do a little wave and a shimmy. He walks the rest of the way over.

Mario

In the morning, I was up for my workout. Minutes after I got rolling in the gym, here came Olga. A first. Olga never comes in to work out, but she looked like that's what she wanted to do. A few minutes later, Letty came in, a regular. Letty faced the mirror and started doing routine stretches.

I stopped long enough to peck Olga's lips with mine. "I didn't mean to wake you," I said. "You didn't get much sleep."

"Neither did you, Amor, or you, Letty."

We smiled all around.

"I want to do the treadmill." Olga walked over to it with a look on her face like it was some kind of alien vehicle. "Not familiar with this model."

Letty beat me over there to turn the machine on and show her the ropes. She saw Olga was ok on it, then went back to the mirror and started doing drills of a variety of moves. She broke off what she was doing, did some more drills with a weight bar, then back to stretches.

I ran through my own stretches and drills. Thirty minutes in, I stopped the kata I was doing, and went over to the rack of heated towels, and tossed one at Olga. It caught on her shoulder and she grabbed it, without missing a stride or grabbing for the sidebars. She grinned in my direction, buried her face in the towel, and draped it around her neck.

"Thanks," she said. She upped the pace and her feet drummed a little faster.

Letty said, "Boss, Olga handles that walker like a pro, she must work out in secret somewhere."

"I should but I don't," Olga said. "Maybe I'll put one on the plane." She smiled but didn't slow her pace. "You two are amazing. Look at the sweat. Amazing."

"Speaking of sweat," Letty said, not finishing her sentence. She was dripping sweat and disappeared into the shower. A few minutes later, I heard the door to the pool room, and figured Letty had decided to cool down with some laps.

I grinned at Olga.

"Alone at last," I said.

"Whatever shall we do?" she said, turning off the treadmill. "Meet you in the shower? I know some moves I'd like to try out."

Before noon, Detective Mullins showed up. We met in my office. He sat at my desk across from me.

"I was in the neighborhood. Sorry for not calling first."

I shrugged. "No problem."

"This man you call the biker has a record of crimes that should have sounded an alarm when we only had the pictures."

"He never left a print behind," I said. "Are you closing the case or are you going to try and find out why he was after me?"

"Can't close the case. We don't know who killed him."

Detective Ramsey Mullins seemed to be a nice guy. There was something about his manner that made me feel he was pressured. Maybe it was the way he sucked down cigarettes. He looked neat and crisp, like he had a military background, but the way he plowed through the tobacco was pathological. No doubt he had a desk full of crimes to solve, with victims more sympathetic than Luca Rossi. Victims who didn't have a criminal record long enough to fill a book.

"Do you really care who killed him?"

"It's murder. Of course, we care. You might be glad to know the coroner says he survived the fall."

"Letty will be glad to hear that."

"That's why I came over," he said. "He was killed some time later by the facial bullet."

"Letty, come in my office," I said into the intercom.

Mullins told her what the coroner determined.

She said, "I knew I didn't do it. Could have but didn't. Glad you know it wasn't me."

"This is a strange case," Mullins said, getting to his feet. "You didn't hear the helicopter before he appeared in your bedroom?"

Letty and I exchanged looks. She shook her head. "Nope. I didn't hear a helicopter until after we were running down the stairs."

"We were…" she hesitated for a few seconds, "…busy."

If there was a helicopter overhead, maybe we were totally involved in each other when it was overhead, probably making our own noise. I should have heard it, but I did not hear anything. I didn't hear anything until the biker alerted me on the patio, five minutes after the sex was over.

"Did you ask the guards on duty about that?" I asked.

"I did. I asked all of them. They heard nothing."

"We get used to the police helicopter flying over. Maybe that's why no one can remember," Letty suggested.

Mullins gave a nod to Letty, shook my hand, and headed for my office door.

Olga was out and missed Mullins. I told her about his visit when she came in the conference room where I was looking over the day's telexes, with Pixie and Letty looking on.

"He survived the fall, amazing," Olga said.

"That doesn't mean he would have survived," Pixie said.

"True," I said. "But he lived long enough to get in the helicopter. Then someone shot him between the eyes and took the time to drop him off at Hollenbeck Park."

"Maybe he was shot at the park," Letty said.

"Stop," Olga said. "The good thing is he's gone now."

"Dead," said Pixie.

"Whoever sent him is not dead," I said.

"Oh Boss, are you saying it's not over?" Letty asked, her voice verging on a wail.

"He's not saying that," Olga answered before I did.

I did not want to contradict Olga, so I didn't add anything else to the conversation. Time flies, and so does Olga. Before I knew it, Olga was gone again.

Here is the heart of the matter: My girls may still be at risk because of me. I know if his loved ones were at risk, Pepe would not have considered the matter finished, and neither would I.

I had been working on a purchase of a hundred fifteen donut shops, located in Southern California, twenty-four of them in Los Angeles. The seller, Calvin Reasons, had pictures of each location along with an accounting package, including sales tax returns to backup the sales reported in the reports. Reasons was a self-made donut baker that started with a hole-in-the-wall in downtown Los Angeles. His source of capital was one hundred fifteen locations, including the real property of each location. This was not included in the bio I was given. He managed this in twenty-two years.

I told my broker to tell the seller's broker that unless I had a one-on-one meeting with the seller, I would drop any possibility of buying. The listing was a buy all, or nothing. The accountant I used to evaluate business packages like this was not my personal CPA, but a friend of his. The donut shop deal was not the first deal he had worked with me on.

"There are forty-one locations that are not doing very well but they are not in the red. Eight locations are in the red. The others are good earners," Rico Munoz, the CPA, explained.

When I finally met with Reasons, Rico's report to me about the losers and winners was my opening.

"Mario, it's all stores or none."

"I know the deal, Calvin. Just want you to know I'm interested and that's why I've spent a ton of money going over the books you've provided for each store."

"That's why I'm here," Calvin said.

Calvin lived in Beverly Hills. He looked like a slightly tanned, slightly underweight Santa Claus, something I guess that might only happen to bakers in health-conscious communities like Los Angeles. He had the full white beard and hair and rosy cheeks of Santa, but his tan and condition was all California. He clearly ate his own doughnuts but managed to burn some of them off. The brokers connected us so that we could talk on the phone and I invited him to come over to Casa Luna to discuss the sale. I was surprised that he accepted. Pixie met him at the door of the house and brought him up to me on the fourth floor. It was a little after ten in the morning and we were in my office, alone, Calvin sitting on a sofa across from me where I was on a twin sofa with a table between us.

His appraisals valued a hundred and fifteen properties at eleven million five hundred thousand. Calvin had the package listed at twenty-five million. Santa had fudged the value a little.

"Can you use any part of this price in cash?" I asked. I saw no expression change in Calvin and that was just great. Who knew how he got his jump start?

"I never thought about that. Why you ask?"

"Well, if there is cash in the deal, it could have something to do with what I am willing to pay."

"Mario, the price is twenty-five million. No negotiation." He picked up his glass of coke and drank half of it.

"You didn't get to where you are believing what you just said."

"Are you saying you will pay my asking price if I accept cash?"

It didn't happen right away but two months later we closed escrow. Ten million through escrow, most of which to pay off his mortgages on the properties and 330 pounds of one hundred-dollar bills, fifteen million.[12]

I only spoke to one person at the management company that LAI used. Raul Gomez. I had once been told Gomez was a Camacho cousin from Bogota who worked for Pepe. We'd talked by phone ever since TJ had finished that building for LAI. He seemed to love the deal. I could only envision that all the donut shops would be showing huge profits in the near future. There was great opportunity to pump a whole bunch of cash for each store directly to bank accounts.

Olga had taken a shine to Letty. I could only suppose she was also taking a shine to Pixie. If not, she was making a great effort at getting to know my team.

When she was back in town, she asked me, "Do you mind if Pixie tags

---

[12] $15,000,000.00 in 1984 had the same buying power as $36,504,047.38 in 2018

along to Brazil?"

"Baby, it's up to her, I'd be surprised if she says no."

I didn't even ask for how long.

"I know she works every day and I just don't want to nab her away from you."

"It's okay, Baby. The work she does is a game of luck. If she finds a small aircraft crash then she works it to convince the victim or victim's family to sign with us."

Pixie was thrilled at the opportunity to go to Brazil. She gave Lainie a call to let her know she was going. Lainie was a freshman staying in the dorm at UCLA.

"You'll have a good time, I promise." Olga said, "I work a lot, but you'll love Sao Paulo and Rio. Wait till you see the Rio house." She looked at me. "We had it redone."

I recalled the home set on an ocean bluff overlooking a sandy private beach. It had been extraordinary when I had been there. I couldn't imagine how they could have improved on it.

"I remember when you and Camila took us to your home in Hawaii. That pad was out of sight," Pixie said.

"It's still there. One day we need to go back," Olga said.

As excited as a little girl at the gates of Disneyland, Pixie called me from the plane's landline.

"Boss, thank you for letting me get away like this. This plane is fucking fantastic."

The next voice I heard was Olga's. "Thank you for letting her come with me. She's great company."

Pixie

Letty gave me the scoop about her trip with Olga. I was really looking forward to having one of my own. After all the flying around with Mario, you'd think I'd get used to traveling. Not me. If I'm lucky, maybe someday, I'd have a plane of my own to hop around in.

Boss doesn't know how often I talk to Jason in London. He always asks me to go see him. I spent a night with him when we were staying at Sami's penthouse in London. He took me to his house, a fucking mansion, that's what it was. I said, "Hey, Jas, I know lawyers make lots of bread, but I never imagined they got paid this well."

He said, "I went to law school, got a license. I did not want my own practice, so I went to work defending insurance companies. I never had to work. It was always a choice. My father was very wealthy, my mother even wealthier. When they died, my sister and I were left with a fortune."

The house was like a palace, too old for my taste but a palace just the same. He didn't give me the tour that first visit. The living room alone is enough to keep a person busy for hours looking at the paintings and artifacts. It reminds me of a fancy hotel lobby though there is no hotel lobby I have ever seen that is as beautiful as the room Jason and I were sitting in.

I wanted a joint so bad. I was nervous. I settled for a glass of red wine. He had some, too. I gulped that glass down much too fast. He poured me more. I knew I should take it easier, but I didn't.

If Olga gets me to London, I'm going to see Jason again.

There were three television sets on the plane. I counted them when we got there. She gave me a tour. After we took off, Olga pulled out several notebooks and took over the table. This is exactly what Letty told me Olga did when they took off.

"Sorry, Pixie, not thinking. I'll move right over here close. I have some stuff to go over."

"Don't move. I'll move."

I moved to the center of the big living room cabin. I sat for a while, but I am not so good at sitting still.

"If it's okay, I'll go watch a movie in the bedroom."

"Si, Amor, you can watch one here."

"I don't want to disturb you."

"Amor, I'll be in there real soon. There's a box under the television with a bunch of movie tapes."

The stewardess, Natalia, gave us a couple of soft sweats that we put on before we took off. Like a queen, I sat on the bed, my back on the headboard and watched Scarface. I love the fuck out of Pacino. Natalia looked in on me every little while. She brought me a coke with a bowl of mixed nuts. Waited on me like a queen.

Olga came in to get me in the middle of the film. I paused it.

"Lunch is served, Amor, come."

Her papers and notebooks were at the table where she was working but our lunch was served on another table in the big cabin.

"You are far out," I told her.

Olga has the most beautiful face. I can understand why Boss flipped over her.

"Did Letty tell you how she played assistant to me when we visited some banks in Paris and Monaco?"

Letty had told me the story a hundred times, but I lied.

"No, tell me."

Hearing it from Olga was a different story. I watched every move she made as she spoke and ate. I had to catch myself, so I wouldn't be staring too much. When she stopped talking, our eyes met for a second.

"Olga, I want to go down on you."

I'd done it before, but this was not at Casa Luna. This was her plane and I was a guest. I just had to say it aloud. Fuck it. Besides, Letty told me she did it, and Olga did it to her.

We stared, still eating, eyes on eyes. Olga did not blush, just smiled.

"Now or later?"

"I'll go down on you right there," I said, "Just tell me it's okay. After lunch, you can work while I do it."

Olga laughed, "Amor, you are so real, I love you."

"I love you, too, Olga."

From the airport that is practically downtown, we took a van with her five security men and a driver that was waiting for us. I said nothing, but I had two guns in my purse, my travel Louis Vuitton purse. In Sao Paulo, I was surprised that we went to a home. A very big home.

One of her guards named Pinto—I've known him since Olga started running around with guards—he always looks at me like he wants to fuck my brains out. I don't lead him on or flirt with him. It's a wonder that Olga, as observant as she is, has never mentioned it. I don't mind someone looking at me like that, but it gets old when it's all the time. Even in the van, he was eating me with his eyes.

"I'm here to pay for this house," Olga said. "Camila bought it. We'll explore it tonight, Si?"

The van pulled up to the front of the house. I counted eight men and women there to greet us, the workers. Olga spoke Portuguese to the help that greeted us. Olga was fucking amazing. Real conversations with them, not just tourist shit like *where is the can? can I have a drink of water?*

"Let me guess. The workers stay with the house?"

"Yes, we agreed to keep them."

"With a house in Rio so close, you must be planning to do business here?"

Olga put her arm around me as we walked through the first floor, a butler leading the way.

"We have business here, long story."

I waited, but it was, apparently, a long story she wasn't going to share. "We've had two plane crashes here in Sao Paulo," I told Olga.

"Oh, so you know Sao Paulo. You didn't tell me."

I smiled. "I didn't want you to take back your invitation because I had been here before."

"Amor, of course I would bring you anyway."

"I was never able to speak Portuguese, but I learned that if I speak slow in Spanish the person I'm speaking to understands me."

"Exactly," Olga said.

The grounds weren't as big, but the house was bigger than Casa Luna. I counted three floors, but it seemed enormous to me.

"It's not as big as Mario's," Olga said.

I counted thirteen bedrooms, and two of them were masters.

"Did you buy it as is?" I knew the house was bigger than Boss's house.

"Yes, as is. Closets and drawers are empty, but by tomorrow all linens will be replaced with new and the house will be ready."

"Exciting."

"Si, Amor. You can have one of the master bedrooms, and I'll take the other."

"Olga, thank you."

We gave each other a wild ride on the plane, couldn't understand why we were going to be in different bedrooms. It was okay by me.

We had dinner at a restaurant that had a giant fig tree in the center. It was so big I had to figure it was a fake tree. The food was wicked delicious, the music was slamming. The rock band entertaining us was on fire with a girl singer who had to be dating somebody in the band, because she didn't sing as good as Jack Fino's parrots. She was what Letty would call a yeller, not a singer. It made me feel good when Olga said that I sing so much better than that girl. And without getting a big head over it, yeah, I think I do. If Letty was here, she'd make me get a guitar and sit here at the table, and strum and sing till they were all coming in their shorts. She's my biggest fan, except for Mario. Looking at all these hot ecstatic Brazilians jumping to the beat and loving the music, I couldn't help but want to grab that mic and go up on that stage and sing to Sao Paulo, so they could jam with me. I almost made a promise to myself to do just that. What the hell. A girl can dream, right?

Mario

Olga ported cash around the world paying for items that Camila purchased. Camila had agents like me everywhere looking to turn assets like diamonds, art, marble, real estate, and business chains over for cash. Most of the groundwork was done before Camila arrived to sign the deal, and Olga arrived later with the cash. LAI seemed to have an endless supply of cash. While I knew of some businesses they were into, I still wondered where all that cash came from. I had three safes in the house, I had eleven million in hundred-dollar bills. One million was mine. Ten million was Camacho money, waiting for me to invest in anything I thought would be good for LAI. I banked the cash LAI paid me. I paid taxes on it. I had nothing to hide.

For breakfast, Miguel had made pancakes and provided a variety of fruit compotes as toppings. If I did not work out like a madman, I'd be pushing three hundred pounds. I looked at Letty across the breakfast table. She was dressed for karate. Normally, she worked out with me or on her own here at the house. I knew she had a class that day. To work her way up to the next belt, she had to attend classes. If we were not out on a case or away on something else, she practiced at Cosmo's a couple times a month.

She slung her purse over her shoulder and put on the big round sunglasses that made her look like a turtle.

"I'll tell Cosmo hi from you," Letty said, heading for the door. "He's not teaching the class, but he always watches me like a hawk. I'll be back in a couple hours."

"We have nothing planned this weekend. When you get back, get us a flight crew for early afternoon and a dinner reservation. Let's fly to Acapulco for dinner at the Mirador."

"Are you serious?"

"Of course, I'm serious. What's the point in having my own plane if I can't decide to fly off at the drop of a hat?"

"Fuck me," Letty said.

Miguel showed no sign of hearing her.

"She is taking after Pixie," I said aloud.

Miguel chuckled. "No sir, Boss. She is taking after me."

She wanted to call right away, but I made her go to class first.

As we descended over Acapulco, Tricia told Letty, "Stash your guns on the plane. You cannot carry a gun in Mexico."

Letty gave her the finger. "I know. I've been to Mexico more than you. Mine are put away. Where are yours?"

"Mine are stashed." Tricia returned the finger gesture, but they were both smiling.

Letty, Tricia, and I disembarked in Acapulco at five in the afternoon and were met by a hired car that drove us to the Mirador Hotel for one of their famous dinners. We drank wine, ate like kings, watched cliff divers spiral from a cliff above the restaurant to the shallow waters below, and saved our applause and whistles for when the divers came up for air. A little after ten, we were lifting off, headed for home in great spirits.

In the plane, Tricia yawned hugely, and asked, "Are you okay to drive, Boss? Because I'm wiped out."

"I'm good."

She yawned again, and I swear I saw down to her feet.

"Are you okay?"

"I'm high, Boss." The next second, she nodded off. I slept for the last hour before we landed. Three and a half hours after taking off, I was driving us home in the Rolls. Letty who had been awake on the plane, slept all the way home.

Tricia insisted she was fine to drive, had to get home. I figured Bill was waiting on her. I had it from Letty that they were not living together.

Letty and I hit the bed. Around four in the morning, the phone rang. I didn't answer. Thanks to Acapulco, and an energetic Letty, I was so tired I could not convince my arm to reach the foot or so to the phone. For once, I had no nightmares of Pixie and Olga getting arrested, shot at, or being in a hijacked plane. At five, I woke up enough to walk around the room and close the blackout curtains, so that dawn would not disturb us. Of course, we got up late.

The personal phone line rang. I answered.

"I tried calling you, Amor."

"I think I heard the ring, but I had just gone to bed. We just got back from Acapulco."

I told her about the Acapulco trip. "Where are you guys?" I asked.

"In Rio. Amor, it's beautiful here."

"How is Pixie?"

Instead of answering, she handed off the phone.

"Boss, I was worried when no one answered this morning. Don't ever worry me like that again, please!"

"At four in the morning you wondered why I didn't pickup the line?" I laughed. "You could have called the main number and the guard would have picked up."

Pixie ignored me, and went on for five minutes about Sao Paulo, the huge old house Olga had bought, and everything else going on under the Rio sun.

Olga took the phone back, and said, "Amor, please don't start seeing Melina like before. She's moving any day. Be friends, but not bed friends any-more, *por favor, Amor, dime que no tengo por que preocuparme.*[13] I'm so jealous of her, I shiver."

---

[13] Please Love, tell me I do not have to worry.

"Olga, I love you. My feeling for Melina is another kind of love. Don't worry about her."

"I'm yours, Amor."

In the morning Melina showed up, taking me by surprise, beautiful, dressed for work, and a sight for sore eyes. I had already worked out. She joined me in the dinette for breakfast, patted Miguel on the back in passing telling him she just wanted coffee. Except for the shock of seeing her, and the fragile feeling that this was our last breakfast together for the foreseeable future, it was like old times.

Almost.

She hugged and kissed Letty. Letty is no dummy. She excused herself and took her plate and coffee into the kitchen.

I kissed her, a kiss that lasted a long time. She didn't push me away.

"I'm moving this weekend, Cuz. Escrow is closed. The new house is mine."

"Congratulations!"

We clicked cups like it was champagne instead of Colombian roast.

I had lived there three years while this place was being rebuilt. I was familiar with the house, she just bought, and its location on what they call Millionaire Row. "I love that house, but the damn street is so busy," I said.

"I'm not going to be sleeping on Orange Grove, Cuz. Love the house."

"It's a great house," I agreed.

Our eyes locked.

"I already miss you," I said. "You've been across the street and I have hardly seen you these past few weeks. Our Sundays, ours no longer. Fuck."

Melina put down her cup and looked into it instead of at me. "Olga called me in the middle of the night last night. She sounded upset. She asked me if we were together." When she looked up at me, her eyes were inscrutable, and she had that faint Mona Lisa smile that she wore like a mask. She returned to staring at the coffee like there were secrets floating in the cup only she could see.

"She called me at four a.m. when I had just gotten home from a day in Acapulco, and I was too tired to answer. When I talked to her a little while ago, she said to be good friends with you but drop the sex."

Melina smiled. "If we weren't as close as we are, you'd never admit what you just told me. That's how I want it to stay, Cuz." Her eyes focused on her cup. "I want us to stay tight even if we don't meet up as we've done for all these years."

"Melina, she and I, we just have an arrangement. She has this thing about you. She heard how close we were to getting married. She considers you a threat. I could tell her to fuck off, but I do love her." It pained me to tell her that. I wanted to be honest, and I didn't want Melina hurt.

"I understand," Melina said.

"We're always going to be tight."

"Cuz, I'm only seven minutes away. Come see me. We don't have to fuck." She gave a little laugh. She sounded bright and cheerful, but when she looked away from the coffee, avoiding my direct glance, I could see unshed tears. We were being so very adult about this, but we were an emotional mess. If Melina could behave like this was normal, so could I.

"Like you said, you're only seven minutes away."

I kept hearing Olga's voice, *Amor, I'm yours.*

She got out of her chair while I was still sitting, and gave me a poke in the stomach, then put her arms around me, sighing into my chest. "I love you, Cuz."

Still sitting, I kissed her. This way she was a little taller. The angle was different, but nice. Her hair was cut in a pageboy, and fell forward in my direction, brushing my face. She smelled of flowers, a simpler perfume than the ones Olga wore. I had to restrain myself from pulling her on to my lap.

Letty did not rejoin us until I was walking Melina to the door.

"Need help moving?" Letty asked.

"I should say yes just for the experience, but I got it covered. A bunch of movers are coming, and I don't have any furniture to move. I'm leaving it all. Just taking clothes, and some of my knick-knacks."

Once again, I wondered what Olga was going to do with everything she had bought from Melina: the house, the contents, all the help. And me.

When Olga returned, Pixie went home to recuperate, and Letty retired to her own bedroom. Melina was forbidden, but Olga had given Letty a green light. As far as she was concerned, Letty never had to go back to her apartment.

"Amor, when Pixie went with me we had a blast. We laughed and had lots of fun. We found something funny in everything we did together, even when we went to the banks. When we'd come out, Pixie always had something to say about who we'd been with."

I handed Olga a glass of wine.

"Pixie is so damn funny, she should be a comedian. She could write a joke book. There were times I had to run to the bathroom to keep from peeing on myself."

I could not resist laughing at Olga laughing.

"I'm glad you two had fun."

"Pixie befriended the pilots, the entire staff in Rio, and even my serious guards who are not supposed to get personal at all. I had no idea what she is like when it was just the two of us alone together."

"Sounds like she was good company."

"She catered to me like you wouldn't believe. Until we got to Rio, she'd massage me till I went to sleep at night. Once we arrived in Rio, I made sure our masseuse took care of her every day."

Though it was the girls who initiated the occasional joint, I usually didn't turn it down. Camila smoked weed like a forest fire, but not Olga. Around Olga, I cooled it. I had been smoking more than before and did not want to get too hooked. She used that math head of hers and calculated every calorie that went into her mouth. Now that I knew her day to day life better, I knew how she used the treadmill with a vengeance to burn off her treats. Olga was trim, but she liked her wine.

We were both feeling the wine. Hammered Tricia would have said, and then I would have called her Tracie. Three sheets to the wind, Melina would have said. Letty would have said we were flying high. Pixie would have said we were shitfaced. Whatever you call it, I was feeling loose, and warm and hazy, and I guess my inner guard was out to lunch. Out popped the question, "Where does the cash come from?"

She took a sip of her wine. She was cool about it for someone who had to concentrate to put her glass down on the table without sloshing it. No reaction in her face. I heard the grandfather clocks, three of them throughout the house, in sync. I heard a song change from (one song) to (another song.)

"I've told you before, my father worked for Pepe's father in the drug business. Pepe's father was at the top of the power chain. Cocaine and heroin. Unlike all the others in his...field, Pepe's father sold his product worldwide. When buyers paid up, the other guys took the cash home. Not the senior Camacho. He stashed it near where it was paid, in houses he purchased, big and small, and sometimes a warehouse. It's a story that has never been made in to a movie."

I laughed with her.

"Stop telling me if it's something I shouldn't hear."

"Amor, we're going to be married. I can tell you. The cash is all over."

"I picture all this cash all over the world," I said.

"When I started doing what I do, Pepe took Camila and me to a small house in Barcelona. It had wrought iron on the windows and two doors. Packages of cash were stashed everywhere out of sight. The basement was filled floor to ceiling with tightly wrapped packages of cash."

"Do you go to these places to pick up money? I sure hope not."

"Doesn't work that way, Amor, not even close."

"Good. I would worry if you were always off to sketchy places." I thought about the effect of time. That money had been stashed for decades. "After a long time, doesn't the money get messed up?"

"The locations are looked after. If there is moisture, there are dehumidifiers, and so forth."

"How can you keep track?"

"Not me. Pepe. He has people everywhere. Every person that works for him answers to him with their family's well-being. Pepe believes it is the only way to keep them honest. He got that from his father. His father was not amazing at keeping track of how much money he had stashed. Pepe has his own methods, and I am part of that system. The cash in Los Angeles and New York is for you and Camila to buy assets with in the United States. That money stays in the states. Money from other countries is not brought to the states."

"Baby, maybe I don't need to know more."

Olga's eyes glinted with mischief. She flung her arms around me, pleading passionately, "Amor, please, let me tell you some more, please." She stopped begging, picked up her wine glass, sipped and set it down, "Where was I?" She flung her arms around me again, laughing, and asked, "Please, Amor, should I continue?"

I put my hands over my ears, "No, no more, enough already."

She picked up my glass with a wobbly hand and handed it over to me. "Okay, drink up and we go fuck, Si?"

"Si, Baby," I said, but my mind was on cash houses and cash warehouses. How many years? Would she lie to me? Like she knew what I was thinking, she did her best to distract me.

During a rest period in bed, I said, "Just one question."

"Amor, I just came so good. Can it wait? I know it's about the dark side," she giggled.

"Baby, just one question. Are you saying that Pepe is no longer doing what his father was doing?"

"You want a lie or the truth?"

"Truth, Baby."

"You really want to know, Amor?"

"I think so," I said, not sure anymore.

"P is not in the same business as his father. Can we get back to what we were doing?"

I didn't know if she was calling him 'Pe' or if the Spanish pronunciation of the letter P was her nickname for him. I didn't ask. My mouth went to hers. I put my hand under her head as I kissed her and thought about how she phrased her answer. I didn't believe her.

Later, she brought it up. "Amor, it should not matter to you where the money comes from, or what business P is in. Nothing you are doing is criminal and you are not going to get in trouble. I promise."

"Baby, I don't want you to get in trouble. Nothing lasts forever."

She sat up in bed and our eyes met. "Wrong. You and me, we're forever."

I nodded. I had no problem with making it forever with her. I loved this woman.

"I'm not going to get in trouble. LAI is a monster company and totally legitimate. When I carry cash, LAI can track it to a legitimate source of income. Please don't worry, Amor."

I kissed her. "I don't believe you," I said into her mouth.

She held the kiss and punched my chest. Maybe she was trying, maybe not. Her punches are like an angry butterfly. Not my words, but it's something Letty says to provoke Pixie.

"I'm hard again," I said. "Can you handle another round?"

She collapsed on her back and raised her arms to me.

"Si, Amor, I need to burn calories."

Chapter 10
July 1983
Bailing out Janice

Mario

Before Jo and Niley had gone to management, my former management company had sent out monthly reports and quarterly reports. Jo had carried on that tradition. The reports were typed out, pages of work. It was the last page that I read, the bottom line, total rents, total expenses, and what was left. All I really cared for was what was left.

Jo had computers in their office, and hired a guy named Harold Tinker to sit with her and Niley and watch them work. Harold was a programmer, and he developed a database that created complicated-looking reports. Manual typing reports was a thing of the past, though they still had to input rents received from each tenant and register every check written for expenses. Since Jo and Niley owned the management company, they kept their own accounting system separate and apart from my rentals. Their income was based on the gross rental they collected for me. They were delighted with the deal and I was also delighted because I loved them. The management company before them used the rental income as the basis for the fees too, but Jo and Niley charged me less than any other management company would.

The reports Jo and Niley brought over to me were fantastic, but after years of their just sending over the reports, I decided to change things. I supplemented the practice with monthly and quarterly Friday night dinners so the whole team could get back together again. Occasionally, TJ sat in, since he was part of the 'family' now. As little work as possible was conducted at these dinners, and a whole lot of chatter, and wine tasting. Before Olga went back to work, I included Olga in one of these.

We sat at the dining room table, all at one end so that it felt more intimate. The buffet was groaning from all the food choices. Miguel had decorated the foot of the table with what he called a 'tasting menu.' A hundred gaily colored paper napkins on a hundred crystal dishes with a crystal spoon of dessert perfectly centered in each one. The dessert cart was filled with untouched pies, cakes, cookies and fruit, waiting to be devoured. I had my eye on a peanut butter mousse.

"I should have never left the team," Niley said. "I feel like I'm missing out on all the fun."

"Mario talks so much about you and Jo that I get jealous," Olga said.

She'd lied, but I didn't contradict her. Niley and Jo were too skilled at reading people to fall for flattery, but I gave Olga brownie points for trying.

Everyone caught up on their recent doings. Letty bragged about her trip with Olga, pulling Olga into the conversation. Pixie interrupted to brag about her Olga trip.

"I told you," Niley said to Jo, "See? We're missing out."

"Nonsense," Olga said. "You have an open invitation to spend a week or longer on one of my trips."

That caused a big fuss, with Jo and Niley drawing Olga out to describe where and when these future trips would be. Miguel sent Sunny in to refill wineglasses, and I took that interruption to talk to Jo.

TJ had finished the addition to the personnel quarters. "As usual, he did a fabulous job. I love your husband."

"We love you, Boss. You are so damn generous. TJ didn't need a bonus for finishing the addition fast."

"Yes, he did," I said.

I recognized that TJ had made the time to deal with a small job like the addition. I knew how busy he was, because his company had signs up all over big jobs downtown. He was a member of the millionaire club by now. I wondered how much longer Jo would want to work. It was not like she needed the money anymore. Jo deserved to be kept in luxury.

"Give me a call the next weekend you spend at the beach house," I said. "He can finish showing me how to surf."

"Deal," Jo said. "We're looking at buying a beach house in the neighborhood, except we never take off enough time to make use of it."

"I highly recommend it," Pixie said.

My team had full use of the beach house, and they used it more than I ever had. But I was glad to provide the perks for my girls.

"Beach house?" Olga asked.

Everyone talked at once, filling her in. Everyone was upbeat, laughing and teasing. Olga participated as though she had been a part of our life for ages.

"Next to Rio, it's a closet," I said.

"It's not a closet," Pixie said. "It's right on the sand in Santa Monica, and it's gorgeous."

"It would fit in the dining room in the Rio house," I said.

"Amor, you took Camila and me there when we went to see the building TJ was working on for us in Westwood. I remember the house. It's cute. I forgot you had it. Let's go back there one day."

When Olga left the next day, Pixie and Letty joined me in the 'his' sitting room off the master bedroom. Letty lit candles after opening a bottle of Argentina red. When Betty came over, she used her portable table in the bedroom for my massage, so we were all together, watching television, drinking wine, and smoking a joint. I enjoyed the massage enough that Betty was deep into her story before I caught what she was talking about.

"...really going through hard times. I shouldn't say anything and that's why I never mentioned it before, but I know how close you were to Oscar. Janice—"

I interrupted her and made her repeat what she had said. "You mean money hard times?"

"I think she's going to lose the house."

I hadn't seen or talked to Oscar's pretty widow for a number of years. We'd talked quite a lot the year Oscar had died, but the calls had slowed and then stopped. For a while, I had been thinking of having her. I'd never acted on it. Betty said she lived alone in the big house. She must have come down a long way from when her husband was alive. His cigars had cost twenty dollars a pop, and his Louis XIII Brandy, a thousand dollars a bottle. Betty said she didn't keep a housekeeping staff any more, just a girl who came in once a week.

"How has she managed?"

"I have no idea. She only calls once in a while, and only when she has cash in hand to pay me. I tell her not to worry about paying me. When she had the bucks, her tips were overboard."

Oscar's death had left the firm in shambles, money-wise. I never asked Tom, the aviation attorney who took over the firm when Oscar died, if they had gotten out of the hole. The firm was still active, so they must have.

"I wonder what I can do to help her."

"I don't know, Boss. I asked her this morning if she wanted me to come over for a massage. I think she took my offer the wrong way, like an insult. I think I fucked up."

"Letty, get me Janice's phone number."

"You got it, Boss."

Letty jotted down the number Betty gave her and left to add the number to the computer phone book. The house now had six computers networked, four of them in the office where the girls worked. Like Jo and Niley, we hired Harold Tinker to program some simple programs, including a phone book. Harold gave the girls lessons on various ways to use the IBM computer. I watched, but my typing was crap. I never learned any of that. Wish I had.

"Please don't mention me," Betty pleaded.

"Of course not."

"Thanks, Boss."

Letty stuck a yellow Post-it with Janice's name and number on it on my end table by the phone. She grabbed my glass of wine from the console, stuck a straw in it, and held it in reach of my face. I know a straw in wine violates etiquette in a big way, but then so would wine drunk while face down on a massage table. I swallowed and enjoyed the buzz, wondering what I could do about Janice. I noticed the clock was approaching midnight, which brought up another subject. I missed Melina. How could I not miss her? She had class and beauty just oozing from her and she was my dear friend I had come to rely on. I consoled myself thinking that we would get back on track without me losing Olga. Wishful thinking.

"Are you still doing Melina at midnight every night?" I asked Betty.

"She's busy settling down. Her schedule is disrupted."

"Tell me about it. How disrupted?"

"When I least expect it, she calls me. Lately, it has been during the day to one of her markets, rarely the same one twice in a row. I take a table and do her in her office. That's working out okay."

"I have to run over one day and see her. She doesn't call me. Olga wants her to keep her distance."

"That girl is always going to love you," Betty said.

"Did she say that?"

"She doesn't have to say it. I know it."

"Want to spend the night with us?"

"You bet, Boss."

I fell into a massage daze, and maybe thirty minutes later, she whispered in my ear.

"Do you want a happy ending, or are you going to wait for the party?"

She knew I wasn't into that kind of happy ending. "I'll wait, Baby."

We all spent the night together. I woke with a full bed, worked out at five a.m. showered and returned to the welcome of that full bed. Betty stayed till lunchtime. The girls went down for a late breakfast, made their personal calls, had a swim, and went to work in the office smelling of sunshine and suntan lotion.

I sat at my desk, feeling about as satisfied as a man can feel. I felt good knowing that my companions had finished as magnificently as I had, or they were damn good actresses.

I met Tom in the building Oscar's offices were in, but now they were in fewer offices on a lower floor. Oscar had gotten into the trust account, intending to pay it back. His death had left the firm with big debts and an upside-down trust account. Luckily for Tom, the client cases they held were money in the bank, worth millions of dollars in huge attorney fees, as long as expenses did not overreach the profits. I had not talked to him in a couple of years, not since I'd been bringing cases to Gonor.

"I understand Janice is in a financial mess and may be losing her home. Is this true?"

"Janice and I are not talking," Tom said. "I send her a monthly check but it's never enough. She calls and screams at me. I can't do more than I'm doing right now." Tom looked at me uncomfortably. "After Oscar died, she called all of the time. You know we had nothing, and the hole we were in was so deep, I wondered how we'd ever dig out."

I looked out the window. The view now was nothing to compare with the one from the penthouse floor above us. "I can see you downsized."

He nodded. "We had to. Two penthouse floors in this expensive building was ludicrous. As for Janice Cooke, she is pushy and mouthy and half the time, she's drunk. She uses language I've never heard a woman use. The trust account is whole, but the cash flow is fucked up. She could care less. I can never finish a sentence with her." He got up from his chair and leaned over the desk. "Those first months after Oscar died, I took nothing. Now there are still weeks there is nothing left after overhead is paid. Janice, on the other hand, gets a check, always. Small sometimes. Late, sometimes. She deals directly with the accountant now."

"This is Oscar's widow," I reminded him.

"Believe me, I know. It is a miracle we made it this far." Tom is a good man and sounded troubled. "Many of those cases are settling for less than we'd expected. There is no guessing what or when a case will settle. I plan to stick it out. Janice is first in line to get hers, as soon as the firm is on a solid footing again. Until then, she should sell the house, take the equity to live on. That's her way out, Mario, but when I brought that up she went crazy on me. I don't know why that house is so important to her."

"Rumor is that she is broke."

"She's unreasonable and confrontational. She leaves the accountant in tears."

I didn't tell him I planned to call her.

We got up, shook hands, and talked about meeting soon for dinner. Oscar had brought him into the firm because I'd requested a lawyer who knew aviation, who would teach us about planes, and he surely did that. I counted him a friend. The past three years had been hard on him. His face was pale, like he'd stopped going outside, and his hair had more gray. I wondered if he was still flying in his spare time but did not ask. I hoped he was still not drinking. When he came to work for Oscar he had been a recovering alcoholic. He taught the team and me enough about aviation to at least bluff that we knew what we were doing.

I had been home for an hour when I had Letty call Janice. I walked down the hall, pacing. When I walked back in, Letty covered the mouthpiece.

"She's either stoned, high or drunk." She handed me the phone.

"It's been so long. How have you been?"

Janice didn't stutter or slur. She gave a mean laugh and did not bother responding in words.

"Really, how have you been?"

She finally stopped laughing. Her voice was so sharp, I'm surprised my ears weren't bleeding. Tom was right about that mouth. She reeled off two minutes of sailor-level profanity before she got to actually saying anything.

"Oscar made millions after millions and died broke. You know why? I'll tell you why. He paid you all of our money for fucking cases. Overpaid you like a fool. His hard-earned money. I remember seeing one check he gave you for over a million dollars. You abused him, and he was stupid and allowed it. You can go fuck off. Why the fuck are you calling here, anyway?"

"Janice let's meet. Let's talk." I should be pissed off over her rant. I should hang up. But I felt bad for her. After all, she'd lost her husband and bread-winner. She made me doubt myself. I wondered, not for the first time, if I had overcharged him.

"Fuck you, Mario Luna. Not one word from you for the three years that Oscar has been cold and in the ground. Now you are calling out of the blue. What the fuck for? If you know what's good for you, don't ever call me again!"

"What does that mean?"

"Whatever the fuck you want it to mean." She hung up.

I hung up the phone and stared at Letty in silence. She'd been screaming loud enough for Letty to hear the whole conversation. That was one angry woman. Neither of us said a word. I walked back to my office and shut the door. I took my time. I sat down, got comfortable. I opened a letter from my stack of unread mail and held it in front of my eyes. The words I read were not registering in my head. I heard my door slam open. Letty stepped inside, arms akimbo and furious. I don't think I have ever seen her look like this.

"Boss, she's drunk or something. If I ever come across her, I will bitch slap her until she passes out."

"Her mouth kicked my ass, no question. Drunk or not, she did the slapping. I shouldn't have waited to check on her."

Letty walked over and put a hand on my shoulder.

"Want a drink or a joint or something?"

"A coke works better."

Why me? I'm low key. I bother no one. Up until I heard her on the phone, I had no idea Janice Cooke was so angry. It made me wonder if I have more neglected friends who are nursing a belly full of rage? More people like Hugo Pliego, an ambulance chaser so jealous of my success in the PI business he sent a killer after me and tried at least three times to put an end to my life, before I tossed him out of my penthouse. At least I knew he was dead, so he wasn't behind the recent attempts on my life. More people had gunned for me, like the Venezuelan lawyers who had kidnapped me, and now were ashes on their coffee plantation. Janice's rage had come from left field. How long had she been living with a gut full of hatred of me? This was the first I'd heard of it.

During my massage that night, I told Betty what happened.

"Fuck, Boss, so you got it, too."

"Does she do drugs?"

"I think she just drinks."

I held off talking to Fino until our regular Wednesday lunch. Fino had been friends with Oscar, had loaned him money for aviation and had been paid five million when Oscar died, insurance related to Oscar's five-million-dollar credit line. Over steak and salad, I recounted the whole story.

Jack said, "I haven't talked to Janice Cooke since I settled the personal guarantees that Oscar and Janice had signed to secure other money not covered by life insurance. I could have taken her to the cleaners. I conveyed the deed I had on the house, leaving her only the original mortgage."

"That was nice of you."

"I don't know if it was nice. It was business. You know the story. I loaned Tom two million to help him hold the firm together. I knew he had to take care of Janice along the way."

"It really is not my business," I said. "But for a while, we talked, Janice and me. I've never seen her like this. I'd hate to see her lose her house."

"Let me talk to Tom and see how much of an injection he can give her. That's where the money should come from."

"Tom says things are tight." I pushed salad around my plate. No steak for me today. My stomach was in knots. "He promised he will try and give her a little more each month."

"Tom is smart. He's pulling the firm out of the hole. They get a lot of business from Carson. Small cases but as you know, those make the cash flow."

"Let me know how I can help."

"Don't beat yourself up. She won't lose the house."

"I feel bad. She said he died broke because of me."

Jack belted out his usual belly laugh. "He bit off more than he could chew. He borrowed from me long before you came along. He's the one who maxed out everything else, and then resorted to borrowing from the trust account. You're not to blame."

He didn't mention his own part in digging the hole, like the hefty interest rates Oscar had been paying on the five-million-dollar credit line and other loans. Two percent on the unpaid balance per month. That's one hundred thousand a month interest just on the one loan. A fuck of a lot of dough. Fino would never admit anything negative to his lending.

As for Tom, if he used up the two million credit line, he'd be paying Oscar forty thousand a month. Add that to his overhead, and it is no wonder he can't give Janice more money. Fuck. Fuck.

Letty was in the office while I called Olga in Madrid. Olga's response did not surprise me.

"Amor, send her a check if it makes you feel better, but it's not your fault Oscar didn't save any money for his wife. Stop stressing. Go to a night club with Letty. Have a little fun."

When I hung up the phone, Letty was standing in the doorway with an eyebrow quirked in my direction. "Well?" she asked.

"Olga said we should go to a club to vent."

I didn't feel like clubbing. I wasn't thinking about club girls. I was remembering Oscar's trophy wife. Oscar was significantly older than me, and so was his trophy wife. She had been a real beauty. I just don't remember her having such a dirty mouth. I kept thinking about her telling me to fuck off.

"Sure, we can go," Letty said, "but you have the diggiest disco right here in the house and I can climb the pole and anything else you want. I can call Pixie to come over and give you a show like you'd never find."

"I'll settle for the wine room."

We didn't drink much and did not smoke at all.

In bed, a different story unfolded.

Letty was the one in my bed, but the one in my head was Janice Cooke as I had last seen her more than three years ago. We had never actually had sex. In my mind, I made up for it. I stayed after the gathering at her house. Oscar's wake. I remember there had been lots of flowers. She was in some widow's wear, something black. Underneath she was in black lingerie, long legs, black stockings, at least in my fantasy. We tore each other's clothes off, and I made her climax on a bed of petals, so many times that there was no room in her for anything else. Afterward, I looked down at Letty, who was panting as if she'd finished a marathon.

"Boss, who were you thinking of?"

"What do you mean?"

"It was fantastic."

"Isn't it always fantastic?"

"Boss, you're the best, but this was inspired." She struggled to come up with another explanation and came up short. "I mean, it was intense. I know you were somewhere else. If I didn't know better, I'd be jealous." She laughed at herself. "I'm not jealous."

I spooned her and kissed the back of her neck. The room was now dark, our dreams waiting for us. I was glad of the dark.

"I confess, I was thinking of Janice."

"That angry woman on the phone? I can't imagine her being the same elegant lady as the one at Oscar's funeral."

"Same woman. Who knew she had such a mouth on her?"

"She did sound passionate on the phone," Letty said, her voice fading away. "Not surprised you fantasy-fucked her. Sounds like she needs it."

I nibbled the back of her neck. Letty moaned. I knew this was a soft spot for her. Letty never made demands of me. Letty wasn't shocked over my Janice fantasy. When she was asleep, I got up, and walked into my office. It was late, around two. I was sleepy. I needed to hear her voice. I called Melina.

"Hey, Cuz," she said, as soon as she heard me. "What's up?"

Not a word of complaint about not hearing from me, and no bitching about the time of night.

"I have a situation," I said. "Need your advice."

"Tell your Cuz," she said.

I told her about Oscar's pretty young widow.

She told me her analysis. "Oscar was her prince charming. His death left her in the lurch. I remember how she was at the funeral, so beautiful and so lost. It must have been hard on her to be by herself. Remember, we used to think she would be okay, that Oscar left her with a safe full of cash. But I bet she would not know how to make it last. She needs a Mario of her own. In the meantime, you should pay her a visit. See what develops."

"In your opinion, do you think Oscar would mind my visiting his pretty young wife?"

She laughed softly, sleep in her voice. "Pretty young wife my ass. She's still five years older than I am, if she is a day, and I'm still ten years older than you. Oscar would mind more if he knew his widow was ignored by all his friends and she had nowhere to live. Olga might object though. You should ask her permission."

"Baby, I don't need permission."

A laugh came through the phone. "Cuz, that's not how I see it with Olga."

In the morning, Betty called. Letty and I had just finished working out. My workout had been a little longer, and I had gone to a separate shower, mostly because Letty had a habit of ending her showers in ice cold water to better rinse out her shampoo. She stepped out to answer the phone. I could see her mouth move, but not hear her talking. She was dripping wet on the marble floor, beautifully naked, nipples tight, probably chilled from that last icy blast she gave herself.

She opened the glass door, so I could hear her.

"Betty wants to know if she can give your phone number to Janice."

I turned off the water. "You must be kidding. Let me talk to Betty."

I got out, adding to the puddles.

"She wants to apologize, but didn't have your number anymore," Betty said, asking for permission to share my number.

"Sure, give it to her."

After that fantasy sex I'd had with Janice last night, I felt a twinge of anticipation, not that she knew anything about it.

I was breakfasting with Pixie and Letty when Janice called.

"Five thirty, Jack Fino called to tell me I had fucked up royally with you and Tom. The sun wasn't even up. I'm sorry." How sorry she was, I couldn't tell. Maybe Fino had strong-armed her.

"I'm sorry I didn't check in on you before," I said. Too little of an apology, and too late. "Oscar was good to me. I owe you more than three years of silence."

I was suspicious. Her anger had been real. That does not vanish overnight.

Wednesday at our weekly lunch, Fino mentioned that he had talked to Janice. He said that Tom confirmed he would send her a bit more each month. I waited a week for the talk to die out at home. I mulled over Melina's advice. I was not keeping secrets but waited till I was alone.

I called Janice Cooke.

"How about lunch?"

"Took you long enough to ask."

"I wanted to invite you three years ago. I don't recall why I didn't. So, what about lunch today?"

"Raincheck on lunch. You know where I live. Come over."

I seriously considered driving the station wagon we use at the house for shopping but why the fuck should I hide my nice car? I took the Rolls and drove myself. The house looked as good as when it hosted Oscar's wake. I didn't expect to see the lawns and landscaping looking manicured. I wondered who was doing the landscaping if she was so broke.

She opened the door herself. Like Melina, she looked ten years younger than her age, probably her late forties. The way she dressed, and the way she wore her hair took years off, too, at least it had the last time I saw her. She answered the door in a bathrobe, though maybe that's the wrong word. When I think of bathrobes, I think terry cloth. Melina would have called it loungewear. It was a black silk number, long, but not hiding much. If you know how silk is, you know what I mean. I kissed both her cheeks, noticing she didn't reek of liquor. No Listerine to mask alcohol either. I followed her to an ornate room that reminded me of Oscar's office only there was no desk. She stood across from me by a leather sofa, and between us was a long granite table with a Lalique tiger and elephant on top. If they tipped during an earthquake, they'd be history.

I turned down the booze and opted for a coke.

"You are no fun, Mario."

She went over to the bar, pulled a chilled bottle from inside the mini refrigerator and reached for a glass hanging upside down from a floating shelf. Standing, I could see myself reflected in the mirrored wall behind her. I could also see the reflection of shelves inside the bar. Her supply of money might be short, but her bar was as well stocked as any night club I've ever seen.

"Ice?"

"No thanks."

She poured herself some Hennessy. "Are you sure I can't get you something stronger?"

"I'm good."

She left the tulip glass where it was hanging, opened the coke bottle and put it on the table in front of me. She walked the Hennessy bottle to the couch and put it down beside the Lalique tiger.

I tipped my cola in her direction and took a sip. "Perfect."

She sat on the couch across from me, the table between us. We talked of Oscar and how we met, how he had offered me five thousand dollars through Carson just to have lunch with him. I did not mention how I'd mistrusted Oscar initially, or how I'd been warned he had some rough characters on his payroll.

"Oscar was a great lawyer, and a better man, but a lousy business person," she said.

"I didn't take the five thousand."

"Carson said you did."

"I didn't realize you knew Carson. Carson and I grew up together. He's a charmer but if his lips are moving, he's lying."

"Doesn't matter to me if you took it or not."

She refilled her glass. I wondered who'd paid for the liquor if she was so broke.

"I'm fine."

She downed the glass, then poured another. I wondered how many shots it took to get her to the state she had been in the other night.

She sipped a little bit of the brandy.

"Carson comes over. Sometimes I ask him to come over." Red bloomed in her cheeks. The mention of Carson must have hit a nerve, or maybe the blush was alcohol hitting her system. "He brings a lot of business to Tom. I'm sure that's where a lot of the firm's money is going to, instead of to me, the founder's widow." She drank a little more. She crossed her legs to show them off. Nice legs. She was wearing fluffy little things, sandals that arched her feet, and bared her painted toenails. They were spindly enough that Pixie would call them 'fuck me' shoes, but they were fluffier than was Pixie's style. I could picture Betty in those shoes because she has that pink boa she likes to play with.

"Carson brings in the business that keeps the doors open," I said.

"At least Carson is good to me, if you know what I mean."

I sipped at my small, frosty bottle of coke. "I don't know about you and Carson, and you don't need to tell me. So, what are you planning to do? Go to work? Do you work now?"

"No. I never finished college," she said.

"Plenty of people work without college. I never went to college at all." I said. "I had enough of teachers in high school."

She nodded. "I was in college, quit because I met Oscar, married him and became a kept wife, with no profession."

"Maybe you'll get married again. Look at Carson. He's on his third or fourth wife," I said.

"Last time we saw each other, I got the vibe that you had the hots for me." She batted her eyes at me.

"Back at Oscar's funeral," I said. "Yeah, but it was too soon."

"All that talk on the phone," she said. "You didn't come over. I figured that was all wishful thinking."

No point in denying it. I nodded. "I had the hots for you. You were beautiful then and you are beautiful now."

She smiled and allowed the silky robe to slide a little off her shoulder.

I was ripe to take her up on whatever she was offering.

"I'll have that drink," I said. The only person I had ever drunk brandy with had been Oscar and it had always been at his office.

She smiled at me like one of those tigers at the zoo at feeding time, and brought a brandy glass from the bar, filling it for me and refreshing her glass. I could see that her mood had changed. She moved like a cat in heat, with her eyes fixed on me. She handed the snifter to me. Our fingers touched and crackled with electricity. Her hand snapped back, and she gave a startled laugh. Then her face got serious again. She shrugged, and the silk robe slipped off and puddled on the floor. She had nothing on underneath.

An hour later, I was in the master bedroom, naked on Oscar's bed with Oscar's widow pumping out an orgasm on top of me. I fucked her for two hours at least and didn't stop until she begged me to stop. I held off on my own release but hit every button she had.

"I knew it would be like this," she said. "I knew it the day I first saw you."

That would have been at Cedars Hospital when her husband was in a coma after being shot. Oscar had been coming to this very house I was in, planning to sleep in this bed I had just fucked his widow in. Maybe I should have felt guilty. Maybe I did feel a little guilty, but I was also feeling satisfied.

We were sitting up in bed. She held her snifter in her hand. Mine was on the nightstand.

"Now that we fucked," I said, "be straight with me. How much do you need to get out of the mess you are in, money wise?"

"Oh, you came to save me?"

"Janice, quit playing coy. Tell me the truth. A few minutes ago, I was fucking your ass."

"You are as vulgar as me." She snuggled up to me, the glass in one hand. "You are better in bed than Carson."

The last thing I wanted to hear about was Carson's love technique. His love life tended to piss me off, like when he'd fucked Melina. Long time ago, water under the bridge, but still....

"Janice, get serious."

She owed eighty-one thousand dollars[14] on her home. She could sell it for maybe five or six hundred thousand, but she didn't want to do that. She had a month or so to catch up on the payments or the house would be sold at foreclosure. She said that Tom was going to start sending her five thousand a month instead of twenty-five hundred. [15] She'd never known any kind of budget until Oscar died.

"Give me a payment stub for the mortgage. I will pay the house off. You will still have to pay the property taxes. Will you be able to manage for yourself with that paid off?"

She set her glass down on the nightstand next to my unfinished drink.

"Why would you do that?"

"Oscar was my friend. You will be okay. Tom will be able to make good, but he's not there yet."

"Tom? That is not going to happen. Over three years, and I see practically nothing."

"I have confidence in Tom. You don't realize how far the firm has come from where it was."

"That's what Jack Fino says, but I don't see it. All I see is twenty-five hundred, once in a while. It wasn't even that much until I went over there to kick Tom's ass."

She wasn't smiling. The corners of her lips had turned down, and there were angry crease marks in the center of her forehead. For the first time, I saw

---

[14] $81,000.00 in 1983 had the same buying power as $204,594.71 in 2018
[15] $2,500.00 in 1983 had the same buying power as $6,314.65 in 2018

what Melina had been telling me about Oscar's not so young widow. Or maybe the past couple years had been really hard on her.

"You are a tiger, Baby."

"I grew up with three brothers. I kicked their asses. If I have to fight for what I want, then I will."

"Let's get back to the house. I'll pay it off, no strings. If things go bad, sell the house and work with the equity."

She rested her face on my stomach and rubbed my abs.

"It would be enough if you can get me out of foreclosure. I should be able to make it if Tom comes through with the nickel a month."

I caressed her hair.

"No. I'm going to give you a clean start, free and clear. I want to do it, Janice. Don't give me a hard time."

"I'll give you a hard time, all right," she said.

A few seconds later her mouth and tongue worked me down there. The explosion I had held off for all of two hours erupted.

I didn't keep it a secret, but I did not discuss it with the team. I did not clear the room when I gave Tricia instructions to get the title information on Janice's house, or when I handed Tricia the cash to pay off the mortgage, foreclosure costs and property taxes if they were delinquent. Letty held her tongue.

Pixie said, "Good move, Boss. Oscar was good to you."

In three days, the house was paid off. That's when I called Janice to tell her I was sending Betty over with the receipt.

Betty had started out as a receptionist in Oscar's office, and Oscar and Janice had been her first real clients. Through the massage sessions over the years, Betty knew Janice better than all of us. I put a package in Betty's keeping and sent her to see Janice. Between you and me, I will admit the package held receipts, the house paperwork, plus a hundred thousand in cash.

It wasn't really an act of kindness. It was an act that made me feel a little better, like I had contributed a little less to the hole Oscar had been in. I had helped him go broke. I had contributed to the financial disaster he left behind. It was like Oscar had been a case junkie, and I had been his dealer. He didn't know how to say no to a new case. Maybe that's just how personal injury is. I remember Jack telling me PI is one way for a good lawyer to go to the poorhouse. It had happened that way for Oscar. It had happened that way to Jake before him. Oscar and Jake had both been PI lawyers, and both lived rich, and died broke. And both of them had been murdered.

I lay on a cushion on my marble spa table as Betty pounded me.

"Boss, she ripped open the envelope standing right in front of me. You should have seen her face."

"I should have sent you with a polaroid to take a picture," I said. "Hey there, it's Candid Camera."

Betty laughed, slapped on some more scented oil, and didn't miss a beat. "She pulled out ten bundles of bank-wrapped cash right in front of me—"

"Ten thousand in each bundle," I said.

"'He must be loaded,' she said. I stood there with a big grin on my face. Then I gave her a session on the house for a whole two hours. When I was done, she got pissed when I told her it was on the house. Insisted on giving me two hundred."

"Was she drinking?"

"She was but she wasn't drunk."

"Thanks, Betty."

"I'm going to avoid her until she calls me. I don't want her thinking I'm over there spying for you. I don't want her turning on me again. She's got a temper."

"She wasn't pissed today?" I chuckled.

"All that money from you, her house paid off. She was killing me with kindness since I was the messenger."

Three days went by and Janice did not call me to say thank you or fuck you.

She must have told him, because Fino knew I had paid off the house plus sent her cash.

"You're a good person," he said to me over lunch.

"Oscar was good to me. What I gave her was a token of what he paid me over the years. I have a feeling she doesn't think I gave her nearly enough."

"Why do you say that?"

I didn't tell Fino that she never called me back, not to thank me, not to cuss me out again.

"From now on, that bitch is on the suspect list," Letty said.

Chapter 11
August 1983
Star

Mario

Midweek I was in my office with the girls looking over some telex messages when Jason called from London. He asked about Pixie, then about the aviation business, and told me he was bored now that he was no longer working. I figured that he was probably lonely without Sami around. As soon as Pixie realized it was Jason on the phone, she snatched the phone from me, and walked around the conference room, twirling the phone cord like a teenager, and chattering with Jason for maybe an hour. I went back to my desk and Letty and Tricia moved to a work station where they each had a computer. After the call, Pixie looked wistful as she walked toward my desk.

"I'm sorry I swiped your call," she said.

"No problem. I know he calls you sometimes, ever since you went out with him. So, how is he?" I asked.

"Bored to death. Thinking of going back to work."

"That would be great. I sure miss his help."

"I think he's kidding around, Boss. He asked me three times to come see him and wanted to know when you give me vacation time. I told him you're a slave driver and there is no such thing as vacation." She giggled.

"You told him that?"

"He didn't believe me. He knows you better than that."

"Go visit him if you want. We have nothing going right now. Take a vacation."

"Fuck, Boss, being in this house is a vacation."

I went around my desk, put my arm around her and kissed her mouth. "I love you," I said. "Not kidding about the vacation. We're not working a case, and Lainie's in the dorm, right?"

"Go see him. He's a catch," Letty said.

"With his money and fact, he's not bad looking." She nodded. "So, he's a catch. So, why's he not just hooking up with someone local?"

"He likes the way you give him head," Letty said.

Pixie gave her the finger but no lip.

Olga had been back from Europe for forty-eight hours and was going to be in town for a few days till she took off for Mexico. We all met for lunch by the pool. Miguel had sandwiches and bowls of chilled fruit for us. When Olga heard about Pixie's London plans, she was less than thrilled.

"Pixie, I wanted you to go to Mexico City with me. I talked with Paulo Ruiz."

"Who's that?"

"Remember when we were in Spain I promised I would talk to a friend in the record business?"

Pixie grinned. "Sure, I remember." Pixie turned to me and—as if I hadn't just heard Olga—said, "Boss, when we were in Spain, Olga promised she would talk to a friend in the record business."

"Paulo Ruiz heads RIALTO, a big record company. I talked to him on the phone and told him that when he hears you sing, he'll be begging to sign you."

"Just like that?" Letty asked.

"Well, she has to go sing."

"Fuck me, really?" Pixie was beaming. "I could dig that."

"What about your trip to London?" I asked Pixie. "You accepted Jason's invitation."

"Go to Mexico City with me," Olga said, "Meet Paulo, dazzle him with your voice and guitar, then I'll drop you off in London."

"Olga, that would be awesome. I can buzz Jason and tell him what's popping. Shouldn't be a big deal."

"Why a record in Mexico?" Letty asked.

"I don't know anyone here in the US," Olga said. "Besides, the market here is flooded. If he likes her, it will open doors. There's a big market for the kind of Spanish singing she does so well. The money is not in how many records you sell. Touring is where the money is made."

"Fucking exciting. I think I'm going to come."

Olga laughed at Pixie's line.

"I already came and I'm just listening," Letty said.

"So cool," Tricia told Pixie. "This Paulo guy will love you and your singing."

I was quiet, but Tricia was right. Melina had always told me that someone would discover her, and she'd be gone. I'd just never thought that Olga would be the one behind the discovery. "I'd like a nice glass of Merlot," I said.

"Si," Olga agreed, all smiles.

Pixie went to Olga, put her arms around her, snuggled face to face, then lip to lip.

"Thank you for the opportunity. I love you, Olga."

Pixie was crying. Letty hugged Pixie. It was a sight, Olga sitting, Pixie behind her and Letty behind Pixie. I watched the emotional moment and felt like hugging them all.

Tricia exchanged a smile with me.

The sandwiches went mostly uneaten. Pixie made her inevitable dive into the pool, splashing everyone, then went up to change. Letty and Tricia joined her, all of them chattering about how Jo and Niley were going to react when they called them in Monterey Park.

When they were gone, Olga told me about the owner of RIALTO.

"He wanted Camila to buy the business several years back, but Pepe is afraid to do business in Mexico. I'm not afraid. I'm buying a house there." She gripped my hand and spoke passionately. "I want to do this for Pixie. When we were on the trip together, I saw she dreams about becoming a star. I can do it for her. She's beautiful, her voice is lovely, she has no accent in English or Spanish, plays any instrument by ear, a natural. She has the talent to actually do what most people can only dream of."

In bed that night, Olga brought it up again. "If I have to buy that record label to get her in, I will." Took me a few seconds to digest what she said. I rolled to face her and nibbled her right ear.

"Let's hope that's not necessary. If Pepe doesn't like Mexico, there's good reason to stay out of there."

"Like I said, if I have to buy RIALTO, I will."

I chuckled. "You don't plan to tell Paulo that?"

She fisted my shoulder. "Think I'm a dummy?"

"Not a chance, Baby."

Olga rolled on top, straddled and mounted me, moving rhythmically. She kissed a pattern down my chest and up again.

I kissed her.

"You are so clever. I know no one who manages as much money as you do."

"I move it. I don't manage it."

I cupped her breasts softly. "You lie. You do it all."

"That feels good, Amor, don't stop," she said, then moved my hands where she wanted them. "My nipples, Amor, Si, like that."

The next kiss was long and passionate, and we stopped talking shop. We stopped talking, period.

"We're going to be in Mexico City five days, max. I'll audition for the heavy dude that owns RIALTO then Olga will fly me to London. Fuck me, I can't stop coming." Pixie told Jason on the phone.

Jo and Niley came to the house to see Pixie off. There were lots of hugs and kisses and tears.

To keep peace in the family, Olga had eight security people instead of her usual six. "Lots of kidnappings in Mexico," she said, "Got to keep Pepe happy. He insists."

"He knows best," I said.

Olga

I don't think I will get caught in the crossfire when I'm with Mario. I don't think someone is coming after me to wipe me off the face of the Earth. I am not so important, but I humor Pepe in his paranoia. Not that I really have a choice.

Pixie is sitting next to me in the back of Mario's Rolls, Tricia driving and Gustavo, one of my guards in the driver's seat. Behind us a Lincoln with seven guards. You'd think I was Belisario Betancur Cuartas, president of Colombia. Pepe wants me safe because what would Pepe and Camila do without me? Lucky me, I'm indispensable. If having the guards keeps him happy, *Que Bueno.*

Mario

In the evening when we were alone in the wine room on the spa level, mellow, listening to music, Letty said, "I think Olga is looking to separate all of us. First it was Melina and now, she is looking for a career for Pixie."

I laughed. "Baby, no."

Letty pouted a little. "Just my opinion. When we were on the trip together she kept saying how nice it would be if I was with her all the time as an assistant. She didn't offer me a job or anything but what a clever way to get me away from you."

"She probably meant it. She came back raving about having you around. Nothing wrong with that." I kissed Letty up and down her neck. She has a neck like a ballet dancer. "Unless you take her up on it."

"I'm never leaving until you open the door and tell me to leave."

I kissed her again. "That's not going to happen."

"I hope she lets me stick around."

My arm was already around her. She leaned into me. "Baby, you can stick around for as long as you want. I just don't want to suck all the good years out of you."

She kissed me and drew back. "Boss, if this is sucking my best years, I don't want to change a thing."

"Letty, you are gorgeous. I don't want you to leave but there is a Prince out there waiting for you."

"Oh Boss, please. I'm not even sure I like boys or girls better. You're the only exception. You, I love."

I kissed her. She kissed me back and before long, we did what we did best.

"What if Pixie gets hooked up with Jason?"

"Like, how?"

"I think he really likes her."

"And you know this, how?"

"I can't say."

She got up to select songs on the juke box. I admired the filmy thing she was wearing, a bikini cover-up without the bikini underneath. Letty is very comfortable in her body. I remember when she was softer, more conventionally womanly, but now she worked hard at her fitness. Her body is toned, and lean, even boyish. To my way of thinking, Letty did just enough. Pixie was even more toned, but she pushed herself hard to be that way. Maybe I miss her curves a little, but martial arts were proving to be a fountain of youth. I had no right to complain when I had pushed them into taking up karate.

So, Letty couldn't tell me where she got her 'news.' There were things I couldn't say, too.

Pixie had confessed to me that she told Jason she'd grown up as a 'corner girl.' He'd been more than accepting and responded with a bout of sixty-nine. I knew Jason had a kinky side. I'd never told a soul that Jason had once sat in a chair to watch Sami and me have sex. I never questioned why Sami had asked me to do it, and now that she was dead, it was Jason's and my secret. Jason had helped get me to where I am in the aviation business. I owe him big time and have no right to judge him.

Pixie had been central to my life since we were teens. I have no right to feel like she was mine, but she was. She'd always been a free spirit though. Over the years, I had allowed myself no jealousy, not even over anything that threatened to split up my family. I would never stand in the way of Pixie's happiness or any opportunity she wanted to take advantage of. I liked Jason very much, but he was an eligible bachelor, a multi-millionaire, or maybe a billionaire. I knew how unique Pixie was, but Jason had access to any woman he wanted. His interest in her would pass. If that was going to break her heart, then I hoped it would never happen.

John Couger started singing *A Hand to Hold On To*. Letty danced her way out of the room. I smelled hot deliciousness in the air, butter, and salt, and realized that she must be in the arcade using the popcorn machine. Before the song was done, she was back with a basket of hot popcorn.

"Boss, you're the hand we all hold on to." She dropped down next to me, scattering a few kernels.

I grabbed a handful of popcorn.

"This calls for a movie. You pick." I handed her the TV Guide, but it sat open on her lap.

"Boss, we're tight, right? Tight enough I can be nosy?"

"If we were married, we couldn't be tighter than we are right now."

"We're so tight, I got to ask, are you going to pop the question to Olga?"

"I'm not so sure we need to be married to stay together."

"It's not like we got heart to heart, but she talks about you. I think she loves you."

"I love her, too."

"But you love all of us, no?"

"Si."

She picked up the TV Guide and pored over the day's listings.

I repressed a yawn. She noticed and suggested what she thought I wanted.

"Would you mind if we take the party upstairs to bed?"

"It's a deal," I said.

She tucked the guide under her arm, and I grabbed the popcorn.

"Forget the TV." I snatched the guide and tossed it to the end table. "We've got a couple of new video tapes. Studio sent them. They're out but haven't been released to the public yet. *Pirates of Penzance* and *High Road to China,*" I said.

She looked up at me with a happy smile and looped her arm around mine. Letty spent more time with me than anyone else. Non-demanding, lovable, entirely fantastic. When she smiles like that, she just radiates happiness and it feels like all is right with the world.

"Perfect, Boss."

"Call me, Mario, Baby."

That smile again.

Pixie was so excited I could barely get her to slow down enough to make sense. RIALTO's verdict was immediate.

"He wants me to spend a week here, and work in a studio with a bunch of selections and if I get in the groove, I get to sing an original. We can break for a few days in London, and Paulo will tell me when to come back and work on it some more."

I could hear Olga in the background. "Tell him how great you did. Don't be shy."

"Boss, I did good, I think."

Letty was on a second phone in my office. "Did you come, you slut?"

"I did. I came so many times."

"Oh, you so nasty."

I could hear Olga laughing. I let them talk.

Almost two weeks later, Olga called from Sami's London penthouse. Of course, Sami was gone, but I would always think of that place as her home. When her plane touched ground in London, Jason had been at the airport to meet them. "Jason took us to the penthouse that your friend owned. Pixie will be staying there."

"I love that penthouse," I said. "Say hi to Ginger and Crispin."

"Amor, they are so sweet. I wonder if I can buy this place."

I explained that the penthouse was part of a trust inherited by Sami's father on Sami's death.

"Jason was the executor of the estate. Ask him."

"I will. When I met him before when you were in the hospital, I did not notice how much he looks like you, except that you're younger and more fit. I wonder if you're going to get salt and pepper like that when you're in your fifties. I sat across from them in his Rolls and watched him hold her hand and stare at her. They whisper to each other. I think he has a crush on Pixie."

It was hard to picture Pixie whispering. She could barely lower her voice. I felt a surge of jealousy burn and swallowed it back.

"I want that flat. It's spotless," Olga said. "The location is fantastic. Place is going to waste. No one lives there."

Sami had wanted to give me the penthouse when she was dying. I wasn't going to mention it.

"You already have that problem with Melina's house."

"I needed to buy that house. Melina was too close for my comfort."

"It cost you six million to move her seven minutes away."

Olga laughed. "I'll let LAI have it, and still have the house at my disposal. For all practical purposes it's a rental property."

"Some rental," I joked, "you know how many apartments I can buy with six million?"

"Amor, stop it, it's done."

"Hurry back."

"I'm going to Madrid first, Amor."

The house would have been too quiet, but Tricia found a strip mall in foreclosure. Letty and I handled a couple of small local crashes that required no traveling. Letty took on a crop duster that had crashed into a full farmhouse after a bad repair job, and I handled a medical evacuation chopper crash caused by a rotor failure. Letty had been spending a lot of time at the hospital with the farm family, all of whom had an assortment of injuries. The pilot had not survived. My case, the helicopter, looked like it was going to be a big deal, but one of those that was going to take years to settle. It had wiped out a burn unit team, and four victims. It was one of those cases that hit me hard. It always does when children are involved—none aboard, but eight kids were left orphans. I was mentally and emotionally exhausted when I got home. Letty and I were in opposite parts of the house, each unwinding in our own way, when Pixie called.

Hearing her voice cheered me up.

"Olga stayed in London for two days. She tried to talk Jason into selling the penthouse, but you know how he feels about that. It's not for sale. I think she was a little irritated he said no. Anyway, when she left, Jason invited me to his house. I had been there before. It's big and damp, and drafty, and two hundred years old, and it is like being inside a fairy tale." Her voice fell to a whisper, "It's not as nice as your house. I do love the modern comforts back in Pasadena.

The bathrooms here are practically indoor outhouses and the water pressure is pathetic." Then her voice rose to a normal level, and she continued. "I have a first-class ticket for a flight tomorrow to Mexico City. I hope Paulo will let me do that single. It's so exciting. It's not like I'm a spring chicken. Fuck me, I'm getting old already, in performer years. And guess what? Jason is coming to Mexico with me! He wants to watch me sing."

"He hasn't heard you sing?"

"Not in a studio. Not with real music. I sing to him in English."

"Baby, you have that gift. I love the way you sing."

"When I get back, I'll sing to you while we do it." She giggled long and hard over that.

"Is that what you been doing in London with Jason?"

"Not going to sing and tell."

"You know, Jason is going to be fifty-one next month. He's all worked up about getting so old."

After she hung up, I got a little down, maybe because Pixie had said Jason was down. I thought about all the people I'd lost, some of whom whose murders had not been solved. Would I make it to fifty with all the attempts on my life? No matter what happened to me, I had to keep my team safe and from being in the wrong place at the wrong time. The world is a dangerous place: Jake shot and killed. Oscar shot and killed. Pixie and Letty followed home from Christmas shopping by loonies who shot up the house. My house torched. The biker going after me again and ending up dead before I had a chance to find out who had hired him. The police were clueless about who was behind all of this. The good thing, no one had made any attempts since the biker turned up dead.

"Boss, where are you?" I looked up to find Letty staring at me from across my desk. "Lolita Blanco agreed to meet with me day after tomorrow."

"So, you're going to Phoenix?"

She nodded. I knew she wanted to do this alone. She'd done everything on this case up on her own. Lolita had lost her husband in a helicopter crash a year ago. Letty found the crash in a telex, Tricia had gotten the contact information, then Letty made contact with the widow.

"Take the plane. If she decides to sign, fly her to Chicago. Take her directly to Gonor."

Three seconds later she was on my lap. I turned us both in my executive chair. My legs were too long to get any real momentum going without bumping the desk and credenza behind it. Letty was so excited over the case and the plane, she was shaking.

"Fuck, Boss. She'll be impressed."

Good news kept Letty from coming home the same day. Lolita agreed to retain Gonor. Letty and the hired plane crew were going to overnight at the Hilton in Phoenix then head to Gonor in Chicago the next morning.

Tricia had brought me paperwork on a strip mall in foreclosure and was waiting for me to hang up with Letty to show off the Polaroids she'd taken.

"Good work," I told her, thumbing through the images. The place was in good shape. It belonged to a widow who wanted to move back to Mexico City now that her American husband had been dead for six months and his estate was out of probate. "I think we'll be able to close on this one fast."

There was no sound in the office but me shuffling photos.

"It sure is quiet with everybody gone," Tricia said. She got up and turned on the radio, then walked over to where I was sitting at the conference table with the pictures laid out in front of me.

"Too quiet," I agreed. "Want to babysit me tonight?"

"What's in it for me, Boss? Driving somewhere? Bill knows the job isn't nine to five. I can drive you any time." She looked at me from under her long, fair lashes. "Or anything."

"Not driving. You won't be able to walk tomorrow."

"Deal, Boss."

"Wait, what about Bill?"

"He's in Colorado on a small assignment. Anyway, we're free agents."

"Should we have dinner in the wine room or in the bedroom?"

"Bedroom, if it's okay, Boss. Are you sure I won't be able to walk tomorrow?"

"Depends," I said, looking at her pretty eyes.

"On what, Boss?" She was playing me, teasing smiles.

"On whether I'm on top or you're on top."

"I'm on the bottom, Boss."

"In that case, you won't be able to walk."

"Cool," she said with a big smile, looking at her watch. "We have a few hours to go. I'll be back. Got work to do."

All the girls were fit, but Tricia was former military. She'd had an athletic physique long before I hired her as a private investigator in Las Vegas during a helicopter case. Sex with Tricia was different, more athletic. She more than held her own. Her torso was lean, her breasts perfect, and she had a tomboyish competitive attitude like she was out to top any move I made. Our bout lasted more than an hour, after which we lay back and stared at each other in the mirrored ceiling above my bed. Of all the girls, only she was a natural redhead, with skin so fair it almost glowed, even now when the one lamp was lit at its dimmest setting. Pixie had been a redhead before but then she's been every color of the rainbow, and sex with Pixie was not like war. I had not managed to knock that chip off Tricia's shoulder, but we were both feeling pretty satisfied. She'd done some Viking ancestor of hers proud.

"Now that the biker is dead, do you feel safe?"

"Luca Rossi was sent by someone. As long as that someone is out there, I can't feel safe."

"I'm glad you feel that way. Don't let your guard down."

"My real worry is you and the girls."

"I'm good, Boss. You already know how Pixie and Letty kick ass. We all kick ass."

"Kicking ass is good but you can't kick a bullet."

"You got to be kidding me, Boss. You know how good they are with their guns. They can outshoot me, and they are trained with so many guns, it's crazy."

"I still worry."

I reached over and turned off the light. Darkness intensified the sound of the clock ticking, distant noises in the house. The sliding door was open, letting in some night breezes and the scent of something flowering, and the sound of the waterfall flowing into the koi pond. Some noisy night birds were out there, owls maybe. We lay there in the dark, the night noises around us, as if our ears could get used to the night and hear better, the same way eyes did. I could not hear Tricia breathing, but my skin prickled with awareness of her. She was as awake as I was.

"Okay, so we fucked, we talked, and you turned off the lights. Is this when you and Letty sleep?"

I rolled on top of her. Her legs went around me.

"You must be kidding. I told you, you wouldn't be able to walk tomorrow."

"Oh yeah?" Her voice challenged me. "Let's see who won't be able to walk. Show me what you got, Boss."

Viking goddess round two.

In the morning, Pixie called from Mexico City.

"I'm jealous. You never sent me on your plane to sign a case. Letty said that the client and her teens were speechless."

"Your next case take the plane."

"I was joshing, Boss. I'm proud of Letty getting that case. It's a good one. The decedent was a big earner, lots of bucks."

"What's the scoop on the record?"

"Boss, I'm going to cut this fantastic original. I love the song."

"Congratulations!"

"The sad news is I must stick around here in Mexico for at least ten days. There's a huge list of stuff needs to be done, including a singing coach. Fuck, I don't need a coach but that's how it's done. Is it okay?"

"Yes, it's okay. Of course, it's okay. You don't need my permission, but you got my encouragement. What about Jason?"

"Jason is going back to London tomorrow. I don't think he likes Mexico City, but all he says is he has urgent business in London. What's so urgent? He's retired."

"Are you going to be okay? Where are you staying?"

"The Alameda Hotel on Reforma. Way cool hotel. I'm fine. Olga said no way I can have a gun in Mexico City. My guns are stashed in her plane. I have a guard during the day and one at night. Orders from Olga."

"That's good, Baby."

"Where is Olga now, do you know?"

"She's in Paris."

"It's a blast flying around with her."

"She likes you a lot, Baby."

"She has to for her to be doing so much for me."

"Baby, give yourself some credit. You are fantastic."

"Did I tell you that on the first audition, I was supposed to sing one song for Paulo?" She giggled. "No one stopped me. I sang six songs one after the other, and when I was done, he got up and started clapping and everyone in the studio did a standing ovation and then followed him over to me to congratulate me, and they didn't stop clapping until Paulo stopped and that was a long time and I was so emotional I couldn't hardly talk, and I looked over at Olga—"

"Wait," I said, "take a breath." But I don't think Pixie heard me.

"... and she had sunglasses on, and she told me it was so that no one would see her tears."

"I picture it all," I said.

"I'm so excited, Boss. I'm sad too. What if I get to go out on tour, what about my job with you?" Then Pixie was sobbing on the phone like her heart was breaking.

I was at the front door to welcome Letty home. I picked her up and she wrapped her legs around my waist.

"It's not like I've never signed a case before, but having your plane was a rush. I love the clients. We're tight now."

Good thing Tricia was available to drive any time anywhere.

"We have something to celebrate. Let's hit the Playboy Club," I said.

Tricia drove, Letty and I in the back seat on a hot date. Tricia insisted on wearing Letty's ridiculous chauffeur's hat.

"What time do you have to go home?" Letty teased Tricia.

Pixie would have turned around in her seat, even if she was driving. Without taking her eyes off the road, Tricia said, "I'm not a little girl and I'm not married to Bill."

"Cool," I said.

We all loved the hamburgers at the Playboy. I had two monster burgers with the works. Letty and I split two bottles of wine, and Tricia had virgin Bloody Mary's with more hot sauce than tomato juice. That girl must have a mouth lined in asbestos. I'm far from being a dancer, but after a few drinks, I danced with both of them at the same time. I could tell they both savored the moment, and it turned into a three-way kiss. There we were on the dance floor, not dancing anymore, embracing, rocking a little. My head spun. Two Playboy bunnies applauded us like we were the floor show. It was a fun night.

"Let's go across the street," I said, pointing at the Century Plaza Hotel.

"Boss, I'm totally okay to drive," Tricia said.

I looked at Letty. "Hotel or home?" I asked.

"Let's go home, Boss. That way Tricia doesn't upset Bill Rush by staying out all night."

"I don't answer to Bill," Tricia said. "And he's out of town."

We went home. It was late or early. A few hours yet, till dawn.

After all that fuss about not being accountable to Bill, as soon as we pulled up, Tricia left for her empty apartment.

Letty and I went to bed.

"Fun night, Boss, thank you."

I caught her laughing in the dark.

"What?"

Letty gave me a peck on the lips, still giggling. "You say you never dance, Boss, but you danced. It was fun."

I probably made a fool of myself dancing, but she was right.

"Get to sleep kiddo," I pretended to be stern, "and quit laughing so hard. You'll ruin my self-image as a playboy and the world's greatest lover."

"Sounds like a challenge," she said, still laughing. I pulled her on top and had to spend another hour or so making sure she had the last word.

Telex news might or might not name those who died in crashes. Even when names appear, contact information remains a mystery. Tricia had become a wiz at finding our persons of interest and kept a collection of private investigator's tools up her sleeve. She knew the ins and outs of legal records and court documents. Among other things, she used my collection of current California telephone books, and blue books. Blue books come out annually, listing names and phone numbers by street. She had developed contacts in many government offices in California and Arizona. She had a growing list of out-of-state investigators who were local to the crash, where ever it might be.

Roger Higgins, a pilot who owned a twin-engine Cessna, was injured, and had been hospitalized for a month. Doctors said he had months of recovery before he could walk again. Originally, Pixie had researched everything about the case, including an article that indicated the plane had recently been serviced by a big franchise operation. In an interview, the pilot/owner said he planned to sue the slobs. He was certainly justified, as both engines had failed. Before she flew off to Mexico, Pixie had showed me pictures of the debris. I thought it was a miracle that he had survived with only two broken legs and serious back injuries. As in the case Letty had just signed, Pixie had followed a lead from a print-out and got Tricia to hire an investigator in Florida to get the pilot's contact information. Pixie was in Mexico City, but gave Letty the go-ahead to make the cold call to the pilot, Higgins. I heard enough of Letty's call to know she had a good chance of getting an appointment with Higgins. I was grinning ear to ear throughout the conversation between Letty and Higgins—a very long phone call. Letty handled herself intelligently. I had no reason to take the phone. Letty was handling it. As soon as she hung up, she bounced into my office and hung on my arm like an excited child.

"Boss, we can see him tomorrow at his home. I am kicking ass!"

"You sure are."

"I told him you're a consultant for the Gonor Firm, and that we would fly over to see him."

"Fantastic, Baby."

"I think it's a good case," she said seriously. "The maintenance included engine work."

"After Miami, we hit Mexico City. Pixie is all over me to fly over there to see her."

"She's on my ass, too. I miss her so much."

We flew that night to Miami and checked in at the Tides Hotel in South Beach. I was getting hooked on owning my plane.

We met with Higgins at his home. Letty was part of the conversation, but I stepped in. Several hours after we got there, he signed a retainer. Higgins could not keep his eyes off Letty, especially when his wife stepped out of the room.

As a pilot, he was curious how we got there, and I told him. As the owner of the Cessna, he was very interested in meeting an owner of a Learjet.

"If I wasn't in this wheelchair, I'd ask you to show me the plane."

"He's not going anywhere just yet," his wife spoke up, nice, but firm.

We went back to the hotel. It was stifling for August. We hit the beach, but it's a different heat from Los Angeles. In hours, we were airborne to Mexico City. It was a carefree week, with a lot of tall fruit drinks with umbrellas, suntan lotion, and bikinis. Letty bought me speedos in the hotel shop. She whistled when I tried them on in the room, but I was happy in my trunks. Olga was in Marseilles but promised to fly in as soon as she was free. She got free really quick, appearing the next afternoon at the hotel where we were staying.

"Amor, I got a suite for you and me. I want you all to myself."

I was game. "I'm hot for you, Baby."

Olga, Letty, and I went to check out RIALTO's studio, and sat in on Pixie's practice sessions. She was geared up with headphones and a microphone, and tons of background mixing equipment. It was like a dream for me to see her there with a group of musicians and getting all the attention of a star. I was so proud of her, my chest felt twice its size. Now and then, Letty sniffed quietly, filled with emotion. I was sorry that Jo and Niley were not with us to witness Pixie ruling the day.

Twenty-two hours after Olga arrived, she got a call from Pepe. She had a brief conversation with him in our suite.

"I have to fly to Bogota to meet up with him and Camila," she announced.

"Is everything okay?"

"Pepe is rarely in Colombia anymore. When he is, he likes us to be there."

"For reals?"

She laughed a little. "I'll see you back in Pasadena."

As abruptly as she arrived, Olga was off in her plane.

Pixie, Letty and I went to a plush Mexican restaurant, La Hacienda, a great big house packed with people. Letty looked with dismay at the long line of patrons who waited to be seated.

"I'm starving," Letty said, sighing and getting in line.

Pixie walked past the line to a host at a podium. Pixie spoke to him quietly. Letty and I hung back a bit but followed.

"What was that about?"

"We have reservations. I called the owner, Fernando. He's a friend of Olga's and the last time we were here, he gave me his card."

"Tell me about my case," Pixie asked.

"Your case. Bitch, I made it happen. What do you mean your case?"

"Boss, tell her I found the case, and its mine."

"Letty, Pixie found the case so it's hers."

Letty made a funny face at Pixie.

"Thanks for handling it for me."

"Thank Boss. He closed it."

To live pianos and violins, we ate *Crema de verduras al carbon, Pesca del dla con infusion de manzanilla, Filete de res en salsa bourguignon al chipotle,* and three *Sorbetes.*[16] The beef was mine. The fish was Letty's. Pixie said she was eating vegetarian until the production was over.

A month later, Pixie's single was released in Mexico City. Her picture was plastered everywhere. At least ten Mexican radio stations were playing her single on a regular rotation. The music crossed the border to the states. On this side of the border, one of RIALTO's partners pushed Pixie and her single. PIXIE *canta Amor de mi vida.* [17]

I was having an early lunch with Olga when it came on the radio. I had Miguel play it on the intercom, so it tuned up throughout the house.

"She sounds as professional as anybody else on the radio," Olga said.

---

[16] Cream of grilled vegetables, Fish of the day infused with chamomile, Filet of beef Bourguignon with chipotle, and three sorbets.

[17] PIXIE sings Love of my Life.

"Olga, thank you for doing this for her. I love you all the more."

"My pleasure, Amor. I knew she had it in her from the very first time I heard her. With that face and body, she's going to make it big, Amor. I'm just as excited as she is, maybe more."

"Is RIALTO fronting all this money to push the record? Payola must be expensive."

"I'm helping out. I bought a piece of her production."

"You should have told me. I can help."

"Small change, Amor. It's my pleasure."

"What did you buy in for?"

"Half."

"Does Pixie know?"

Olga shrugged. "She does, but she doesn't care how the system works. I don't even think she cares about the money she may make."

"She's not in it for the money. She loves to sing."

"She loves the attention, Amor."

"I hope not too much attention."

When we were fifteen or sixteen or so, Pixie had shown me everything there was to know about sex. She had never hidden her life as a corner girl, not from anyone. When Pixie first started signing cases with Jo and me, we were at a client's house and the husband of the injured lady we were interviewing followed us out to the car and asked Pixie if she was still doing the street stuff in her off time. She laughed it off. Pixie always said it was a small world out there. I hoped her history would not come back to bite her.

When her song was done, I had Miguel turn off the radio. Letty, Tricia, and Pixie tore down the stairs, chattering in excitement from hearing Pixie's song announced by the local disk jockey.

"If this works for me," Pixie said, "I'll get Lainie to cut a record. It's genius how RIALTO works it, releasing in Mexico and spreading the word there, then crossing the border."

"The genius is you." I hugged her. "I've never seen you so happy."

She sniffed. "Boss, that's not true. Being with you is happiness for me. Being with the team. It's all happiness for me."

I thought again about that client who had remembered her. He had not been a jerk, but I did have concerns about her history coming out. I was worried she was in for a fall. We talked about it. She was not concerned, though.

"Everyone who matters already knows," she said. "And anyone who might be offended, well, I don't give a shit about them." She tried to make me forget about it, but it preyed on my mind.

RIALTO bought time in an LA sound studio, and Pixie recorded Amor De Mi Vida in English, LOVE OF MY LIFE. DJs argued on the air and took audience surveys on what version was the best. Even the English audiences seemed to like the Spanish version best.

I had always taken Pixie's singing for granted. She always sang old ballads. She'd never had any formal training, but now she had confidence. She'd picked up a lot from the recent studio work with professional musicians. On her own, she wrote the lyrics of her second single with RIALTO, about an abandoned little girl named Baby, raised by a kindly lady in a house of good time girls, and how Baby grew, and learned to sing for her supper, and how instead of a mother and a father, it was the love of the audiences who kept her warm. When she sang that song, there was not a dry eye in LA county. Her public embraced her. Rolling Stones interviewed her, and she admitted she'd written that song *Baby* about herself. "My best friend was worried that people would not accept me because of my history. I'm the one who grew up in a house of good time girls. So that's why I had to put it in a song." The public was in love with her, and she could do no wrong.

Her first single sold a million records in two months. She hired a driver to get her around, a guy named Raul. Raul lived at Melina's old house in the servant's quarters. He just kicked back until Pixie was in town.

Her second single got to the top of the charts within a month of its release. Pixie technically moved in with me, but as a test, went on tour for one month as the act introducing Los Lobos. She called me at home every night, and on the weekends, Lainie flew across country to be with her, until the month was over. Pixie's fan base was growing so quickly that I had Fino find me an entertainment attorney. Larry Miles knew the record business, had connections galore and made his clients, including Pixie, pay him well.

"Olga is really my manager," Pixie told Larry Miles. "What I need you to do is to make sure the contract I end up signing with the U.S. company is in my best interest."

"I have a lot of connections," Miles told us.

"Call them," Olga said. "Let's get our girl on the road."

Olga was sitting pretty, making half of what the record company in Mexico City was making on Pixie, whatever that was. She deserved it. She never told me how much the payola was running but I was sure it was a bundle of cash. Pixie was a total unknown and suddenly the most listened-to radio stations on both sides of the border were playing her songs. It took *mucha lana*[18] to get that done.

It felt like months since I'd seen Melina though she was only seven minutes from my house. We talked on the phone maybe once a week.

"It's not like I'm married to Olga."

"No, but, she's living with you."

"Her residence is the world-at-large," I said.

"Don't you have enough pussy at your house?"

"I miss your pussy, period."

"I miss you, but I don't want Olga to put a hit on me. I don't trust her or her family."

"You said we would always be friends, and Olga said we should be good friends."

"I did say that. I said it before Olga paid me six million for my house.

---

[18] Lots of money

For all I know, she's having me watched."

"Is this Melina I'm talking to?"

"It's me."

"I think you're just saying that because you want a way out. Maybe you got a boyfriend."

"No boyfriend, but when the opportunity strikes, sometimes I take advantage of it."

"Baby." I was all wound up to convince her. I still felt a rush of jealousy at the thought of her with someone else.

"Cuz, stop it."

It looked like I had to keep my word to Olga and not mess with Melina. That's okay. I loved Olga, a different kind of love, like for keeps. But I loved Melina for keeps too. And Letty. And Pixie. I don't know why I should have to choose when I love them all, all for keeps, all differently.

Betty came over for my massage at eight. We set up in the spa. I had worked out before sunrise, and after dinner, swam laps for an hour. Her massages seemed to have the best effect after workouts, so my body was ready for her. I was relaxed on the table and she was a half-hour deep into our session when she spoke up.

"Boss, I am doing Janice's massages again."

"How is she? I haven't seen her since I paid off her mortgage, though she called me to come over a couple of times. Last time she called, I was in Mexico. What's new with her?"

"She put her house up for sale."

"What?" I tried sitting up, but Betty pushed me back into place. I can listen as well lying down as sitting up. "Go on."

"I did her this morning. She had a hangover and called me to come over fast. I saw a sign out front."

"Did she say anything about it?"

"Not a thing."

"She has no mortgage or unpaid taxes. That should give her some cash to squander."

"You don't mind that you paid it off, and now she's selling?"

"Why should I have an opinion one way or another? It's her life."

The television was on, and I was halfway listening to some old movie with Jimmy Stewart. She worked on me for another hour before she said anything else.

"I can go upstairs with you tonight."

I looked over at the clock. Near the end of the movie. I knew it had to be close to midnight.

"What about Melina?"

"I did her at a market today."

"Better for you, I bet. Years of that midnight massage appointment had to be a bitch."

"No way. Work is work, and I love her. And she's generous, like you."

"She pays as much as I do? Looks like I have to start paying you more."

"I didn't mean anything by it, Boss. With you, I also have Pixie, sometimes Olga, Tricia, Jo and Niley. With her, it's only her."

Betty was smart. Before she'd gone into becoming a massage therapist, she'd been a paralegal at Oscar's office. I remember that she'd made the change because she wasn't into desk jobs. But she had gotten plenty of experience at Oscar's office. It occurred to me she could put some of that experience to good use.

"With Pixie's new career change, I've been thinking my team is just Letty. Tricia still provides support when I need her, but she prefers information and property hunting. How in love are you with your clients?"

Her hands on my body didn't stop but I had her attention.

"Are you saying I could be on the team?"

"You worked in a law firm for a long time. You know the business."

"That would be so exciting. What would it pay?"

"We could work that out. When you get up to speed in a few months, you'd be making the same percentage as the rest of the team. Think about it and I'll think it out, too."

"I'm interested, Boss. I know a girl named Tangles. She went to school with me. I could introduce her to my regulars."

"What kind of name is Tangles?"

"Nickname for her hair. Boss, she's gorgeous."

"Bring her by. Let me meet her. Maybe you can do four hands on me?"

"Sure, I'll do that. I don't let roosters in my pen, but if you'll hire me on the team, I'm game."

"I understand."

Her point of view reminded me of my feelings about Carson. I brought him to the ambulance chasing business back when we were kids in school, when I had been getting cases for a lawyer named Jake. Carson crossed the line and started faking crashes. I booted him from Jake's team. On that day, he became my competitor. Since those days, we made up, and I ended up giving my contacts to the firm Tom Jones now runs. Using Betty's terms, his rooster wasn't in my cage because I moved on to aviation.

Tangles

I have three regular customers that I do massages for. By regular I mean, they call me when they want a massage. I don't have them on a set schedule. I have business cards and an ad, but money is tight. When I get no calls, there's no gas money, no food money. It sucks. I thought about working in a massage joint, but I hear they get busted a lot for sex. I don't want to get busted. I know a girl who was caught giving a guy a blow job and got sent to jail. They sweep everyone off to jail. In school they told us the same thing, so I watch my p's and q's. I'm a newcomer. I'm not exactly first choice at getting hired.

My first regular wants to put his hands on my legs while I massage him but nothing else. He helped me get my second regular who wants a happy ending, but he gives me an extra twenty for it. I got to eat, got to keep gas in my car. The third regular was a referral from my first. He just likes a firm massage.

Betty and I aren't real close or anything, but I was happy to hear from her when she called me. I met Betty in massage school. She already was working but came back to learn some new techniques. She's a good-looking chick and told me right from the start that my looks and my figure would put me over the top. It's been six months since I got that license and I ain't going nowhere.

"I barely have enough for gas."

"Sorry things are that bad. Come meet me at the laundromat. I'll cover gas money, no sweat."

The laundry was practically empty. I spotted her across from a row of avocado appliances. She was reading a section of newspaper, and wearing bright pink leotards and sneakers, hard to miss. I also spotted a quarter on the floor. I popped it into a vending machine to get a pack of gum. You know that saying beggars can't be choosers? It was the only thing that cost a quarter. I ain't complaining. When I walked up, I saw she was watching three full washing machines do their thing.

"What's up?"

I sat on the bench beside her and she talked up seven regulars that she does every week, all in one house. She going on about some guy named Mario and his girls like Charlies Angels. I unwrapped the gum and tried to follow what she was talking about.

"I'm going to be working full time for Mario. I do his workers most times. I thought you might want to take over my clients."

My stomach was growling. I folded up two sticks of gum and shoved them in my mouth. When I heard her offer, instead of the gum, I bit the inside of my mouth. I wasn't sure I heard right.

"What was that again?"

"Say what again?" Betty asked.

"Say that again, you want me to do what, take over your clients?"

"Exactly."

"You mean it?" I grabbed her hands. "Really? You're not kidding?"

"Why would I kid? Look, you have good hands. I remember how we used to practice on each other. You're good. I think you'd fit in pretty good with this group. I didn't think of asking anyone else."

I was just sitting there, not believing my luck.

"If you don't want to, I don't know who else to call. Are you interested?"

I realized she was waiting for me and blurted it out. "Hell yes."

She laughed at my excitement.

"Betty, pinch me, pinch me." She didn't pinch.

"So, you're in?"

"I'm in no matter what."

"They will love you, I know it."

"What do I give you? What's this gonna cost me?"

"Not a thing."

"What gives?"

"Look, they are my friends. I want them in good hands. Don't make me look bad, do your best, look good, be sure you smell good and are totally clean. Sometimes you have to drop your clothes."

I knew it was too good to be true. "I will have to fuck these clients? Are they creeps, or what?"

"It's not like that. They're swingers, open sex, your choice. There's Boss and his team. There's Melina. She's at midnight, six nights a week, a hundred for a two-hour massage."

I said, "That's three times the going rate. For that, I'll fuck them all."

Betty shook her head. "My other clients, I will walk you through them until they get used to you and you never know, you may lose a client but so what. The income just from Boss can be more than from the rest."

"I'll fuck them all," I told Betty, filled with excitement.

"You got one guy, Boss. The rest are girls, beautiful, like you and they swing with each other."

Betty looked at me with a questionable look.

"I will tongue them to death," I said.

Betty broke out in a big smile and hugged me.

"I'll do you, too," I told Betty.

"Do me righteous with my clients, Tangles. That's all you have to give me."

I went home with three hundred dollars that Betty said was a loan. My first stop was Big Boys. I ordered a double cheeseburger, a side of fries, a side of onion rings and a coke.

Chapter 12
February 1984
Baby Sings

Mario

Pixie's first album was released in February simultaneously in Mexico and the states.

The plan was for her to promote the album on tour. Mexico and parts of South America. Later, a second tour in the US.

Olga told Pixie, "Your popularity in Latin America is pouring across the border. It will be more so when you finish the first tour. Radio reps will be on the disc jockeys over here doing what they do to keep you on the air while you are down south."

Olga was referring to payola, money to the DJs to induce them to play Pixie's songs and to promo the rising star. I listened, offered nothing. This was Pixie's and Olga's business.

Pixie's singles were kicking ass. The new album included the songs from the singles including the autobiographical one she'd written herself, plus eleven originals that were written for her.

Pixie told everyone who would listen that she was just taking a break away from the team. She believed her singing career was a fluke, that she was just a flash in the pan, and that a singer whose career began in her mid-thirties did not have much of a remaining shelf life.

"You will rise and stay up there," Olga told her.

"Baby, I agree. Look what you have done in months," I said.

"Olga and Paulo did it. All I did was sing a couple songs. Thank you, I love you," she told Olga, hugging her.

Pixie's tour went for several months, and when she got back, she stayed in Melina's old house, as Olga's guest. She bought a blue Rolls Royce, a red Porsche 911, and replaced Lainie's Camaro with the practically new Porsche that she already had. Her driver Raul was thrilled to be driving the new car.

Tangles took over Betty's massage business, and that included taking care of Melina.

Melina had no complaints. "I do miss Betty, but I don't get a daily massage anymore. When I do, it's at a market during the day. Tangles is not a bad masseuse. I asked her if you fucked her, and she just smiled."

"Baby, why ask her something like that?"

"What does Olga say about this new find?"

"There's nothing to say. I put Betty on my team, just good business. She speaks Spanish. Tricia doesn't. Tangles is just our masseuse. She's done Olga a couple times."

"I can tell you she's not shy," Melina said. "She does a full body massage."

"If you're uncomfortable with it, I'm sure you told her."

"Cuz, I'm not uncomfortable," she said, laughing.

"I'm glad to hear," I said.

"Cuz, you are still young and so is Olga. If you guys are serious about each other, and plan on kids, better do it before the window closes."

"What window?"

"You want to be sixty when your kids are nearing twenty?"

"I told that to Olga once, and she shined it on."

"Do the math, Cuz. Better hurry."

I still wanted Melina. "What if I come over to the market and we can do it like we used to, on your conference table."

"I don't have a conference table in Montebello."

"If you did, would you say come over?"

Her answer was silence. I tried again. "Baby, if I take a walk, I can pick up any girl and bring her home and fuck her. Why are you turning me down?"

"Don't be so sure of yourself. When's the last time you picked up a chick that you brought home and fucked?"

It had been ages. I was always home or away on a case or working to acquire assets for LAI. The rest of my time I spent with what remained of my team.

"I should marry Letty," I said.

"Marry the one you love," she said.

But I wanted them all. Loved them all. Once again, I wondered why I needed to get married at all?

Olga, Letty and Tangles were rolling around my huge bed. Tangles was easy, single, carefree, knew how to please both sexes, and had no limits. When I found out she was rooming with two other girls in Hollywood, I had Jo hook her up with an apartment of mine in Monterey Park.

"My entire team and now Tangles is okay with having it with either sex. What are the odds of that?" I asked Letty. "Did Tangles want to fit in and figured she had to have group sex?"

"Boss, Betty picked her because she thought she'd be a good fit." Letty laughed at her own choice of words. "Look, Tricia doesn't like group anything. When she's with us, she lays back and loves getting her pussy taken care of, but she gives nothing back."

"Who else is like that?"

"Nobody else on your team. Boss, you know I had been with more women than guys when I started working here, I told you that. It's a bonus for you, right? Don't you like it?"

"Like what?"

A burst of laughter. "You are putting me on, Boss."

I wasn't putting her on. I liked the sex as it was, but I had to wonder when I saw Tangles was equally as comfortable with me as she was with Letty.

Tangles moved to Monterey Park, minutes from my house. Jo set her rent at half the going rate, $125 for a two-bedroom apartment.

"Mario, your massages are free from now on. You took me out of the dumps. I've seen some hunger filled days. Thank you."

I kissed the top of her head. "Tangles, you have a business. You will be paid for all the massages you do here. You owe me nothing. Betty is the person who helped you, not me."

Pixie started her U.S. tour and called me daily from wherever she was.

"I have a nine-day break. I told Jason I'd fly to London."

"Enjoy my favorite city," I said.

"I don't know that I love London that much, but I do love the penthouse and that's where I'll be staying again."

I said, "You have fans chasing you around now, and no security here in the states like you do elsewhere, so please be careful."

"Boss, I still pack my guns. You know I can kick-ass. Don't worry about me."

When I talked to Olga that night, I brought up my concerns. "Why don't you have at least one person traveling with Pixie on this tour?"

"Amor, she doesn't want a guard. I told her she should at least have Raul travel with her. He just sits around doing nothing when she's gone."

Raul was a chauffeur, not a guard, but I went with the flow. I'd learned the hard way with Bruno Bruno that a real guard needed certain training. "What did she say?"

"She doesn't want company. Do you know something I don't?"

"No, she's fine. Going to London."

"I sent a plane for her," Olga said.

"That's good, but expensive."

"She's worth it, Amor. I want her to feel as special as she is. A private plane gives you that lift. I still get it when I board my plane."

"I wish you were here," I said.

"I wish I was there, too. Where is Letty?"

"In the kitchen baking a cake."

Olga laughed. "She loves the kitchen, huh? I guess it runs in her family."

"She makes a mean pastry."

"Night, Amor, I adore you."

"Love you, Olga."

Tangles' beat up jalopy often left her stranded. I had Letty take her to a VW dealer to pick up a new car. I had Jo work out a payment schedule that the management company would collect monthly. In my opinion, Tangles overreacted.

"I love that little bug! I'll pay you back, Mario. I love you, and I'm going to devour you."

Letty said, "Hey bitch, not so fast. You just got here."

"I'll do you, too," Tangles said.

Letty stared her down like she was thinking it over, making Tangles sweat before she agreed.

"Deal. And Boss gets to watch."

Tangles gave a little orgasmic moan, that I'm sure wasn't put on. After years of Pixie, I could almost hear Pixie's voice say she'd just come. My eyes met Letty's and I had the feeling we'd just had the same thought.

After some big acquisitions for them, I was making a whole lot of money from LAI. A thousand apartment units needed tens of thousands of dollars in renovation, but they were a block from the beach in a solid gold location. Jo's husband got the job of fixing it all up. I knew TJ would do a superb job. I figured LAI's management company would be funneling rental income to their bank accounts even though more than half of the units were vacant. I could have been wrong, but in the long run, it didn't matter. The deal I made was a good one and I was paid well for bringing in the asset.

Camila dropped in, coming from Colombia on her way to Madrid. She advised me to invest in gold.

Olga had another angle on the same issue. "I prefer sitting on the gold instead of having some third party sitting on it."

"You've always been the untrusting type," Camila said.

"You mean like gold bars?"

"Any kind of gold. Gold coins are easier to store. Depositories will have bars."

"I'll look in to it." I said.

Olga took my hand and kissed it. "We'll look in to it."

It was the first time that I could remember that Camila and I had met for more than several hours and never hit the bed. Things were changing. Maybe the change was Olga.

"I love seeing you too so happy," Camila said. "Why don't you get married already?"

Olga looked at me. "We're good. We don't even talk about it anymore."

"Do it. Married couples can't testify against each other." Camila said.

I could not tell if she was kidding. If it was meant as a joke, it wasn't very funny.

"True, Sis," Olga said. "But don't say that because he'll start with the paranoia."

I felt like the cartoon guy from that magazine with the folding back page. What, me worry? "What paranoia? Me, paranoid?"

"He's a worrier. Just doesn't admit it," Olga said.

"I only worry about you, not me. I'm not doing anything wrong or illegal."

"Are you saying I'm doing something wrong or illegal?" Olga punched me.

I didn't give it much thought right away, but that conversation lingered in my thoughts. Olga never mentioned marriage after Camila left. Then Olga left town. I put off my plans till she returned.

I presented her with the ring Sami had given me on her deathbed.

I didn't go down on my knee or knees, nothing like that. "Olga, will you marry me?" I went straight to the bottom line.

"I'll marry you, my love. I adore you." Her reply was fast. I barely got the words out before I had an answer.

She knew who Sami was and had met Jason, had spent two days in Sami's penthouse in London, but she didn't know about the huge diamond ring. I told her how much the ring meant to me, that Sami had worn it always, and just before she died, she gave it to me. As I told her, my throat locked up, and I wiped my eyes with my sleeve. The memory of Sami filled my head and heart. Olga listened silently to my explanation, her eyes on the ring as I slid it on her finger. She looked from the ring to my eyes, and I felt like I was drowning in her. We polished off a bottle of Merlot and tore up the sheets in my bedroom.

Afterward, Olga was making marriage conditions.

"Amor, you can fuck anyone you want, but promise me you will never have sex with Melina."

I wasn't sure I liked a woman telling me what I could do, not even Olga. Still, I wasn't going to spoil the moment. Besides, the Melina thing was nothing new. She had made it clear before. I wondered at the fixation she had on her.

"Baby, I haven't touched Melina. I can count the times I've seen her and those were chance meetings. She's never been back here since she moved."

I felt henpecked. "What about you?"

"I will fuck anyone I absolutely have to if it is business, and I have to do it to open or close a deal. I'll never fuck anyone just to fuck, like you do."

"Ouch, Baby. That hurt."

She bit my lip. "Supposed to hurt."

I wasn't happy about this concept of her fucking to accomplish something, but if I expected freedom, I had to give freedom back. Balling was no big deal to me, and not to Olga either, unless it was Melina and me.

So now we were engaged, but we didn't set a date.

"When I get back, we have two decisions. Do we want a big wedding and when?"

"Don't take the ring off, Baby. Even if you have to fuck someone to accomplish something."

"You make it sound so tawdry." She looked at the ring. "It is the most beautiful ring I have ever seen."

"You would know, Baby." Letty had told me about the ring she wore when she visited some of the bankers during their trip together. Letty said it looked as big or bigger than this one. I thought of the diamond she paid six point five million for in New York that I never got to see.

I had never had the diamond appraised. Melina had figured it was worth a million or a little less. Without a real analysis it was very difficult to know.

"Do you have it insured?"

"No. It's been in my safe since Sami died."

"Don't insure it. I'll take care of it later. I don't plan to take it off, ever."

The last hand who had worn it all the time was Sami. She never took it off.

"Do you mind that it came from Sami?"

Olga blinked, candlelight in her eyes.

"Not at all. Sami was very special to you. Jason told me how she wanted to give you the penthouse."

"Jason told you that?"

"He did. He likes you very much."

"I like him very much, too."

"You know he's gay?"

If I had been swallowing my wine I would have choked. "No way, Baby." She was wrong.

"Amor, I've been around. He may be closet gay but he's gay. He seems fond of Pixie."

I thought of Jason sitting next to the bed while I had sex with Sami, pouring wine for us so we could drink when we came up for air. I thought about all the times he stayed overnight when I was visiting Sami. Every time he was there, I was kicked out of the master bedroom. I knew behind the door; he and Sami had torn up the sheets. But, it's not like I saw them in action.

"He's not gay," I said.

I could tell she disagreed. She didn't like to lose an argument. I could see she had not let it go.

"I think he's adorable no matter what."

If he was gay, why would he be wooing Pixie? It didn't matter if he was gay or not. He was a friend of mine, and a friend he would stay. I just didn't want Pixie getting hurt.

Chapter 13
Early May 1984
Butterflies are Free

Mario

A Boeing 737 crashed minutes after taking off from Madrid headed to the Virgin Islands. My team—Letty and Betty—made preparations to head for Madrid. Tricia was performing her magic at home. Her miserable Spanish made her more valuable in Pasadena than in a Spanish-speaking country. Juan and Valita were already in Madrid making preparations for our arrival. We were doing this one without Pixie, who was on tour, Pixie who was on the phone with me.

"I feel so bad that I'm not going with you. Fuck me, Boss, I'm sorry."

"Baby, we've had a number of crashes since you've been away. I miss having you with us, but don't stress. Stay in touch. Believe it or not, Betty is pinch-hitting for you."

"Changes," Pixie sighed over the phone. "Oh, Boss, I miss you."

Letty was on a roll. She had seen Jo in charge, then Pixie. Now it was her turn. On her own, she scheduled the flight crew to man my plane, made hotel arrangements for Juan, then contacted him to act again as my advance man. I heard her tell him to make sure we were in a good hotel close to where the airline had stashed the families of the crash decedents. I considered it a bonus that Juan's wife, Valita, was going to be working with us in Madrid. Valita was fluent in Spanish which made her being there a plus. I still had strong feelings for that luscious woman who had helped me stay alive when I'd been kidnapped in Venezuela. Valita had been a housekeeper for the kidnappers but was more of a slave than an employee since whenever she'd managed to leave, they fetched her back. You would not believe what we went through to get her away from that coffee plantation.

"We need to find another person for the team."

"Eventually."

"Tangles would be great, Boss."

"Tangles took over Betty's massage business. Let's not involve her for now."

Tangles took over Betty's client list, so Melina was not her only client. However, it was the thought of Melina's massages getting disrupted that led me to tell Letty to wait.

Our rooms at the Madrid Hilton had two singles attached to my suite. Letty and Betty showed the bellboys where to put their luggage in the singles as I walked in stockinged feet from the open bedroom to the sitting room while talking to Olga on the phone. The cord was pretty long since there was only the one phone that I was carrying. Practically the entire outer wall of the suite was glass, providing a stunning view of the expressway and sunny Madrid traffic. At least the weather was great. The interior of the hotel was an atrium, each floor providing a view of the ground floor dining room, a study in black and white.

"Wall to wall cars out there," I said to Olga on the phone.

"Wall to wall planes here," Olga said. "I'm going to be flying to Cape Town."

"That's not a usual stop, is it?" I asked. I didn't hear her response. The girls came in, making a lot of noise, distracting me.

"I'm starving. Let's go eat somewhere Spanish," Betty said, returning to my sitting room.

I put my hand over the phone and explained, "In Madrid, except for the hotel, eateries are open only during certain hours. In other words, if you want a sandwich—" I looked at my watch. "—at three in the afternoon, forget it. Nothing is open."

Her face fell.

"There's a restaurant downstairs," Letty said, solving the problem. "Let's unpack and check it out. Then we can come back up and get some practice in. Boss, you want anything?"

"Nothing heavy. Dinner will be around seven. Surprise me," I said, returning my attention to Olga. "We got here way too soon. Sometimes it doesn't matter, but here in Madrid it matters."

This was far from my first case in Spain. At least the executive suite package gave us access to the executive lounge and a decent workout area and spa.

"Go home and come back later," Olga said.

"Baby, we're already here. The accommodations are acceptable. Betty hasn't been with us out of the country before. She's followed Letty on a local case or two, but that's really a completely different experience. She really had no experience in what we will be doing. I feel sure we won't be wasting the time. Doesn't change that it is still too early to do anything with the families."

"Why are you complaining you got there early, then?"

By the time the girls got back, Olga was off the phone. I heard them approach all the way from the elevator and down the hall, chattering in Spanish. Before they knocked, I opened the door. Letty had her hands full with three plates of sandwiches. Betty carried a package of cokes, a loaded ice bucket and some small bags of chips. Everything went on the small table in the sitting room. Betty and I sat down. Letty walked into the sink area and brought back four paper-wrapped glasses. Club sandwiches, canned cokes, more cokes in the full ice bucket in the center of the table. Just like home.

Betty took a big bite and sighed. "I am still looking forward to real Spanish food."

"We can get Paella somewhere at mealtime," I said. "Get recommendations from the concierge. We're going to be here a while."

"No time for chatter, Betty," Letty said seriously. She turned to me. "Mr. Luna, the Gonor Firm has aviation specialists who have the financial means and expertise to give your case the representation it deserves. They will direct this expertise against all the responsible parties. Who knows so early who is responsible, so the investigation is going to take a long time. There may be multiple responsible parties that contributed to the events that caused the crash."

She looked at Betty. "Go ahead. Repeat what I said."

I ate my sandwich while I watched Letty grill the hell out of Betty. I could hardly chew. I was so busy grinning ear to ear listening to her. I could think back to other days, other teachers and students. Letty had learned her stuff. I was proud of how she handled herself and waited patiently for everything to become second nature for Betty. There was absolutely no reason for me to intervene. About the only suggestion I had would have been to run through this again with Valita. But I didn't interrupt. Besides, this was not Valita's first rodeo with us.

After a day or two, Letty hung out with Betty and Valita at the hotel where the families were being housed by the airline operator. Normally, I would be there with them, but I was not raring to go the way I usually am. I couldn't identify what was holding me back. Maybe it was easier acquiring assets for LAI, not having to engage wounded families facing death. Maybe the business was getting to me. It was a business, and it was professional, but there is no way to stay emotionally aloof.

The next evening, it was still too early to get really involved. I had paid two visits to the airline's hotel looking in on the girls, and checking in with Juan, but I spent most of the day at the Hilton, working out and in the spa. The masseuse did not measure up to Betty or Tangles. At seven, we went to a local restaurant for Paella, which thrilled Betty to no end, then the girls retired early.

I was surprised by a knock, but I figured maybe Letty had called room service. I pulled on the jeans I had been wearing earlier, and opened the door to a tall, fashionably dressed woman carrying a small garment bag. Olga.

"You sounded bored and terrible last night. I had to see you."

I carried her straight to the bedroom.

"Make love to me all night, Amor. No sleeping. I need you."

I wanted to thank her for coming but put it into action rather than words. While we were rolling around, making a mess of the room, I saw Letty come in, but when she saw who was with me, she quietly slipped out. We stopped for a breather. I poured us each a glass of wine and asked the question that had been on my mind.

"I thought you were going to...where was it..." I wracked my brain and came up with her destination. "...Cape Town?"

"I am. I just came here first."

"Why Cape Town? There's a lot of chaos going on there."

"Business, Amor. I have a lead. I expect to come away from there with diamonds."

Even before she was my fiancée, I loved her. When I love someone, I worry. She was flying into a lion's den and acting like it was nothing. I could not sit here and twiddle my thumbs. "I am coming with you."

"Are you serious?"

"Damn straight. What clothes do I need?"

"Keep it simple," she said.

In the morning, I had a meeting planned with Juan, Valita, Letty and Betty. It was as good a time and place as any to let the team know what was going on. But first I let Letty take the lead and give a report of where we stood, retainer-wise.

"We've made four casual contacts, Boss," she said proudly. "Betty and I made three, and Valita is working on a family of ten."

They were sitting shoulder to shoulder on the couch, and one by one, each talked about the potential clients. Juan talked about a couple of local lawyers he'd sussed out for me. Ricardo Munoz was a lawyer I'd worked with before, a slim man with a bit of a temper. Jason had suggested him to me a couple of years ago. We'd gotten ninety-five retainers on a 707 crash in 1978, retainers we brought to Oscar and Tom. If there was a possibility Munoz didn't want to work with Gonor, I felt it was smart to have an alternative.

"Hold off on making appointments with them," I told Juan. "I'm going on a hop with Olga. I will be back at the end of the week. I'll call you when I get where we're going. Letty don't kill anyone while I'm gone but do protect Betty and yourself."

"Boss, no worries."

On her show-off kick with a little leap, her toes touched the top of the bedroom door.

"Letty, you are so hot when you do that," Olga said.

"Get some cases," I said.

Carrying Olga's valise, and a duffle of mine, I headed for the door, Olga leading the way. I felt a bit of the old excitement as we headed down the hall to the elevator, two of her guards behind us. In the lobby, four plain clothes gorillas greeted Olga, then me. We took two cars to the airport.

"Fuck, you don't need me." I was kidding. I wanted to go.

She took my hand.

"I do need you, mi Amor."

Olga was in another of the LAI planes, one I hadn't seen before. This one was configured with twelve seats behind the cockpit, then a curtained-off sitting area with wide seats and a sofa. Behind that was a good-size cabin with a bed big enough for me to sleep on, and I'm six feet five.

"We have a crew of four captains, two stewardesses, and my seven *moscas*."

I laughed at what she called her body guards. Flies.

"Who is the extra guy?"

"Julio is a diamond expert."

"Right, you said we were going to Cape Town to buy diamonds."

"Si, Amor, seeing is believing. We have twenty million. Let's see what that buys."

"Fuck me," I heard myself say.

"You sound like Pixie." She laughed. "Don't get all paranoid on me. Everything is going to be okay."

"That's a lot of diamonds you're trying to buy."

"If we're lucky, Amor, Si."

We strapped in seats for the takeoff, then when the captain gave the go-ahead, went into the bedroom.

"Fuck me, Amor."

Just to hear her say it was a tremendous turn on for me. At thirty thousand feet or whatever altitude, we were flying high. Every little while we hit some turbulence, but that just improved the ride. Olga's screams did not bring the guards storming the cabin. After a while, we went to the sitting area for food. Doesn't matter how much money you have. There's no way to serve great cuisine on a long flight. It might start off as cuisine, but hours later when it's warmed and served, well, you might as well settle for ham and cheese on toast.

"At least we got exceptional wine," Olga said.

"This kind of reminds me of the Bahamas trip with you and Camila, remember?"

Olga was looking out the window at the patterns in the clouds below us. She was drinking more of the wine she liked, but put down the glass, and turned away from the window to face me, with her arms crossed around her chest, and a half-smile on her face.

"Sure, I remember. The yacht, the house. It's all there. We should go back sometime."

"The yacht was more like a ship than a boat."

"A hundred twenty feet. It's a ship," she said, her eyes meeting me squarely. "Ask me. I know you want to."

"Ask what?"

"Ask me what happened about the two bums who pulled guns on Camila."

"I wasn't even thinking about that."

"Mentiroso," she said in Spanish.

"Hey, I'm not a liar." I tried laughing it off. She left her seat and got on my lap and made me laugh for real. Started tickling.

"Mentiroso."

"Okay," I gave in. "So, what happened?"

"Not a thing. The family sold us the property just as they had committed to do."

The *pendejos* who had tried to strong arm Camila had ended up dead. I did not know if the shooter had been Camila, Olga or one of the guards. I did know we'd left the Bahamas faster than I'd have thought was possible, and I had always wondered what had happened to the bodies. Probably taken out to the open sea and dropped off as shark bait.

Cape Town was always in the news, bombings, piracy, and mayhem reported daily. It was not a safe place to be, and I was not happy about Olga being sent here. We landed at a private airport. I was half-expecting to see the chaos first-hand before we ever left the airport, but from the windows, nothing alarming appeared.

"I thought Camila made the deals and you paid?"

"Yes. Why you ask?"

"So, where is Camila?"

"She has come and gone already. No need for her to wait around."

The customs officer had been dispatched from the main airport. From the time we'd notified him, he took thirty minutes to reach us, a medium-sized man in an ill-fitting uniform with food stains around the chest and stretched out of shape by his generous paunch.

In sing-song English, he introduced himself as Siyabonga Naiboo, and asked if we had anything to declare. With a flash of white teeth, he glanced left and right as if pretending to search, but not bothering to open compartments.

"We have nothing to declare, Mr. Naiboo," Olga said.

I thought of the twenty million dollars somewhere on this plane. The customs agent flashed his bright smile again. It took less than five minutes for our passports to be stamped, and we were allowed to deplane.

"Did you know that customs guy?"

"I've never been here," Olga replied.

I held Olga's hand as we walked down the stairs, guards behind us. At the foot of the stairs, we were greeted by a young man who bowed sharply to Olga.

"Welcome to South Africa, Miss Olga. My name is Mismo. Miss Camila described you exactly."

She matched his toothy smile. I did not know if it was because they did not know each other, or because of local customs, but there was no hand shake.

"I show you the way, Miss Olga."

Olga didn't know this Mismo either, but he'd obviously known who to look for. She was the only woman in our group. Two of the guards moved beside Mismo. We followed to the only other plane on the tarmac, a Boeing 747.

"Please follow me up the stairs."

I would have held back. "What is this?"

"It's okay, Amor," Olga said reassuringly, and took my hand like I was a child.

I walked into the plane with some misgiving, not knowing who waited inside nor if we were going to be flying somewhere else. I wondered why the guy we were meeting had chartered such a big plane, but Mismo said it belonged to our host. It turned out to be an executive jet. I'd been aboard plenty of executive jets, but never one so huge. We were greeted by a hostess in a white uniform whose name I did not catch, something foreign, a mouthful. She led us past textured gray wall panels to a small elevator. She pushed a few buttons, and we went up a level. It was cramped for me because I am not a small man. I had the feeling I was in a conference hall rather than a plane.

The hostess hooked her finger around a small knob and slid open a curved door revealing a room not unlike the executive lounge at the Madrid Airport Hilton, except that all the seats had seat belts. Supersized squarish furniture, modular, upholstered in white leather. Four distinct social areas. There was also a bar that looked fully stocked behind glass doors, with all the glass bottles and glasses locked in place. If my own feet had not carried me inside a plane, I would have believed I was in someone's home. Agog is not a word I use, but I was agog. I had no idea a plane could be like this. I was itching to see the rest of it.

I was so wrapped up in the plane, I failed to notice our host until he took both of Olga's hands between his own, and kissed them, then he kissed her on each cheek, and ended with a friendly hug. He was somewhere in his fifties, dressed comfortably in jeans and a cotton shirt. He had a huge diamond on one finger, but no other adornment.

"Thank you for coming to meet me."

I was still in the dark about who he might be.

"I am grateful that you came to meet me," Olga said.

Mismo disappeared. Olga waved away her guards. Julio, the gem expert, stayed.

The mystery man extended his hand to me.

"Mario Luna," I said. "Pleased to meet you."

Julio also got a handshake and greeting. It was all very polite, but not so polite that we would be getting a tour. I caught glimpses of armed guards, men similar to Pepe's.

"The pleasure is mine. Call me Johnny."

Olga and I sat on a mink draped loveseat wide enough to sport three sets of seat belts, across from an identical seat where Johnny sat, with a table between us. Then Julio left us.

I found it difficult to stop staring at our surroundings. Johnny did not feel like a threat, but threats rarely announce themselves. I did not let down my guard. I experienced a wave of tension. I hated to be adding this new possible threat, this Johnny on top of all my other stresses. I tried listening to Johnny and Olga but my mind kept wandering off. I mentally added this unknown man to my list of potential threats—whoever was behind the attempts on my life. She was not talking with me, but I felt the heat of Olga's thigh pressed to mine. It was only a matter of time until we would be married, and who knows what. A baby to worry about. I had to put an end to this mysterious enemy. I did nothing, but suddenly wished I could tuck Olga underneath my arm and get out of Africa, get out of the whole iffy business, just to protect her.

For a long while, Johnny and Olga talked about diamonds, then our host led us down another hall to a conference room where Julio had his magnifier in his eye, as he inspected diamonds. I saw he had a camera he was using to photograph each diamond, and a legal pad where he was taking notes. A security camera was trained on him and the surface of the small table where he was working. The large conference table was set up for formal dining. The three of us sat, and the hostess served us a meal. It wasn't reheated food either. Johnny and I had porterhouse steaks that must have been grilled in the plane's kitchen. Olga had a sizzling rack of lamb. After about five hours, we were escorted by two sets of guards—Olga's and Johnny's—back to Olga's plane. I missed the part where the actual diamonds were exchanged for the cash, but maybe that was part of Julio's responsibility. I wouldn't be surprised if diamonds need chain-of-custody protocols just like legal documents. That twenty million in cash weighs over four hundred pounds so it wasn't going to be in a briefcase. I never saw the exchange.

"The meal was fantastic, and his wine was to die for," Olga said. "He gave us a couple of bottles, so we can keep the same buzz going on the way home."

As she stashed the wine in an ottoman, I didn't ask what customs would say about the wine, and I didn't disagree about the meal; but I've had good steak all over the world. The plane is to die for. I had no idea the 747 was ever outfitted into executive jets. It is a massive plane, prohibitively expensive. I did know the plane because of my interest in aircraft, but there had never been a 747 crash, so I didn't know as much about it as I did many others.

Siyabonga Naiboo paid us a return call.

"Leaving so soon?" he asked, then again asked if we had anything to declare. I noticed that he had changed his shirt, and that Olga did not say word one about the wine. Again, Mr. Naiboo glanced left and right as if pretending to search. His teeth flashed, as if his inspection was a joke. In a way, I guess it was. I wondered if Johnny or Olga or both of them had paid him off, or if he was just naturally easy-going and conveniently near-sighted.

"We have nothing to declare, Mr. Naiboo," Olga said. "As you can see, we were not here long."

He gave her a formal little bow and left. He was barely out of the plane, when we were taxiing, ready for takeoff.

"Don't we still have the cash? We done here?"

I hate to state the obvious, but we were already off the ground. So much for my African adventure. I was not displeased though. I was glad we were out of there without having any personal encounter with the famed South African chaos. "So, what happened to the lions and tigers and elephants?" Relief made me a bit too jolly.

"If you want, we can always come back to South Africa for a safari."

"Baby, why Cape Town? Why not some other airport in another part of the world?"

Olga took a gulp of wine and licked her lips. "This was Johnny's call. I'm not sure where he met with Camila, but he has some control in Cape Town."

It was my opening. I could have asked about the diamonds. Always, so many unanswered questions. Where were the diamonds right now? Where was the twenty million? How did it get to Johnny? I didn't ask. Olga can be fantastically evasive when it comes to certain answers. My future wife remained a mystery to me.

"So back to Madrid?"

"All done with diamonds," she said. "My next stop is Geneva if you want to join me."

If my abrupt leaving of Madrid could be called a plan, I had planned for a week in Cape Town. I had the time to spare.

"Sure. I can buy clothes. If we leave the airport."

Olga was so elusive. I had seen Olga's expert inspecting the gems and assumed they were aboard. I wondered if Geneva was where we were delivering the cash.

We did leave the airport, but I did not shop much. Geneva had the air of a small town, lots of old streets, flags, and they rolled up the streets at night and on Sunday. No night life to speak of but there were lakes, and mountains and cathedrals. Olga went off on her own for an hour twice during our stay, once at the beginning, and once just before we left. Once, when we were eating lunch at a café, a fiftyish year-old guy approached our table. It was coolish, in the sixties, and he was well-dressed, but looked hot in a wool suit. Graying fair hair, well-fed, not particularly healthy looking. Pasty complexion of someone who rarely left the office. He carried a pocket handkerchief, and frequently dabbed his sweaty face with it. I pegged him right away as either a lawyer or a banker. Olga introduced him as Alexander Müller, a banker who worked across the street.

Two brief meetings were the extent of her business. We took in a couple of tours but got to know our honeymoon suite very well. I never took my new pajamas out of the package I bought them in. All too soon, we were back aboard Olga's plane on the ground in Spain and saying goodbye.

"I have to go to Bogota, but first I'm going to stop in Pasadena."

I had thought the Camacho's were getting out of Colombia, so I had to ask. "How is the move from Colombia going? You said you only had your house, Camila's house and the two main residences."

"That's correct, Amor. The new government is turning out friendlier than Pepe expected. We are not rushing, but we are still getting out. My trip to Bogota will be quite short, a few days."

"What house are you going to be staying in Pasadena?"

"Casa Luna, of course. My fiancé's home."

I kissed her. "Our home, Baby."

"Si, Amor, Si."

Olga dropped me off in Madrid, and took off to New York, then Pasadena, even though I would not be there.

Seven days from when I left Madrid, I was back with my team. I wanted the low-down, first thing.

"We did good," Letty said. "Five retainers signed and some serious prospects. You know how it goes, Boss. As women in Madrid, we can only do so much. Your presence will make it so much easier with these macho types, and Juan just doesn't have the authority. We were thinking of having a group meeting. You speak, take questions, we get signatures."

"You did a wonderful job. Five retainers in the first week is great."

Letty said, "Thanks, Boss. Betty and I think it's pretty good, too. Ricardo Munoz is cool. He was okay working on a handshake till you go talk to him and sign something formal. It's not really a handshake, but he is okay with the deal you had before. It can stand, or you can go make changes."

"Each case requires a new deal to be signed, even if the terms are the same as in the past," I said. "His last deal was with Oscar. He must have gotten paid by Tom to want to deal again. Does he know this is another firm, and that Oscar died?"

"We explained all that," Letty said impatiently. "Boss, how was Cape Town? Did you take a safari or something?"

I did not want to talk about Cape Town. "Turns out, we went to Geneva."

"And how was Switzerland?" Valita asked.

"Mountains," I said. "Old Protestant cathedrals. Narrow streets. Sweaty bankers. Decent accommodations." I opened my suitcase and dropped a couple of the hotel's scenic postcards on the table with our lunch. "I'll be going with you this afternoon."

Geneva with Olga revitalized me. We handled business in Madrid. We took six weeks, but Gonor was happy with our results. I was glad to be home, though Olga was not there waiting for me. She called from Milan after I had been home for a few days.

"Amor, Casa Luna is just another big house when you are not there. I'm leaving Milan in two hours. I'm on my way."

There was a gas shortage, but either jet fuel wasn't in short supply or shortages didn't matter to Olga.

That night, Letty slipped out of my bed. It was dark, but my eyes were accustomed. I saw her put on a silk nightgown and robe and open the door to the hall.

I sat up in bed.

"Where are you going?"

"To my room. Go back to sleep, Boss."

She left the door, and returned to me, bent down and I felt her lips.

"You're engaged now," she said.

I reached for her, but she slipped away.

Hours later, with my eyes still shut, I heard the house alarm disengage, and the door to my room open. Olga's distinctive Jo Malone fragrance filled my head. I felt her body move against me under the covers, naked. Instead of my morning workout, Olga and I stayed abed till ten. I called Miguel with our breakfast order. We had breakfast on the bedroom balcony, the canvas canopy protecting us from the late June sun.

Letty

I love Olga and I want to believe she's for real when she tells me the same. She ain't no rattlesnake. Rattlers rattle before they strike, and I don't think she's the kind that gives a warning. Only I don't know with her is what's for real or what she thinks is for real. Like how she is fixed on the idea Melina is a threat. What's keeping her from thinking that I am a threat? Because if in her head, I become a threat like Melina, she'd have me snuffed. Those security guards of hers, all she'd have to do is drop the word, and I would be history. I don't want my future full of sleeping and showering with my guns to keep her hired creeps from carrying out an order like that. Better now to keep it cool and give them their space. He wanted me to stay in bed with him and he knows she could arrive tonight. She knows I sleep with him but finding me in bed with him all snuggled up? I don't think so. Knowing she's on her way, I'm not pushing my luck. No way, Jose. Good thing I did get out of there before she arrived and good thing six lavender scented candles stayed lit to absorb the smell of our sex.

Chapter 14
Late June 1984
Plane Talk

Mario

Breakfast this morning was quiet, just Olga and me. We'd stayed in bed late. The team was already up in my office, working. We were in the nook, Olga facing the garden, I was facing her.

"An operator from Chile asked the manager of our airline if we had a plane he could lease for a while. Pepe personally got involved and spoke with the Chilean president of the airline, and bang, he rented out one of his planes for a year. I penciled it out for him. It's going to be so profitable, he is thinking of selling off the airline instead of expanding it. He's got this idea that leasing planes to operators is more lucrative."

"Doesn't the airline make money? Why would he get rid of it?"

"When he owned only a few planes, it was easy to check the bottom line for a profit. Now, it's become a bigger business, more complicated. There are restrictions not only where your home base is, but also where you fly. As you would say, it is a pain in the ass. I don't know if leasing planes is a big deal or not. On paper for that one plane, it's a winner."

Olga reached for the decanter Miguel had left and filled her demitasse.

She offered to pour me some, but I picked up my cup of regular coffee and took a sip.

"Like leasing a car?" I asked.

"I don't know how car leasing works here. The Chilean Airline that rented the plane painted their livery on the fuselage and pays Pepe a monthly rent. They signed a twelve-month agreement. The Chilean operator provides their own crew, their own insurance. Pepe just rented the plane to them."

"I've had cases where the plane that crashed was leased from another operator. The rental included crew, insurance, everything, and the owner is responsible for maintenance. They call it a wet lease."

"I'm strictly a numbers girl, Amor. Above my head. Sounds funny, wet lease. Is there a dry lease?" She laughed.

"Actually, there is. In a dry lease, the lessor provides an aircraft without crew, without staff."

She shrugged. "At first he was talking about dismantling the airline and leasing the planes out one by one. Camila reminded him he paid a lot of money for his routes. He's not a fool, he won't just let the airline go. I ran the numbers for him. He'll sell."

The airline was healthy, successful, and profitable. Leasing out the aircraft might be a start for a leasing company, but not necessarily an advantageous one. Dismantling it and selling off a whole airline piece by piece would mean a loss. And when all of the planes, i.e the assets were leased out, then what? The concept bloomed in my head. It was the same as all of Pepe's other businesses I was hunting for him in the US. The airline had a finite fleet, with no guarantee what they had was what would sell, and when they were gone, he would need more.

Who sold used planes? Would sellers accept green cash for the aircraft so I could get in on the deal? I made a snap decision. "He's better off selling the airline if he's serious."

"Yes, Amor, that's what I said. It takes Pepe some time to come around."

"If he sells the airline with the fleet intact, he'll have to buy planes that he can lease out. That is, it will free him up to select the planes for the buyers."

"Amor, yes, that's what I suggested."

With only my used tiny jet plane to go by, I had little perspective on the cost of planes. If mine was worth more than the million I paid for it, an airliner would be a bundle more. "How much does a DC 9 like yours run?"

"Lots of factors are involved. Everything is tracked by hours. Every time a plane fires up an engine and takes off, it is logged as a cycle. You have flying hours for the plane, flying hours for engines, age of the plane, age of the engines, maintenance, that kind of thing. Millions for sure. If I had paid for the planes, I would know, but Pepe purchases them."

I decided to ask Jason about plane values. Olga had set me off on a day-dream, or maybe a pipe dream. If Pepe was launching this new line of work, I wanted in on that income, maybe by buying planes for Pepe and getting my ten percent from getting the seller to accept cash. I am wealthy, but far removed from the Camachos, and the likes of Olga's diamond merchant Johnny, the super-rich who can sink millions after millions into refurbishing airplanes. It was going to cost Pepe a bundle initially, but once his jets were leased out, profit would be rolling in. Theoretically, it would be like my apartments, except the difference between the monthly rental of an apartment vs a jet plane is astronomical. I made a wild guess that his present fleet had been purchased for cash in South America cash. If Pepe decided to go through with this venture, I would help him realize he needed me to help him find the planes the operators wanted to lease.

Wednesday, I spent an extra hour with Jack at the PDC, where he talked a lot about the ins and outs of plane financing. Pepe was way ahead of me. Fino said Pepe called him for input. I should have known.

I had a lot on my mind when I got home. I saw Tricia, Letty and Betty around the pool having lunch, waved for them to stay where they were, and climbed the stairs to my office with the intention of examining a Boeing sales brochure I had picked up. Jack had promised his secretary would fax us a plane price list if he had one. I hoped it would be waiting on my desk, but it was not. There was, however a brown paper-wrapped box, postage stamped and addressed to me. I slit open the envelope attached to it, and a piece of stationary and a business card fell out.

> Dear Cuz,
> I hope you do not feel neglected. I was at a benefit recently and met a corporate distributor for Motorola whose card I am enclosing. I got a deal on the attached package, so I am sending this to you. I bought one for each of my store managers. After all the aggravation you have endured with your car phone, I know you will just love this. Consider it a late birthday present from last year or an early one for next year. I have given Dennis your name, in case you are interested in getting more of these magical things. They take all night to charge, and they only run for thirty minutes but you don't have to fool with the operator. Take care of yourself.

The note had no signature, but only a phone number. I knew whose number it must be. Only one person on earth called me Cuz.

I cut the paper and found a device inside that looked like a souped-up walkie talkie. Motorola's DynaTAX 8000X cell phone was the newest thing, and it was heavily in demand. I took it out of the box.

The phone in my car looked like a princess style phone, small, and pretty compared to a regular rotary phone, and had a dial that was only for show. When I lifted the receiver, I pressed a button, and would ask for the mobile operator, and identify myself. If the mobile operator said, "Go ahead mobile 998," she would dial the number while everyone with a phone could listen in. The business end of the phone lived in a suitcase stashed in the trunk.

I picked up the device. It was not nearly as small or as pretty as the princess phone in my car, but it was self-contained, no separate suitcase carrying the works. I could see why people were calling it a brick. I plugged in the charger but was too impatient to wait overnight. I dialed Melina on the new phone to thank her.

"I knew you'd love the phone. Don't worry, I put it in your name. Do you miss me?"

"I do miss you, Baby. Want me to come over?"

"I'm working, Cuz, but don't write me off."

It was the first time I ever caught her at her market on the first call. I could see already that the cell phone would be making a huge difference in my life. It was good to hear her voice, but we barely talked for a minute. Both of our phones needed charging.

When Letty came back upstairs, I had her call the number on the business card and order a dozen at almost four thousand a pop. I had her put all the phones in my name. She came back to tell me the dealer said each minute of talk would cost big time, incoming and outgoing. I scoffed at the warning and had her go through with it. After all, for years, I had paid dearly for my car phones for nothing.

"There must be a way to have extra batteries that can be charged outside the phone," I said.

"I got it, Boss. If I have to, I'll find someone to make us battery chargers."

"Good-girl, Baby, go."

I tested out the phone some more, called Letty in the office ten feet from me, delighted there was no mobile operator to deal with like I had put up with for years with my car phones. Unlike the car phone, the brick had a push button pad that worked.

A Mr. Dennis delivered the phones to me before the sun had set. He gave no discount for the volume purchase, but he gave me an extra charger for each phone and promised to see what he could do about buying extra batteries.

Pixie was living between my house and her rooms across the street, though I knew she was coming up on another concert tour. I gave her a phone and Mr. Dennis's card. She needed phones for Raul and Lainie.

I gave phones to Letty, Niley, Jo, Tricia and Betty.

I dialed Olga. She was off again. I didn't even know where to.

"I love this!" I said. "I'm on a brick. I bought a bunch of them."

"Save me one, Amor. I got one registered in New York." She gave me the number, and I wrote it down. "Camila and Pepe will have theirs in a couple days."

Letty programmed all of the cell numbers on auto dial on my cell and on all of the home phones. The cell had room for ten-digit numbers, but a redial memory of thirty lines.

"I'm not carrying these big things around, Amor."

"You must. I want to stay in touch."

"I was joking, Amor, of course."

The phones were a challenge for me. I tried figuring how to beat the battery limit of thirty minutes of talk time. When I was away, I carried them in a briefcase. I bitched about the problems: hang-ups, dropped calls, terrible reception in some places. But I liked that I could be reached when I was not at home, that I didn't have to go to a phone booth to make a call, and not having a mobile phone operator publishing my call over the public airwaves.

During my massage that night, Tangles thanked me enthusiastically for the phone I gave her.

"Melina gave me my first phone, then I gave several people phones. I hardly hear from Melina anymore. Is she seeing someone?"

"I doubt it. Boss, that lady is so busy with work. She's married to Marron's Markets."

I figured Tangles wouldn't tell me anyway.

Two months later, I was as enthusiastic about the bricks as I had been when they first came out. Being able to be in constant touch was like smoking. Addictive. But I did not talk about everything on the phone.

Case in point: I was about to make the September installment on units being remodeled in Long Beach. I made that cash payment myself, at least until TJ's remodel was done, when the finished units would be handed over to Pepe's local management company's office. I went into the safe and counted out the pile of bills. Something caught my eye. The bills were dated from the late seventies and early eighties. It was troubling. Olga had told me the cash had been warehoused by Pepe's father before he died. By the late seventies, he was already deceased. I doubted he was warehousing cash posthumously.

The discrepancy was still on my mind when Olga called from Lima.

"Amor, I'm just getting to bed. I needed to hear your voice."

"I am about to hit the sack too, but glad to hear from you. Any news?"

"Pepe leased my plane out for two years to the government of Venezuela. They fell in love with it, as is." She laughed with excitement. "Wait till you see my new plane."

"What did you get?"

"Another DC 9. I'm coming home while they do an inside makeover. Engines have very low mileage."

"Fuck, that was a quick deal. You only left a week ago."

"It was in the works. I forgot to tell you, Amor. I'm sorry."

"Baby, anything else you forgot to tell me?" I was kidding, but not really kidding. If that cash was warehoused, those bills were being warehoused posthumously.

"You know everything, Amor."

As much as I wanted to ask about the cash in my safe, I held my tongue.

Olga flew home in her new plane. To surprise me, she hired a limo to fetch her from Ontario while the refurbishing company picked her plane up from Ontario Airport. I wanted to talk about the cash but did not greet her at the door with it and held off until after we had a significant reunion in bed. We didn't speak about business for all of twenty-four hours.

The next morning, I woke up alone because she had gone down for a swim in the outdoor pool. Even though it was in the upper eighties today in mid-September, and the indoor pool would have made more sense to me, I know Olga had been flying around cooler, overcast Germanic countries and missed the sun. I skipped breakfast and worked until noon while she sat oiled up on a chaise and soaked up some sun and some Steven King book about a pet graveyard. About two, she sent Miguel up with a message to meet me for a late lunch at the pool.

"I think not the pool," I told Miguel. "How about the sunroom over-looking the pool."

I walked out to meet her and escort her in. After the dazzling sunlight, inside, she looked pale and washed out. The sunroom was set with minimal fuss—glass dishes on a glass table. Nothing to mar the view. Miguel laid out a simple lunch. A couple of grilled burgers for me, and a salad for Olga. A big boat of French fries sat on the table between us. She never asked for fries, but had a tendency to eat half of mine, so Miguel planned accordingly.

I pulled out a couple of bills and placed them on the table.

Olga laughed. "Big tip for Miguel?"

"Baby, a question."

"Ask away."

"It's no big deal. Don't get excited."

"I never get excited, Amor."

"I noticed the dates of the bills."

"I don't understand."

"Most of the bills were late seventies and early eighties."

"So?"

"You said money you moved was old money from Pepe's father. That man has been dead a long time."

"Amor, why would you check the dates on the bills?"

"I did not check the dates. I paid an installment on the units being re-modeled in Long Beach. When I counted it out, I noticed."

She stopped eating. "Amor, what do you want me to tell you?"

"The truth, whatever it is. I want to know if the cash I'm using to buy assets is hot. I need to know if it is going to come back and burn me."

She pushed away from the table and stared at me. I reached over and took her hand.

"What are you afraid of?" she asked.

"We're getting married, Olga. I'm not afraid of anything in this world. If there is trouble, I need to see it coming. If there is a risk, I need to know it."

"You want to know if the money is from drugs? You want to know if Pepe is a drug lord?"

"No, not at all," I lied.

"Amor, you asked me before and I told you, the drug business died when Pepe's father died. The labs in the jungle were closed down. The business taken over by others."

"Baby, I love you enough to let it go, but that does not explain the dates on those bills. It does not jive with your story of the warehoused cash."

I went back to work, and she went out to shop. We spoke no more about it until that night in bed. I had resolved to say no more about it, but she brought it up. I was deep inside my fiancée when she said, "Amor, I promise you will never be hurt for what you do for LAI. If anyone ever questions the cash, we will step in and provide any explanations they need."

This was not news. Though she'd said this before, I had never let a situation like that come up. When a seller resisted taking cash, and I knew it was going to be an arm-wrestle, I walked away from the deal or bought it with bank funds. I had never put LAI in the position of having to step forward to explain the cash transaction.

"Trust me, Amor. I will never do something to get you in trouble. You are my life now. I adore you. Pepe loves you. Camila loves you. You are family."

I said nothing, but I kissed her. Our teeth rubbed, then our tongues dueled. It was so hot, so real. I loved this woman.

She flew out the next morning. Something in Colombia.

The question about the dates on the currency was left hanging.

Olga

If I didn't love him, I would let him know what I think of his constant interrogation. He's so damn suspicious. Making more money than he ever has with LAI and he keeps digging, keeps insisting to know and at the same time, insisting he doesn't want to know. Mario is crazy suspicious. If Pepe knew he was like this, Pepe would not be happy. Mario should take me at my word. When I tell him not to worry, it should be enough, not this constant question of where the money is coming from.

My stewardess Natalia is beautiful in her white short-shorts. The red halter she wears shows off generous breasts. Her shoes are standard issue, plain and white. Her shaved head shows off her elegant long neck and jawline. So sexy. Spanish is her first language, so I speak to her in Spanish. "You like the new plane?"

She handed me a Coca-Cola in a bottle the way I prefer it.

"Lavish and impressive. Do you love it?"

"I've only been in it for an hour, haven't bounced on the bed yet. Come with me. Let's check it out."

The seat belt signs were still on. Coke in hand, I led the way. Natalia followed right behind me.

The carpet is way plush, a deep, dense pile saturated in color. The bed is the same standard king-size, the headboard blue-tufted, subtler than the white one. The bathroom and shower are a little bigger. The bedroom television screen is bigger, and all brand new.

I sat on the bed, then lay down fully clothed, exactly as I had been when leaving Casa Luna. I gave the bed a little buck, and found it firm, soft, offering less bounce than a regular bed.

"Got time for a massage?" Natalia asked.

"Do I need to take my clothes off?"

"I can do it for you if you give me permission to get on the bed."

"Silly lady, you come here." I patted the comforter. "When's the last time I told you how gorgeous you are?" I asked as she removed my shoes and moved on to another article of clothing. I lay back to let her undress me.

"When you came on board."

She smiled. A big smile. "You are too kind, Miss Olga."

Our eyes locked. I raised up my arms. She moved close. I put one hand on her right cheek, the other on her left.

"Smile again," I told her, our faces close. I find her big eyes and dark skin a turn on.

I moved my right hand between her legs. Her smile grew as I felt it getting hard, though it was not as big as Mario's. If I looked, I would see the bulge in her tight shorts. We rolled around, play-fighting for dominance, and the extra pillows and comforter hit the floor. I went somewhere else, not on this plane. *Pixie is hitting high notes, Niley is on top of me, Letty next to me, Mario is fucking me, my hands are rubbing his head, her head. Mario has hair.* I opened my eyes to watch Natalia's big eyes as she fucked me, deeper and harder.

When Natalia was back in her uniform, she carried in a pitcher of lemonade and a bed tray with a pile of finger sandwiches fit for an afternoon tea. I was on the bed watching Flash Dance and paused the tape as she put the food in front of me.

"I know you wish I was a guy," I tell her.

"Did you enjoy?"

"Very much." I went for a sandwich. She poured me a glass of lemonade, then placed the pitcher on the night stand.

"Amor, when you are totally sure you want to fully jump the fence, I will give you the money for the surgery."

Her smile lit up that cabin.

"Get a plate and join me." I patted a spot beside me where she had been earlier. "Good movie. Should I start it from the beginning for you?"

I should be working on my report for Pepe, but I am playing hooky. If Mario asks, I will say it is business. "Amor, I only have sex if it's the only way I can get what I'm after, always business." I love him so much, but his bed is always filled with women. I'm entitled.

I don't know why she's so shy now. She sure wasn't shy earlier.

"Eat, Amor," I say. "Relax, enjoy the movie with me." She only brought one glass. I hold it to her lips so that we can share the lemonade.

Mario

August came and went, marking a year since RIALTO discovered Pixie. I found I missed her tremendously. When we rolled into September, she was in the midst of her Mexican tour, calling in every night to touch base. When we talked, I laughed. No one had as foul a mouth as Pixie, but she just talked that way. She even sang a song that was all cursing, in Spanish and English. It was impossible to hear it without laughing.

"I make good bread when I do concerts here, but the cell reception is shit."

"I been calling you, so now I know why I can't get through."

"They have a fucking long way to go to perfect these fucking things."

"I'm happy with my bricks, but I'm looking forward to when they have a longer talk time."

"I can't wait till we can deep throat on the phone."

"What was that again?" I wasn't sure I heard that right.

"I miss you, dude. RIALTO is flying me home midweek. Raul is picking me up at Van Nuys. I'll let you know when I get home. We gotta fuck soon. Can we, Boss?"

"Hey, you been calling me Mario. Why back to boss?"

"Habit. Is your fiancée around, or are we going to be able to do it?"

"You're on the okay list."

I had the original painting of Pixie that had been used on her album cover. It was an exact likeness. I walked over to the wall of my office where it hung next to the black and white photograph that had inspired it. She was still Pixie, the girl I'd known since we were kids, but also Pixie the star, singing to huge audiences, a marketing tool in Mexico and South America to sell concert tickets. She looked twenty, not a day older.

"Have I told you today how proud I am of you?"

She giggled. "I forgot. Have you done it with Melina?"

"I haven't even seen her. She's blacklisted." Actually, she was the whole blacklist.

"Not good, Boss."

"Hurry home, Baby."

"I just came thinking about you, Boss."

Letty and I were in slippers and jeans about to unwind in the wine room. Tricia and Betty had gone home, and Tangles was with another of her massage clients. At nearly eight, the phone rang. I took the call which was from Raul, Pixie's driver.

"Mr. Luna, I am at Van Nuys Airport."

I didn't know Raul well enough to read the tone of his voice, but he was shaky. It was alarming because he would have no good reason to contact me.

"She's not there yet? Is something wrong?"

"The terminal manager said the plane is forty-five minutes late. They can't reach the pilots."

Chapter 15
Early September 1984
Close Call

Mario

"I'm on my way."

I stood, and pulled Letty along with me, explaining as we headed up the stairs to the main landing.

"Pixie's plane is late and can't be hailed. We're going to the airport."

"I'll call Lainie. Wait a sec."

"Call from the car. Let's go."

I waited while she ran up to the office and got our phones and their chargers. She raced down within two minutes, barefoot, shoving the phones and my shoes at me. A pair of her sandals dangled from her fingertips. Beside the front door, she dropped them on the floor, and hopped on one foot as she slipped the first one on. She grabbed her phone back, hobbling ahead of me as she worked her other shoe on. Her purse hung heavily from her shoulder, stuffed with whatever she'd thought we'd need, a trick she'd picked up from Jo. I worked my feet into the open, untied running shoes. Letty grabbed my hand before I was done.

"What're you waiting for? C'mon, Boss."

I took the wheel, Letty beside me. Lainie's number was on auto dial.

"Maybe her phone is not charged. It just rings," Letty said, dialing another number. She listened for a moment. "No one picks up at her dorm room, either."

"Keep trying."

"Should I call Auntie Carmen?"

"No way."

I waved at Quito to open the gate, pulled out of the driveway, and turned down my tree-lined street. It took real effort to keep from gunning the engine and breaking all speed laws, but I did not need a ticket.

"Can I call Jo and Niley?"

"Yes."

By the time we reached the airport, Jo, Niley, Tricia and Betty were aware and headed to meet us. Reception was difficult from the car. Each time Letty tried to reach Lainie's phone or dorm room, she was disconnected.

It was dark. I found the first parking spot and pulled into it, stopping with a sharp jerk. The parking lot light illuminated Letty's face as she stepped out of the car. She looked small and frightened.

"Hope for the best," I said, stopping long enough to tie one of my shoes.

"She's okay," Letty said, her chin held high. Her eyes were brimming with tears, but she was not crying. "She has to be."

We found Raul seated a few feet from the doors to the tarmac where the plane would park once it landed.

"Any news?"

"No," Raul replied. "Let me take you to the manager."

Letty and I followed him. Just inside the small office, we passed a cabinet packed with files and airline journals, several shelves of health-oriented junk food, six-packs of carrot juice, pickle juice, and the like. A small trash can beside it needed to be emptied. Letty picked up a sesame-carrot chip wrapper off the floor and tossed it on the top of the pile. Two bright orange vinyl chairs faced the manager, who was behind his desk with his back to us, facing a stack of technical equipment, all engaged in active operations on the counter against the back wall, a dizzying array of flashing and beeping gizmos, and intimidating monitors. Though he was not an air traffic controller, the dashboard looked to me as busy and complicated as a pilot's. He spun his rolling chair to face us at our entrance, loosely tangling him in cords. He was about my age, thick glasses, dirty blond, furrowed brow, losing his hair, and was wearing a headset with a springy cord plugged into one of the machines, maybe a radio. He mumbled something into his mouthpiece, then pulled off the headset detangling himself, and tossed it on top of the device it was connected to.

My plane was housed at another terminal at this airport. Everyone knew everyone. He always seemed worried about something, so I could not gather much from his stressed attitude.

"Louis, what's the word on Pixie?"

He did not reply immediately. It seemed like it took a long time for him to get up. He is not a big man, maybe five foot eight, densely built. Not muscular, precisely, but he consumed a lot of 'health' food. We shook hands. He nodded to Letty.

"I'm monitoring the calls from the tower." He gestured toward the headset behind him. "No response. They left Mexican airspace over an hour ago then went silent."

"So, they are on this side of the border?"

"I'm sure of it. We have an alert out, no sightings."

"No report of flight plan change?" Letty asked.

"I wish," Louis replied. "Have a seat."

I complied. "Letty, go in the hall and get Olga on the phone. Bring her up to date."

Letty walked into the hall. I heard her voice as she talked, indistinctly. Could not make out the words. I got up to shut the door. No need to upset Letty any more than she already was.

I turned to Louis. "Ninety minutes. Something is terribly wrong?"

"I'm not going to bullshit you, Mario. You have a plane, you know. Ninety minutes is a long time to be incommunicado and out of radar reception."

He unplugged the headset from the device, and the line of communication he had been monitoring was amplified over a set of speakers. Interference, static, tinny voices. We heard spurts of a random conversation between some unknown pilot and the tower. The noise was disquieting.

Jo and Niley arrived together, opening the door, and bringing Letty with them, then Tricia and Betty minutes apart. Louis pulled hall chairs in to his office and we all sat facing his desk. The palms of my hands were sweaty.

When my phone rang, I opened the door and stepped into the hall to answer it. I did not close the door. Letty was right behind me in the portal, her hands laced into a fist clenched at her chin, covering her mouth, almost like she was praying. Her eyes were terrified and fixed on my face. My heart stopped painfully with a hard jolt as Pixie's voice came loud and clear over the line.

"RIALTO's mother fucking plane could have killed me and the crew. You won't believe where I am."

Everyone stood. They must have heard. A rush of noise came from the office. I barely registered Letty's look of relief but pushed her inside the office so I could shut the door.

"Thank God you are all right."

"I'm on the phone in the Commandant's office." Her voice was muffled for a moment as she talked with someone in the room she was in. "Make that the General's office. Don't be upset, but I called Lainie first to let her know I would be late arriving home. My fricking brick is dead. We made an emergency landing at Edwards Air Force Base out in the desert. We lost power, one engine. I thought I was dead. Fuck, Fuck. We were flying low, braced, heads down. The pilots saw a runway and landed. We're lucky we didn't get shot down. You should have seen the horde of dipshit dickweasel MPs that raced to surround the plane with their fucking guns out like dicks at a circle jerk. They had the pilots facedown, flat on the tarmac, arms behind their heads. Someone screamed 'Everyone out, hands up.' I couldn't have taken those stairs with my hands up, not in my heels. I came out on the first step with one hand on the rail, and one hand up and said, 'Sorry boys, I can't put both hands up or I'll fall on my ass.'

One of them said 'I don't believe it! It's Pixie!' They were all like puppies, a bunch of screamers at the back door of a hillbilly concert hall. I was so fucking glad to be back on the ground I could have fucked all of them. I had to remind them of the pilots so that they'd let them off the ground. It was so stupid. It was obvious from one look at the plane there was an uncontained engine failure and we had just made an emergency landing. I made one of the fanboys get me a camera, so I could take my own pictures of the fucking engine intake blasted all to hell. Don't worry, Boss. I used up two rolls of film, seventy-two pictures. We got this."

My mind wasn't on crash cases, but I couldn't really see Pixie taking RIALTO to the cleaners on this. I opened the door to the office, though everyone had heard her voice and announced, "Pixie is okay."

Raul was crying. It was hard to make out his words.

"Mr. Mario, I go get her. Where is she?"

They all pulled me in, clustered around. We were all crying like babies, even Louis, who barely knew Pixie. Tears poured down my face. I don't fucking know why. I should have been happy. Relief I guess. My throat was a knot. I could hear Pixie whistling and fussing, trying to get me back to the phone, but I was wound into the middle of a giant hug.

"The plane landed at Edwards Air Force Base," I managed to say.

Louis took a tissue and passed the box around.

I said into the phone, "Pixie, I can fly in and get you."

Louis put his hand up and shook his head. "No way would you get permission to land at Edwards Air Force Base. You need a week for permission paperwork to go through."

"No need, Boss. MPs are taking me and the crew to the Best Western in Mojave. They will get a room there. I will snooze till sun-up and take a taxi or rent a car. Mojave is eighty miles from Pasadena."

"Are you sure?"

"I can drive eighty miles. No sweat. See you soon, Boss. Love you."

Pixie was a big girl, no question but I took over.

"Raul is going to head out to Mojave. He will have his cell. Try and get yours charged where you're going."

"Sounds like a plan," Pixie said.

In the lot, Letty said, "I called Olga back, let her know Pixie was okay."

That was good. I hadn't thought to call Olga.

Letty and I got in the Rolls, Letty at the wheel.

"Thank God she is ok," I said. "I really thought the worst."

Letty and I were asleep when the intercom woke me, the guard at my gate letting me know Pixie was arriving. It was three thirty. Night lights were on, but the house was dark as I ran down the flights of stairs. She stepped out of her car that Raul was driving and ran into my arms.

She pushed me to arm's length, gave me a frantic look, then jerked back into a desperate hug. I heard her mumbling into my shoulder. "I'm fucking alive. Fuck, I thought I was dead!"

"Thanks for the rescue from Mojave," Pixie told Raul. "Go home. I'll be there in a minute."

I lifted Pixie in my arms and bounded three flights up to my bedroom where Letty was sound asleep.

"Hey bitch, I'm home. Wake up." Pixie giggled, sitting on the edge of the mattress.

"You slut," Letty muttered. It took a few seconds for events to register in her sleepy brain, but I could see when the light hit. She sat up and smothered Pixie with kisses.

I expected Pixie to spend the few hours till morning with us, but she said she had too much to do. Letty and I walked her across the street. Raul was at the gate waiting for her. After another round of hugs and kisses, Letty and I walked back to Casa Luna.

There is something about fright being an aphrodisiac. The crisis was over, but Letty and I went at each other like animals in heat. I actually howled when I came. Letty laughed at me. I could feel her tears on my chest, not bad ones though. Tears from laughing too hard.

The morning news aired Pixie's emergency landing, the story no doubt circulated by her agent. Miguel had gone shopping before breakfast, and over my breakfast eggs, he told me that a crowd of reporters was staked out by her gates.

After my workout and breakfast, I went up to the office. I'd given Tricia and Betty the weekend off, but there was a six-inch stack of property analyses Tricia had compiled for me to go through.

Pixie did not pick up her cell phone when I called, but she picked up the house phone.

"You have a bunch of reporters out front."

"I'm going to see them when I'm done getting ready."

"Getting ready?"

"I got up looking like an ageing rag doll and I have that whiplash thing. I spent an hour in the hot tub getting over it. I'm almost ready to face the horde. Want to come over?"

"Not a chance. You come over when you are done."

"I told Paulo Ruiz I will quit if he ever put me on a fucked-up jet again. We're going to sue the shit out of them, right?" She laughed, but her voice held the edge of panic.

"At least now you are home and safe. From now on, I can send my plane."

"You are sweet, Boss. Let him ante up the bread. They have a bunch of planes and they're making big money off me."

"It's a good thing I didn't reach Lainie last night," I said.

"You tried calling her?"

"Letty called and called. Never got an answer."

"Boss, I left her in Mexico City. Reception sucks there. She's not using the cell much. I reached her at the hotel."

"What's she doing in Mexico City without you?" This was news to me.

"You know she flew out on weekends to duet with me on the tour, right? Paulo has been at me to get her to do some test recordings. They like her. She's doing good."

"What about school?"

"I'll tell you when I know. She wants to sing. She's working on some music degree anyway. She dropped my name, and the school said they can work around her schedule. Fuck, if she quits, there's nothing I can do. She finished high school. That's a hell of a lot more than I did. I'll be over, Boss. I want to talk to you about if I should break my contract with RIALTO. I have other offers."

I hung up, wondering what Olga would have to say about that. I did not have long to wait. Olga called the next morning. I caught the call in my dojo downstairs, after the work out, before the shower.

"Amor, talk some sense into Pixie for me," Olga said from where ever she was. She sounded irritable and surprised. "She wants to drop RIALTO."

I held the phone in one hand and scrubbed at my sweaty skin with the workout towel that had been hung around my neck, then tossed it in the hamper. I could barely hear Olga.

"Baby, she barely mentioned it. I don't know anything about what was going on in her head." I walked over to the audio controls and turned off the music I'd been working out to. I need not have done that. Her voice rose. Olga was irritated.

"She's under contract. She's making good money."

"I'll talk to her."

"Gracias. It would be embarrassing for me with RIALTO if she got legal with them."

"I got it, Baby."

"It's not like they put her on a plane knowing she was going to have a problem in it. They don't want her dead, they need her alive."

She was right. "I got it, Baby. I will talk to her."

"Amor, thank you."

I cooled my head off in the shower and pulled on some jeans before I walked across the street. I rang the doorbell at the gate and the housekeeper came on the intercom. The gates swung open. Before I got to the front of the house, Pixie was walking towards me.

"Boss, what a surprise."

She fell into step beside me, our arms linked.

"Pix, do me a favor."

"Anything."

"Stop talking about leaving RIALTO. It would be embarrassing to Olga."

She leveled her gaze at me, her eyes serious but twinkling. She stopped walking.

"Okay, but it's going to cost you."

It was the way she said it that made me laugh. I knew her so well.

"You gotta fuck me for three hours."

"One condition," I said.

"Anything."

"At my house, not here."

Pixie made a funny face.

"As your fiancée would say, Si."

Olga called after she sent a plane for Pixie to resume the tour in Mazatlán.

"Amor, thank you for talking to Pixie. What did you tell her?"

"You know how volatile she is. She was just mouthing off. She didn't intend to embarrass you."

"I love that girl." Any irritation I felt coming off of her had vanished. I could hear her smile through the phone.

"And I love you. When you coming home?"

"Sooner than you think. I'm so wanting to be with you."

Chapter 16
Late September 1984
Impulse

Mario

Instead of coming home after the tour, Pixie and Lainie caught a ride with Jason. He picked them up in Mexico City in his new Falcon 900. I heard about it after the fact, when Pixie called from London.

"I didn't know he had an interest in executive jets."

"I've been telling him to spend some of those millions he has," Pixie said. "It's not for me. I want him to have a good time. Boss, he has so much money you wouldn't believe it."

"I know," I lied. I knew he had a lot of money, but no clue what he was worth, just as I had never known what Sami was worth. That kind of thing had never mattered to me.

"Lainie and I are going to stay at the penthouse. He wants us to plan a trip together, anywhere in the world that we want to go. I'm encouraging Lainie to pick, since you've already made me a world traveler."

"That's fucking great, Baby."

"It's good for Lainie."

"It's good for you, too."

"Fucking A, it is," she said boisterously, then her mood shifted drastically. Her voice lowered, turned solemn. "Now that we have these cells, Jason calls all the time. I think I talked to him every day of the tour, even though the reception in Mexico is fucked. Boss, I think Jason wants to get serious."

"Serious like in...?"

"He mentioned engagement. Just like that, Boss. Out of the blue. But I can't believe it. Why me? With the street history I have, why would he want me for keeps?"

"Do you love him?" I thought about Olga saying he was gay. I had never mentioned that to anyone.

"Boss, I love you. I love Lainie. I love Auntie Carmen. I love the team."

"And Jason?"

"I like him."

"Enjoy the trip. Whatever happens, happens." I thought of how Olga would take to the idea of Pixie on vacation and changed the subject. "Have you got anything coming up with RIALTO?"

"I do, but I'm waiting while they do a big build up. I love touring, but only as long as we keep the tours short, no more than a month. Next one is going to be thirty cities in thirty days. Lainie will cut a single in the next couple months. They had to rush with me before I wither on the vine." She giggled. "They're spending a lot more time grooming her than they did me. Lainie is still a youngster, and they're grooming her for pop."

I didn't like the idea of grooming. I knew from Olga that 'grooming' meant they were shaping their images to fit what the label thought the fans would like. Pixie was perfect the way she was. Letty too, for that matter.

It was Miguel's day off. I was sitting on a stool at my kitchen island, the daily newspaper open in front of me. I was not working, just glancing over the headlines, and enjoying the moment. Maybe Jo had already flown the coop, and Pixie was about to, but Letty was in my kitchen making cookies. She had spooned about half of the cookie dough on to trays. I grabbed a chocolate chip and tossed it into my mouth. The bowl on the counter held enough for two more trays of cookies, at least.

I started to bring up Pixie's plans, but Letty cut me off. She knew about the trip before I told her. She put two loaded pans in the hot oven. The scent of baking butter, brown sugar, and chocolate filled the kitchen and my head.

Letty said, "Lainie is making a list of places she wants to visit. Exciting as all fuck."

I nodded in agreement. It didn't sound like a bad idea. "I tie myself down here in Pasadena waiting for the next crash, waiting for the next big deal I can land, waiting for Olga to come home. I'm always waiting, burning up my life. Maybe I should make my own list."

"Why would you need a list, Boss? You always do what you want. This is Lainie's first time to have the money and the opportunity to see the world." Letty kissed me lightly and touched me with her floury hands. I was getting a little intoxicated by the scent of cookies baking.

She continued. "You're feeling bad about Pixie and Jason and hiding it. I know because I feel it too. But maybe Pixie is lonely, and for sure, Jason must be. I don't want to be a downer, so I haven't mentioned my feelings to Pixie either. We already went through this when Jo got together with TJ. I'm so proud of you, Boss." She pulled me close into a hug, her white hands branding my black shirt.

"Letty, call me Mario, already."

She put her hands on my cheeks.

"Mario, I get so horny when you call me Letty in that tone of voice." I thought of Olga claiming she gets chills when I call her Olga.

The oven's buzzer went off, startling us both. Letty found the oven mitts and pulled out the cookie trays.

"Gorgeous," I said. I wasn't talking about the cookies. Okay, I wasn't talking *entirely* about the cookies.

I stood. In a single motion, I swung Letty around to face me, and plucked off the oven mitts, tossing them over my shoulder. She laughed. The cookies could wait. I caught hold of her hands, kissed her fingers, one at a time. My jeans and her panties hit the floor. Her legs locked around my waist as I picked her up. Our bodies knew exactly where everything went. She gyrated deeply, shallowly, deeply again. We were just getting started. I was enthusiastically geared up, endurance-wise, for the long haul. I walked, then found a convenient cabinet to lean against. Around us, pots rattled wildly to our beat, like music.

Olga walked in the kitchen. Surprise.

Her arrival was sudden. One second it was just Letty and me, the next, it was Letty, me, Olga and Olga's mood. The three of us frequently shared a bed, but going by the fire shooting from Olga's eyes, this was a little different. Like a dummy, I just stood there in the kitchen, Letty's naked legs wrapped around me while we were still engaging in acrobatic sex. My black t shirt carried the tracks of Letty's hands. Letty's blouse was half buttoned, her skirt shoved to her waist. Olga didn't look shocked, but I felt her anger flash over me like the first wave of a forest fire.

"Oh, I'm sorry," Olga said. "Should I come back after you finish?"

Letty was fearless, versed in firearms and karate. She could have held her own with Bruce Lee (if he'd still been alive) but her confidence had evaporated, and her face was frozen in sheer panic. She dropped to her feet, her hands tugging her short skirt down to conceal her bare ass.

"I'll be back," she said in a strangled voice. She snatched up her panties, turned off the oven, and left the kitchen at a run.

I didn't reach for my shorts or my jeans. I opened my arms for Olga.

Color filled Olga's cheeks. She turned her back and took a few steps toward the door. She jerked to a stop, then turned crisply to face me.

"I need a shower," she said, then proceeded on her way out of the kitchen.

An hour or so later, my cell rang. It was Letty.

"Where are you?" I asked.

"I'm in my room. Just out of the shower. I think Olga is in the spa. Should I go to my apartment?"

"No need. You live here. If you want to go to your apartment, go, but only if that is what you want. You don't have to."

"Oh, Boss. Fuck, I thought I was going to have a heart attack. She's your fiancée now. Maybe she doesn't want this to be going on."

"Go back to the kitchen and finish baking the rest of the cookies."

"For reals?"

"For reals. I want cookies. Two trays are not enough. I want all the cookies."

She gave a broken laugh. "Okay, Boss."

"You got your gun?"

"I always have it nearby." She got the joke and uttered a tiny laugh.

I went down to the spa where Olga was in the sauna. I stood silently by the glass door.

"Come on in, Amor."

I was glad to hear the 'amor.' The sauna thermometer was at 165 F. I grabbed a towel to sit on, dropped my clothes, and walked into the blast of heat. I sat, and she scooted next to me. I put my arm around her sweat-slickened skin.

"Kiss me, Amor," she said. "Tell me you love me."

"I love you," I said.

"I adore you."

"Are you okay?"

"Why the kitchen? What if the help sees you? Miguel?"

"Miguel is off today. The help is back in their quarters."

"Amor, you are a sex maniac."

"This is not news. You knew this."

Her face was wet with sweat. Maybe tears, too. "If it had been Melina I would totally be mad."

"It wasn't Melina. Please don't be mad at Letty."

"I love Letty." She gave me a quick kiss, then said, "You can fuck her, but do it in the bedroom. Now I have a mental picture engraved on the back of my eyes of you two going at it in the kitchen like a couple of otters."

"I love you, Olga. I'm sorry you didn't see it coming."

She gave me a look. Bad choice of words.

"I almost did see you coming," she said drily. "Amor, make love to me right here, right now. Get in me like you were doing it with her. Amor, Si, *Apurate*"[19]

We weren't in the kitchen, but I did my best to comply. Olga did not complain. We both exploded, then looked each other in the face, gasping. She was flushed from the heat. Me too, probably.

"It's hot in here," Olga said.

Maybe it was just relief from the release of tension, but we caught the giggles, and in a flood of laughter, escaped from the sauna, and jumped in the icy jacuzzi. I swear I heard us sizzle when we hit the water. It took a while to cool down, but when we did, we chased the cold with the hot jacuzzi. Gradually, our laughter died down. I noticed my engagement ring, Sami's ring, where I had put it on Olga's finger. I kissed her left palm, then kissed the ring.

"You are my only real love, Olga."

Like saying it made it so.

We walked out of the spa in our robes and climbed one flight of stairs toward the mouthwatering aromas of brown sugar, butter, chocolate, and peanut butter. In the kitchen, Letty looked up from two sheets of peanut butter cookies cooling beside four sheets of tollhouse already cooling on the island. She blushed. I wasn't surprised to see her there, not because I suggested it, but because Letty handles stress by cooking.

Olga walked over. Put her arms around Letty. Kissed her lips.

---

[19] Hurry up

"I love you," she said to Letty.

"You gotta be pissed at me."

"I'm not pissed. You knew him before I did."

Letty slid a spatula around one tray, and then the other, balancing one of each confection on the spatula. She held it out, offering them both to Olga. "Cookie?"

We all laughed.

Olga accepted the peanut butter cookie and sniffed it. "I've never had one of these," she said. She handed the chocolate chip cookie to me. Letty's face was a mask.

The next morning, Olga and I had breakfast in the bedroom, but not in bed. Letty and Caro served us.

"I missed you last night," Olga said to Letty.

Caro did not bat an eye.

"You're a tease," I said to Olga.

They left us alone. I bit into my crispy bacon.

Olga spooned her grapefruit. "Amor, I spent two days in Geneva again. Remember Alexander Müller, the banker I introduced you to when we were there?"

I nodded. I remembered the guy.

"He's good to take four, five, sometimes six million cash and put it on deposit for me."

"You never told me the details."

"He's a drop. We have millions in the bank there. Anyway, once in a while, he gets balky. I had six million to drop off and the bastard gave me a bad time. I had to fuck him to get him to agree."

"For reals?" I stopped eating. I pictured the guy. Remembered him sweaty in his suit, mopping his face with a fucking handkerchief in sixty-degree weather. He was no Prince fucking Charming.

"I told you I would only do it for business sake, not for pleasure."

"How often?"

She didn't answer. She took another bit of her grapefruit, chewing in slow motion.

I repeated myself a little louder, hating the sharpness in my voice, "How often do you have to do this with him?"

"It has been a long time since the last time. Amor, he comes in five minutes. It's over like that." She snapped her fingers.

"Are you telling me this because of Letty and me yesterday in the kitchen?"

She put down her spoon. "No. Not at all."

I wasn't sure I believed her. She could be making it up, or maybe it was something she had not been planning to tell me at all.

"Do you do it in a hotel? A back room at the bank? A car, or what? Do you do it standing up? Leaning over a wall? On a bed? Did you do it with him when we were in Geneva together? Do you take the ring off?"

"No, I don't take the ring off. Amor, you and I, we have an open relationship. Don't ask for details you don't really want to know."

I swear I could see the kitchen scene with Letty replay in her eyes. I picked her hand up, kissed the palm then the ring. "I love you, Olga."

"I adore you, Mario Luna."

Letty

She's seen me fuck his brains out and him fucking my brains out plenty of times, but after the kitchen clusterfuck, and after they had spa sex, they ate cookies in the kitchen like it was the Geneva fucking Cookie treaty, but she took his fucking peanut butter cookie. Doesn't she know those are his? I don't know if that was on purpose or a mind game, but my mind is sure fucked. I had a terrible night. All night, I was awake, waiting for fireworks. If she went off, he would have it out with her. If he went off, no telling what she would do. So, I heard nothing but silence all night, then this morning she tells me she missed me in their bed last night. What the fuck? I saw her face when she caught us in the kitchen. She was pissed off as fuck. That doesn't just go away.

So he's somewhere with Olga, I'm working in his office, Betty is working at the conference table and Tricia is out messing around with property deals. It's almost one. I punch in Pixie's number. If she's still in London, it's almost nine in the evening. She answers.

"What are you doing?" I ask.

"Duh. Talking to you. What's up? You miss me?"

I tell her about the kitchen drama.

"Oh, fuck-me, that's so hot," Pixie said. "She's a slut like all of us. You traveled with her like I did. She's a flirt and I think Natalia services her, as needed. The way I see it, more power to her for taking it the way she did."

"It's not really how she's taking it. I think she's pissed off and hiding it," I tell Pix. "And who gives a shit about Natalia. We all service Queen Olga."

"Dumb ass, you don't know that Natalia is a Lady Boy?"

Betty has stopped working and is staring at me through the glass. I realize I have been sitting here for a few seconds with my mouth open. I get out of his chair and turn my back to the glass so Betty can't see my stupid face. "You mean that beautiful girl has a dick?"

"Exactly."

"I don't believe it. I would have noticed. I've only seen her on two flights but–"

"I sure would let her bone me. She must have a ding-a-ling as big as Boss."

I laugh out loud. Can't help it, with Pixie.

"You don't think she's putting on about not being pissed?"

Pixie says, "Doesn't matter if she's putting on. Tell the dumb ass at the gate to announce who is headed for the house. What the fuck. It's his fucking job."

"I didn't hear him on the intercom. He is supposed to announce."

Pixie giggles. "Yeah, too busy fucking, like the night the helicopter dropped off that asshole. You two heard nothing."

"Bitch, don't bring that up. We were done five minutes before we heard him."

"It's all old news now, anyways."

"We got calls coming in. I'm in the office, I gotta go. Miss you, Pix. And when you come back, make the fucking pilot run the checklist twice."

"See you when I see you, kiddo. Miss you like my own right hand."

Mario

With Pixie away, her chauffeur Raul had very little to do. I had him take Olga to the airport, her senior security guy in the passenger seat and a Lincoln with her other five guards trailing behind. I made it through the day, working. Betty and Tricia left. Miguel served dinner to Letty and me, alone, again, in close quarters. He served us in the wine room. It was a regular meal, nothing fancy. Great red wine from Argentina in monogrammed stemware. I had a hamburger, Letty a grilled cheese. Real napkins. Paper plates. After we were done, Letty made a joke about washing dishes, tossed the linen in the spa hamper and the plates into the trash.

"Want to know a secret that's not a secret?" Letty asked.

Of course, I did.

"I think Tricia's Bill is opening a PI office in Alhambra."

"I've been hearing that for a year."

"I think it's happening," said Letty.

"Good. I hope he does well. I like him better in an office than in the FBI."

"If Tricia moves in with him or him with her, or if they get married, I have this feeling she'll go work at the office with him."

"Did she say that?"

"No, but I feel it."

"It's not like she's my driver anymore. Her work on the properties is really outside services, not payroll anymore either."

"I know, Boss."

"If she goes with Bill to an office, we won't have her here all the time. I'm sure she'll want to continue the income from the work we give her."

"She might not want to travel on cases," Letty said. "Can you live with that?"

"I can live with that. We don't take her to Spanish-speaking countries anyway, but I don't want to lose her entirely."

The television was playing the movie Rain Man. The Caesar's Palace scene. Letty was engrossed, lying on her stomach on a floor pillow a foot from the TV.

.   "I'd love to see that place."

I couldn't help myself. "You know, Letty, if I had any brains at all, I'd ask you to marry me." I had mentioned this so many times before that I was lucky to be engaged to just one person.

"So sweet," Letty said gently, not indicating if she would say a hypothetical yes or no. She got off the floor and on my lap.

"I can go down on you while you enjoy your wine, Boss."

She slid from my lap, and knelt on the floor, her head resting on my knee. I pulled her up, remembering the tone of her voice when she'd talked about Lainie taking advantage of her opportunity. What was it she had said? 'Exciting as all fuck.'

"Rain check," I said. "I got an idea."

Her eyes grew big in anticipation. "Tell me."

"Get us a crew together ASAP. Let's fly to Vegas."

She reached for the closest phone.

We arrived in Vegas at midnight. I had twenty thousand in hundreds in my pocket, enough that a bulge shows even under the sport jacket.

To reduce the bulge, I gave ten thousand to Letty, who had one of those purses that hangs from the shoulder. She secured the purse to hang across her chest like a sash and put the cash in there.

We hit Caesar's Palace, where Letty stood behind me while I played black jack. I love to win, but after three different tables, I was down two thousand dollars.

"That's it for me, Baby. Let me watch you play the slots." She gleamed.

An hour later, she sighed up at me and said, "Boss, I'm done. There's no winning. No doubt they are fixed."

"I don't think they're fixed, but odds favor the house. You can't beat the house. House always wins." It was something Tricia had told me when I hired her the first time, back when she was a freelance private investigator living in Las Vegas.

We took a cab downtown. At three in the morning, the lights were incredible, bright as daylight. The city never sleeps.

"I should have brought a camera."

"Cameras are for tourists."

"Boss, we are tourists."

Two hours later, give or take a few, we settled in our huge and gorgeous penthouse suite, worth every bit of its five hundred a night price. It could have been the one in the movie. Our view of the so-called strip sported fewer lights than what we saw downtown but was still spectacular. Olga called my cell in the morning, waking me up. I said where we were, making nothing of it. She was in Geneva again. We slept until three in the afternoon and shared a fancy-ass brunch delivered to the room by some stiff, self-impressed, overdressed waiters working hard to fulfill our every whim. An hour later, we were on my plane, headed to San Francisco. A private car arranged by my crew agency delivered us to Nob Hill to our penthouse suite at the top of the Fairmount Hotel. Olga called as we were checking in. I told her where we were. She was still in Geneva. We talked for about four minutes. I managed not to ask about Alexander Müller.

At the gift shop, we bought a pair of suitcases, planning to fill them with clothes to wear to the fancy restaurants we hit during our four days there. As I talked to the concierge to get the lay of the land, I noticed exactly where Letty was looking in the lobby jewelry store window showcase. After we got settled, we rode around on the cable car, down to China Town, then to Fisherman's Wharf. We shared a massive porterhouse steak at the Mark Hopkins Hotel next door to our hotel.

"You are spoiling me rotten, Boss," Letty said. Her big eyes were bright with happiness. She was in a Diane von Furstenberg label black dress we had just bought. From the waist to hips, it was fitted, shirred. Buttons marched waist to the hem. The fabric must have been cotton, but it moved with her and looked soft, and touchable. The sleeveless top bared her slim arms, which looked somehow naked. I decided to do something about that. Her dark hair was in the kind of loose waves that Pixie used to sleep in pink curlers to achieve, but Letty had done nothing but run a brush through it. She looked comfortable, at home in her skin, and somehow managed to be the most elegant woman in every posh venue we'd visited.

I stared at the beautiful girl who had bloomed before my eyes over the years, feeling like I was seeing her for the first time. I wanted to tell her, again, that she was burning up the best years of her life on me but didn't want to ruin the moment. After dinner one night, we were walking past the jewelry store in the lobby as we had a dozen times before. I took a detour and went inside. Letty followed.

"Let me see that diamond bracelet," I pointed at the store shop window. I'm pretty sure it was the one she'd been looking over.

Letty put it on and held it out for me to admire. The total weight of the diamonds, 18 carats. A platinum block bracelet with graduating size diamonds all the way around.

"Olga is going to love this," she said, sighing a little.

"Olga has a jewelry box bigger than your apartment, and it is full. This is for you."

She was speechless. Her eyes beamed, then brimmed over with tears, and she hugged me so hard I had to pry her hands loose.

I told the clerk she would wear it out. Paid cash.

On the way to the airport, she asked, "Boss, why? This trip. The suites. The bracelet. The clothes. Everything. Why?"

"Why not? You deserve a hundred of those bracelets, a hundred trips like this."

"It was so much money, Boss, God, I can't believe it." She looked down at her wrist, turning it this way and that, looking at the play of light.

I felt real fucking good that we had split on a moment's notice. I felt happy.

When I got home, Olga was in Cali, Colombia.

"Where are you?"

"Home. In the office. This afternoon, going to check out a chain of beer joints for LAI."

Reception on her cell was scratchy, so bad that she called me back from a land phone to the house phone. For half a second, I felt like she was calling to check on me.

"Amor, is there anything about Letty I need to worry about?"

"Not at all. Why?"

"The trip. It's romantic. Impulse sex in the kitchen. It's like more than just fucking."

"It's unwinding, Baby."

"I adore you, Amor. Please don't break my heart."

"Never. You are the woman that I truly love."

We ate again, paper plates in the wine room. Crabmeat Louis. Fancy name for a heap of fresh crab on shaved lettuce, with thousand island dressing. Melina would have insisted on serving it on china. Olga would have insisted on eating in the dining room. Letty liked the paper plates because that joke about washing dishes and throwing them away had made me smile. Still, however it got in front of me, it was good. Miguel sent down a shaker of a lemon cayenne pepper mix I like. Letty had a sorbet for dessert, and I had so much peanut butter ice cream that I worked out after dinner for an hour. When I was done, showered, and back in front of the TV, Letty told me she got a call from Olga.

"No shit?"

"No big deal. Not the first time she called. She said that you said you needed to unwind and asked how the trip was."

"And?"

"I told her we had fun."

I hugged her. "We did have fun, Baby."

"First, she catches us in the kitchen, now she's no doubt wondering about this trip we just took, like verifying that you needed to unwind."

"I'm not worried," I said.

"Okay, then me neither. But let's not do it in the kitchen anymore." We smiled at each other.

"Kill-Joy, that's what you are," I accused.

Letty turned serious. "I love her, Boss, you know it and she knows it. But I don't trust her. I think she would turn on a dime against me if she thought our thing was serious."

Olga

The flight from Cali, Colombia to Bogota is just a hop, under two hundred miles. My security detail took off to their homes, relieved by six other familiar faces. I had them fetch my luggage from the plane and went to my lovely home. I had to see Pepe in the morning at the big house. Camila would not be there.

A family of four attends to my home. Diego, Alicia, Lucia and Marco Restrepo. Lucia is twenty-one, her brother Marco, twenty. The deal is they keep the six thousand square foot house ready for me and my guests without notice. That meant food, fresh daily change of linens in the bedrooms and fresh towels in the six bathrooms, etc. Food did not go to waste; the family could take perishables and restock what was taken. Freezer items were rotated every three months, even though I knew the food could last a lot longer than that. The rules that I had put in place were the same for all of Pepe's houses, though the staffs can vary. I know Pepe keeps gardeners in some of his properties. The exterior of my house, landscaping and pool were contracted out.

Away from the main house was a small home for the Restrepo family with room for four more people to live if I needed more crew for a longer stay. I figure if I had to come home to a locked-up house, there would be no reason to own that house or call it mine. For the workers, it was good. They had a job no matter if I was there or not.

Most of the friends I grew up with had left Colombia but there were still a handful of friends here. I didn't see them often and there would be no time to meet up with them on this trip. I planned to see Pepe tomorrow and take off the following day.

I soaked in a fantastic tub that is the center piece of my ensuite bathroom. It's round and very Roman, but the Roman's didn't have jacuzzi jets in their fancy marble bathtubs as I do.

Lucia wasn't married yet. When I was there, she was my attendant, looked after me, prepared my tub, laid out my clothes, there for anything I needed. I should have been content. My bathtub was overflowing with bubbles, and she was sitting on a chair a few feet from the tub.

"You are so pretty, Lucia."

She spoke Spanish. "Gracias, Senorita Olga."

"Olga is good enough, I've told you before."

Lucia smiled.

"A pretty girl like you. Do you have a beau?"

Lucia shrugged shyly. "I like working here. I don't want to leave."

"Amor, there's room in the house for your husband. Don't let that stop you."

The smile again. "Thank you, Senorita."

I turned off the jets of streaming water, and the bathroom became quiet. I stepped out of the tub, bubbles clinging to my skin. Lucia wrapped a big towel around me. I walked to the shower, letting the towel fall into her hands. I prefer she doesn't stand right outside the shower door because I feel like she's rushing me. She returned to the chair to wait for me to step out, so she could wrap me in a fresh towel and help me dry off.

My hair is short so drying it with a hair dryer takes only a few minutes. My stomach growled. I turned off the dryer and ran my fingers through my hair.

"Lucia, I'm starving."

"My mother is waiting for you to tell her what you'd like to eat. What would you like?"

"Amor, have her get me a crab cocktail and avocado, plenty of it. Then I'll decide what else."

"I will tell her now. Do you want to eat in the kitchen?"

Instantly, I pictured Mario and Letty, fucking in the kitchen.

"Dining room," I said, sharper than I intended. I softened my voice. "Good, Amor, go. I can dress and be down there in twenty minutes."

The door shut. I went to the chaise and leaned into it. I don't want to think about food and kitchens. If I think about it, I am still upset. I can still see them going at it. I don't like that he fucks her in the kitchen. What is he doing in the kitchen when she's baking cookies? He's never in the kitchen like that. This trip to Las Vegas and San Francisco, a honeymoon? Why the intimacy? Agitation made me get up.

I went to my suitcase. I opened it and saw it was the wrong one, one I brought from Casa Luna and had stashed in the plane. I recognize the things inside as from after a day of shopping in Los Angeles. I keep extra clothes in the plane for when I need them. The clothes are rolled neatly with great care in the way Letty does. I could not help thinking of her. I want to wear these things, not leave them languishing in the closet for a year, so I decided not to unpack. I picked a dress from the closet and put it on. It was not as fresh as what is in the suitcase but there's no one here to impress but me. Letty would not have let my clothes get so stale. I should be thinking about my man Mario, but here I am thinking about Letty.

It hit my head like a ton of bricks. Letty likes women. She's not out to marry him. Letty is not Melina. She has never come close to marrying him. I've seen her kiss Pixie and how Pixie kisses her back. She loves Pixie. And the way she goes down on me, no hesitancy. She's better at that than Pixie. I don't believe she loves him like Melina loves him. The open relationship with Mario made me free. I could have had somebody. I wished I had someone to sleep with tonight. I didn't want to think about Mario and Letty anymore.

Mario

I didn't know what Jason is worth. Less than Pepe, certainly more than me. Not that I'm a pauper. I could jet around the world in my small jet without touching the income from my apartment rentals. I now had fourteen hundred apartments and Jo and Niley employed ten to help them manage the rental properties. Even though I was paying hefty taxes, income from aviation and LAI commissions added up. I paid taxes on the cash I was receiving from LAI, banking it. I only kept a million in my safe that belonged to me.

With the economy bouncing up and down, banks loved me for my balances. And since banks only insured for one hundred thousand in case they went broke, I spread around my largesse. At last count, I used twenty-two banks. Seven of them had over a million dollars each. I bought savings bonds and put money with my stock broker that Melina had introduced to me years ago. I had bank accounts with small balances in many countries where I had worked cases. Nest eggs, like the one in Paris. When I'd sold my partner Simone my share in her bakery, I did very well. I left the money in a Paris bank. I wasn't trying to be another Pepe Camacho. During crash cases in various countries, it was just easier to have a local bank. No one could be Camacho rich.

November was approaching. I got to thinking about people I knew, and it occurred to me my old school buddy Pélon had a birthday coming up. I had not talked to him in a long time, but I did not want him to think I had forgotten him.

"Letty, when you talk to Pixie again, see if she has Pélon's address in San Quentin."

"San Quentin?"

I realized Letty didn't know Pélon, who was doing life for murder. "He's someone I grew up with. You fed his mother on the first Thanksgiving you worked for me. Little woman. Big hair. Remember her? I want to send him some money."

"Sorry, I can't remember a guest from a party in 1977, but I'll check with Pixie, Boss."

From my desk, I watched Letty's animated face as she dialed several times. After Letty made it through to Pixie, the call lasted a long time. When she hung up, I joined her.

She poured us each an iced tea from the carafe Miguel kept supplied.

"I got a twenty-minute earful from Pixie about Pélon. He was her protector when she worked the street. Your best friend."

"Protector might be a little of an exaggeration, but Pélon was fierce. He had a hair trigger temper and a dozen brothers built like forklifts. I don't know if he ever stuck up for her," I said. "But he was always an angry kid, and nobody messed with his friends. Pixie and I, we were both his friends. All the gangs steered clear of our neighborhood." I remembered confronting a bully or two on my own. I'd never needed to hide behind anyone. Cosmo's karate lessons had saved my life.

I was a bit jealous hearing that Pixie thought of Carson as her protector. If anything, I had been her protector. I was losing my team, little by little. I missed Pixie being around, her cussing up a storm all the time. I missed her voice. I missed her jumping on me.

Letty brought me back to Pélon.

"She told me how you went to San Quentin to visit him."

That visit had been about Melina. The brother of the guy who had shot her father had been up for parole. Pixie and I went to see if Pélon could do something about it. As I recall, Pélon made sure the guy was involved in riots and fights whenever he had a parole hearing come up. Made him look like a trouble-maker so he kept getting time added on to his sentence.

"Did you get the address to reach him?"

"She's going to fax it to me in the next day or so. She didn't have it on her."

"When you get it, send him a money order for one thousand dollars with a note, Happy Birthday."

"Will do."

"Where was Pixie?"

"Venice. They've been there ten days and haven't gotten tired of it." Instantly I thought of Fae. I put the iced tea down on the table and shut my eyes. I could still see her face.

"You okay, Boss?"

"I was just remembering Venice."

"Going by that look on your face, you must have loved the hell out of Venice."

"I lost a girl there, once."

"How do you lose a girl?"

I told Letty about Fae, the little French girl I'd met in Venice. I had been twenty-seven, she twenty-five, and down on her luck, or maybe running away. Our language barrier had not stopped me from falling madly in love with her. Remi, the Hotel Danieli concierge, had been our go-between. We were only together a couple of weeks, but it may have been the most memorable relationship of my life. She disappeared in Rome. I had frantically searched for her to no avail. Sometimes, I still wonder where she might be now.

At lunch, Jack asked, "Have you set the big day?"

"Haven't even talked about it."

"She's always on the road. How does that go over with you?"

"We have an agreement. It's okay. One day it won't be like this."

"I don't know what Pepe will do without Olga handling the money."

"Jack, don't tell me. I don't want to know."

Jack changed the subject.

"I worry about you." Jack signaled the waiter to refresh his sparkling water. "So many unsolved crimes involving you."

"I think that all the time. If someone wasn't after me, I would not have full time guards, a manned gatehouse, dogs walking the property, a gate, four-teen-foot walls, and security cameras."

"With this bastard dead, it could be over?"

"I seriously doubt that whomever went through the trouble of choreo-graphing this biker's actions is going to stop just because he's dead."

"Could it be the biker killed Bruno?" Jack asked.

"I remember when you said there was no connection." I worked on my steak.

"Conjecture. Until we know for sure, it's a guessing game. How would I know."

"Jake and Oscar have been dead a long time and still nothing," I said.

"Torching of your house as well." Jack carved his steak.

"I try not to think about it," I lied.

"I agree, Mario." He made a face, sipped his water, and put down the glass. "How about we do something different? A little wine instead of this sparkling shit?"

I smiled. "I'd love an Argentinian Pinot Noir."

"I'll flip you. Merlot against Pinot?"

"I bet neither one of us has a coin in our pocket, so I yield. Merlot. You pick it."

A few glasses later, Jack mentioned, "I just took a case. Gilberto Laso. It's been in the news. The guy claims the DEA kidnapped him out of Colombia and brought him here for prosecution."

"I haven't been following it. I didn't think you were taking cases?"

"If it's criminal and big enough, I take it."

"Don't blame you."

We clicked glasses.

"Did they really kidnap him?"

"The DEA claims he came voluntarily. My client says he was hand-cuffed, masked, and put on a plane that landed in Miami."

"How do you go about proving something like that?"

"I'm more interested in proving that he's not guilty of the charges they arraigned him for. I'll be busy on this one."

"If you're busy in court, who's going to make the loans to lawyers in need?"

"Who else? I learned how to walk and chew gum long ago."

I raised my glass, "Cheers, my friend."

Chapter 17
Early November 1984
Behind Closed Doors

Mario

Olga came home and wasted no time in getting me pissed.

"Baby, why did you tell Letty to go home for a couple days? She lives here. It was you that told her not to leave when you're here. Did you forget that?"

"I didn't forget, no. I didn't plan on telling her to go. She has an apartment, Amor. She works during the day with Betty and Tricia. I didn't tell her not to come during the day. I just saw her, and...it was an impulse."

"I told her to get her ass back here. This is a big house. She doesn't have to sleep with us."

"Amor, you are upset?"

"We made a deal. Letty would live here."

"Okay, Amor." She changed the subject, like it was all over and done. "So, what have you been doing while I was gone."

"Other than the trips to San Francisco and Vegas, just the usual thing. Looking at some beer halls for LAI. Lunch with Jack Fino yesterday."

"Fino is representing a friend of ours. Gilberto Laso."

"He told me. I didn't know Laso was a friend of yours."

"Family friend. Gilberto has been in the drug business for years, all the way back two generations."

"Baby, don't say that too loud. The prosecution will call you as a witness."

Olga laughed. "It's no secret. The secret is how he keeps it so far away from himself and his family that they've never arrested him. Not once."

"Do you think they really kidnapped him?"

I had to get up. I paced over to the window, and looked out, then came back and stood beside the couch. I was interested in Olga's topic, but I was still fuming at her for telling Letty to leave.

"Don't you think he was?"

I shrugged. "I don't know. I haven't much followed the story."

"Well, if he was kidnapped, I hope Jack can prove it. If he can prove it, they have to return him to Colombia."

"Is he wanted in Colombia?"

"Not that I know of. He's friendly with this new government, so I don't think he's wanted by the police."

"Don't be mad at me about Letty. I do love her. I just wanted us to be alone. She has you every single night of the week."

I kissed my fiancée. "You're always gone. Imagine how fucking lonely I'd be if Letty wasn't around."

"Are you serious?"

"Serious as a heart attack. Why are you surprised?"

"Amor, you have money, a Rolls Royce, this huge house. You could go out, bring new girls home. I would not care. Really, I would not care."

"You would not care? In this world that has a deadly sex disease?" She did not meet my eyes. "Baby, are you heading to blacklisting Letty like Melina?"

"Blacklist? What is that?"

We made it through the night with no other argument. The next day, Olga was down to one more night at home. In one more day, she would be flying off to Barcelona.

She had to bring it up again.

"Did you really have to give her that diamond bracelet?"

Talking to Olga was like playing poker, and I don't even know how to play good poker.

"I've given my team many gifts. Rolex watches, cars, mink coats. All sorts of things. What about the bracelet?"

"That girl is a *chingaquedito*[20] but I didn't know it until now."

"Baby, next time she's down between your legs, I'll remind you."

"Do you hear yourself?"

"Yeah, our first argument."

"I don't want that bitch around here when I'm staying here."

"Olga, this is my house. We're not married. You have a house across the street."

"Imbecile!" [21]

I thought the next thing she would do is take off the ring and throw it at me, but, that didn't happen. I had never seen Olga mad at me before. I had never seen her mad before. Not since Camila introduced us, in December of 1977, right after the fire at the Palomar hotel.

I could have run after her. I didn't. Fuck it. This wasn't about Letty any more. I wasn't about to have anyone tell me what I can do and cannot do in my own house.

Olga spent the night at her house. I didn't call her. She didn't call me.

"I feel fucking terrible," Letty said.

"Why did you tell her I bought you the bracelet?"

Letty blushed and looked at her wrist. "I haven't taken it off since you gave it to me. She saw it, made a comment and asked me if you bought it for me. I told her yes. She didn't ask for details. Sorry, Boss."

I looked at Letty. "Are you really sorry?"

---

[20] Scheming, two-faced

[21] Idiot

"Sorry that I got her pissed at you. Sorry that she looked at me like I was dirt. Not sorry that I told her the truth."

"You told her that to get even after she told you to spend the night at your apartment?"

Letty looked at me with big eyes. "I was not thinking of that. Maybe. I don't know."

"It's okay, Letty. We made a deal that you could live here. She's not changing that deal, and neither am I."

"Boss, my apartment is nice. It's cleaned once a week even though I don't live there. The sheets are changed, fresh towels in my two bathrooms. Almost every dollar you pay me goes in the bank and stays there. Don't feel sorry for me, I'm totally cool, Boss."

"Come over here." She got up from the sofa across from me in the big living room I hardly used, and stood in front of me, practically knee to knee, with an uncertain expression as if she did not know where to go. A lost puppy. I pulled her beside me, but she sat stiffly on the large couch. I did not like to see her like this, uncertain, after it seemed she'd matured into someone more confident.

"I should leave until she's on a plane tomorrow," she said in a small voice.

"Hide?"

"Not hide."

She had been avoiding my gaze, but now looked directly at me. I could see nothing but sincerity. *Chingaquedito*? I don't think so. Not by a long shot.

"I don't want to be trouble for you," she said.

I put my arm over her stiff shoulders and kissed her lightly on the forehead. "I'm sorry she hurt your feelings."

I thumbed away her tears as she talked in a soft voice.

"I felt horrible that she turned on me. She has never looked that way at me. Like something to scrape off her shoe."

Something in her expression reminded me of Melina. Melina was fearless in all her doings, but she had been scared of the Camachos from the moment I told her I'd met them. From the first, she feared them about as much as I liked them, or at least as much as I liked their lifestyle.

"Did she scare you?"

"Boss, please. I felt like kicking her ass. I pictured it. She must have seen it in me because she backed off and said that of course I could come to work during the day."

I did not feel much like eating, but we went into the wine room, and had dinner. Miguel gave us a cheese soufflé so light it almost floated off the plate. It went perfectly with Argentinian red wine. Letty was back to herself.

"You can't blame her, Boss," she said, a little drunkenly. "She loves you. How could anybody help loving you? I know she loves you. Why should she put up with me or anyone?"

"Because we have a deal. That's why."

"She's a swinger but now that you're engaged it may be different in her mind."

"She's a swinger," I said. "She understands how it goes." Swinging was just...I don't know...loving. It had no commerce to it. It was just people getting intimate, feeling good, feeling together. I thought of how Olga slept with men in the course of her work. If she wasn't a swinger, it made that sex seem so calculated, made it seem even worse. She admitted sleeping with women, Camila included. She said those encounters didn't count. What bullshit.

Letty and I went to bed that night as we always do when we're alone. Maybe half an hour after the lights went out, she kissed me before slipping out of bed.

She spent the night in her bedroom.

I must admit that I expected Olga to come to me during the night and then we could apologize to each other. No such luck. Fuck it.

Jo and Niley brought over their computer-generated reports and stayed for lunch. Miguel fixed a shrimp salad. It was too cool to eat outside, but Betty, Tricia and Letty joined us in the sunroom. Everyone concentrated on the food. It was delicious, as always, but everyone was quiet.

Jo pushed away her plate and looked around at everyone. "Who died?" Jo asked. "Is this because Pixie is off slumming with Jason?"

"No one is pouting about Pixie except me. We all want her to be happy," I said.

No one said anything. Letty got up. "I'm going upstairs to make some calls."

Jo watched Letty leave, then narrowed her gaze at me. "What the fuck happened? Who shot her puppy?"

"Olga did," Tricia said. She looked over at me. "I'm not saying any more. It's not my beef. I'm not mixing in."

Betty didn't know what was going on but shoveled in two shrimp and stood up. "I'm going up to work. I don't like to think of Letty up there alone. She looks upset."

"Thanks," I said. "I don't think she should be alone."

Tricia and Betty went upstairs to comfort Letty and gossip. I called Miguel on the intercom and told him to bring the girls their desserts and coffee upstairs on the conference table.

"Sure thing, Boss," Miguel replied. "As soon as I bring yours."

He arrived with coffee, a tray of brownies and cookies, gave Jo and Niley a fond hug, made quick work of clearing the table, and went up to serve the girls.

"I sure miss you being around," I said to Jo. Her voice was a breath of fresh air. I told her what had happened with Olga. Her reaction to the Vegas, San Francisco trip. The bracelet.

"Olga's no Melina," Niley said.

Melina was my best friend. I hadn't been with her in ages. We barely talked.

"I am over Melina. If she really wanted to see me, or talk to me, she'd be here."

Jo looked at me and shook her head. "Melina has always accepted you for yourself. She would do anything for you, even stay away. She knows her presence will bug Olga, and if she's bugged, it will spill over on to you." Jo put her hand over mine. "Letty's not just some shadow following you around. She and Miguel have made you their family."

"Letty has done nothing wrong," I said. "You know this. I know this." Olga did not know this, and she was making Letty feel guilty about being herself.

Olga

I felt depressed and helpless, and much of it was the argument with Mario. I wanted him to follow me across the street. Of course, he did not. So, I flew off to do Pepe's bidding, Pepe is just another man who is angry with me. Always for him, it is work, work, more work. I was miserable. I was depressed. Still am. I could not make it through the Barcelona meetings without crying so I flew home. Not Pasadena where my Mario dream is haunted by Letty, but home. I kept thinking that he would leave me for Letty, and if not for Letty, because of what happened with Letty, he would go back to Melina. At home I hid from the world. The phone rang and rang but I didn't answer it, nor did I answer my cell phones. It would be the bankers whose meeting I missed. It would be Pepe, angry. It would be Mario, telling me that to have him I had to have Letty too. Now Letty stands between us like a wall. It wasn't my heart that was broken. It was my pride. My ego was shattered.

Felicia was with me every minute, comforted me when I cried Mario tears. I talked to Pixie in Rome. Pixie can be a good listener when she wants to. She tried to assure me about Letty, but I know the two of them are tight. She'd never say a harsh word about her.

I had been home three days when Pepe arrived. He walked in and caught me alone. The last person I wanted to see.

"Why are you not answering the phone? Why didn't you keep your appointments in Switzerland, Barcelona and Paris?" He was furious.

"I'm sick, Pepe, *perdoname*," I told him in a soft voice. I was crying. I was sitting on the edge of my bed, I looked up at him, and repeated, *"Perdoname."*

I felt the slap. It was so hard, I tumbled on to the floor, face down, my breath knocked out of me. Before I could turn, I felt his belt on my back, my shoulders. I was on fire. I don't know how long, but finally, he backed up. I managed to get on my feet, shaking, I stood in front of him.

"This time you went too far," I screamed at him at the top of my lungs.

He slapped me so hard, I was knocked to the floor again.

I looked up at him putting his belt back on.

"I hope your mother in heaven saw what you just did to me. Your mother loved me. You crossed the line. Get out of my house."

"I stay as long as I want to stay," he laughed. The bastard laughed again and battered me with kicks. A blow to my stomach, I wanted to throw up, but curled into a ball. I stayed like that till Felicia crept in like a quiet mouse, leading me to the bed, where I stayed curled up till Camila called. Camila would understand. Her voice brought me to life. I talked for five minutes without letting her get a word in. I told her everything that had happened.

"Amorcito, he had to be drunk. Amor, I'm so sorry, Amorcito."

"I did not smell liquor," I said through tears. "I'm not a punching bag. I will not put up with this. This ends now."

Pepe returned the next day. It would have been stupid to tell the guards to block his entry to the grounds and to my house. They were his guards. He paid them. He pays everyone.

Felicia sat on a chair next to the bed where I was sitting up. When he walked in, she jumped like a mouse but stood her ground.

"Get out," he told her.

I got to hand it to Felicia, she was shaking so hard I could see it, but she did not move.

He told her again to get out. Poor Felicia did not move. Before she died from fright, I said, "Felicia, it's okay, come back when he leaves."

She gave me a look of terror, pity, and regret, and fled.

"He has a name," Pepe growled.

"Pepe, you don't scare me. Look what you did to my face! You think I can go see bankers when I look like this?"

It hurt but I got out of bed and dropped my nightgown to the floor. "Look what you did to me." I had bruises all over, marks on my back, across my neck and shoulders and a bruise the size of a football across my stomach.

Pepe stared, turned without a word, and walked out of my bedroom. Felicia let me know he had driven away.

Camila called to see how I was. I told her again what happened.

"Amorcito, I will take care of this," Camila said. "Stay home and recover. I talked to him, he told me how he hurt you, he feels bad."

"Imagine how I feel," I said, and I hung up. I could not tell Mario about this. This was what it meant to be Camacho. Always alone.

There are hospitals, but I did not go. Felicia and her mother prepared ointment. The bruising would disappear eventually, but it would take weeks. Letty hardly seemed important now. I wished I could talk to Mario, but that would set him and Pepe at odds. I couldn't risk that. Can't risk Pepe seeing Mario as an enemy. Pepe's enemies do not live long.

I can't take a sleeping pill because I had four glasses of wine. I'm lying here in the dark bedroom in Bogota. Camila is in Turkey, Pepe the barf bag psycho is in Cali.

Mario

Pixie called from Rome.

"Boss, what the fuck is going on there? Olga called and told me Letty is all over you and trying to split you two up."

"Do you believe that?"

"Fuck no. I know Letty better than that."

"You should have told that to Olga."

"I sure the fuck did tell her. Olga was crying. I've never heard her cry."

"Really?"

"We were on the phone. I didn't see her but that's how it sounded."

"I told her Letty was staying here. She stomped across the street, and left Pasadena without a goodbye," I said.

After I hung up, I called Olga on her cell. I wasn't sure if she had landed in Barcelona or if she was in Spain or had changed destination. No answer.

Betty, Tricia, and Letty were working in their space next to my office. I looked over rental reports Jo and Niley had brought over. I called Olga's answering service, the one in Colombia that always had access to Pepe, Camila, and Olga.

"She's in Barcelona," an operator told me. "I'll tell her to call you."

A few minutes later, they returned the call.

"Mr. Luna, Olga told me to tell you she would call when she had time. She's very busy right now."

"Too busy?"

"Yes, that's the message she told me to tell you. I'm sorry, Mr. Luna."

So. I was given the brush off. I wondered who she might be fucking in Barcelona. Another sweaty banker? It was a petty thought, but it was mean of her not to respond, and I could not help feeling mean right back in her direction. After all, I had called her after Pixie told me that Olga had been crying. My good intentions soured on me.

At the end of the day, I dialed Tangles and told her to come over. I needed a massage.

Tangles did me first then Betty and Tricia.

"I remember when I had this gig," Betty said. "Now I get to go home early."

"I thought you liked being here late with us."

"Boss, I was just poking at Tangles. Want me to stay?"

"Stay," Letty urged. "Boss needs to relax."

We commenced relaxing by smoking some of the pot that Olga kept us stocked with. No telling where it came from, but according to Pixie, it was the best of the best. I can't tell the difference. As big as I am, you'd think it would take a lot for me to feel it. I don't recall everything we did, but we were all pretty wiped out, and woke up upstairs in my big bed.

I was counting the days since Olga left for Spain. Days I had not talked to her. I did not try to reach her. At least Pixie stayed in touch. She called me around dinner time in LA, which meant it was close to midnight in Rome.

"Boss, I'm having a blast and so is Lainie. This is more fun than singing."

"You gotta be kidding."

"Yeah, I'm kidding. Nothing is more fun than singing in front of an audience. I come and come." She giggled.

"Is Jason happy?"

"He's a quiet guy, but he laughs and seems to enjoy being with us. It's embarrassing all he does for us. If I didn't know better, I'd say he has a crush on Lainie."

"Come on. How could he look at her when he's got the original, you?"

"I have eyes. I see things."

"Not long ago you thought he was going to propose to you."

"Once he saw Lainie, I got flushed," she laughed.

"She is a prize," I said with a chuckle.

"Yeah, she is. Like her mom." She changed topics. "Any word from Olga?"

"Nope."

"I haven't heard from her since before she called you, crying. Not a word. Her service gave me a message that she'd call me when she had time." I felt a bark of laughter come out, but not the fun kind.

"She'll come around," Pixie said in a soft voice, her trying-to-comfort voice.

"Think so?"

"Yes. Maybe she's waiting for Letty to move."

"She's not talking to us. She wouldn't have a clue if Letty moved. And anyway, Letty's not moving."

"Boss, marry Letty, already."

"If I was really wanting to get married and had brains, I would ask her."

"Fuck me, Boss. That's totally cool."

"I miss you, Pix."

"Oh, Mario, I miss you, big time."

"I miss you more," I said.

"I'll check you out tomorrow, Boss. I think I better give Jason some head, so he'll go to sleep. Be in touch. Love you."

I hung up the phone and laughed.

Pixie

I told Mario I had to hang up to give Jason head. I lied. I go down on him, but he doesn't get it up. "It's not working," he always says. "Get a thing and I'll do it to you." He meant a dildo from a large adult toy trunk he keeps in a dressing room off the master bedroom. One night, I was sitting up in bed, legs crossed, he was flat on his back. I finally asked him.

"Jason are you gay? If you are, far out. I'll still be with you if you want but tell me."

The most I got out of him was 'I have a temporary problem.'

Jason seems to enjoy watching me playing with myself. He eggs me on but gets no erection. He just wears a big smile, even laughs sometimes, happy laughter. What the fuck? He has a huge collection of X-rated movies. Tubular for me. I can get off watching. I don't have pegged what part of a movie revs his engine, watching pussy or the guy who always pulls it out, so the film catches the orgasm.

Now that Lainie is with us on this trip, he invites me to join them for dinner, but I can tell I would only be in the way. Lainie is young. I never told her I thought I was falling for Jason. I wondered why he'd be interested in me since I told him from the start about my life as a street girl. Seems like a hundred years ago but I don't hide it, fuck it. It's common knowledge ever since I wrote that song, and Rolling Stone interviewed me. He buys me gifts, expensive gifts. He listens to me. He went out and spent millions on a plane that I suggested he buy. He kisses me. He hugs me when we're in bed, he cuddles, but he's not loving at all. He doesn't fuck me, he doesn't eat me. What the fuck am I doing here? I should be back at RIALTO before they boot me off this gravy train I'm riding. Fuck, I just got the career of a lifetime rolling. What am I doing here? Now I brought Lainie here. She's so innocent she scares me. I mean, she knows my history, but she doesn't know what it's like. She doesn't know how men can be. I've seen the worst of it, and I'd go through hell to see she never has to. But Lainie, she's dazzled by the sideshow Jason puts on for us. The expensive hotels, gifts, flying around in his plane. I can't just leave her here.

Mario

A lawyer I had worked with on a crash in Mexico City called me with a lead on a medical helicopter crash. He knew one of the families and arranged for them to meet with me. I took my plane to Guadalajara, Mexico to handle the case with Betty.

Letty went shopping. Grocery shopping that is. When I first hired Miguel and Letty, she had no assigned job in my household, so she did the shopping. Pretty soon she was buying for the entire household, everything that was needed in the kitchen and everything else. After she became part of my team, Miguel took over that duty. He used the station wagon that I kept for that purpose, but sometimes Letty went along for the ride, taking the opportunity to chat with her uncle. I missed having Letty along, but Betty was the newest of what was left of my team, and I wanted her to get the bonus, if we signed the case, and the experience. We spent half a day with the family of the passenger, and the other half of the day with the family of the deceased doctor and staff. The only person I did not sign was the wife of the pilot, on the off chance that the pilot was blamed. That could cause a big-time conflict of interest with the passengers and Gonor. During the day, my cell had died, but I thought nothing of it, other than to kick myself for forgetting to bring a charger, or extra phones. It was great having my own plane. We returned to Van Nuys airport about twelve hours after we had taken off that morning. I drove us to my place, pulled in, and waved to the night guard. Betty kissed me good night and walked to her car. I let myself in the house. I was starved. I went straight to the kitchen surprised to find Miguel and Letty in there drinking coffee. Letty jumped off the stool where she was sitting and came at me, arms open.

"Boss, I been calling all your numbers."

"I took one phone and it went dead early in the trip."

"Miguel, I'm starving. How about an omelet with the works?"

Miguel got off the stool. I saw right away that he was hurt.

"Did you guys have an accident or something?"

"Kind of," Letty replied, pulling away from me.

It was clear there was some hesitancy to tell me, so I gave them more time and asked an easy question.

"Who was the last one in? I noticed the alarm wasn't on when I opened the front door."

"My doing, Boss," Miguel said. "When you're not here, we're not as careful as we should be. I'm sorry. It will not happen again when I'm in the main house this late and you are not here. I promise."

Miguel washed his hands and put on his chef jacket.

"What is the big secret?"

"An omelet with the works coming up, Boss. How about some cinnamon rolls?"

He did not wait for an answer but put a pan under the broiler. While Miguel was cracking, separating, and whipping eggs, and keeping an eye on the cinnamon rolls, Letty poured me a cup of coffee. The scent of toasting cinnamon rolls was intoxicating. Miguel flipped them on to a plate for Letty to place in front of me. I cut the first big one with a fork and knife, chewed, sipped coffee, and looked at the two clouded faces watching me. "Good," I said. My response did not ease them one iota. "Now you tell me what's going on. Both of you are ignoring my question. What kind of accident were you in? You look okay but not okay. Shoot."

Miguel had a slight limp. Letty was untouched, but her left hand looked swollen. I could not tell if she was favoring it.

Both of them started talking at once. Letty had driven Miguel to Montebello, the closest of Melina's markets to the house. They picked up some take-out burritos inside, shopped, and packed up the wagon. They returned the carts to the store and headed back. As they were passing a parked car, it pulled out. If not for Letty, both of them would have been mowed down.

"Letty saved my life," Miguel said, "I would have been hit, but Letty was too fast. When she jumped out of the way, she shoved me so hard I ended up under the next car over. I landed hard, but the stupid car didn't hit me."

Letty said, "The driver of the car was a young Latin dude with a hat. He should have gotten out to see how we were, but no, he just sat there behind the wheel, with the car running. Staring at me like he'd never seen a woman in blue jeans before. He didn't come close to an apology, even when I got right up to his open window."

Miguel broke in. "The security guard who patrols that lot was hotfooting his way to us. We needed help. I was yelling at him to hurry."

Letty interrupted. "This creep in the car tried staring me down, smiling like he was really heavy. I gave him the finger. Bastard."

"That's when the guard reached us," Miguel said.

"He saw the guard. By the time he stomped the gas, I already had his fucking neck squeezed between my hands. My feet were braced against the car door and when I straightened my legs, he fucking flipped out of the moving car to the pavement. I landed on my back with him on top of me," Letty laughed, as tears rolled down her face.

I stopped eating my cinnamon roll.

"On top of me for three seconds. I rolled him over. You should have seen the look on his face!" she said, still laughing.

"It was crazy, Boss," Miguel said. "He'd gassed the car, and it pretty much rolled off without him, ramming two parked cars."

"So, you're okay," I said.

"We're okay," Letty said. "That's the end of it."

"That is not the end of it," Miguel said, contradicting her. "She was on top of him, right? Dodging everything he put out. He tried to punch her, but he missed, again and again. Letty got off him and the moron came after her. She pounded his chest like a punching bag, bang, bang, bang. And he had a good six inches on her, Boss. He started wheezing, 'Fuck, get your hands off me, bitch.'"

Letty could not win a fight with me, but I knew from experience that she could defend herself against me. We'd practiced so many times, she had muscle memory of all her moves. She'd be able to wipe the ground with anybody who didn't know what she did about martial arts. She'd been duking it out at Cosmo's for years now, and Cosmo is the best. He'd been my karate master since I was ten.

"Letty slapped him in the face. Fast, Boss. Her hands were a blur. She said 'Call me bitch, bitch? This is bitch slapping, bitch. Who put you up to this? You aimed for us like we were bowling pins.'"

"The security guard was there," Letty said. "Or I'd have done more than break his nose."

"Then the cops got there," Miguel said. "By the time they were out of their cars, the security guard had the guy in handcuffs. The guard was a witness, so we didn't have any cop trouble. And the cops said he was in a stolen car. Called the kid Kenny Campo."

"Proud of you both," I said. I clapped Miguel on the back and got up to kiss the top of Letty's head.

Miguel fussed with the omelet, adding the cheese, peppers, other things, and plating it. I didn't want to even think that this had been a deliberate act ordered by someone. But stranger things have happened to me and those close to me. My mind raced. Had this been planned? I pulled her out of the chair and gave her a full-on hug.

"I'm sorry this happened to you both."

Miguel answered, "It was just a kid, Boss. Joyriding in a stolen car."

"Joyriding in a parked car?" I said, dubiously.

"I don't think he intended to run us over."

"No point in speculating. The perp is in custody," I said. "We'll get to the bottom of this."

"We had considered not even telling you," Letty said.

"Of course, you had to tell me." I kissed her head again.

"Boss," Miguel said, indicating the plate he had just put at my chair.

I sat without complaint. "How about some peanut butter for the toast?"

Letty had a jar in front of me in seconds. I caught her eyeing the jar with a naughty smile, a signal that Letty's mind had moved out of the parking lot and into the bedroom.

"Does Melina know?"

"Yes, she's called three times. I assured her we were fine."

"Did she ask for me?"

Letty made a face and shrugged. "No."

I felt like Melina had abandoned me. "We should sue the market for failure to provide adequate security for their customers."

"Oh, Boss, stop. You wouldn't sue Melina, and neither would we."

I bit into peanut butter covered toast. Peanut butter, my comfort food. It hit the spot, but there was still a hollow feeling somewhere around my chest.

I told Miguel to take a day or two off till he felt better, but he looked insulted and claimed to be fine. He left the main house for his quarters. The alarm was set. Letty and I went to the spa. In the shower, I saw a mass of nasty bruises covering her back, shoulders, and buttocks. She had hit that pavement hard.

"Baby, this has to hurt."

"I get more bruised up during a workout at Cosmo's."

As true as that was, I still felt bad how she got hurt. I pulled her away from the rainfall shower head, kissing her bruises, making a gentle path to her face.

"I know that in your own way, you love me, Boss." She reached out and touched the scars left by bullet wounds from two attempts on my life.

She laughed unsteadily. "Aren't we a pair?" She matched me kiss for kiss.

Letty

How totally bitching would it be if Olga sent Boss the ring and disappeared from his life? I'm a sicko to think like that. He loves her, and she loves him and if she doesn't come back, he'll be heartbroken and that's not what I want. I don't want him for myself. I only want to be with him. I don't want this bitch chasing me out of the house, away from him. I want to be near him. I want to breathe the air he breathes. I want to watch him sleep and wake up with him in the morning. I want to keep sweating with him in the gym during our early morning workouts.

I know she's vindictive. She reminds me of a karate match against a dude who has more belts than me. The look I see when the dude is after me, and when I take a fall, the satisfaction on the dude's face. My read on the Camacho's is they are vindictive. At first, when that car pulled out and almost hit my uncle, I saw

Olga. If she wanted me dead, she'd get one of her guards to sneak up and do me. One thing for sure. That guard better be really fucking fast, because I'm fast.

I send you good vibes, Olga, wherever you are. Don't fuck with me. I don't care how many guards you have around you.

Mario

It had been twenty-one days since Olga left Los Angeles. I had stopped calling her after getting the second-hand brush off from her answering service. I really was not expecting her to call back. I thought she would just show up whenever her mad wore off. But that was not her way, I guess.

She made the call.

"Amor, I can't stand this. We can't continue like this. I am having a horrible time."

"I miss you, Olga." If I told her I was having a horrible time, it would be a lie.

"Amor, I adore you with my entire heart and soul."

"Where are you?"

"Colombia."

"Again?"

"Been at my house for a week."

"Baby, home is here."

I heard a sniff.

"You said my home was across the street." She was quiet for a moment, then said, "How I treated Letty was wrong. I was so jealous. I never thought I could be so jealous over a man." Sniff. "Only once before, I was jealous over a woman Camila wanted too much. That was because I love Camila." I had seen the two of them in bed. It was not just sex between them. In the past, there had been times when I had been with Camila and Olga when I felt like the third wheel.

"Amor, Letty can stay and live with you, with us, it's okay. I understand.

I will apologize to Letty. I will bring her a present, so she will know how much I love her."

It was not the right time to mention the market incident. I would leave it up to Letty if she even told her at all. If I mentioned it now, Olga might take it as an accusation, and that was not a door I was going to open. There was no way Olga was involved.

I told Letty about my conversation with Olga.

"I don't need for her to apologize. It's okay, already."

"Play it by ear."

"Boss, don't worry about it. I got it. I'll be nice."

"Nice?"

Letty gave me a look. "Yes, nice."

Olga

I took the time I needed for the bruises to heal. The inside part of me that Pepe bruised would never be patched up. As many times as I have let it slide, never again. He would never know I got back at him where I knew it would hurt. The first thing I did was short a deposit by three million dollars and put it in my own account. If he ever raises a hand to me again, he would pay a price, and the currency would not be money.

On the day I left for Pasadena, Felicia handed me a paper bag with several rubber bands around it. As he had done before, Pepe had sent me money. Twenty thousand dollars. I handed ten thousand to Felicia and insisted she take it. The rest I gave to Natalia for her surgery. I told her to take off for three months, and I would fix it, so she was paid for the time off. Natalia did three things for me on the long flight to Pasadena. She kept me fed with special food from the catering company. She massaged me, softly. I was still so very sore. I wouldn't be in Pasadena long. Just one night, but that would be long enough to make peace, and set everything aright. The stomach bruise was not entirely gone, but if I did not flaunt myself around, I figured Mario would not notice. Natalia noticed, and she kissed my entire body after my massage. Natalia made love to me, beautifully. Afterward, I held him for the last time. "Are you sure you want to get rid of this treasure?" I asked.

Mario

Olga called after she landed. "I'm just deplaning. Shouldn't be long. I can't wait to see you."

"I'm anxious as all hell," I said.

I hovered downstairs till I got word from the guard she was through the gates, then I went outside waiting for the limo to drive up. Her guards were all in the car with her. I put my hand up, so the driver would not come, but one of her guards opened the door before me.

"Amor, Amor. I'm home."

I picked her up and cradled her. I kissed her for a long time before I carried her inside the house. I paid no attention to the guards getting out of the limo, two of them staying near the front door, the other four headed to their quarters in the back residence.

"Any luggage?"

"Just my purse."

We kissed again in the entry foyer. Betty, Tricia, and Letty came down the steps together to welcome her home.

When I let her down, the first one she embraced was Letty. We all walked into the living room.

"Wine?" I asked.

"Si, Amor," Olga replied.

They exchanged talk and smiles. Olga gave Letty a package while I was doling out the wine. The two of them were quiet and civilized, as calm as if no blow-up had happened between them. Silly of me to think that. They never had a blow-up. They barely exchanged words. The blow-up was between Olga and me.

Later in the day, after Olga had settled in, and was in the shower, I went into my office. Letty was in the conference room. She saw me through the plate glass that separated the two spaces. Letty showed me the present Olga had given her, diamond hoops that were lovely on her. She turned her head, so I could see them better.

"It's embarrassing that she brought me a gift so expensive, or a gift at all for that matter."

"It's okay, Baby."

"I know, Boss. She's over it now. I feel it. She kissed me, and a kiss like she gave me doesn't lie."

"You'll have to demonstrate," I said.

"I will, yes." She kissed me lightly. "Enjoy your fiancée, Boss."

And she was gone, probably to her room on the floor below.

After the lights were off, the plan with Olga and me was to snuggle and sleep.

"Amor, don't be mad. I have to leave early in the morning."

I sat up. "What? You just got here."

She sat up, too. "Pepe is pissed off at me."

"For what?"

"After our argument, I slacked off completely. I cancelled all the stops I had to make and just said the hell with it and flew to Colombia. I have much to catch up on."

"Oh, Baby."

We settled into the bed, swallowed up in covers, embracing, our faces inches apart.

"Amor, seeing you was my top priority. I had to straighten out the Letty situation. One day we will have all the time in the world."

"I got it, Baby. It's cool."

She gave me a wet kiss, and I returned it.

"Do you think we should sleep or…?" She reached between my legs, her touch awakening me.

"Looks like this could be ready in a minute, Si?"

"Si."

At eight in the morning with Raul behind the wheel, Pixie's Rolls was waiting for Olga outside the door to my house. A guard held the back door open for her. As usual, Olga's Mercedes with her other guards would follow. Olga was planning to keep the Mercedes parked at Ontario Airport till her return.

It was cold. I was in sweats. Neither of us had slept. She waived breakfast, settling for coffee only, and got into the limo in a full-length mink coat and bedroom slippers.

"I'll sleep on the plane, Amor. Please go to bed and do the same."

Olga was beautiful. She was looking a little thinner, maybe even fragile. I don't know what it was. Maybe the morning light. I came close to saying I'd go with her.

I went straight to the gym. Letty was already there. I worked out for an hour, showered, put on fresh sweats. Betty and Tricia arrived at their usual time. We had breakfast at ten.

"A detective from Montebello Police called me about the parking lot thing," Letty said.

"What are they charging him with?"

"Grand theft auto and possession of a gun. I never saw the gun."

"Fuck," Betty said.

"Apparently the gun was under the seat. The detective wanted to know why I beat him up so bad."

"You got to be kidding."

"That's what I said. I told him he tried to fucking run us down. A broken nose is nothing. The guy was throwing punches at me. It was self-defense. He said if I pressed charges of attempted bodily harm, it may be hard to prove that he backed the car out intentionally to hit Miguel and me. I told him he wasn't backing out. He was flat out facing us and we saw his eyes. I also told him that Miguel and I were not planning to file a complaint, even though we gave the police on the scene a statement of what had happened."

"Good move. If we want to get even there are better ways," I said. "We don't snitch."

"Boss, they could have been badly hurt," Tricia said.

"It's okay. I'm not in for testifying. Besides, he's not going anywhere with car theft and a gun charge pending, especially with him being a felon out on parole."

"They will send him back to prison, but it won't be because you put him there," I said. "Fuck him."

"Letty, you sure?" Betty asked.

"I am sure I'm not testifying in court. If I want to get even, it's like Boss just said, there's ways. I'm not even that pissed at him."

I smiled at her. "Good girl, Baby."

"I just am not a hundred percent convinced I got to the bottom of if he acted alone."

Tricia finished eating and stood. "I'll go up and check the telex."

"I checked it when I came in," Betty said. "There was nothing."

"I got one early. One advantage of living here," Letty said, showing us all her pretty teeth. "It's a Piper. Engine stall or something. Pilot killed."

"So much death. We do so much of this, and we don't squirm when we talk about death," Betty said.

"Hey, wait a minute. Just because we don't squirm doesn't mean we don't feel," I said roughly.

"I didn't mean anything by that. Sorry, Boss."

"You never get used to it," Letty said. "What if that engine failed because someone fucked up? A product defect? A mechanic screw-up? Do you think the one responsible is going to seek out the widows and admit it?"

I kept eating. I was hungry.

At two in the afternoon, Tangles came over to give me a massage.

"You're a lifesaver," I said, lying on my big bed. I was paying a physical toll for my sleepless night. "Sorry for having to do it in bed today but I know I'm going to fall asleep. I don't want to crash on the massage table."

"Boss, no problem. And with the mirror above us, so cool."

I remember smiling and not much else. When I woke up much later, I was under the covers, basking in the fireplace's warmth. I opened one eye and saw Letty watching me.

"I love watching you sleep," Letty said.

"What time is it?"

"Time to go back to sleep."

"Get under the covers then."

I didn't have to ask twice.

I didn't get up at five to work out but slept until the phone woke me at nine something. Letty was not in bed with me. I don't know when she left.

"Amor, are you up?"

"I slept like a log. Where are you?"

"Milan, at Pepe's house. It's almost five thirty in the afternoon here."

"Did you sleep?"

"I did, Amor."

"Are you there to see Pepe?"

"No, Pepe is away. I'm going to have dinner and take a sleeping pill. I have an early morning meeting at a bank."

"Thanks for stopping by," I said.

"Amor, I wanted to stay longer."

"I didn't mean it the way it sounded."

"Good, Amor."

As I was hanging up, Letty walked in with a tray of food, followed by Caro with the bed tray.

"Morning, Boss. Bed or table?"

"Bed, please."

Caro flipped open the legs and placed the oversized tray in front of me. It was an outsized white-painted wooden tray, a design Melina would have called shabby chic, with a rim to keep anything on it from sliding off. The legs were tall enough to easily fit over me. Caro double-folded a plaid cloth over the surface before Letty placed the dishes. Miguel had rolled the silverware into the linen napkin, like a restaurant service, and provided another napkin folded like a bird of paradise, intricate enough that I always thought twice about unfolding it.

Breakfast smelled delicious. I could make out the fragrances of bread, coffee, bacon. Toasted brioche. I leaned against the headboard and looked at the different dishes Letty uncovered. She handed the silver warming cloches to Caro, revealing a single place setting of the gold-rimmed Wedgewood Melina had given me a few years ago, and two of the cups.

"Unless Letty needs something else, I think that's all, Caro."

"I'll put the cloches and the dishes in the dumbwaiter when we're done," Letty said.

I thanked Caro, and she left. Letty crawled up on the bed next to me, sitting with her legs folded under her, and buttered my toast.

"I thought you went to bed with me last night?"

"I did. Stayed all night. I got up at six, worked out, showered, checked telex, then helped Miguel in the kitchen."

"I'm tired just listening to you."

I noticed the diamond hoops as she poured me a second cup of coffee. She had her diamond bracelet on her right wrist, Rolex on her left.

"Looking good, Baby."

She gave me a peck on the cheek. Actually, she secured my coffee on the end table, straddled my legs, and leaned over the tray to give me something more than a peck. After a few minutes, she returned my coffee, and—after she snagged the extra cup and poured herself coffee that was half milk—resumed her position at my side.

"Did you and Olga talk while she was here?" I asked, dipping my crust into egg and biting into it.

"Nope. She gave me the present and kissed me. That was it. Did she say anything to you?"

"Not a word. I think that's the way Olga handles a crisis. Presents. Fast exit. Done."

"You went to sleep during your massage," Letty said.

"I was so tired."

"How you feel now?"

"I'll be fine after I shower."

"No workout?"

"Too late. I can afford to skip one."

She made a face at me. "Chicken."

I could see that Cosmo's gung-ho attitude had rubbed off on her, as it had on Jo, Niley, and Pixie. "Maybe you can give me a workout later."

"Deal, Boss."

I finished up. Letty got up from the bed and kissed me. She picked up the tray and headed for the dumbwaiter in the office.

"Have a good shower."

I watched her walk away. What a fox. Why me? Why am I so lucky?

I did not have a check from the last crash case we'd handled. Since Gonor leveled with me about the money shortage, I respected him more than before. Fino knew already I needed a backup attorney in case Gonor got to a point where he said stop sending cases or I felt he was drowning. Gonor was established as an aviation attorney so I could pass out brochures of past and present cases he had handled. I always tell the families that they can't just hire any lawyer. They need an expert in aviation to properly represent them against experts that the insurance carrier retains. Another lawyer had to have the same credentials or there would be no expertise to sell. Aviation experience is a must. Fino either couldn't find another lawyer for me or he was resisting my closure with Gonor, although closure wasn't what I planned.

I was in my office going through my mail. I had Letty doublecheck before I called Gonor.

"I'm not losing any sleep over it, but I don't have a check on that last case."

"Mario, I'll check with accounting. Did you call them?"

"You know I don't like to go around you. Have them mail me the check."

"You got it. Keep them coming."

Seeing the dishes from my breakfast had waked up something in me. Olga was in Milan, soon off to Turkey. I loved her, but I needed to see Melina. It had been ages. It didn't matter that Olga didn't want me to mess around with her. It was up to Melina. Maybe she would show me the door like she did before, that would be okay. I was having trouble dealing with Olga making orders that I not have sex with Melina.

I called Melina on her cell. "What's your schedule? Treat you to a burrito."

"Cuz, you so sweet. I'm in Hacienda Heights. Come at noon. I'll have the cook get us two giant porterhouses."

"I'll be there. Excited to see you."

"Ditto."

"That's my word," I protested.

I'd never been to the Hacienda Heights market, but had no trouble finding it. I drove myself.

Like her other markets, it was huge. Like her other markets, her second level office had windows with a good view of the entire public area. I did not know the personnel here, but the building's format was familiar, making it easy to find her. I climbed the stairs to find a small reception area behind which was a hall which presumably led to a couple of other offices.

A woman behind the desk stood when she saw me. She looked less like a secretary and more like someone you'd find manning a booth at a flea market: pale, studious-looking, hair cropped short, big earrings and lots of bright colored bracelets.

"Mr. Luna," she said, "Ms. Marron is expecting you." She would have opened the door for me, but I was there first.

"You look beautiful." I picked her up as soon as I saw her. She hugged me. We kissed long and hard.

"Missed you, Cuz."

"I missed you more."

"Don't say that." She thumped my chest.

I looked around after I set her back on her feet.

"I like this office. Nice big couch."

Her Echo Park market couch and also the conference table had borne us to joy many times.

She licked her lips, then reached for the door knob. Locked the door.

"This is where I receive my visitors," she said.

We fell on to the couch. She did not say a word about wrinkling her business suit. In minutes, we were naked. It had been a long time since we'd been together. We both climaxed in a fury under five minutes. It was good. It was very good. We sat up, leaning into the cushions and each other.

She smiled. "I needed that, Cuz."

"I have needed you." Our eyes locked. "This reminds me of way back when," I said. "Remember those first nights we spent together? We sat up all night in the apartment you decorated for me and shared our whole life histories. You inspired me to move out of a crappy rental into that Bunker Hill high rise. Seems so long ago. Back then, it was just Jo and me finding car crashes for Jake. That was right around when I brought Pixie in, and before I brought Niley in. You and me, against the world. Man, I thought we were so glam in our hot pads."

"Bunker Hills *was* glam. And remember, soon as my first market was built, you brought Niley to me. You set up Niley with that gift basket business from her garage," Melina laughed. "She had some great ideas. She inspired us to move into a new arena of catering, but I was glad when you added her to your team. You were the best neighbor. Nobody knew my name back then. I was just some orphaned girl with an inheritance and a dream."

"An orphan with a law license. And I was just some orphaned guy raised by his aunt, with a pocket full of ambition, and a couple lawyers who trusted me."

She hugged me. "What I remember is that you tried so hard to act like losing Tanis didn't tear you up. She got shot, and you blamed yourself. You had a broken heart, and I wanted to be the one to heal you. I wanted to make it all better."

"You did that, Melina."

No matter how much time we spend apart, when Melina and I get back together, it feels like we had never separated. We buttoned each other's buttons, and talked about our past until we were presentable, then Melina hit the inter-com.

The steaks were huge as promised, served on white bone china on a table in her office.

"We can't do this too often," she said. She might have been referring to the steak and her slim figure. She might have been referring to the sex.

I nodded. "We used to go for hours the second time around, and not come until we were ready."

"I'm up for seconds," she said softly, "if you are."

I touched the plate under my steak. "Remember that Wedgewood set?"

"The gold one with dragons?"

"That's the one," I said. "Ate breakfast on it this morning. The dragons told me it was past time for me to give you a call."

She sighed a little. "Have you set a date yet?"

"No date." I felt like I was apologizing, though I did not mean to. "We were going to set a date, then nothing happened."

I told Melina about the Letty situation. How Olga had been jealous, and then apologized. Turns out, she already knew. Pixie had told her.

"Why did you agree on my coming by today and not before?"

"Because you called me. Olga doesn't want me around you, but you and I, we're still tight, Cuz."

"That's who you are now? You let someone else draw a red line you don't cross?"

"You're going to marry Olga. I am not going to mess that up for you."

"When I see you, like right now, I don't know what the fuck I want more than you."

Melina didn't reply. I could see in her face so much that she was not saying. We ate in silence. I knew that Melina would never marry me because of our age difference, and I knew I would never just move in to her home nor she move in to mine.

The next day, I was in my office when Olga called from her plane about to take off from Turkey.

"I'm headed back to Milan, Amor. I miss you."

"I miss you, too."

"Amor, you never talk about Melina anymore. Is she okay?"

"She's fine. I had been wondering the same. I went over to her market in Hacienda Heights and had lunch with her."

"Say hi to her for me."

I wondered if Olga was having me followed. I changed the subject. "Are you coming home for Thanksgiving?"

"I'm sorry, Amor. I have business."

"I'm not much of a Thanksgiving person," I said, recalling one Thanksgiving when I threw a big dinner in Casa Luna One, the one that was torched. Melina and I had held it together.

In bed that night, I told Letty about my talk with Olga.

"You think she has someone watching you?"

"It is not like I ever see anyone. I check my rear view mirror a lot, just because I've become so careful. Fuck, maybe there's a bug in my car."

"So, what? You told her you did see her. If she already knew, that was a great answer, no?"

"It was the truth. If she had asked me if we fucked..."

"What would you have said?"

"I would have lied. She's made it clear that if I have sex with her, I'll break her heart."

Letty moved to my lap. She was naked. We both were. One could say she took advantage of the situation, but it is not like I resisted.

"Naughty boy," she teased me, not only with her words, but also moving her body in just the way I needed most in that moment. "You went over there to take care of business. Where did you do it?"

I kissed her. "You are so dirty, Letty. Sometimes you remind me of Pixie."

"Tell me. Long time since you and me and Melina...I dug watching you two." Sometimes when Letty laughed, it was like a funny gurgle.

I remembered my afternoon with Melina. Before and after the steak. "Couch," I said.

"Boss, if you don't have the energy tonight, we can snooze or watch a movie." Still on my lap, she kissed my neck. I could feel her soft pubic hair on my growing centerpiece.

I slid off the bed and she rolled off me on the mattress. "Boss, what gives?"

"Got to shower, Baby." I could smell Melina on my skin.

As if I had conjured her, later that night, Pixie called. I could hear loud music in the background, but Pixie walked away from it, shutting the door so the noise dimmed. We were on a land line, so the call could be longer than thirty minutes.

"We're in Amsterdam. I told Jason I had been here twice with you on cases, but we came here anyway. Maybe it was the lure of waffles," she giggled.

"You sound happier than you did the last time we talked," I said.

Silence.

"Pix?"

"I want to go home, I want to get back to work. Jason shines me on. His attention is totally on Lainie."

"Baby, you went from giggles to sounding desperate."

"Not desperate. Fed up."

"Then split."

"I'm going to put up with it a little longer. Hopefully, I can take Lainie back with me. I want to get her situated at the house."

"You mean at Olga's house?"

"Yes. I haven't signed off on the deal yet, but Olga said I can lease the house from her, as is, with all the help. She also said that even if we don't make a deal on the lease, it's a good idea for Lainie to move in. She can commute to the studio in Hollywood and fly to Mexico City in three hours when they need her at RIALTO."

"Sounds like Olga is doing you righteous," I said.

"Yeah, is that sweet or what? Olga said to box up Lainie's stuff and move her in. Told me to move out of the guest bedroom and into the master bedroom."

The master bedroom where Melina and I spent our Sundays for so long. Seemed strange to hear Pixie say this. I am not sure why.

"Sounds like a plan, Baby. I'm glad this Jason-Lainie thing doesn't seem to be interfering with your relationship with her."

I heard a long sigh. "Not yet."

"Let the chips fall where they fall, Pix."

"I am. I don't need Jason, and Lainie needs me. She's a big girl. She doesn't want to finish school. Fuck it, nothing I can do. I'm stuck here watching her head for heartbreak, unable to do anything about it. Parenthood sucks."

"Pix, you have one more apartment to rent," I said, only half kidding. If she moved across the street, she'd have the better half of her duplex to rent out now.

"I need it as a backup," she said, laughing. "I may need it some day when the bubble bursts on me."

"Not a chance, Baby. Bubble is never going to burst. You are rising. No limits."

"Boss, stop saying things like that. I just came. Damn, I'm all wet."

I laughed. "Still my same nasty girl."

"Forever your girl. Yeah, Boss. Never going to change."

"I love you, Pix."

I heard her sniff.

"Love is not a strong enough word to express how I feel about you, Mario."

It was the first time since I was eighteen that I had a Thanksgiving without Pixie and Lainie in on it. Melina begged off. She couldn't make it because her markets were open for the first time that year and she planned on visiting several of the locations during the day. The stores were going to close early so the employees could get home, but she didn't plan on quitting early. I was not entirely convinced she had business reasons.

Melina said, "Johnson and I are having dinner at the Echo Park store. I'm having a feast prepared for us."

Olga

It is very difficult for me to pretend like he didn't beat me up. I must be strong because I've always been strong. I just clipped him for another million today and a million yesterday, that makes five million, and I'm not done yet.

If he touches me again like that, even if he just slaps me like he's done for years, I won't let him get away with it again. No more Miss Doormat for me. I wish I had the skills that Pixie and Letty have. I don't have karate and I don't have guns, but I have money. With Pepe, money is the key to the kingdom. Money doesn't just talk with him. It sings, and dances, and it's the whole shebang. It's the only thing that matters to him, the only chink in his armor.

Has he ever slapped Camila around? They've argued in front of me like a couple of feral cats, but I've never seen him get violent with her. Would she have told me? I don't think Camila would have kept it secret. I don't think she could be as complacent as I am pretending to be.

Melina

This nonsense of me dressing like a bank manager needs to go this coming year. I've been doing this so many years. It's getting old. I envy women who wear jeans, simple stuff, comfortable. Look out New Year, change is coming. I have nothing to prove that I can't prove while being comfortable. I don't have anyone to answer to, so I might as well please myself.

Thanksgiving at Aunt Carmen's, if I attended, would result in another argument between him and Olga. I hate to do it, but I will stay away. I should feel good that the bitch was jealous enough to give me six million for my house. That's two million over market value and then the market for a house like that is limited to a handful. I'm sad not to be sharing Thanksgiving with him, sad to break our tradition. Mario doesn't understand that tradition means nothing to that fiancée of his. She wants to erase everything that came before her and rewrite him in her image.

I have Gilberto cooking a turkey for Johnson and me. Special stuffing and a prime rib with all the trimmings. I told him to stay thirty minutes after closing and set it up for me up here in my office then he can leave. I have six hours to go. The stores are so busy. I should have opened on Thanksgiving from the start, but I wanted to give the employees a full day off. Paying double time and letting everyone off at six gives everyone a chance to get home for Thanksgiving dinner and extra cash for working the holiday.

There's really very little for me to do right now. I'm at my desk, alone. Each market has a manager, and managers have assistants. The assistants have heads of departments who handle the day to day operations. Everyone has their own little thread, and they all manage to make knots that only I can untie. I walk over to the glass windows overlooking the packed market. The meat department is humming with activity, a double line of people waiting with a number on a ticket that will be called when there is someone ready to help them. The kitchen, my pride and joy, has seven lines, depending on what the customer wants to buy. Aisles of food from Mexico, hundreds of items made in the states that the chain markets have on their shelves. My produce department is as big or bigger than any statewide chain store. My bakery is a delight to watch, a long line of customers holding their tickets waiting on cakes, pies, pan dulce, cinnamon rolls, and cream puffs.

My decision not to marry Mario because I am ten years older, how stupid is that? Not stupid at all. When I hit sixty, he's fifty. If I make it to seventy, he's sixty. I could never bear to wither away while he is so much younger, and so vital.

I see Betty on the monitor, here to play masseuse for me, a special favor because I don't know Tangles well enough to ask her to give up two hours of her Thanksgiving. A two-hour massage will cut the time to closing.

"You look fantastic," I tell her.

"Melina, come on. Jeans and a sweater."

"I like Tangles, but I miss you."

Betty smiles. Pats my hand.

"You should have let Johnson bring the massage table up those stairs."

"Good exercise. It's a good way to get my workout."

I lock the door to my office, undress in the bathroom, and by the time I come out, it's not dark but just right. The table is waiting, the blinds are down, the lights are out.

"I miss the candles and the ambiance," I tell Betty.

"Close your eyes, the ambiance will sweep in. Want soft or rock?" I hear the music from her little portable tape player as she switches it on.

"Soft, please. Are you having dinner with Mario at his aunt's place?" I ask.

"I'm invited but I passed, going home."

I know she has had trouble with her parents. "Maybe you should drop in on your parents?"

Betty starts working on my back.

"I didn't tell you. They moved to Oakland."

"Really, why?"

I could feel her shrug.

"Even if they were here, I wouldn't go over."

"That bad?"

"That bad. Letty told me you weren't going over to Aunt Carmen's?"

"I'm having dinner here after the store closes, then going home to relax. Can I convince you to stay and eat with us?"

"That's a sweet offer. I'm going home to relax, too."

"Tell me you will be alright?"

"Melina, you are the sweetest person I know. I promise, I will be fine."

"Okay, I'll shut up, so you can concentrate on my body."

"Precious body," Betty says. I feel a little tiny bite on my right buttocks.

"Feels good. Do the other side," I tell her.

Mario

Niley and Jo did their own thing for Thanksgiving, but we talked by phone. Betty would have come, but she called it off, said she had a bad cold. Letty said she was lying. There was no cold. I did not ask. Tricia was spending Thanksgiving with Bill. She didn't volunteer details about their dinner, and I didn't feel it appropriate to ask.

Miguel had plans with one of his boyfriends. All my household help had plans of their own. I wasn't sure what they were doing for dinner but figured Miguel had fixed them up.

That left Letty and me to spend Thanksgiving with my Aunt Carmen. Letty was dressed to the nines and wore her mink. I was in jeans, a sweater Aunt Carmen had given me, loafers, and one of my winter jackets.

"You two look so lovely together." I pretended not to hear. It was Aunt Carmen's theme for the evening. She dropped that line so many times that I stopped counting. Subtle, she's not.

Letty blushed.

"How come Olga did not come?"

"Auntie, I told you, she's working."

"No one works Thanksgiving."

"Olga is out of the country in some country where they don't have American Thanksgiving." I know I overdid the sarcasm, but Aunt Carmen appreciates sarcasm when she hears it. She can dish it out, too.

"I invited Melina to come but she blamed it on work, too."

"More food for us," Letty said, piling stuffing on her plate.

We laughed. With just us, it was a shorter dinner than usual. We were out of there by seven thirty. After dinner, Letty and I returned home. Three of my guards were around the gas fire pit across from the driveway, though they weren't all on duty. The flames were beautiful, surrounded by countless landscape lights, trees, and shrubs. Quito didn't usually work nights, but he was in the guardhouse with two of my German Shepherds. No one was in the main house, but it was lit up as if there was a party going on. Letty went around dimming or turning off lights as we moved toward the staircase.

At the foot of the staircase I pulled her gently toward me.

"I don't think I told you how beautiful you look tonight."

"Aw, Boss, thank you. Are we smoking or drinking?"

"Your choice, Baby."

"Let's get stoned."

"Deal."

We smoked in my bedroom. The TV was on, but we weren't really watching, thanks to the weed. Letty went to her bedroom to get ready for bed. The fireplace wasn't on, but the house thermostat was perfect. I was still a little too full of Aunt Carmen's Thanksgiving dinner and started for the bathroom to take a shower but stopped in the door and looked behind me, toward my end table.

I had a feeling.

I looked at the phone and then it rang. Ten minutes till eight. It rang a second time. Letty yelled out that she would get it. I waited for Letty to yell that it was for me. She did not yell.

She ran in.

"Mario."

The way she called me by name, I knew it wasn't good. She was white-faced, and her voice sounded broken. I froze. My imagination stopped, my head filled with a black fog of anxiety and expectation.

"Something terrible."

"Who was it?"

"Julio, a security guard at Melina's market in Echo Park."

I felt a chill.

"Who?" *No please. Not Melina.* I could not get another word out of my mouth.

"Melina and Johnson were shot in the parking lot." Letty was crying. "A helicopter flew them to a hospital. Julio doesn't know where."

Since the age of ten, I had been taught never to panic, but this was Melina. I was panicking. I gripped Letty about the arms, one hand on each of her forearms.

The phone rang. Letty had to elbow me in the chest to get through to my brain. I let go of her. She answered the phone and handed it over to me. It was a man, talking before the phone was at my ear. I struggled to understand him. His was the voice in the nightmare in language that was not quite understood.

"Mr. Mario, it's Julio. The police officers told me they are taking them to Queen of Angels Hospital here in Echo Park."

"Did you see Melina? Was she alive?"

"Miss Melina and Johnson were alive when they left."

I slammed down the phone.

"She's at Queen of Angels. Let's go."

"Boss, your jacket, shoes."

I must have put on the jacket and shoes, but I don't recall doing it. Time lost meaning. We were in the car. I had to slam on the brakes to avoid hitting the slow-opening gates. I heard noise, sound of nothing blasting my ears. A buzz of silence. We squealed through the city, running lights, screaming tires.

"Easy, Boss. I know you don't want me to drive."

Queen of Angels is where they had taken Melina after her car accident in front of the Grand Central Market in downtown Los Angeles. That was the day we met. I don't pray often, but I was praying that my knowledge of her would not be packaged so neatly. Let me not lose her now.

In my head, a litany ran. I know Letty talked to me, but I could not hear beyond the dialogue in my head. I raced through the streets. God, please don't take her away, please, God.

"Who could have done this?" Letty asked.

She asked more than once. I heard her belatedly, as if from a long distance. It was hard to focus. Hard to keep my voice normal.

"Julio said some guy in the parking lot."

My mind was racing. No suspects yet, only facts. I knew how Olga felt about Melina. Only a dumbass would not consider Olga a suspect. But Melina had always been afraid of a guy who was in jail, the brother of her father's killer. I remembered all the people I loved and lost. I thought of Tanis, Niley's sister who had died in my arms. I thought of Sami, victim of a terrorist bomb in London. I could not lose Melina this way. Why does death follow me around?

I pulled up to the ER entrance and got out.

"Park the car and find me inside."

Letty slid over to the driver's seat.

The Cuz thing started between us here at this hospital. I told hospital personnel that I was Melina's cousin. A lie. Neither of us had known how important she would become to me.

My eyes were full of tears I refused to shed. She had to be okay.

I made it to the desk, interrupting everything.

"Melina Marron," I said. "Shot. Where is she? How is she?" There were three people in line. I towered over them. No argument.

Someone behind the desk answered. A voice. I didn't register who. "She's going right to surgery. You'll need to wait there. Someone will be out to talk to you."

Two policemen came through an unmarked door by the desk. They could have been there for any reason, but I went in where they had come out. I saw a doctor. I used my size and my confidence like a battering ram and did not give him a chance not to answer. He didn't brush me off.

"My fiancée was shot and brought here by helicopter. I need to know about her. There was also her driver."

"She's in critical condition. Going into surgery in a few minutes."

"Is she going to make it?"

He pointed at a doctor walking towards the surgery doors. Big red sign. Medical Personnel only.

"She's the doctor you want to talk to."

I reached the doctor as she got to the doors. They opened in front of her.

"Doctor, my fiancée has been shot. I was told you will be attending her."

If she had gone through, I'd have followed her, but she stopped. She wore a pin on her white coat.

Patricia Haines.

She didn't brush me off.

"Yes, I have to scrub up."

"Is she going to be okay Dr. Haines? Can I see her?"

"She's very unstable. She has bullets in her chest and maybe her stomach. Follow me."

I walked behind her.

Melina was on a bed, three nurses around her. "You got about two minutes. She is out but you can see her. I'll see you after surgery."

I picked up her hand and kissed it. "Melina, can you hear me? Baby."

Melina's eyes were closed but the edges of her lips curved up in a smile. I felt my tears fall. Two nurses moved a few steps away. The third was on the other side of the gurney, pressuring a wound so it would not bleed.

Melina's eyes were still closed. Her fingertips moved slightly, beckoned me to move close. She whispered in my ear, a breath of sound.

"Don't talk, Baby. I love you. Save your strength."

"Listen to me." Her voice was a thin breath. "Everything I own is yours. So glad you came to see me before I go."

"You're not going anywhere," I said, trying to force my will on fate. I was ready to do some serious bargaining with God. "You're going to live. Promise."

Her eyes opened. She looked up at me, her lips a shade of blue paler than the sheets. "For you, Cuz, anything."

Melina

I'm clinging to a wall. I look down and I can barely see green grass far below. If I let go, I will die. I need to be strong, need to hold on but I'm losing my grip. I don't want to fall. I don't want to die. I hear his voice, telling me to hang on. I'm losing my grip, but I can't disappoint him. Fingers slippery, and such pain everywhere. Can't keep my eyes open. So tired. I feel my eyes close, hands relax but the wall comes with me into the darkness.

Mario

I stepped aside as four nurses moved her from the bed to a gurney. I could not see her anymore, blocked first by nurses, then behind another door on her way to surgery. A Latin nurse was last to leave.

She touched my shoulder. "Stay positive," she told me.

I nodded, wiping away tears. "Do you know about her driver Johnson?"

"I'm sorry. He didn't make it."

I shook my head. Johnson had been my long-time friend, once the doorman of the apartment building where Melina and I had lived.

I met Letty in the main waiting room and went to another waiting room near surgery. We were the only ones there.

I spent way too much time in hospitals. I could not count the number of times I'd been here, meeting the families of people dying inside. I had the words in my head again, the prayer or maybe just pleading with God. *God, please don't take her away, please, God.*

I had pleaded this way when Sami had been dying, too.

"I got a chance to talk to her." I leaned my head against the wall, my eyes shut as I pictured Melina pale and weak and surrounded by nurses and doctors. I felt tears run down my face.

"Tell me she's going to be okay. Oh, God." Letty's voice cracked.

"Johnson didn't make it. The nurse told me he was DOA."

Letty hugged me. I did not open my eyes. It was midnight, four hours since we'd gotten the news. I heard Letty dial and reach Olga and tell her I would call her later. She reached Jack Fino. Letty told the team to stay home, promising to let them know as soon as we had news. She followed up until her brick ran out. Then she used mine. Then she used one of the pay phones in the hall.

The waiting room got quiet. I opened my eyes and saw that Letty had managed to fall asleep.

My aunt had always told me if you really need something to happen, ask the Virgin of Guadalupe. I was praying with all my might. I closed my eyes again and prayed to the Virgin of Guadalupe.

Virgencita por favor, salva a Melina, por favor, Virgencita, no te la lleves.[22]

I left Letty in the waiting room asleep and went into the hospital's little chapel. It was late, and no one else was there. I walked up to the altar. It wasn't anything fancy, but it brought back memories of when I was a boy. I stopped, turned around, and walked back to the entrance. It was a tiny chapel with a red carpet leading down the center, stained glass, candles, a big wooden cross. I got on my knees, and that is how I went to the altar, on my knees. It was only a short distance.

I prayed to the Virgin of Guadalupe.

If only you will help Melina get well, if she survives, I will fly to Mexico City and enter the church and pay you homage.

I have not begged so hard for divine help since I was a boy, but I prayed as hard as a man can pray.

My friends and I have a stash of men's magazines we circulate between us, naked pictures, sex pictures. Boys will be boys, in spite of aunts. Aunt Carmen found a magazine, and now I find myself on my knees, crawling to the altar to beg for God's forgiveness. I feel the rough old carpet through the fabric of my trousers. I hear people whispering and rustling in the pews. I feel their eyes on me. I inhale the dust of the old church in my nostrils. The path down the side aisle stretches on forever. All the Catholic kids are watching—Japanese, Mexican, and American alike. Carson is in a pew, giggling though I had covered for him. It was his father's magazines which were responsible for my humiliating crawl. But the crawl is something else. Now my heart is aching, dying. The mag-

---

[22] Virgencita please save Melina, please Virgencita, do not take her.

azines are nothing. I pray for Melina, my heart heavy with the weight of her soul. At the altar, the priest awaits, his face stern, blank, expressionless. I whisper to him, "I am sorry for these sins and all the sins of my whole life." Somehow neglecting Melina is one of those sins. "If only you will help Melina get well, if she survives, I will fly to Mexico City and enter the church and pay you homage." The blank expression clears. The ancient face smiles down at me, beaming, kindlier than I have ever seen him in my life, beams of light coming from him like he is a candle or a sun. The light hurts my eyes, and I force them open, finding myself in the dim hospital waiting room in a metal chair beside Letty.

I was not the boy I had been, but I hoped the dream was a sign that God and the Virgin had not forgotten me.

Around five in the morning, Melina's doctor found me in the waiting room.

"It's touch and go," Dr. Haines said. "She lost a lot of blood. You can donate if you want. There's not a shortage, but it always helps. And it will make you feel better, like you are doing something. You don't need to match her blood type. The blood bank will give her the credit. I am hoping the sutures in her stomach will hold. She's in recovery being monitored closely."

When the doctor left. I hugged Letty. I trusted my dream that felt like I had made a deal.

"I think she's going to make it."

"Yes, she will, Mario. She's strong."

I was frustrated at being able to do nothing. I followed the doctor's directions. Letty and I gave blood, but it hardly took any time at all. We returned to the waiting room.

At six or seven, I was advised that Melina was back in surgery. I was wracked with anxiety and snapped at Jo when she came by with a picnic basket for us packed with turkey sandwiches and frozen cans of coke. She came wearing sunglasses to hide her puffy eyes. Miguel brought by a thermos of turkey soup and I snapped at him too. Not knowing the shooter made me even more upset.

We were no longer alone in the waiting room. Seven people had joined us, each of them sitting in their own pain-filled bubbles, worry written on their faces. Letty and I went to the cafeteria to get coffee, shared our sandwiches and soup with two of Melina's store managers that I knew from years ago when I partnered with Melina in her first market. I did not share my dream.

"I didn't know you were here," I said, shaking hands, introducing Letty to Marco and Bub.

"There's a bunch of us in the main waiting room," Marco said. He had developed a paunch and an indoor complexion since I'd last seen him. Bub still looked the same.

I brought them up to date.

"What time do the stores open?" I asked.

"In about an hour, at six."

"All the stores should open as usual."

"It's covered," one of them said to me.

"If you give me your numbers, Letty will call with updates."

"Just one number is all you need," Bub said. "We have a phone tree."

"Good idea," Letty said. She went off to the pay phone and told Jo to organize a phone tree on our end.

Time was crawling. We'd been there for over twenty-four hours. Dr. Haines found us in the surgery waiting room and woke me from a sound sleep. My bones felt like one of those collapsible clothes racks, with an impossible number of twisted joints bent the wrong way. I looked up at her bleary eyed, wondering why she didn't look as exhausted as I felt.

"I think we fixed the bleed. She has a better chance now." She smiled at me gently. "Go home. I promise to call the minute there is any news. She's going to be out for hours. I may have to induce a coma to keep her still."

When I awoke from a similar coma in London, Melina had been there for me. I had not been shot, but I had been injured in a bomb blast. I was reluctant to leave, but with some persuasion, agreed to go home. On the way out, we ran into Pixie's driver, Raul, in the main waiting room.

"She's out of surgery. We're going home for a while to clean up, maybe get a few hours of shut eye."

"Boss, I drive you. I have Pixie's car here."

I was so tired, I put up no argument. It was dark outside, but he was wearing sunglasses. He took them off when we hit the parking lot. In the harsh light, I saw his eyes were swollen. I was too tired to talk, but heard Letty bring up Johnson. I had not known that Johnson had taken Raul under his wing. Raul was broken up over Johnson's death. It hurt to remember that my old friend was gone. I left my car at the hospital. Letty and I dropped off to sleep as soon as we climbed into the back seat for the short ride home.

"Wake up, Boss," Jo said. I opened my eyes to find her in the back seat. Letty had already gone into the house. I found myself leaning on Jo, more for the comfort than the physical support. I found my entire team crowded just inside the door. Their hugs and kisses disturbed my weak control, and I found myself in tears. I was glad Cosmo was not there to see me so shattered. Even if I can break a stack of cinder blocks in one chop, he would have shamed me for my lack of control.

I ended up in the spa where I dragged myself through cycles of hot and cold, wet steam and dry heat broken up with the icy jacuzzi, with Letty next to me, both of us too anxious to sleep. Betty and Tangles gave Letty and me massages with instructions to wake us in two hours. They waited four. While we were out, someone put our phones on to charge. A full charge takes ten hours. Good thing I owned six.

Before I left, I had to call Carson. He would remember the name that was eluding me. It was almost six a.m. I had a feeling I knew who the shooter was, but I couldn't remember the name of the asshole Melina had always feared would be released from prison and come after her. I called Carson from my office, waking him up from a sound sleep.

"Hey man," he said, yawning into the phone. "I heard about Melina on the news."

"They took three or four bullets out of her, but she has a hell of a will to live," I said. "You remember when Pixie and I went up to San Quentin to see Pélon about the guy who broke into Melina's father's store?"

"One of the Vicario brothers. Bruno was the one who survived."

Bruno Vicario. I remembered the name. No connection with Bruno Bruno, my former security guard. Vicario's brother had shot Melina's father during a robbery. Melina had used the store's gun to shoot back. At least she'd killed the bastard. Too bad she hadn't killed them both.

There had been no news from Dr. Haines, and I hoped no news was good news. Six hours after we left the hospital, we returned. Raul drove all of us in Pixie's limo, not only Letty and me, but also Niley, Jo, Tricia, and Betty.

Letty brought six of my cell phones in a briefcase. Four of them were fully charged, and she had also brought several chargers. At the hospital, I met with Melina's attorney, Carlos Munoz. He was a senior citizen, gone from gray to white hair, but he was as canny and wise as I remembered him a decade ago. He had been Melina's father's lawyer since he set foot on American soil, and after her father's death, he had steered her (and her inheritance) toward her current prosperity. I understood his sense of responsibility. Melina had considered him close as family. Her mother had died when Melina was young, and she had witnessed her father's murder in his own store. Her last relative, an aunt, had left Melina alone in the world right out of high school. Carlos had found her a probate lawyer, and had helped manage the insurance money, and the cash from the sale of her father's assets. Melina had put herself through college at USC and then law school, graduated, passed the bar, and took off for Europe for six months. When she returned, she had an accident, and that was when we met. I pulled her out of her little car just before it went up in flames. Where her father's small store had once stood, she built a market from the ground up. We became partners in that store. Our friendship had weathered the break-up of our business relationship, and plenty of disagreements and misunderstandings. We'd had rocky times, but always weathered them. I prayed we would weather this.

"Melina will pull through," Carlos told me. "She's strong."

"For sure," I agreed, hoping she was strong enough.

"In case it doesn't go that way, you will have to take control of the markets and her other assets until you decide what to do with it all."

I interrupted him.

"I am not going to talk about that, Carlos. She's going to live."

"She would be angry if we don't discuss it. I waited for you to arrive. I knew I would find you here."

"Okay, we have discussed it. It is enough."

Carlos continued as if I had not stopped him. "The managers will take care of the stores as they do now. They know you are who will take control if—"

"We are going to stay positive," I interrupted again. "I will hear nothing else."

Carlos filed a release and consent that had been prepared long ago.

"We are putting her in a medically-induced coma," Dr. Haines said. "I don't think it will be long. Normally we do this for brain injuries but in her case, I want her to be motionless. The bullet did some serious damage in there. Three bullets were bad, but we got them out and everything is sutured up. It's her stomach we're working on. Damage from the fourth bullet."

The doctor's down-tilted light amber eyes were very kind. Her skin had a yellowish tone, probably a fading tan that was not helped by reflected light from the green walls of the room we were in. A surgeon's cap covered her dirty blonde hair, but I had seen it earlier in a pony tail. A mask hung loosely around her neck. The doctor's coat was gone, but she was in brown scrubs.

"Thank you, Doctor. I know she's in good hands."

She looked from me to her hands, and back. "May I be entirely honest?"

My heart lurched, as I feared the doctor was going to share some terrible thing about Melina's condition. I swallowed. "I expect nothing less."

"This hospital is very old, and we don't have everything we should. There is talk they may shut the place down. I don't know Miss Marron personally, but I know of the big market she has here in Echo Park and heard about a number of others she has all over town. If she were my family, I would relocate her."

"Doctor, what is the very best place she should be?"

"Cedars. I could get in a big jam over—."

I interrupted her.

"Do you have privileges over there? She already has a very good doctor."

She shook her head.

"I regret you won't be there."

She handed me a card. "Call this doctor. He can arrange to move her by helicopter or ambulance. I'll discuss that with him. She's in a coma, so now may be a good time. I am worried about the next three or four days. She's better off there."

Feeling a huge surge of gratitude, I clutched both of her hands, and could have kissed them. "Dr. Haines, I owe you." I could not resist pulling her into a hug. She patted my back lightly, like a butterfly, and pulled away.

"No worries, Mr. Luna. It's my job. I will brief him. Dr. Stein is the best there is. Give it thirty minutes, then call him."

When I was in the car crash business, I did all the hospitals except for Cedars. Most of those patients were professionals who didn't need any help finding a lawyer to get them compensation for someone rear ending them or making a left turn in front of them.

My team pointed out what I already knew, that Oscar had died at Cedars during surgery, and he too had been in a coma. Melina wasn't having surgery. She'd already had two surgeries. I trusted her doctor. I respected the nerve of her advising me to move her from that hospital.

I walked out to the car with my team behind me, and we huddled inside as it heated up. It was cold enough that we could see our breath. I was thankful for my warm jacket. I brought them up to date, then made the call. Three hours later, Dr. Haines, a nurse and a paramedic rode in the ambulance with Melina to Cedars-Sinai Hospital. I walked with her through the hospital from the room to the ambulance, surrounded by a cluster of nurses, doctors, and orderlies. She was pale and unconscious on the gurney, bundled under blankets, bristling with tubes and gadgets. I dispersed the team.

"Letty and I will stay in touch."

"We're temporarily moving into Casa Luna," Jo said.

"Good. Miguel will keep you fed."

Letty drove us from Angels to Cedars. I returned Fino's call.

"Cedars is the best. Good decision," Fino said.

I called Olga.

"Amor, I've been waiting to hear from you since Letty called last night," she said. "How is she?"

"Too soon to tell."

I cried. Olga cried. At least I thought she cried. I just wasn't sure what to think.

The phone went dead. I called back again. I wanted to believe that my fiancée had nothing to do with this. And why was I even thinking that way?

After Melina was safely established at Cedars, I left Letty there, and went home for a shower and a change of clothes. While I was getting ready, Pixie arrived.

"You're a sight for sore eyes," I told her. I brought her up to date, and we both broke down a couple of times. "Did Jason come with you? Where is Lainie?"

"She's asleep at the house. Not at home. At Melina's. I mean, Olga's. We dropped Jason off in London and came as quick as we could."

"Thanks for coming."

She hugged me. "Please don't thank me. I love her."

Having Pixie around was a great comfort. Officially, she stayed with Lainie at Olga's house, but most of her time was split between my house and the hospital, waiting for Melina to be waked up. RIALTO was getting cranky about getting Lainie back to Mexico City, and for Pixie to get ready for the Spanish tour pushing her next album. Neither of them was budging until the doctors gave a favorable report. Jason sent his plane. I promised she would get daily reports.

Dr. Haines drove to Cedars daily to check on Melina. The internist in charge, Renaldo Stein, was Dr. Haines friend.

Niley was at the hospital, and I was at home when Renaldo called to say Melina was in the process of being weaned from the coma meds and off the respirator. She'd been out for almost a week. He said if all went well, it would take anywhere from twelve to seventy-two hours for her to wake up. I waited twelve hours before I went in again, determined to be there when she woke up. I arrived around four p.m., but she did not rouse till four a.m., during that time when nurses go around disturbing people with early morning tests. An orderly had left the door open, letting in the noise of someone down the hall making a racket. I had been sitting in ICU in a miserable excuse for a chair and saw Melina open her eyes. She saw me first, and then glanced at the IV bottle and the tube running into her arm, bruises everywhere from someone's attempts to find her veins.

"What the fuck?"

That was the first time since the shooting that I had the feeling she was going to be okay.

Six days later, Melina was moved from the ICU to a private room. Letty and Betty were manning the telex without me, and Tricia continued checking out properties for me. My team went back to sleeping at their own homes, but I did not much notice their absence since I was spending most of my time at the hospital.

Chapter 18
December 1984
Recovery

Mario

Melina's private hospital room looked like a florist's shop. I had brought in an arrangement every day for several days, hundreds of Marron Market employees and managers were sending them, and there were three potted California poppies from Mayor Tom Bradley who had made speeches at the grand opening of each of Melina's markets. My recent arrangement was on the bedside table, two big rubber trees had been moved to the hall, some were crowded on the window ledge, and the rest were blanketing every surface including the floor. Most of the deliveries were piling up at the nurse's stations. The bed was made with gaily patterned Burberry sheets, and a stack of extras on standby for changes. Only Cedars Sinai Hospital allowed such things as personal linens like this.

"Patricia, how fucking long am I going to be on this bland diet?"

It was not the first time that Melina used choice words.

"I'd say another two weeks."

"I hate you!"

Dr. Haines smiled. "You don't hate me. I dug those mean bullets out of you and went back in to patch up the leak in your tummy."

"Sadist! What the fuck did you use? A rusty spoon?"

Melina was feeling better.

"Yes ma'am. That's exactly what I used. And sewed you up with barbed wire to keep you on your toes." Patricia could hold her own with Melina. "I will see you this time tomorrow, Melina. Try not to burn the ears of your orderlies too much."

Dr. Haines beckoned me into the hall.

"Sorry, doctor. She does have a mouth."

"I am glad Melina is feeling better," she laughed. She and Melina had struck up an instant friendship even though for Dr. Haines, it had to be like doctoring Lenny Bruce.

"What are you doing out there? Fucking in the hall?" Melina's voice carried from the room.

People up and down the corridor hurried off, some of them smiling, some of them turning red.

Dr. Stein was an older man. He did not have Patricia's sense of humor, so Melina's mouthy attitude gave him a rough time.

"I can get all this medical attention at home. I'll hire a nurse, two nurses."

"Be patient, Miss Marron. You will be home soon."

Melina

For years I have been expecting this bastard to be released from prison and come after me. I became a marksman and have carried a gun for over ten years. I always said, as long as I see it coming I can handle anything, primarily referring to the brother of the dirtbag who killed my father, who I killed minutes after. I let my guard down, and I almost went to my grave, and poor Johnson is dead now.

I'm so happy to be alive and so sad that Johnson is dead. I'm supposed to be happy that I didn't die. I'm bursting with anxiety. I'm used to days full of work. Lying around is killing me.

My hairdresser, Lupita comes in the morning to wash and blow dry my hair. Yesterday, Miguelito did a manicure and pedicure that took two hours. My nails were a disaster.

I still have tubes but not as many as before. I get up and walk four times a day, hauling around the tube tree that's on wheels, up and down the hallways. A nurse walks with me. The doctors limit my walks to ten minutes, still afraid of my stomach acting up. That bastard will pay for putting me through this and especially for killing my friend, Johnson.

When I asked, both doctors cringed at the thought of me getting a massage, but finally approved Tangles to massage me, but only my feet. When Mario comes in to see me, he kisses me. My libido is killing me. Will I be able to fuck again? When?

My brain seems fried. How would I know my brain is fried?

I got a call from Olga.

"Melina, when you get released from the hospital, come back to your house, I'm not there, Pixie is seldom there and Lainie, well, she's absolutely never there."

Mario had invited me to come stay at Casa Luna. I gave Olga the same answer I gave Mario. "Jo tells me my master bedroom will be ready, and the gym will be retrofitted." TJ had the specifications from an independent physical therapist that Cedars recommended. I knew TJ was working day and night to get it finished.

I have a way to go before they let me out of here. At least I am finally off the liquids. I've been dying for food I could chew.

Two days from now, Christmas. I feel bad that Mario didn't put up a tree and has no plans to have a party as he has in the past. He told me there's next year. Yes, there is next year but we never know if we'll be around. Things can change in a split second.

Mario

In the weeks since she'd been shot, I had met with LAPD officers three times. Initially, I was told there were no suspects. What else is new? The detectives were finally allowed to see her. Detectives were low on the totem pole.

I sat in on the detective's interview at Melina's request. They had very little to tell. Melina and Johnson had been shot without warning. Melina's purse was missing, and Johnson had no wallet. Police assumed the shooter had been there to take their money. I had a different opinion. If it had been a hold up, wouldn't thieves have demanded the cash first? I think the theft of the purse and wallet was a cover.

I'd given the cops Vicario's name on my second visit with them. On the third visit, they said that Vicario had been out for almost a year, with only a few months left on his parole. He had an alibi for the shooting. I was pissed off, because the authorities were supposed to notify her when he was released.

"Ease up, Mario, whoever made that promise may have retired or died. It's been a long time."

"You're right," I conceded.

Melina said that the parole board should have let her know he was granted parole. They used to write her when he had a parole hearing scheduled.

Kito, head of the personnel office for all her markets, employed a domestic agency to fill eight live-in jobs at Melina's home. When I heard that the interviews were going on, I recommended that she take all her employees left behind with the sale of the house to Olga. Olga would no doubt be happy to be rid of them and hire a staff of her own. Melina would not do that. "I made a deal with Olga and that's that."

Melina was finally released from the hospital seven days into the new year. I wanted to drive her home. Kito had hired six additional guards to protect her house to join the two guards who were already working. She would be accompanied by them as soon as she was well enough to leave the house.

"Cuz, I hope he gets through my guards. It will be my pleasure to kill him."

"Baby, you don't even know if he did it."

There was nothing I could say. The police had one suspect, a dummy named Conway Sneed who had held up an off-duty sheriff coming out of a downtown market. Bad choice of targets. She disarmed the guy and took him in, and his gun.

The detectives told Melina, "The weapon is a 38, same as what was in your robbery. We are running ballistics now."

"It's a different M.O.," I said. "This guy asked for the goods. The guy who shot Melina shot first."

The detective gave me one of those looks like, like stay out of this.

Every time she met with the detectives, Melina insisted, "Vicario did it. I don't give a fuck about his tight alibi, the pictures of him and family having a Thanksgiving Dinner at the same hour I was shot."

I suggested to Melina that when she first came home, maybe TJ should stop working for a few weeks to stop the noise and dust. She wouldn't have it.

"Not a chance, Cuz. Noise doesn't bother me and the rooms where he is working are totally protected with air tight enclosures."

You'd think that my fiancée would have been with me for the holidays or for my birthday which falls on New Years Day. She knew I didn't put up a tree and planned no festivities. But still I figured she'd fly in. She was a no show.

She gave me her excuse three days after my birthday, January 3rd. "Amor, I'm giving you space. Don't you see that?"

"Fuck the space," I said. "I want to see you."

"What about Melina? Doesn't she need you?"

"Don't go there, Olga."

"Amor, get in your plane and come see me, or I'll send you a plane to pick you up. I don't want to return until I know Melina is herself again."

I hung up on her.

I told Melina about my conversation with Olga.

"You've been around me for almost two months. She didn't want you around me at all."

"Wrong. She didn't want me to have sex with you."

Melina was up and around in her house, walking slow, but feeling right at home during the remodel. She was always part of the action.

Melina would be going back to work soon and although she would not admit it, I knew she was anxious about Vicario coming back to try and finish the job. Again, I wasn't convinced it was him. It was time for me to go eye to eye with this creep. In late January, I sent Tricia to obtain Vicario's address and to sit on him for a couple days.

"He lives in a first-floor efficiency apartment and has an old Chevy that he parks in front of his place. He works at the Goodyear plant in ELA. I checked the inside of his place and took Polaroids for you, but there's nothing of interest. No weapons. A TV, no phone, nothing in the fridge. Lives on fast food. He gets off at five, has something to eat, home by seven. His car is a junker, gives him trouble, but he gets it started and goes home."

That night when Vicario got home, I was waiting inside his little shabby hole of a place. I was positioned between his college-sized refrigerator and the door, leaning flat against filthy coffee cup patterned wallpaper as the door opened. The bulbs in the outside hall gave off enough light to show he was in a bulky sweater and jeans. He was about five foot nine. That gave me about eight inches over him. Before he kicked the door shut, I saw thick features, short cut hair like he was military which I know he had never been. Streetlights blared through the window enough for me to watch him chuck the sweater to the floor, and sail past me, toss his keys and a fast food bag on his coffee table. In a gray sleeveless undershirt, he sat down in the dark on his Goodwill couch that had seen better days, shucked his shoes and used his remote to turn on the TV. That gave off some light, enough to see he had some shoulder, chest, and arm development. He was buff, no doubt from lifting weights in prison. Crude prison tattoos marked up his arms and back. He got up, and faced his efficiency kitchen, which meant he was facing me. He saw me.

"Who the fuck are you?"

He came at me at a rush. I grabbed a wrist, and let his momentum swing him around, slamming his back against the door. I loomed over him. He snarled at me, jerked and jabbed me in the jaw. Not some pushover, then.

I punched him in the stomach, and as he bent over, his arm around his belly, answered his question.

"I'm your nightmare, mother fucker."

"I don't even know you," he wheezed. "I got nothing for you to steal. Who the fuck are you? What the fuck do you want?"

I grabbed him by the neck. The apartment flickered between dark and darker, the frigid night lit only by streetlights from outside, and the small black and white television.

"Let me tell you a story. Tell me if any of it sounds familiar. It started off when you and your fucking brother robbed a market many years ago. Your brother killed the grocer, then got shot by a girl. The grocer's daughter. Her name was Melina. Remember her?"

I reached over and hit the light switch, turning on an old light fixture, two bare bulbs hanging from the ceiling. Now he could see me clearly, and I, him. He was looking pale. I adjusted my hold.

"I asked you a question."

"That was a long time ago. I did my time, ese."

"Have you looked Melina up since you got out?"

"No fucking way, ese," he babbled.

I squeezed.

"Back off, *pinche puto*!" [23]

"Did you know someone shot Melina on Thanksgiving?"

---

[23] Fucking scallion

"How the fuck would I know?"

I kept him pinned against the door but eased my grip a little.

"Did you shoot her?"

"I swear I didn't do her. I was at my mother's for Thanksgiving with the whole family. Thirteen of us. The dicks showed up, interrogated my whole fucking family. Fucking pigs took our Thanksgiving pictures."

"That doesn't prove shit to me. I think you did it."

Vicario was scared. Still, he grinned at me, mocking and vicious. "I miss my brother. She deserves to be dead. But I got word a long time ago from a dude in the Q not to make any moves against that bitch or I'd be a dead man. I never put a hand on her."

"What dude? You mean Pélon?"

"Yeah, him. Pélon nixed it, or I would have wasted her soon as I got out."

I squeezed again. "You don't have to worry about Pélon having you done. I will kill you myself."

"That bitch deserves to be dead, but it won't be by my hand."

I squeezed his throat again till his face turned an ugly shade.

"You are as guilty as your brother for killing her father. I should just kill you now."

"I did my time," he managed to say.

"And you will never send anyone, right?"

His mouth moved soundlessly.

I loosened my grip again to hear him. "What is that?"

"I hate that bitch. I hope she dies, but if she does, it won't be by me or any of my people."

I let go of his throat and took a step back. He got a good breath in, and lurched at me, swinging wild. I punched him so hard he bounced from the wall to the floor and passed out. It took all my self-control not to kick him and be done with the bastard forever. I left him curled up on the floor.

I was not convinced of Vicario's innocence, but was not as sure of his guilt as Melina was.

It was the first time that Melina came over to Casa Luna since she moved away from her home across the street. I told her about my visit to Vicario. She wasn't happy.

"Cuz, please don't do that again. Damn, I don't want you to get in trouble."

"I had to do this," I said. "I had to see him, had to let him know he would not get away with anything."

"Cuz. I have plans. Let me handle it."

"Plans?"

"All I need is for Olga to show up now and go crazy on us," she said. She reached in her purse and pulled out her Beretta that I had seen many times in the past. She set it on the coffee table. I could tell she was on her way to a full recovery.

"Is that necessary?"

"You bet it is, I don't trust your fiancée."

If Melina had not been caught off guard, if she had faced the gunman and shot her assailant, what then? But that isn't what happened.

Melina said, "I got a call from the detective about the guy they picked up. The ballistics came back. It's the gun. It's the fucking gun."

Miguel had left a carafe on the table, and a container of steamed frothed milk. She poured milk into her coffee. Her preferred eating and work routine had always been erratic, and before the shooting, that milk might be the only nutrition she had before dinner. She was under doctor's orders not to work forty full hours a week at her markets, but Melina has never been the best at taking orders. I slid one of my pancakes on a plate and shoved it in front of her. She gave me a wan look. She had always been slim, but after her recent recovery, there was a leanness to her. Sure, it enhanced her beauty, but she still had to eat more. The bullets had wreaked havoc in her digestive system.

"Go ahead, you know I hate to eat alone." I said nothing until I saw her take a token bite of pancake and chased it with milky coffee. "I don't believe it," I said. "The guy had a different M.O."

"Detectives don't think so either. I was told the robber says he found the gun in a trash can downtown in Los Angeles."

"That's a long way from your market in Echo Park."

"They have him charged with the robbery attempt on the off-duty cop and waiting for the district attorney on whether they will charge him on my thing." She made her right thumb and forefinger into a 'gun,' aimed it at me and pantomimed the shakes. "I was told he's an alcoholic with the shakes. They don't think he could have shot me and Johnson." Her voice quivered a little as she said her driver's name.

"What a fucking mess," I said, putting my palm over her gun hand, and putting the fork in it, waiting for her to take another bite. She scooped and swallowed a bite quickly, to get it out of the way of the conversation. "I'm sorry, Baby. They going to get back to you?"

"Yeah, the detective I talked to will call me back soon as he knows. He wanted me to go for a lineup, but I told him I saw nothing. Neither did my guard inside the market."

Something had been bothering me. That whole thing about inheriting her markets. I had to bring it up.

"You never told me about your move to leave everything to me if something happened to you."

"Took you long enough to mention it," she grinned at me. To think that I had almost lost her. I did not want to think of a world without Melina in it.

"Took me off guard. I could not bear for you to die."

"We're all going to die. You're the only family I have, Cuz."

"I would have died right with you under the stress of all those markets you run."

"No, you wouldn't. You'd sell them."

"You wouldn't have cared if I sold them?"

"I wouldn't be here. What's the difference?"

I shook my head. "There's a difference. It's your life's work."

She shook her head. "I have millions in the bank, and I'd have more if I stopped opening more markets. I could sell the markets like that!" She snapped her fingers. "I would get bored and just start some other business. Some new challenge, but one I wouldn't have to babysit. Maybe I'd steal Pixie and Lainie and give RIALTO a run for their money. That would be so much fun." She laughed at my shocked expression. "By the way, are your affairs in order?" she asked.

"Of course not," I said, sticking my tongue out at her. "I'm going to live forever." When I was seventeen, Harry had drawn me up a will leaving everything to my aunt, and later Oscar had changed it for me to a living trust.

In February, a U.S. Drug Agent was kidnapped and murdered in Mexico, his body discovered soon after. President Reagan had a lot to say about that tragedy. The federal government pledged to crush the ones responsible. Olga never mentioned it and neither did I.

In March, I had Letty go out and buy an album by one of my favorite female singers, Whitney Houston. I invited Olga to meet me on the sixth in New York to see Mike Tyson make his professional debut. I wasn't into boxing, but I did like this loud mouth. I had him pegged as an up-and-coming winner. I didn't enjoy the sport on television, but in person was a different story. Olga couldn't make it to the Tyson fight in Albany. I took Letty with me, and Betty for company for Letty. The fight was great and so was the trip.

"Do I get to sleep in the middle?" Betty wanted to know.

"You wish," Letty said. "We're coming right back after the fight."

Later in the month, I sat through the academy awards with Melina in her media room. We watched the whole thing on a projection screen with oversized theatre chairs that were also recliners. It was a first for us. She wasn't working until midnight anymore. Amadeus won best picture.

"You and I are such squares," Melina said. "We don't go to the movies."

"Speak for yourself. I go to the movies," I lied. Why go to movies? I could get my hands on movies before they were in the distribution pipeline. I knew plenty of Hollywood movie guys from my years of Los Angeles car crashes. A movie buff would turn green with envy over my movie library. I hardly had explored it myself, but Letty and the girls had their own popcorn-filled movie nights in my screening room downstairs.

"Did you see Amadeus?"

"No."

Melina gave me the finger and stuck her tongue out. I knew she was better.

Olga spent zero days in Pasadena in January, four days in February, seven days in March, four days in April. In spring, Pixie returned from her Spain tour. Olga leased her the house and servants. Five thousand a month[24] included the help.

Pixie loved the deal. "Fuck me, Boss, that is sweet." After her five-year lease, if she wanted to keep the staff, she had to pay them. The strange part of the deal was that Pixie had an option to buy the house at the end of five years for four million dollars, as is, all contents included.

"That's two million less than she paid for it," I said with some surprise.

"I know, Boss, and she knows I know. Olga can be strange." She giggled. "I like this kind of strange though. If things go well for me, I'll buy the house."

When I brought the house deal up to Olga, she gave me her explanation.

"I'm going to make a lot of money on Pixie and Lainie. Giving her a break on the price of the house is just giving back some of what I know I'll make from them."

---

[24] $5,000.00 in 1984 had the same buying power as $12,168.02 in 2018

"I love you," I said. "That's very generous of you."

Lainie cut her first single in Mexico, then another single in Los Angeles. She was not an instant success, but disc jockeys were playing her two records. Lainie and Pixie arranged month-long tours singing together and lived in the big house when they weren't traveling for RIALTO.

All that time, I had been a monk, at least, with Melina. Melina didn't want me.

In five months, I had not had sex with Melina. She begged off each time I tried to get things moving, and I didn't push. I was afraid I'd hurt her, physically or emotionally. Maybe she was afraid of that too.

If not for Letty, I don't know what I would have done. I don't mean just sex. Tangles was always game and so was Betty, and if I got out of the fucking house, there were plenty of women, if that's all I wanted. Olga had reminded me of that, though I knew what I could do without her telling me. I loved Olga. She was a strong woman, and smart. She carried secrets that made her seem elusive and mysterious, but when I came home, Letty was always there for me.

It was best Olga had not set a date. If Olga brought it up and pushed it, I would not say no. Still, it was on my mind that Letty should be wearing the ring I had given to Olga. Letty was my day and night.

More turbulence struck my team. Betty could not handle the deaths. I wanted to talk her out of the changes Betty wanted to make but did not.

"You do great with the families."

"I know, Boss, but I can't deal with the deaths, and the grief just—"

"No need to explain. I can see it in your face."

"Boss, I love the traveling. I love the money, and since I don't want to leave you in the lurch, I already talked to Tangles. Her Spanish is perfect, she's a knockout, and she's a people person. She is dying to dive in."

"And what will you do?"

"Go back to massages. Tangles and I have worked it out."

Letty was not happy. "You should have said something. We spent all those hours training you." I wasn't sure what was going on there. Maybe Letty felt left out of the loop, or maybe she just liked working with Betty better than Tangles.

"I'm sorry, Letty. Don't be mad. You were a good teacher."

"You'll still be on the team," I said. "We might even take you on some cases just to be our masseuse."

Letty leapt to her feet. "If it was up to me, I'd cut you loose Johnny on the spot, right the fuck now."

"Easy, Baby, Betty is one of us."

"I thought so. She came in, learned the business. Who the fuck knows? Maybe she'll hook up with someone and become competition."

I couldn't believe this was Letty talking. I thought I'd have to step in to save Betty from an assault. Letty seemed furious.

Now that Melina was getting much better, my sex drive was back with a vengeance. Betty was smooth and good, but Tangles was still mysterious, a riot, in and out of bed, very like Pixie but without the cursing.

Tangles anxiously awaited the next plane crash, so she could get some training in. She filled Betty's spot. Massages went back to Betty. Small crashes came in, and Letty, Tangles and Tricia handled most of them. Betty and Letty didn't appear to have any friction, but Letty passed on the massages. I figured she would get over it.

I heard Letty one day with Tangles. "I will kick your ass if you pull a Betty on us. I swear, I will."

Tangles laughed. "What, am I joining a gang or something?"

I walked in as Letty grabbed her by the neck. If Tangles had been training in karate, the scene would have been okay. Letty and Pixie always went at it, but I knew it was not serious.

What I broke up that day was serious.

"Boss, I'm sorry. I'm a little crazy."

"Self-control. Work on it."

"I promise, I will. I already apologized to Tangles, even promised to give her head."

"You didn't." I said.

"I didn't. It took me a very long time for me to earn my spot in the team. I'm not sorry."

"We need her. Train her."

Chapter 19
May 1985
The Virgin

Mario

"I can't handle the fuzz any longer," Melina said. "Got it, Cuz? Get rid of your PI tracking that asshole. I have two ex-cops watching him, 24/7. It's a waste of money."

I was surprised because I thought she had not known anything about Charles tracking Vicario. "How did you know?" Charles was a private investigator that I had hired to keep tabs on Vicario. The deal was, I paid him for ten hours. He watched him from the time he left work.

"I have my ways. I should have mentioned it before this. Pull him off."

I just nodded.

"I love you for all you do for me," she said.

"For years you been doing for me."

Melina got in her car for Paul to drive her to her Echo Park market. Paul was a tall, husky guy who only used to drive her on Johnson's day off. She planned to visit three markets that day. She kissed me through the open window of her Rolls Royce, then waved goodbye. The car pulled away. I went home.

It took her five months to gain the weight she'd lost and a lot of good people to get her back on her feet. More than two doctors, two physical therapists, nutritionists, exercise classes. She was becoming very close with Patricia Haines. Patricia lived in Hollywood Hills and was a divorcée with a nineteen-year-old in college.

Olga was back. I came home from a fast trip to Fresno, California to close a deal on one hundred apartments for LAI to find her in my bed, a welcome surprise.

"Amor, let's make this our year," Olga said to me, "Melina is well now. Can I have you back?"

"I've been here, Baby. You're the one that's been absent."

She punched my chest making a funny face. "I was just giving you space."

"That's behind us now, Melina is on the road to a full recovery."

"I've gotten a lot done," Olga said. "I've put a lot of money away. We are going to be so rich."

"Baby, you are already very rich."

"I want to be richer." Then she said, "Amor, tell me you love me."

"Olga, I love you. I have missed you."

"Thank you, Amor. I adore you."

"I've been so afraid you'd call me one day and tell me you wanted Melina instead of me."

Olga was back but only for a week. She flew off, leaving me ready to work. I found myself leaning more than ever on Letty. A big case had not come along while Melina was recuperating and my acquisitions for LAI had suffered a drop because my head wasn't there. The Fresno apartment deal I just closed had been a close call. I almost lost it. But just as Melina was back, I was back. I was ready to dig into the pile of choice properties Tricia had for me. It was a big stack, and I'd have to weed out the ones that were still available. The Fresno deal had been one of them. I spent a full day working through properties, and found a couple I was interested in. I'm not much behind a desk, so the day wore me out. I skipped lunch, and then worked out at seven. I could never get the work-out right unless it was at five in the morning, but I tried. I suffered a guilt trip when I skipped the morning routine, but also, it fouled up my energy for the whole day.

Letty and I went down to the wine cave. We played in the arcade for a while. We were alone in the house. Neil Diamond was not as hot with the public as he had been a decade ago, but I still loved his stuff and played it all the time. The sound system was extraordinary. Where we were, the juke box played, amplified throughout the wine cellar. I had another juke box in the disco next to the arcade and spa, and even the intercom had primo speakers.

Our glasses clicked. We had our first drink of the night.

"Love this stuff." Letty licked her lips. I think she did that because she knew it got my attention every time.

"Are you and Betty okay now?"

Letty made a funny face. "Yes, Boss, we're straight."

A week into May, Pixie invited me over for shrimp salad tacos. There was a nice repast laid out on Pixie's patio prepared by the chef she'd inherited from Melina and Olga, albeit fixed not as much to my taste to what Miguel would have put together. Lainie mentioned that it was nearly Mother's Day.

"I wish I'd known my mother," Pixie said. Lainie hugged her.

"Me too. Though I will always appreciate Aunt Carmen," I said.

"You know who else lost her mother early? Melina." Pixie said.

I knew Melina had not been an infant when her mother died. She had been older than that, and had always celebrated the holiday, even though her mother was gone. Or because her mother was gone.

I visited Melina at home. It was impossible for her to limit her work hours to forty a week, but Dr. Haines had been insistent that she limit her hours. The truth is that she brought work home with her, anything that she could handle in her own home office. She had faxes and an assistant at home, and I suspected she was working far beyond the hours she was allowed. She chafed bitterly at the restrictions. I only cared that she felt well enough to assert her will. That was important. I practically had to drag her outside, but once we were outdoors, Melina took me into the garden to see the new plantings. We linked arms, and, of course, strayed from the path.

"I'm going to Mexico," I said, getting to the point. "It is not a case. I have to make a little pilgrimage. I made a promise to the Virgin of Guadalupe. My aunt always told me to pray to her if I ever really needed something. I asked her to save you. And she did. So, I have a promise to fulfill. I have to bend my knee to her."

There was silence. Melina took my hands. I'm pretty sure she was too choked up to say anything. She rarely cried, but she was doing just that right now. My eyes got moist in sympathy. I cleared my throat, and my voice came out gruffly. "I'm flying to Mexico City the day after tomorrow to keep my promise. Dr. Haines handled the surgery, but the Virgin was at her side. The Virgin is the reason you are breathing now."

"Mario, did I ever tell you at my parents' home we had two beautiful statutes of the Virgin? Most of the time, a candle was lit in front of them."

"You want to go along?"

"Wouldn't miss it. I will clear my plans and join you. I love you, Cuz."

"And I love you."

"I know you do."

My Learjet 35A had been configured for eight passengers plus a small jump seat for a flight attendant. The only place to lie down was a three-seat sofa but it was a joke to imagine myself lying on it. The sofa and the other five seats were wide for a small plane, upholstered in brown suede. We flew to Mexico. Melina, Letty, Jo, Niley, and me.

When Olga landed in her big plane in Van Nuys or Ontario and not at LAX, she had to pay for customs to send out an officer to clear the passengers and the plane. This airport in Mexico City, had two customs officers on duty for private planes. I recognized Olga's plane two planes away from mine. At the nose, OLGA was spelled out under the icon of a sun. Her arrival was not a co-incidence, but I wondered who she'd talked to to coordinate her timely arrival.

As we stood in customs, Olga, Pixie and Lainie were waiting for us. It was a happy reunion. Olga gave Melina what appeared to me to be a loving hug. Melina was receptive and all smiles. They exchanged kisses.

"Who told them we were coming here?"

"I did, Boss. Hope it's okay. I didn't think they'd be here. Did I fuck up?"

"You didn't fuck up," Melina whispered.

The only concern I had was Olga and Melina, but they had just hugged and kissed.

In two Cadillac limousines, we went right from the airport to the Basilica of Our Lady of Guadalupe in Mexico City. During the ride, Olga said she had been there many times before. Melina had been there with her mother when she was a little girl. For the rest of us, it was the first time.

As we passed it, Olga said the new church was always packed and accom-modated over ten thousand people. It was round and massive and had been built on the site of an older church in the mid-seventies, so it was ten years old. We climbed the stairs up the hill to an older chapel called the *Capilla del Cerrito*. Everyone except me walked inside. I entered on my knees. The center aisle was a solid mass of people, enough that I had to stop every now and again while someone moved out of the way. I was not as disturbed by my surroundings as when I was a boy because I was wrapped up in the prayers running in my head. The wall of people around me blocked my view, but I was physically aware of the ancient floor stained and worn smooth by countless generations before me, the venerated age of the walls, the soaring ceiling, the walls covered in religious art. These details were more comforting than the jeering kids from my child-hood. I did not wait to pray, but in my head all the way I was thanking the Virgin for the miracle of Melina being alive. At the altar, I bowed my head and felt a wave of comfort. I remembered the dream I'd had the night Melina's life had been in the balance.

We went outside the church where candles were sold, loaded up on them and came back inside to light some of them, then went up the stairs to the top overlooking the shrine where the Virgin had appeared. There was a small chapel there as well, roomy enough to accommodate a lot of people and it too, was packed. We lit the rest of the candles there, got more candles outside, and went back down the concrete stairs to the new church and lit candles there too.

When we returned to our cars, we huddled and recited the lord's prayer and the Hail Mary. Among us there were no dry eyes.

It was not a trip for lingering. We went straight to the airport. All of us boarded Olga's plane and we were served a delicious late lunch catered by Olga's favorite restaurant and served by almost as many stewards as there was of us. We drank Dom Perignon.

Pixie, Lainie and Olga headed back to Guadalajara where Pixie and Lainie were holding a concert the following day. Olga was headed to Uruguay. The rest of us took the three hour twenty minute flight to Van Nuys aboard my jet.

"I love the plane, Cuz," Melina said. "I remember when you opted out of accepting Oscar's plane as payment. Too expensive to maintain."

"So far, it's not that bad. We use the hell out of it for my business."

We were all headed to Pasadena, but Melina's driver Paul picked her up at the airport. Jo and Niley rode with Letty and me back to Casa Luna where they'd left their cars. At home, Letty and I thought we were alone again, but inside we found Tangles.

"I thought you two might want a massage," Tangles said, wide awake and energetic in spite of the lateness of the hour.

"You're not our masseuse anymore," Letty said.

"I'm an all-around. Boss is paying me. Got to do something."

"I'm in after I shower," I said.

"You can do me in the meantime. I'm not showering for you, bitch."

Tangles winked at me.

"Spa, or bedroom, what's your pleasure, ma'am?"

Chapter 20
June 1985
Beat Down

Mario

Olga was in Pasadena for a week.

"Amor, I hear there is a blood test now to find out if a person has AIDS."

"I heard the same. It's really for people who donate blood, to check if they are okay."

"I didn't know," Olga said.

"Hey, there must be something to it, if the test determines your blood is okay to donate to a blood bank, then you must not have AIDS."

Olga smiled. "Makes sense to me."

We looked at each other.

"I don't go outside the group, Baby. You do," I said.

"How dare you," she said, though she did not sound angry. "I will always tell you when I have to do it for business sake. Let's take the test, Amor."

I wasn't fucking anything strange. Blood test? Fuck! What happened to spontaneous sex, orgies?

I hated the tragic disease going around that threatened us with life without sex. I had never touched base with the girls on sex lives in a world where

AIDS existed. There were many factors now. Jo was with TJ who for all I knew was fucking someone during all those hours out on construction jobs. Niley for years said no one stayed long after they found out she had four kids, but the point was that she's dating. Tricia was fucking Bill. Who the hell knew who he was fucking? Betty, certainly, a free spirit, was back to massage work and fucking others. Tangles was a fox. When she went home at night, she had to be fucking others. Letty hardly ever left my side. She wasn't fucking anyone else. Melina, by her own admission screwed around whenever she felt like it, but except for that once in her office, I hadn't had sex with her in a year.

Olga

He's so open about who he has sex with. Why do I keep telling him that I only fuck if it's business? What gives him the right and not me? It's my fault for covering it up from the start. I doubt those old bankers I have sex with have AIDS, but how about Natalia? How do any of us know who has it?

By now, Natalia is a girl all the way. She won't be fucking me anymore. I'm dying to see her when she returns to work. I've seen it all but never have I seen what they did to Natalia. She's so brave to go after what she wanted. First those lovely breasts and now the main event.

Letty

Boss told me to get a nurse to come over and give all of us a blood test. I'd seen a blood shortage announced in the paper by a blood bank in Pasadena and thought that would be a good place to start. When I called, I only got an answering machine. I drove over there, finding a small free-standing brick building with vans in the parking lot, and a couple of cars. Inside, this guy in a white doctor's jacket was typing at a computer. Sandy hair, glasses, nametag said Danny. He had a forgettable face. Four people were in the waiting room scribbling away on clipboards.

"How come you don't answer your phone or return calls, Danny?"

The guy got up and walked over to his side of the counter. He pushed a clipboard in my direction. I ignored it.

"How can I help you?"

"I'm looking to arrange blood tests for about ten people who want to make sure their blood is okay to donate."

"When you donate, we test you first."

I didn't feel like announcing our business to the room.

"Call me on my cell when you have time." I slipped a folded hundred-dollar bill across the counter to him with my card. He hesitated for a split second, then snatched up the bill and card as slyly as I had passed it to him. I walked out to the car. He called promptly, and we made the arrangements. The results were personal and confidential. There was one test called ELISA, and if anyone tested positive, it would be followed by a Western Blot test. If anyone had been exposed in the past eight weeks, it wouldn't show up in the test.

Danny arrived at Casa Luna at ten the next day. Olga, Boss, Me, Pixie, Lainie, Jo, Niley, Betty, Tangles, and Miguel had their blood drawn; then he left for Montebello to test Melina. I gave Danny two hundred, and the laboratory bill went to Boss.

"If it's personal and confidential, if any of us has it, how will the others know?" Tangles asked.

"We have to agree that the results will not be kept secret from each other."

"Agreed?" Olga asked looking around.

Everyone agreed.

We were all clear.

"How do we know about Melina?" I asked.

"She'll tell me," Boss said.

If any of us had been exposed in the last two months, it wouldn't show up in the test, so the blood test, if it really works, is bullshit. The results are for that very time and date that blood was drawn. Anyone that likes to fuck is at risk.

Mario

The first thing I did when I heard about the quake in Mexico City was check Pixie's tour schedule to make sure she was safe. She called not long after.

"Boss, did you hear about the 8.1 earthquake in Mexico City?"

"I did. I was worried and checked to make sure you were in London. Where is Lainie?"

"She's here in London with me. I ain't going back to RIALTO for nothing."

"We're going to have a big one in LA one day, too."

"Scares the piss out of me."

It's not what she says, it's how she says it that makes me laugh.

"Pix, if you don't have anything going for a couple of months, come home. I miss you."

"I wasn't going to make this trip but Lainie wanted to come and I want to be around them as much as possible. If you know what I mean."

"Pix, if they want to fuck, they will fuck."

"I know. He doesn't fuck anyway. I'm hoping he tires of her and she wakes up and realizes he's way too old for her. She's going to be ultra-fucking-famous, if she wises up. She's dazzled by Jason's wealth. I used to get diamonds. Now Lainie gets them. You should see the necklace he put on her a day after we got here."

"Pix, you have your own stash so don't begrudge her. It's Lainie already."

"I don't begrudge her. I'm just saying what a prick he's become. I'm in the penthouse and Lainie is with him at the mansion most times."

"You said you didn't like his big house," I reminded her.

"I don't like it, so how can Lainie like it? Fuck-me, what a drag."

"You just want to be in London," I said.

"Not really. I'm lonely when I'm here, but, I keep busy. I shop on Jason's credit card. It's not like I don't have my own money. But fuck him. He dropped me like a dead fish to romance my daughter. It's so screwed up."

Pixie was a difficult person to understand but I understood her. I didn't quite understand the part that Jason doesn't fuck anyway.

Melina called twice before we had a good connection.

"I'm not sure the picture will fax well, but I've sent you something I got from my two guys that are watching that bastard."

That bastard could only be Vicario.

"I'll call you back on my cell," I said.

"Call me in Hacienda Heights. Land line is better."

Tangles and Letty were going over teletype messages on the conference table. I went to the fax machine, also in with the telex machine. The fax was a slow process, and was still printing as I walked in. The image was not very good, but clear enough for me to recognize Carson coming out of Vicario's apartment.

I slid the faxed image on the conference table and took a seat to call Melina.

"This picture." I picked it up and looked at it closely. There was no mistaking who it was. "This is Carson."

"Sure is."

"What the fuck connection would he have with this bastard? When we went to see Pélon, he was gung ho to broker a kill on this guy for you. I nipped that in the bud or you'd still be paying him and Pélon protection money."

"Don't remind me of that," she said.

"Have you gotten anything else on this guy?"

"Nada. It's the first thing I've gotten in all this surveillance. All that son of a bitch Bruno Vicario does is work, eat, and go home. No one ever visits him. He's never been seen with a woman or even a guy."

Looking at the picture was pissing me off. Letty noticed and came around behind my chair to see what had my attention.

"The picture doesn't show Vicario," I said. "Did you get a shot of him going in?"

"Yeah, but not enough to make out."

"Did he break in?"

"Vicario let him in at ten minutes after eight last night. I have fourteen pictures. When I see you, you can check them out if you want."

"Will do," I said, "Be careful, Baby. Is there anything I can do?"

"Cuz, I got it totally covered." She hesitated. "Let's not mention this to the cops in case you talk to them."

"They haven't been in touch with me in ages. It's you they would call, not me."

"I haven't heard a damn thing since the district attorney said he was going to hold off filing the case against the alcoholic until later. They have plenty on him for now to keep him in the slammer. They can bring him back when they have more evidence that he shot me and killed Johnson."

Tangles and Letty got excited over a case that came across on the telex before it was on the news. On June fourteenth, a group hijacked a plane carrying one hundred fifty-three passengers from Athens to Rome. I asked Gonor if he wanted the cases.

"Should I try to sign up some of the passengers? They must be traumatized."

"Mario, pass this one up. This kind of case is so unique that I wouldn't even know how to pursue it." Gonor chuckled over it. I don't know what he thought was funny.

"It's TWA, an American operator."

"Pass, Mario," Gonor said.

"Forget it," I told Tangles and Letty.

On July third, I agreed to go to the movies, the first in a long time. Niley, Jo, Betty, Tangles, Letty and I left Casa Luna and went downtown together to the Los Angeles Theatre to watch Back to the Future. We drove down in two cars. Melina and Tricia were not with us.

Afterward, when I came by to see her, Melina coaxed the spoilers out of me, and mentioned she had hired two additional private detectives to watch Carson.

"A prudent move," I said.

Where Carson was concerned, I don't know how I managed to control my temper. The last time Carson got me seriously mad, I had sneaked over to his place and left him in a bloody pile. My fists and I itched to do it again. If I beat the crap out of Carson, at least he would spill the beans so I would have a clue what the fuck was going on.

Melina continued to surround herself with protection with no plans on cutting back. Vicario wasn't smart enough to get through Melina's line of protection, and he didn't have a helicopter at his disposal. If Vicario had not been the shooter, who else could it be? The guy in custody who held up the off-duty sheriff? Neither Olga or me, believed the drunk to be the shooter.

When Olga was in town, she said, "We should tell Pepe about this suspect. He has his ways of taking care of things."

I didn't doubt Pepe had a handle on a way to take care of 'things.' But if it was that easy, why didn't he help with the mystery of who killed Jake, who killed Oscar, who torched my house, who killed Bruno and who had sent the biker after me?

I had a whole lot of unanswered questions.

I was in bed with Olga after a long weekend. We'd had so much sex already we should have been worn out. We were still doing it but slowly.

"Amor, do you ever think of her when you are making love to me?"

I was on top. My mouth found hers and we had the longest kiss. I never answered the question. Because she brought her up, a movie of Melina played in my mind. I truly loved Olga but who knew if it was in me to settle down. If I didn't know what I wanted, who would?

Olga left with her troops. An hour later, I got a call.

"Amor, I thought I was going to die."

"What happened?"

"The pilot aborted the takeoff. He got a weird signal in the cockpit. It scared me."

"Where are you?"

"Van Nuys. Don't come. It's a false alarm. Please don't come. I almost didn't call you."

"Baby, are you sure you don't want me there?"

"If it's serious, we won't take off. I'll come home. I'll call you either way."

When Melina had been shot, it crippled me for months. I wasn't the one shot, but it was as though it had been me. Now, waiting for Olga's call, I realized what she meant to me. I suppose I need an awakening every once in a while.

She called back to tell me the problem had been a French instrument on an American plane. "From now on," she said, "I'm landing in Ontario. Van Nuys runways are too short for this big plane. We don't have a chance in an emergency. I found that out today. I adore you. I'm going to lose you in a minute, kisses, *querido mio.*"[25]

My plane was small and perfect for Van Nuys but not perfect for her planes. I had always wondered why they let her land there.

I told Letty and Tangles about the aborted takeoff.

"And she went on anyway?" Tangles asked.

"She's in the air by now."

"Olga doesn't look it but she's strong," Letty said.

"Stubborn like steel," I said. "I don't know if she knows how to be afraid. She said this scared her, but I couldn't tell by her voice."

The work day was done. Miguel was going to be feeding us in the wine room. I was still feeling restless. Letty was good at deciphering my mood. The

---

[25] My love

wine room is on the same level as the spa, and that is where she called me from.

"Come on, Boss. Let's get some color back in those pretty cheeks of yours."

Tricia had gone home to Bill already. Tangles was in socks and shorts, and had three wine glasses out waiting for something, probably Argentinian red. I followed the sound of Letty's voice. Tangles followed me but stopped just outside the workout area. She knew to keep her distance.

Letty was in position. She bowed to me. I bowed to her. I took a playful swing, knowing what she would do. She blocked me and positioned herself to strike back.

"You so sexy," I said.

"Maybe I should take up karate," Tangles said, from her safe distance.

"Too late," Letty said.

"You started way late, too," Tangles said to Letty, "I'm only twenty-five."

Twenty-five sounded so young now. I remembered when I had been that age. The years were flying by. Still, I had no wife. No children, at least none that that I knew of.

"If you want to take up karate, I'll introduce you to Cosmo," I told Tangles. "Betty never really got into it, but if you're interested and you have the knack, it's a good thing to be able to defend yourself." Cosmo did not hold classes himself any more, but he went to his studio every day. As far as I could tell, he was as spry as ever. I did not go to see him often. It hurt to see how the neighborhood had gotten shabbier every year, and I could barely stand to see the building that had once held Harry's offices. Harry had been the lawyer who got me started looking for car crashes when I was fourteen.

On the weekend after my morning workout and a shower, I arranged to come over to Melina's. She'd done a lot of the police investigators' work for them. She was leaving for work at nine.

"Maybe you need to share this with the cops?"

"I don't have anything solid yet," she said. We were in the breakfast room and carried our coffee cups with us into her first-floor office, done up in her up-scale version of shabby chic.

"Let me show you the new stuff."

Eight by tens were in a pile on a vintage black and gold table she was using as a desk. I spread them out to look them over. The pictures were better in person than via fax. Carson was caught going to different houses, sometimes alone, sometimes with a companion, probably part of his team. He was signing cases, car accidents, just as I had done years ago before I sold my contacts to Oscar, who gave them to Carson. A series showed Carson getting out of his car at a high rise a few blocks from the building I had bought from TJ for LAI, and another in the same series getting back in his car. No pictures caught him in the lobby, only a car attendant who handled the vehicles.

"My guy paid the lobby man," Melina said. "Carson visited Janice Cooke."

"Janice Cooke. Hmm."

"What does that mean?"

"A while ago, she told me that she saw Carson from time to time. He was her boy toy. Something along those lines."

"You never told me that."

"The position I put myself in was nothing to brag about. I gave her the money to get on her feet and paid off the foreclosure, so the house was clear and free."

"I remember that."

"All over a guilt trip that I put myself in and she helped me be in."

"That's the part you left out."

The office door was open. One of Melina's staff came in with carafes of coffee, cream, and foamed milk, and placed them on a rolling silver cart. Melina glanced at her watch, and toward the woman. Late forties, short blonde hair, wide pink headband. The uniform she was in was of white cotton, plain, no buttons anywhere I could see. It looked more like scrubs than housekeeping uniforms. Melina gave her a nod, and she nodded back, before disappearing down the hall.

"We don't know if Carson was there to fuck or what. I can't see a connection with Janice and you."

"You were there when I met her," Melina said.

"It was when you came to Oscar's funeral with me." I looked down at the photos. "Carson is dirty. If there's an angle somewhere, Carson is going to find it."

"But why would he visit Vicario?"

"I knew Carson would remember the guy. He never forgets a deal. Remember when you first met him and wanted him to do the hit? He was intent on getting Pélon to hit Vicario for you. He wanted a piece of that action, and he was royally pissed off when it fell through. When I pushed it to fall through." I looked up at Melina. "When you were in the hospital, I couldn't remember Vicario's name. I called Carson. He could have visited Vicario just because I brought up his name."

"It's a guessing game right now, Cuz."

"You don't look worried," I said.

"I'm not. I will find out who did it. I still say it was Vicario. Don't give a shit about his alibi, or the so-called Thanksgiving pictures. Cops screwed up."

In the old days, when Carson crossed the line, I used to sneak into his place and teach him a physical lesson, the only thing that ever sinks in with him. At the time I was blaming him for things he hadn't done. Not that he was innocent in general, just innocent of what I thought he had done. I had fucked up. Eventually I apologized, and we had made peace. I found myself in the same position, again having to press Carson. Times had changed, though. This time, no skulking around. I called him.

"Can you come over? I need to talk with you?"

"Ese, about time you invited me to the new pad."

My security crew knew I was expecting him. After the guard let me know he was driving in, I was there to see him out of his car and let him in.

He arrived well dressed in jeans and a nice sport coat, driving in his newish Corvette convertible. Carson was a good-looking guy with a tan that might have come from his topless car. When we'd been kids in school, the girls had loved him. He had always been a hard drinker, a hard smoker, but skirted the murderous violent nature that had put Pélon away. That and several divorces had left some wear and tear, but I could still see in his face the boy he had been. He had a convincing quality of sincerity, but the sincerer he seemed, the bigger the lie he was covering up.

He embraced me as soon as he was in reach, then looked around, his expressions fleeting.

"Are you selling dope or something? Fuck, this is fucking amazing. Guards, dogs, ese, you can't be doing this just on plane crashes."

I gave him the top down tour, rushing it so there was no time to linger. The girls were in the office with their backs to the door, coached not to turn around to greet him.

"Hardly seems your office without Pixie," he said.

I nodded, rushing him through the guest level, and the main floor. We walked down one level. He walked a few steps ahead, and when we got to the gym, he turned to face me, I slammed him down. I didn't punch him, but he went down on his back.

"Notice there is a mat under you," I said, standing over him.

"You invite me to you house for this, ese? You crazy?"

When he started to get up, I put my tennis shoe on his chest, leaned down, casually retied my shoe. It was new. I took my time.

"I want to think we're still friends. I don't want to beat your ass, but you know I will."

"What is it, ese?" he asked, sweat blooming on his brow, not from this air-conditioned gym.

"Why you seeing Vicario? What you got going with Janice?"

Carson turned red. He looked up at me from his spot on the mat. I leaned over him, my face about a foot from his.

"You fucking following me or something? You a cop now?"

"Answer me."

"Those things aren't connected. Pélon told me to look up Vicario. Gave me the address. Janice, I go there to fuck. Now that she has money, she pays me."

I'd get to Janice paying him later.

"How the fuck are you in contact with Pélon?"

"I visit him every couple months."

"Why?"

"Man, it's not like he gives me a choice. He's always got some threat in his pocket that he's willing to...."

I nodded. That was Pélon's way. Carson was still talking.

"...told me you sent him a grand, told me to tell you it was about time you remembered him."

I put my foot on the floor and extended my hand. Carson took it and I pulled him up. He gave a little cough and brushed off his chest. His shirt was spotless. I started for the door.

"Where are we going now?"

"To the wine room."

"A minute ago, you're ready to fuck me over, and now you take me to the wine room?"

Carson and I went back a long time. I really didn't want him to play dirty with me or Melina or anyone around me. I didn't want to be at war with this old friend.

Inside the wine room, I switched on the lights, turned the rheostat full blast. Usually the room was at twilight, never this bright. Our shadows were harsh and dark in this light. Lots of illumination in this room casting lots of shadows.

I poured myself a glass of wine. He wanted a Bohemia. I provided him an iced mug.

"You a punk, ese, slamming me on the floor and now you all nice."

"I'm not done yet. Tell me about Pélon. When did you see him?"

"Two weeks ago, Saturday."

"Why Vicario?"

"Vicario ain't ever met him in person. Pélon is in isolation in Quentin. His *vatos*[26] handle it in there. When Vicario got parole, Pélon made it clear not to fuck with Melina or he'd be dead meat."

"That still does not explain why you were there."

"I'm trying to tell you, ese. Vicario owes him ten grand. Now he's out, the deal is he starts paying the ten Gs. For not putting him down like the dog he is."

Pélon would do that. He lived on extortion, I was sure.

"And you went there to...?"

"I got a thousand from him. I can show you four postal money order stubs for $250 each, all sent to Quentin to deposit in Pélon's account. The first payment."

Carson poured the dregs in his mug and drained it. I tossed the bottle in the trash and got him a chilled Bohemia and a fresh iced mug. His eyes strayed around the room and returned to me. He studied my face.

"Punk motherfucker," he said with the hint of a grin. "What is going on? Why you following me?"

"I'm not the one following you."

Whatever he was, he wasn't stupid. "Melina thinks he shot her?"

"Do you know who shot her?"

"Fuck, ese, no fucking way. Why would I know?"

"Your opinion then. Do you think Vicario did it?"

Carson shrugged, a thoughtful expression on his face. "He would be mo-

---

[26] dudes

tivated to do it if he could get some money for it. If there was a big payoff, and if he believed Pélon wouldn't get wind of it. He ain't got shit. That job he's got, he can barely make it and he has this *deuda*[27] with Pélon. Got to pay a G every three months. He had a year to make first payment but ain't no more extensions. That's hanging over his head."

"Why's he got you collecting? Why not one of his boys?"

Carson smiled. "If he sends one of his boys, he's obligated to pay them a share. I'm free."

I looked at Carson. I could see him clearly.

"If you lie to me, I will beat your ass," I said.

"Ese, for once, fucking trust me. On my mother, man, I just told you everything. If Pélon knows I'm spreading his business, even to you, he ain't gonna be happy."

"He'll never know it from me."

Carson downed the rest of the beer. I got up, gave him another, and sat down again. I picked up my full wine glass, swirling it, watching the play of light in this bright room. I had more questions.

"What about Janice? She's not that old or fucked up that she needs to pay for it."

"Ese, I'm not in her head. I guess she doesn't want a relationship. She wants sex. No obligation. When she wants sex, she calls. I ain't the only one."

"Who else?"

"Who the hell knows? She doesn't tell me. I fucked her for free until she sold her house. Now she gives me a hundred.[28] I ain't turning down cash. I take it."

"Her dead husband's firm is supporting you. Why the fuck do you take money from her?"

"I deliver cases for the money Tom pays. I keep that place moving with cases. It's all business."

---

[27] Debt

[28] $100.00 in 1985 had the same buying power as $234.12 in 2018

I had once kept Tom moving with cases. My mind did not want to go there, so I changed topics.

"What's the connection between Janice and Vicario?"

Carson looked at me like I had grown a second head, or giant ears.

"Ese, you crazy. Those two don't know each other."

Two beers later, I walked Carson out the front door, and stood on the steps as he got in his flashy fast car, the embodiment of his dreams. It was weird having him so close, while he was so far away, as far away as our childhood.

"Next time, we meet in a public place, ese," he said, starting the car and gassing the engine.

He gave me the high sign. I gave him the finger. Some things never change.

"I wish you would have let me handle it," Melina said the next morning. We were back in her office. It could have been a repeat of the day before except the photographs had been put somewhere out of sight.

"Baby, I grew up with this mother. I may not know the private parts you know but I know his brain."

She ignored the private parts. "If you believe him, I'm back to square one."

"Pélon has a hook in Vicario. Carson was there collecting a debt, but I don't know why Janice would pay for a fuck. I believe the sex, but I'm not sure if I believe she paid him for it."

"One day maybe I'll have to pay to get fucked," Melina finished her coffee, then looked at me.

I took her free hand and squeezed it gently.

"I'm never going to charge you," I said, keeping my face straight until I had to laugh at her expression.

"Asshole."

"It's been too long," I said.

She looked at her watch. I knew it was time for her to head for work. I walked with her through her front door. Paul had pulled her car to the front steps beside where I'd parked my Rolls.

"One day, when your fiancée is ten thousand miles away," she said.

"She's about five thousand miles away right now. Will that work?"

"No."

Letty, Tangles and I went clubbing in Hollywood. I was in jeans, the girls in shorts, boots and designer tops. Tangles was wearing clothes Letty had loaned her. They were the same size. Luckily, they were getting along. The club was hopping, busy for a Wednesday night.

"I should buy a club," I said. "Wonder if there's any money in it."

"Boss, buy one for LAI. You'll get all the perks and none of the headache," Letty said.

When Pixie was out of town, I had a deal that I could use Raul when I needed a driver. She offered the limo too, but we three were okay in my Rolls.

Our third stop was Whisky A Go Go. It was hard to get good wine at Hollywood Clubs, but wine is what we drank.

"I wish we could bring our own bottles when we go out."

The girls chimed together they'd do that next time. Not word for word, but close enough.

"You wish," Letty said doing a hundred and eighty degree turn. "Ain't bringing a bottle in to one of these joints."

When I came out of the rest room Letty and Tangles were dancing together to a slow song. They were smiling at each other. I should have been prepared for it, but the girls went wild in the back seat of the car on the way home. I wished we had brought the limo. For all those hours, I never thought about business. I didn't think about all the mysteries that needed to be solved in my life. I didn't think about Carson or Pélon or Vicario. All I wanted was a fucking escape from reality. The wildness continued in my bedroom for hours. It derailed my five A.M. workout but by seven, I was in the gym.

I should have been hung over from nasty wine, sore from the sex. Instead, I worked out with mysterious energy. Olga had wanted me to go clubbing but she told me that in hopes I would not get serious with Letty and just bring home one-night stands. I believed that the Letty thing with Olga had passed, for good, maybe because Olga believed that Letty wasn't looking for a husband or maybe because Olga knew Letty wasn't going anywhere.

Chapter 21
July 1985
Riana

Mario

"Heads up, Amor. In case you're in the kitchen making cookies with Letty, I'm on my way home. Be there in a little bit."

"No cookies," I said. "You sound cheerful, Baby."

"Always, Amor. I'm coming home to you."

"Hurry."

"I got a surprise."

"Tell me."

"You'll see, Amor."

A few moments later came the call from the guard at the gate, telling me about the two cars entering my driveway, my fiancée and the car with the guards trailing behind her. Olga emerged from the rented limo dressed to kill in what Pixie used to call 'Betty Davis red', the color that draws every eye in the room. She was done up, designer from her hair to her toes. She did not look like a woman who had just flown from Barcelona to Miami for customs and refueling, then nonstop home. I pulled her off her feet, and into an embrace that got us lost in time. I was instantly wrapped up in sensation of Olga back in my arms, and her tongue in my mouth. I looked up from kisses to see a someone on the bottom stair of my front porch, someone tall and slim, lightly dressed in a plain sleeveless dress with a wide white stripe down the front, and definitely no un-derwear. Except for the glitter of diamonds on her arms and neck, everything else she had—purse, carry-on, shoes, belt—was a golden-orange in a hue scantly warmer than her skin, artfully designed so it gave the impression of nudity. Her features were small, her eyes and hair brown, lush, and luminous, and her lips painted a bright hot red.

"Amor, this is Riana. Surprise!"

I extended my hand, but Riana opened her arms. We hugged, and kissed both cheeks European-style under Olga's smiling eyes. I shook hands with the guards as they made a last check in with Olga, before speeding off to some hotel to wait for their next summons.

Letty came out of the house and was quickly introduced and embraced. Letty took a large Louis V suitcase from the driver, carried it inside, and must have handed it over to someone else. A moment later, she returned for Olga's briefcase.

While I was playing host, Pixie called. "Boss, I'm home. Can't wait to see you."

In the background, I heard Lainie, "Yeah, Uncle Boss, wait till you see. You won't recognize me."

"Oh hush, brat."

"Home as in across the street?"

"Still at Van Nuys Airport. In Jason's plane. He's back in London."

"Olga and her friend Riana arrived earlier."

"I know," Pixie said. "We're going to party, Boss. I'm so fucking happy to be home."

I was happy for her. The instant we hung up, the duty guard at the gate called about congestion in the neighborhood.

"Boss, you might check the video monitor for the west camera out front."

"Anything wrong?"

"It's a circus in front of Pixie's gates. I guess they are reporters. I didn't think she was there."

"She's on her way from the airport."

I felt excitement for Pixie and Lainie. I felt good that Pixie and Lainie were together, considering the daily talks with Pixie about Lainie and Jason. Olga represented them both and was pushing for Lainie to do a short tour on her own. The mother and daughter thing had been fine to help launch Lainie, but they were going for different styles of music, and different audiences. Olga parroted the marketing geniuses at RIALTO.

Everyone crowded into the sunroom chomping on tapas, talking about going for a swim. I whispered to Letty to keep it going and went upstairs to the office. I shut the door and looked at the monitor facing Pixie's gates at the crowd the guard had mentioned. I did recognize a couple reporters and there was at least one TV van that I could make out. There were also two distinct groups of fans. I could guess who was there for Pixie, and who for Lainie. It did not take long for Pixie's limo to pull up with Raul at the wheel. I did not have a clear view of her, just enough to know that Pixie was busy being herself, with the windows open, accepting things and signing autographs as fast as she could write. It was strange to see all the fans, because in my heart she was still just Pixie, the girl from my childhood, but I know the acceptance of her fans meant a lot to her.

Pixie insisted we get together at her house that night. We waited till the crowd cleared to cross the street. Pixie was a sight for sore eyes, and Lainie was all grown-up. Lainie had started calling me Boss, too, about half of the time. She still called Aunt Carmen *abuela*.[29] Lainie had reinvented herself, and did a little spin in front of me, showing off. The new look should not have surprised me, since Pixie did it all of the time. I knew RIALTO had wanted to control her look, Olga had called me once about it, despairing, and railing over Lainie's

---

[29] Grandmother (Spanish)

stubbornness. Lainie, of course, had rebelled bigtime. They wanted long dark hair? Red lipstick? Full makeup? Her hair was in a short bob, the kind of look that had gotten her mother her name. It had been bleached to a Marilyn Monroe blonde, but with her creamy skin, the look was more Audrey Hepburn's pixie-cut phase. The minimal make up showed off that same incandescent beauty she'd inherited from her mother.

"Boss, you dig my hair?" Lainie asked.

"HOT, Baby, hot."

Pixie shook her head, smiling. "Stop flirting with your Uncle Mario."

"He's not my Uncle, mom."

Pixie gave her an expressionless look.

"I like being Uncle Mario."

Pixie whispered in my ear, "Down boy. She could be your daughter."

I put both hands up to show hands off, like she'd pointed a gun. I was even a little shocked. Even all dolled up, I could only ever see Lainie as a kid. Pixie should know she shouldn't have to warn me off. Not that I took the idea of being a parent seriously. If Pixie thought I was the father, surely, she would have said so in the beginning, when she'd moved in to my aunt's house. We'd decided a long time ago that I was not Lainie's father.

We sat down to a basic American table. Her know-it-all chef prepared hamburgers, hot dogs and pastrami sandwiches with all the trimmings—overboard on the available trimmings, actually. No one went for caviar on their burgers, but the variety of mustards and ketchups were a hit. The fries and onion rings were fantastic. I couldn't recall a similar meal at Melina's, but then the chef was just catering to Pixie's simpler tastes.

"I've been dying to eat a hamburger and a hot dog. Fuck me," Pixie said, her eyes rolling in exaggerated bliss. She took a huge mouthful of a massive hamburger that totally filled the dinner plate.

"Totally killer eats, mom. Off the hook," Lainie agreed, munching away. "And we didn't even have to sing for our supper."

Pixie, Laine and me, and of course, Betty, Jo, Niley, Letty, Tangles, Olga, and Riana sat around the dining room table stuffing our faces. Tricia could have been there but maybe she was secretly pissed at Olga for not making any secret about getting the jitters around her boyfriend Bill. Pixie and Lainie talked music, then Olga brought up her latest scheme.

"I'm thinking of a Lainie concert at Olimpico Universitario in Mexico City. Capacity is fifty-five thousand."

Pixie said, "She's just starting. That's a big forum."

"I'm thinking free admission," Olga said, smiling at her own idea. "RI-ALTO can put together a group to accompany her. She can sing her own songs."

"How does Lainie make money off that?" Pixie asked, Lainie nodding in agreement. We were sitting around the dining room table. Melina's custom-made dining room table, massive but not as big as mine.

"One day, it won't be free. If we pack the stadium, the press will be all over you. The publicity will be worth every penny that it costs me to make it happen."

"Why just you? Doesn't RIALTO put up part of it?" I asked.

"Paulo takes risks, but he may balk at doing something this big, so soon for Lainie."

"I'm in," Lainie said. "Fuck the money. Imagine me singing in front of a crowd that size," she covered her mouth like she was ready to scream.

Pixie said, "You never did that for me." She pretended she was in tears, a napkin covering her eyes. Everyone laughed except Lainie.

"Mom, you can sing with me, if Olga does this."

"No," Pixie said firmly. "If we do this, it's your show, Lainie."

All the household help was serving that night and looking after us. Raul, her driver was running bar and pouring champagne and wine. Riana was drinking margaritas. I don't know what time we walked home. Jo and Niley stayed at Pixie's, too drunk to drive. Betty and Tangles came over to my house and stayed for the same reason. Riana settled in a guest room no one else had claimed, the first one ever to use it. Olga and I went to bed alone. We probably did it, but I don't recall. I woke at five, showered off last night, and returned to cuddle in bed. When I opened my eyes next, the clock said it was eleven ten.

Olga pulled off the lingerie she was wearing, not that it came close to concealing anything. She'd already showered at some time and returned like me to laze in bed. We savored each other as we kissed, morning breath notwithstanding.

"Amor, tonight, we bring Riana in here with us, Si?"

"Deal," I said, feeling something coming awake. When we were talking again, Olga told me about Riana.

"She's the daughter of one of my bankers in Barcelona. The father is Felipe Carrera. He owns the bank, lots of money. When I'm there I normally see her. We go out to dinner and we've slept together."

"She's single?"

"She's married, separated over a year. Rich family."

I tickled her. "How well you know this banker?"

"Amor, when I first hit him up to let me make cash deposits, I had to do it a couple times but that was long ago."

"You say it like it's nothing," I heard myself say.

"Amor, it is nothing. I douche them away, and all is back to normal. Besides, how is that different from what you do every night right here in this bed with others?"

"Sorry," I said, "I said that without thinking."

Olga kissed me. "Please, no sorry needed, Amor."

We were lying there in the dark, blackout curtains pulled tight, too lazy to ring for food. Olga whacked me lightly on the chest.

"Hey, that hurt."

"It didn't. You're superman."

"Riana knows I fucked her father twice and could care less."

"Riana is a pretty one," I said.

"She's a horny bitch who likes coke, but I made it clear that the ground rules for her coming here were that the only thing she could do was pot and booze." Olga reached between my legs.

"We don't have coke," I reminded her.

"I know, Amor. You know I hate coke."

Two days later, the whole crew left for Las Vegas to take Riana who had never been. Olga, Riana and I were in my plane. Everyone else was in Jason's. Olga deposited two hundred thousand with the cashier at Caesar's Palace to an account of hers that I had no idea she had. We had never been to Vegas together. We got connecting VIP suites in the newest tower. No reservations, but then whales never needed any.

I had been to Caesar's with Tricia and once with Letty. That first trip, I'd had a nice suite. This one was top of the line like the one I'd shared with Letty, out of this world extravagant. Too bad no hotel that I had ever been to have a double sized king size like I did at home. Still, it was big enough for the three of us. It was also big enough for them to work out together, though Cosmo would never have put them in the same class.

Jo and Niley had their own suite. Pixie and Lainie shared a suite. Tangles, Betty and Letty shared a two-bedroom suite. Since Tangles had taken up karate, (and Betty had too, sort of) they were all getting along. Letty and Pixie were incredibly strong, fast fighters with fabulous agility. Pixie would lose that agility unless she kept working out, but her new life would probably interfere. I did not ask Lainie if she was working out when she was on the road. She already had one black belt. At her age, that was a total achievement to be proud of.

Before this, I had not seen Betty, Tangles and Letty working out together, but I knew Letty liked being top dog. She had whispered to me after their first or second class that Cosmo had suggested Betty and Tangles try Jazzercize instead. According to Cosmo, Betty wasn't interested in martial arts, but was a cheerleader during the class. Tangles had no aptitude for karate, but I thought she was game for trying. The truth was that these days, I had a measure of peace of mind from having good security. I had forced the karate and gun expertise with Jo, Pixie, Niley and Letty, but really felt the need for them to become lethal weapons had passed. Maybe I was being overly optimistic, but that ship had sailed. I guess what really mattered was that they were all getting along.

"You don't mind being in there with them? I wish you were in my room."

"Boss, I'm cool," Letty smiled.

During dinner that night at the Bacchanal, gorgeous belly dancers pranced around in very short costumes, and massaged our backs during and after dinner. Betty and Tangles got a big kick out of being on the receiving end of massages. We drank wine from silver goblets, and the music was so loud everything vibrated. We laughed the night away.

The hotel phone rang, and I blearily answered it, first registering an urgent note to Tricia's voice, and then realizing I was in the Caesar's Palace hotel room with the two passed-out women next to me, who had slept through the first ring. I took the phone into the bathroom and closed the door.

"Go on," I said. I pulled on the bottoms of my pajamas and ran my fingers over my short-cropped hair, gazing at myself in the mirror, not really seeing anything. I was still drunk from the night before. I had a history of partying hard in Vegas and was living up to it.

"Turn on the television to CBS network news and call me back."

I went into the den, found the channel, and caught the tail end of an interview. I had missed the first part, something about a guy in prison. I had no idea what it was about and called her back.

"What's this about, Tricia?"

"You got a call from Detective Mike Sanchez, Boss. They know who killed Jake." She reeled off Mike's number. I scribbled down the number on hotel stationary, and returned the phone to the bedroom, ignoring the snoring bodies of my companions. I felt numb doing it, but walked out in the hall, and banged on Pixie's door.

"They know who killed Jake," I said. "I don't have the details yet."

I found myself on her couch, getting sucked into the past.

My mentor Jake and his wife had been brutally murdered, and the crime had never been solved. He had been the second lawyer I'd worked with, but he'd held a special place in my heart as the guy who had come to my rescue when I'd been eighteen years old in jail on a trumped-up drug charge. As soon as he discovered my knack for getting clients for Harry, he'd taken me under his wing, leading me to becoming a better—for lack of a better word—ambulance chaser.

Chapter 22
October 14, 1974 (Eleven Years Ago)
Vigil

Mario

"Jake is dead," Jeff said. "Killed during a break-in."

I found myself in an office chair without any real sensation of sitting there. It was one of those awful moments that happens and then suddenly, nothing else is ever the same. The world shifted on its axis.

"Lupe, the housekeeper, found the house broken into," Jeff said. "Let's meet. I don't want to do this on the phone."

Jeff and I met at the Pantry. I don't remember driving there or walking in. Jeff was already seated when I arrived. We ordered coffee and comfort food that neither of us felt like eating. Jeff and I both ate. The food was ashes in my mouth.

Jeff explained what had happened.

"Lupe knew something was wrong immediately. Every day, she had to enter the security code as soon as she came in. But today when she got there, the alarm wasn't on." Jeff told me how Lupe had arrived at seven in the morning, her usual time. The family dog, Barkly, was lying dead on the kitchen floor. When she screamed, no one came to see what she was screaming about. She was the only one in the house who was alive.

"Lupe dialed 911 from the kitchen phone. She waited on the line as the operator had instructed. Usually she delivered a tray with coffee, toast and orange juice to the master bedroom because Jake and his wife had coffee together in the morning before Jake left for the office. Lupe did not fix a tray or go up-stairs. The 911 operator told her not to leave the kitchen, but to wait there on the line until help arrived. The first police car was in the driveway in minutes. The cops had Lupe stay in the kitchen as they went through the house. They found Jake and his wife Michelle, dead. The second floor was intact. It appeared, at least at first glance, that nothing was taken. The security system was off. No one knew why."

"I'm shocked," I said. Grief hadn't hit me yet. What I felt was disbelief, and numbness. I had heard the words and knew intellectually that Jake was dead. I was running on borrowed time. I'd have to keep busy. If I had free time, my mind would go there, and as soon as I thought about it, I'd be wanting to curl up into a ball somewhere. Too many people depended on me to let that happen.

"Me too," Jeff said. "I'm having trouble getting my head around it."

"Okay," I said. "Listen, I've got a couple clients to interview and probably sign, but now, I don't know..."

"Sign them," Jeff said.

So that's what I did. I don't know if it was legal, strictly, but I was still taking the cases to Jake's firm, so what did I, a non-lawyer, know? All I knew for certain is that when I went home to meet with Pixie and Jo to give them the bad news, I had two signed retainers in my pocket.

"Now what?" Pixie asked. "What else can happen? Tanis, Harry, 'Nando, Jake. You were almost on the dead list, Mario. What next? Who next?" She clutched at me frantically.

I put my arms around both. They both leaned into me.

"Now we roll with the punches, Babies. We got each other." Their grief spilled over me. That's when I felt it. I felt their loss. Their sadness. I felt the loss of Jake, the fucking, aching, bleeding hole his loss made in my life. The pain hit, and along with it, a fierce need to protect my team. Who am I kidding? It was no team. These girls—Pixie, Jo, Niley—they are my family, my life. I had to say something comforting.

"This isn't the time to talk business," I said, "but it's something I need to do right now. I've always been my own man. Lawyers like Jake and Harry depend on me, on us, for the business they have in their office. It's not the other way around. Please don't worry about tomorrow or the next day. Let tomorrow come. Whatever happens, we'll be okay. I have money. I have rents coming in from my apartments. I can and will take care of you, no matter what happens."

They protested my leaving, but I had to go. I needed to be there if there were going to be decisions made. As I drove in, I thought about the situation. Jake had five lawyers in his firm. It was my understanding that they were not partners. Jake owned it all. Jeff was only a two-year attorney. The others surpassed him in years and experience. Archibald Graves and Lorne G. Crutchfield had been with Jake since the time when the practice had been all criminal, and they were as old as their names sounded. Of the other two attorneys, one was a four-year. His name was Tim Todd. The other was a six-year named Ken Harvey.

When I got there, I found only a skeleton crew. Rachel was working, and an office worker Jo probably knew but I didn't. Jeff and I met in the larger conference room, minutes later joined by Graves and Crutchfield.

We shook hands and offered each other condolences.

Jeff took me aside, and said, "Archie and Lorne have a successor agreement that basically means they will take over the firm. The agreement was executed two years ago before I came on board."

We sat down.

I didn't know a damn thing about a successor agreement, but it appeared that although Jake had had no partners when he was alive, he had his death covered.

Lorne said, "If no agreement existed, the clients would be put through a mess of red tape. The State Bar sometimes steps in and takes over the firm. That's a mess." I didn't know Lorne very well, but he seemed like a good guy. I know that Jake had liked him.

Archie's mind was still on the finances. He said, "I don't know how we'll be able to afford the huge case load we have unless we can start settling cases right away for the cash flow. We're going to work with Rachel on cost-cutting where we can."

"It's complicated," Lorne said.

Jeff was silent all this time. Our eyes met. I could tell he was in the same boat I was in. For all he knew, he could be out to lunch when they were done doing the cutting.

Archie continued. "Lorne and I are in position to keep the firm going for a while. Hopefully Jake's attorney who prepared the successor paperwork will tell us what Jake provided for working capital. We'll have to see."

I stood. "Jake and his wife lie murdered in a morgue. We have no idea who the killers are. Even so, I am sure Jake would have wanted you to step right in and take the reins of the firm without delay."

The three attorneys nodded in agreement.

I had retainers with me. I put them on the table. "I assume you don't want more new business. At least not at this time."

"I don't think we can handle what we got," Lorne said. "Rachel gave us an idea of what you have been getting paid as cases come in. These expenses, well, we could never afford that."

I picked the retainers back up, folded them, and stuck them in my inside pocket.

He damn well knew it wasn't expenses. I was paid contingent on what I produced. Yes, it was a lot of money. I got paid sometimes as frequently as three times a week. I had overhead. Almost every person who sent me a case was used to getting a cash gift from me.

I shook hands and gave Jeff, Archie, and Lorne a hug.

"We'll talk again," I said.

After this meeting, I was more anxious than sad, and uncertain of my next move.

I loved Jake, and I would grieve. It was a good thing that my heart and head weren't connecting yet. I had to figure out what to do. The only thing I had figured out was that there was no time for me to collapse. I had to keep it together.

Chapter 23
July 1985
Vegas

Mario

I looked up from the floor I'd been staring at to find Pixie, Niley and Jo had gathered close around me. I was still on the couch in the girls' suite, with Mike Sanchez's phone number clutched in my hand. Jo dialed and stuck the phone in my hand.

"Mike, you broke the case?" A cold case, eleven years cold.

He brought me up to date. He gave a name to the shooter. Jaimz Battaglia.

"Con Sneed, the thief, was trying to plea bargain with the DA on an unrelated grand theft charge. His statement implicated someone as Jake's shooter, Jaimz Battaglia. He is doing time now in Folsom on another crime. Battaglia had gotten away with Jake and his wife's murder. The story sounds plausible. Sneed knows everything about the house and gave up details how they got in. All of it jives with evidence gathered at the time. The District Attorney will agree on a deal that will send the actual shooter straight to the gas chamber on conviction."

Outside of this room, none of our present companions knew Jake's name. Jo and I both sucked it up and let the Vegas trip play out without bringing everyone else down though the two of us were knocked back into grieving mode. Jo had had an office at Jake's, so she knew him well, but Pixie and Niley had not worked closely with him. We stayed at Caesars through the fourth of July blow out. Vegas does holidays big.

Jake's firm had dissolved some years back. I'd been pretty friendly with Jeff until he called to say he was moving to San Francisco. Without meaning to, I lost track of him when he hooked up with a big firm, I assume in San Francisco, where he did not have to worry about the financial bullshit he had inherited after Jake passed away. I felt an urge to talk to him but didn't try to track him down after I got the news about who killed Jake. No need to stir up that painful mess. I did talk with Jack Fino who had known Jake, too. He and Jake had never been pals, but we talked about the cold case coming to a close.

He came up as a topic during one of our Wednesday lunches. Our meetings weren't as regular as they had been, only about once a month. We were still friends, but we were both busy with numerous irons in the fire. In addition to all of his financial interests, Jack had his criminal client Gilberto Laso. I did not want to lose track of Jack though. He was a good business resource and a friend.

It wasn't like I was getting broody, but I was spending more time than I usually did thinking about the past. Of course, my past had a lot of unanswered questions worth thinking about. I tried to believe that the cops had it right, finally, with Jake. After Jake's death, I had been left with no lawyer to work with. I sold off my sources to Oscar, the lawyer Carson had been working with, and flew off to Europe to find myself. On that eventful trip, I discovered my good friends Sami, and Jason; and Jason, who was working aviation insurance, had led me to learn about aviation cases. I came back from Europe raring to go and proposed to Oscar that I find aviation cases for him. He was gung ho for it. But then Oscar had been murdered, too. Finding the answer about Jake only reopened all the other questions, and all the old wounds. I still lived with the mystery of who had killed Oscar, who torched my house, who sent the biker with a shotgun after me on the freeway, and who sent him back with another guy to ram my Rolls, nearly killing Olga, and who killed the biker after he survived the fall from my balcony.

Olga and Riana spent two more weeks in Pasadena before taking Riana home to Barcelona.

At the end of July, Tricia came in my office with a cup of coffee for each of us and sat down on the office couch. I judged by the placement of the mugs on the coffee table that she wanted me to sit beside her. I could tell she had something to say. In typical Tricia-fashion, she got right to it.

"I plan to work with Bill out of his office. He's got commitments from two corporate clients in Los Angeles."

"If that's what you want," I said.

"Boss, I will have plenty of time to attend to anything you need from me, and frankly, I can always use the bucks."

I agreed she would continue to work on a case by case basis and bill me for the work as she had when she first started with me.

That night, Letty and I were on the balcony. The balcony door to my room was open, and we were reclining, just out of the shower, air drying. It was a hot night. End of July, no breeze. On summer nights, there is something primitive and vital about being on the fourth-floor balcony in the middle of the night, the air soft against our skin. The night rang with the calls, hoots, and cries of night creatures broadcasting their lives. It was easy to feel what this land had been like before we humans had civilized it.

"I keep looking up to see if some bastard is going to rope it down here like the fucking biker did," Letty said with a little laugh.

"If you hadn't been coming so loud, we would have heard the helicopter," I teased.

"It was your fault, Boss. You were pounding away like a jack hammer."

Letty sat up, the two-person recliner that held us creaking as she shifted.

I rested my palm against her back, just for the contact. She gave her short cut a furious scrub with her towel, then let the terrycloth fall loosely around her shoulders. She fingercombed her hair, and said, "Boss, I told you Tricia would be next to leave."

"You were right, Baby." I nodded, though neither of us had needed a crystal ball to see that coming, what with the relationship with the FBI guy, and his new agency. I'd been through something similar, with Jo and Trent Joel.

"My hair is dry enough," she said. I followed her inside to the bed. We left the balcony door open and the sound of the night followed us in. Our eyes were accustomed, but it was still too dark for the mirror above my bed to be interesting. Letty flopped on the mattress, center stage, asking, "Did you have fun with Olga and Riana?"

I didn't answer, just rolled next to her, tickling her here and there until she went from giggling to helpless laughter. I flipped her on her stomach, and she flipped me right back. In a split second, she had pinned me down on my back, both of us still laughing.

"You're getting good, Baby."

"Wanna fight me, Boss?"

"Looks like I'm already pinned," I said softly.

I could have pulled away and reversed our positions, but Letty was slick and naked, writhing, and incredibly arousing. Fighting was the last thing on my mind. It really wasn't unusual for wrestling in bed to become foreplay between us.

"Fuck me, I win," she said.

"Okay."

Lainie went back to Mexico City to fulfill one of the conditions of her future success with RIALTO, to continue working with her own singing coach. Lainie now had two records and was still training. Pixie had not needed as much training before her first record. I didn't ask why Lainie needed lessons if she sang so well. After Lainie's departure, Pixie was at my house more than her own. Pixie had dinner with Letty and me every night and slept with Letty and me until she left for London. I guess you could say we were all getting addicted to massage. Betty came over daily. Sometime Tangles insisted on pitching in to help Betty or to give me four hands massage. Tangles was a paid member of my team, working during the day with Letty on teletype news and going out with us when we went on a crash. She no longer was a masseuse, but she wanted to do this, and I loved it.

Lainie had been gone for two weeks, two weeks that had gotten me accustomed to having Pixie around again. I was sad to see her go, and I could see Letty was just as sad.

The night before Pixie left for London, she and I were on the balcony. Letty was inside on my bed, asleep. We were listening to an owl and a woodpecker, and who knows what else was out there. Neighborhood dogs, maybe coyotes. We had raccoons, squirrels and opossums, but who knows if they ever make a sound. My five watch dogs only barked if there was some threat out there. I asked Pixie how it was going with Jason.

"He says he loves Lainie and loves me, too. A total weirdo."

"Why, kind of how I am."

"Boss, I think he wants to marry Lainie. The shit about loving me is because he thinks he needs to make me feel good."

"He treats you good," I said.

"He does. Notice I have his plane," she giggled. "I'd be lying if I said I didn't love that man, weirdo or not. He asks for very little, but I think losing Sami left a hole in his life that he can't fill. I asked Lainie if they fuck."

"You don't need to tell me," I said. "I don't need to know about Jason's love life."

"She says it's none of my business. I figure he likes guys. Nothing wrong with that but if I'm right, why this serious thing with Lainie? At this point in his life, why would he need a beard?"

I shook my head. "If you don't know, for sure I don't know. What is the plan now that you are leaving tomorrow?"

"A month in London, then I have a Brazil tour. Brazilian's love me." She giggled. "I got RIALTO convinced to do one-month tours. Fast paced, but I get to come home in between."

I was going to miss that giggle.

Pixie was already settled in London for the month when I let her know that I arranged a Venice trip with the agency that rented me my pilots.

My plane had a range of about twenty-five hundred miles and pilots needed to sleep so many hours. It wasn't the right plane to go from Los Angeles to Venice, but it was adequate. Venice in August is in the eighties.

"Reminds me of how we complained about fuel and rest stops when we'd cross the ocean in Oscar's plane. That seems so long ago." She giggled. "A Venice trip is cool, Boss. Be sure and stop by London if you can. Lainie will be here starting next week. You haven't seen Jason for ages."

"For now, it's just Venice. I haven't taken the plane that far. It's exciting for me."

"I could have Jason's crew pick you up. His plane has more range than your Lear."

I laughed. "If I told Olga I was doing this, she'd send a big plane. I want to do this."

Tangles and Letty and I boarded my plane. I had two pilots with over ten thousand flight hours, one third of which were in Lears and Falcons. The relief pilot had fewer hours. Having a third pilot on board meant that one of the cabin seats would always be occupied by a sleeping pilot. The good thing was that his seat faced forward and not us. I didn't call Olga until we landed in Washington, D.C. to refuel.

"Amor, if you're bored you could have come with me," Olga said.

"I'm not that bored, but I do miss you."

"I get chills when you say you miss me," she said in Spanish. "I didn't drop off Riana. We're in Madrid. She wants to keep me company."

"Baby, that's good for you."

"You know how naughty she can get, Si, Amor?"

"Si," I replied, remembering.

Olga never commented about my two companions.

"I'm so fucking excited, I'm trying hard not to come," Letty said, I think deliberately, reminding us both of Pixie.

Tangles could not stop thanking me.

We landed in Tessera at Marco Polo Airport, Venice's airport on the mainland four nautical miles north of the city. Seeing Venice below us brought back an unexpected rush of memories, and a longing for Fae.

Chapter 24
August 1985
Venice, Italy

Mario

"Head for your thoughts, Boss?" Tangles asked.

I had phased out into the past again remembering Fae. I looked down in surprise to find Tangles lying across my lap. We were on the suite's living room balcony on an outdoor loveseat that reclined. Wine glasses were out, half filled. The balcony overlooked a canal that was straight out of the sixteenth century.

"Tangles, he's day dreaming. Leave him alone already."

I called Olga from my cell, I was surprised how good the balcony's reception was. I told her we were outside in the heat, drinking wine, and I was thinking of her.

Olga

To Letty, Mario must be more than just her boss, her friend, her lover. I feel it. She's with him all the time. I feel better when they are on a trip like they are now in Venice with Tangles, not alone with each other. I must not let myself be jealous. Does me no good, and it makes me look bad if I show any signs of how I feel. A beautiful girl like her. Why no boyfriend? It's like she's under his spell or the other way around. Why do I crave this man so much? I've had tall men like him with as big or bigger cocks. What is it about him?

Riana was nude. "Let's get high," she said. "Are you sure you have no white powder?"

"Positive."

I know she missed her coke but settled for cannabis.

"Maybe in the cargo bin?"

Riana teased me, but it was the kind of teasing that was more dangerous than amusing.

"Don't let anyone hear you say that." I told her this gently and softly.

"I had to ask. Don't be mad."

I kissed her. She closed her eyes. Mine were open. She returned the kiss.

"Okay, a joint."

I'm not crazy about pot. I get a buzz easy. Everything gets unreal and dull. Everything that's important fades away.

"Amor, light one up. I'll be in bed by the time you take two tokes."

Mario

The top floor suite we had was a beautiful space, but not huge. The living room balcony was perfect for people-watching. The steamy August weather didn't stop the crowds any more than it stopped us. We wore shorts, sandals, and the girls were in bikini tops, not much more than teasing bits of string. The girls were incredibly sexy. Tangles had the more conventional figure, a tiny waist and an ass that was killer. Letty was just as curvy but athletic, her abs and lean biceps enhancing her physique. When we hit the tourist spots, the girls went just as they were, in their bikini tops, shorts and sandals, though often they were heeled sandals. All I added was a sleeveless shirt. Of course, when we went visiting the local churches, we wore the conservative outfits church policy demanded.

Nine days from the day we left, we landed in Van Nuys, a short trip comparing to a work trip when sometimes we stayed for months in a foreign country.

I never made it to London.

Letty called everyone to let them know we were home.

"I'm fucking jealous," Pixie said on her call back.

"I'm jealous of you over there in London. I was getting used to having you around again. Now I have to share you with Jason," I said, a second later adding, "and thousands of fans."

"He's not interested in me. He's with Lainie all the time."

"Pix, if you can't handle it, come home."

I heard a sob.

"Pix, are you getting soft on me? Are you crying?"

"I'm depressed."

"What's wrong?"

"The release of my album is on hold until I go back on tour. That's not the problem. They like to push the album with the tour, but they did it this way because I insisted on keeping the tours down to a month instead of three months at a stretch. I'm hoping Olga swings something soon to get Lainie out on the road. I don't want to leave her in London. He might convince her to marry him."

"She's an adult, Baby."

"Jason is old enough to be her grandfather. She doesn't need that. She's vulnerable."

Days after that call with Pixie, Quito called to say someone was headed up the driveway to the house.

"Who?" I asked him, but he had already hung up. I almost called him back, irritated that he wasn't doing his job.

I went down to answer the door myself. For a second, I was swept back ten years in time. I was delighted to see Pixie, looking just as she had when she was twenty-two. Her hair was short, what she used to call a boy-cut. No media was stalking her. It was so good to have her home.

"Don't fuss at Quito!" Pixie said. She knew me too well. "It's my fault! I wanted it to be a secret."

"Best surprise I've had all month," I said, though I still planned a word with Quito. I could imagine all sorts of little disasters with my good friends being able to drop in unannounced.

She'd flown in Jason's private plane, so no one knew she was here. She leaped into my arms in a gleeful hug.

Letty laughed at the length of her shorts and said she could see her pubic hair.

"I have no pubic hair, bitch."

I knew they loved each other. The chatter between them was how they expressed affection. Sarcastic banter had always been Pixie's way, and when Letty first joined us, she'd picked it up. Letty made Pixie welcome, then went upstairs to finish a project she'd been working on. It was late in the afternoon, and the downstairs smelled wonderful. Pixie pulled us into a breakfast room scented by the pastries Miguel was baking. He came out of the kitchen smelling of butter and cinnamon and gave her a big hug.

"I need black coffee," Pixie said. Miguel retreated to the kitchen, and Pixie continued, "Couldn't sleep on the plane. I think RIALTO wants to cut me off. The tour delay, the album delay. The hurry-up to get Lainie out on the road on her own."

"Have you talked to Olga?"

"Olga is in love with Lainie. She's going to be the big hit of all time, here and in all of Latin America."

"Her songs are different from yours."

"I know. I'm traditional, and she's pop. At least, that's how they're marketing us. It's not like we can't do each other's music."

I gave no opinion, skipped the coffee and went straight for wine.

"What makes you think Lainie would marry Jason?" I asked. It was just the two of us, and I didn't know if Pixie was going to let everyone know how she felt.

"Mario, she's in love with Jason's money. Don't know why though. Her career is going to make her rich beyond imagination. I just don't want her making some kind of mistake."

"Pix, if she makes a mistake they get a divorce, big deal."

"Why go through with that?" Pixie asked.

I hated to say it, but I did. "You said he was kinky?"

"He is. He likes to watch. He doesn't go down on me, takes me an hour to get him hard if I'm down there trying to give him head. He wants to watch me get myself off or to have a chick and me get it on. That's the price of the money that goes with him, the rich boyfriend that lets me use his plane like it is my own. I guess that's why I can still say he's my boyfriend even though he's hooked on Lainie."

"Does Lainie know this?"

"She sure doesn't know it from me. She stays at his fucking castle most times. Neither of them answers the fucking phone. The head maid picks up and says they are not available. After I talked to you, all I wanted was to come home."

Pixie had a pastry straight out of the oven and sucked down two cups of strong black coffee. Before it was dark outside, we moved to the wine room. After a glass of wine, Pixie yawned, and excused herself. I passed Letty and Tangles chowing down on popcorn in the media room.

"Join us," Letty said, patting the recliner next to her. Tangles was on her other side, chowing down on fragrant buttered popcorn. "We're watching an unreleased movie called Top Gun."

The popcorn smelled tempting, but I hadn't had dinner yet, and I knew there was a porterhouse waiting for me.

"Not tonight. I want to see where Pixie went off to."

I went up to my room and found her passed out on my turned-down bed, dead to the world. It was just eight o'clock. I took off her shoes, covered her, turned the temperature down the way she likes it and shut the door.

I went into the office and told Miguel on the intercom to start the steak, that I would be down in a minute, and took advantage of the quiet moment to call Olga. She said she was in Lisbon. Portugal is eight hours ahead and I woke her up.

"It's okay, Amor," she said sleepily, "I can pretend you are here with me in bed."

I told her that Pixie had arrived earlier and had a list of things she blamed for being depressed. One of them was the cancellation of the Brazil tour and the delay of her album.

"Amor, the tour is not cancelled, it's coordinated. The album, it gets released when she's in Brazil. She knows that."

"I feel better now that you told me this. She's going to be here for a little bit. I think she feels like she's reaching forty soon and may be over the hill."

"Did she say that?" Olga scoffed. "It's ridiculous. She looks like Lainie's sister. And as for her music, it's more folk than pop, and folk singers have a permanent shelf life."

Pixie's songs were mostly in Spanish. I believed her US following was mostly in the Latin American community, but there had been some cross-over. The local Mexican newspaper, La Opinion had something about Pixie every day. They push local celebrities hard. Channel 34, the only Spanish speaking TV station in Los Angeles, covered her regularly on their news reports. She was more buff than was fashionable in Latin American countries, but she had a big following in spite of not being a macho man's ideal. And why not? She was beautiful, her songs were great, and she played different instruments while on stage. I saw her once with a microphone in one hand and a trumpet in the other.

"Love you, Olga."

"I love when you call me by my name."

"Did you come?"

"I can if you want me to. Riana is with me."

When we disconnected, I felt good that Riana was with her. It balanced out how I had Letty, Tangles, and, for now at least, Pixie.

Olga

I'm no better than my fiancé. Riana, asleep now, goes out of her way to please me. I know she would prefer to have a man in bed with her than a woman. Now that I have Mario, I know how she feels. I've thought about getting a guard to service us, but I don't have the heart. If Pepe found out, he would kill the guard. I settle for Riana's caresses. She doesn't want my gifts. Her family is rich. She has it all. Her husband has been calling, but she tells him to stop bothering her. She asked for my advice.

"If you love him, go back to him. You had to love him, or you wouldn't have married him."

"I did love him, but he's the one that turned me on to drugs. He's always high on something. I can't live like that. With all the dope he has laying around, I can't control myself. He's cruel and uses my money to buy the shit. He says he buys it all for me, but that's not true. To him, I'm just a wallet he gets to fuck." She moved into my arms and gave me a hard hug. "Olga, thank you for taking me with you. If I'd stayed at home, I would be overdosed by now."

The hugs turned to kisses. Everything between us comes natural for me, after all my years of playing on both sides of the fence.

Chapter 25
August 1985
Guadalajara

Mario

Chartered out of Dallas, Texas, a Falcon Executive jet carrying a family of six crashed in downtown Guadalajara. The preliminary investigation revealed that the plane was following too closely behind an airliner that was descending to land at the international airport there.

"Have you ever had one like this?" Tangles asked.

"I haven't even heard of one before. Both planes were flying low. The wake of the big plane was so tremendous that it caused the Falcon to go out of control and crash."

"Wake, exactly what is that?" Letty asked.

"Wake turbulence. You ever been in a motorboat, and watched how the water moves behind the boat? It's the same turbulence, except in air, you can't see it. Must have been extreme to throw the plane out of control. The pilots should have known how dangerous it is to follow close behind any plane and air traffic control must have been sleeping. What a tragedy."

Five people on the ground were killed and eleven were injured. Aboard the plane, parents and their kids were traveling to Guadalajara for a wedding.

The children were two boys and two girls, ages seven, eight, ten, and twelve. The mother's parents lived in Guadalajara, the father's in Dallas. Siblings were in Dallas and Mexico. The survivors' locations were significant because it would be the survivors who signed the retainers.

Before we went out on the case, I got feedback from Gonor on his opinion of whether it would be worth it.

"I wonder if there is enough insurance to pay for the tremendous loss of life, injuries and property damage," I said.

"Sign what you can. Worry about insurance later."

"Exactly my plan," I said.

Normally small aircraft crashes were resolved fast, that is, either the family of those who died signed with us or turned us down. The actual legal resolution of the case would be somewhere down the road at the far end of the investigation. The deceased parents were probably big earners, since they were both doctors in their early forties. Even if there was insurance, another crucial question would be how much they were worth to the surviving family. That could be a lot if the doctors were supporting the parents or siblings, but that would be something else to worry about later.

"I think we go after the people who died on the ground, and the injured. Let's let some time pass on the passengers."

Tangles asked why we should wait.

"It is delicate for us to solicit here in the US, and it's too soon to talk to the family in Mexico. Let's find out who was on the ground. We can help pay for funerals or anything else the families might need."

"Got it. I'll call Juan. You want him to be the first to hit the ground?" Letty asked.

"Yes, but only if he can get on a plane, immediately."

Juan was not full time for me. He had an independent private investigator practice in Puerto Rico but would drop anything else he was doing to run for me. I paid better than any assignment he had going.

Seven days after the crash, Letty and Tangles took my plane to Guadalajara with plenty of cash on hand, enough to help the families who asked Juan for help with expenses. We had no retainers yet, but that would come later. I felt there was no catch to advancing this money to the needy families. Insurance companies after this accident dropped the ball. They weren't on the scene spreading around money, and they should have been. Of course, I was glad they weren't there because that left the opening for me.

Airliner crashes were different. The operator advanced decedents' families a small amount of money right after the crash, as long as they could establish the recipient was the principal heir or heirs. The advance would be deducted from any future compensation that they would pay, directly or through an attorney representing the family.

As Olga and Riana were finishing up a week in Pasadena, I could not fly with the girls, but was planning to join them before too long. Pixie was back in London, and Lainie was back in Mexico City.

Before I left, Pixie contacted me with concerns over Lainie.

"If you get a break in Guadalajara, fly over to DF[30] and have a talk with her, please."

This was Pixie asking for a favor. "I'll make time," I said.

Three days after the girls had gotten to Guadalajara, I landed in Mexico City for lunch with Lainie. We met at the Paloma Restaurant at the Alameda Hotel, ten minutes from RIALTO.

They seated me at a window overlooking the city, primo restaurant real estate at a prominent table near the front. I was glad I was already there when Lainie arrived, so I could see her make an entrance. She got the royal treatment. Maybe everyone did not know who she was, but plenty of people did. I saw diners look up from their food, noticing and whispering as she was escorted to my table. It was late August, and she was dressed for the stifling hot weather in a sleeveless, white dotted yellow wrap around dress that was made of some kind

---

[30] Mexico City, D.F. (Federal District)

of soft, flowy cotton, and flat yellow leather sandals. As she walked up, it was like a ray of sunshine had walked in the dark dining room. I saw her take off big round sunglasses and drop them into a huge floral purse that would have done Jo proud. Speaking of pride, I felt so proud that my chest got tight. I couldn't have been prouder, even if I had been her actual uncle rather than just an honorary one.

I stood as she got to the table, and she grabbed me enthusiastically, squealing, "Uncle Mario."

I pulled out her seat as if she were a grown-up. I know she is one, but she still feels to me like a little girl playing dress-up, the same Lainie she'd always been, even with the new white-blonde hair. She looked a little surprised to get the grown-up treatment, but grinned like we were playing make-believe, and sat down catty-corner from me.

The server asked us about drinks.

She glanced at her watch, and said, "I have a couple of hours free, but I don't want to waste it. I'd like to order now. I want a hamburger and fries."

"Make that two," I said. Paloma was a fancy restaurant, but their hamburgers were almost as good as Miguel's. I ordered a bottle of red wine for us to share. Good wine. Back home it was a hundred dollars[31] American per bottle.

Lainie was bubbling with enthusiasm and caught me up on what it was like spending her days in the sound studio, taking lessons and recording drafts of songs.

"They make me study and practice five hours a day or more, but I love it. I'm getting to be a real powerful singer." To demonstrate, she hit a couple of notes I recognized from her first release, and the sound cut through the restaurant noise causing a stir. She had a lovely voice but was unexpectedly loud. The people who hadn't already noticed her stopped eating and turned to look. Someone started clapping. She got up, did the queen wave, and took a bow, then sat back down. It took a while, but people went back to eating. I was a little taken

---

[31] $100.00 in 1985 had the same buying power as $234.12 in 2018. (American)

aback, but after all, she is Pixie's daughter. I could imagine Pixie doing exactly the same thing, even before she got famous.

We both felt a little rumble, not enough to make the wine ripple in our glasses, but the vibration was there. We looked at each other, smiling, connecting over the familiar experience.

"Aftershock," I said.

"Just like home," she said. "I hate these tall buildings. I hate earthquakes in these tall buildings."

"How's the house you are staying in?"

"It's fabulous. Not as grand as yours and mom's, but grand." The house was in Chapultepec, the Beverly Hills of Mexico City. "When I'm here, I have a complete live-in staff, a driver, a maid and two guards. One is always on duty. Olga picked out the staff too, and it is part of the deal. I don't know if she's going to charge me rent or charge RIALTO for everything. No matter, I'm cool with whatever she decides."

"This must be the house she said she's buying?"

"That's another house. I've seen that one, not far from the one I stay in."

"Who owns the house you stay in, RIALTO?"

"Boss, you don't know much about your fiancée," the mom giggle. "House belongs to Olga."

"I'll have to check the house out," I said, not surprised.

"Yeah, it has a boss master bedroom. I never counted how many guest rooms. A bunch," she winked. "Uncle Boss." She laughed.

"You're not flirting with me, are you?" I said, not sure how to take her reference to the bedroom. As Pixie's daughter, she'd had the run of any house I'd ever owned, not that I'd much noticed when she was around.

"No sir, I would not dare," she said with mock humility and sarcasm bordering on Pixie's. "I don't know how many times Abuela told me I was named for your mama, Elena."

I felt the need of a change of subject.

"You are keeping up with your karate?"

She found my right hand and squeezed.

"Yes, Sensei," she said, giving me a little bow of her head before she released me.

"That's a pretty good grip you got," I said, meaning it.

"If I can make the time, I may get a second belt, but not for a year. I do have a room set up to work out in while I'm here, but there's no Cosmo around. If I make it in music, I may have reached as far as I'm going in karate."

"You have time."

"If you would just stop thinking like we're blood relatives…" She was staring at me; Pixie Junior was staring at me.

"Lainie, you're a flirt," I said with a grin. I could see why Jason would be head over heels for her. Pixie had the same look and manner.

A sommelier showed up with the bottle and glasses, made the usual fuss over uncorking, tasting and pouring, then the waiter came and loaded up the small table. We ate and drank for a few minutes.

"I know why Mom sent you," Lainie said, breaking the silence between us. "We had a fight."

"She didn't say anything about a fight."

"No? She didn't say she's all worried I might steal Jason from her?"

"Be nice," I said softly, eyes on hers. "Your mom doesn't think that at all."

"Then what does she think? Why did she have a hissy fit?"

"She's thinking of you. Look, I love Jason. He's a good friend. He met your mom through me. It's just that he's so much older than you."

She took an aggressive bite of burger, chewed, and wiped her lips with a linen napkin. She put the napkin down in her lap.

"He is so rich. Maybe as rich as…" She thought for a second or two. "… Pepe Camacho."

I chuckled. "I don't think so," I said. "No one is as rich as Camacho."

I really didn't know the kind of money Jason had, but I had moved many Camacho millions and knew a portion of how many millions Olga moved around. No one had the kind of money Pepe had.

She took another bite and looked up at me slyly.

"You want to know if I slept with him?" she asked, with a challenge in her voice.

I shook my head. "Nope."

"Well, I have slept with him."

I was careful not to react. I concentrated on the food.

She giggled at my reaction, or the lack of it.

"He didn't fuck me. We're not platonic, but I don't think he fucks." She covered her mouth. "Sorry, I know he's your friend. Sorry, sorry, sorry."

I raised my hand. "I didn't hear anything." I raised my glass. She raised hers. Click.

We chased the burgers and wine with scoops of rainbow sherbet.

"I love Mom. You know that?"

"Of course."

"She just has to give me some slack."

"You don't need slack. You're an adult. On the other hand, if you are going to live in her house, she is entitled to make rules or have rules."

"I know, I know."

"And it is childish to do something just because you can, especially if it is going to hurt her."

She rolled her eyes at me.

"I agree with your mom. Don't be so blinded by his money," I said. "Pretty soon, you're going to have more than all of us put together."

She gave me a huge grin and set the sherbet aside. "You ain't kidding, Uncle Boss. My two songs aren't doing so bad right now. One day when I'm on tour all the time, wham, money will pour in." She looked a bit dreamy but only for a second. "But, Jason, he has millions, and he swears he loves me."

"Do you love him?"

"I don't know."

"Word of advice," I said. "Be smart with the jewelry."

It was a two hour plus lunch. Other than learning that Jason didn't fuck her, I don't think I accomplished a thing. She didn't say they didn't have sex. I did squeeze a promise out of her to call Pixie to mend fences.

A driver I hired to pick me up at the airport took me back to my plane. On the short hop to Guadalajara, I could not help but think of the old days in ELA. Before I brought her home to my aunt, Pixie had grown up in a brothel.

Oscar used to pay a crew to hang around and wait. Since I owned my plane, if I wasn't going home right away, I sent the crew home. I was in Guadalajara for a little over a week and signed the families of all the decedents and all the injured on the ground. I didn't try to sign anyone connected to the plane. The family of two doctors doubtless had lawyers of their own, maybe not aviation expert attorneys but they would never admit they weren't experts. I knew how it worked.

On September 19, 1985, I was back at home with my usual routine, up at five in the morning, working out for thirty minutes until Letty joined me for an additional thirty minutes. We showered, jumped in the indoor pool, and did ten minutes of excruciating laps. The staff kept stacks of fluffy white towels by the wet area entrance. I did not hear or see her walk in, but Caro was standing beside the pool holding a house phone in one hand and a couple of towels in another.

"It's Miss Olga," she said. "Urgent."

I climbed out of the pool, swabbed myself with the towel and took the phone. Letty swam to the pool steps and sat there watching.

"Amor, there's been a terrible earthquake in Mexico City. The phones are out everywhere. Television stations here are broadcasting radio from Mexico City. Apparently, that's all there is right now."

Chapter 26
September 20, 1985
All Shook Up

Mario

Pixie was still in London. I only had to worry about Lainie in the earth-quake zone.

"Mexico City is two hours ahead of Pasadena. It's only eight something there. She's at the house?"

"Yes, but I'm worried. The quake was about an hour ago, still too early for her to be up and gone from the house."

"Where are you?"

"I'm in Rio. I'm going to get a crew together and fly over there."

"I'm closer than you are."

"You may not be able to land."

"I don't think so," I said. "I'll call you back."

Caro was still waiting to carry the phone away. Letty only heard my end of the conversation, but it was ominous enough to get her out of the pool.

I gave Caro the damp towel and the phone, and she left the wet area, winding the cord as she went.

"What's up in Mexico City, Boss?"

"Bad earthquake. Get on the phone and call Lainie till you reach her."

"God, I hope she's ok," Letty said, "I just talked to her last night. Only for a second though. She was going out the door to a dinner date at a hotel or something."

I dropped my wet trunks. With a towel around my waist, I took the stairs two at a time to my office. I walked in on a couple of the house lines ringing. I picked up the first line and got Jo.

"I got to call Pixie in London," I said, putting her on hold.

Pixie was already on the other line.

"I was just going to call you."

"That fucking city and their fucking earthquakes. They say it was stronger than the one in May, maybe an eight. I can't reach Lainie!"

"We're all trying. Olga is flying there from Rio. I'm flying in the instant I get a crew lined up."

She was crying so hard that I could barely make out her words. I hate feeling helpless, and helpless is what I felt.

"I'm so fucking far."

"Is Jason with you?"

"Nah, I'm at Hyde Park.[32] Haven't see him in three days. I tried calling him. No answer."

"Wish you were here, Baby. Trust me, I'm working on getting in touch with her."

"She should be home. She doesn't leave the house till after ten. Oh, God, I'm so worried. Call if you hear anything, please."

As I was hanging up, Letty walked in in a cloud of chlorine with tousled hair, still wearing a sheer bathing suit coverup and carrying some sweats for me that she probably grabbed from the spa. I accepted the sweat pants and slipped

---

[32] Sami's former penthouse

them on. In the minute she had been in the office, I'd seen her redial twice.

"I get this no circuits signal. Can't get through," Letty said, with her cell to her ear.

"Get me two pilots. Going to Mexico City in two hours."

"I'm on it."

She went into the conference room, plugged the cell in to charge, and started dialing on a landline.

I turned the television on in the office and in my room. News showed the live images of local reporters and still photographs with voiceover of radio reports on the scene. No live video. The one television station that was operating in Mexico City was working on being able to transmit. Ham Radio operators were broadcasting news to the outside world, but no one knew how reliable these reports were. Channel 11 Los Angeles was replaying visual clips of the May earthquake with radio voiceover. No images on the current quake. As I walked through the house, I turned the news on in every room. No station had anything to show.

"Reports are that the buildings of the Commerce Secretariat, the Justice Department and other agencies have been totally destroyed," one reporter said.

Letty brought me bad but not unexpected news.

"Boss, the agency says all flights to Mexico City are cancelled. We can't get pilots for a trip there."

"So much for flying."

"Lulu said the airspace is restricted."

I nodded. My mind was racing.

"Call Louis at Van Nuys. Get him to have someone to let us know the instant planes can land in Mexico City."

"Already did that, Boss," Letty said.

Pixie called again at four London time. "I just want to know she's un-hurt, and that she's not leaving the house."

"I want the same, Pix."

"I don't know where the fuck Jason is. I keep calling but can't get through to his cell, and he's not home. I called to arrange a flight to Los Angeles but he's in the plane somewhere. No one tells me shit."

"Easy, Baby. You stay there for now."

"Okay."

She was crying when she hung up.

After hearing the news, I figured phones were dead for the time being. Tangles was on the house phone steadily dialing the Mexico City house and Lainie's cell. I didn't tell her to stop trying.

Olga called. "Amor, any luck?"

"Impossible to get through. The television stations don't even have live feeds yet."

"Same here," she said. "Pepe's got two men getting on a helicopter for me right this minute in Acapulco. They will land up in the mountains of Guerrero. A car from there to DF takes under five hours. Taking the helicopter will cut that time down by about three hours. That's the plan for now."

Pepe had told me for years he wouldn't buy a house in Mexico because he didn't trust the government, and always left me with the impression that he would never do business there. I didn't ask what Pepe had going in Acapulco and in the mountains of Guerrero that he could arrange for a car to wait for two men in a chopper, but it seemed awfully easy and convenient for someone who refused to do business there. I didn't ask. None of my business.

"Olga, thank Pepe and thank you."

"I'll call Pixie and tell her," Olga said. "The house Lainie is in is solid. It has withstood many strong earthquakes in the past. Don't worry."

"Great, I will let the others know."

I couldn't imagine how congested the city and highway must be, or the condition of the roadway after a quake.

"One thing is for sure," Letty said. "Lainie must also be trying to get in contact."

"Sure," I said, being as upbeat as I could.

"Dinner at the hotel last night doesn't mean she was there at seven in the morning."

I stopped what I was doing and looked at her.

"Any idea who she was having dinner with? What hotel?"

"She didn't say. We only talked for a second. She was on the way out the door."

Pepe was in Bogota, Colombia, with access to a shortwave radio, and relaying what he heard to Olga in Rio and Camila in Rome. Olga was calling me periodically with those updates in advance of what was being released on network news.

"Pepe says downtown Mexico City is crushed, buildings collapsed and there are terrible aftershocks."

"Why doesn't the helicopter fly somewhere close to the house?"

"The airspace over Mexico City is closed for everyone other than emergency, military and government agencies. Amor, this is a good plan. The chopper should be landing soon, then it's just a car ride."

"The streets must be a mess. And the traffic..."

"A minute at a time, Amor." Olga was calm.

I stayed in the office going through the motions of working, but I wasn't even close to accomplishing anything. Pretending things are normal does not make them so. It wasn't even eleven and Letty asked me if I wanted a drink or a joint.

"No way, Baby. I got to keep it together."

"Sorry, Boss. I just thought."

When I opened my arms, she moved against me. Tangles got up from her seat at the conference table and came at us.

Jo and Niley arrived, and Betty soon after. Melina surprised me and showed up. We were in crisis mode. She sat beside me on the couch in my office, and took my face between her hands, her eyes inches from mine. I could feel her intense concern.

"I'm sorry, Cuz. Stay positive. Lainie is a smart girl. She's fast. She's not just going to stand there and let something fall on her. No bad vibes allowed."

I hugged my dearest friend.

Miguel kept a steady stream of coffee flowing and brought up home-made donuts that were wasted on us. No one touched them. Melina stayed for over an hour and spent most of that time on the phone with Pixie.

"She's fine," Jo said.

"Fricking right," Niley agreed.

I wanted them to be right. I relived the lunch I'd had with her last month in Mexico City. I remember we'd felt aftershocks. What kept replaying in my head was what she had said about hating earthquakes in tall buildings. When I thought of her words, I got anxious.

If Lainie was home when the quake hit, chances were she would be fine. Surely home was the most likely place for her. I'd never asked if the property was a single story. I didn't think it was a four-story house like mine. Was I thinking how being taller made a building more dangerous in a quake? Was I thinking that when the big one struck Los Angeles, my house was more vulnerable than a single-story house? I was confident TJ had built my house from the ground up to withstand even a bad earthquake. I remembered how Lainie had said Olga's place was grand, but not like her mother's place, and not like mine. I kept hoping it was a single story and built by someone like TJ.

I sent Jo and Niley over to Pixie's house to bring the household help up to date with what we were doing to try and reach Lainie. When the girls came back, they told me that Pixie hadn't called.

"No question she's distraught."

When Pixie was still a teenager, she'd found herself pregnant and home-less. She came to me distraught when she'd been evicted from the only home she'd ever known after the death of the woman she called Nana. I brought her to Aunt Carmen, who made Pixie move in. My aunt took her under her wing and delivered Lainie a few months later. Pixie kept living with my aunt for years after I moved out, and I had always thought it a good thing that neither of them were alone. Even after Pixie was renting an apartment and working for me, she never really moved out. Lainie was always at Aunt Carmen's and so was Pixie. My aunt had to be taking this hard, but that did not come across when we talked about it on the phone. All I could hear was how Aunt Carmen's faith in God kept her positive. Maybe it was my aunt who inspired me, but I asked the Virgin of Guadalupe for help once again.

The hours went by with no news.

I prayed that Lainie was safe and unhurt. I prayed for all those who lost their lives. I prayed for those who were injured. There were no numbers reported of the casualties. News reports were still not official, all from a single Tijuana station. Channel 13 was the only operational station in Mexico City. Local stations were passing on enough of the live shots to give a sense of the devastation. Tall buildings I had admired last month were rubble now. The whole corridor on Reforma was a shattered ruin. Reforma, the street where I met Lainie for lunch.

I didn't drink hard liquor but the images that made it through were enough that I had to take a shot of brandy. I hadn't done that since Oscar had been around. The more I heard of the earthquake, the more shattered I felt.

Olga called with word from Pepe's men. "Lainie was not at her house. Her chauffeur took her to the Hotel Regis for dinner and told him to go home. Her instructions were that she would call him to come get her if she needed him. She never called."

"Okay," I said. But in my head, I was thinking it was not okay.

"Amor, I told Pixie about this before I called you. She's really torn up about it."

"Of course. I'll call her when we hang up."

"I don't know if I should head to LA or go direct to Mexico City when it's open to air traffic."

"I don't know if I want you in Mexico City with the aftershocks that are being reported," I said.

"I have to be there. I need to find her."

"Let's stay in touch. When I get an all clear, I'm going. I have a crew on standby."

Pixie could not talk. She was inarticulate. Our calls were silent, and then she would say 'call me back' only to sit in silence and pain on the next call too, both of us holding the receiver like it was a life line.

Work was only pretend business. As soon as we heard Lainie's last known location, we watched for images of the Hotel Regis, and saw everything but. We were glued to the coverage. Miguel brought breakfast, lunch and dinner to us as we sat in front of televised news. Disaster piled on disaster. Then delayed video clips showed up. The Hotel Regis had collapsed then burned.

We sat in silence, horror in the air.

"I refuse to believe that Laine was in that hotel," I said. I pictured her sunny presence. She could not be gone, and not gone so horribly. No one spoke. I understand that. It hurt to breathe. Had she stayed the night with whoever took her to dinner? I prayed but the only one who knew it was God.

The phone rang. It was just after twelve noon in Los Angeles, twenty-nine hours since the earthquake struck Mexico City. I was in my living room with my entire team, still waiting for a green light to depart for Mexico City. We were all so tense, the ringing made us jump, everyone fearing the call with bad news. My former and current team members had spent the night. Everyone had showered, eaten a late breakfast and gotten ready to leave.

Letty answered. "Pixie, Boss."

"We are ready to bail out of here, but no clearance yet," I said to Pixie.

"She called me!" Pixie said, her voice full of emotion.

"She? She as in Lainie? Lainie called?"

Everyone in the room hopped to their feet.

"She's in Buenos Aires." The dam of emotion in her voice broke, and Pixie started crying. I felt tears come to my eyes.

I took a deep breath. Two. Managed to respond. "Baby, I'll wait for you to calm down."

"I am calm," she said, her voice anything but.

"Lainie is in Buenos Aires," I said to the room. "She's okay."

The room exploded in cheers, whoops, exclamations, and shrieks. I waved for them to shut up. They ignored me.

I raised my voice over the clamor. "Stop, I can't hear Pixie," I said, and spoke into the phone. "What took her so long to call?"

"She didn't know about the earthquake and called me as soon as she heard. Want to know why I couldn't locate Jason?" She didn't wait for a response. "The prick went to Mexico City, the city he said he couldn't stand when he was there with me, and he came back to London and left me there."

"Jason was in Mexico City?"

"She spilled the beans. Said they were going to have dinner at Hotel Regis where Jason had checked in but Lainie suggested they go over to the Alameda for dinner."

"The Alameda where I met Lainie for lunch," I said.

"Wait, let me finish."

I sat down. The team sat around me on the sofa and on the floor, trying to hear Pixie. Pixie had stopped crying. The team had started crying. Soft small sobs they tried to hide.

"I'm dying to hear. Fucking happy as hell that she's okay."

"They eat at the Alameda, then he talks about Buenos Aires. He loves the food. They go straight to the airport, get on his plane and head out. They go to sleep in Argentina, tired, and have no idea about the earthquake."

"At least Lainie is fine."

She started crying again.

I did not want to hear Pixie cry. I wanted to laugh, because Lainie was not buried in the rubble.

"Baby, calm down," I said. "She's alive."

"That mother fucker, Jason."

"Pix, do you really care? You don't love him."

Sniff. "That fucker, flying to Mexico City for a date. Bastard."

"Thank God he did. He got her out of Mexico City before the quake."

"I'm coming back to LA."

"Want me to pick you up?"

I heard a watery little giggle escape. "I'll be there before you know it."

I started dialing, and told a couple of people, including Aunt Carmen, that Lainie had been found safe, not in Mexico at all. Olga called to let me know she'd talked to Pixie and Lainie. Raul called me. It sounded like he was in the middle of Whiskey A Go Go with all the shrieks and music.

"I booked Pixie a first-class ticket," he said, in a raised voice. "She's leaving London in three hours."

"What's the noise?" I asked.

"We are celebrating the good news."

Pixie returned to Los Angeles to the house she rented from Olga across the street from me. Lainie went from Argentina to London with Jason. Pixie and Lainie had always been close, and were acting like nothing was wrong, but I know neither of them were talking with the other.

They got separate invitations to participate in a short tour with a long list of famous stars to raise money for the people of DF, and they both accepted the gig. Letty got her hands on footage that showed them at the event, walking down a red carpet together arm in arm, like they were as close as ever. At least for the cameras, they buried the hatchet.

Camila came to visit me on business, warning me a week in advance. Camila was just as beautiful as ever, and knew it. After the hugs and kisses celebrating her arrival, Letty and Tangles disappeared to the office, and we went down to the wine room.

"Amor, do you want to make love first or after business?"

"Hit me with business, first. Let's get it out of the way."

"Pepe wants you to find airplanes for sale, on the same basis as you do with properties. Paying the seller green cash."

"Olga tells me he's renting out planes."

"Amor, he leases them on a yearlong contract, the longer the better."

"Is this LAI?"

"We have a company just for the leasing of aircraft. It's called Global Aircraft Leasing, GAL for short."

"Nice."

She smiled her familiar smile. I had explored her mouth with mine many times before.

"Pepe will operate the company for a while. He's very much in love with the idea."

"I hear he's spending more time in Milan."

"He's always there. GAL's offices are there. GAL is looking to lease re-conditioned airworthy planes to small airline operators all over the world and we're open to the idea of leasing out new aircraft."

"Amazing," I said with gusto.

"Pepe is amazing," she said.

"No question," I agreed.

"Amor, we need airplanes. Pepe is considering selling the airline, so he can concentrate on building the leasing business as big as possible. Operators all over the world dump some of their planes. Just as many need planes, but they don't have the big money that it takes to buy. Pepe feels this is the perfect place to be."

"I told Camila this reminded me of my apartments only this is huge income. When you get enough rental income coming in, it gets very interesting."

She got out of her chair and straddled me, arms around me, her lips up close to mine.

"Amor, we know you are good at getting anything you go after. Are you interested?"

I rolled my eyes. "I'm in, Baby."

We kissed. Long kiss.

"Do you miss me?"

"I miss you," I said.

"When are you going to marry my sister?"

We both knew Olga was not really her sister. It wasn't complicated. To the world, they pretended to be sisters. But they were lovers.

"We don't talk about it anymore."

"Marry her, Amor. She is madly in love with you."

She gave me another kiss, her fine ass, moving just enough on my lap.

"I love her very much as well."

I hugged her tightly, rose from my chair with her cradled in my arms, and took the elevator to the fourth floor. I closed the door with my foot and placed her on my bed.

"I need to shower, Amor."

"You can shower after," I said.

After the charity tour, Pixie returned to Pasadena.

"I thought Lainie would come back with you," I said.

"Jason sent the plane for her, the bastard. If I didn't know better, I'd say that prick cast a spell on her."

"Have you heard from him?"

"He calls at least once a day, but I hang up on him. I refuse to talk to him."

"Whatever is going on will wear out," I said. "Don't burn your bridges."

"You should see the diamond necklace she wore on the tour, the bitch. Bigger diamonds than the one he gave her before."

Pixie has always been volatile, but she doesn't mean half of what she says.

"Baby, don't call her that. She's your daughter."

"So, what? She's acting like a slut."

That night, Letty, Pixie, and I sucked down a lot of wine and smoked enough to get good and stoned. I hate that word stoned, but when I have trouble getting on my feet, I gotta call it like it is.

Now that Pixie was in town, she and Letty worked out daily in my gym, burning up two hours. It always brightened my day. Their karate workout was a joy to behold. They were like dancers almost. They chased their kata with boxing, punching the bags in a fast, fierce, amazing rhythm. Pixie had started up boxing a long time ago, and was far ahead of Letty, but Letty had such a competitive nature, she drove herself on. It probably helped that she was living with me and worked out every day. I sparred with them. The challenge for me was to push them to their limits without any injurious contact.

Chapter 27
November 1985
Singing Boneyard Blues

Mario

Around seven, Melina called to ask me about the upcoming holidays. I'd gone to my room to get comfortable after telling Miguel to fix me a late and lazy dinner. I held the phone between my shoulder and my ear and sat down on the edge of my bed to peel off my shoes and socks.

"What are you planning for Thanksgiving?" she asked.

"Going to Aunt Carmen's this year," I said. I tossed my keys on the tray on top of my dresser and my jeans and shirt vaguely toward the bathroom door where there was a hamper. "Olga won't be here. I don't plan on hosting a big thing. Are you going to come with us?"

"I'll let you know," she said.

With a little bit of a shock, I remembered she had been shot last Thanksgiving. It did not seem like it could have been a whole year since getting the call from the security guard, the beginning of that nightmare. "I insist you come with us," I said. "You are not spending Thanksgiving at work."

She did not argue with me but said something I never expected.

"That bastard has been following me."

"Who? You mean, Bruno Vicario?"

"Who else?"

I heard lots of random noise in the background. "Talk louder. I can barely hear you. Where are you?"

"Echo Park."

"Where is he?" I got up and grabbed my pants and jerked them back on. I got my keys from the dresser. "Are you in trouble now? I'm on the way."

"He's not here now, but he's been tailing me. I have the investigators still watching him. As soon as he got off parole last week, he broke his little routine of going straight to and from work. Now, he's following me in that jalopy he has. The bastard."

"I'll go kick his fucking ass."

"Don't you dare." Melina's voice rose on the phone. I could hear the noise of the grocery around her. She was in the market, walking around. I heard shoppers, employees, a store announcement calling the dairy department to the back for a delivery.

"He's not going to get close enough to hurt me. My security people got it covered, but I'd like him to try and get me."

"Baby, what are you talking about?"

"Mario, don't you dare let him know I am on to him." She never called me Mario.

"Then why are you telling me? You gotta know I'm going to erupt. I'm not making you any promises. I cannot sit by and do nothing."

"I can't sit by and do nothing, either. Don't mention this to the girls, or Tricia."

"The matter is under control."

"What does that mean?"

"It means go back to work and let me get my work done over here. I love you, Cuz."

She had protection, not just her gun. Melina was adamant about me staying out of it. Not that I always listen to her. It's not like I had her permission when I went to see Vicario last time. I could have told Carson to notify Pélon what was going on, but I didn't trust Carson.

For the time being, I was focused on my new project, which was finding planes for Pepe. Retired and unused military aircraft is stored in California and Arizona in large desert areas referred to as boneyards. I called Tricia and asked her if she wanted an assignment to find an airliner boneyard. She came up with one in our own backyard, in the Mojave Desert, an area only an hour or so away. I missed having Tricia around, but her moving on might be a good thing. My finding businesses for LAI might be coming to an end.

It had been in the seventies during the day, but the temperature dropped about twenty degrees after dark. Just before dusk, Tricia arrived at my office in a no fuss turtleneck, belt, boots and jeans, her usual refreshing self. Her long hair was in a pony tail. She put the boneyard map, a report, a folder of information and articles, and a card for my rolodex on my desk.

"How you are doing at your new office with your hubby?" I asked.

"He's not my hubby."

"Are you still fucking him?"

"Sure."

"If you are fucking him, he's your hubby."

"I was fucking you and you weren't my hubby. He's my boyfriend and my business partner."

"You want to bill me or take cash now?"

Before she answered, I pulled out two hundred from my pocket and gave it to her.

"Here's a tip."

"Boss, that's more than what I was going to bill you."

We hugged, then I sat at my desk. She blew a kiss and was gone.

I thumbed through photos of some of the planes and laughed, high on the potential of this new aviation biz. I had no idea how many planes qualify for what Pepe might want, but I was starting my plane search in the desert.

I'm not a paranoid man, but I know better than to trust Carson. I decided he would not be my middleman in talks with Pélon. I know men like Pepe keep a hierarchy between themselves and their criminal connections, but I'm not Pepe. Pélon was a murderer, but we had grown up close as brothers. I was going to talk to him myself. I called Letty to my office from where she was manning the news tapes.

"Remember Pélon? You sent him a thousand dollars in San Quentin?"

"Sure."

"Find out if he can get visitors and if there is a process to get approval."

"I'm on it."

The last time I saw Pélon was years ago when I came up with an attorney and Pixie to discuss Melina's concern that Bruno Vicario would be paroled soon. On that trip, I asked Pélon to fix the surviving Vicario brother, the one who so terrified Melina, so he didn't get out anytime soon. Pélon loved seeing Pixie. She too was part of the old crowd, but even if Olga had not just sent a plane to fly Pixie to begin her record-pushing tour of Spain, I would not have asked her to join me. If word got out to the press that she was visiting someone in San Quentin, there would be no good outcome. It would hurt her fanbase, her record sales, and heads would roll. And I am sure Pélon would milk the situation for whatever it was worth.

Early on a Thursday, Letty and I flew up in my plane. The car and driver that delivered us from the airport to the prison had been hired for the day. The visiting area at San Quentin was practically unchanged from how I remembered it. The common meeting might have been painted, but it still had stainless steel tables with four attached stools. The guard told us that physical contact was not allowed, or we'd be kicked out. Maybe more people visited during the weekend, but today only four other tables had visitors.

Of course, Pélon was still a short little guy, but he was square and firmly on the ground, if you know what I mean. He was led in wearing a khaki shirt and trousers with black loafers, and I'd have recognized him anywhere. I could tell by his tight shirt that he was buff. He still had the moustache he'd had when I saw him last. We are the same age but being here had taken its toll on my friend. His dark hair was threaded with white.

"Hey, this isn't so bad," I glanced around the room. The Hilton, it wasn't. Nothing here but walls, floor, steel furniture, and guards, and the merged scents of sweat, cigarettes, bleach, and pine cleaner.

"Punk," he said, grinning. "*Carnal*,[33] you forgot me. Haven't seen you in years." He looked at me with those eyes he still had, hard brown eyes that could bore a hole right through you.

"Guilty," I admitted. "Sorry about that."

"Hey, thanks for the bread[34] you sent. Been nice if you wrote me a letter with it."

"No excuses, man," I said.

His eyes moved from me to Letty.

"Ese, it's okay."

"This is Letty, my assistant."

"Hey Letty, you look fine."

She smiled. "You look pretty fine, too."

"Carnal, she's only been here a minute and she's flirting." He gave me a big grin that reminded me powerfully of him as a kid.

"I keep up with some of what you are doing from my *jefa*[35] and Carson. Carson doesn't know shit."

I wasn't sure what he wanted Carson to know. Aunt Carmen, Pélon's mom, and Carson's mom were all friends going back to when I was about four, when we'd moved into the neighborhood across from Hollenbeck Park. We had grown up together.

---

[33] Brother

[34] Money

[35] Mom

He flirted with Letty for a few minutes and flexed his muscles for her. She flirted right back. Then I got to the bottom line, told him about Bruno Vicario.

"His alibi passed the cops' smell test. They did not arrest him. I went to his house to waste him, but he convinced me that he hadn't shot Melina or killed her driver. He told me that he had orders from you not to mess with Melina."

Pélon listened intently. He had been the same way as a kid growing up. Intense.

"I ain't met the dude in person, but I sent him word. Melina, she gave Carson money to handle that dude in here then she said not to do it. I figure we even on that point."

"She has no idea I'm here."

"Why you here, Carnal?"

"I promised Melina I wouldn't get involved. So, I really don't know. I just know I didn't want Carson as a middle man. Figured it was about time I see you in person again."

"She ain't worried?"

When I ignored the question, he kept talking. "Bruno owes me a lot of bread. I don't want him dead." He clasped his own hand. "If he does her harm though, he's dead. Ain't a favor to you or her. It's the price for ignoring an order."

"Do you think he shot her and the driver?"

"I ain't out there so I can't say. I will send some soldiers to remind him to stay away from her, and to lean on him about the shooting."

"They can't mention me. They can't tell him Melina knows he's following her."

"I got it, Carnal."

I nodded. "Thanks, man."

"Carnal, do me one."

"Anything."

"Lay five G on my *jefita*.[36] It will go a long way for her."

"Done," I said. "Sorry I haven't thought of helping her out on my own."

"Ese, she will refuse the help. You know how she is. Push it on her. Make her take it. She comes up here to see me on the bus, then turns around and goes back on the bus because she can't afford to stay in a hotel."

His mother Ida used to babysit me while my aunt worked, and when I was older, she was there when I came home after school. I remembered her as a little woman who wore her hair big, back in the days when they did that. I bet she probably still saw Aunt Carmen in church. Aunt Carmen drove past twenty churches to get to the one she'd been going to every Sunday for the past thirty-five years. I bet Ida was too proud to let on she was hurting for money.

The boneyard was a storage facility for airline operators who at the moment did not need the planes but wanted to store them somewhere. It was also licensed to work on almost every commercial airliner being operated in the United States, as well as a final destination for unused planes and others destined for scrap or parts. I took a ride to check it out and found a lot of aircraft there, some being scrapped, but mile after mile of them were intact. Planes had to go somewhere when airlines went under, or didn't pay their bills, or when banks repossessed planes.

Kinko gave me a tour of his facility. He introduced himself as the manager, and he was the one who pointed out a hundred or so intact planes available for sale. He was proud of the shop he was running on site.

He was a tall, thin guy with a bushy moustache, who would have looked natural selling cars. He had on a light suit, and even though it was only sixty-eight degrees, he worked up a sweat while we were walking the grounds. He took off the jacket when we went inside a hanger where crews were working on a couple of planes. The metal building trapped the heat, though it was cooler than outside, and even cooler still in Kinko's air-conditioned office.

---

[36] Mommy

"If you bought a plane for yourself, we would refurbish it according to your specifications, and make certain it was certified as airworthy. It can get expensive to refurbish or for some of these planes, to do the bare minimum to get them back in running form. It can run into money just being stored until it is sold or needed by the owner operator."

Kinko gave me an inventory of the planes that might be for sale. He checked off the repossessed ones. Banks would sell their repossessed planes in a heartbeat.

When I got home, I called Pepe in Milan and ran it past him.

I am lucky that Pepe travels everywhere but the United States, so that I can act as his agent here.

"You have a nose like a hound dog, Amigo. Fax me the list of planes we may be able to buy."

"The sure things are the bank-owned repos. Not sure how open they will be to cash."

"Send me the inventory. I have cash I need to use, but we can worry about how we pay later. This leasing business can be so profitable, if we have to, we can pay through a bank. I need planes."

I wanted to ask how much more cash there was. The question I could not ask was why the money was newer than it should be, a question Olga didn't answer when I asked.

"What's in it for me?" I asked.

Pepe had his answer ready. Same cut as on the businesses. "Ten percent of the purchase price. If it's over one million, you get five percent."

"What if I can't get the seller to agree to accept green cash?"

"Same deal. I need planes."

"What about refurbishing the plane?"

"I've had dozens of planes gutted and redone. I know how that works. We'll get to that when we get there. The plane has to be airworthy. You get ten percent of the out the door price we pay for the plane one million or under, five percent if it's over a million. I trust you. Continue to get me the best deal possible."

"Count on it," I said. "I love this deal."

"You should, Amigo." He laughed at his own humor. "When are you two getting married?"

"Don't know. I'm ready," I lied. Maybe I lied. I did not know. I lived in a tornado of shifting feelings. I loved Olga who never wanted to set a date. I loved Pixie who laughed at marriage. I loved Melina who ran from marriage. I loved Letty who had never considered marriage.

"You don't plan on asking Olga to stop working?"

Olga had told me she needed four or five years to work before she stepped away, but I wasn't getting into that.

"Olga has her own mind."

"That she does, my friend. I hope I will be calling you my brother soon, no? Marry her."

He laughed again. I joined in the laugh, unsure if this was pressure or just talk.

"Fax me the list," he said. "I am anxious to see what's available."

I drove downtown to the Pacific Dining Car for a meeting with Jack. When I met up with him, I usually wore a suit to mirror how he dressed. Sure enough, he was in a three-piece suit. I wore faded jeans, a cashmere sports coat, t shirt, and black loafers, all Versace.

"It's winter," he joked when he saw me. We hugged.

"I ran out of the house as is."

As soon as we ordered, Fino got to the reason he asked me to lunch.

"Gonor is in trouble."

"Money trouble?"

"Yes."

"And I suppose I'm the problem?"

"He pays you a lot of money, Mario. He owed me nothing when I introduced you. He's into me for over five million."

That's what Oscar had owed Fino when he died. Oscar's life insurance had paid Fino off. I made a joke. "Do you have him insured?"

Jack put his fork down and reached for his sparkling water.

"Come on, Mario. This is serious."

"What do you want me to do? He wants the cases."

"Cut the upfront payment. Take a percentage at the end of the case," Fino said.

I put my fork down.

"You know the story, Jack. I'm not a lawyer. It's a handshake deal. If something happens to Gonor, nobody will give a fuck that I am owed a cut of cases I took in to the firm. I lost my ass with Jake."

Jake used to pay some up-front money, but the carrot was supposed to be a percentage of the cases I gave him. That was before aviation. For him, I worked car crashes, bus crashes, some big train cases.

"He only owes me for one case right now," I said. "He can pay me when he can."

"He knows I was going to see you about this. He told me that the check is in the mail."

"Great, then he owes me nothing."

"Mario, you can afford to wait."

"More cases mean more overhead," I said. "You know this, Jack."

"He wants the cases. He loves the caseload."

"So did Jake and Oscar," I said, "and recently I have been feeling like I was a big part of their having to use the trust account as a line of credit."

"Since when do you care where you get paid from?"

"Jack, please don't ask me to do this as a favor. I don't want to do it."

"You have no one else to send the cases to," Jack said.

"May I remind you that I asked you to recommend an alternative law firm a while ago? You never did," I said. "I'll wait until I have someone, or I'll go back to Gonor when his cash flow can handle more cases."

"Mario—" his voice rose slightly.

I cut him off. "Jack, to begin with, I don't have a plane crash that just happened and the small stuff I drum up for him, he can do without. Believe me, I'm doing him a favor."

"You're just saying this because you got a new deal with Pepe." Jack was upset. I should know that he's in constant touch with Pepe.

"Nothing to do with that. I have Pixie and Tangles working every day looking for small cases until the next big one."

"What will they do now?"

"Jack, please. I'm not going into a partnership with Gonor, I'm not a lawyer."

We hadn't ordered and even if we had, I seriously doubt that Jack would have done anything different. He got up. I watched him walk toward the entrance and out the door.

The waiter came. Instead of ordering, I handed him a twenty. "I'll be back, Jimmy. Don't write me off."

"Not a chance, Boss."

I wasn't sorry. I was pissed off. Jack was trying to muscle me, and that's not going to happen. I don't know Gonor well enough to say I love him like I did Harry, Jake, and Oscar. To be honest, Harry and Jake pretty much raised me from a kid. Oscar loved me like I was some kind of ambulance chasing prodigy. He made me feel like I was God's personal gift to him. Gonor was a different situation entirely. Jack had introduced us, and knowing Jack, the introduction had been well-thought-out as well as self-serving. Jack's bread always falls Jack-side up.

Gonor was too far away for us to rub together day to day, which meant I never really got to know him. I respect him for not being afraid of pushing forward, but his seed money can't be on my dime. PI lawyers chase blue sky. Always, the next big one will be the saver of the cash flow problems.

I got nothing to bitch about. Jake died and couldn't make good on our percentage deal, and I lost my shirt. Oscar died, and he owed me nothing, because we didn't have a partnership. Gonor, if he really mailed me the check, once it cleared the bank, he owed me nothing.

Except for Harry, all the lawyers I have ever known believed aviation cases were worth tons of money. Before my first aviation case, Tom Jones had assured me that aviation cases were worth a bundle. He gave me the green light to go out in the world to get them. I only did what I was asked to do. My team and I spent countless hours, days, weeks, sometimes months building relationships to get those retainers. I twist no arms to get paid what I ask, and I am paid big bucks up front for every case I bring in. I'd heard whispers that cases did not always turn out to be worth as much as anticipated. No matter how good or how bad a case appears, you can't predict its value. It's a crap shoot. On top of the game of chance, years go by before cases settle, and as time passes, expenses pile higher and higher. After the case's overhead—expenses and whatnot—is figured, the firm does not necessarily net as much as predicted. I am mentally prepared for the day a lawyer comes to me and says he can't pay me as much as we agreed. When that happens, I plan to listen and to negotiate, but so far, not one lawyer I've done business with has ever done that. This situation makes me think of Tom struggling on two fronts: to keep the doors open and to pay Janice. If the cases had settled as expected and in a timely way, the lawyers should be swimming in money. I never intended to hurt Jake, Oscar or Gonor. If it is too much, why don't they argue with me when I set a price? Or just stop taking cases from me?

"Boss, you are being too hard on yourself," Letty said, after I had explained why I was feeling down. "Jake is gone and so is Oscar. They were your friends. They were huge professionals. They knew what they were getting into."

I nodded, almost feeling better.

Then the sarcasm hit. "What you plan to do? Give them a rebate?"

I looked at her like she'd just fucked up. Once in a while, she did have an acid tongue.

"Sorry, Boss."

"No need to be sorry. I didn't tell you the punch line."

"What?"

"Jack got so pissed off that he got up and walked out of the restaurant."

"Did he stick you with the bill?"

I was sitting in the living room in a deep huge chair. Instead of answering, I laughed and closed my eyes. She dropped on my lap and hugged me.

"Let's get stoned."

I went for Merlot instead.

We kept talking. "If Gonor owes Jack more than five million, the interest is more than one hundred thousand a month. Way I see it, Jack wants me to wait to get paid until a case settles so he can continue to get his monthly interest from Gonor. The whole reason Jack recommended Gonor to me was that Jack saw Gonor as a potential money pit. He wanted to hook him into one of those pricey loan agreements."

"I got it, Boss. Jack's an asshole."

She squirmed on my lap trying to reach the clasp on the back of her bra. I unhooked it for her.

"He's a business person. I think I lost him as my friend."

"If that's all it took, the friendship between you sucked." She was feeling the wine, but she was right. I'd wait and see.

"Are we out of business?" Letty asked.

"Letty, you and Tangles aren't going anywhere, no matter what."

She rolled around so that she could kiss my face. She took my cheeks between her hands.

"Boss, I have so much money saved, you don't need to pay me. Seriously."

"I love you," I said, my lips finding hers.

"Tangles, she has no money, Boss."

She wiggled a little and managed to pull the bra from the sleeve of her shirt. She gave a sigh of relief and comfort.

I sighed. "Letty, did you hear what I said? Neither of you are going anywhere. You know I can afford to pay you, so stop it."

She pulled back a little, and saluted me, her bra hanging from her little finger. "Yes, Boss, got it."

I held her close, our glasses on the table. She switched on the TV remote and rubbed her leg up and down mine.

The day before Thanksgiving, my thirty-foot Noble fir was delivered. It looked like it had been sculpted by Michelangelo, if he had ever carved a tree.

"I will have to find a way to save this tree after Christmas," I told the delivery guy. He laughed at me and pointed his crew to where I wanted the tree placed.

"When we cut a beauty like this one, we plant a hundred more in its place," he said.

"You got to be kidding," Letty said, sorting through boxes of ornaments and tinsel. She had gathered the rest of my staff, including Miguel and Tangles, and set them to decorating the tree.

The delivery guy winked at her and scoped her out.

In Melina's big limo, we went to Aunt Carmen's for the planned Thanksgiving dinner, Letty, Melina and me. The big surprise for us all was that my aunt had invited Pixie and Lainie, and they'd flown in just for the occasion. We drank to Johnson who used to join us for Thanksgiving. It could have been a maudlin evening, but because Lainie and Pixie were there, we were all in stitches over the stories they told. It was clear they weren't getting along quite as well as usual. They were both drinking and trying to top each other's stories. I never saw them actually speak to each other though they were seated side by side, and at one point back to back. At least they didn't argue. Of course, there were sober moments too, when we prayed for Johnson, and all expressed thanks and relief that Lainie had not been in the earthquake.

"Truth is," Lainie said, "I can't stand Mexico City now. If I was scared of high rises in earthquake country before, you can't imagine how bad it is now. It sucks bigtime because the hotels on tour..." she shuddered. "No penthouses are on the ground floor. And RIALTO always puts me up somewhere flashy so there can be pictures, so I keep staying in tall buildings. The Alameda where we had lunch," she looked at me, "was flattened."

"The hotel where fuck-face-wanker-asshole Jason checked in was also flattened," Pixie said. "Lucky for you and him, you were on a plane to Argentina."

It was on the verge of getting ugly. Lainie turned her chair from facing the table to face Pixie. Letty got up for a platter of something and inserted herself between Pixie and her daughter.

"Sweet potatoes?" She scooped a ladleful on Lainie's plate and without moving, another on Pixie's, and dropped a yeast roll on both plates.

"Thanks," Lainie said, her voice sarcastic.

Pixie said nothing. Lainie said nothing else. Letty stayed there, making it clear she wasn't moving until Lainie and Pixie let it go. For once, Pixie didn't add anything about Jason, though I could tell by her stormy expression that the words were tickling the tip of her tongue.

Melina was unusually quiet.

Lainie talked about Mexico City after the earthquake. Pixie told the story about the emergency landing at the US military base. For me, it was a good night. Aunt Carmen brought out an assortment of pies: apple, pumpkin, chess, chocolate icebox, and peanut butter. Pixie and Lainie might be divas now, but they still cleared the dinner table, and loaded the dishwasher. An hour later, Aunt Carmen handed Lainie Tupperware full of sandwich fixings for her flight and was insisting everyone take home packages of food, and all the pies.

Lainie started for the door ahead of us. It was good to see her give her mom a hug before she headed back to Jason's plane at Van Nuys Airport, then off to London.

In the open door of her Monterey Park house, my aunt clung to me in a lingering turkey and cinnamon-scented embrace. She did not go inside afterward, but stood there letting the warm air out, and saw us off, watching us yacking away, going to the cars.

Raul was standing at the passenger's door of Pixie's car, waiting to take her home. Pixie hugged all of us and gave me a kiss from wine-flavored lips.

"See you tomorrow, Boss. I'm here for three days."

"Come to the gym in the morning so I can kick your ass," Letty said.

On our way back to Pasadena, I sat in the middle, Melina on my right, Letty on my left. I kissed one, then the other.

"Have fun?" I asked.

"Beats last year for certain," Melina said with a genuine laugh.

"I will never forget that phone call from the guard at your market," Letty said, covering her mouth with her hand.

"We're not going to talk about last Thanksgiving," I said.

Melina pinched the top of my leg, then reached between my legs where Letty's hand was already fooling around.

"Stay the night," Letty said to Melina.

"I got to work tomorrow. Early call as usual, and there's Olga."

"Olga's in Milan," Letty said.

I urged her to join us but knew Melina wouldn't stay the night.

"So how long do you think this little beef will go on between Pixie and Lainie?" Melina changed the subject.

"This is new to me. Pixie never stays pissed off with anyone, much less her daughter."

"It's over Jason. It's stupid," Letty said. "He's too old for both of them."

I was surprised to hear that from Letty. It was Melina who could not get past being ten years older than me. Our age difference had always bothered her and had probably kept her from marrying me. I wondered if the issue with Jason was the same thing, or was it something else? If Lainie was taking this to the extreme just to make a statement to her mom, I wasn't sure what that statement was.

"Seems to me they should both be grateful to be overnight sensations. They should be seriously happy," Melina said. "I don't know what they are fussing about."

"I should have stepped up to settle this crap," I said.

"Tomorrow, Boss. Pixie's coming over."

Melina insisted that her driver pull up to the entrance of my house. We drove through the gates, and past the guardhouse. The guard waved at us. I heard barks at a distance, though I did not see the second guard walking the German shepherds.

We drove up to find Pixie's car rolling to a stop just ahead. She was out of the car before her driver could get the door. Paul got out and retrieved my aunt's food packages from the trunk and handed them over to Sunny. Letty was out of the car, greeting Pixie like a long-lost friend, as if we hadn't been with her twenty minutes ago.

Melina kissed me, then kissed me again. The spotlights here and there by the entrance did dramatic things with the planes of her face. She was lovely. I could not tell if she was troubled, but she seemed tired. Maybe the dinner had exhausted her. Not the dinner alone. Being the workaholic, she was, of course she'd worked all day.

"Looks like you got Pixie for the night."

I kissed her, again. "Miss you," I said.

"Ditto."

"Hey, that's my word." We laughed.

I was reminded daily that it was shopping season by the Christmas tree in my atrium.

"Don't let anyone follow you home from the parking lot," I reminded Letty of when two shooters had followed Pixie and Letty back to the house. I had defended my family and sent one to the hospital and one to the morgue. The survivor ended up in prison.

"I was a novice at self-defense back then," Letty said.

"I got my gun," Tangles said.

"You don't have a permit for that."

"Melina said she would get me one."

"But you don't have it yet."

"It's okay, Boss. She can always hand it over to me." Letty had a gun permit for years, thanks to Melina. I heard Letty scolding her like a mother hen for not filling out the permit form yet.

If it wasn't business, Tangles ignored my directions, much like Pixie always had. She stuck her tongue out and followed Letty to the elevator. I stayed in my office when they went off to buy Christmas decorations at a nearby Christmas store that was open all year.

Christmas this year was going to be big. Olga promised to be there.

"Amor, Camila and I both are going to be with you for Christmas. So exciting."

"Can hardly wait, Baby."

"By the way, Amor, I hear you and Jack Fino are on the outs?"

"He walked out of the restaurant and left me there with a menu in my hand like a fool. He got pissed because I don't want to do a partnership deal with Gonor."

"I think he's going to call you," Olga said.

"My answer will still be no."

I learned that Olga's house in DF made it through the earthquake without a crack. Lainie was still in London, but Pixie was staying in Mexico City while she was cutting a single, a festive ballad with a rush release just before

Christmas.

"I know nothing about the record business but it's too close to Christmas. How can they get the record out in time?"

"For all I know, it's a token release this year, then they shelve it and release it next Christmas. I think what they want is to give the disc jockeys something new of mine to play, and this is perfect for Christmas."

"Makes sense," I said. "Not that I know that business."

"These aftershocks are horrible. I hate this city. Did Olga tell you that the house she was planning on buying collapsed?"

"She didn't tell me."

"Well, I saw it. It pancaked, and it was practically new."

"Olga has her secrets," I said.

"At least she hadn't paid for it yet."

Pixie promised to come home for Christmas, and to think about making up with Lainie.

Pixie

I enter his office. Enormous, modern, and cold. All glass and steel. He asks two assistants to leave, I stand across from him, the desk in between us. Paulo is fiftyish, half a foot shorter than Mario. Tabloids say he's in his forties, but I know better. He wears a suit well. He's almost still a hunk. A little chunky but he carries it off.

"Pixie, I believe the album is finished. I need you here for a couple more days to make sure."

I nod and smile. His eyes are reptilian. He watches me like he's the iguana and I'm the butterfly he's having for lunch. I've had a lifetime of that look. I have been bent over this desk before. I politely clear a few papers out of my way and lean over the desk, my palms flat, my arms stiff.

"It's fine, Paulo. Is that all you want?" I manage to say it without being at all suggestive. Okay, I know the position I'm in is doing all the talking. He's sitting, and I am eye to eye with him.

"How would you like to have dinner with me?" He sounds a little choked up, maybe developing a stutter.

I'd love to get out. He doesn't want to hear the truth. I want to go home. I'm stuck in Olga's Mexico City house from the time I leave the studio until they bring me back. The city is still pretty rubble.

"Your wife may not like that."

"You are very important to the studio, and she knows it. Actually, she's a fan of yours."

"Really?" I don't have to be clairvoyant to know he doesn't want dinner. We've played out this scene before. I'd rather not drag it out. I'm not cynical. I'm practical. "Are you sure it's dinner you want or something else, Paulo?" I lean closer.

He gets up from his macho leather chair and comes around his ornate desk. He gets behind me and I feel a kiss on my right cheek through my clothes. I feel his hands on my ass.

I'm not stupid. I am a special project in this studio of Paulo's, but I am lucky to have the opportunity. Olga has pressured him. He's had her on this desk too, according to Olga. I have a long way to go yet, to be where I want to be, and this man can make or break me. A man like him, he wants this, needs it to stay interested. I look over my shoulder, coy, pretending this is my idea.

"Paulo, what's your pleasure?"

Big executive that he is, the man every wannabe singer would do anything for to get a shot at getting signed by him, he blushes.

I change my angle, shove a bunch of stuff off his desk. It smashes to the hard floor, making lots of noise. I get flat on my elbows and forearms, lay my head on the cool wood. I spread my legs, arch my back. I hear him gasping, his breathing heavy.

"I'm ready for you, Paulo."

I hear his belt and zipper.

"*Querida.*" He's not even inside me yet. He flips up my skirt, uses a letter opener on my thong so it falls to the floor in two pieces. His hands roam my ass. He moans. He holds my waist, then moves one hand to my right hand and the other to my left. I think of sex with Mario and Letty and have an instant orgasm as soon as his cock enters me. No doubt he figures he made that happen.

Two days later I am delivered to Van Nuys Airport in a two-year-old RIALTO plane, Paulo's personal plane. Now I need to convince Lainie to come home for Christmas.

Mario

In the Mojave Desert at the boneyard managed by Kinko, I struck pay dirt on three planes. I paid Tricia to film them, and sent Pepe the videos, one of each plane. Tricia wasn't a videographer, but she was good at anything she tackled. The videos came out great.

"Pepe, sorry it can't be a green cash deal."

"*Está bien, me da mucho gusto, el video que me mandaste de los aviones está muy bien.*"[37]

I wanted this purchase to be perfect and drove out to the desert four times. I got to know the planes and toyed with the idea that the planes talked to each other at night, knew they were bailing from the desert and were excited to be flying soon. I kept Pepe current on the inspections. The covers they put over the planes preserved the windows and engines. Kinko told me the planes could sit under this kind of cover in the Mojave for years preventing wear and tear.

"They can use seats," I told Pepe. He laughed.

"I have an operator who will take them as is as long as they are certified."

---

[37] It is all right, I'm so glad, the video you sent me of the planes is very good .

It was a good point. Why put money in if the lessee was satisfied?

Except for it not being in cash, the deal was perfect. Two weeks before Christmas I closed the deal to buy three repossessed Boeing 737s from the Bank of America, conditional on their being certified as airworthy in the US, but otherwise as is.

Tangles looked over Letty's shoulder when she was getting papers together for my accountant.

"Christmas money," Letty called it.

"Just from one deal," Tangles said, her mouth hanging open when she saw the figures.

"That's Boss," Letty said proudly. I was a little embarrassed.

Fortunately, Pepe was pleased.

Chapter 28
December 1985
Christmas

Mario

Pixie called when she got in from Mexico City.

"Boss, I'm across the street. Be over in a couple hours when I unwind. Lainie will be here day after tomorrow. She's staying with me."

"Cool on both. Anxious to see you, Baby."

Olga and Camila arrived on December twenty-second. The next day, we drove out to the boneyard where I introduced them to Kinko.

Camila was mesmerized by the tremendous area filled with planes.

"Amor, you are a jewel."

"He's my jewel," Olga said, her arm along mine, our hands clasped.

"*Que paso con nuestro?*"[38] Camila asked. She was talking about me, but her eyes were on the boneyard.

"*Hermanita,*[39] he's mine, but I share."

I ignored being the topic of conversation. We were here for the planes.

"Figure this," I said. "All of these planes got here on their own. They flew

---

[38] What happened to ours?

[39] Sister

here and landed on that runway over there." I pointed to the 8,000-foot runway.

"Is that true?"

"I'll verify that with Kinko, but I believe so."

"Find more boneyards, Amor. Pepe can use all the planes you can get him. Word is out. He has inquiries coming in from countries so obscure he has to look them up on the map to figure out where they are." Camila laughed.

"Are these big airline operators?"

"Now it's startups with not too much capital. If they can convince Pepe they are genuine and have a chance of making it, he'll give them what they need and carry the paper."

"No bank?" I asked.

Olga laughed at the question. "Amor, Pepe is a bank."

"A dummy question," I said.

Both girls put their arms around me.

"Next time we come out here, let's fuck in one of the planes," Camila said.

"I'm in," I said.

"Si," Olga said. "But our planes are comfier."

"Roughing it is good once in a while," I said.

Camila laughed. "You're so spoiled, Amor. What do you know about roughing it?" I didn't know if she was talking to Olga or me, but Olga took the challenge on my behalf.

I did not respond but Olga jumped right in, "Hasn't he told you how he grew up? He started working at the age of ten."

I opened gifts Christmas Eve with Olga, Camila, Letty, Pixie, Lainie, Tangles and Betty. I had tried to get Aunt Carmen to stay the night, but she went home early. We sat in the living room with the double twelve-foot doors open to where the Christmas Tree was located.

Olga had insisted on handling the gift buying. She gave jewelry that cost more than I would have spent if I had done the shopping. Letty received an Elgin gold necklace watch and chain with a diamond bezel. Pixie and Lainie got identical diamond bracelets with five engraved heart charms: Mario, Olga, Camila, Auntie Carmen. The fifth charm on Pixie's bracelet was Lainie, and on Lainie's, it was Mom. Tangles and Betty both got one carat diamond studs.

I gave Olga the fourth Rolex watch I gave her since we met and gave Camila a watch also.

"I'm sorry the gifts are so boring," I apologized.

"Here's another boring gift, Amor," Olga said, covering me with kisses.

"And another one," Camila said.

More kisses followed. There was a lot of that. Letty had typed up a coupon book for the girls, offering walks on the beach, picnics, massages, and assorted g-rated options. Olga gave me a Wurlitzer juke box that I put in my office. It was similar to the one in the wine room and disco, but with different color bubbles. Some delivery people interrupted the opening—some guys Melina had sent over to install her gift, a new machine for the arcade—a flight simulator. Aunt Carmen came over late Christmas Day escorted by Senor Chapo. Both were dressed in Hawaiian shirts under their winter coats.

Letty had planned the Christmas party, which was a low-key play-it-by-ear event. I had a fun house. Guests could get lost in it or could hang out in big rooms with lots of people. Letty hired bartenders and servers to roam with appetizers and drinks. Miguel provided a buffet spread that was out of this world.

Jo, TJ, and Jo's teens were there.

To my surprise, Jack Fino showed. We hugged. Never mentioned what happened.

"Looks like a fun night," Jack said. "Good thing I didn't give Chuck the day off." Chuck was his driver. Jack introduced the knockout he brought with him. Jane. We never got a last name.

"She's a hooker," Pixie whispered to me.

"A knockout, Baby."

There were faces from my distant past. Pélon's mom, Carson's mom, Carson and his current wife. My aunt was escorted by Senor Chapo, who now had an impressive head of silver hair that may or may not have been his own. Aunt Carmen was sixty-one now. Her hair was dark brown, and she looked good for her age. She and Senor Chapo had just gotten back from a week in Hawaii and wore the tans to prove it. Carson mingled and shared small talk but didn't mention Pélon or Vicario, for that matter. Early in the evening, I saw Ida, Pélon's mom standing apart. She was tinier than ever, and still wore her hair in a huge do that reminded me of a giant spider. I took the opportunity to give her the envelope with five thousand dollars. She seemed flustered. I told her to put it in her purse, and to wait to open it when she got home. Aunt Carmen walked over around that moment and interrupted her protestations.

Our guests included Pixie's entire staff. My staff worked but they had a lot of help from outside vendors hired by Letty, and they were probably looking forward to their annual Christmas bonus. As usual, Miguel had made way too much food, so the staff had a party buffet waiting for them back in their residence.

Niley brought seven kids and a guy she introduced as Tony. Tony introduced three of his children, who were also teens. I recognized Niley's four, which included Tanis's two kids who were actually adults. They shook my hand and called me Uncle Mario, and looked so much like her, my heart stopped for a moment. Tanis had died in 1972, thirteen years ago. It was hard to realize so much time has passed, but kids are a barometer of time.

I whispered to Letty, "I didn't know about Tony."

"It's just a date," Letty said.

Tony apologized ahead of time for his kids.

"No worries," I said, and led him and all the teenagers down to the arcade. When we walked in, the popcorn machine was going, and Sunny started handing out cokes from the dispenser down there. Going back up, I picked up some red from the sommelier we'd hired for the evening. The disco ball was flashing in the wine room, turning the room festive. The juke box was playing, and Tangles and Letty started dancing to get something started down there. I brought my wine glass upstairs. My Cuz, Melina, my love, caught my eye. She was looking so damn good. She came in a black velvet sheath that fit her like a glove.

Before I said anything to Melina, Olga took me aside. I think her tongue had been lubricated with wine, so I took it with a grain of salt when she said, "Amor, Melina has recovered. She doesn't need all the attention you've been giving her until now, okay?"

I smiled. "You so jealous, Baby."

"And don't you forget it." She waved her glass wildly. I gave her a dramatic kiss and she forgot about bitching. She's not as big a ham, but she likes being the center of attention almost as much as Pixie does. I was pretty sure she'd like the kiss, anyway. Staking her claim.

Melina waved from across the hall, walked the rooms and made conversation, then joined the group circled around Pixie. The floor had been cleared of everything but two tall stools. Pixie was in the center of it all, singing, and strumming a guitar. Lainie was beside her, asking for requests.

In the white guest room on the third floor of my house, I got a chance to sit for a quiet moment and talk to Melina over a glass of wine. She looked very dramatic, against the room's fluff of white ruffles, chintz, and whatnot. White marble floor, white curtains, white pattered wallpaper, white waist-high beadboard. And there she was, lean and sleek as a mink in her black velvet.

"Did you confront Vicaro by any chance?" She quirked the dark slash of her brow in a challenging way.

"No way. You said to stay away."

"My people haven't spotted him anywhere near me or following me anymore."

I thought my visit with Pélon might have something to do with that.

"You got to be careful," I said, seriously.

"I am careful. Notice I don't lay my purse down anymore." She winked. "Cuz, it's Christmas. I promise, nothing is going to happen to me."

"Where are your guards?"

"My driver packs a gun and a shotgun in the front passenger side on the floor. At home, I have three people when I'm there. Day shift, night shift. Same as before."

"Good, Baby. I feel like I'm in a fortress over here with guards and dogs. I wonder if it's not overkill."

"It's overkill if you can see it coming, but you don't always see it coming."

"You're right."

A week ago, I had given Letty carte blanche to go on a gift-buying spree. She'd taken Jo and Niley to Robinson's Department Store, like the old days, and told me later it had been a blast, and the best present I could have given them all. For the party, Letty had hired the actual Robinson's Santa Claus who handed out those gifts to everyone there. If he wasn't the real deal, he was close enough to fool Mrs. Claus and Edmund Gwenn. Four carolers circulated around the second floor where most of the guests congregated to chat and gnaw on a buffet that kept getting refilled. Olga and I took seats in chairs that had been arranged in front of the Christmas tree. Melina introduced the head mariachi that brought eleven other musicians, all dressed in black with beautiful hats and silver buttons on their jackets. They stood around the Christmas tree and played for almost two hours. Pixie sang two solos, Lainie sang one, then they sang La Paloma together.

Olga asked, "Amor, do you love me?"

I kissed her, the second public kiss of the night that said I love you.

She whispered in my ear, "I adore you, Mario Luna." She raised her left hand and kissed the ring I had given her.

Olga and I drank a lot of wine, Camila stuck it out with champagne and both ladies had gone outside several times so that Camila could take some hits from a joint. With hours of that and the excitement of the great celebration, we were dead sober. Maybe we just thought we were sober. That night I shared my bed with Olga and Camila. It was not the first time I had been with these two women at the same time, but it was a night that went beyond fantasy. The only low note was that Aunt Carmen reminded me that I would be thirty-seven on New Year's Day. I wondered how much longer my testosterone would hold out. I wondered if my dick would shrink as I got older. That would be so gruesome.

The day after Christmas I woke up tired. No way was I going to work out. With the blackout drapes closed, I could not tell the sun was up, and had to look at the clock to check the time. Eight a.m. Olga and Camila were sound asleep, and by the time I returned from the bathroom, they had crossed the bed to embrace each other, still asleep. I didn't put up a fight to get back in the middle, just got on my side of the bed. I was just passing out when the phone rang three times, my private line. I did not answer it. I heard a light knock on the door, and when I looked up, I could just make out Letty walking in. She was dressed and looked fresh as if she hadn't had a drop of liquor the day before.

She came to the bed and whispered in my ear.

"Melina says it's important. Call her right away. She's home."

It had to be important or Melina wouldn't be calling me at eight in the morning after a party. I followed Letty out of the bedroom to her room. She dialed Melina and handed me the phone. I sat on the edge of Letty's bed, and she sat beside me.

"Mario, something has happened to Vicario. I'm sure of it."

Her words zapped me awake. My mind shot straight to Pélon, my visit at San Quentin, the money for his mom.

"Explain."

"Lou, the PI I have watching Vicario at night, said that this morning at ten after five, a car pulled up and four guys hopped out. The driver sped off to a parking spot along the curb. No plates on the car." She spoke clearly, slowly. I said nothing. "Lou says they didn't barge in. He believes one of them knocked on Vicario's door and when the door opened, in they went. Lou's camera never got a shot at their faces. They were wearing jackets, jeans, knit caps. At five thirty-two, the car drove off. Lou swears there were four heads plus the driver. He figures they went out a back door and over to a neighbor's, then to the waiting car as though they knew they were being watched."

"Melina, speak up. You're fading."

"I'm not fading, I'm just thinking. I have a feeling something happened to this bastard."

"Like what?"

"I feel like he's dead."

"Did you send the four guys over there?"

"Get serious," she said, her voice louder. "I've been waiting for him to make a move, so I'd have the pleasure of shooting him. He was a participant in my father's murder."

"I know, Baby. I'm sorry I said that. Now what?"

"Lou's relief will be there in an hour. He wants to know what to do: if they do nothing, call the cops, knock on the door, or what?"

"It's a stupid question," I said. "Lou doesn't know if something bad happened."

"You're right, that's why I called you. I need your input."

When Melina had wondered the night before why her people reported that no one had been tailing her any more, my first thought had been that it was Pélon's doing. Now this. Pélon had said he would send soldiers to speak with Bruno. Were these the soldiers?

"Here's my input. Tell Lou to leave. Call off the relief."

"Why?"

"Just in case."

Melina caught on.

"I'll call you back. I'll call Lou on my cell right now."

Letty's eyes were wide open. She had heard it all. "Fuck me," she said.

I ignored the Pixie line. "How come you're up?" I asked.

"I been up. Pixie came over at six, and we did our thing, worked out, got in the sauna, took a shower then she ran back home. I got dressed, then the phone rang. Anything else you want to know, Boss?"

I gave her a light kiss on the lips, before going to shower in the spa. I heard the phone. Through the glass door, Letty gave me the message that it was Melina.

"I'll call her right back."

Twenty minutes later, I called Melina.

"Why do you make me wait so long, already?"

"I was in the shower. Now I can think. Did you call Lou?"

"I followed your suggestion. Lou left, and he called off the relief."

"How the fuck we going to know anything?" I said, not thinking.

"Are you sure you're awake?"

"I'm awake. I think it was the right move to get your hired gun out of there, just in case."

"Just in case what?"

"Just in case something bad happened."

After I hung up, I was curious enough to consider going over to Vicario's house but that would be fucking stupid. If Olga and Camila weren't here, I would get in my plane and go visit Pélon.

I just had this feeling.

I called Melina back and caught her in the car on her way to one of her markets.

"Let's lay low. Keep your guns close. You don't need to watch his house."

"I'm not afraid at all, Cuz."

I laughed. "It's Cuz now? Earlier it was Mario."

"Thanks for being there, Cuz. I love you."

"Melina, when you came so close to dying last year, I went crazy. I'm so happy you are here with me, even if you aren't here with me."

"I understand. Thank you, my dearest friend. I love you. Always have."

The stores would be absolutely crazy the day after Christmas, but Camila and Olga wanted to go shopping in Beverly Hills. Tangles bowed out. Raul drove Pixie, Lainie, Camila, Olga, and Letty to Beverly Hills. Two cars loaded with guards followed. I was happy to stay home. I told Tangles to take the day off.

"Boss, let me stay with you. I never get any quality time with you."

I smiled at my newest team member.

In the family room, we sat on the kid leather sofa that was twelve feet long and very deep, in front of the eight-foot fireplace that had a fire going. Miguel brought us hot chocolate and a jar of chunky peanut butter for me.

Tangles stirred her chocolate and tapped the jar with her spoon.

"Boss, you eat so much of that stuff. Is it really good for you?"

"It's good, Baby, and I need the energy."

I dipped my spoon in the jar and held it to her lips. One thing led to another. We stretched out on that sofa, and it embraced us as we embraced each other. It was not my first time with Tangles, but it was the first time with only Tangles.

The fire was a glorious fire but not half so glorious as her luscious body on top of me.

"I could learn to love you very fast, Boss," she whispered before her lips met mine, again.

On the way up to work after breakfast, I passed Tangles and Letty in the great room, and heard Tangles say, "My folks always take down the tree the day after Christmas."

"Mario keeps his up till after New Year's," Letty said.

I walked in to my office to a ringing phone and picked it up. I pulled open the curtains to let the sun shine in, but the sky was so grim and winter gray I nearly closed them again. I tend to pace when I am on the phone, and crossed the office to the door, turning, and contemplating the window from a distance.

"I just got a call from the detective who investigated my shooting. Remember him?" Melina asked. It had been two days since she pulled Lou from surveilling Bruno's house. I could hear a man's voice asking for a price check, canned music, and white noise. She was calling from one of her stores.

"I sure do. What did he want?" I picked up a page Tricia had dropped off early this morning. A list of US airports that had space set aside for boneyards. She'd also brought some real estate foreclosures she thought I might want to see. I thumbed through them, not really paying attention.

"Not much. Just to tell me that Bruno Vicario was found dead in his car."

"What?" I tossed the papers aside and sat down at my desk.

"He said it appeared to be gang related. He had over a dozen stab wounds."

"Damn. When? Where?"

"This morning parked in front of his house. He said my case is still open. The D.A. doesn't want to file on the homeless guy who had the gun. They are still hoping to find the shooter. Detective said the autopsy will reveal if he was killed in the car or put in the car after he was stabbed."

"Are you okay?" I asked.

"Perfectly fine, Cuz."

"I'll talk to you in person about this, okay?"

"Sure."

I hung up the phone, and saw Letty and Tangles walk into the office with their morning coffee. I watched them go about their business, but I was thinking about Bruno Vicario. The guys who went in to Bruno's had not left him dead inside the house like we feared. This must have happened after Melina called off the surveillance. The exact time was not important. What was important was that my gut told me Pélon was behind this.

Olga and Camila were still here. Staying so long was a first for either of them. A week for Olga was really long. More than two days for Camila would break a record. I did not ask how long they planned to stay. Camila slept in the guest room she preferred except for when she joined Olga and me.

Betty was over daily with her portable table, and doing massages on the spot, where ever we were. If we were watching a movie, Betty was in there doing one of us. If we were in the wine room, or swimming or in the arcade, it was the same. She didn't always leave at night, either. Betty spent a night with Camila.

Over coffee the morning after, we were all sitting at the breakfast table. Miguel had fixed waffles and was also taking individual orders for eggs. Camila had eggs Benedict. I had scrambled. Olga had a white only omelet. Letty casually told me that she and Camila had, as Letty put it, "a real good time."

I couldn't remember the last time I celebrated my birthday with a birthday cake. I was frequently away on New Year's Day, my birthday. I never really had a birthday party and I didn't have one this time, but on New Year's, except for my aunt who was at home with a cold, I had all the people I loved around me. Olga, Camila, Melina, Pixie, Lainie, Letty, Jo, Niley, Tangles, Betty, and Tricia. TJ was there with Jo. The guy I met on Christmas that had been with Niley was a no show.

Miguel and Letty fixed a five-tier cake, huge, and beautiful and filled with a luscious chocolate. When lit, the candles for every one of my years looked like a bonfire.

There were no formal invitations, but that night, Olga, Camila, Letty, and Tangles ended up in my bed. Letty had lit more than a dozen candles to augment the blaze in the fireplace. We were feeling good from champagne, wine, and the joint we passed around. I felt inspired and decided to make each lady there with me reach an orgasm they'd never forget. I wanted to please them. I started with my fiancée, kissing her body. I worked her body with my lips, my tongue, turned her over on her stomach, then rolled her face up again. I was physically aware of the three girls watching us. Olga moaned, asking me to mount her, but I didn't stop what I was doing until she exploded with a loud scream.

I moved on to Camila, starting with her feet and moving up the tender landscape of her body like I was Christopher Columbus in search of the Indies. I had just discovered a route to the new world when I heard Tangles burst out. I could not believe my ears.

"Olga, you nothing but a slut bitch whore!"

I stopped and with a glance of apology to Camila for the interruption, sat up. Olga looked shocked. I patted her hand. Tangles leaped to her feet, naked as all of us. Her hair was smooth and perfect, but in the firelight, she looked crazed, and flushed, and her eyes were bloodshot. Her mouth twisted into an ugly shape and she looked at Olga like she was a snake or rodent. All the while Olga shrank against me, like she could hide.

"Hey," I said, "What's going on, Tangles?"

"How can she lay there and watch you do what you are doing? Doesn't she care? Your fiancée is a whore."

Tangles was high as a kite, stoned like a kite, drunk as can be, not sure what I should think. I grabbed her by her wrist, not hard, and pulled her to sit on the bed.

"Tangles, come with me," Letty got between us, still sitting on the bed, but with her feet on the floor, her arm extended to Tangles. She took Tangles hand, but she shook her off.

"Fuck you," Tangles said.

I could not recall a situation like this anywhere, ever. The crisis sobered me up, or at least shot down my high so I thought I was sober. I got to my feet, as Letty, too, got to her feet beside me. I did not think she'd hurt Olga physically, but still. If she was going to attack, she had to get past me and Letty. Camila was frozen there like a stump.

Letty grabbed for Tangles' wrist again, but Tangles shook her loose. She did not lunge as I had expected, but grabbed her own ears, pulling off diamond studs. She threw them at Olga.

"Slut, I don't want these."

Chapter 29
January 1986
Fisticuffs

Mario

I was standing in front of Olga, braced for an attack, but Letty went on the defensive.

She gave Tangles a chop behind the neck. Tangles fell forward, limp as a hundred-pound bag of flour, over Letty's shoulder. Letty grabbed Tangles limp arm in the fireman's carry. She gave a little stagger, but righted herself, and took some careful steps out of the bedroom.

She stopped at the door, and without turning to face me, said a little breathlessly, "I got it handled, Boss. Go back to bed."

"That little girl is jealous," Olga said, as calm as if nothing had happened. She groped around the bed collecting the earrings, and put them on the night stand, then stretched and settled back in the sheets.

"Amor, that girl has the hots for you," Camila said with a little laugh. "*Vente Amor, por favor sigue lo que me estabas haciendo.*" [40]

Olga and Camila were shoulder to shoulder on the bed, then Olga scooted away and patted the space she had just made for me.

---

[40] Come here, love, please continue doing what you were doing to me.

"Amor, get over here. I want to watch."

I couldn't help but wonder how they could be so fucking calm. I went back to Camila, and started where I had left off, and came up for air some time later. "I need a drag," I whispered.

Olga who does not smoke much lit another joint and passed it on to me. I passed it to Camila.

"Do you ever get personally involved with your team?" Camila asked, barely audible as she held the smoke in her lungs.

I shook my head, not sure what she meant. My team was my family. How much more involved could we be? "Tangles hasn't been with me long enough to really know me."

I remembered the afternoon in the family room on the sofa. That was just a fuck. She came, I came, we kissed. She loved it, I loved it. But that's all it was, just sex.

"I'm sorry. This has never happened before."

"Poor Letty. It blew her night, too. Wonder if she's with her?"

"I'm sure she is."

"Did you see how she knocked her out, then threw her over her shoulder?" Olga asked, laughing.

"That was so funny. I sure don't want to get Letty mad at me." Camila was high again.

When Camila had left for the guest room, leaving Olga and me alone, I found myself filling the silence with repeated apologies and kisses.

"Amor, it's okay. She was drunk or something." Olga shrugged.

Until the next morning, I didn't think about Vicario lying in the morgue waiting for an autopsy. I didn't try to figure out who killed him. I felt good about Melina's promise that she would keep the guards and not take anything for granted. I felt no guilt that I had not shared that I had visited Pélon in November at San Quentin, nor my suspicion that Pélon had something to do with Bruno Vicario's fate. She was safe. That's what mattered.

The guard gate called when I was getting out of the shower.

Letty walked in just as I dried off.

"Wow, Boss. What a way to start a morning." She leered at me, playfully.

I was naked, drawer open, underwear in hand.

She was in jeans and a sweater, but I leered back. I heard Olga turn the water on in the second shower in the master bedroom. I dressed as we talked.

"Boss, Quito says they have a guy out there who wants to see you."

"Who?"

"Don't know. He rang the gate bell. They are holding him at the guard-house."

"Have them walk him to the front door. I'm on my way."

When I opened the front door, I saw the guard next to a young man in his mid-twenties, dressed in worn khakis, a faded sheepskin-collared denim jacket, and a knit cap. His combat boots were far from new but had a high gloss. Letty was at my side, looking him over. She glowed with confidence this morning, no doubt from successfully defusing the Tangles situation, not to mention lugging Tangles to my fourth-floor elevator draped over her shoulders like a mink stole.

"They call me Easy," the young man said, giving me a smile that showed he had all of his teeth. He extended his hand. "Pélon sent me."

We shook hands. I told the guard to leave.

"Come in."

"Easy, what do you mean Pélon sent you?"

"Just that, Ese."

Letty maneuvered herself so Easy was between us. We stayed in the foyer by the entry doors.

He took a small white envelope out of his jacket and handed it to me. "When you listen to this, do it in private. It's a present from Pélon."

"How did you get my address?"

"The package was given to me with this address, Ese."

He gave me a cocky grin, like he was telling me something obvious, then turned around to face the door he'd come in, ready to go on his way.

"Easy, need some bread?" His head swiveled to the side to look at me. He nodded.

"Whatever you can spare."

Easy was clean cut. He reminded me of when I was growing up, the care of my khakis and my shoes. I never wore combats but my shoes, old as they may have been, were always shined.

I looked at Letty, and she double-timed to the den and returned with some bills. I gave Easy five hundred.

"Merry Christmas, man."

He and I tapped fists.

He looked at Letty, his fisted hand out, waiting. She looked at me for confirmation, and bumped fists, then walked him to the front gates.

I dumped the envelope into my palm, and a small tape recorder fell out. I ran up to my office on the fourth floor, locked the door, pressed the play button, and adjusted the sound. At first the voice was muffled. I listened to a few voices, and one referred to Vicario, and spoke his name aloud. My one meeting with Vicario had been strained. How could I be sure I was listening to Vicario?

> *"Last year on Thanksgiving night I was at my Jefe and Jefa's house. At seven I told everyone I was going to get beer and I drove to Marron's market in Echo Park. I knew the market would be closed. A person I know works there and she told me that after closing, Melina and her driver were going to have dinner in the market. I wanted to catch her when she came out. The parking lot only had two cars. One was a limo.*
>
> > *"Ese, who is this mystery person that works there?"*
> > *-Pause- "She's a cousin. She hates the bitch as much as I do."*
>
> > *"Where did you park?"*
> > *"Half block away, I could see the side entrance from my*

car."

"Don't slow down, ese or you dead right now."

"After long time, I saw the door open. A store guard stood there. A big, tall dude walked past the guard, followed by Melina. I got out of my car and moved toward the parking lot. The guard went back inside, closed the door and I couldn't see him anymore."

"You got the word from Pélon not to mess with this woman. Why were you there. Why?"

"She killed my brother. I hate the bitch. I swore I would do her. Pélon ordering me to leave her alone? Fuck Pélon. I hate the bitch. I been paying Pélon the money he asked for. Why the fuck not leave me alone?"

"He sent you word to not fuck with this woman. Nothing else matters, ese."

"Finish, ese, or your whole family dies tonight." The voice was deep, and I could hear another voice, maybe more in the background.

"How I know you ain't going to kill them anyway?"

"You don't."

"Why should I tell you shit then?"

"Ese, I told you, Pélon said we ain't messing with your family unless you lie."

Other voices. Crazy laugh.

"You die anyway, Puto, and you know it."

-Pause- Random noise. A fight in the background. Flesh on flesh.

-Pause- "I ran up behind them. The dude turned around to face me. I shot twice, and he went down. The bitch turned to face me. I got her three times. I got his wallet and took her purse. In the car, I found a gun in her purse. The bitch had a gun."

"What did you do?"

"I dumped the guns in two trash cans downtown. Later I got rid of the wallet and purse. My Jefe and Jefa ain't never been the same since my bro got killed. It been a whole many year, ese."

"You be with your brother in a few minutes, ese."

Laughter.

The tape went silent.

I wanted to hear it again, but I needed more time for that. I opened the small safe where I keep my personal stuff and put the recorder inside. I walked to the door and unlocked it then back to my desk to digest what I had just heard. I needed to hear it again but not now.

I was so deep in thought, I didn't notice when Letty walked in. I looked up and she was just...there.

"Boss, are you alright?"

"Sure. Why?"

"You're white as a sheet."

"Baby, you are getting color blind." I got up energetically. "Come on, let's find the girls, I'm starving."

I had to wait to tell Melina. I couldn't do it until Olga and Camila were gone. Besides, I had some thinking to do. At our late breakfast or brunch or early lunch, Pixie and Lainie joined us, so there was a bigger than usual group eating and chattering.

Olga asked where Tangles was, then started to explain to Pixie. She glanced over at Lainie and hesitated.

"Go on," Lainie said with a grin. "Think I got virgin ears or something?"

"We were in bed together last night and Tangles went off on me," Olga said.

"Off on you?" Lainie asked.

"What you mean off on you?" Pixie asked.

Olga explained.

"She left early this morning," Letty said, between bites. "She is totally embarrassed. I think she's going to quit."

"Get her on the phone. I'll talk to her," Olga said. "No harm done."

"She doesn't have to quit," Camila said, good humoredly.

Letty looked surprised.

"I like Tangles," Olga said.

"I haven't tried her, but I like her massages," Camila said.

"You are a nympho," Pixie said with a giggle.

"Amor, do I look like a nympho to you?"

"No way," I said.

"My baby sister is not a nympho," Camila said, pinching Olga's nose.

"I always figured you had orgies in your big bed with that huge mirror on the ceiling," Lainie said.

Lainie looked right at me, giggling like her mother, then she shook her head, and wagged her fork at me. "Swinging with more than one woman isn't safe. Got to be careful."

"Boss, say something," Pixie said to me.

"I have no clue what you are talking about," I said with a straight face. My mind was on the tape. Had Vicario been telling the truth, or had that confession been beaten out of him? I think Melina might know. Not that she was well-acquainted with the brother of her father's murderer. Melina had not heard or seen this dude in almost twenty years.

I caught a shift in their conversation when it all came to a halt. They were all looking at me.

"What?" I asked.

"Disneyland or not, Boss," Letty said softly into my ear. She looked at me with concern. She'd shoved her plate away, half eaten. I saw her expression change. She aimed a big smile in Olga's direction. It was like watching someone put on a mask.

On my other side, Olga was beaming, oblivious to my state of mind.

"Amor, let's go to Disneyland. I have to leave the day after tomorrow and I've never been there." Olga was all smiles.

"Bravo!" Camila said.

I had to talk to Melina in person. I had to let her listen to the recording, but that would have to wait.

Lainie wanted to go to Disneyland too, but a plane was picking her up at four that afternoon to begin a one-month tour in Mexico, beginning in Guadalajara. Pixie, on the other hand, had two more days before she went on her album tour, starting in Sao Paulo. They speak Portuguese there, but they love her Spanish music. Or maybe they just loved the way she looked. Pixie looked like a wet dream, more beautiful than ever now in her late thirties.

Olga and Camila talked to Tangles on the phone. Olga said she was crying, apologizing. She passed on Disneyland.

We had a blast and got home at midnight.

Soon, it was back to just Letty and me.

As soon as Olga's plane was in the air, I met with Melina. She listened to the tape three times. She cried.

"Why didn't you tell me you went to see Pélon?"

"It was my way of protecting you."

"The tape sounds scripted," she said.

"You heard the voices on the tape, asking questions, pushing him to answer. I think it's real."

"Are you going to see Pélon again?"

"Not right away, but I plan to."

We sat in silence for a long time.

"I suppose it is best I didn't do the killing."

"I agree, yes."

She blotted her eyes with a tissue. "I don't know why I'm crying. I should be celebrating. All these years I worried about that asshole coming out of prison and coming after me."

"Long time," I agreed. "What made you believe he would be after you if he ever got out?"

"I had to appear in court a number of times when he went to trial. When I took the stand, he tried hard to stare me down. His hatred was clear. He also ran his mouth in the courtroom."

"I'm sorry for asking."

"It's okay, Cuz. For years I stayed in touch with the parole board. I wrote them letters. I even appeared at his first parole hearing. I objected to their giving his application for parole even the slightest consideration. He was right there when I did it."

I thought the only reason Pélon would have offed him would be if Pélon found out that Vicario had been the shooter who almost killed Melina, but I said, "Pélon told me if he found out that Vicario had done the shooting, he would off him, not as a favor to me, or to you, but because he disobeyed an order." I also thought about the five thousand I'd just given Pélon's mother. Vicario owed Pélon a lot more than the five thousand. Killing Bruno would cost Pélon that income. Thing is, when we were kids, Pélon and I were like brothers. He'd always been a fierce little guy, and fiercely loyal. That was the biggest difference between Carson and Pélon. Carson would sell his own mother's teeth right out of her mouth. Pélon would aim that hair trigger temper of his to defend anyone he called a friend from the slightest insult.

"An order?"

I gave her a light kiss on the lips. "He ordered Vicario to keep his mitts off you. Baby, that's the way they work. Pélon is way up the ladder and this guy was down there somewhere on the bottom rungs."

"What about the guy that brought you the tape?"

"He said he's called Easy. He brought me the tape in an envelope with my address on it. Don't know where he got the address. I've never given my address to anyone. Maybe Carson gave it to Pélon and he passed it on. I don't know. Doesn't matter."

"I think it matters, Cuz."

Melina and I stared at each other in silence.

Tangles was at the house when I returned from seeing Melina. When I walked in my office, she and Letty were in the twin leather chairs pulled up to my desk. It was the first time Tangles had been there since she'd pitched a fit. I'm guessing she'd timed her return to be after Olga flew out of the country. Her hair was its usual mass of curls, and she was in her usual jeans and t shirt, but her eyes looked haunted, and she was holding her mouth in a tight line.

"Wait here," I said, then went to my bedroom end table to fetch the envelope that held her earrings. I returned, took my seat, and pushed the envelope across my desk to Tangles. "Olga left your earrings."

"Boss, I'm so fucking sorry."

I raised my hand to stop her. I didn't want to hear it, but she went on anyway.

"Letty told me everything I did. I didn't remember."

"How could you forget that?" I thought back to that day. I did not remember her drinking so much that she would be a black-out drunk.

"I been taking speed since I was in massage school, working a job and keeping up with long classes learning massage. Not street drugs, it's a diet prescription. An amphetamine. They make me a little on edge, but it's okay as long as I don't drink too much. Boss, it's a piss ant excuse but that's what happened. I lost control. I was out of it."

Judging by Letty's expression, she believed her. I sat back in my chair, glanced at them both. I believed her too. It explained the sudden explosion. But it was still an excuse.

"Are you going to keep taking the pills?"

She shook her head. "I'm fucking done with those mother fucking pills. I swear to you."

"I'm going to hold you to that." I pointed my finger at her, something I never did to anyone, much less someone I liked as much as I liked her.

"I'm going to start working out. Letty thinks it will help clear my head. I'll never get as good as she is, but I'm going to clean up my act. I swear, Boss."

When she came around the corner of my desk, I turned my chair to face her and opened my arms. She wrapped her hands around my neck, hugged me and kissed the top of my head. I hugged her back. Letty didn't move from her chair but sat silently watching with teary eyes.

Letty and Tangles went downstairs to work out. Melina's call caught me at my desk.

"I haven't been able to figure out who the cousin is. I have seventy employees at this market and I checked every application. I see no connection to the Vicario family, no one by that name. I'm going to put Lou on this. He's worried that he didn't report the guys that came to see Vicario that morning."

"Lou knows that the guy wasn't killed that morning. He checked."

"It will be okay. Lou has a future with me and knows it. I may make him head of security for all the markets."

"For all we know, it's not a cousin. It could have been anyone he knew, no connection to the family at all."

"I thought of that. On the tape, Vicario said that this mystery woman hates me too. I hate having someone working for me who hates me."

"Could it be someone in another market?"

"No one in another market would have any idea that the Echo Park chef was cooking for Johnson and me or that I planned to eat after the store closes."

I met with Letty and Tangles. "It's a waste of time for you to be looking for crashes. I've got no place to send them."

"Sounds like Gonor is still out," said Tangles.

"He is," Letty replied before I did.

"Maybe you can help me finding planes for LAI."

"Boss," said Letty.

"Yeah," agreed Tangles. "Boss, I don't want you to fire me. I can take a pay cut."

"No pay cuts and no getting fired," I said.

"What do we do then? It's ten and we got all day."

"Get Harold Tinker to up your lessons to three a week instead of one."

"Boring," Letty said. "I already know what I need to know."

"Waste of your money, Boss. I'm damn good in WordStar. Anything you want typed, I'll get it done for you in no time."

I didn't ask what WordStar was.

"Then help Miguel fix lunch."

"Are you serious? We just had breakfast."

"What if we just kick back for today only and think about it?" Tangles suggested.

"I love you guys," I said.

"We have pussies," Tangles said. "We're not guys."

I had planned to wait to go to San Quentin, but the matter was too urgent. Letty and I flew down and had to wait anyway. The guard at the reception desk looked Pélon up and told us he was in disciplinary status and for three months couldn't have visits other than his attorney of record. I doubted the guard knew what Pélon had done, or if he would tell me if he did know. I didn't ask. But Letty did.

"The reason is never explained," the guard said, flashing us a brief glance at his clipboard.

We went straight back to the airport and headed to Van Nuys. Two hours later, we were back at Casa Luna and walked in on Tangles busy with tele-type printouts.

"Hi guys. I think I got a helicopter right here in Palmdale."

"We're not taking any new cases," Letty said.

"Well, I have to keep busy doing something. If I go in the kitchen Miguel will throw me out. Want a massage or should I help the gardener cut grass?"

"I got to take a nap," I said, surprising myself. It was only two in the afternoon, but I felt beat up.

When Letty woke me, I thought I had only been asleep a few minutes, but the clock at my bedside said it was after seven. I woke up so disoriented, I had to check the calendar. Ten days into January. Check. Evening. Check.

"Boss, let's go. Just got a call from Tangles. She just shot someone in her apartment."

I shook my head. "Say again?"

"Let's go."

I had gone to sleep fully dressed down to my shoes. I followed her down the stairs, double time to my car. Letty took the wheel.

"Talk to me," I said on the way to the apartment.

"Tangles said when she got home, a girl was in her apartment and attacked her. Maybe it was a burglary. I don't know. We were barely on the phone a minute. Anyway, Tangles shot her. That's all I know."

Three Alhambra police cars were parked in front when we arrived. If there had been an ambulance or paramedics, they were gone by the time we arrived.

At the door, a cop stopped me.

"Crime scene, sorry. What's your business here?"

"The person who lives here works for me and is also my tenant. I own the building."

"What's her name?" the cop asked. He was well under six feet and had eaten more than his share of doughnuts.

I couldn't remember if I ever heard Tangles' real name.

Letty spoke up. "Teodora Martinez."

The cop wasn't impressed. The stub of a mangled toothpick hung out of his mouth. "You have to wait. She's being interviewed."

"Is she okay?"

"By okay, what do you mean?"

Since the cop was being a wise ass, I didn't push it. "We'll wait."

"Is that your car?" He jerked his head in the direction of my Rolls Royce

where it basked in the street lights.

"Yes."

It was at least an hour before we saw Tangles. I was getting pissed at the wait, so it was a good thing that he asked no more questions. She emerged with two uniformed cops who greeted a team of five plain clothes officers.

Tangles hugged me with one arm and wrapped the other around Letty. When she pulled away, I saw bad bruises on her face. Blood clotted around her nose which was clearly broken. Her face was swollen, and one of her eyes was blackening.

"Can she leave now?" I asked the cops who had come out with her. "She needs medical attention. Why didn't you call the paramedics?"

The tallest of the cops stood as high as my shoulder. He faced me.

"Let's see some identification. Who are you?"

I took out my wallet and handed him my driver's license.

"I'm the owner of the building, and she works for me."

Another cop took my license and checked the picture, his eyes darting at me like a nervous bird.

"Luna, for your information, the paramedics and ambulance were here to take the woman who was shot to the hospital. Miss Martinez refused medical attention at that time." He handed my license back.

"Got it. Can she leave?"

"Where will she be? The detectives will want to speak with her. This is a crime scene now and the crew in there will be here for hours."

I gave him my address. We left with Tangles and drove silently through the night. I felt fucking horrible for her. We were silent during the short drive home, with Letty driving. I sat in the back with Tangles, my arm around her. I am sure she was feeling upset. As for me, I was raving mad, but not sure at what or who. The diamond studs Olga had given her glinted as we drove down the street. I had a feeling that the attack was because of Olga. It was fucking horrible for me to think of that, but if there's one thing I've learned, it is that if you fuck with a Camacho, there is going to be payback. And she had fucked with Olga. I hoped my leap of intuition was wrong.

Eventually, I broke the silence.

"What happened?"

It all came out of her in a rush. "I got home, turned on the lights and this bitch belted me, a hard punch. I saw stars, I swear. I got knocked to the floor. She kicked me in my stomach, hard enough that I puked on her foot. I managed to get to my feet and she punched me again. I felt a gush of blood from my nose. She slammed me in my eye. This time when I went down, I could barely see, but I felt around for my purse. I took the gun out and shot the bitch."

"Did you kill her?" Letty asked.

"I was ready to."

"How many shots?" Letty asked.

"Just one. Nailed her in the right knee. Cunt went down on the floor, crazy in pain, left a lot of blood on the carpet. I kept the gun on her while I called 911. I was ready to blow her away, but she pleaded for me not to shoot. I kept my gun on her till the cops got there. The cops have my gun now."

"Did you tell them you were carrying it?" I asked.

"No. I told them I keep it in a drawer in the living room where she got me."

"You're in the clear," Letty said with clear relief in her voice.

"You got a good look at her?" I asked.

"About thirty. Dishwater blonde cut short with a mullet. Brown eyes, I think. Coarse features. She had on a winter jacket, so I didn't see her upper body, but she has fists like a man. Bitch wore boots. When she kicked me, I thought I was going to die. Boss, I was lying on the carpet puking my guts up, not able to breathe. I saw my purse, and I knew that even if it was the last thing I was going to do, I was going to shoot her."

"You did good," Letty said, slowing to a stop at a light. There was substantial traffic around us, but we were in a private bubble. As gently as I could,

I kissed Tangles' forehead and each of her injuries. The bruised eye, the broken nose.

She winced and looked down as if she was embarrassed at being overpowered.

"You stay at the house for a while."

"Thank you, Boss." She was trembling, and her teeth were chattering.

I pulled her against me. She was probably in a state of shock.

"Let's go to Huntington Memorial ER," I told Letty.

"Five minutes away," she replied.

"Boss, I don't need a doctor. I'm okay."

"I'm worried about your stomach. Do it for me," I whispered.

She clutched at my jacket.

"Okay, thank you."

I pulled out my cell and dialed Melina.

As Letty was parking at the ER parking lot, I said, "Letty, soon as we go in, call the doctor that did the plastic surgery on Olga and Tricia, tell him we need him over here for a nose problem."

"Boss, I don't want surgery on my nose," Tangles said as she got out of the car.

"Be brave, Baby. You'll be asleep and not feel a thing."

"He's kidding you. You need that checked by an expert, so it heals right."

"How do you know it's broken?" Tangles asked.

"Baby, it's broken." I said.

When the doctor left the curtained ER cubicle, Tangles showed us her stomach. After twenty-five years of karate and judo workouts and tournaments, I've seen my share of contusions, but her bruising was some of the worst. It looked like a purple and black map of Russia.

X-rays showed no damage, but the doctor warned that X-rays do not show soft tissue damage. He wanted to do an MRI immediately, and again in a few days.

Michael Bisko, a cosmetic physician, showed up to set Tangles' nose.

"You don't need surgery," he told Tangles. "In ten days or so, maybe two weeks, you'll be good as new. If not, come see me."

"You're the best," I told the doctor. "Thank you for coming so fast."

"We both live in Pasadena," he said. "We got to take care of our own."

We shook hands. Letty kissed his cheek. Tangles said, "Bill the hell out of me. I have great insurance, Doc."

The ER doctor said Tangles could go home.

"No pain pills," Tangles told him.

"I will write the script, and if you can manage without them, good for you."

Letty called the nursing agency, and within an hour, a nurse showed up. Letty and I tucked our invalid in bed.

"You make me feel like a princess," Tangles whispered.

"Go to sleep, Princess Tangles," Letty said.

Caro kept the nurse supplied with ice for the ice packs.

Letty and I retired to the master bedroom like a married couple would probably do. We moved like animated robots, if robots can be exhausted. This time, I managed to take my clothes off. We looked at each other in the mirror above the bed, our energy sapped. I would have sworn I was too tired to sleep, but I blinked, and it was nine in the morning.

In the afternoon when Olga called from Lisbon, I told her about Tangles' altercation, and that she was here at the house with a twenty-four-hour nurse at her bedside.

"She's going to be fine," I added.

"*No sé qué decir, me siento terrible. ¿Quieres que me regrese?*"[41]

"I always want you to return, but not because of Tangles. She's going to be fine."

---

[41] I don't know what to say. I feel terrible. Do you want me to return?

"What do the police say?"

"Nothing yet. It hasn't been twenty-four hours. Tangles believes she interrupted a burglary in progress. She's probably right."

Three days later, a detective came by to see Tangles. Medium brown hair, black Buddy Holly glasses. He was one I'd never seen before, a small non-descript man. Without the glasses, his face would be hard to pick out of a crowd. After we sent the nurse down to Miguel to grab her lunch, Tangles asked Letty and me to stay in the room. Her left eye was the color of an eggplant. The map of Russia that crossed her abdomen was also mostly eggplant, with shadings of gold and green, not that the detective got a look at it. He shook our hands, and introduced himself as Sam, no last name mentioned, though it was on his badge.

"Have a seat," Letty said. "Do you want something to eat or drink?"

"Thanks, but no thanks," he said.

Letty and I sat in chairs that had been moved on either side of the bed when we'd been playing gin across Tangles' bed last night. A couple of card decks were on her bed stand, and an abandoned game of solitaire on a TV table beside the recliner the nurse had been using. Sam's lips pursed, and looked a little impatient, as if he'd have preferred to stand, but took the seat he was offered.

"I hope you are feeling better Miss Martinez. It is Miss?"

"Call me Tangles. Everyone does."

"Miss Tangles—"

"Just Tangles," she said.

"I have the report taken after the incident," he said. "Officers found no sign of forced entry. Did you have the door unlocked?"

"Not a chance," Tangles said in a low voice, with a slight shake of her head.

"Was anything missing?"

"Nothing that I noticed. I had eight hundred dollars in a kitchen drawer, and it was still there."

"How long do you think she was there? Had she just gone in? Could you tell if anything had been rummaged through?"

"I couldn't say. When I went in, the lights were out. I didn't see a flashlight when I held her at gunpoint after I called 911."

"So, she might have just gone in, then you surprised her."

Tangles shrugged. "I can't respond to that. For all I know she was waiting for me. That's what it felt like. An ambush. I can't believe she was in my house. I've never seen her before in my life."

"She had nothing with her, no identification," Sam said. "She told the hospital she was Imelda Flores and was booked under that name. Her prints came back with nothing to show. A ghost."

"Is she in the hospital?"

"First hospital, then jail. Currently she's out on bail."

"How much was her bail?" I asked.

"Twenty thousand."[42]

"That tramp was burglarizing my house and had twenty thousand for bail? Who bailed her out?" Tangles' face flushed. She rose up on her elbows in indignation, winced, and fell back against the pillow.

"I talked to the bail bondsman before coming over here. He says he got twenty-two thousand cash from an old man that came to his office. Bondsman made an easy two thousand commission for posting a fully collateralized bond." He got up.

"Well fuck me and the horse I rode in on," Letty said.

The detective said, "Excuse me?"

Letty waived her hand, "Talking to myself. Sorry."

The detective looked at Tangles, "I'll be back. I'll let you know the moment I know something."

I left Letty with Tangles and walked the detective out. We passed the nurse waiting outside the door, holding a coffee mug and a paper bag with food I presumed Miguel had fixed for her.

---

[42] $20,000.00 in 1986 had the same buying power as $45,109.61 in 2018.

I told her she could go back in.

"I like the way you take care of your employee," Sam said.

"She's a dear friend. One small favor, detective," I said. "Can you get Tangles a picture of the assailant?"

"Her booking picture?"

"Yes."

"It's public. I see no problem. I'll get it for you."

We shook hands. From the door, I leaned against the frame and watched as he walked to an unmarked black Plymouth that had seen better days. Before getting in, he stopped and looked around. "You're living in Fort Knox, here. Gates, guards, dogs, cameras." He pointed at the one security camera in view that was aimed at my front door. "Why so much security?"

"So that I don't have to call someone like you. No offense." I grinned.

"None taken." He grinned back at me. His bland face had a couple of surprising dimples.

I would bet a stack of hundred-dollar bills that as soon as he got back to the precinct, he'd be looking me up. I gave him a little more of an answer. "To keep those with bad intentions away from my property."

The detective laughed, got in his car, and drove away.

The follow-up MRI the doctor had taken showed nothing significant. Tangles insisted that her nurses be discharged after seven days. The nurses left, but I told Tangles it was too soon for her to go home. She and Letty went by Tangles' apartment and got more of her clothes to put in the closet. Letty told me that having Tangles over felt like a slumber party.

Olga called daily. Now that I owned a plane and was in the plane acquisition business, I better understood the cost of fuel and maintenance for a plane like hers. Fuel prices were skyrocketing. The expense of keeping it running had to be outrageous. I thought that Pepe must not be thinking straight. When I'd first met him, he'd flaunted his planes and wealth, and I'd considered that he was eccentric. The flamboyant eccentricity was part of his charm, but even he should be practical. There were far smaller birds out there to get Olga and Camila around, even with the guards. An enclosed full-size bed separated from the rest of the cabin was hardly worth the expense.

I learned she was now traveling with Riana.

"Riana is good company. With her, I don't feel so alone."

"You have the guards."

"Amor, don't be mean. The guards, they keep their distance. You know that."

"Baby, why do you and Camila need such big planes to get around?"

There was a pause so long that I thought I had gotten disconnected.

"Why you are wondering? We love our planes," she said defensively.

"There are more economical means of transport out there. Some of them very posh. I've seen some gorgeous executive jets that have a range to cross oceans and then some."

"You mean like your plane?"

"My plane doesn't have the range I'm talking about."

Olga was silent.

Wishing I had not brought the subject up, I forced a laugh. "I promise I'm not trying to sell you a plane."

"Ever the salesman," she said with a sigh of relief.

It took a while for Tangles to go from eggplant to lavender to a light yellow, but when she did, she started working out with Letty in my gym. In that same time, Imelda Flores disappeared. She didn't show in court for her arraignment. Her bail was forfeited, and a warrant issued for her arrest. Her disappearance was an inspiration to Tangles to work harder, and to think of karate practice as more than Jazzersize.

One question had been bugging us all, and became the topic during the late lunch Letty, Tangles and I were taking. A simple meal. Cups of tomato soup and club sandwiches.

"Do you think someone sent that bitch to hurt Tangles?" Letty asked.

I toyed with the idea. "The cops said she had no gun."

"She had her fists," Tangles said. "And who was the man who walked into the bail bond office and dropped off twenty-two thousand cash to bail out the puta? She didn't show in court. Her prints came up with nothing."

"I've heard vengeance stories," Letty said emphatically, taking up her tall glass of sweet tea and gesturing with it in my direction before she ever took a sip.

"What stories?"

Letty narrowed her eyes at me. "The last time Pepe got pissed off, he firebombed a plantation."

"There's a little more to it than that," I said. "Pepe and I suspected that the bastards who ordered me kidnapped in Venezuela were also responsible for killing Oscar."

"Boss, I know the story," Letty said.

"I don't," Tangles said. "I'm listening."

"I had been kidnapped. Oscar asked Pepe Camacho to find and rescue me, so he did, and we met for the first time. The kidnappers were lawyers, wannabe Venezuelan aviation lawyers. They did about five years in prison, not for the kidnapping, because those charges would never stick, but on drug charges. After they bribed their way out of hard time, Oscar was shot. We never knew for certain, but the lawyers might have been responsible. Pepe sent ten men to the lawyers' coffee plantation to check things out, mostly to see if they were holed up there. His men did not return. Pepe flew out, found his men dead. That was when the plantation was burned to the ground."

Letty broke in. "Pixie told me the lawyers were competitors on a case you were on, and you flew to Caracas to see it for yourself they were dead."

"I never did see their bodies," I said. "Their plantation was sure as hell gone to ash. But this has nothing to do with Tangles getting attacked in her apartment."

"Maybe Camila or Olga were not as cool as they pretended. Maybe one of them sent that tramp to teach Tangles a lesson." Letty said, not letting go.

"Baby, Olga is my fiancée. You can't be thinking about her that way."

"Okay, how about Camila? Olga and Camila are lovers. Maybe she's protective."

Tangles said nothing. She sipped her soup with a stony expression.

"Letty, back off," I said. "Let's put an end to that kind of talk. There's no proof."

She made a face, then apologized. "Sorry, Boss."

Melina called.

"The chief who gave me my concealed carry permit is dead. Now I must deal with the sheriff. No telling how many blow jobs this favor is going to cost me." Tangles would be getting her permit to carry just as Letty, Pixie, Niley, and Jo have.

"She has to get her ass over to Olga's house and use that shooting range."

"I think she's been doing that weekly since she bought the gun," I said. "With Letty and when Pixie is there, the three of them go at it."

"I'll get feedback from the sheriff."

"Baby, thanks." We laughed, but I never knew with Melina, how much of this was a joke, and how much was real.

"I know that the coach is no longer on my payroll, but Letty can teach her," Melina said.

When Olga and Riana arrived on Friday, Olga was eager to talk to Tangles.

"I have to meet up with Pepe on Monday in Milan. Where is Tangles? I want to see her."

"Letty and Tangles are in Utah. They went to video an office building I'm working on for LAI."

"You really are out of the aviation crash business?"

I hated to think I was. "For now. I need a lawyer with money and aviation experience."

"Amor, you don't need the income from that. Good idea to have the girls helping you like Tricia used to do."

"Tricia still does some work, but not as much," I said.

"I'm leaving Sunday," she said. "Will they be back by then?"

"Unlikely," I said. I was glad to have Olga back and glad that Olga wanted Riana in bed with us, but I was also glad that the girls were away. I knew the girls would be back before Olga left, but I didn't feel like letting her know that at the moment.

Chapter 30
March 1986
Fortune Springs

Mario

Melina told me she'd hit a roadblock.

"Lou said he ran into a dead end. No name is tied to the cousin working for me. I think that was bullshit," she said.

"How would he have known you were still at the market after closing? Maybe it wasn't a cousin. I guess you can't bring in the cops. They'd wonder how you know this. By the way, I just bought new cell phones. The NOKIA is small and has longer battery life. Have you seen it?"

"I saw an ad in the newspaper, let me know if you like," she said.

"I'll buy you one."

"Thanks, Cuz."

"Box up all the bricks. I hate those things," I said to Letty.

"I saw a flip phone by Motorola," said Tangles. "I don't think they are out yet."

"Boss, those are smaller than Nokia, but Nokia is sleek."

The Nokia was a great improvement. It almost fit in my pocket.

It was past time to see Pélon. To avoid another pointless trip, Letty called San Quentin. Pélon's disciplinary status had been extended.

By the end of March, I had purchased seven planes for Pepe's leasing company. If the demand for planes held true, I was on my way to making a lot more money on planes than in property acquisitions. In June, Kinko arranged for me to have a tour of the Boeing plant in Everett, Washington. Kinko was certainly well connected. The public had tours, but our private tour was led by an upper level representative named Roseanne Smith. I suppose they hoped that the leasing company I was buying planes for would someday start leasing new Boeing planes. Pepe dispatched Camila to take the tour with me. We each came to the tour in our planes, she in her Boeing 737, me in my modest jet. We had permission to land at the Boeing runway. It was just another runway, but still, I found it exciting. I had this feeling of being important. In my big house I never think about the grandeur I am living in. I want to believe that I'm the same person who found a job at age ten and hustled ever since. I knew good things were going to come from this leasing business.

In a crisp suit and tie, Camila looked head to toe like the executive that she was. She played it cool around Roseanne, but in spite of how blasé and unimpressed she looked, by the way her hand gripped mine, I knew Camila was excited. I guess I looked like myself, whatever that means. Though lately I lived in blue jeans, I wore a navy-blue suit tailored for me in New York during one of my trips. It was good I wore what I wore. Washington was still cold.

My business card had only my name and phone number, but Roseanne asked few questions of me. I was certain Kinko must have already informed his contact that he had brokered planes through me to GAL. Roseanne took us around the immense building in a four-wheel motor cart, a little bigger than the carts I kept for the help to drive to their lodgings at the back of my estate. The 747s built inside were enormous, each plane with its own space.

I knew one thing for sure. If we ever bought directly from Boeing, we weren't going to pay for it with green cash.

Camila, Roseanne, and I had lunch in a private dining room. We discussed the leasing markets in Europe and South America—especially South America where Camila and I knew Pepe aimed to corner the market. We made our interest in the South American market clear, and that the location of the GAL office in Milan meant nothing. Roseanne got Camila talking about her plane, and asked Camila to show her the interior. Camila agreed.

When Roseanne took us out to our planes, she dropped me off first. I kissed Camila, shook hands with Roseanne and watched them drive off to Camila's plane. I did not stick around waiting for Camila to leave. Ten minutes after I boarded, my pilots got a clearance to take off. I looked out the window at the enormous Boeing compound as we sped down the runway and took off. Nothing but blue sky ahead.

Camila was on her way to Rome. Olga was already there with Riana.

"Amor, I'm sending my plane for you. Even Pepe will be here. All of us will be going to Mass together, and we will be sitting in the second row because there are too many of us."

"Too many of us?"

"I want you to bring Letty and Tangles with you. Camila asked that you please invite Betty. She likes her."

I remembered when I had gone to Mass at the Vatican with Camila. The following year, though Olga and I had front row seats, we ended up staying in bed and not using the extremely hard to get tickets.

I called Letty and Tangles in to my office and told them about the upcoming trip.

"Of course, you don't have to go," I said. "If you do go, all this talk about my fiancée or her sister having anything to do with that attack has to go in the shit can. If this is too hard for you to do, tell me now, because not only will you not go to Rome, you may not be working for me anymore."

Letty's eyes opened wide. Tears appeared. No sound.

Tangles grimaced, but her answer sounded honest. "Boss, I have no proof where that tramp came from. Even if I knew it was your fiancée or her family, I'd be scared to death to bring it up."

I was ready to slam her with words, but her lips trembled. I didn't want to kick her when she was down.

"I'm surprised you would hold my job over my head like that. It's not like you." Tangles said.

I stared and let her speak. Letty was still silent, wiping tears. The way her lips were clenched together, it was like she was afraid if she opened them, a whole torrent of things I didn't want to hear would gush out.

"I can't handle this gossip another day," I said. "Olga is wearing my ring, and you will respect her. If you want to talk to me about it again, bring evidence."

"Letty, did you get what I said?"

She nodded. "Loud and clear."

"Let me know tomorrow if you are going with me."

I was feeling irritated at my team and took the elevator down to the entry level. It wasn't my intention, but I drove mindlessly, and ended up at the Whisky a Go Go in Hollywood. Everyone at this club has an expensive sports car, so my Rolls just fit in. A twenty to the attendant insured that my car would be on the sidewalk in front, ready for me when I came out. I had to wait twenty minutes for my seat at the bar. I ordered Merlot, took a sip, and asked for a Pinot Noir. Like a dummy, I always ordered wine, knowing it wasn't going to be up to par. I put a hundred on the bar. Whisky a Go Go is not known for their wine. Whisky a Go Go is known for the night life. I felt a woman's hand on my back. Small hand. Expensive perfume. I remembered back when Olga told me I should go out clubbing and pickup chicks. She'd said it when she was jealous of Letty. I saw no reason not to take her at her word. After all, she screwed her bankers, and Riana.

"Hey, sit over here with me, and I'll buy you a drink."

I turned to check out the owner of the husky voice propositioning me. The bar's lighting didn't show much detail, but I could tell she was slim, curved in all the right places. She had on a sheer top over a black lace teddy that showed a lot of the tawny skin underneath. Her straight dark hair was pulled back in a loose ponytail, with a few stray strands hanging down her cheeks. Dark lashes and brows. She had a way of tilting her head when she looked at me that was steaming hot.

I got to my feet. She looked up. Way up. I'm guessing she was about five feet six inches, shorter than the girls on my team.

"You are one tall one."

Her table was in front by the stage. I followed her there, where a lingerie-clad girl was dancing to *Live to Tell*.

"Jenny Singer." She put her hand out for a shake. I bent slightly and kissed her on her hand, and on both cheeks. She smiled, and we sat down. The bartender sent my Pinot Noir and my change with a waitress who got the tip.

The loud music was an obstacle to chat, but we did the best we could. We moved our chairs side by side, so we could talk in each other's ears. I was already half in love. I loved Jenny's scent. I loved the way she held her glass. I loved the honey-gold salon tan of her skin. I loved how she sipped her Margarita. She was nursing the drink. I had no clue why. Maybe she didn't want to get drunk. I had no driver with me, so I too was taking it easy. Jenny had me mesmerized.

"I have a beautiful pad up Sunset ten minutes away. The view is to die for."

"I'd love to see it," I said. "Any husbands, boyfriends, girlfriends for me to worry about?"

"No. I'm sure you could handle it if there was."

She wrapped both her hands around my arm.

I whispered in her ear, "Is this business or pleasure?"

She dimpled, amused. I was glad to see a smile. That meant she wasn't offended.

"By business, you mean am I a hooker?"

I felt like the loud music hid my embarrassment. "I didn't say that."

"Two hundred[43] for the night."

I whispered. "That's a fucking bargain, Baby. Tell me when you want to leave."

I couldn't remember the last time I had paid for sex. Probably during my six months in Europe, years ago.

Jenny had a cute, brightly colored Jaguar. I followed her car up Sunset Boulevard to a small, squeaky clean house. A huge window in the living room looked down on the glitter of Hollywood's thousands of lights. Dazzling, really.

She didn't ask my preference but prepared me a Margarita. "That's all I have," she said. "It's damn good. Please try it."

She kissed me. I was on her couch, an ordinary loveseat, beige fabric, nowhere near as deep or tall as my own, but it was comfortable just the same. She sat on my lap facing me. We both sipped. The end table was topped in some kind of polished stone, convenient for holding the Margaritas when our mutual exploration got too heated. A splash or two or three got licked up. Her smooth, unexplored skin was spicy and tasted like a mixture of honey and adventure. The second drink found us in her blue lighted bedroom.

It was exciting to be out of my element, to be led to this strange bed, to bathe in this blue ambiance, to lie on this stranger's king-sized mattress so much smaller than my custom-made one. In the ceiling, a small but a very pretty gold-leaf framed mirror—the kind of mirror you hang on a wall—looked down at us. I wondered how it was mounted to the ceiling. It was a fleeting thought that was chased away by the vision of her body as she dropped the wrap around skirt and slid the silk shirt off her shoulders. She left the sheer black lace teddy on. I

---

[43] $200.00 in 1986 had the same buying power as $451.10 in 2018

captured and sucked on her nipples through the silk and surprised a passionate breath out of her. I watched as she lit four candles, and then she climbed on top of me. I woke at five, my workout time at home. I dressed as she slept, leaving my business card and five hundred dollars on the night stand. On the way home in the dark, I wondered how many men visited her, how much she made a day or month. The Jag she drove and this house she was living in could not be cheap.

On my way home, I saw a Winchell's Donut Shop. I got a cup to go and a selection of doughnuts to take home. I walked to the car with a buttermilk doughnut between my teeth, the box in one hand and the coffee cup in the other. The doughnut was long gone when I got home. Letty and Tangles opened the front door to the house as I drove up. I got out of the car, box of donuts in hand. Letty wrapped her arms around me, Tangles on the other side. She ended up carrying the doughnuts.

"Boss, we were so fucking worried," Letty said.

"Boss, where the fuck you been?" Tangles was sounding like Pixie winding up for a rampage.

"You didn't answer your cell," Letty said, squeezing my butt as we walked in the house.

"You guys should be asleep."

"We were too worried to sleep," Letty said.

I laughed.

"Not funny," Letty pinched my dick.

"Ouch."

"I smell a woman," Letty said, with humor. "You scored." From the tone in her voice, I half expected her to high-five me.

We all walked up the stairs to the master bedroom. As much as they begged for me to tell them where I had spent the night so that I came home smelling of perfume and sex, I did not tell. Eventually they quit asking.

"Boss, we're packed for Rome," Tangles said.

"All good, Boss," Letty said. "Really."

Right before we left for Rome, Jenny called me on my cell. The girls were getting the luggage to the car. I took the phone with me to the balcony outside of my bedroom and shut the door. She'd called to thank me for the five hundred dollars.

"You must be loaded," she said. "You're such a hunk I would have done it free."

"You're so hot," I said, "I'd have paid twice as much and thought nothing of it."

"You did pay twice as much and then some," she said.

Olga's plane landed in Ontario with a crew of two pilots, one relief pilot and two flight attendants. No guards. Betty took us up on the invitation to come along.

"This is so bitchin'," Tangles said. "To think they travel all over the world in this flying palace."

"I'd wear a strap on and fuck Camila every day and night if I could ride in this fucker with her," Betty said.

"This is Olga's plane, not Camila's," I corrected Betty.

"She told me she had one, too," Betty said.

"She does."

When we leveled off at thirty thousand feet, we took the bottle of wine and four glasses to Olga's bed in the main cabin. We sat on the bed, drank the great wine and crashed in each other's arms. It was a squeeze, but tight quarters are okay in these conditions.

Pepe had flown in from Milan and was there when we arrived. I had been to his Rome house before. Pepe introduced a friend named Caprice, a hot girl from Italy who couldn't have been older than twenty-five, if that. He and Caprice gave the team a tour and told the girls that the house had twelve guest rooms, and three master bedrooms. Olga saw me and pulled me into the room we were going to be sharing, so I did not finish the tour. Jenny wafted through my head, a secret memory as Olga and I had a leisurely reunion in the most luxurious bedroom I'd been assigned in in this villa, so far, one of the master suites. It made me remember how the first time he introduced me to Camila, Pepe had warned me if I slept with her, I had to marry her. Now, it seemed to me that Camila would be sleeping with Betty. I wondered what Pepe would have to say about that.

It was cold in Rome that morning before Mass. Before leaving the house, Olga took coats out of a guest closet and handed minks to Tangles and Betty. Letty had her own mink that I had bought her way back when. I had a full-length cashmere jacket and a scarf. A heated executive bus delivered us to the Vatican where we were escorted through security. Pepe, Caprice, Camila, Olga, and I were seated in the front row; in the second row, Letty, Tangles, Riana, and Betty.

I whispered to Olga, "How did you get this many seats?"

She did not answer aloud. She gave me the scratch gesture, her thumb rubbing the tips of her index and pointer fingers. She did not say how much.

Pepe looked over at Olga and me with a smile on his face, as if he were sending us his approval.

During the service, the parts of me that were covered were fine. My face grew cold, and the tips of everyone's noses were turning rosy. I wondered if under his robes, the Pope had thermals on to keep him warm.

There was something very emotional about attending a Mass at the Vatican. About a million people were behind us.

Everything is closed in Rome on Easter Sunday. At least, that's what I'm told. I didn't find out for myself because we didn't go out. Back at the house, a buffet awaited us. The tables were groaning with Italian food, and servants were running back and forth supplying everyone's needs. One thing I noticed, and maybe it was a small thing. Pepe set himself between Caprice and Letty.

During dinner, Pepe wondered aloud about the faint bruising remaining around Tangles' left eye. It had been a casual question, but it awakened the topic of Tangles' attacker. Camila and Olga pressed Tangles to tell her story, and she complied reluctantly. She glanced in my direction and I nodded for her to go ahead.

I observed the way Olga and Camila listened to Tangles' brief anecdote about the trespasser who hurt her so badly. For the life of me, I could not see any guilt at all in the faces of these women. I only hoped that Tangles and Letty saw what I saw. I wanted them to be confident that neither Olga or Camila had anything to do with the beating.

After we had eaten, Pepe and I went in to the library to talk.

"Thanks to you and other investments we've made over the years, LAI has a lot of money in the banks now." He laughed. "The bakery you got for us is clearing five hundred thousand a month. Imagine that."

There was no way in the world the bakery was making that much money, but I understood what he meant. The management was injecting cash to the actual sales of the busy business. I smiled.

"That's great, Pepe."

"We still have a lot of cash we want to bank. Please keep your eyes out for me. However, the main business now is to find planes. Doesn't matter if we can't pay with cash. I need inventory."

I nodded. "I have feelers out, and plan to travel wherever there is opportunity," I said.

"Thank you, Mario."

"On the contrary, thank you."

I felt like Pepe was a genuine friend. It had been years since he freed me from the kidnappers that had me captive, but he had done that as a favor to Oscar. Now, it was about Pepe and me. I wasn't sure if he liked me more now that I was engaged to Olga whom he considered his sister. Pepe was not blind and certainly not naïve or stupid. He had to know that Camila and Olga were in love with each other and that they had female lovers, here and there. I was all set to marry Olga. It didn't bother me one bit that she was flying around with Riana, sleeping with her, and finding sexual satisfaction. As for whatever else I did not know, secrets don't stay hidden forever.

On our second night, Olga told me, "Camila has Betty, Tangles and Letty in bed with her."

Olga and I were in bed. It was dark. I was barely awake but happy to hear the news. I hoped that meant my team's crisis was over. At the moment, I did not care who sent the burglar or if the burglar was just there to steal. I only wanted the suspicions against Olga to go away. Maybe one day all secrets would be revealed, like the mystery of Jake's death. After all, after years of not knowing who was responsible, the cops had finally come out with the killers of Jake and his wife. I hugged my fiancée from behind, like a spoon, kissed her neck and savored her scent. I think I said, "I love you," just before I knocked out.

Pepe was the hosts of hosts. My fiancée ran the eighteen-household staff like there was nothing to it. In the disco room, Pepe had belly dancers at night and masseuses during the day just waiting to be needed. Betty, who always spent hours massaging us, was the recipient of two-hour massages, as was Tangles. The hospitality reminded me of Sami, may she rest in peace. We stayed four days in Rome, every night an unforgettable feast.

Olga and I did not share our bed with anyone else during our stay. My team was having a great time smothered with the good life, except the one thing that Pepe didn't have in this house was a big spa like mine. He did have a gym, a steam bath, and a sauna, but nothing to compare with Casa Luna.

The holiday drew to a close. Olga and Riana took off for Rotterdam. Camila left the day after, headed to Lisbon. In Pepe's plane, Letty, Tangles, Betty, and I accompanied Pepe and Caprice to Milan. The plan was that we would drop them off and head home in his plane. Pepe suggested that we stay a day in Milan to check out the GAL offices, and visit his home.

"Milan has lots of memories," I said, with a laugh.

"This is where you shacked up with two models before my time," Letty said.

"Right." One of the girls and I broke the dining room table while doing it. Lots of memories.

I could understand why Pepe spent so much time in Milan. His home there is a palace. My Pasadena house was huge, but Pepe's Rome house was bigger. The Milan house was the biggest of all his residences I'd seen so far.

We stayed for three days in Milan, visited the impressive offices, and had a blast in the house. We did get out to see bits of the city and all the tourist venues, but always headed back home to the disco at the house that Pepe's staff had ready to go twenty-four hours a day and continued until whatever time the guests pooped out. Caprice didn't seem to be a swinger. Through it all, I had the feeling that Pepe liked Letty. I'd noticed little things, ever since he'd sat beside Letty our first night here.

Chapter 31
Tuesday April 15, 1986
Tangled

Mario

Pélon could have visitors again. I didn't want Letty to witness the exchange with Pélon, so I flew up alone. I was relieved that his visiting had not been restricted to a glass window and phone after his reprimand. The visiting area was the same as when I came up with Letty, steel tables and stools.

"You been a bad boy," I said. "I tried to see you and you were under disciplinary something or other."

Pélon shrugged and gave me no details of what led to his loss of privileges, but got right to answering my questions. He spoke in a low voice because there were other visitors sitting at tables not too far away. He and I sat opposite each other. Physical contact is forbidden.

"Vicario did the shooting of your friend," Pélon said, "You got the recording, right?"

"I did. Thanks."

"Scumbag motherfucker owed me."

"I'll take care of that."

He nodded. "Give my Jefa ten when you can spare it." He winked and grinned.

"I'll handle it. It's a gift, not a payment for anything."

"Ese, I told you, if he got gone, it wouldn't be for you or your friend."

"I got it," I said. "In the recording, he mentioned he's got a cousin or something in the store. So, we know Melina has a snake in her own stomping ground."

"Ese, you know I don't know what was on the recording, only that he copped to the shooting, and copped out on me."

"In the tape, he says that someone in the market gave him details that Melina would be there late that night. Anyway, that was over a year ago. Maybe she has moved on."

"Can't help you there, ese, but if you or Melina have any blowback from Vicario's family, let me know." He pointed his finger at me.

"I didn't know we had to be worried about the family," I said.

"Always worry about the family. Look at Vicario. He gave his life trying to get revenge for his brother."

I nodded my understanding. "Are there any brothers left to worry about?"

"Nah. I was going to waste the whole family if that mother fucker lied. I think we got the truth. Ese, nothing going to happen." He grinned at me. "I miss you bringing eye candy, man."

"No need for Letty to hear more than was healthy."

The conversation moved on to safer topics. He asked about Aunt Carmen, Carson, and Pixie. He mentioned Pixie had sent him tapes of her live performances, and referred to her as our *carnalita,* as I guess she always will be. He was jazzed over her getting to be a star. "Never would have guessed that she would have such a big career change. I did not see that coming," he said. "I don't even remember her singing, back when we were kids." I told him about the earthquake in Mexico, talking about Lainie's close call without mentioning Jason, and about Pixie's flight disappearing.

When our time was up, I said, "I would give you a hug, but you know the rules."

"Carnal, you always been and always will be my carnal. No hugs needed." He winked. The wink was something new. "Take care of my Jefita."

"I'll do it right away," I promised.

When I landed in Van Nuys, I called Melina's cell phone to find out what market she was in. Montebello. I drove to see her.

I walked the stairs to her office. Though the details vary from store to store, she always designs her office on the second floor with a huge one-way mirror overlooking the store, with a tapestry black-out curtain to cover the glass when she wants the lights on. Her desks are always set against the far wall, facing the store view, though the desks themselves change frequently, and she passes her hand-me-downs to employees' offices. The matching buffet was probably a gussied-up file cabinet, the desk of finely crafted walnut. Behind it, in her designer suit, she looked like a banker and not the owner/manager of super markets. I hugged her, put my hands on her fine ass as I pulled her against me, both of us standing.

"You're a sight for sore eyes, Babies. I thought you said you were going to stick to comfortable jeans. I'm glad you changed your mind." The shimmery fabric of her caramel colored suit, probably silk, was no obstacle. I could feel her heat against me as our welcome took a serious turn, leaving me with a hard ridge of growing craving. Her fingers clutched at my shirt, and for a few pulsing moments, it seemed the old hungry Melina was back. She stepped back stiffly and turned away. When she faced me again, she was all business, except for a flush of color blooming in her face.

"That felt good," she said. "When you leave, do it again."

We sat on her sofa.

"I was just with Pélon. He winks goodbye now, since hugs are forbidden."

"You can communicate a lot with a wink," she said.

I relayed the entire conversation.

"I believe as he does, that the insider must have been here, but she's gone now. We concentrated the search on current employees."

I told her about the family thing that Pélon mentioned.

"Way ahead of you. He has two sisters, thirty-four and thirty-seven. His mother doesn't work. She's fifty-seven. His dad works as a mechanic at a Ford dealer in Glendale. The two sisters are married, out of the house and have kids. I have a full run down on them and their husbands. Looks like a stable family with two weirdo sons who were robbers and killers."

"Smart move that you have the run down," I said.

"Got it covered, Cuz. I'll have my security guy fax it to your office." She smiled. "Want to eat or drink something?"

"I would, but I have a phone conference in an hour on the home phone about three planes I'm trying to get."

"Does Pepe know how lucky he is to have you?"

I got up. "I'm lucky to have Pepe, Baby."

"Let me give you the ten for Pélon's mother."

I kissed her. "I'd rather take it out in trade on another day."

"Think my pussy is still worth that much?"

"Baby, your pussy is priceless."

She beamed. That compliment had struck home, and it was only the truth.

I hugged her and squeezed her ass again.

"I miss you," she said, our lips barely touching.

"Ditto, Baby."

She punched my chest. "Don't use ditto."

"I miss you, too, Baby."

She walked me down the stairs, passing a plainclothes guard who must have been a football player at some point in his life. Because we were in full view of a security camera and the guard who followed us to the exit, our goodbye kiss was g-rated, and I didn't squeeze her butt.

I watched her walk back into the store. She looked at me over her shoulder, as come-hither a look as I ever saw, and gave me a wink full of sex and promises. I knew she was thinking of Pélon and his wink, but hers said a hell of a lot more, plus it made me laugh.

"You said it, Baby." I said it aloud, but she was already gone.

Toward the end of April, a couple of weeks after we had returned from Italy, Betty was still talking about the time she had. It was early in the morning, around seven. I'd already worked out and showered. From the spa, I could hear the girls kicking each other's asses in karate practice. Betty winced every time there was a slam or a smack that echoed, though I told her time and again that it sounded worse than it felt. I kidded Betty about becoming a chatterbox.

"I don't remember you being such a talker during a massage."

"Boss, so mean." She gently slapped my butt.

She went from massaging to running the edge of her long nails up and down my back, legs, and feet. It always made me twist away because it tickled so, but I loved it. It was all good, but the best was when she did my ass. It had nothing to do with sex, just that the way she used her nails was stimulating. When I had a restless night, Letty used her nails like Betty did until sleep took me over. I guess when she did it, it was soothing.

"I forgot to mention, and maybe I shouldn't..." Betty said, hesitating.

I waited. "Mention what?"

"I did Janice yesterday. That lawyer friend of yours was there."

I hadn't seen Janice in ages and didn't plan to visit. "Which lawyer?" I had to narrow it down. Half the lawyers in Los Angeles call me by my first name.

"The one that's been in the news lately. He's representing that guy from Colombia who was kidnapped and brought here to stand trial."

"Allegedly kidnapped," I corrected. "Jack Fino?"

"Yeah, that's him."

I sat up on the table.

"Boss, we're not done."

"Have you ever seen him there before?"

"Not at the apartment where she lives now. At her other house, yes. Why?"

"What did he do when you started the massage?"

"Soon as I went in, he totally shined me on. He left."

"When did you meet him?"

"You had a dinner here or something, Thanksgiving or was it Christmas? Yeah, it was Christmas."

"What was he wearing?"

"A nice suit, something a rich guy would wear in court. Boss, lie down. Relax. I shouldn't have said anything."

"I am glad you told me," I said. I didn't know why this felt important, but it did.

I yielded to Betty's request and went back to lying on my stomach. She started massaging my neck.

"Please go back to the nails."

She resumed. I tried to surrender to the sensation, but the feeling that I was missing something about Jack hanging out at Janice's kept interrupting the moment.

In May one morning, I asked Melina to get her new head of security to call me back.

"I need some work done," I said. "Do you have anyone available?"

Of course, Melina wanted to know why I wanted one of Lou's guys. I kept it short.

"A small assignment that I don't want to give to Tricia." Tricia's guy didn't like surveillance work, plus if they were found out, Tricia's involvement made it a direct line back to me.

"A secret?"

"Baby, you're the most mysterious woman I've ever known," I said.

"Bull, Cuz. I'm an open book. Your fiancée is the mysterious one." She had long questioned the wisdom of my working with the Camachos. I let it drop.

Maybe it was unwise to take the chance that Fino would find out that I had put a tail on him. There was little that went on that he missed. He was a close friend of Janice, who I didn't trust at all. When I thought of her, I kept hearing how she bad mouthed me, blaming me for her husband dying broke. But I needed to know what the connection was, if it was sex, or something else.

Lou sent me Arthur Moore. I met him upstairs in the conference room by my office. The girls had the radio on and were going through tapes. They got up from where they were working at the table to shake his hand, then went to their workstations. Art was about my age, reasonably fit, and showed up in jeans and a brown polo shirt. He had worked with Lou on the Bruno Vicario surveillance, looking after Melina. Medium height, medium brown hair cut short enough that I couldn't tell if it was straight, wavy, or curly, but not so short that it screamed law enforcement or military. He looked kind of average, with a roundish face on the verge of needing a shave. Nothing about his features struck me much, probably a good thing for a guy whose profession was all about not getting noticed. I led him into my office and closed the door.

"Jack Fino. This guy is a big-time attorney and a good friend for a long time. I need to know what he has going on with Janice Cooke." I gave him extensive details in a low voice.

"What do you suspect?" Art asked.

"I don't have a clue." I shook my head. "It surprised me to no end to learn that Fino was at her place a couple of days ago."

"Are you trying to find out if they are having an affair?"

"I could care less if they are fucking. If that's all they have going, great."

I told Art about the unsolved arson of my house, and the unsolved murder of the investigator named Bruno Bruno, who had been killed on his way to tell me who was behind the arson. I told Art how I had had no contact with Janice after Oscar's burial, and then when we did talk she accused me of taking advantage of her husband and leaving him broke.

"I felt so bad, I gave her enough money to get her out of the jam she was in. I took her house out of foreclosure and paid off the mortgage, so that she owned it free and clear when she sold it to move where she lives now." I told him about the biker I had a couple of run-ins with, how it was the same one who showed up when a truck rammed my car, sending Olga to the hospital. I told him how the biker dropped in to my house at night, when he fell off the balcony into my koi pond, how he did not die from the fall but when they found him, someone had executed him by planting a bullet between his eyes.

I made certain that Art understood the assignment was not intense. No one's life was on the line. I didn't want a team to work day and night like Melina had them do with Vicario.

"Handle it yourself," I said. "Take your time but be careful. This guy is the sharpest tack in the box. Nothing gets past him, and he absolutely cannot know you are tailing him or interested in him."

Fino was a criminal lawyer with vast power and a host of shady connections. He had business, whatever it was, with Pepe. I'd always had suspicions that he was attached to some kind of mafia, though I had never had any doings with him that were anything less than spotless.

After Art left, I joined the girls at the conference table. Of course, they had questions. I didn't answer them all.

"Why do you need another investigator?"

"It's something I don't want Tricia to handle," I said.

"Fuck, must be top secret," Tangles said. "All hush hush," she whispered.

"You're such a drama queen," Letty accused.

Tangles scooted her chair so that she could look past Letty who was between us. "It's not because of me, is it?" she asked, her voice urgent. "You're not sending him looking for Imelda Flores, are you?" She fidgeted with the paper tape, her anxious eyes never leaving my face.

"No, I didn't send him looking for her, but that's not a bad idea." I nodded, thinking. "Maybe I should put that on his to-do list."

She kept watching me with that haunted expression.

"What's up kiddo?"

"It's May already. The break-in was back in January. I've been here four months. It's past time I pack my racks and tacks and head on down the tracks. If I was Olga, I'd be pissed off."

"Do you want to go home?"

She took a minute or two before answering. "Not really, Boss."

That night, Letty and Tangles were in the arcade when I talked to Olga on the phone in my bedroom. I took advantage of the privacy and brought it up.

"I want Tangles to move in."

"Fine with me, Amor, but, why?" Olga sounded perplexed.

"I don't want to worry about her."

"She has a gun and a permit and she's working out with Letty, isn't she? You think someone is after her?"

"I doubt it," I said.

"Amor, no problem from me. Will she keep her apartment like Letty has kept hers?"

"Yes, like Letty."

"Do it, Amor. Does she know?"

Sometimes, Olga totally surprised me.

"No."

Olga laughed. "Amor, maybe she won't want to live with you."

"If she doesn't, it's okay."

To me, Letty was an open book. Though we had not discussed it, I knew

Letty liked having Tangles around—that was half of the reason I was going to ask Tangles to stay. The other half was just how Tangles being here the last four months, she just fit in. I was alone upstairs, and paged Letty to join me. I certainly didn't have any obligation to consult with her. I had a strong sense of how she felt about things, anyway. When she came up to the fourth floor, I told her I was thinking of telling Tangles to stay.

"Hallelujah," she said. "Good move, Boss. She's coming up in a minute. She was just finishing up a game."

"Good," I said. "Let's ask her when she comes in."

So that's what happened.

Hearing the invitation, Tangles lost the hangdog expression she'd been wearing all day and jumped on the bed between Letty and me. She flung one arm over me and the other over Letty.

"I've been wondering when you were going to show me the door. Oh, Boss, thank you."

"Where's my thanks?" Letty asked.

Tangles looked from me to her. "Don't look at me. I'm hitting the shower," I said, leaving them to their moment.

"We still read the telexes," Tangles said, picking up a handful of discarded tapes and letting them drop into the trash. "We're missing out on some good ones."

"Boss, she's right. Of course, just because we have the telex doesn't mean we're going to hit a home run and get the families to sign with us," Letty said. "I think you should shop for a lawyer."

"I'm not sure I want to," I said. "I'll think about it. In the meantime, let's work on planes. Let's find operators who have planes they want to sell off."

"We're doing cold calls," Tangles said. "We need to order phone books from other cities."

"Just keep calling information."

"Maybe we need to go to the library to find out where some of these operators have their home offices," Letty said.

"That's using your head. Keep thinking about it. Don't mess with plane crashes for now. And find more sources of planes being marketed, like pilot magazines with ad sections. See what newsletters plane brokers send out."

Letty was taking notes of what I was saying and put down her pencil. She looked at me intently. "What are we going to do when the next big airliner crashes?"

That was a very difficult question for me. "At the moment, we have no lawyer, so I would pass it up."

"I don't believe it," Letty said.

"Believe it, Baby."

"Try it on, Boss. I think it will look good. If it fits, I can get it in more colors."

Without the girls' shopping addiction, I'd probably run around naked. Letty shoved a shirt at me, canvas, heavier than what I would normally wear in the summer. I liked the two rivet-type snap pockets, though, and it wasn't always going to be May. I guess I'm lucky the girls like to shop and have taste I can tolerate. I shucked off my t shirt, pulled on the canvas shirt, and spun in a circle, model-style.

"Funny, Boss," she said, her hand brushing my pecs before she did the snaps. "It looks good. How does it feel?"

Sipping from a can of coke with a straw in it, Tangles walked into the conference room. She bent down and picked up my t shirt before she narrowed her eyes at us. "What'd I miss?"

I didn't have to answer. The phone rang, and she jumped to answer it before Letty.

"Casa Luna, Tangles speaking," she said. After a second she held the receiver out to me.

"It's Jack Fino," she said, covering the mouthpiece.

I took the phone and walked with it toward the window. I had not been to lunch with Jack since he'd walked out on me. Though the ice between us had been broken when he showed up for my Christmas party, things weren't back to normal between us. At least, it was civil. Since then we did talk on the phone, but that was it.

"You got me," I said. "What do you need?"

"You got a lawyer yet?" Jack asked.

"To tell the truth, I haven't been looking."

"That's because you're making big bread buying planes."

"I miss the action of running after a case, but we haven't had a big crash."

"Let me know if you change your mind about Gonor. We can come up with a better deal than what we talked about."

"Jack, if the deal includes me taking all or part of my money when the case settles, I'm not interested."

There was some silence. I could practically hear the cogs and wheels spinning in Jack's head as he tried to come up with something I'd agree with. "If you could get your costs up front, would you wait for the rest?"

"I have a plane. That's a cost, Jack. If I don't get that as part of my expenses up front, then I'm still rolling the dice on something more than just the case."

"I think we could work that out. As you know, I have a plane, and know what it costs to operate."

"I'm not saying I'll do it but check with Gonor. See what he says."

"I don't need to check with him. He's right here. I'm in Chicago at his office and you're on the speaker."

"Hi, Mario, this is Les Gonor. We're doing better. Cash flow is better. I miss the cases, even the smaller cases your girls were bringing in."

"The bigger your caseload, the greater your office expense," I reminded him.

"He knows that, Mario," Jack said.

"If I don't pay you when a case settles, you can throw me out a window or off a balcony. I won't put up a fight."

They laughed. I didn't.

"Since we're being really frank here, I have to point out that if I go for this, the only benefit is that it gives Gonor the ability to continue paying you the monthly interest on his credit line with you which I imagine to be over a hundred thousand a month."

They didn't laugh.

"If you do this, I'll cut the interest rate to 1.5 a month," Jack said.

"How will that help me?" I asked. "I'm glad for Gonor, but what's in it for me?"

"That will help my cash flow in a big way," Gonor said. "Make it easier to reimburse you right away for the costs that with the plane expense can get expensive."

"What if your percentage is thirty instead of twenty-five?" Gonor asked. "I could handle thirty percent if it is on the back end."

We talked for another thirty minutes before I agreed. Without Pixie around, queen of the eavesdropping committee, the girls had moved to their workstations. Harry had installed a contact management program that interfaced with my contacts with a set of letter templates. The girls were really getting into computers. I tapped Letty's shoulder.

"Boss, this is great. I've typed up a letter to go out to the plane brokers, and Tangles is typing in all the broker addresses we got from the library's plane magazines. What's up with Jack?"

"What's up is we're back in business with Gonor. He covers expenses, including the plane, up front. We get thirty percent on the back end."

"Net or gross?" Letty spun her chair around to face me. "Better be gross."

I laughed. "If they cover the expenses, I'm happy with net."

"If you're happy, I'm happy, Boss," Letty said, though she was shaking her head.

"I hope you don't lose any money and that he pays you, but I'm happy you ironed that out. I feel funny getting a paycheck and not really doing anything," Tangles said.

"You're doing something," I pointed to the broker database she was building. "I like that attitude. Come over here and let me give you a hug."

"Hey, Boss, how about me?" Letty asked.

I opened my arms wide enough for both of them. We stood in a huddle, all smiles.

"It's good to be back in business," Letty said, somewhere below my left pocket.

"You can say that again, sister," Tangles said, somewhere below my right. She snapped one of the pockets closed and snapped it open again. "Hey Boss, I like your shirt."

Tangles and Letty were monitoring a Cessna crash in Reno, Nevada. They faxed the available details to Tricia to work it up. After Tricia sent contact information, the girls waited two weeks and called the families of the two passengers. One thing led to another, and they got an invitation to visit to talk about the possibility of pursuing a case against the manufacturer. The preliminary assessment said that the engine had failed. The plane was under a year old.

"What are you going to do while we're away?" Letty asked, being her usual nosey self.

"I'll find something to do."

"Come with us, Boss. It could get interesting on the way there and back." Tangles grabbed my arm, as if she were trying to drag me along.

I didn't join them.

They took my plane. It's not that I didn't want to be involved in plane crashes. It was good practice for Letty and especially good for Tangles who didn't have that much time in with us. If we got the case, cool. If we didn't get it, well, that's the way it goes.

The girls were gone, and so was Olga.

I found Jenny's phone number, dialed it, and got an answering machine. Pixie was still away so I called Raul to drive me to Whisky a Go Go. On my way there, I got a call from Jenny.

"Stranger, what you got going this fine Friday night?"

"I was going to ask you the same thing?"

"I'm yours," she said. "Want to come over?"

"I was headed to the Whisky."

"We don't need the foreplay. Come on over, okay?"

"Not sure I can find it. Last time, I just followed you there. Give me that address again. I have a driver."

I pictured Jenny, the dark flow of her hair, the slash of her brows against her honeyed skin. I'd be a liar if I said I didn't think of the AIDS epidemic that was still some what of a mystery of who could get it and from where. I had read that it was advisable to use rubbers, but I'd never bought a rubber in my life.

It was dark. Finding her house was becoming a problem. Raul had to pull over and study the Thomas Guide.

"Found it, Boss."

When we pulled up, Jenny was standing in the open doorway looking twice as lovely as I remembered in jeans with rolled up cuffs and a baggy white shirt.

I got out of Pixie's Rolls. I saw Jenny was impressed by the vehicle.

"Shit, you must be loaded. How many of these do you have?" She hugged me like we were old friends. I hugged her back.

"Send the driver away. I'll drive you wherever you want to go."

"I may not fit in your car." Her Jag parked in the driveway looked like a toy car to me.

"You'll fit, big boy."

I relented. The last thing I wanted was to worry about the driver hanging around.

"Raul, if I need you, I'll call you."

"Sure, Boss."

Jenny heard Raul and laughed. "Boss is it?"

I didn't reply, just followed Jenny to her den. The loveseat had fond memories for me. We shared one big Margarita, two straws like a couple of teenagers.

"Jenny, let me take you to dinner."

"Are you hungry?" she asked.

"Not really."

"Let's chill." She put on a big smile. "Boss."

I carried her to the bedroom.

"I love the way you smell," I said.

"Is that what brought you back?"

We necked. In the middle of necking, I felt something strange, the rubber Jenny was putting on me. She made it part of the foreplay, but I guess with her line of work, she was scared of making babies. Once I was inside of her, I forgot about everything but the sex.

With the passenger seat pushed all the way back, the ride in the Jag wasn't so bad. Jenny chattered the whole trip, telling me how she moved from Maryland, couldn't find a job in LA, then started hooking. I thought of Pixie's history. Sure, she'd made a bundle singing songs about it, but her story wasn't mine to tell a stranger.

When we pulled up in front of my gates, I stuck my hand out and waved at one of the cameras. The iron gates opened inward.

"You are rich," she said, emphasizing each word. The guard was out of the gate house when Jenny drove up. Quito peered through the driver side window past Jenny at me.

"Evening, Boss."

I knew I was showing off, but I liked this girl. It didn't bother me that she would know where I lived. I seriously doubted she would ever be part of my team, but stranger things have happened. She stopped her car behind my Rolls parked in front of the house.

"Another Rolls? How many do you have?"

I just laughed and opened the door. From the living room, I dialed the intercom number for Miguel. "Hate to do this to you at fifteen minutes after midnight," I said.

"Boss, I'm wide awake." Ten minutes later, Miguel appeared in his whites.

"Miguel, this is Jenny. I'm thinking we're both pretty hungry."

Miguel smiled, and bowed his head. "Miss Jenny, pleased to meet you."

"I feel like steak and eggs," I said. "Jenny has been starving me now for hours."

"Right away, Boss. What will Miss Jenny like?"

"What you got here, a restaurant?" she laughed.

"Anything you wish," Miguel said confidently.

"Eggs and bacon?"

"Of course. Boiled, poached, fried, scrambled, Benedict, Sardu, omelet, quiche—"

"Nothing so fancy. Plain old scrambled would be great," she said, laughing.

"Anything in the scramble? Cheese, onions, caviar, beans, curry, spinach, other vege—"

"Cheese is fine," she said, interrupting breathlessly.

Knowing Miguel, I knew what was coming.

"Cheddar, American, queso fresco, ricotta, gruyere, blue—"

"Cheddar is fine, any cheddar, anything you already have open is fine, really," she said very fast.

Miguel nodded, keeping his face serious. "I will make many trimmings for you."

"I had to stop him," Jenny said, grinning. "I thought he'd go on forever with the choices."

"He will," I said. "But to be fair, Miguel has an excellent memory, and you won't have to tell him again unless you want a change."

"Good to know," she said.

We moved to the family room on the same floor, and I walked over to the bar to open a bottle of Merlot.

"I can make you a Margarita?"

"No way, Boss. Wine is fine."

We sat ourselves in the dining room at the ridiculously huge table, not at opposite ends but directly apart from each other. Miguel moved the massive floral centerpiece to the buffet. The rheostat for the lights was dimmed so low that it made a buzzing noise, and a pair of candles flickered between us, but not blocking the view. Just before he brought out our food, he set two place settings at one corner, so we could sit more intimately. Before he returned, I got up and pulled back one of the chairs for Jenny to move to. I moved the candles to our new location and lit a third before I sat myself at her right shoulder.

"I can turn the light up if you wish," I said. "In a restaurant with dim lighting, I always worry why they are hiding the food."

"No, this is very romantic," she said, her voice faint.

Miguel brought me the one steak sauce I prefer. For trimmings, he used the spoons he sometimes takes out for a tasting menu, a presentation that rests on a stairstep frame, usually set up on the buffet, but he put them to Jenny's left. There were cheeses, and sauces, chopped vegetables, fruits, jellies, and marmalades, at least two dozen choices for Jenny, each in its own spoon. He also brought out a basket of tender crisp hot croissants, and butter molded into fanciful shapes but soft enough to spread.

I could see Jenny was impressed.

While Miguel was in earshot, I said, "You should see what he can do when he has time for a little preparation."

"I can't even imagine," Jenny said, her voice faint, her hand over her heart.

I skipped giving her the tour. It was nearly one when I led her to the elevator. As we stepped out on the fourth floor, I turned toward the master bedroom. The door was open, and the light streamed down the hall in a welcoming fashion.

"Oh my," she said.

She looked wide-eyed at the bed. I led her past it to the round table in the sitting room where we sat, but not for long.

"I have never seen a bed that big, ever."

She got up and studied it and looked up at the mirror. She looked at me over her shoulder. I was still at the table.

"Oh my. You are really, really rich."

"I'm comfortable," I said, following her to the bed. "I'm sure you've been with friends who had bigger houses."

She laughed up at me with those kissable lips of hers. "Friends? I've had a whole lot of tricks, but they normally don't take me to their homes."

"Jenny, how old are you?"

"I'm thirty-one but I tell everyone I'm twenty-eight." She sipped her wine. "I know I look older."

I shook my head. "No way."

I stepped away to open the balcony door to the outside. The breezy May night was around sixty degrees and would make blanket cuddling cozier.

A shelf in the bedroom holds a couple dozen tea lights in hurricane candleholders. The candles were usually Letty's doing. I looked at Jenny in the bed, and switched off the light, then in the dark, went over to light the candles with a long match designed for a fireplace. She got up and helped me to light and place them around the room. The candles, in their tall hurricane glasses, were safe from the breeze from outdoors, and provided a lovely glow. I looked at

Jenny in that candlelight, wondering when she'd taken off her jeans. She did nothing that I could see, but the large shirt she was in slid down her body to puddle on the floor. She was so lovely licked by the candlelight, I was torn between watching and having her. She took that choice from me, and moved to the bed, and put out her hand, reaching for me.

I gave her a walk-through of the house at eight when we got up. We did the spa tour together: steam, sauna, freeze dip, then shower. She passed on breakfast but had two cups of coffee, claiming to still be full of eggs from last night. I walked her to her car, and gave her two thousand in hundreds, folded very flat. I palmed the money to her even though we were alone.

"Thank you," I said.

She pushed the cash back into my hand. "I can't take the money. You made me feel so welcome in your home."

"There's two thousand there," I said. We had a little tug of war, each trying to give the cash to the other. It fell on the pavement.

"Generous, but no." She was not bluffing. "Thanks for making me feel so special," she said. I gave her a big hug and kissed her.

"You have overhead," I said. "You should take the money."

She ignored my words, opened her car door, and got in. Her window rolled down and she peeked out with puckered lips. "Kiss me, big boy."

I did not pick up the bills until she had cleared the gates.

The afternoon after Jenny left, Letty and Tangles returned. We sat at the conference table as they gave me details about the case, including that the surviving family members were female.

"Fuck, Boss, we didn't sign it," Letty said with a grim look.

"It's okay," I said. "I don't always get them either."

"All is not lost. They are thinking about it," Letty said.

"I think it's a girl thing," Tangles said. "Just my opinion."

"Guys, they listen to a woman. But with women, it's usually the Boss who closes," Letty said.

I wasn't arguing. In all the years I worked with a female team, we got a lot done. "The last two you went on, you signed," I said. "Relax, already. Let's have dinner and some wine."

Letty and Tangles exchanged glances.

"Wait, Boss," Letty said. "Tangles wants to tell you something."

"Shoot," I said, focusing on Tangles.

"It's like this, Boss. I been thinking about your generous invitation to live here. I'm grateful to you and Olga, but I want to move back to my apartment."

I started to get up. "Fine. No problem." Maybe my voice was a little curt.

"Boss, wait. Let her finish," Letty said.

I sat back down. Tangles continued. "If I stay here, then I'm running away from whoever came after me. I will always be afraid to live alone. I got to go back, face my demons. I don't know self-defense well enough to do shit, but I'm really good with my gun. And thanks to Melina, I'm legal now."

"I understand. Do you want to move into another building?"

Tangles declined. "I'm not running away. Olga and Camila went out of their way to make me feel comfortable in Rome. I feel guilty for believing they sent that tramp after me. I must have been warped to think that."

If Tangles only knew that I had immediately figured the hit was Camacho, maybe she'd feel less guilty. I didn't enlighten her.

"Even if I go home, Boss, I'll stay anytime you want me to stay. I'll give you head and spread out for you anytime you want me."

Letty laughed.

"Dirty cunt."

"Are you mad, Boss?"

I looked at her, at her beautiful almond-shaped, almost Asian eyes.

"I'm not mad at you."

She got up and ran around the conference table, and from behind my chair, blanketed the back of my neck, my head, my ears, my cheeks with kisses.

"Thank you, Boss."

The next day, Tangles moved out of Casa Luna. The plan was that she would still work with Letty at the house and go to her apartment when she was done. I could live with that because I did not really fear for her safety. The first night back in her apartment, I called her twice, once before bed, and later when I was in bed with Letty.

"You must miss me," Tangles teased.

Letty yelled into the phone, "Only that you aren't down there doing me, bitch."

I shook my head. Pixie never left. Her mouth lived here with me in Letty.

I was in the office when Kinko called to say he was getting eight planes from Australia from a domestic operator who cut his fleet after he lost half of his routes. "He can't get shit for the planes over there, so he's bringing them here to store or sell."

Letty and Tangles were at the table with their morning coffee but had not gotten the tapes yet. The machine was racketing away, audible behind the closed door. The girls were watching me and listening to my end of the conversation.

"What kind of planes?"

"Your favorite kind, Boeing."

"Boeing, what?"

Kinko laughed. "Does it matter?"

"Get serious, I'm over here coming in my pants with excitement."

Letty opened her eyes wide when she heard me say that.

"Two are 747s. Let me get them in, and we'll take a look," Kinko said.

"Why bring them here? Let me fly over, and see them, and buy them direct."

"If I arrange that, how will I make any money?"

"I'll pay you. What you think?"

"Mario, you are better off having them here. If they need something done, I can do it here and you won't look like such an easy mark to the seller."

"You're right. I'll take real good care of you. Let me know when you get them."

After a long three weeks, the planes finally arrived at Kinko's. His report took two more weeks, but by then I had already been there twice to check them out. I sent videos of each plane to Pepe.

I took Kinko fifty thousand cash.[44] We sat in his stuffy office in the front corner of a hanger. Through the door, I could hear crews working on planes. Lots of noise, banging, dropping tools, and the buzz of power tools. I reminded him, "I want you to know that you will always make more money with me than with anyone else for any inventory we want. This fifty is to show you how real I am. I don't need receipts. All I ask is if you tell me a plane is worth a million, make certain it's the truth. I may be a novice, but I learn fast."

Kinko tapped the paper bag with the cash. He smiled and said, "Don't learn too fast. You won't need me anymore."

"I'll always need you. You're the one with connections."

"With this kind of cash, I say you're the connected one."

"We're both connected," I said. "What I need from you is inventory and expertise. The sellers will pay you a commission, and I will be paying you, too. You're my insurance that I don't get screwed overpaying or buying a piece of crap that somehow got a certificate of air worthiness. Get it?"

"Got it."

"Good."

"Give me two days. I'll figure out what these mothers are worth, and

---

[44] $50,000.00 in 1986 had the same buying power as $112,774.02 in 2018

you can make your offers based on that. I ain't going to fuck you."

Every time I returned from the desert, my Rolls was covered in dust. I hated a dirty car. As I drove in, I dialed Letty up in my office.

"Baby, I'm back. Get someone to get the desert off my car."

"Right away, Boss."

I went in the kitchen and came out with a jar of peanut butter and a spoon and headed up to my office to check my mail. Lately I'd been using plastic spoons, so I could toss them when I was done. Tangles was reading teletypes, looked up and smiled. Letty was already inside and came across the room and sat in front of my desk. I shuffled through the stack of letters, bills, and junk.

"How's the Mohave?"

"Way hot, Baby. Good thing you didn't go. I have to shower." I tugged at my collar to emphasize the heat. I scooped out some peanut butter and wagged the spoon at her, "But first I need a bit of energy. How's Tangles and the apartment situation doing?"

"She said Jo sent maintenance over to put on a new deadbolt."

I glanced at my wall at three blown up mug shots of the muscular, masculine-looking blonde who had attacked Tangles. One more was in the conference room opposite the floor to ceiling bookcases. They were staying up until I had answers. There was still no word of her. She seemed to have disappeared into thin air.

Chapter 32
June 1986
The King is Dead

Mario

At breakfast, I noticed a bruise on Tangles' cheek. Tangles' trespasser was my first thought.

"What happened?"

"This morning, I feinted when I should have blocked," Tangles said, one step behind me on the stairs.

"Baby, take care of that pretty face." I glared at Letty who was walking at my side.

"It wasn't me, Boss," Letty said. "She was at Cosmos. No mercy over there."

Letty and Tangles both laughed.

"I'm making gladiators out of my team," I said. Pixie has five belts to her name, Jo and Niley four, Letty three, and Lainie has her first. Not that Lainie is on my team.

"Better a gladiator than a punching bag, Boss," Tangles said, and walked to the teletype room.

"Couldn't have said it better myself," I said.

Letty followed me into my office, and I sorted out some papers I wanted filed, and a copy of Kinko's plane reports. She was wearing a short-sleeved top, bright yellow and white stripes, white culottes that looked like a skirt, and matching flats.

"Fax these to Pepe's Milan office," I said. "I talked to Pepe the other day. He said he's in love with Tangles' hair," I said to Letty. "I told him that I thought I caught him eyeing you."

"Me?"

"He said he likes you both. I told him he can't have either one of you." I lied about what I said but it's what I felt.

"Good, Boss. Pepe is okay as a friend, but I won't give him head."

I didn't ask what Tangles thought. No point in yelling through glass and across the forty-foot conference room. When she came out of the teletype room, I waved her in.

"I talked to Pepe and he told me he has the hots for you and loves your hair."

Tangles plopped down in the chair next to Letty. "Really? Boss, what else did he say?"

A week later, the values of the planes from Australia were pinned down. The asking price for the six planes was forty percent more than Kinko recommended we offer. It was a lot of money. The 747s were the biggest part of the sale. Pepe said he had an operator who would lease them.

The planes I had purchased earlier in the year had been less money, a deal I had worked with Pepe on the phone. This time, he wanted me in Milan to discuss this purchase.

"I have a seven-year-old Boeing 707, a four-engine job, totally redone as an executive jet. I'll send it for you."

"Pepe, I can take my plane. I don't mind the fuel stops."

The 707 was not nearly as big as the 747 I had been in with Olga in

Cape Town, but it is a huge plane for just a couple of people to fly around in. With all the hunger and want in the world, I felt guilty thinking of how much money was burned to keep it in the air. I kept that to myself. It's not like I would win an argument with Pepe, or that if he switched to something economical, he would use the savings to feed the hungry and house the homeless.

Pepe laughed. "No arguments, Mario. I will send the 707 for you tomorrow. I haven't leased it yet. I bought it from an Arab from Kuwait. Long story."

"They aren't making them anymore?"

"No, they're not, and it's a shame. They are marvelous. Bello." He paused, then added like an afterthought though I was sure it was not one, "Mario, bring Tangles with you."

"Sure, she'll love it."

"And of course, bring whomever you want. Wait till you see the bed. Olga and Camila would kill to get this plane."

We were dining on grilled brie sandwiches and tomato soup. The girls loved the soup, or maybe they just loved the dishes of trimmings. Tangles dumped in the whole bowl of the goldfish crackers. Letty had added torn basil, fresh ground pepper, and croutons. I skipped the soup and had a four-inch thick round filet of beef wrapped in bacon and grilled over smoke. I told the girls about the upcoming trip at dinner.

"Pepe asked specifically for me to come along?" Tangles asked.

"He did. And I invited Letty," I said. But we were both watching Tangles.

"Lighten up, Tangles," Letty said. "You've gone the color of..." She searched the table. "...Miguel's tomato soup."

Tangles ignored her. "Boss, what about Caprice?"

"I have no idea what's in his mind. We're only going for a couple of days. I have to get back and buy these planes."

When I let Olga know I was going to Milan, she apologized.

"Oh, Amor, I know. I'm leaving for Lima. I won't be able to join you."

"Why Lima?" I wanted to see her. Lately she had been making fewer stops at home.

"Camila is about to close a deal. I must come right behind her to take care of things. I love you. Miss you."

"Ditto, Baby."

I could hear Riana in the background. I had a stupid thought. If Olga and Riana would get married, I could marry Letty.

That night, Letty and I had at least an hour of hot sex and were taking a breather. Her head was on my chest. We were sweaty, breathless, panting.

"Baby, I'm not asking but would you ever consider marrying me?" I asked.

Letty laughed, a put-on laugh for sure. "No, Boss. I'm never getting married."

"Ouch, that hurt, Baby."

She laughed more and poked me in the side.

"Not like I could say yes anyway. You have a fiancée, Boss."

We showered, and came back to bed, spooning. The thought still drifted in my head of how like a married couple we were, except we never tired of each other. I had the feeling that under the right circumstances, I could convince her. The night was too warm for the balcony doors to be open. The bedroom thermostat was set in the sixties at night, so we were cuddled up tight in the dark.

A long time passed, and Letty said, "I can feel you not sleeping. Did something happen?"

"No, nothing happened." I tried to figure out the last time I saw Olga. In Rome. Easter weekend. We were already into June. It felt like forever. It seemed like a long time not to see someone I was affianced to wed.

"I love you, Letty. Really, I love you."

"Not as much as I love you."

The girls were so cool butter wouldn't melt in their mouths. They sashayed into the 707 like the luxury jet was their given right. They held off going bananas until after the pilots disappeared into the cockpit and the two flight attendants took their seats in a separate curtained area. The bedroom had a king-sized bed that stretched nearly the full width of the plane. It was white on white, with luxurious linens, probably a goose-down comforter, and the windows to the left and right gave us our view of the clouds. We went to the main cabin where I sat across from Letty and Tangles, a table between us. The table was probably mahogany, laid out in a full place setting with fine china and stemware. The seats were like living room chairs, deep cushions and upholstered in a figured ivory satin with fleur-de-lis in a paler ivory embroidery. As soon as I saw the upholstery, I remembered Melina rejecting a similar fabric as being too hard to keep clean, otherwise I'd have no idea what to call it. These cushions were new and spotless. To our left, across a spacious aisle, a huge couch in the same fabric stretched the full length of the table and chairs, with several pillows. Behind Letty, a partial screen separated us from the next room where there was another grouping. Of course, the girls had to sit in every seat, and try out the bed.

By the time we touched down in Washington D.C. to refuel, we had eaten an early dinner, gone through two bottles of wine, had sex at 30,000 feet and had fallen asleep. We had a shower aboard, but water is not plentiful. We limited ourselves to one brief shower each.

A car delivered us to Pepe's. When we got out of the car, Pepe greeted us at the foot of the marble stairs leading up to his front portico. He hugged me first, then Letty. When we walked in to the house, Pepe had an arm around Tangles' waist. Caprice was nowhere in sight. I didn't know if she was still in the picture, or if she had just been his girl of the week. I didn't ask. If he had wanted us to know, he would have said something. We were fed a buffet-styled meal and given our own rooms. Letty and I each slept alone.

In the morning, I met with Pepe in a room he used as an office. On the way, we'd passed servants carrying breakfast trays to the girls. I sat down at a huge antique table, and a servant came in with a coffee carafe, and bowls of Italian bread and butter. Pepe apologized for the 'continental' breakfast and said I could have anything I wanted when we were done. The office was about what you would expect for Pepe. Everything that would be gilt everywhere else was solid gold. Lots of antiques. A decent bookcase, but not as fantastic as the one in my conference room. Marble floor, antique Persian rugs. Hot and cold servants jumping at his every whim.

"This is more than fine," I told him.

At a gesture, servants slipped out of the room, including one or two I hadn't realized were there.

He sipped at the strong Italian coffee—all coffee in Italy is espresso—and got excited talking about the plane project.

"Eventually, I will have a group of banks pool the money to buy the planes and we will lease the planes as partners. When we start buying planes for fifty million dollars, newer planes, and new planes, we will need the funds for such a giant investment. If things are as good as I anticipate, we need billions of dollars."

I had never thought of those big numbers.

"I take chances with the operators who are leasing from me. They are not necessarily startup companies, but they are short of cash. The airline business is treacherous. That's why I got rid of my airline. Banks are particular about who they finance a lease for. I will do like Fino does with his loans to lawyers, put up a portion of the loan, and investors put up the difference. When the interest payment comes in, we will divide it up after expenses, of course. In this case, the other investor is the bank, Follow me?"

"Yes, Fino puts up sixty percent and his investors put up forty. When the interest check comes in he takes sixty percent of the money and distributes the other forty percent."

"A bank will look kindlier at a company if they know that I am putting up part of the money. I don't need a damn bank, but when I reach the limit I place on myself, then I will need to off a piece of each lease, not of the company. The company will not have a partner. Each lease is a partnership on this end. The operator leasing the plane pays GAL and doesn't need to know who is putting up the money. For all purposes, GAL is putting it up."

"I get it, sure."

"Riana's father owns a bank. He already offered to get a group of banks, a consortium that can finance everything GAL will ever need. I normally don't meet bankers, but now that Riana is flying around with Olga, I have had direct communication with him."

"Love it," I said. Olga had admitted to me she'd slept with Riana's father before to get him to agree to accept large cash deposits. And although Olga had told me many times that she loves Riana's companionship, now that I knew her so well, I felt that taking Riana under her wing was to get the banker involved with the aircraft leasing company.

"Now, let's talk about the deal on these planes. I suppose there is no way to pay in green cash?"

"I haven't talked that part yet because I need to get to a number they will accept. The planes are consigned to Kinko. I can ask him. I gave him fifty big ones to make sure he stays loyal."

"Good, good. I'll give that back to you."

I had not figured I'd get it back, but I didn't put up an argument.

In short order, Pepe and I worked up a price we would pay if the deal was bank to bank, and a larger amount if the sale was all cash. My commission would be five percent.

Our meeting left me feeling all charged up. Pepe, no doubt, saw it in me. I saw it in him. In spite of our intense excitement, we both had more espresso. It went very well with the bread. I had planes on the brain and was not quite anticipating the change of topic.

"I like Tangles very much. Do you have a problem with me and her? If so, tell me."

The question took my mood down a notch. "Olga and I are engaged," I said. Pepe's expression did not change. "Pepe, Tangles doesn't belong to me. She has a mind of her own." I laughed just a little.

"Good you said that. She slept with me last night." His laugh boomed.

Nice of him to ask after the fact. But I felt guilty for the thought, because he'd asked me to bring Tangles, and I'm not stupid. I hope she didn't feel pressured.

Fuck, I had a feeling. I wasn't sure I wanted to lose Tangles.

"I haven't seen Caprice?" I asked since I'd been wondering about her since we arrived.

"She's shopping in Madrid."

Very convenient.

Pixie called me from Pasadena.

"I was excited as all shit to see you guys and you're not even here. I find out you're in Italy. When you coming back?"

"Not even a hello?" I laughed.

She laughed. "Hello. When the hell will you be back?"

"Look for us in another three days. Olga said your tour was great."

"I hate living out of suitcases, I'm too old for this shit."

"You love it."

I heard a sigh. "I do. Hurry home, Boss."

"Where is Lainie?"

"She's winding things up on her tour, then flying to London. Money hungry bitch."

"Baby, I know you don't mean it. Why you call her that?"

"Oh fuck, I don't know. I love her so damn much."

"That's better," I said. "Get some rest. We'll be back soon."

I asked Letty if she had talked to Lainie.

"All the time, Boss. She has two or three more nights, and she's taking a month off in London."

"Pixie's home."

"She called me when she landed, and I told her we were in Italy."

"She's wigged out over Lainie and Jason," I said.

"Maybe because he asked Lainie to marry him."

"What?"

Letty did that exaggerated nod. "Yep. Lainie told me, and Pixie confirmed it."

"Well, at least they're talking to each other. I mean, Pixie and Lainie."

"I think Pixie is jealous, not of Jason going with Lainie but about Lainie picking up where Pixie left off."

So, Olga's talk about Jason being gay was bullshit just like I first thought. When she'd first mentioned it to me, I thought maybe she came to that conclusion when he turned Olga down. The complaints from Pixie that he didn't fuck, and Lainie telling me she had not fucked him, what was all that about? If she was alive, what would Sami think about Jason cradle robbing Lainie? But that was not a valid thought at all. If Sami was alive, Jason would still be adoring Sami and working, not trying to fill the emptiness in his life.

I finished my business with Pepe right away, but we still stayed four days from the day we arrived. We boarded the 707 again, back to California. The pilot announced belts could come off. Twenty minutes after we took off, we were served an early dinner. The girls sat across from me. The stewardess brought us our food from the galley, course by course, and though the table was big enough to accommodate all the dishes, she carried each plate off as we finished.

"I don't know why I'm so starved," I said after a salad and shrimp. "I ate constantly from the time we got to Pepe's."

"With me, it's the plane. Soon as I'm on board, I get hungry," Letty said.

"Boss, I'm sorry I caved so easy to Pepe," Tangles said. She tore into her shrimp cocktail.

The stewardess brought us massive bowls of Fettuccini Alfredo. She did not mix it at the table as they do at Alfredo's, but that didn't matter as I was pretty sure our meal had been catered by Alfredo's.

"I don't know what you mean."

Letty made a face at me, slurped a long noodle, and said, "It's obvious. She means that she sucked him off and fucked him in every which way every night we were there."

"That mouth," I said. "Letty, we should rename you Pixie."

"That would be an honor. I love Pixie."

Tangles said, "Fucking-a. Letty's right. I did it all. I'm sorry if I embarrassed you by being so easy. Maybe I was blinded by who he is."

"Stop hiding the gift he gave you," Letty said.

"But don't get mad, Boss, please."

"Why would I get mad?"

Tangles unbuttoned her shirt's top button, revealing a diamond drop.

"It's pear shaped. The man is crazy to give me this. He said it's five carats."

Letty said, "I already told her I want half the diamond." She hooted with laughter, coughed, then claimed she'd snorted a noodle. Tangles whacked her on the back with an impact that shook the table. When Letty got her breath, she whacked Tangles back. It was like dining with the two stooges.

"I'm engaged to his sister that he adores. He knows I have no legitimate claim on you or Letty," I said.

"Boss, wait. Tell me you aren't mad and that you like the gift," Tangles said, pleading. She was holding the diamond, slightly pulling it away from her upper chest so it was really visible.

"I love it," I said. "If he got to your pussy, you deserve two or more of those things."

Tangles said, "Boss, you *are* mad at me."

The expression on her face made me laugh. "I don't know diamonds, but you're probably wearing a house around your neck. That could be anywhere from fourteen thousand to half a mil."

She blanched, and then held the stone up close to her eye.

"Really? I had no idea."

"Lucky bitch," Letty said.

"Don't say that."

"I'm joshing, Boss. She knows it."

The girls' friction never rose to the level of an argument. They hugged and kissed, and I heard something like "I'm stoked for you, sweets," then their attention switched to their plates.

One of the attendants served us Château Mouton, no doubt a gift from Pepe. Coming over, we had not had Rothschild. I toasted to everything that was good, including Melina, drunkenly sad she was not with us. After we polished off two bottles of wine, I got up to stretch and hit the bathroom. When I returned, the girls were ready to move either to the sofa or the bedroom.

"Are you sleeping with us or are you on the couch?" They wanted to know.

All three of us hit the bedroom.

"I'll take a sniff," Letty giggled. "See if there's any trace of Pepe."

"No way!" Tangles swore, turning to me. "Boss, I promise, before we left I did a number on myself. I am so sanitized, you'll never know I was with anyone else."

I put my hands up. I wasn't touching the Pepe topic with a ten-foot pole.

I was so full, I should have been uncomfortable, but the wine knocked me out. Well, it knocked me out after I felt I had sufficiently wiped any memory of Pepe from Tangles, and I had Letty singing to the high heavens. The girls were my gems, and I made sure they knew it. In the seventies, it was cool to have sex just to have sex, no strings, no catches. Maybe it was a hangover from the sixties, with the whole free love doctrine. Everybody didn't feel that way, but most young people who were on board made it clear how they felt. Free love was one thing, but it was entirely separate from the idea of having a one and only true love. I was convinced that Olga was my one and only true love.

The 707 landed in Ontario, California about 40 miles from Pasadena. I expected Pixie's driver, Raul would be there to pick us up. I didn't expect to see Pixie until we got home, but there she was, waiting.

"You look fantastic," I said, picking her up and spinning her around with me. She'd been under the blade of some mod-crazed hair stylist who left her with an unsymmetrical haircut, shorter on one side, and streaks of blonde in her sleek dark hair. When I set her on her feet, she spun around to hug Letty and Tangles.

"Those shorts are up to your belly button," Letty said, laughing.

As Raul stacked the trunk, I sat myself across from them in the Rolls, my legs stretched out. We were rolling in a few minutes, the partition between driver and passengers closed.

"I dare you," Letty said.

Pixie, in the middle, unbuttoned her shorts and wiggled out of them, saying, "Eat me, bitch."

Tangles howled in laughter.

Pixie looked at me. I shrugged.

"Okay, but I want twenty autographed albums. You got it, bitch?"

When I was a kid of about ten years old, the neighborhood boys had a stash of adult magazines left behind by fathers who were long gone. We passed these around, looking at naked women and pictures of couples having sex in different positions and weird places. You can't imagine how much trouble that soft porn got me into. I never guessed that as an adult, I could sit there in a car and watch two of my best friends submitting to each other as Pixie and Letty were doing. Sure, they loved each other, but this was sex, just for sex and laughs. And that was just wonderful.

"Can you see, Boss?" Tangles asked between laughs.

"No, it's too dark."

"Liar," Tangles said.

It was pretty much hard to miss, with Pixie's leg bent over my shoulder, and Letty crouched half on Tangles, half on me, like I was part of the furniture.

For the next four days, my house rang with laughter. We did no work and hung out together twenty-four hours a day. Tangles and Pixie sent Sunny running home to pick up clothes. We ate and celebrated Pixie's homecoming, and slept together Thursday, Friday, Saturday, and Sunday. Once or twice, Pixie cried a little, still down over the Jason-Lainie situation, then with some help from us, she'd bounce back.

A RIALTO music video with a cutoff-clad Pixie singing and playing the trumpet had been a smash hit in Latin America and had shown impressive sales in California and Arizona where Capital distributed the VHS release. I had not seen it before.

"You look so fucking hot," I told her after watching the tape. Three times.

"You do look hot," Tangles said.

"Bravo, bravo," Letty chimed after the first showing. "Gangbang!"

Pixie plays every instrument you put in her hands, but I had never heard her with a trumpet. In the tape, she dances and alternates between blowing the horn and singing, so fit and vital, it's hard to believe she's in her late thirties. I think she owes that to what it takes to keep at level five in karate. When she'd first started with RIALTO, some reviewers said that Latin men identified muscles on a woman as manly, but no one was saying that now. In those shorts, the tiny waist, and a tiny cover on her breasts, she was savagely sexy.

Pixie split early Monday for a meeting Olga arranged at CAPITAL Records in Hollywood with the President of RIALTO to discuss pushing her music aggressively in the United States. Lainie already had three single Capital releases sung in English.

Through Kinko, I submitted a written offer on behalf of Global Aircraft Leasing to the operator in Australia for the bank to bank price that Pepe and I had worked out. The cash price could not be put in writing, but I had to let the seller know we were willing to pay millions in cash for these planes. I brought it up to Kinko, though I hardly knew him well enough to discuss it.

"It is possible this could be a cash deal. How do I tell that to the sellers when I can't put it in writing?"

"I'll tell them on the phone. What's the price if they do it?"

I gave him the cash price.

"They owe money on these planes. Not sure all cash is going to work, but I'll speak to the guy I'm dealing with in Sydney."

"Kinko, you the man."

"You the man," Kinko said. "Chill. Lots of people use cash to buy planes through me."

I had had no idea. "Got it," is all I could say.

I didn't consider how Australia is 17 hours ahead of California. At ten p.m., Letty and I were engrossed in something of a naked wrestling match when the phone rang. I answered. You can't take your attention off Letty for a second. She flipped me. One bedside lamp and an alarm clock clattered to the floor, but I managed to hang on to the phone.

"This is Chuck Morrison," a strange Australian-accented voice said. "Is this Mario Luna?"

"It is." I released my grip on Letty's torso, and she pouted for about three seconds, then got off the bed to right the clock and lamp, both undamaged.

"Kinko told me I could call you direct. I own the planes you're interested in." He gave a short bark of laughter. "My company owns the planes, but I am the company."

Kinko had not mentioned this guy would be calling me. I tried to ignore Letty, who had turned her back to me, and was standing just out of reach, writhing around, doing that thing that looks like someone else is hugging you. Hard to ignore.

"I am glad to hear from you."

"I read the written offer that Kinko faxed over. It's not acceptable. I want to discuss this other offer but prefer to do it in person." He coughed. "Sorry about that. I smoke."

"Come on over," I said without a pause. I patted the bed. Letty sat. I put my finger up to my lips, so I could listen to Chuck.

"How's day after tomorrow?"

He landed at the Ontario airport. Kinko picked him up and drove him to my house.

Kinko had not been to my house before.

When they arrived, it was eleven p.m. which put Chuck at two p.m. Sydney time. My staff was up and ready for anything. I called Miguel in from the kitchen, and he offered to prepare anything they wanted. They settled for appetizers and martinis. I drank wine. Letty tended bar and served us as we sat in the den. Tangles brought out tray after tray of Miguel's appetizers. Shrimp and cocktail sauce. Crabmeat on rounds of toast. Fried stuffed olives. Jalapeño poppers. Shish kabob skewers of filet and bell peppers. Grilled oysters. His homemade potato chips. Rounds of mashed potatoes that had been piped into little mounds and toasted till crunchy. Miniature apple tarts. Trays filled the coffee table in front of my oversized couch. Kinko and Chuck were parked on the couch, and I on the opposite side, on a chair. I could see my guests were blown away, Kinko by the poppers, and Chuck by the grilled oysters and shish kabob.

Chuck was a big guy like me, well over six feet. For being sixty-eight, he looked good.

"I can tell by your house that you can afford whatever we talk about," he said. "I can use cash because the airline is in terrible shape right now. They cut half my routes. The government just tossed my renewals in the shit can and left me out in the cold. Not sure how much longer the business can weather the storm."

I listened. Letty refilled Kinko's martini glass, and he drank and listened. Letty and Tangles glanced up the stairs, like they were asking if it was time for them to go, but I waved them to sit. They each grabbed a tiny apple tart and sat nibbling it on wing chairs on either side of the coffee table.

"I can pay off what is owed on these planes from my accounts and give you title without a problem. The cash, if I can get it all in cash, I can use to tidy up some holes—"

I interrupted him. "Chuck, you give me title for the planes and I'll give you the cash. I don't need to know what you do with it."

Chuck smacked his lips. I did not know if it was over the deal or Miguel's savory filet. He took a sip of his martini and did not torture me by making me wait. "Okay then. With the price you offered, if it's cash, I won't even play hard ball."

I smiled. He was hooked. All I had to do was reel him in. "Tell you what. When you go home tomorrow, I'll send you off with a ten-million-dollar deposit, so you know how real the deal is."

He smacked his lips. This time I could tell it was for the savory transaction.

"You got a deal, son."

Letty showed Kinko to a guest room. Tangles showed Chuck to another guest room. I showed myself to my own bedroom where Betty was waiting for me with the massage table up and ready.

"Boss, it's so late I figured you wouldn't want to go down to the spa."

"You figured good," I said, tired as all hell. "But no table. Bed."

I shed my clothes and belly-flopped on the mattress. My head hit the pillow, and I was out. I don't have a clue what happened after that.

In the morning, I picked out two oversized duffle bags from my luggage room and packed them with cash. Chuck and Kinko left early with about 220 pounds of cash. Hundred-dollar bills. Ten million dollars.

"I'll keep my end of the bargain within a week of my arrival back home. I will have to come back for the cash at that point." He gave me a hug. "Good doing business with you, Mario. And thank you very much for your hospitality. I owe you."

I smiled. "My pleasure, Chuck."

Kinko smiled, and gave me a fist bump, then touched his heart with his fist.

I did the same.

I caught Pepe on his cell at six p.m. Milan time to tell him we had a deal, and that I had emptied my safes of Camacho money. Although a million of my own money remained in the safe, I deposited my income to my main accounts spread around Los Angeles.

"There's plenty where that came from. You are a genius," Pepe said.

"I got lucky," I said. "Let's celebrate when we close the deal."

Chuck had ten million dollars[45] on a handshake. If I had been worried, I would never have given him that much money. It was important to show him that I was real, and the company I represented was just as real.

Thirty minutes later, Olga and Camila called. Conference call. Olga was still in Lima, Camila in Rio.

"Amor, you got both of us," Olga said.

"I wish I had you with me in bed," I said, though it was nearly ten in the

---

[45] $10,000,000.00 in 1986 had the same buying power as $22,554,803.29 in 2018

morning, and I had long since finished breakfast and was up in my office.

"I close my eyes and pretend," Camila said, laughing.

"Pepe is so happy, Amor. You are fantastico!" Olga was ecstatic.

Two days later, Pepe called with a proposition. "Mario, do you love that plane I sold you?"

I didn't know what was coming. "I love that plane. Why do you ask?"

"I have someone who would like to lease it for two years, maybe longer. I can probably get you twenty-five thousand a month."

"I'm listening," I said. "Math says that I won't have back what I paid for the plane in two years."

Pepe laughed. "Mario, if you get it back in two years, you still have a plane worth a lot of money."

"That will depend on how many hours he puts on the plane," I said.

"I can see you don't want to lease it. I thought you might want to buy something with more range."

I had about a million in the plane. At twenty-five thousand a month, my return would be thirty percent each year it was leased out at that price.

"Are you there?" Pepe asked.

"Here's a deal for you, Pepe. Give me 1.25 for the plane, and you lease it out. I make a profit right now on the plane and you make a profit by leasing it."

Without hesitation, Pepe said, "I'll give you 1.25 cash."

"Cash is fine," I said.

"I'll find out if this guy wants it for sure. Send me a video."

Olga called with her own advice. "Amor, lease the plane. Pepe is giving you an opportunity to make the nice return. You need a loan?"

"Thanks, Baby. I don't need a loan."

Two weeks later, instead of selling, I leased out my Lear. The paperwork went through Pepe. The leasing company would take five percent of the monthly rental for handling and I would get the difference.

Kinko had nothing that would work for me, but he called friends and found me a two-year-old 1984 Dassault Falcon 900B with an interior that I fell in love with. Everything was brown, manly. I wasn't certain I wanted to dish out this much cash or if I should lease it or buy it with bank financing. With Tangles and Letty along for the ride, I took it to San Francisco and back, and toyed with the idea of closing the deal. It was a step up from the Lear. I loved the fact that it had a range of four thousand miles.

With no notice, Olga showed up. She called when she landed in Ontario. We stayed in bed for twenty-four hours, just the two of us. Her pal Riana slept in a guest room and Letty in her own room.

"Let's go see the plane," Olga said. "Falcons are so boss. Excited for you, Amor. What is taking you so long to close the deal?"

"I don't know," I lied, not disclosing my indecision.

We didn't take it up in the air, but we loved in it, and Olga said she loved it. I called the dealer but not until I consulted with Pepe for the second time about what he thought of the price.

"I'll arrange for a wire for the entire amount," I told the dealer. "Fax me the wire instructions and the invoice."

I figured I could always finance it and get most of my money back if that's what I wanted to do, but for now I was liquid enough to dish out 2.3 million for the plane. Olga stayed close to me during this visit, so I didn't consult Melina. Letty brought me the fax. "Send it to Lola at the bank. I'll send her instructions in the morning."

Letty was excited.

"Far-out, Boss. Fuck-me, that plane is so fucking cool."

In the morning after breakfast, I went up to my office while Olga showered. At 10:30 a.m., I called Lola at the bank giving her a heads up about the outgoing wire I needed.

"Must be a pretty good deal for you to put out that much money."

"I love it," I said.

"We could have financed it," she said. "Still can?"

"Maybe later. If I need money, it's like having a pink slip for a car, right?"

Lola gave a little laugh. "Yes, almost. Just a lot more money."

I wrote out the instructions as Lola told me. I waved Tangles to come into the office. She came in with a mug of coffee for me and set it down on my desk.

"Morning, Boss."

"Where's Letty?"

A few beats after I asked, Letty popped her head in from the hall.

"Right here, Boss. I was handling something with Olga before she got in the shower."

"Monkey business?"

"Nothing like that."

I handed the paper with my signature to Letty. "Fax this to Lola."

Letty read what I handed her. Tangles, the snoop, read over her shoulder.

"That's for the plane? Oh, Boss, I can't wait to go somewhere again in that beautiful plane," Tangles said.

"Send the wire."

Letty didn't send it. She was just standing there.

"Boss, you're too late," she said, handing me back the paper.

My first thought was that it had been sold to someone else. I felt confused. I looked at her. "Late?"

"Boss, Olga wired the money about twenty minutes ago. That's what we were doing."

"What do you mean? You mean she paid for it?"

"She said she wanted to give you a present, and this was perfect."

I stared at Letty, then at Tangles then at Letty.

"Boss, did I fuck up?" Letty asked.

I shook my head. "No, not at all." I was feeling a little shell-shocked.

"Some present. Fuck," Tangles said.

"If Pixie was here, she'd swear she came after hearing something like this," Letty said.

"I'm the one that's going to have the orgasm," I whispered.

On July 4th I had planned to put on a bash at the house, but on July second, I was on my plane with Letty and Tangles headed to Amsterdam where a plane overran the runway and crashed in a field, killing at least twenty-one people, and injuring over eighty others. Though the tragedy occurred in June, it wasn't until the first of July that Juan had cleared the way for the team and me to start canvassing the hotels where the victims' families were being housed by the airline operator. Fifteen of the decedents were from Amsterdam and the surrounding area. Most of the injured were also locals.

"I had cases here before," I told Gonor on the phone, "and practically struck out with locals. Don't expect too much. The family group did not want to make much noise. They wanted to give the insurance carriers room to make them direct offers and avoid litigation."

"Get the case," Gonor urged with enthusiasm.

"You know the deal we have, but this could be a big one. I said could be, nothing is a sure thing. Are you sure you can handle the expenses and the weight it will add to your overhead?"

"Get the case," he repeated.

I told Letty and Tangles, "I don't have high expectations of the Dutch families. We'll do the two hotels, but our goal is the families that live in other countries. Juan is working on getting the details of those families. I know we usually work cases for a couple of months, but we'll be out of here in two weeks. I'm not wasting all of July in Amsterdam." What we needed was the one case to break the ice. With one case secure, others fall to us like dominoes.

"If we're lucky, those families will still be here at the hotel," Tangles said.

"Not if the bodies have been turned over to the families," Letty corrected. "They'd be back home or on the way home for the funerals."

The good thing is the weather was good. Low seventies in the day, fifty and change in the evening. Not too bad for a place I remembered as being very cold on my last two trips.

Although the morgue is not always where we get the details of the decedent and family, that's where Juan made a contact. It turned out to be a winner in Amsterdam. I put my sights on one family from Mexico City. Three of their loved ones perished. Juan provided the contact details and confirmed that the bodies had been released, and that the husband had flown them back to Mexico City. I sent Juan to Mexico City to do the advance work. If I came out of this with only the family in Mexico City, it would be a win for me.

"Don't give up on us," Letty said. "I have Lionel Lucas who lost his wife. They were on their honeymoon. He's only twenty-three. He's a local, but he's talking to me."

"I have a couple of men that have connected with me, too," Tangles said.

"Nothing wrong talking to the women, too," I reminded them.

"We do, Boss, but here, it's harder than anywhere else," Letty said.

"Holland is tough. I remember that I hit a wall here before," I said.

"Then why are you spending the money to be here?" Tangles asked.

"For the families that need the help of Gonor's law firm in Chicago to get them maximum compensation."

"If I have to spread them, no problema," Tangles said.

"These people are mourning," Letty said, "but I've done it before. Not in exchange for a signature on a retainer."

I covered my ears. "I don't want to hear it."

"Oh Boss, come on. How about you and widows? You never done it? Don't pull my leg," Letty said.

"Never," I lied with a straight face.

"Well, I'll be damned," Tangles said, and stuck her tongue out at me.

"You probably will," Letty agreed.

We had been in Amsterdam for under two weeks when Pixie called on her house phone.

Earthquake.

"I thought the house was going to collapse. I just had fallen asleep, a little stoned, but I have never run so fast. I was down the stairs and out the front door in record time."

She had been at home in Pasadena on July 13th during the 6.0 earthquake somewhere near Palm Springs.

"Baby, I wish I had been there with you. We'll be home day after tomorrow."

"I went over to your house. Everything is fine there. Seems intact. TJ already came by and checked."

"Thanks, Pix. Miguel says the same. Everyone is shook up though. Stay calm for the aftershocks."

"We've had a bunch already," Pixie said.

"The house you are in has been through these many times, and it's still there. Probably safer than my house."

"Your house is brand new," Pixie said.

"I know, but it's four stories. If you feel better at my house, get your little ass over there. I can't wait to be there with you."

"Hey, Boss," Pixie giggled. "What you mean my little ass? I got a fine ass. You should read some of my fan mail."

"No one knows that ass better than me," I said, mirroring her mood change.

"Hurry home, Boss. My fine ass is waiting for you."

I called Olga to let her know Pixie was hanging in there.

"Amor, I talked to her last night. I just heard about the earthquake. This world will crack in half one day."

"Hopefully not in our lifetimes," I said.

Letty came into the hotel's master suite. We were in a three-bedroom unit, each bedroom with its own attached bath. Letty hovered by the door like a bee deciding whether or not to land on a nervous flower. She clearly had something on her mind and had waited for Tangles to fall asleep before joining me.

"Boss, I gotta tell you something."

Her serious tone threw me off. With no idea of what to expect, I patted the mattress beside me.

"Something bothering you?"

"Not me, precisely," she said. She was wearing socks, and an oversized t shirt that barely reached the top of her thighs. Her short hair was pulled into two tiny pigtails.

"If not you, who?"

"It's not my secret to tell, but you have to promise not to say a word."

I sat up in bed and tossed aside the editorial section of the Sunday New York Times, which I'd picked up at the hotel's magazine stand. "This is starting to sound serious. Your secrets are safe with me."

Letty settled on the cloud of extra pillows next to me and carefully removed her socks, putting them on the bed stand. The spread was folded down to the foot of the bed. She always did that to everyone's beds at all the hotel rooms we'd ever been in, as she devoutly believed hotel bedspreads carried every germ created since Eden, and that they were rarely, if ever, washed. The same feeling extended to hotel carpeting, hence the socks, and her treating her perfectly white, perfectly clean socks as if they were radioactive after she'd walked with them across the floor.

She stretched out on top of the blanket, her bare feet brightened by the same raspberry nail polish as on her fingernails. She stared at her toes as she talked. I stared at them too.

"Lainie said she's going to accept Jason's proposal of marriage. She's anxious about breaking the news to Pixie."

Whatever I thought she was going to say, it wasn't this. I spoke carefully. "Pixie feels Jason is too old for Lainie. I know she wants Lainie to marry for love." I was surprised, but I didn't yet know how I felt about it.

Had it not been for Tangles and Letty, I would have not signed a single case in Amsterdam. Between them, they signed four families. In each case, it was a male survivor of the victim or the person who called the shots for the family. Maybe I didn't try as hard as I used to. Shame on me. My head was into plane leasing.

We flew direct to Mexico City with one stop. My plane originally had seating for fourteen passengers, but I'd sacrificed some seating for a forward bathroom. The girls stood easily but I had to remember the ceiling was only 6'2", so I couldn't stand up straight. With just Letty, Tangles and me rattling around all that room, it was pretty cool. The captain and co-pilot stayed in the cockpit. The relief pilot had a jump seat right outside the cockpit door. If we had a flight attendant on the crew, she would have used a seat in the forward cabin, where there were three seats arranged in a conversational grouping. Tangles and Letty and I spent the trip at the center grouping at the table and on the bed. The aft cabin had come with two three-seat divans facing each other, but I kept the partition up, and preferred the bed configuration to divans. The bed stretched all the way across the plane. Sure, the bed was a little short for me, but the three of us slept on it easily. It was not having to stop and refuel that felt like the biggest luxury. I kidded Olga that my bed was as big as the bed on her plane.

"You wish, Amor, your bed is a crib compared to mine."

Juan set up a meeting in Mexico City with Santiago Solis. His wife Isadora and two children were the decedents. He was barely managing to hold it together between moments when he was transfixed by grief or crying inconsolably. His heartbreak reminded me strongly of my panic when Pixie's plane had been incommunicado, when we'd all been quietly convinced it had crashed somewhere. I related strongly to this man, who would never get a call from a military base that his beloved Isi and his girls had made a safe emergency landing. Never again would he hold his Isi, or rock his children to sleep. Never again would he wake to his wife's smiling face or share her counsel or her bed. His grief tore into me, into a private vulnerability that never heals. I could understand why Betty gave this up. Never in a million years can one get used to being so close to so much grief.

We met at his very nice modern house that had been built for a family, now an airy shell filled with sadness. He was an architect; and we already knew his wife had also been an architect who only rarely took on projects, so she had time to raise their two daughters. He led us toward his kitchen for coffee. The kitchen was open to the family room where we passed a painting of two beautiful young girls in a garden. I knew one was named Isadora for her mother, and the other was Isabel. Santiago introduced them to us as if they were still alive, calling the older girl Dora, and the toddler Bella. I could hear the love in their names, and nearly broke down myself.

The bright sun-lit kitchen had a window wall looking out into a pretty shaded patio with curvy white wrought iron furniture. The white Formica breakfast table nestled in a bay window nook of light and more windows, overlooking a garden with a central bird bath fountain, and wild masses of tropical greenery so brilliantly green they hurt my eyes. I sat at the table as Santiago poured a fresh pot of coffee into a carafe and brought it to the table.

"Let me do that," Letty said.

He sat.

She brought us mugs that were out on hooks, colorful mugs, that looked like they'd sprouted in that garden outside. She found cream in the refrigerator and put it in the creamer. Sugar and spoons were already at the table.

"I am alone," the husband told us, in a way that sounded like he was broken now and would never be fixed. He watched a little helplessly as Letty poured coffee for everyone.

Instead of sitting, Letty knelt next to the widower and put her face on his upper thigh, her hand clasping his. Tangles stood behind his chair, her hand on his shoulder. There was silence between us. Letty knew that words of comfort don't work. The grieved must cry. Tangles had not worked out what needed to happen, but her instincts were good. She moved when Letty moved, was quiet when Letty was quiet, talked when it was appropriate. I watched my two stars, but my heart bled as I listened to Santiago weep over Isi, Dora, and Bella.

Juan flew back to Puerto Rico with fifteen thousand dollars I gave him. The girls and I boarded my plane for home.

"Let's get out of here before they have another big one here," Letty said.

"Dummy, haven't you heard what's happening at home?" Tangles asked.

"Fuck you, bitch. If I gotta be stuck in a shaker, I want it on my turf. I don't care if it's fucked up. It's how I feel," Letty told Tangles.

The flight from Mexico City to Van Nuys is a short three hours and change. I was exhausted by the emotion I'd been feeling, and went back to the cabin, took off my shoes and crashed on the bed, glad of the extra padding on the mattress. The pilot came on to let us know we should have our seat belts on, and we'd be taking off in five minutes. My mind skittered away from the overwhelming grief of Santiago Solis. I thought about Olga and Camila. Planes like this would be perfect for them, could land in more places than the big things they flew around in, could save them a bundle in fuel. Why did they need so much plane? It was silly, extravagant, wasteful. Sometime after I fell asleep, the girls came to bed and spooned me between them. The comfort of their embraces seeped into me, even though I did not wake until we landed in Van Nuys.

At home, I found my answering machine had several calls from Arthur. I called him back hoping he had more details on what was going on between Fino and Janice Cooke.

"Arthur, what's up?"

"Is it okay to talk on the phone?"

"If you got something, come over for a late lunch by the pool. I haven't eaten today, and I'm ravenous."

Late July in Pasadena is hot. We met outside under an awning and a fan, both of us in shorts. Miguel brought us a series of cold drinks. Iced tea. Frozen pineapple blended with ice and coconut cream. Frozen fruit salad. Grilled hamburgers. The girls were eating inside in the air conditioning. I'd told them this was a business meeting.

"I have an opportunity to bug Janice's apartment, at least two maybe three rooms. I'm getting nowhere watching Fino. He's not been to her apartment since you put me on this. She gets out a couple of times a week to visit a hair salon and a nail salon."

"Maybe there's nothing," I said.

"I can pull out, no problem."

I thought for about ten seconds. "Can they trace the bugs back to you?" I asked.

"No trace. I have to monitor but we never have to retrieve the bugs. We just leave them."

"How about the phone?"

"I can do that," Arthur said. "If I just do phone, I don't need to get in there."

"Do phone," I said. "Thirty days."

By the last week in July, the plane paperwork had been completed, and Olga had come and gone, leaving behind a boatload of money. Three of her guards carried in laundry bags filled with paper-bound bundles of cash. I did not bother with the safes, just had them put the money in my office supply room. I must admit I was a little nervous, though not about theft. I was concerned that the cops could show up. What would I tell them? The good thing was that the money would be gone in just over twenty-four hours. Chuck from

Australia arrived the next day for the rest of his money, coming equipped with his own duffle bags and suitcases. Chuck showed up alone as I had instructed. The two of us carried the bags to his rented station wagon.

"I have men back at the plane," he said. "Wish I could stay longer and let your chef impress me."

"You have time for a steak, I feel sure."

"I hate to eat and run," he said.

"Rain check on the fancy dinner," I said with a chuckle. "Let's see you take down Miguel's porterhouse."

The planes were certified as airworthy. I used my regular agency to supply pilots to deliver the first three planes to an operator in Sao Paulo, Brazil where they would be painted to match up the rest of their fleet. Pepe sent GAL pilots to fly the other five planes to Milan. Olga delivered my five percent commission in a duffle bag.

"Baby, let me pay you back for my plane," I said.

"How dare you, Amor." She pretended to be angry, but I couldn't take her seriously when she grabbed my dick. "That was a gift from your fiancée who adores you." She released me long enough for us to get to my bedroom. We spent the next day abed. Riana and Letty were on the third floor on their own.

"Pepe and Camila keep asking me when we're going to get married," she said, after she came up for air the first time.

"I'm ready."

"Me too, Amor."

We didn't touch the subject again but fell into round two, or maybe three. Who's counting?

Miguel brought in tea and cakes at four in the afternoon. We ate naked on the balcony with the doors shut. We had to follow up the July heat with a cool shower. The balcony table was cleared by the time we were out.

I could not resist bringing it up again. "Baby, why don't you get the bigger version of the Falcon to fly around in? The Falcon is heaven in a plane. My bed is as big as yours."

"You wish." She laughed. "Why you ask this all the time?"

"I just wonder why you want to be flying around in that big plane."

"I brought you all that cash for the Australian. I need a big plane."

"Give me a break. You don't need an airliner for that. Do you have something in the cargo hold?"

"Amor, please, *no me chinques,*[46] she said with a laugh.

There she was again, being evasive. Her evasion convinced me that something was in the cargo hold. I had seen the cargo hold doors were always opened for the customs officer who came to check passports. I'd seen those holds before, always empty, a lot of room, space to transport tons of something more profitable than air. Would Pepe use his own family, his two knockout jetsetters, Camila and Olga, for transporting more than just cash? I felt acid burn its way down my stomach, and deliberately refused to chase that thought.

"Amor, I'm right here. Where are you?"

I snapped out of it.

"You need to ask?" I nibbled a path down her body, little bites and kisses, devouring her. She went wild.

"I'm happy Riana's your companion. I hated when you were always flying solo. How long will she be free to travel with you?"

"I guess she'll get tired one day, but so far, she's happy. I know her father is happy to have her out of his hair," she laughed. "Not that he has hair."

I nibbled on her ear and whispered, "How come you haven't asked her to come in with us this trip?" I patted the bed, indicating the bed-bound flight we'd been on.

"Oh, you bad boy. You will make me jealous."

"It's you I love, Baby."

She kissed me. "Tonight, let's invite Letty and Riana to come in with

---

[46] Stop messing with me

us, Si?"

"Si," I agreed. "How about Tangles?" I was pretty sure they'd buried the hatchet, and her answer confirmed it.

"Si, Tangles. Tambien, Amor."

Maybe we were taking Letty and Tangles for granted. Maybe they didn't care to join us. Unless I was worried about something, I was always horny. Being horny was my normal. I knew Olga loved Camila and slept with Riana like I slept with Letty, every night she was away. That was her normal.

I talked to Pixie frequently, and so did Olga. Pixie was on her second week of flying around the U.S. doing television and radio interviews to promote her latest VHS album, the one with her playing the trumpet. Capital worked differently from RIALTO, insisting the star make appearances to promote the latest release. They had agreed to distribute her latest cut in VHS and vinyl. If Olga and I were together, she'd hand me the phone when she was talking to Pixie.

"I'm living out of a suitcase again and not getting paid for it," she complained into my ear. "At least when I'm on tour, I get paid."

Beside me, Olga mimicked Pixie complaining, making me laugh aloud.

"Not funny, Boss."

After Pixie hung up, Olga and I moved our party to the shower. We each lathered up our huge mesh shower poofs. Whatever the hell they are, they make a shitload of lather.

Pivoting in the water so it streamed down her back, Olga said, "Has Pixie told you that Jason proposed to Lainie and she accepted?"

"No, damn, really? When?" I pumped some extra surprise in my voice, and lathered my hair, handing the shampoo bottle to Olga.

"Not sure. I'm surprised you don't know. Letty talks to Lainie a lot, doesn't she?"

I nodded. We rinsed off the shampoo. Back to the soapy poofs.

"I heard it from Pixie earlier today," Olga said. "She was not happy about it."

"I hear her complaints about the air travel. Nothing about Lainie and Jason," I lied but not sure why.

"I think she's accepted it. It won't last. Jason is gay. Lainie is not going to give up fucking," Olga said, smiling.

"Jason is not gay," I said. I didn't see what she was smiling about.

"We've had this conversation before, Amor. He's gay and wants Lainie for appearances. He has a name to protect. He needs a wife."

I shook my head, sprinkling water like a dog. "If that was true, he would have married someone a long time ago, not wait until after he retired."

"I don't know. Maybe he was married before."

"I don't think so. He never mentioned it, and neither did Sami."

"I hope Lainie doesn't stay away too long. The public is a fickle bedpartner. It forgets fast, especially when you are just starting out, like she is."

"Whatever makes her happy," I said, meaning it.

"Of course, Amor."

"So grumpy, Amor, why?"

"Never grumpy."

By now, I'd frosted her whole body with an inch of lather and she had covered me up to my neck. We looked like soapy yetis.

"I adore you, Amor."

"I adore you, too," I said, running my hands over her slickened skin. I took some time to get her screaming my name.

Pixie was still full of complaints and vinegar when she got home three days after Olga and Riana left. Letty and Tangles were upstairs working. We had a little karate workout together and were following up in my breakfast room with coffee and pastries. Have I mentioned Pixie has a sweet tooth and eats like a horse? I don't know where she puts it. She has abs like a wrestler but her middle's about as big around as a number two pencil.

"That fiancée of yours works my fucking ass off," she complained.

"It's probably Capital."

"Capital my ass. She's the one riding me like a donkey. She calls me twice a day from wherever she is. Did you hear about Lainie?"

"I did, but not from you."

"She'll get a snoutful of the Englishman, then come running back home."

"Are you sure? Olga thinks the same thing."

"She must know that marrying him is an arrangement for appearances. He likes the female body. He enjoys watching, but he won't fuck me, and I know he's not fucking Lainie."

"Ouch, Baby. Live and let live, right? I don't need to see into Jason's bedroom."

She shook her head. "That's my Baby. The world can go fuck itself. All I want is for Lainie to be happy. And how happy will she be in a farce of a marriage?"

Pixie left to have a day at Capital but was back that night after dinner. I was sitting on the sofa. Letty was next to Pixie across from me on another couch. Tangles was upstairs in the office. Pixie came around the table between us and sat on my lap. I cuddled her. Her arms were around my neck, hugging me. I looked at Letty still across from me.

"I'd like a few hits of a joint," Pixie said, releasing her hold on me, but still parked on my lap.

Letty didn't say a word, but sprang off the couch, and ran up the stairs, off like a genie to hunt down some pot.

I always gave my team bonuses but there was no fixed amount. I gave Letty and Tangles eight thousand each as a bonus for Amsterdam.

"Boss, I get a paycheck once a month. No need for the bonus," Tangles said, trying to hand me back the envelope holding the cash.

"It's not like before when you got paid Johnny on the spot when we turned the retainers in," Letty said. "We talked about it. You have to wait for your money from Gonor now."

"I hope Gonor gets around to paying, but that's on me. You earned it. I pay you. This is the way I've always done it, and there are not going to be any changes."

Now that the deal was made with Gonor, there was no reason for Jack and me not to go back to having lunch, if not weekly, at least once in a while. It didn't happen, though. We continued to talk by phone. I doubted that Jack would know about the wire tap or being followed by Arthur. Arthur had a reputation of being too smart for that.

"I sent Gonor a good case from Amsterdam," I told Jack. "I billed him for the expenses, and I'll wait for the cases to settle to get paid on the percentage."

"You have nothing to worry about," Jack said. "He'll pay when the money is due, and he told me this morning he was mailing your expense check."

"Great," I said, "Got to feed the kitties."

"I didn't know you had cats?"

I laughed.

"I don't have cats, but I have four badass dogs."

I heard his hearty laugh.

"I'm sure you are doing well enough with our friend in Milan to feed the whole bunch of you and then some."

Tangles had gone home. Over dinner, Pixie said she had an early call.

"Capital wants me to kick around some new songs." She ate the dinner Miguel had prepared, joined us in the wine room but headed for the door early.

"I'm going home to take a sleeping pill," Pixie said. Letty and I got kisses before Pixie let herself out.

Letty and I were walking back to the wine room when the front gate came on the intercom. Even over the loud music, I heard the urgency in Quito's voice.

"Boss, something is going on with Pixie. I'm headed out there."

I dashed out as fast as I could manage, Letty at my heels. There were no visual clues to what might be going on, but my gates were open. In the seconds it took me to reach the street, I saw my second guard with his gun out at the gates, and Pico the dog handler with two bristling dogs. A street light beamed down on Pixie and Quito standing over a handcuffed man, face down on the asphalt. Quito's foot was on the man's back. An old yellow Camaro was parked along the curb, just feet from Pixie's gates, engine running, headlights on, driver's door standing open.

"What happened?" I asked, feeling frantic and full of adrenaline.

Letty didn't ask but ran straight to embrace Pixie who was in the Zenkutsu Dachi stance facing the prone man.

"This pig tried to punch me out and put me in his car," Pixie said, over Letty's shoulder.

"Are you hurt?" I asked.

"He's the one not okay. Prick isn't going anywhere."

"Cops are on their way, Boss," Quito said, moving aside as I rolled the guy on his back. He spit a mouthful of blood at me but missed. Blood was drizzling out of the side of his mouth and his long nose was crumpled. His hair streamed past his shoulders in a tangled bush around a triangular face, with a broad forehead, thick brow ridge, wide-stretched dark brows, and tiny pointed chin.

"Motherfucker is lucky I didn't shoot him," Pixie said, looking down at him over Letty's shoulder. Letty was still hugging.

"Bitch," Motherfucker said. "I only wanted to fuck you, bitch."

At the would-be rapist's words, Letty turned to glare at him.

The cops finally arrived, put Motherfucker in the car, and the paramedics attended him in the patrol car's back seat. He wasn't seriously injured, but he'd be hurting and would need a dentist to replace two front teeth.

One of the cops did a doubletake, flashed Pixie a big smile and said, "Hey, Pixie, I know you."

Pixie did an instant kick that would have broken his nose if she hadn't pulled back. Then she took a bow.

"Didn't know you kicked ass like this." He was impressed. He bowed back. I knew why he was impressed—Pixie is crazy limber.

She smiled at the cop and gave him an autograph. She yelled past a paramedic in the process of stopping the attacker's nose bleed. "You lucky, mother fucker. Lucky, I didn't kill you."

Pixie stayed with us. I put her in a guest room and Raul brought her a sleeping pill to knock her out.

"Boss, I'm fine. He was just sitting there, parked by the gate. I got to the street, and he ran out of the car like his ass was on fire. Never got close enough to put his mitts on me. His eyes were screaming crazy way before he was in reach."

Letty and I stayed in the room until she went to sleep.

My detective friend Mike Sanchez called the same night to tell me about the thirty-one-year-old perp. He went by the name Cliff Puckett. He had done seven years for rape and got out just three months before. He was on parole but since he had skipped out from the halfway house five days earlier, he was already on his way back to prison for violating the terms of his parole. We talked a little about bringing an assault case against him.

Quito told me that when Pixie passed the guardhouse, he opened the gates for her. On one of the monitors, he watched her crossing the street. When he saw the guy jump out of his car to rush her, he made the intercom announcement to me, and ran out to find her going to town on her attacker like there was no tomorrow.

"Boss, if I hadn't gotten out there when I did, she could have killed him. She was slapping and kicking him like he was a rag doll. You can see it all on the security video, when I got in the picture and cuffed him, he was trying to crawl back to his car. I never seen nothing like it," he said. His words sounded shocked, but his expression was admiring.

I talked to Camila who was in Paris, and Olga in Colombia. Olga beat herself up about it like it was her fault, and not the fault of the would-be kidnapper/rapist.

"I must be crazy not to have protection for her living in that big house, with the help living in their quarters and only Raul in the main house. Raul can't defend her. What was I thinking?"

"Don't be so hard on yourself, Baby. Pixie can defend herself and she did."

"In Mexico she has 24/7 protection. So does Lainie. Should be the same here. I'm going to fix this tomorrow, I promise. I'm sorry, Amor. I know how you love her."

In the morning, Pixie was off to the studio. The story was already at the bottom of the LA Times front page. No pictures. Letty fielded calls from Jo, Niley, Betty, and everyone on the block. My aunt showed up at my door with a gift basket of food. Everyone local read about it in the LA Times and in the afternoon in the Herald Examiner.

Pixie called me at noon.

"These fuckers at Capital really dug the story. When I got there, they had TV cameras out to film an interview. They want me to go out and do interviews telling this story to every seedy morning DJ from here to the east coast. Anything for publicity. Bastards."

Everyone called. Jeff, the lawyer from Oscar's firm called from San Francisco to confirm that Pixie had been the girl he knew from my team. Fino called after reading about it in the paper and wanted to know how big the guy was.

"He wasn't a big guy but much bigger than Pixie." I said, "She's got the skills. She can take down just about anybody, especially when she sees the danger coming as she did."

Fino's hearty laugh went on for at least thirty seconds.

"I love it," he said.

He was still laughing when we hung up the phone.

Gonor in Chicago called in the late afternoon.

"I heard it on the radio on my way to court. Is she okay?"

Melina didn't call. She showed up that afternoon, her first appearance in ages.

"I drove over here from Echo Park when I got to the newspaper today. Where is she?"

"She left for the studio at six this morning." I told her the story.

"She needs guards. She's a celebrity, hello?"

"Got time for a quickie? Been a long time." I said.

I got that great wet kiss.

"Never in this house, Cuz. You want my pussy, come see me at home or at work."

I got instantly hard at the suggestion. "You're just teasing me," I said. It had been ages since we did it.

"Maybe, maybe not, Cuz."

Pixie got back from her long day and wanted to do something different.

I suggested the club, kind of hoping we would run into Jenny. If we did, so much for the secret.

That night, Raul took us in Pixie's stretch limo to Whisky a Go Go. We'd been there about an hour when people were noticing her, asking her to do a song. Raul fetched a trumpet and guitar from Pixie's trunk, and she did three numbers for an appreciative—if drunken—audience.

Sometime during those performances, I saw Jenny to our left at a front row table with a middle-aged guy. I looked later, and she was gone. I did not see her come or go. All I knew for sure was that she didn't walk in front of us. The brief glimpse started pictures of Jenny running through my brain. I pictured her in her small house, and in the bed that I shared with my companions, even when they were practicing their nubile aerobics on me.

"Did I tell you I came when I was smacking that dipstick?" Pixie asked out of the clear blue, following up with a giggle.

"You lie," Letty said with a whack on her ass.

"I believe it," Tangles said.

I knew she was pulling our legs. She loves to play an audience. She made up a little song about Cliff Puckett kicking the bucket. I should have written it down when I heard it, but I was laughing too hard. It had pluck it, suck it, and fuck it in there too. Letty had to run to the bathroom to keep from wetting the bed, she was laughing so hard.

"You need to put that in your next album," I said. "Maybe talk to a lawyer first."

On the last day of August, Pixie was with us at my house watching television when the program was interrupted with a news bulletin.

In the Cerritos city limits, two planes dropped out of the sky. An Aeronaves flight from Mexico collided with a Piper coming from Torrance to Big Bear and crashed into a Cerritos neighborhood. The air traffic controller in contact with the flight 498 did not see the Piper on radar. When they impacted, the Piper was flying under Visual Flight Rules, and not in radio contact with any air traffic controller. The Piper fell onto an elementary school playground. The DC-9 blasted a residential neighborhood, destroying five houses, and damaging seven more.

Pixie grabbed my hand and pulled me off the couch.

"Come on! We've never had one this close. Let's get over there."

"We cannot get close to this one," I said. "We can pray for the victims, but we can't get near the crash site. It just happened. You think they are going to let us get near the site?"

Pixie sat down, deflated.

"Boss, we used to do the trains and bus crashes at the hospitals. What gives with this plane crash?"

"Too close to home."

"Should I get Juan over here?" Letty asked.

"Yes. Book him a hotel near the airport. Can't come over here."

"Why not?" Tangles asked.

Before I had a chance to respond, Tricia called.

I told her, "This is an international flight. The Feds might get involved. I don't want to be slammed for soliciting. We keep our distance."

Tricia said, "Boss, I can use the extra money. Want me to work it?"

"Yes, but just you, not your partner."

"He's busy anyway, Boss. I know what to do."

"Juan is flying in from Puerto Rico. I don't want you working together." I wished that Tricia knew Spanish well to handle it, but she did not.

"She's not going to talk to the families anyway, just get us details," Letty said.

"I got it," Tangles said. Pixie made a face at her.

It was reported that the left horizontal stabilizer of the DC-9 had sheared off the top of the Piper's cockpit, with grisly and horrific consequences.

"Not sure how this might help you," Melina told me over the phone. "But I know the wife of the Mexican consul general. She shops at the Glendale market. Seems to me that Mexican citizens aboard that plane fall under the protection of the consular office in Los Angeles."

"Baby, I'm lost." All I knew of the consular office in Los Angeles was that it was on Olvera Street. I did not know what their function was other than maybe promote tourism for Mexico. I told that to Melina and she laughed.

"Cuz, where you been? The consul general is appointed by the President of Mexico. At least I think that's how it works. They are heavy. There is a consular office in every major world city and probably a number of offices in every state here. I'll make a call or two."

The news about the crash was grim. All sixty-seven people were killed, and fifteen more on the ground. There were no numbers for how many were injured on the ground.

The next day at noon, I walked in to the consulate office for my appointment with Martin Suarez, the consul general. He was a very distinguished looking middle-aged man. Behind his desk was a photo of the president of Mexico. At the right of his desk, a Mexican flag, at the left, a US flag. Both reached from the ceiling almost to the floor.

We shook hands, and he invited me to take a seat.

"I understand you are not a lawyer, but you are an aviation expert who represents a law firm in Chicago."

"Yes sir, that's correct."

"Mr. Luna, we have an attorney that represents our office," he said in perfect English. "When a Mexican national needs legal assistance, we send him to our attorney. Why would we want to refer a family to a lawyer in Chicago?"

"If your lawyer is an aviation lawyer, by all means, he should step in to represent the families of those who died and those who were injured. If he is not an aviation lawyer, we should talk more about this."

He leaned forward at his desk, his eyes steadily meeting mine. He seemed to get interested right before my eyes. I continued, "What is important is that the attorney you recommend be expert specifically in aviation law."

The consul nodded. "You have a point."

The meeting went on for twenty minutes. We left it that he was going to check if their attorney was an expert in aviation. He would get some background on the Gonor law firm and let me know his decision in a few days. We exchanged business cards.

His office was not huge or grand like those of the attorneys I knew, but I did feel power vibrations. Maybe it was the flags, his manner, his perfectly trimmed mustache, his immaculate grooming. I could feel the weight of his government behind him. His three-piece striped suit was too hot for my taste for an August afternoon. I supposed he mostly stayed in his office, and in his air-conditioned office, the suit was appropriate and impressive.

I called Melina from my car and gave her the update.

"His lawyer is no aviation expert," she predicted.

"Do you think he'll admit it?" I laughed at the thought.

"I'll stay in touch with the consul's wife. She wasted no time getting her husband to get you the appointment."

"That's for sure. Love you all the more, Baby."

"Are you going straight home?" she asked, her voice low and hungry. It hit my ear, stirring some hormones.

"Where are you?"

I only felt the guilt trip up front, because I knew how much Olga didn't want me to do what was about to happen. Still, I knew she did whatever she wanted with whoever she wanted when she was out in the world. Thirty minutes later, I was in her office at the Montebello market behind locked doors, naked on her sofa. This was not going to be a quickie. We did it once with the lights out, overlooking the store, and once with the lights on, and the blackout tapestry protecting our privacy. We pulled the couch into a bed so that we had a bigger playground to roll around in. Our times together had lately been few and far between. We had lost time to make up for. We broke for a meal and fell together on the bed for a rematch. Okay, several.

The next day, the consul's assistant called, asking if I could run over for a meeting right away. The deal was that the consulate would assign the cases to their local counsel, and the local counsel would refer the cases to Gonor. I arrived, waited for the local attorney to come join the Consul and me, then we all got on the speaker with Gonor. The whole thing was signed, sealed, and delivered after five hours.

Signed, sealed, and delivered did not mean automatic retainers. The families were not obligated. They had the right to hire their own attorney of choice. Only two of the Mexican families opted out of the consulate's recommendation to have Gonor handle the case.

The accident was a collision that killed everyone on the commercial liner and the three people in the Piper. The only survivors were eight people in the Los Cerritos neighborhood where the plane fell.

None of the passengers had survived, but I had a letter signed by the local attorney and stamped by the consulate office that we could interview witnesses on behalf of the Mexican Government who had the responsibility of looking out for the rights of their citizens. In addition to the Mexican families we met through the consul, the letter got us in to talk to survivors. In the hospital, we met the eight injured, all of whom were local residents of houses damaged by the crash. As they began to mend, we met them outside the hospital in their temporary housing. To be honest, the letter gave us no actual authority over anyone not a Mexican citizen, but it had what Letty called 'street credit,' and was as good as a key. It didn't hurt that we were representing so many decedents.

"You need to let me give you something for this," I told Melina. "I could not have done this without your introduction to Martin Suarez."

"You crazy or something? Offering me money, Cuz?"

"How else can I repay you?"

"You mean you don't know?" That hoarse giggle of hers was the Pied Piper of laughter, impossible to hear and not join in.

Fino knew of the deal made with the Consulate. October first fell on a Wednesday. We met for steaks at PDC and talked. It had been many Wednesdays since we'd had lunch. I had just finished signing what we believed was the last consulate-related case that wanted in. Fino was still defending the drug dealer claiming to be kidnapped by the government. It can be annoying to talk to a lawyer. They clutter their sentences with 'allegedly this, and allegedly that', especially when they know their clients are guilty as hell. Not that he said anything that was off the record. Besides, I was more concerned with Gonor's reliability than Fino's legal track record.

"I hope Gonor doesn't let me down," I said.

"Long ways to go till settlement. Relax. You get your expenses up front now. What's the risk? He's good for it. And he loves the case." Fino laughed confidently. Big booming laugh.

"He loves all the cases," I said.

"Yes, he does. He's a lawyer. What you expect?" Fino asked.

The case had consumed a lot of time without disrupting our lives with a three-month international huddle. The running was done by my team. It was unusual to have a big local case right on our turf. Since it was local, I could simultaneously handle searching for planes. That turned out to be a good thing too, because Pepe called me daily with leads for planes he wanted me to check up on, or to ask me if I had anything new since the day before. I was on the phone with Kinko daily, too.

Kinko was a rich guy. He wasn't just the manager. He owned the whole damn thing. With over a thousand desert acres housing aviation equipment, and enough qualified personnel to man his repair hubs, he had money coming from all over the place, but he certainly loved my cash. When he didn't have a plane I was looking for, he scouted his sources. Many were the times he found a diamond in the rough for me that was worth purchasing. In the aviation market, I was just getting rolling.

Melina hosted a dinner at her house with the consul, his wife, and my team. The consul and his wife were impressed with Melina's house, and our dinner table conversation was a mix of Spanish and English. Entertaining stories flew back and forth. Unsurprisingly, the couple were brilliant guests. Martin Suarez was a tremendous connection. I don't often have the chance to get cozy with someone with the ear of the President of Mexico, and I did not lose any opportunities to strengthen the connection. On Halloween, I reciprocated with a masquerade party and invited the consul, his wife and many of his staff that the team and I had worked with and gave the consul's assistant a box of invitations, so they could invite anyone they wanted too. Just for the hell of it I invited Janice and Jack, though not as a couple. Melina was a no show, Olga was in Marseilles, and Camila in Milan with Pepe. Janice showed up dressed like a witch. She was pleasant but spent most of her time with Betty since she really didn't know anyone other than my team. Pixie and Lainie showed up, Lainie sporting an engagement ring the size of a tennis ball. Okay, maybe not quite that big, but it was huge.

Letty asked, "Boss, why invite Janice?" Since I decided to do it, she and Tangles had asked that a hundred times.

Jack didn't show, but he called the afternoon before the party.

"I'm going to take a rain check. Don't be mad. I've been tired lately."

"I'll miss you. Nonsense about mad."

I had wanted to see if Jack and Janice spent time together at the party, but that wasn't going to happen.

The consul and his wife understood masquerade parties and had come dressed in splendid Flamenco costumes, but were mystified by the first and second floor full of friends in Halloween costumes. When they asked for a full tour of the house, of course, I showed them. They seemed a bit mystified at the house, too, but I knew we would become good friends.

Miguel outdid himself with a groaning buffet of delicious food that looked creepy, trays of hors d'oeuvres looking like eyes, frogs, caviar labeled goblin eggs, and other unsavory things. Letty and Tangles went overboard decorating the whole house to look like a haunted mansion by calling in some Hollywood set designer that Tangles used to massage. Pixie loaned her staff to help move furniture around, put dust-cover costumes on the furniture, fetch and carry, cook and serve. My staff and hers had worked together so much, they worked like one team. If there were any rumbles of rebellion, they never got past the kitchen door for me to hear.

The main thing was that the consul and his wife had a blast. I knew we were going to be fast friends.

The day after the party, Betty was over giving massages. I was still bushed. I was on a massage table in the spa. She always started with me face down.

"Baby, you must be tired, you were here late. Are you sure you're okay to work now?"

"Totally ready, Boss. You sure know how to throw a party," Betty bubbled. She had been one of the last to leave.

"I'm sorry you got boxed in with Janice. Couldn't help but notice."

"She didn't seem to know many people. I did the floor a number of times and just ended up there."

"You think she's still drinking a lot?"

"I'm in and out of her place in an hour so I really don't know much. She always smells of booze, especially in the afternoon. She wasn't drinking much at the party, but maybe that's just because she was driving herself. Sorry to be so gossipy."

"I'm asking," I said, my laugh muffled by the headrest.

"There is something I should say if you're asking," she said, working her nails at what I loved most.

"Tell me."

"She's so jealous of you that I don't think it was a good idea to invite her."

I moved to a sitting position to face her.

"What did she say?"

"Boss, lie down, and I'll tell you."

"Okay, tell me." I settled into position.

"She said that everything you got is with her husband's money. She wanted to see the whole house, but I told her to ask you. I didn't feel right walking her through. I figured it was enough that she floated between the first two floors."

"Does she think I retired after Oscar died?"

"She didn't say that. Just that everything you have came from money her husband gave you."

I sat again, pulled her over to me by her waist and kissed her. A meaningful kiss.

"Thank you, Betty."

"Wow," she said, though it was more of a long, drawn out wow that went on for ten or fifteen seconds. She batted her eyes at me, pretending to be coquettish. "Am I staying over?"

A couple of days passed. The retainers were safe with Gonor, and I was able to focus my time on finding planes again, though Tricia did let me in on a couple of real estate deals that looked promising.

Arthur called.

"She called him thirty minutes ago. Want me to come over?"

"Are you at the office or out?"

"Office. I monitor from here."

"Transcribe the tape. No need to be perfect. Fax to me."

Tangles brought me the fax after lunch. I don't know if she was curious about it, but she didn't ask.

Janice: He didn't invite you to the party?

Fino: I passed, too tired, too much on my plate to dress up for a party. I didn't know he invited you.

Janice: I wasn't going to go but I wanted a look at the mansion I keep hearing about from you and my therapist.

Fino: Who is your therapist? Didn't know you had one.

Janice: I'm my own therapist.
Fino: It's a big house.
Janice: I didn't see it all, but I saw enough. The bastard used Oscar's money to buy everything he has and left me in the gutter.
Fino: He's made a fortune on his own that has nothing to do with Oscar. You are not in the gutter. He got you out of foreclosure, paid your mortgage off in full and sent you a hundred grand. It's not his fault you blew it all.
Janice: I don't know why I bother with you.
Fino: Because you have no money.
Janice: You took Oscar's money, too. Charging him all that interest then taking the insurance money I thought I would get.
Fino: Same old story. I have heard this how many times, too many times. Change your tune. This one is old.
Janice: Fuck you, Jack.
Fino: Call me when you aren't drunk. I see you started early today.
Janice: I hate you, Jack.
Fino: Laughter.
Click.

Tangles and Letty only knew Art was working on something for me but had stopped asking what it was. Only Melina and Arthur's boss knew.

I hoped Janice kept on as Betty's client. She was my only entrée into Janice's life. I felt sure that something was going on with her.

On the plane-buying front, Pepe had called twice to egg me on. "A new 767 just came out so be on the lookout for any operators dumping the older models. We can use them. I have a big operator in Peru who is looking to lease three 767s."

"I'll start hunting. I never handled a crashed 767, but I know the plane.

Not sure that says anything. It's a big plane."

"Boeing is always best," Pepe said.

I laughed but didn't share what was so funny with Pepe. With Pepe, what he wanted right now was always best. Last week when an operator was looking for an Airbus, Airbus was best.

Pepe was enthusiastic about leasing out these planes. I was glad to hear it, because it cooled my long-held suspicions. Oscar—rest his soul—had never said it outright, but implied that Pepe had kept his father's drug operation alive and shrouded through so many layers of anonymous corporations that it could never be traced back to him.

Pepe was deeply into GAL leasing aircraft. He also had that giant management branch of his massive LAI corporation running his cornucopia of commercial enterprises, office buildings, apartment buildings, tortilla factory, bakery, soccer stadiums, liquor stores, carwashes, retail stores, shopping centers, etc.... And those were just the ones in the Los Angeles area. He had hundreds, probably thousands world-wide. When would he have time for dealing with a cartel?

I dialed Kinko and set him to hunt for fresh meat. 767s. He faxed me a list of possibles before the end of the day.

Instead of a Thanksgiving dinner, Olga and I planned to meet in Rio for a week, alone. I had missed Thanksgiving before because I was away on a case, so it wasn't like this was a first. I gave my Aunt Carmen plenty of notice and the girls were on their own.

I visited Melina at her North Hollywood market for lunch in her office.

I smelled mouth-watering steak. She met me at her office door, and we had our usual torrid greeting, a full body-contact kiss and grope that had both of us panting and ready for more. The table—which we had been known to use as a platform for our sexual gyrations—already held some mean porterhouse steaks, still sizzling, grilled for us by her catering kitchens.

Instead of sex, we sat down to eat.

"Any Thanksgiving plans?" I asked.

She gave me a look. "Thanksgiving will never be the same for me. It's been two years since I was shot by Bruno Vicario. I'm okay, but as far as I'm concerned, the holiday died."

I told her I was going to be in Rio. She took the news without a whimper.

"Cuz, a break in routine is good."

"You're not sitting at home alone, are you? I'm sure Aunt Carmen has a chair with your name on it."

Her face flushed.

"I have a Thanksgiving dinner invitation, thank you very much."

"Really?" I put down my fork and looked up.

"Dinner with a liquor rep named Armando. Actually, his parents."

I set down my knife and stared. "I don't believe it."

"Believe it, Cuz. I've been seeing him, if seeing him means he's been at my house a couple times for Sunday brunch."

"Sunday brunch? Our Sunday brunch?" Before Olga, Sunday at Melina's had been our exclusive territory, a weekly bacchanalia that was uniquely ours. "Baby, you let this dude in your house?"

"He's a good guy. Never married. Almost my age and he's sweet."

"You can't do this," I heard myself say. "Are you fucking him?" I grabbed my glass and gulped to shut myself up. My mouth had developed a will of its own.

She raised her wine glass of sparkling water. I had no choice but to raise my glass and click. I didn't drink again, though.

"With your track record, you got some nerve." She giggled. She took a slice of her steak and waved her fork at me.

"What about this Armando?"

"I've fucked him twice. Want details?"

After a pause, I swallowed a bite of steak that had grown into a huge lump and was stuck in my throat, along with a bunch of gall. "I hope it works for you."

"I didn't say I'm going to marry him. But what you're feeling now, I probably feel about you and Olga."

After we ate, we made no move to have sex. When we said goodbye, it was like a couple of nuns parting. I wanted her, but there was Olga, and now, apparently, Armando.

"I love you, Cuz."

"Ditto," I said.

When I got in my car, I called Jenny.

"Are you busy?"

"For a hunk like you, never."

"Jen, if I see you today, you can't turn down what I give you like the last time."

It took me almost an hour with traffic to get to her house. It was strange to see her in the afternoon.

We drank two margaritas before we went to her bed.

I was pumping away. She put her hands on my face.

"Where are you? I like it hard but..."

I had been too rough. I got up, and stood by the window, every part of me clenched but one. She coaxed me back to bed, but I was limp.

She kissed me. "Something is going on. Tell me what it is."

I could not tell her, but eventually I got hard again. I made sure she was satisfied. I left money on her table. When I left, I felt I had taken good care of her as she had done for me. I don't know if it was Janice or Armando, but I was still feeling unsettled.

As Thanksgiving week approached when I had to leave for Rio to meet up with Olga, I did not want Letty to be alone. I told her, "As always, you have the run of the house. It is still your home away from home, even on Thanksgiving."

"Boss, totally cool letting me stay here."

I laughed. "Let you stay here? You *live* here. I'm sorry that Pixie will still be on tour," I reminded her.

"And Lainie is in London and won't be back for two weeks. If I get lonely, I get on the cell. I'm going to be fine. Betty will be around if you don't mind."

"Of course, I don't mind. What about Tangles?"

"If she doesn't go to her mom's, she'll come. Miguel will be off, but I can do a turkey in my sleep. Go have your Olga time. Take a minute and look out for yourself. Stop worrying about all of us."

Letty packed two suitcases for me, way too much for a week.

"You have two jars of peanut butter, and a package of plastic spoons."

My Falcon got me to Rio. I found it lonely to fly that many hours alone and filled most of the flight with broody thoughts about this interloper Armando. It had been two weeks since Melina told me she was seeing him. I was still processing it. If she married, things between us would change. No question, I'm a selfish prick.

Olga and Riana arrived in Rio a day before me. It was supposed to be our week alone. If it were going to be fair, I should have had the chance not to leave Letty alone. Thing is, I liked Riana. I did not want to make her the focal point of a disagreement, so I let it pass. She seemed lonely.

"You didn't bring Letty and Tangles?" she asked.

I would have loved to have brought them, but the plan was for Olga and me to be alone for the week. All I said was "They had things to do."

I had been to the Rio house a number of times, paradise on a bluff that overlooked the Atlantic ocean. For two nights we stayed in. The third night, we went clubbing. A jeep with five security guards followed the Mercedes we were in.

"I'm glad to see you don't lighten up on the security," I said.

"Amor, in Rio, you can get kidnapped faster than in Venezuela or

Colombia."

I gave her a look.

"I'm sorry, Amor, didn't meant to bring up your kidnapping."

I laughed. "That's far behind me. Thanks to Pepe, I'm here."

"You were kidnapped?" Riana asked.

At Olga's insistence, I told the story while we were en route. I was in the middle, my hands on Olga's and Riana's knees as I repeated the tale of my kidnap and rescue. One at a time, the guards followed us into the club. I suppose they felt they were being discreet.

A day before Olga and I were planning to leave Rio, I was in swim trunks, and Olga was topless as we walked down to the sandy beach. Though it was getting cold in Los Angeles, here in Rio it was eighty degrees. The sand felt like hot powdered silk, but not burning hot. The path to the beach was a long one, as the house was built on a bluff.

"How will our lives be different when we get married?" I asked. "How do you envision our life together?"

We held hands. Beneath our feet, the sand changed from loose and dry to hard packed, and finally at the edge of the waterline, it was damp and did not support us. Our feet sank in, leaving craters of footprints the waves filled with water.

"I see two children in our lives. I see us traveling together instead of alone. I see us cutting others from our sex lives when the first baby is born, maybe before. I see us being so in love that our friends will envy what we have between us. With all of my heart, that's what I want."

We stopped. We faced each other, the water to my right and Olga's left as the trailing edge of waves washed over the tops of our feet. I could feel the ocean breeze soft on my skin. All the fish in the sea were out there, all the birds overhead. A flock of black-beaked seagulls swooped around us with shrill cries cawing their hunger, and then moved on.

"Are you ready to give up the chase?" I asked.

"Eventually, yes. What about you?"

"If you do it, I can do it," I said.

"Kiss me, Amor."

I lifted her, cradled her. Her arms went around my neck. Behind me, I heard the sound of clapping. I turned to look, taking Olga with me.

Riana. Also, topless. "Bravo," she said.

The Rio house was just another of Pepe's residences. Olga did not tell me he would be there during our stay, and I did not discover he was there until one of his assistants found me coming inside after an early morning beach workout. He led me to a table in a room off the kitchen where Pepe was drinking the local espresso latte Brazilians call *pingado*, and breakfasting on a basket of cheese rolls they call *pão de queijo* and a bowl of sliced papaya. One of the kitchen helpers brought me a cup and I poured my own. The espresso is strong enough to stand on its own without a cup, but it was a treat for me to drink it black.

He had good news about GAL's latest development and was on a high. The girls were still sleeping while he and I had an early breakfast.

"The bank consortium is good to go. Used or new, the sky's the limit."

I knew he was talking about the banks Riana's father had put together.

"Fantastic!"

"GAL will be bigger than LAI. You will see, Mario. You are part of it. I cannot do this without you," he said.

LAI had been around a whole generation before the Camachos' coaxed me into shopping for businesses for them. Being here in its beginnings, I felt more a part of GAL. I was surprised to learn that Pepe was planning to fly back to Milan that same day.

"He flew from Milan just to see you," Olga said. "He loves doing business with you."

I have to say that made me feel real good.

Olga and Riana separated when she boarded her plane and I boarded mine. Just as my cabin door was closing, Olga rang me on my cell from her plane, fifty feet away.

"Amor, I need you right now."

I love spontaneous anything. She did not have to ask twice. Nursing a glass of wine at the DC 10's bar, Riana waved me on to the cabin where Olga was waiting.

December 1986

An airliner crashed in Russia, the second in as many months. Gonor had called me about it.

"I've never had a case in Russia," I told Gonor. "Visas are hard to come by, and this plane is an Antonov, made in Russia."

We passed on the Antonov, but Letty and Tangles flew to Seattle, Washington to meet with a widower. His wife had piloted and crashed in a new Piper Cub back in October. The plane was under a year old and had less than 400 hours in the air. The preliminary buzz was that the engine failed.

Meanwhile, Kinko kept me busy looking at planes.

While Letty and Tangles were in Seattle, Pixie came over to keep me company.

"Olga went overboard on my house security. I hope she doesn't think I'm footing the bill for all of it. One of them followed me over here."

I nodded. I knew about the waiting guard. Quito had already called it in, and I had him invited to this side of the gate.

"Want to drink or fuck, Boss?"

"Both," I said. I got up from my chair. "Let's hit the wine room."

"Good deal. You have the best wines, ever."

"That's Melina's doing," I said. "I knew zero about wine."

"I remember," she said, a faraway look in her eye. "So, what do you think about her boyfriend?"

"Never met him. She had Thanksgiving dinner at his parents' house."

Pixie giggled. "If he's what she wants, I hope she marries him."

"I know what you mean, Pix."

I opened a bottle of Chateau Mouton Lafite intending to pour it in a snifter to breathe. Pixie took the bottle and expertly poured. She lit the fireplace, then she turned on the juke box and spent a minute going through the list of 45's packed inside. I laughed at her selections, all of them either hers, or Lainie's or the two of them in a duet.

"You are handy, Baby."

She smiled and sat on my lap.

"I miss you," she whispered, resting her face on my chest.

"Baby, you are killing them out there. How can you have time to miss me or anyone?"

"If I didn't have my cell phones, I'd go crazy. I'm not ever going to fuck a fan. And the team that travels with me...they're RIALTO suck-ups, not friends. I'm so fucked without getting fucked."

I laughed a little.

"Not funny," she said, giggling.

Betty arrived when we were on our second bottle.

"Set a table up in here," Pixie told her, "and do Boss, first."

"Be right back," Betty said, and headed to the spa for a table and linens.

"How often do you talk to Lainie?"

"Every day. Even if I hang up on her or she hangs up on me, there's always the next day. I call her, or she calls me like nothing happened."

I heard a suspiciously juicy sniff.

"Baby, don't cry."

"I'm not crying," she said, tears rolling down her face.

I did not think she was in love with Jason. I knew she was feeling hurt, but I did not know if it was from Lainie usurping Pixie's place in Jason's life, or Jason usurping Pixie's place in Lainie's life. Betty and I convinced Pixie to go first. She dropped her clothes and got on the table. The music kept playing. Off and on, Pixie was quiet, or singing in harmony with herself or Lainie. The only other sound was Betty's expert hands working their magic. We had the whole night ahead of us. It was one of those moments when everything is just perfect.

When December tenth came around, I still had not ordered my Christmas tree. I was up in the air about the coming holiday.

"What's your schedule?" I asked Pixie at breakfast.

"I'm free after the twentieth," Pixie said, "I'm in, whatever you want to do."

"Let's go somewhere for Christmas."

Letty clapped her hands.

I tried expanding our party. Niley and Jo passed on the invitation. Niley was working a new boyfriend. Jo and TJ had plans to have all the kids over for some quality time. I knew better than to ask Melina. She would say she was busy with work or had plans with Armando, and, if she said yes, what would I tell Olga? Tricia said no, too. Her stuffy boyfriend didn't socialize much. It was just as well because Olga would not have wanted him around bogging up Paris where we were headed.

On December twenty-first, I left Casa Luna in the capable hands of my household staff and security personnel and headed to Van Nuys Airport to my plane. Letty, Tangles, Pixie, and Betty flew with me. Olga, Riana, and Camila planned to join us at the George V, Paris.

The luxury hotel was as festive as my house would have been. The first-floor garden area had ten decorated Christmas trees, plus a monster fir about the size my tree had been last year.

Olga got us rooms on the same floor. Pixie had a one-bedroom suite as did Riana. Letty, Tangles, and Betty were in a two-bedroom suite, one bedroom with twin beds, the other with a king. Olga, Camila, and I were in the two-bedroom presidential suite, a feat Olga no doubt managed by arriving early packing a bundle of cash. The bellman showed us the one-bedroom suite reserved for Pepe. It had a parlor as big as the parlor in the presidential suite.

"Pepe will be arriving on the twenty fourth," Camila said.

"Where is your security?" I asked.

Olga shrugged. "Throughout the hotel but only at night will one of them be near the door."

"Mine are here, too. But, we have Pixie and Letty, don't need our guys," Camila said, laughing. "Pepe will also have security. They have rooms on another floor."

"Is Pepe in Rio or Milan? I haven't heard from him in a couple days."

"Neither. He's in Bogota closing the sale on the house."

"I never got a look at that place."

"It's just another great big house," Olga said. "But it is a gorgeous great big house."

"Goes back years in our family," Camila said.

"In Medellin, Pepe and Camila have another house as big as the one he is selling in Bogota," Olga said.

"I have so many friends there. My roots are there, and yours, Camila."

"I need a smoke," Camila said. "Most of our friends left Colombia, Amor."

We all hit the Champs Elysees and shopped, sometimes together, other times separately, then catching up at the *Galeries Lafayette,* two huge buildings with everything one could ever want to shop for, like a French Harrods. The PLO had blasted the buildings last year, but they remodeled and were open again.

Olga and Camila gave Letty, Tangles and Betty thirty thousand francs each[47], and told us we had reservations downstairs in the main restaurant for

---

[47] In Dec. 1986, the exchange rate was 6.3725, making the cash equal to $4707.72. $4,707.72 in 1986 had the same buying power as $10,618.17 in 2018.

dinner on Christmas Eve and for brunch on Christmas Day.

We were sitting around in our suite. Riana came in to join us. Olga was beaming and dressed head to toe in some kind of close-fitting red cashmere that was devastating with her coloring.

"You look happy," I told Olga.

"This will be a treat for us," Olga sighed.

I kissed her. She nibbled my lips.

"I adore you, Amor. I am so happy."

"Enough," Camila said, "I'm getting jealous. And impatient. I wish Pepe could have come earlier, but of course he just had to wait till the 24th."

"You know how important it is for him to close this bit of business in Colombia," Olga said with a touch of annoyance. "He'll get here when he gets here. Today is the twenty-third. It's not like you have long to wait."

"Okay," Camila said, equally annoyed. She walked over to the window and stood looking out with her hand on the glass. "It's too cold to smoke on the balcony. I need a hit or two to pass the time."

Olga said, "The garden is below us. They would smell it. Don't go out there. Go to Pixie's room and smoke," Olga said. "Don't stink up the place here."

"You act like you don't get high." Camila griped and fidgeted and made no move to head to Pixie's.

Olga relented.

"Light up. You'll do it anyway."

Camila lit up.

Our suite had at least a dozen ashtrays. Smoking tobacco was no big deal. I don't know if smoking pot at the Four-Seasons Hotel in Paris would be tolerated but fuck it. Camila couldn't care less, nor Olga for that matter.

"Let me have some," I said as though I loved the stuff.

"Amor, no," Olga said.

"Baby, a little weed is good to cool your jets," I said.

"Okay. Give me some, too." Olga reached for the joint. She took a deep hit, and said, "Pixie should be in on this."

She called Pixie and told her to come over.

"You're all alone over there. Get your *culo*[48] over here."

Pixie didn't come alone. Letty, Tangles and Betty arrived with her. Riana was already with us. We stayed in, keeping room service busy. The music was on low and we had the TV on a French dubbed version of *It's a Wonderful Life*.

At eleven, Camila's cell phone chirped. We all heard it.

"I hope it's Pepe. He should have left by now," Camila said, pulling her phone from her purse.

I was looking forward to talking to Pepe about the upcoming GAL purchase. It was supposed to be a vacation, but I'd still brought the latest list of potential planes Kinko had lined up. Pepe might be calling from the Bogota airport or from Roissy. I was eager but there would be no point in meeting him. He would already have arranged transportation to the hotel.

"This is Camila," she said. She listened for a moment, and asked, "Who is this?"

Her expression changed to one of irritation and from irritation to despair.

"What's wrong?" Olga asked. "Who is it?"

Camila screamed.

I jumped up. We were all on our feet.

Camila dropped the phone on the floor and went down on her knees on the carpeting, bent over, sobbing.

Olga picked up the phone.

"This is Olga. Who is this?"

She listened for a moment in silence. Her face twisted. A tear spilled from her eye and ran down her cheek. "Diego, I can't talk now. Stay ready for my call."

She went down next to Camila. The two of them hugged and sobbed.

---

[48] Ass

"What happened?" I asked.

Olga looked up at me, pale with shock, her eyes big, her voice clogged with tears.

"Pepe's plane was shot down as it took off from Bogota."

I went down on my knees, and put my arms around them both, Camila and Olga. I felt shock, and my heart twisted like it had suddenly forgot how to beat.

Olga and Camila clung to me, and I held them hard against me, as if there was something I could do to absorb their grief. I could not think in that moment of Pepe never coming to see the plane list I was holding for him. I could not think of him at all. I was watching two strong women come apart at the seams, beyond all comfort. Olga pushed me away, screaming, and beat on my chest, screaming "Why Pepe?" then clung to me harder than before. Camila hung on to me, too, but was talking to Pepe, telling him he should have come on time, and if he'd been on time, this never would have happened. She went on and on, words to a dead man who would never hear them.

I said nothing. My mouth was full of words, but none of them came out. My head was too full of the idea of the end of Pepe. I didn't have any platitudes to offer, and don't think either of them would have heard me anyway. Grief was something I'd been through a thousand times or more, families broken down by shock and tragedy. The only way through the grief is time, and crying, and mourning. Nothing I could say or do ever worked to calm anyone. I couldn't throw out any life preservers anyway, because I was sucked into the well of despair. Pepe had been a good friend. My affection and love for Olga and Camila ran deep. I felt a shade of anger crisping on top of my grief. How dare someone shoot down his plane?

"Caprice too?" Letty whispered.

I shrugged. We knew only that Pepe was dead.

I don't know how long we were there, Camila and Olga and I, kneeling on the floor. Pixie put a box of tissues beside us. I grabbed one and pulled an arm free to wipe at Olga's face, then Camila's, but when I tried to stand, they clutched at me. I was down there with them till my legs went numb.

Pixie, Letty, Tangles, Betty, and Riana had returned to the sofas and chairs, everyone in tears. *It's a Wonderful Life* was still playing, the sound off. Camila and Olga were the center of silent attention.

A sharp knock at the door did not get through to Olga and Camila. Letty handled it when room service came and went, leaving a feast at the table. No one touched it.

"Boss," Letty said sharply.

I saw her holding out a brandy. Somehow, I pulled away, and found myself on the ottoman, swallowing the drink at one gulp. I remembered Oscar. He always went for the brandy. Only during a crisis did I ever drink the stuff. He used to say the wine I liked was like a young girl, but his brandy was like a complicated older woman you would not bring home to introduce to your mother.

I went to the bar. I took up the bottle of Armagnac, refilled my glass and poured its harsh burn down my throat. I filled two more glasses and took them to Camila and Olga, who ignored me at first. Olga looked at her hand with the brandy glass in it as if she had no idea how it had gotten there. She gulped it down and got Camila to swallow hers. Pixie took the glasses away. It did not seem as if the brandy had helped at all except perhaps to break the embrace between Camila and Olga.

I put my arm around Olga and gently lifted her into a deep comfortable side chair. I returned for Camila who resisted at first, then put her arms around me, with a bewildered expression. I set her down in another side chair. Pixie returned with two more brandies. They slowly sipped, hands trembling, still crying. I could no longer see them. The team had circled them with towels and tissues. I had pulled up a straight chair opposite them.

"I have to call Diego back," Olga said.

"Let him know we are going there," Camila said.

"Who is Diego?" Riana asked.

"He handles security for Pepe in Colombia."

"Please hand me the phone," Olga said, looking at Letty.

"You can't go," I said. "It isn't safe. You said Pepe's plane was shot down."

Olga looked at me blankly, not arguing. I wanted to know the details of what had happened. I watched as Olga picked up Camila's little black book to find the number and dialed.

"Hello, Diego," she said. She listened for a few moments, her face wearing a tortured expression, then said, "No more of this. Tell Mario."

I took the phone and listened to the details. Pepe had Caprice with him, three pilots, two flight attendants and six security people. A single rocket fired from a shoulder launcher took the plane down as it lifted off the runway. Diego and nine men who had come with Pepe to the airport witnessed it and cornered the single terrorist. He was shot and killed when they tried to take him into custody. Diego said when he was cornered, he yelled at Diego's men with a Colombian accent before he opened fire, then he was shot dead.

"Is it safe for Olga and Camila to be there?" I asked Diego.

"The army has great respect for Pepe and his family. This was not our government, not our military."

"Diego, I need an answer. Is anyone after Olga or Camila?"

"Pepe had good relations with the new government. He would have left two years ago if that was not true."

"Answer my question, Diego!"

"I don't know but I will find out. Maybe it is old history, related to Pepe's father."

"I don't care about old news," I said. "This happened today. What's to prevent whoever is behind today's attack from going after Camila or Olga?"

I couldn't hear what Diego said. Camila snatched the phone from my hand. "Diego, we will let you know when we will arrive."

She listened to his end of the line, started crying again, and handed me the phone back.

"What did you tell her?" I asked Diego.

"Until twenty minutes ago, the plane was still burning. Not sure what will be recovered."

I heard Diego's voice break. He was crying too.

It was well after two in the morning. We had gotten several glasses of brandy into Camila and Olga, and they were both nodding out in their chairs. I carried Camila to one of the bedrooms and returned for Olga and put her on the other bed. I don't know who went in to take care of Camila, but someone undressed her, and made her comfortable. Riana went back to her room and so did the others. I went to bed and found Olga in a night gown. I embraced her as she slept.

In the morning, no one cared it was Christmas Eve. I convinced Pixie to take my plane back to Los Angeles. Betty decided to fly back with her and keep her company.

"I will stay with her, Boss, no worries."

"I don't want you photographed in Colombia," Olga told Pixie. "I'm not sure how the media will treat this."

Nothing I could say could convince Letty to join Pixie and Betty flying back to Los Angeles.

"Boss, you will need me. I know I can help you and Olga."

Olga hugged her. "Amor, I love you," she told Letty.

At noon, we reached the airport. I had been brooding. My dreams had been full of crisis, of burning fields, houses, and planes, and a confused mess of attempted shootings, and car crashes. I had woken up with my dreams telling me the world was full of dangerous, unsolved shit that was all connected to me. I suddenly felt protective again of my team. There was a reason I was keeping my house secure.

"Stay at my house," I told Pixie and Betty. "I think I have better security.

Not that you need it, but let's not ask for trouble."

With only a skeleton crew, Camila's plane left for Mexico City. I wondered why she didn't have the plane flown to Colombia where we were going. Tangles, Olga, Letty, Riana, Camila, and I flew to Bogota in Olga's plane. Olga and Camila's security people were also on board. We talked on the long flight to Bogota.

"Thank you for being here with us," Camila said.

"Who do you think was responsible? Diego says it goes back to your dad."

"Diego is full of shit. All those people are dead."

"Everyone loves Pepe," Olga cried. "He was charitable and generous to everyone. Everyone who had their hand out got something from Pepe. It couldn't have been anyone with a grudge against Pepe."

Camila could not hear a word against her father, and Olga was deaf to the possibilities that Pepe might have made enemies. I was getting nowhere with them.

For years, I 've had to take drastic steps to keep from getting killed. Compared to Pepe, I was a pea in the pod. Pepe was a giant. I only knew a tiny bit of his business. Certainly, there were people who wanted him dead. I remembered when he had told me he torched the lawyers' coffee plantation. All buildings and residences had been demolished, and anyone who had not fled was killed when his helicopters dropped bombs. Actions like those make enemies. Diego had said that the terrorist was a single person who took down an airliner with a single rocket. Who would know where to hire a person like that? Someone well-connected. Someone with cash. Someone with power.

It was almost midnight. I didn't know we were going to land at an army base until we started our descent. Diego was there to meet us as we deplaned. Camila was first down the stairs, followed by Olga and me. On the tarmac, I counted eight military cars packed with fatigue-clad men that I assumed were soldiers. A man in an army jacket held open the door to a Mercedes limousine. Our luggage was carried to the trunk of a car ahead of ours. We had two lead cars, four door Cadillacs loaded with men and behind us were the cars I had seen on the tarmac.

"Miss Camila's house is ready for you," Diego said.

"Pepe sold the main house. It was the largest," Olga said in a low voice. "Camila's house is bigger than mine, with nine bedrooms. We will be good there."

Letty and I were in the jump seats facing Camila, Olga, and Tangles.

The back of the car was dark, scantily illuminated by the surrounding headlights. We could have been anywhere. Not much to see in the dark but the shades of cars.

"Do you feel safe with the security I see everywhere?" I leaned forward and took Olga's hand.

"Amor, I have absolutely no fear. I'm at home here."

I was not so sure, but it was not the time for me to be a wise ass and remind them their brother had been killed twenty-four hours ago.

"Bravo, *hermanita*," Camila said.

Camila's residence in Bogota was a modern construction right out of Architectural Digest, loaded with huge glass walls and concrete, two stories but taller than my four-story home. There were several master suites on the first floor. In the morning, Olga walked me through, and pointed out the suite Camila used, the one Pepe had used, and the one that was hers that we were sharing. The level above us had six bedrooms. Letty and Tangles elected to share, and Riana was by herself. All the suites had a glass wall facing a spectacular view of the city, even though we were only about a third of the way up the incline. Through the window, Olga pointed out the bulk of the estate, which was at the foot of the mountain, with a strip going up to this property. A wooden staircase went down the property to extensive gardens on the flatland.

"Pepe always said 'Acreage on a mountain is like owning nothing,'" Camila said, pushing a sugar bowl across the table to Olga who was drinking coffee. Camila's plate held some *queso fresco* and she was drinking *aguapanela* made from sugar cane. She stirred the *aguapanela* but did not drink it.

"That's why I was able to build on this property. He didn't want it."

The first level of the property was open, with a kitchen, great room, living and dining room all sharing the view of the city. The mountain side of the property had a small pool and sitting area.

I saw Tangles and Letty had already been at work. A stack of several local newspapers sat on a counter, discarded. The girls were nowhere in sight, but articles had been torn out, and Camila passed them around.

"Tangles and Letty, they make apologies to you," Camila said. "They are in back swimming. They wanted to get in a workout and couldn't believe it is in the seventies here."

Newspapers, radio, and television were all reporting that federal authorities were investigating the death of Pepe Camacho, his fiancée and staff aboard an airplane that was shot down. The Camacho's spokesperson said that Pepe was in Bogota to close the sale of his house in Los Altos to Cristobal Munoz, former mayor of Bogota and that he had been flying to Paris to meet his family to spend Christmas together.

We were seated in the dining room. The buffet held a big breakfast spread with local breakfast dishes like milk soup, chicken tamales, *caldo de costilla*,[49] and a variety of *arepas* topped with tomato and cheese. I had black coffee. It's impossible for me to eat during a crisis. Pepe's remains were being extracted from the burned plane, and that was crisis enough for me. Though we were all on edge, I had not seen a tear from Olga or Camila since we landed in Bogota. They were not going to cry in front of others, determined to present a unified front.

---

[49] Beef rib soup

"I haven't heard a thing about papa y mama, or our history," Camila said. "No speculation of who gave orders to the man who shot down the plane."

"Thanks, no doubt, to Matias," Olga said.

"Who is Matias?" I asked.

"Our lawyer here. He's been around since my father's time. He was once the number two for the president," Camila explained.

"The man just keeps going. I don't think he will ever die," Olga said.

"Thank God for that," Camila said. "He's the only one with influence enough to control the press. I will ask him to come over."

Olga and I went down the mountain and explored the grounds. When we got back, Camila was waiting in the great room with news. The phone had been ringing off the hook all day. One of the calls was from the former Mayor of Bogota, the buyer of the house that Pepe had been in Colombia to sell.

"He wanted to offer his condolences," Camila said. "He said that everything was ready for signature. Everyone was at the house to sign before the notary. Pepe asked Munoz to step out of the room to speak privately, and Pepe told him he couldn't sell the house. It was just too sentimental. He could not sell our heritage, our family history."

"Good for him," Olga said, dry-eyed, but there was life in her voice. "I am so glad he did not sell."

"Me too," Camila said, literally jumping for joy. She lunged over to Olga and they danced around hugging each other, chanting together, "He didn't sell the house!"

In a calmer tone, Camila said, "If I change my mind, Munoz will buy it. Pepe must not have told Diego about not selling. We could have stayed there."

"If you like my house," said Camila. "Wait till you see that house."

They launched into anecdotes, fond memories of the house they'd spent so much time in. It took a little while to settle down, then Olga said, "I think it's time we talk about the funeral."

I would have expected an outburst of tears as they started discussing funeral arrangements, but that didn't happen. Even though Camila was the head of the family now, it was Olga who spoke, and Camila who agreed, point by point.

Olga said, "Pepe will be buried on the grounds of the house he did not sell."

"Next to my father and mother," Camila said. "If we bury him there, I can never sell the house," Camila said to Olga, looking at her as if they were the only people in the room.

"Never, Hermanita," Olga agreed.

"On the property?" I asked.

"The estate is more than a hundred acres. There is a private family cemetery on the property," Olga said.

When I first got to know Camila, she'd told me her father had molested her. When her mother found out, she had shot him then turned the gun on herself. In the years I had known Camila, she had never again talked about it. Olga never mentioned it to me. I wasn't sure she even knew that Camila had told me.

That night we had dinner with Mattias Castro, the man who had managed the press. I know the girls said he was old, but he came across as much younger. He was lean, and tanned, his hair silvery, and his brown eyes crinkled and glinting with humor, even in this time of grief. He spoke with a strength and intelligence that impressed me to no end.

"I think it is a good idea that you sell the house and consider selling the other house in Medellin."

"Why?"

"When your parents died, we almost lost the house to the government. Your father owned the house. Property records had not been recorded properly. Taxes were underpaid for years. The government presented pages of reasons why they were entitled to take possession. I audited the records and corrected things and made notations of what needed to be cleared up. Pepe paid off the taxes, brought everything up to date, and then he paid off everyone with their hand out, so they would go away. There have been many changes in government since then. No one since has bothered to come after the house, but it is bound to happen again, now that Pepe is gone, more reason. A huge property like that raises many questions. Pepe was going to sell because he could cut possible risk right now and walk away with eighty million dollars American. Both of you are American citizens now. Your assets are no longer in Colombia. Get rid of the house here and in Medellin. If you want to keep your own residences, keep them. There is no cloud on their titles. The big houses are a different story."

I still hadn't seen the house. Eighty million dollars.[50] That's a lot of bread.

"I am not going to sell," Camila said. "Maybe the Medellin house, but not the one here. If Pepe had wanted to sell, he would have sold it. He changed his mind. I am going to honor his wishes and not sell the house."

"You know best."

Olga got up and walked around the back of his chair, put her arms around him and kissed the back of his head. Matias chuckled.

"I love you, Matias. Thank you for all you've always done for the family. My own mother and father loved you very much as well."

He reached for her hand, and pulled it to his chest, patting it.

Camila moved next to Olga, kissing Matias, and thanking him in kind. It had been about forty-eight hours since they had been sobbing on the floor of the Four-Seasons Hotel in Paris.

The gates of Casa Camacho were two football fields away from the front of the residence. Green lawns with fountains like those I had only seen in Las Vegas adorned the lawn outside the gates. The guardhouse stood outside the gates blocking even a view of the property. The day before the funeral, we stood outside the house.

---

[50] $80,000,000.00 in 1986 had the same buying power as $180,438,426.35 in 2018.

"This is like something royalty lives in," I said, looking up at the vast old building.

Camila said, "The government tried and failed to prove my parents were in the drug business, time and time again. They always came up empty handed. You would think my parents would hide their wealth like many of their friends in the same business. Instead, they lived in this big house. Everyone knew they controlled thousands of acres of jungle, jungle that yielded tons of rubber and cacao that my parents paid big taxes on, and that appeased the authorities. No one could ever prove that on top of that legal rubber and cocoa, tons of drugs were ever cultivated, processed in hidden labs, and shipped to retailers. If you asked anyone, they speculated that the Camacho were wholesalers."

"Wholesalers?" I asked.

"A wholesaler grows the stuff then processes and ships it to retailers who sell it," Olga explained.

"They could have never made the money they did just being wholesalers. They were retailers in countries most competitors never bothered to go to or send their product to. My father was the go-between between Camila's father and the jungle operations. He was the man behind the scenes that no one ever saw. When I was orphaned, Pepe's father and mother took me in and treated me like family, sister to Pepe and Camila."

"You are my sister," Camila said, extending her hand. "Everything I own, you also own, I love you, Hermanita."

"And I love you," Olga said.

It took two hours to tour the forty thousand square foot house. I tried to persuade Camila and Olga that we could do this at another time, but they insisted. Three swimming pools outdoors. One indoors. A staff of thirty lived on the grounds. There were ten gardeners. Three men did nothing but tend the fountains. Between the men at Camila's and here were more than forty guards.

If Bogota was so safe, why all the muscle?

It wasn't any of my business, but I wanted to say what a waste of money it was to keep all those people working. The upkeep involved in maintaining the main house and all the other quarters had to be sky high.

Olga and I had not had sex since Pepe's death. That night, we lay in bed and talked in the dark.

"We have no more businesses in Colombia. Nothing obvious anymore, but we do have millions coming from here every month. The expense of the property is more than covered by that. In case you were wondering why we allow so much overhead here," she said in a low voice as though there were someone else with us. She kissed me, a wet kiss.

"I never gave it any thought at all," I lied, wondering if she was a mind reader. It had not been that long since Pepe had moved the hub of his airline out of Colombia. I had known politics were behind his move, but politics can cover a lot of ground. Clearly, what was obvious was Olga was telling me something, *nothing obvious* going on in Colombia anymore.

"Amor, I know you so well." It was a tiny laugh, but it was the first laugh since we lost Pepe.

"I love you, Olga."

"Amor, you know how I get when you call me by my name," she sighed. She turned to face me. "You know how I adore you." We kissed for a moment before she turned away and cuddled next to me.

I went to sleep holding her, wondering how many millions were coming out of Colombia from their not-obvious business. A sane person might run away from secrets like those the Camachos kept, but I loved Olga. Nothing else mattered.

When we left Colombia, all of us left the same way we got there, Olga's plane. The plane stopped in Mexico City where Camila, Olga, and Riana took Camila's plane from there to Rome where they planned to spend several weeks together with a stop in Barcelona at some point to drop off Riana.

On the way home from Mexico City with Letty and Tangles, it felt like it had been ages since I had spent any time with them alone. It wasn't about the sex. It was their company.

Epilogue

The funeral left me exhausted. By January tenth, I was in Pasadena, dark and sad over Pepe's death. We missed Pixie by three days. She'd left for Mexico City to prep for a South America tour. Fino had flown to Bogota for one day for the funeral. His appearance reminded me to monitor what he might have going with Janice. When I called Arthur, he reported there had been no contact whatsoever.

"Cut monitoring Janice's phone, and let's shelve this for now," I told him. It wasn't over. I didn't have answers, but saw no point in listening to calls no one made. I told Betty to stay in touch with Janice.

Since I'd been home, Olga didn't answer her cell. I heard once from Olga and Camila when they arrived in Rome, then nothing. That didn't bother me. They would surface when they surfaced, as they always did, as long as no one shot them down, too. Kinko's list of available planes was no longer burning a hole in my pocket. I didn't know if I should still be looking at planes. I folded up the list, stuffed it in an envelope and put it in my safe. The sight of it made me physically ill.

"The plane situation is on hold," I told Kinko. "I have no idea where we go from here."

The miserable weather, and the gray skies seemed fitting. The head of LAI and GAL was dead. LAI businesses lived on. That cornucopia of business still pushed booze, sheltered families, filled Mexican menus, and baked their way to profits, all the while hiding secrets that had gone to the grave with the man now six feet under in Bogota. I felt ice around me, inside me, sadness, and darkness. I couldn't focus on anything, but spent hours in the gym in endless repetitions till I left pools of sweat behind. Like when I had been trapped in a warehouse on the coffee plantation, I filled the hours working out. The trap was the same, only now the walls were not concrete blocks and miles of forest; the walls were the constantly ticking seconds, tick, tick, ticking on, separating me farther from the friend who had changed my life without revealing his secrets. Hours would work through me in the gym, with me repeating moves till my muscles ached and my breath hurt. Letty braved my anger to make me stop, dragging me to the shower, washing me like a child while she held me to her heart. I could not accept that Pepe, the man who'd had it all, was dead. After we'd been in Pasadena for seven days, my phone rang.

"Pack your bags mi Amor," Olga said. "We have plans to make. "You're coming to Milan."

About the Author

George Hatcher is an entrepreneur with a gift for business and storytelling. Whether he's traveling the globe as a consultant/strategist for lawyers in high profile wrongful death cases, running one of his many enterprises, or at home with Molly amid the birds and cats in California, he's always got his eye on the next project. He does a whole lot more than what is mentioned here.
 A longer bio is on his website at: www.georgehatcher.com/bio/bio.html